THE TOBACCO LORDS TRILOGY

Margaret Thomson Davis left school at the age of 16, working as a children's nurse and having a variety of other jobs before achieving her ambition of becoming a writer. She has had 15 novels published, many of which have been best-sellers, over 200 of her short stories have appeared in newspapers and magazines in Britain and overseas, and she has also written an autobiography. Active in a wide range of literary and other societies, Margaret Thomson Davis is in much demand as an entertaining and informative speaker.

MARGARET THOMSON DAVIS

THE TOBACCO LORDS TRILOGY

THE PRINCE AND THE TOBACCO LORDS
ROOTS OF BONDAGE
SCORPION IN THE FIRE

EDINBURGH
B&W PUBLISHING
1994

First published 1994
by B&W Publishing, Edinburgh.
Copyright © Margaret Thomson Davis 1994.
The Prince and the Tobacco Lords © Margaret Thomson
Davis 1976; *Roots of Bondage, Scorpion In The Fire*
© Margaret Thomson Davis 1977.
The moral right of the author has been asserted.

ISBN 1 873631 33 2

British Library Cataloguing in Publication Data:
A catalogue record for this book is available from
the British Library

Cover illustration:
Detail from *Mrs Scott Moncrieff*
by Sir Henry Raeburn
Photograph: by kind permission
of the National Galleries of Scotland

Printed by Werner Söderström

THE PRINCE AND THE
TOBACCO LORDS

This book is dedicated to the following good friends, in appreciation of their kind and generous help with my research: Mima Walker, Highlander Allan Walker, and Margaret and Mairead McKerracher.

Chapter 1

Regina wondered if it could be morning. The house was black and still. The harlots were quiet upstairs. Not even Blind Jinky's stick scraped the wall. Only the excited squeaking of the rats penetrated the wooden doors of the hole-in-the-wall bed. She eased her arm from under the plaid, stretched it over wee Gav and stroked her mother to make sure she was still there.

Jessie Chisholm snapped into wakefulness at the feather touch.

'Gav? Regina?' Her hands groped for them.

'Mammy,' Regina said, 'I thought I heard the bellman.'

Gav punched her. 'I was sound asleep. You're always wakening me.'

'Wheesht!' his mother whispered hoarsely.

After a while Gav exploded, 'Och, she's just blethering again!'

'Will ye wheesht!'

The sporadic ringing scratched the air from far off and obliterated the bellman's words. But gradually as he approached Tannery Wynd they were able to make out what he was shouting.

> 'The Pretender and his rebels
> Are surrounding the toon.
> If the redcoats don't stop them
> They'll be in Glesca soon.'

With hardly a pause Moothy McMurdo roared on and a vivid picture of him took colourful shape in Regina's mind: the tattered green frockcoat, the orange breeches, the buckled shoes and the cocked hat jammed on a head thrown back and only a huge open mouth showing.

> 'Auld Jock Currie deid last night.
> They poored in potions. They bled him tae.

3

But auld Jock Currie jist spluttered away.'

'I'm going to join the Highlanders.' Gav bounced up excitedly. 'I'm going to be a Highland rebel like my grandfather.'

'No, you will not,' Jessie said.

'Why not?'

'Because there will be fighting.'

'I can fight. I fight every day. The other boys are all for the Glasgow Volunteers and the English King Geordie.'

Regina sighed. 'You're only ten. The Highlanders don't want wee boys. Anyway, the redcoats won't let them come into the town.'

'I'm big as you and you're twelve.'

'Be quiet, the pair of you, or I'll open the door and let Blind Jinky and Spider in.'

This immediately silenced the children, who feared nothing more than the twisted skeleton of a man who lived in the adjoining house with his long-legged and ragged-toothed dog. Many a painful bite they had suffered from the animal.

Their mother jerked into a crouching position.

'There's the college bell now. Five o'clock. Time I was up.'

She flung back the tartan that covered the three of them, punched open the doors of the bed and groped for her crutch.

The smell of peat smoke became more pungent and mixed with the stench of the dunghill outside. Regina began coughing and shivering, despite being fully clad in her striped woollen dress and apron. She tried to cuddle into Gav for warmth, but he pushed her aside.

'I'm getting up. I'm hungry.'

'You too, Regina. You've not to be late for school,' Jessie said.

It always puzzled Regina why her mother was so set on her going to school. It was different with Gav. He found his lessons a challenge and despite the fights he got into with the other boys he seemed to enjoy attending school. She hated it. She hated the dominie and the constant floggings he meted out, not only to her but to all the children. She abhorred the violence, the pain, the cries of distress that had become part of the dismal room in the

4

hovel where the dominie lived and taught. Her whole being shrank away from ugliness or cruelty of any kind.

'I don't want to go to school.'

'Think yourself lucky you've the chance, lass. With schooling you can have a better life than me.'

'How?'

'Never mind how. Do as you're told. I'll poke the fire and light a candle.'

Gav scrambled over the edge of the bed and dropped on to the earthen floor, but Regina remained propped on one elbow watching her mother's bent figure in the flickering gloom.

Jessie's skirt hid the fact that she had only one leg, but everyone knew the reason she hopped about with the help of a crutch.

Many's the time Regina and Gav had listened in horror to the story of how Jessie's mother had been burned for witchcraft and how Jessie, as a wee girl, had been tortured with the boot to make Granny Chisholm confess. Her leg from foot to knee had been put in the iron cylinder while the hangman drove in wedges with a mallet till the flesh and bones were crushed to pulp. Granny Chisholm had confessed to try and stop the torture, but later when the flames were crackling up she screamed out: 'As the Good Lord's my witness, Jessie, I'm not a witch and never have been.'

Regina screwed her eyes shut to blot out the awful picture, but it became worse. It switched characters and revealed a vision of her own mother tied to the stake. Flames leapt up to redden the huge frizz of hair, the pocked face, the wild dark eyes. And in terror beyond all terrors Regina saw herself being tortured. Her leg was forced into the boot and the hangman's mallet donged like all the bells in Glasgow in her head.

No amount of schooling could stop that.

'Regina, will you get up? You lazy wee devil,' Jessie scolded. 'The porridge is nearly ready. There's no milk. Do you want a wee drop ale in it?'

'I'm cold, Mammy.'

'Enough of your whispering and whining. Get up and speak up.'

5

'She's the same at school,' Gav said. 'The dominie's always flogging her.'

Regina slithered to the floor.

'He flogs you too.'

'I'll flog the pair of you if you don't find your bowls and spoons and start supping your porridge.'

The icy clay knifed between Regina's toes as she raced across to where her bowl was kept on the shelf beside the ingle-nook fire. She was not afraid of her mother, although there were other children in the town and even grown-ups who gave Jessie a wide berth. The children were nervous of her harsh gravel croak and a swipe from her crutch. Grown-ups thought she was mad because sometimes she could not remember things and became confused.

When Gav asked her to tell the story about Prissie Ramsay and Granny Chisholm, she shook her head and said, 'Who are they? I don't know what you're talking about. Away with you.'

It was Prissie Ramsay who told the ministers and the baillies that she had visions and knew who the witches in the town were. It was she who pointed the finger at Granny Chisholm.

Or when they asked Jessie to repeat the story about Grandfather Chisholm, who had fought for the Pretender's father and the Jacobite Cause in 1715, she knocked them impatiently aside with: 'I know nothing about that.'

Even questions about how Granny Chisholm lost her house and all she possessed, and had to tramp from the Highlands to Glasgow in order to make a living for herself and wee Jessie, were shouted down at times.

'I'm not a Jacobite. I've never set foot in the Highlands. Glasgow born and bred like everyone else. That's Jessie Chisholm.'

Yet she was in no way like everybody else. For one thing she did not speak with a Glaswegian accent. Through the hoarse voice, another remnant of the torture she had suffered, came the strange lilt of the north. Sometimes in her maddest moments the Gaelic took complete possession of her and no one could understand a word she was raving about.

But nothing could make Gav or Regina afraid of her. They

6

recognised that underneath the wild exterior their mother loved and cared for them.

They were afraid of the harlots and the soldiers in Blind Jinky's house or in one of the two houses upstairs. Afraid of the bawling and cursing and fighting and the stamping of Jinky's feet and his fiddle scraping and Spider snarling like all the fiends in hell. The harlots and Blind Jinky were always trying to persuade Regina upstairs into what her mother called their 'dens of evil'. Once one of the drunken soldiers pounced on her and roaring with laughter held her prisoner while Blind Jinky, equally drunk, fumbled his hands up her skirt. Despite Spider snapping at his heels, Gav had rushed to her rescue, his fists flying, and Jessie came stumping rapidly after him, cursing and cracking Blind Jinky's and the soldier's heads open with a sharp rock in one hand.

Every night, returning from school or from playing on the Green after school, they took their time going up Saltmarket Street and along the Gallowgate. They only began to run when they turned into the Tannery Wynd, in case one of the soldiers or the harlots or Blind Jinky and Spider would be hiding there. Choking for breath, they raced towards the tenement building with its crow-stepped gables and windows sunk deep into the walls. Jutting out on either side was a wooden staircase leading to the upstairs flats and on the front were two doors for the downstairs houses. They hurled themselves against the door on the left and it never failed to open and tumble them into the safety of their mother's arms.

Some nights their mother had to shout her stories to drown out the terrible sounds from upstairs. Sometimes she sang songs to them or she questioned them on their catechism.

But now the rest of the building was quiet and Jessie muttered to herself as she doubled over the pot hanging on a chain over the fire and peered into it and jerked a wooden spoon round and round.

Soon, the three of them would slip silently from the house, the children cowering close to their mother until she secured the door. Then they skittered nervously along in front of her in the dark, all the time listening backwards for the rhythmic splash of her crutch on the quagmire of Tannery Wynd.

The Old Coffee House Land was the name of the tenement building situated at the corner of Saltmarket Street and Trongate Street. It commanded an excellent view of the business centre and the market place where four main streets intersected. Gallowgate Street cut across from the east, where the Glasgow Tannery was situated. High Street ran down from the north from the Cathedral. Saltmarket Street came up from the south and the River Clyde. Trongate Street came from the west. It was on Trongate that some of the most handsome buildings in Glasgow—indeed in Scotland—could be seen.

In daylight, from his bedroom window, Adam Ramsay could view the Tolbooth across the road with its crown-like spire, grated windows and outside stair. Next to it the Town Hall and the Exchange were resplendent with Doric columns and arches opening into shops below. These covered arcades, or piazzas as they were called in Scotland, skirted both sides of each of the four streets whose centre formed the Cross. But it was Trongate Street that boasted the equestrian statue of King William, the hero of the Boyne, the Inn Steeple and the Old Guard House with its colonnaded front projecting into the road. At the far end, past the tenements in which lived many of his friends, was the short square steeple of Hutcheson Hospital. Then on the very western verge of the city there stood the last building. The Shawfield Mansion was separated from the street by a high stone parapet with iron railings on the top. Beyond this stretched wild country and only the occasional cottage or inn like the Black Bull, until the village of Anderson or across to the other side and the village of Gorbals was reached.

Ramsay felt irritated every time he thought of the Shawfield Mansion. It had recently been acquired by John Glassford, a fellow tobacco merchant. Glassford was a reckless extravagant fellow and no good would come of squandering so much money. What was wrong with the tenements? If a tenement was good enough for the Earl and Lady Glencairn and the Earl and Lady of Locheid and the Earl and Lady Glendinny, his other tobacco colleagues, why should it not be good enough for John Glassford?

He was riding high at the moment with his twenty-five ships and his shares in about as many companies, but the man was a gambler and a sinner and would come to a bad end.

Trongate Street was dark now, but the watery glimmerings of day had begun to etch against the black cloth of the sky the huddle of houses that was Glasgow.

Ramsay swung away from the window and peered from under bushy brows at the figure of his son who was still dressing. Douglas's long lean figure melted and swayed and wibble-wobbled in the light of the candles.

'Are you no' ready for the reading yet?' Ramsay flung his arms behind his buttocks and slapped the palm of one hand down on the palm of the other. 'You're worse than your sister. Vanity. Vanity.'

Douglas gave his red shoes with their outsize silver buckles a final pat of pleasure before straightening up.

'Will you be going for the mail, Papa, or shall I?'

'You ken fine I like to collect my ain mail.'

'Ah, well, I'll just slip into my dressing-gown until after breakfast. To save you waiting any longer,' he added hastily.

'It's wicked to have candles burning in every room. Do you think I'm made of money?'

Douglas tidied his eyebrows with a wet pinky. Then he flipped the pigtail of his wig outside the collar of his damask dressing-gown and plucked at the cuffs of his shirt until they frilled out of each sleeve before bowing and making a sweeping gesture towards the door.

'After you, Papa.'

Ramsay's head, enormous with long curly black wig and three-cornered hat, thrust forward as he walked and he continued to thump his hands behind his back.

A candle guttering in the lobby panicked into life as he swept past and into his daughter's bedroom.

Annabella was in a state of undress, having no hoops under her gown and no wig covering her hair. Not even padded, it smoothed close to her face, then back over her shoulders in ringlet curls. Beside Annabella's perky blonde head was the lowered one of Nancy the maid.

Ramsay called: 'Where's Big John?'

'Comin' comin', maister.' Big John Binney came lumbering noisily, cheerfully, into the room and stood with his head screwed as low as possible into his shoulders so that he would not bump it against the ceiling.

'And Jessie?' Ramsay lifted a candlestick from the table and held it up.

'Right in front of your eyes, Merchant.' The washerwoman's crutch thumped and scraped nearer.

'Stand still and listen to the word o' the Lord. Job, chapter 14.' He replaced the candle and settled himself at Annabella's table with the Bible open in front of him.

' "Man that is born of woman is of few days, and full of trouble . . ." ' Trouble indeed, he thought gloomily, with the Pretender and his rebel army poised outside the town and the Glasgow Volunteer Regiment away helping the redcoats to defend Edinburgh. Glasgow had no walls, no arms, no army, nothing to protect it. If the Highlanders did not murder them all in their beds, they would rob and plunder the town. One way or another they surely meant ruination.

' "For now Thou rememberest my steps; dost Thou not watch over my sin?" . . .' He wondered if this present trouble was being heaped upon his head as a punishment for his sins. As if he had not enough reminders. His eyes skulked round the room. The washerwoman's pocked face hung low with shadows and the faint beginnings of light from the window silvered her tangle of hair. She could only be about thirty-four but she looked seventy. She had been eleven years of age when her mother was burned and he had been twenty. He remembered his twentieth year very well. That was when the devil had come and taken away his sister Prissie.

Prissie had the same round perky face as Annabella, the same blue eyes, the same mischievous love of practical jokes, the same fiendish temper. His eyes closed.

'O Lord,' he prayed, 'let it be fatherly chastisement flowing from fatherly Mercy and Grace. Grant, O Lord, for the Redeemer's sake that these afflictions both spiritual and temporal with which Thou are visiting me, may, by Thy Blessing, be the means of strength and grace. May they purge me of all corruption and make the consolations of the Gospel more precious. May they wean my heart from a present world. May they produce in me the peaceable fruits of righteousness to the Praise of the Glory of Thy Grace.'

The six o'clock gun exploded his thoughts. The post-horse had arrived from Edinburgh. He forced himself to finish the reading in the same solemn measured tone as he had begun: ' "But his flesh upon him shall have pain, and his soul within him shall mourn." '

'I'm away for the mail, Annabella. See that my breakfast's on the table before I come back.'

'Yes, Papa.' She flounced round on Nancy. 'Well, away you go and get it ready. Don't just stand there.'

Nancy was absently playing with a lock of her hair, twisting it round and round her finger. She slid Annabella a look from under a raised brow before slowly sauntering from the room. Big John followed her with guffaws of laughter and lustful eyes for the sway of her hips and the flash of white ankle and foot.

Ramsay's jaw muscle jammed forward. He would have to lecture these two in the ways of righteousness. A terrible responsibility had weighed on his shoulders since his wife's death. There was no use trusting the moral or spiritual welfare of the servants to either Annabella or Douglas. Annabella needed the most careful watching herself and Douglas was too busy trying to be a fashionable fop, and wooing Griselle Halyburton.

He swung on his cloak and strode from the house. The landing and the spiral stair in the round tower attached to the back of the building was dark and crammed with sleeping people, tramps and beggars and orphan children. He kicked them aside to make a passage for himself.

'Out o' the way, you lazy devils!'

The air outside frosted his skin and breath. Quickening his pace, he bumped into another hurrying figure.

'Och, it's you, Provost.'

'A good morning to you, Ramsay.'

Andrew Cochrane smoothed his cloak closer as if he was

11

comforting himself. 'My mind's not on where I'm going.'

Ramsay measured his step to that of the Provost.

'No better news then?'

'They keep telling me that troops are coming but they've not come yet. And as I said in my letter to the Lord Justice Clerk— we in Glasgow can expect no favour from the rebels.'

'If they'd even let us have our own men. It's a disgrace. This town has always been the most loyal in Scotland.'

'Most loyal,' the Provost agreed. 'Quick to raise two volunteer regiments the last time and as quick again.'

'And this is what we get in return.'

'They just refused to believe me. I've read Mr Crosse's letters over and over again until I've got them off by heart. "I received your Lordship's communication", he wrote, "and I cannot imagine that the Highlanders can be so far advanced as Carlisle on Tuesday last." And as usual he gave me the same assurances: "You may depend on it that the protection of the town will be first looked", and "You may be sure that everything will be done toward the preservation of the town", and "Lord Glencairn will be with you tomorrow!" '

'Aye, and now where is he, and Lord Home, and General Blakeney and all their battalions? A damned disgrace, Provost.'

Cochrane's skin was as fair and as delicate as a woman's and he had fine dark eyes, but now his face was grey and his eyes looked haunted.

'Ramsay, I still can't get over it. After all their promises—to announce they were going to march to Edinburgh! "We heartily compassionate your case," they said, "but cannot make it better and therefore we commit you to the protection of God Almighty." '

'Commit us into the hands of Highland savages. That's the damned truth of it,' Ramsay grunted, 'and may the Lord God have mercy on us all.'

'Fresh herrings at the Broomielaw!' Moothy McMurdo roared with all his might to make himself heard above the noise of the bell he was energetically thrashing about.

12

'The bonniest fish you ever saw.
Fresh herrings at the Broomielaw!'

His head well back and his hat jammed down, he surrendered himself completely to his job.

'Thomasina Galbreath
Makes dead clothes
And everybody knows
She's the town's best mantua-maker.
Thomasina Galbreath wants me to say
This verra day
She's got an ell of new satin
Tae make dress and pattern
For anyone willing to pay.'

Jessie stopped for a minute to rest on her crutch and listen to the bellman. Despite the crisp air, that made clouds of each breath, she was hot and sweating. It took a desperate energy and concentration to do her job, hindered as she was by the lack of most of one leg and her dependence on a crutch for balance. But she managed to hump the washing down to the river in a sack slung over her shoulder. Then instead of hitching up her skirts and tramping on the washing as the other women did, she crawled around rubbing and scrubbing and squeezing at it before spreading it out on the grass to bleach and dry. Only it never dried so easily and quickly in the winter.

Then, of course, there was not just the Ramsays' washing to fight with. She worked for the Halyburtons as well. She was on her way there now along Trongate Street to the tenement in which they lived across the other side from the Ramsays, near the Guard House and opposite the Tron Church.

The musical bells of the Tron burst into lively competition with the bellman and heralded 11.30 and time for the merchants and tradesmen to adjourn to their favourite taverns for their 'meridian' of ale or brandy. They began pouring into the street, the tobacco lords swaggering along in their large wigs and three-cornered hats and satin and velvet knee-breeches and coats and silk stockings and shoes decorated with glittering stones. The tradesmen all kept at a respectful distance in their short cloth coats and blue bonnets or tam-o'-shanters.

In the middle of the street a fat woman in a filthy cloak and mutch crushed past Jessie singing lustily.

'Fine Lunnon candy! Good for the cough and the cold and the shortness of breath—come, buy my Lunnon candy!'

Ignoring her, Jessie hurried towards Locheid's Land, the tenement building owned by the Earl of Locheid where the Halyburtons lived. They had a bigger household than the Ramsays and Mrs Halyburton was a bit of a targe.

Glasgow Green was not good enough for her washing. It had to be taken all the way to Woodside Fields and the burn outside the city where she insisted both water and air was sweeter and cleaner.

The tobacco lords were pacing the plainstanes, the only piece of pavement in the whole of Glasgow. Flagstones were laid along the front of the Town Hall, the Tolbooth and the Exchange Coffee House next to it and no one except the Lords of the Plainstanes dared put a foot on them.

Jessie spied young Douglas Ramsay greeting another young tobacco lord with kisses on both cheeks. The other scarlet-cloaked, silver-wigged gentlemen were greeting each other with bows and kisses too. Only Douglas's father did not seem to enjoy the custom. Each time he received a kiss he irritably swiped at his face with cuff or handkerchief.

The sight of Adam Ramsay never failed to disturb Jessie. One minute she could be hustling about her business. The next minute she was thinking about how she was going to get all the washing attended to before it was dark, or planning to make sure she would be home in time for wee Gav and Regina. Then she would look at Adam Ramsay and something about him would scatter her wits. Secret doors in her mind creaked open. Weird shapes danced out. She twittered hysterically at them, wild for them to go away. Then only a desperate burst of energy would chase them back behind their secret door again. She would hop madly about laughing and shouting and swearing or she would rub and scrub at the washing until it tore to shreds in her hands.

But now she hurried safely past with only a sideways

malevolent glance in Ramsay's direction.

She climbed the narrow turnpike stair at Locheid's Land with difficulty. The crutch jabbed deep into her at every hop and step. The Halyburtons had a four-roomed and kitchen flat above the warehouses where they stored their tobacco. The young maid Nell opened the door, but showed no interest in helping to shift the mountain of washing into Jessie's sack.

Out again, breathless and with Mrs Halyburton's warning ringing in her ears: 'Now make sure you take good care of my precious linen, Jessie, or I'll get Hangy Spittal to lock you away in the Tolbooth.'

Hopping and skipping and tittering and cursing, the stone-heavy sack thumping her shoulders, Jessie left Trongate Street, passed the Shawfield Mansion and made for the wooded place outside the town.

Chapter 2

Gav and Regina stretched up on the balls of their feet, their bare toes digging into the icy earth. They peered close to the window, every now and again rubbing at the glass so that they could see what was going on inside the room. Jock Currie's dead body lay in his coffin in the centre and on seats around the walls some of his friends who had been watching the body all night sat silently drinking.

Gav and Regina should have been at school, but the dominie had been called away and they had been sent home for a few hours. Nothing would induce them, however, to return to the notorious Tannery Wynd until they were certain that their mother would be home from work and at the house to see them safely in. Their mother was employed as washerwoman by two of the tobacco families in the town, and no doubt these same families would be here at the funeral service because Jock Currie had also been a tobacco merchant.

It was then that Regina caught sight of Mistress Annabella, daughter of one of the families her mother worked for.

'Gav, look! Isn't she beautiful?'

Both children gazed in awe at the young woman who flounced from a sedan-chair outside the house and posed, straight-backed, chin held high and fan flicking, while a maid arranged the skirts of her wide hooped dress. The gown glowed like an orange sun but could not compete in radiance and vivacity with the face above it. An air of expectancy sizzled around the woman and Regina felt that just by looking at her life had become more exciting.

But Gav's attention had returned to the inside of the house.

The room looked warm and a table near the window was crowded with bottles of port wine and sherry wine and whisky and bread and cheese and cake. Gav's mouth watered and he felt so hungry he could not bear to look. Turning away, he shivered

16

and stuffed his hands in the pockets of his jacket. His mother had bought the jacket from a rag woman and it was several sizes too big. His hat had originated from the same source. It had once belonged to a farmworker and was the colour of a newly ploughed field. The bashed crown and wavy brim were man-sized and dwarfed Gav's face. The hat would in fact have fallen down and completely covered his features had it not been held up by his hair, which was thicker and curlier than most cauliflower wigs.

'Come on, Regina,' he said.

'You know we can't go home before Mammy. Do you want the harlots or Blind Jinky to get us?'

'Not home. Back to school.'

'We won't be able to get back in yet. Anyway, I want to stay and see all the lovely clothes. Look, there's more people coming.'

Gav scowled. It was not so much that he wasn't interested in the fineries of the funeral guests but that he secretly feared the tobacco merchants, with their lordly ways and their gold-topped canes which didn't hesitate to smash you out of their way if you dared set foot too near them. Many a painful blow had he received from old Jock Currie when he had been alive and strutting along this very street with his scarlet cape billowing out behind him.

Now Jock Currie was dead and the funeral guests arriving at his house in Saltmarket Street were being received in absolute silence. Eventually the minister said Grace, then a series of services began, services of food and drink, mainly drink. The first service consisted of bread and cheese with ale and porter. Next came a glass of rum with 'burial bread'. Pipes of tobacco were passed round as the third service. The fourth was a glass of port wine with cake, next a glass of sherry with cake, and a glass of whisky. The seventh service was a glass of whisky. Then when another guest arrived another Grace was said and the services started all over again. The deceased had been one of the first men to trade in tobacco after the Union of Scotland with England in 1707. Before that, English laws had prohibited Scotland from trading with the Colonies. The powerful tobacco merchants of England had cause to bitterly regret Glasgow's

17

freedom to trade as their competitors. No one had dreamed that a small and remote town in Scotland would within two generations completely capture more than half the tobacco trade in Europe. They had wrenched it from the powerful rivalry of London, Bristol and Liverpool merchants in whose hands it had been for over a century. It was a tremendous achievement and had launched Glasgow as a merchant city with fast-growing trade and industries. To transport the tobacco Glasgow began building ships. Then, rather than see the ships sail empty to Virginia, Glasgow manufactured goods and filled the holds with every kind of article the colonists needed. They became linen manufacturers. They had manufactories of woollen cloth, stockings, shalloons and cottons. They started sugar houses and distilleries. They made nails and spades, earthenware and shoes and boots and saddles and an ever-growing number and variety of other products. The goods were bartered for tobacco and the merchants dealt with the planters direct, they or their agents sailing up the rivers to the plantation landings and exchanging the goods for tobacco on the spot.

Now many of them had started their own stores in Virginia where the planter could get credit and make his payments in the form of tobacco. The tobacco barons had always been astute. No payment was made to the manufacturer or shopkeeper in Glasgow until the ships safely returned with their valuable load of tobacco, most of which was destined to be shipped off to France and other parts of Europe.

There had been none more astute than old Jock Currie, and his colleagues had turned out in force to pay their last respects to him. Some of their wives and families had come too. They filled the musty, seldom-used dining-room to capacity. The hooped skirts of the ladies vied with each other in width. Some women had skirts the width of the room and their padded hair touched the ceiling. Not an inch of floor space was visible. The room was a rustling satin sea that began to sway and undulate alarmingly as the services of wine and whisky were repeated again and again.

'Where's the body gone?' Regina said. 'I can't see it any more.'

Gav shrugged. 'Probably they're tramping on it. I don't care.'

Somewhere in the midst of the sea stretched the body of old Jock Currie, no longer watched, but jostled and jerked and squeezed with complete disregard. By the time the funeral procession was due to start the company was in spate with chatter and gusty with hilarity. A riot of noise exploded from the tenement building with the beadle leading the way cheerily ringing the 'dead bell'. Regina and Gav followed, skipping along as best they could.

The graveyard was up at the top of the High Street beside the Cathedral and the mourners ambled along Saltmarket Street, past the Cross and up High Street under the terrible stress of concentrating on keeping their balance.

Some of the ladies were nearly lost to the procession when they swayed left at the Cross and along Trongate Street. They were rescued and pointed in the proper direction and duly rewarded their rescuers with deep tottering curtsies and eyes ogling over fans.

At times gentlemen bumped into one another, bowed in formal and graceful apology, only to have their cocked hats fall off. Then heads clashed and bodies bounced about in efforts to retrieve the hats. People jostled and fell one against the other like packs of cards. Eventually the graveside was reached. Profuse apologies were made to the grave-digger, who had been hanging around in the cold, purple beak dripping icy water down to sour blue lips as he leaned in readiness over the shovel beside the waiting grave.

'About time tae. I'm fair nippit! Where's auld Jock?'

'In his coffin to be sure,' answered MacFuddy, the chief mourner. 'Now get him into the earth as fast as you can.'

'Where's the coffin?'

The mourners gazed around and staggered about in search of the deceased, but no coffin could be seen.

'Damnation!' roared MacFuddy at last. 'The old devil's still back at the hoose!'

The grave-digger laid down his spade.

'Is this no' hellish!'

'Now, now, ma man,' the beadle hiccoughed. 'We'll have

none o' your foul language on this sacred occasion. We'll no' be long in hashin' back for auld Jock.'

Giggling now, Regina and Gav ran after the company as it tottered back down the High Street. Hoops bounced from side to side, showing flashes of yellow or white silk stocking and high-heeled shoes with pointed turned-up toes. Men's cloaks puffed out and wigs went askew to reveal bald heads.

Once in the house again, it was obviously felt that a few more services could be only right and proper. This routine being accomplished, the ladies sank gratefully on to the floor and the procession, now just a vague crush of men, returned with Jock Currie to the graveside and thankfully dropped him in. Then they came back to Jock's house for shortbread and whisky and much talk and hilarity.

By this time Regina and Gav were too exhausted to care what the guests were doing any more. When William Halyburton at last sailed towards Trongate Street accompanied by his fellow Virginia Merchant Adam Ramsay, the two children were huddled in the back close just concentrating on trying to keep warm. Halyburton and Ramsay had been suitably drunk in order to show their respect for their deceased friend, but now the effects were fast wearing off and they were able to journey home without too much difficulty.

'You know, Ramsay,' Halyburton boomed out, 'Jock Currie would see the funny side of that.'

Ramsay pulled at his nose.

'Aye. I can just hear him from the other side. "Well, it didn't take you rascals long to forget me!" '

Halyburton's laugh rumbled up from a mountainous body.

'Poor auld Jock!'

'Nothing poor about him. It's a blessing the Lord gathered him. He's well out of it.'

'True. There'll be no Highlanders up in heaven to bother him.'

'I wish we could be sure of that, Willie. But God is the Great Forgiver. Maybe he'll think a few of them have said their prayers well enough.'

'Fiddlesticks! Not even the Lord God could understand their

Gaelic jabber!' He gave his cauliflower wig a chug to straighten it. 'Would you no' like to come along and take pot-luck with me and my family?'

He turned and made a signal to a bevy of ladies following at some distance behind.

'Come away, come away. Put a jerk on there!'

Turning back, he addressed Ramsay again. 'It's my lassies I'm worried about.'

Ramsay thumped his Malacca cane on the ground as he strode along.

'I've had much soul-searching these past weeks about why I didn't join the Volunteers.'

'Damn it, man. Where would you be now if you had? In bloody Edinburgh.'

'Aye,' Ramsay agreed. 'Better to be in Glasgow.'

'Any time, Ramsay. Any time.'

'Somebody's got to keep the wheels turning.'

'The Provost's done his best. We've all done our best. It was us that drummed up two battalions, six hundred men in each, remember.'

'Aye. The Pretender and his rebels are going to love us for that.' Ramsay's mouth twisted. 'Glasgow's always been his verra favourite place. Especially after us being just as quick to do the same to his father.'

'And were we no' right?'

'Of course. Of course. What I'm angry at is the way the English have handled the whole campaign and how they've rewarded our loyalty.' He spat to one side.

'My God, Willie, the rebels marched a hundred and fifty miles into hostile territory in terrible weather and in the face of two armies capable of annihilating them. But they've no' been annihilated, have they? Even yet the Highlanders keep turning and beating them. Out of five thousand I hear they've only lost forty men and that's with sickness and everything else included. The trouble is the English are too afraid of them.'

'Weel, weel, Ramsay, they're a fearsome sight for somebody who has never clapped eyes on them before. It's a wee bit different for us having had a few come doon to Glasgow every year as cattle drovers. We've seen a few of them at the markets.'

'Aye.' Ramsay nodded and slid his friend a sarcastic look. 'We've seen a few of them.'

Nancy the maid kicked open Annabella Ramsay's door to reveal Annabella in nothing but red silk stockings and silver garters from which dangled purple tassels. Beside her was a young man busily unbuttoning his breeches.

Leaning her back against the door lintel, hands on hips, Nancy surveyed the scene.

If she had been caught having a naked frolic with a man she would be whipped through the town or, at best, pilloried at the church and made to stand Sunday after Sunday in a sackcloth gown with a card proclaiming her sin hanging round her neck.

Life was so damned unfair. Why should she be kicked about and have nothing to look forward to in life but washing floors and emptying chamber-pots and dancing attendance to a spoiled mistress like Annabella? She was as clever as her and as beautiful. Indeed, if she could dress in flattering gowns like Annabella she would look even more striking than her. Despite the shabby petticoats, many a gentleman's attention had already strayed in her direction and more than once a pretty compliment had been paid to her black hair, her violet eyes and her shapely figure. She was taller than Annabella and more voluptuous.

Staring derisively at Annabella's apple buttocks and breasts, she said:

'He's coming.'

Annabella squealed.

'It can't be Papa. He said he was going to the tavern after the funeral. He's always there for hours.'

'Expecting somebody else?'

'You impudent wretch.' Annabella stamped her foot, making the tassels dance a jig. 'Don't just stand there. Help me to dress.' She flapped her hands at the young man. 'Away with you. Away with you!'

But already he was hopping out, tugging on his shoes with one hand and striving to plunge the other into his coat sleeve.

Nancy scooped up the low-bodied petticoat and Annabella

clung round her neck to balance herself as she hopped into it.

'Losh sake,' she wailed.

'Hold still till I fasten it.'

'Hell and damnation.'

'Now the hoops.'

'They'll bump into one another on the stairs.'

'I warned you, mistress. Come on, here's the skirt.'

'Damnation! It's monstrous of Papa to come so soon. Was ever a poor female in a more distressed situation?'

'He'll nab you yet. Take a grip of your fan.'

The outside door banged and Ramsay's heavy tread approached the bedroom.

'Young Robin Bicker's just hared past me on the stairs.'

Annabella worked hard at her fan to cool her crimson perspiring face while at the same time attempting to appear wide-eyed and innocent.

'Annabella, has he been here?'

'Yes Papa. Looking for our Douglas. I told him if he found Griselle Halyburton that's where he'd find my brother, silly lovesick fool that he is.'

Ramsay studied her thoughtfully.

'Willie Halyburton has invited us to supper.' He jerked a thumb towards the wig perched on its stand in the corner. 'Get your head on.'

'Och, papa, can I not go the way I am. Is my own yellow hair not devilishly bonny?' She tossed her head, making her long curls fly out and over her shoulders.

'Enough of that. You're about as vain as your brother and fine you know Mrs Halyburton's a stickler for the proprieties.'

'To hell with Mrs Halyburton and the proprieties.'

'Watch your wicked tongue. You're needing a good bleeding, my girl. Or a Sunday on the cutty stool. Have you been learning your Catechisms like I told you?'

'Yes, Papa.'

'What is the Chief End of Man?'

'Man's Chief End is to glorify God and to enjoy Him for ever, Papa.'

'What rule hath God given to direct us how we may glorify

23

and enjoy Him?'

'The word of God which is contained in the Scriptures of the Old and New Testaments is the only rule to direct us how we may glorify and enjoy Him, Papa.'

'Aye, well . . .' Ramsay said. 'Just you keep that in mind. Now do as you're bid or you'll stop here until bedtime copying out every testament in the Bible.'

Annabella flounced round, her skirt seesawing. She hated wearing a wig. It was a fiendish nuisance. After a while it felt like an iron pot full of boiling water on her head. It inhibited movement too. Having her own hair built up was not quite so irksome. And she had such pretty hair. Once it was brushed up all round and secured firmly over some padding it looked more attractive than any wig, especially when it was decorated with bunches of curls on top and strings of beads.

Her father said, 'I'll tell Big John to get the lanthorns ready.'

'Am I not to have a sedan-chair, Papa?'

'It's a fine dry night.'

'But the streets are filthy. My shoes and skirts will be ruined.

'Wear your pattens to keep you up off the ground then. I'm not wasting money on a sedan-chair on a night like this when we're just going along the road for a bite of supper.'

Annabella pouted. It would be no thanks to her father if she captured a husband. Men were afraid that her father was too mean to supply a decent dowry. She hated his dour face, his melancholy prayers and his boring Bible readings. She longed to be away in a house of her own with a man of her own; a gay dashing devilish rake of a man.

With a sigh she crumpled on to a chair and allowed Nancy to fit the wig on. There was not much chance of such a man being at the Halyburtons'. Mrs Halyburton's son Andrew was fat and short-sighted and always had an itch or a cough or a snuffly cold, or all three. She wished the soldiers would hurry back to town. It was deadly dull without them. She felt unbearably restless. Unsatisfied emotions careered wildly about inside her.

'Losh sake, Nancy. You're so slow I could scream. That'll do. Give me my cloak.'

Ignoring Annabella's command, Nancy took her time finishing

24

arranging some curls on the wig. Often she took a perverse pleasure in being awkward and causing irritation to Annabella. To be excruciatingly slow and subtly impertinent gave her a strange sense of power over the other woman.

'What's all your rush?'

Suddenly Annabella giggled.

'I've a secret assignment with Willie Halyburton. After supper we're going to steal through to the kitchen and fornicate in front of the fire.'

'You're fit for it.'

Annabella's giggles whooped into laughter. 'Aye, but Willie Halyburton's not. Although no doubt he'd like to. I can't imagine him getting much joy from his cold fish of a wife.'

Her spirits never sagged for long and with energetic bouncy step, despite the weight and height of her wig, she joined her father and they followed Nancy and Big John from the house. The servants each held a horn lamp in front of them. The lanterns were lit by smoky tallow candles and their flickering light sent shadows leaping like giants in the stair. Once out on Saltmarket Street Annabella picked her way with more care. The iron-ringed and wooden-soled pattens that protected her dainty green shoes crunched and clanged into lumps of frozen earth and dung. They turned into Trongate Street and crossed to the opposite side so that they could walk more easily along the plainstanes. But once past the Tolbooth and the Exchange their feet wobbled once again over dirt and around dunghills. Annabella screwed up her nose and agitated her fan. Obviously Stinky Rab, who was supposed to clean the streets every night, had, as usual, not done a very good job.

'These streets are a disgrace,' she called out as loudly as she could, knowing it would annoy Nancy, who was ashamed of Stinky Rab and her other brother, Daft Jamie. Daft Jamie always followed Stinky Rab's cart and foraged amongst the rubbish and ate cockroaches and beetles.

'I'm sure they haven't been cleaned for a week. Some people are just too lazy and stupid to do a job properly.'

Ramsay glowered round at her. 'Hold your tongue.'

'But it's true, isn't it, Papa?'

'I'm not deaf. Enough of your ranting and raving. Try to act like a lady for once.'

She longed to smite him with one furious blow, but knew better than to try it. Once she had struck him in a temper and had the blow immediately returned and with such force it had felled her to the ground and knocked her wig off. Afterwards she had been imprisoned with him in her room, forced to kneel with him in solemn prayer. 'Forgive us our wicked passions, Lord God Almighty, chastise us, stay our hand . . .' The praying had gone on for hours and had been worse than anything else.

She relieved her feelings by throwing her fan at Nancy and rejoiced that it clipped her on the back of the head. Big John, grinning through the darkness, picked it up and gave it back to her. Nancy never even flinched or turned round and Annabella hated her. Often she suspected that if Ramsay had any feelings for anyone they were for Nancy rather than his own flesh and blood.

The lanterns intensified the gloom rather than relieved it. Glasgow was devilish black but not silent. From deep in tenement buildings came muffled sounds of revelry; faint screeches of laughter, sudden swells of busy talk, scraping of fiddles and rhythmic thumping of feet. The great bell in the college tower donged to mark nine o'clock and the end of the students' day.

Annabella wondered about all the life and merriment going on behind the muffling wall of darkness. She longed to be part of it. Sometimes she felt she would die of the restrictions of mind and body her father subjected her to. As far as her father was concerned her only recreation ought to be the earnest studying of the Bible. He had read to her from that book so often she was sure that one day she would have the whole thing off by heart. If they weren't reading the Bible they were praying, and, oh, what long and melancholy prayers they were. Surely God must be bored to distraction by now. She certainly was.

The Halyburtons lived above their warerooms and entry had to be made through an archway, alongside one of the warerooms and into a close at the back. The close led to a turnpike stairway hardly wide enough to take Big John's shoulders.

26

'Make way for my lady and gentleman!' he called to the tightly packed human debris on the stairs. It shrank back and snaked upwards into the shadows in front of him.

Annabella held her nose with one dainty hand and manoeuvred her hoops sideways with the other until she reached the first landing and Willie Halyburton's door. It was opened by their young maid Nell whose pale face and hazel eyes looked sly in the shifting light. Their old maid Kate, who was jealous of Nell, came bustling from behind her, piercing the darkness with her shrill voice.

'Come awa' in. Come awa' in.' Then, with a punch at Nell, 'Do ye no' even ken how to make folk welcome?'

Annabella swept past Kate with much swishing and rustling of satin. She could never understand how Mrs Halyburton could thole having such an ugly old crone in the house. Kate was a hunchback with bald patches in her hair and eyes that were nasty slits in layers of tough leathery wrinkles and a nose that was huge with a black wart on the tip.

The Halyburtons had a dining-room but this was never aired and seldom used except if extra special company were coming from a distance. Normally they just entertained in the bedroom like everybody else.

Annabella envied Mrs Halyburton's bedroom. It had a four-poster bed with orange and gold damask curtains and the walls and the ceilings had remnants of old paintings and designs on them. By the light of the candelabra on the table she could discern rich shades of blue and green and purple and yellow and red-brown.

Mrs Letitia Halyburton came forward to greet them with rigidly straight back and hands clasped primly beneath a long bosom. 'Aye,' she said with a nod, 'Mr Ramsay. Mistress Annabella.'

Annabella flounced down in as low a curtsy as her wig permitted with much fluttering and swooping of arms and fan. 'Madam.'

Despite the enthusiastic curtsy, or perhaps because of it, Mrs Halyburton pressed her lips tightly together in disapproval. Devil take her, Annabella thought, and turned her attention to

27

the other occupants of the room. There were no young men, she noticed with acute disappointment, except her own brother Douglas and the Halyburtons' son Andrew. Fat, short-sighted, messy Andrew; scratchy, eye-blinking, breathless little bore. She swept towards him with head in the air and arm outstretched. His white cauliflower wig bent low over her hand as he kissed it, his spectacles clinging to the tip of his nose.

'A terrible time we're having, Annabella, eh? A terrible time.'

'Indeed we are, Andrew,' she agreed, not having the slightest idea of what he was talking about. He was always grumbling and wheezing on about something.

He scratched his head, his cheek, his neck.

'Would you take a pinch of snuff with me?'

'That would be a prodigious pleasure.' She frisked her weight from one foot to the other and stretched out her arm again. While Andrew searched for his snuffbox she admired her fine creamy skin and the silver lace drifting down from her elbows and her neat wrist with its silver bangles. All wasted on fat fumbling Andrew, who was hopelessly in love with Sukie, the daughter of the Earl of Locheid who lived upstairs. At last he found the snuffbox and managed to convey a pinch from it on to the back of her hand and then a pinch on to his own.

'Losh, Andrew, that's a handsome snuffbox you've got there.'

He indulged in a rapid scratch behind his ear.

'I had it made special and I was thinking of getting Lady Sukie one made the very same.'

'She'll be uncommonly pleased. I'm sure.'

With graceful sweeping gestures they both swung their arms inwards, sniffed daintily from the backs of their hands, then snuffed and heaved and jerked and sneezed in wild abandon.

Annabella dabbed at her face with a lace-edged handkerchief.

'And where is Sukie tonight, Andrew?' But before he could answer, old Kate the maid screeched from the doorway:

'The supper's on the table. Will ye a' sit doon and no' waste it? I canna stand guid food being wasted.'

The old manservant, Tam Bogle, pushed past her.

'Away to your place in the kitchen, woman. You ken fine it's

28

my job to see to the table.' Then, turning his attention to the company: 'Weel, ye heard what she said. Sit doon!'

The table was resplendent with, on one side, a haunch of venison and a baked pudding, in the middle, partridges and larks, and along the other side veal collops.

Mrs Halyburton issued sharp orders.

'Mistress Annabella—you here beside Andrew. Mr Ramsay over there between Mistress Griselle and Mistress Phemy.' She flicked an impatient fan at her two daughters and they hurried to take their chairs. Then she nodded towards her husband. 'The gudeman at the top of the table.' Another flick alerted Douglas. 'You at Mistress Griselle's other side.' Gratefully he obeyed. 'And you, Glendinny,' she favoured the Earl with a small smile, 'beside me, sir. And your gudewife at my other side.'

Lady Glendinny was a skinny waxy woman like a long candle that was slowly melting down.

'My faither used to say about our auld maid, "For the first ten years she was an excellent servant. For the next ten years she was a good mistress but the third ten years she was a perfect tyrant." '

Old Tam, who was pouring wine into her glass, laughed heartily and nodded.

'Verra good, ma'am. Verra good.'

Mrs Halyburton rapped him on the arm with her fan.

'Watch and no' spill the wine.'

'Have I ever skailt the wine before?'

'Are they no' a worry, Murn?' Ignoring him, Mrs Halyburton addressed Lady Glendinny, who sighed deeply in agreement.

'Aye. Aye.'

'I've warned Jessie Chisholm—you know, the washer-woman—"The next time you take my washing to The Woodside," I told her, "you hurry straight back here—never mind hirpling away to your own place." She's always in far too big a hurry to go home, that one. But, I'll stop her yet.'

Chapter 3

'Hur skelpt about, hur leapt about,
And flang amang them a', man,
The English blades got broken heads,
Their crowns were cleaved in twa then.'

Jessie's song kept time to the thump and heave of her crutch. Exhilaration lightened the load of herself. The washing had been cleaned in the sparkling water and first a wintry sun had bleached it and then a gusty wind had made a surprisingly good job of drying it. All she needed to do now was to scoop up the linen that was whitening on the grass like patches of snow and stuff it into her sack. There was no need to worry. She would be in time for Gav and Regina. Despite her grumbles about coming to Woodside, she enjoyed being alone in its peacefulness with only the whispering of the water and the lonely soughing of the wind.

But dusk was creeping down and she would have to leave. Better to be early than late for the children. Yet it was because of them that she hesitated.

There might be some nuts left in the woods. They seldom had the chance to taste anything except oatmeal in one form or another. A few nuts would be a real treat. For a minute, leaning on her crutch, she gazed uncertainly into the trees and bushes. She was nervous in case brownies or fairies or wood-kelpies might be lurking. Still, she was ready to brave anything for the sake of the pleasure on her children's faces and making up her mind she plunged forward. It was past the nutting season and she could find very few and she had just decided to abandon her search when she spied a hazel shrub with some clusters of nuts on it. It was deep in a thicket but she struggled towards it. Then suddenly the world split open, sucked her down, whirled her round and spat her out. She landed with a bump that jarred every bone in her body and every tooth in her head. Then she

30

floated through a long empty tunnel of time before gradually gathering her wits together and getting her bearings.

On peering round, she discovered she was squatting at the foot of an old pit. It obviously had not been worked for several years and its subterranean passages were choked. Far above her head the bushes through which she had fallen had tangled together again, making a closely knit roof. The pit was about five feet in diameter and at the bottom of it all around and over her crawled great quantities of reptiles, frogs, toads, large black snails, slugs and beetles. Wild-eyed, she jerked back, flurrying at them with hand and crutch.

Then suddenly a much greater horror felled her. She saw a vision of wee Gav and Regina racing along Tannery Wynd, reaching the house and finding the door locked and no one to admit them to safety.

She clawed at the earth walls with her crutch in a fight to get up and once up she sent shouts for help spiralling towards the roof. Then she listened. There were no answering voices. Nothing but the hollow measure of water dripping, and the swishing, hissing and scuttling at her feet. She strained louder cries from a dry sandpaper throat until her voice, despite her tenacity of purpose, rasped hoarsely down to a whisper. Panic flurried through her mind, opening and shutting doors.

She was a wee girl, alone in Glasgow. Everywhere there were enemies. She remembered the faces of the people who had watched her mother die in agony. Big-eyed, eager faces, faces enjoying a day's entertainment at the Fair; solemn sanctimonious faces, gloating faces.

She saw Adam Ramsay and his sister Prissie. They had been there.

Half laughing, half weeping, Jessie gave a hop and a skip. And another and another. Round and round she went, but could find no solace, no escape.

They were coming at her with the boot. They were holding her. She saw the hangman.

'Jessie! Jessie!' her mother called out.

Her mother always kept the cottage clean and neat. There was always a fire in the hearth. Her mother sat peacefully at the window with the Bible on her knee. She wore a white apron and a white mutch. Tiny round spectacles perched comfortably on her nose. Often she gazed out of the window. Then she said calmly but with ill-concealed pleasure, 'Aye, Jessie. Here's the gudeman.' Then she got up and stirred the pot hanging ready over the fire.

The gudeman wore the belted plaid and was big and bearded with rough-gentle hands and voice.

'My bonny Jessie.' Proudly he hoisted her in the air. 'My bonnie wee bird.'

The house was gone. Burnt too. By men with fiery torches. Her mother, hiding among the heather, had wrapped her plaid around them both so that she could not see. But she had smelled the smoke and the burning. She remembered the smell of the burning.

The pit was dark yet not black. Grey ghosts swayed about. Sickly moonbeams seeping through the tangled roof ebbed and flowed. She called again desperately but hopelessly. No one would come through the woods at night. It would be dark in Tannery Wynd. Gav and Regina would think she had deserted them. She skittered and splashed about whimpering to herself between curses. Regina would panic. Gav would struggle to put on an act of bravado. He would try to take charge. But he would not know what to do.

Somewhere, deep in the woods, an owl hooted. Was it the witching hour? Were they creeping out from the shadows to have a coven with the devil by the moon's eerie light? Could she hear them chanting?

> 'In the pingle or the pan,
> Or the haurnpan o'man,
> Boil the heart's blood o'a toad.'

She shrank against the wall, eyes bulging.

> '. . . Hawker kail and hen dirt,
> Chow'd cheese and chicken-wort,
> Yellow puddocks champit sma'
> Spiders ten and gellochs twa . . .'

'Jessie! Jessie!' her mother called out.

> 'Half a puddock, half a toad,
> Half a yellow-yeldrin',
> Gets a drop of the devil's blood,
> Ilka a May morning.'

'As the good Lord's my witness, Jessie, I'm not a witch and never have been!'

Her father had a red beard and long red hair. He wore a blue bonnet that was round and flat like a giant griddle and had the white cockade on top that proudly proclaimed his Jacobite loyalties.

'I am going away to fight for my "King across the water", Jessie. King James, God bless him. You be a good wee lass and help your mother look after the cottage until I get back.'

The cottage was a white bird nestling on the side of a purple mountain. The wind soughed and sighed and moaned around it, like the wind was moaning now.

'The gudeman's no coming home any more, Jessie.' Her mother took her down the mountain, far away, to the city of Glasgow and a cellar room in a tenement building.

> 'There's the tree that never grew,
> There's the bird that never flew,
> There's the bell that never rang,
> There's the fish that never swam.'

Her crutch thumped among the frogs and toads and beetles, swirling them into a crazy dance. She jigged along with them, screeching with laughter.

> 'Prissie Ramsay had a vision,
> Witches she can see
> Not me.
> Not me.
> Prissie Ramsay she accuses,
> Her finger points to whom she chooses,
> Not me.
> Not me.'

Suddenly she stopped. She listened. She thought she heard a snapping of twigs like feet approaching the thicket. But no. It was only the wooden web high above creaking and cracking.

She was alone. Her mother was gone. Someone else lived in the cellar room. She was alone in the streets of Glasgow, not knowing where to find food. Not knowing where to sleep. Not knowing what to do. 'Gavie?' she cried out. 'Regina?'

'Give us a gentleman, Letitia,' William Halyburton called across the table. Dutifully his wife raised her glass.

'The old Earl of Locheid.'

Everyone raised their glasses.

'The old Earl of Locheid.'

Halyburton gestured to the manservant Tam to refill his glass.

'The Lady Locheid.'

Everyone called in unison after him before draining their glasses again, 'The Lady Locheid.'

'Lady Sukie,' Andrew Halyburton burst out excitedly before anyone had time to have their glasses topped up. Everyone laughed while Tam shuffled round the table as fast as he could, muttering:

'Him and his Sukie. And her no' caring a sheep's heid about him.'

'How's your courting doing, Andrew?' Glendinny's blue eyes beamed mildly from over his huge twisted nose. 'Is there no news of you getting wed yet? It's time there was a wedding about the place.'

Andrew scratched at himself in confusion while Tam filled up his glass and repeated, 'No' a sheep's heid!'

'Hold your tongue, man,' Andrew muttered.

'For a' the clamjamphrey you give her.'

'Hold your tongue!'

Annabella glanced roguishly in Glendinny's direction.

'There's quite a bevy of unmarried ladies here, sir. We would deem it a prodigious favour if you'd wish the next wedding on us.'

'Weel, I declare! It's time a sonsy lass like yoursel' was

married, right enough. Ramsay, have ye no' some man in mind for your bonny lassie?'

Griselle and Phemy bent over their glasses but stole looks at each other and giggled. Griselle primly with pursed lips like her mother. Phemy like a beaky little bird. Annabella fluttered her handkerchief and rolled her eyes.

'Losh, Papa's too busy with his money-making Virginia to think of his poor Annabella.'

Ramsay eyed her sternly.

'I agree with Glendinny. It's time you were wed. I've already had a word with the Reverend Blackadder.'

'That's uncommon kind of you, Papa. But I really do feel one ought to have a husband in mind before speaking to the minister.'

'The minister's the husband I have in mind.'

Griselle and Phemy nearly choked with suppressed hilarity. Annabella grabbed her fan and flicked it into rapid motion. She kept her chin tipped high and her back straight.

'Indeed, sir? Well, such a husband has never entered my head.' Pox on them all, she thought, and flung herself wholeheartedly into hiding her extreme agitation.

The Reverend Blackadder was worse than her father. At least Adam Ramsay was a tolerably good-looking man. But the minister, with his long cadaverous face, was like some monster disgorged from the hell he was always roaring on about. 'The everlasting fire is waiting for you. No friends, but furies; no ease, but fetters; no daylight, but darkness; no clock to pass away the time, but endless eternity; fire eternal is always burning and never dying away. That is the horror that is waiting for you.'

It would be hell indeed to be married to such a man. In her mind she suffered the torment of his face pushing nearer and his long skeleton fingers stretching out to fumble with her clothes. Pox on him. She would see him damned in his hell before she would entertain the preposterous idea of such a creature defiling her.

Letitia Halyburton addressed Ramsay: 'You, sir, should have an older woman relation living in your house to chaperon and keep an eye on Mistress Annabella.'

35

'Oh, aye, aye. You've said that before. And I've told you before I've no old female relations.'

'An old servant, then?'

'I've enough servants.'

'A respectable woman?'

'And enough mouths to feed. I'm no' made of money and this is no time to be taking on extra expense.'

Annabella tossed back her head in a gay trill of laughter.

'Madam, a respectable widow might ensnare Papa into marriage and what a to-do that would be.'

'Mistress Annabella!' Letitia's words were icicles cutting across the table. 'You are too perjink and disrespectful. You need someone to discipline you. The minister should do very well!'

'The minister might do better to discipline himself, madam. The monstrous way he rants and roars and splutters and spits in the pulpit—it's a miracle the man does not choke.'

'No, it's no' a time to be taking on any extra expense,' Halyburton boomed out. 'You're right, Ramsay. It's no' a time to be doing anything except wait until we see what this rascal of a Pretender is going to get up to next.'

'He's going to rob us. You can be sure of that, Willie.'

Annabella mimicked wide-eyed distress. She fluttered up her hands.

'Losh and lovenendie! They might even rape the women!'

'Let's hope and pray, Mistress Annabella, that respectable women are always treated with respect. Let's hope, too, that the rebel upstarts will never have the impertinence to put foot in our town.'

'My auld faither,' sighed Lady Glendinny, 'fought them at the '15 rebellion. He said the Highlanders acted like savages. They flung off their clothes and came louping and screeching and waving their swords over their heads. Stark naked they were. The English just turned and fled at the sight of them.'

'That was in battle, Murn,' Letitia corrected primly. 'They're no' likely to come loupin' naked in here.'

'A pity, madam.' Annabella fluttered a mischievous glance around. 'It might have been uncommonly diverting.'

36

Anything would have been better than sitting in such boring company. She longed for the great sights and adventures of far-off places like Edinburgh or even London. But there were no coaches from Glasgow to London and very few from Glasgow to Edinburgh and even that was a long and dangerous undertaking. Before setting off for either city everyone had to make their last wills and testaments and put all their affairs in order, and say earnest prayers for their safe deliverance from the perils of the journey.

But some brave men had made such adventures on horseback. Mr John Glassford, her father's merchant colleague who lived in the elegant Shawfield Mansion, had ridden to London.

He said there were not even any turnpike roads until he and his companion came within one hundred and ten miles of the city. It sounded fearfully exciting because there was only a narrow causeway and sometimes they met a string of pack horses, from thirty to forty in a gang with huge packs on their backs, the leading horse wearing a bell to give warning to travellers coming in an opposite direction. Mr Glassford and his companion did not have space to pass these beasts. They were forced to plunge into the rough pot-holed earth at the side and often found it extremely difficult to get back on to the causeway again. Then there was the danger of highwaymen, masked gentlemen of the road who stole money and jewellery and even kisses from lady travellers.

It was said that Prince Charles and his Highlanders had marched that same incredible journey, to Edinburgh and far beyond it to England and back again. They must surely be magnificently strong and daring men. She frisked out her fan. Hell and damnation, she would rather take a savage Highlander than the Reverend boring Blackadder!

The school was a room in the dominie's cottage at the foot of Stockwell Street and Bridgegate Street. Both streets ran from the river. Stockwell went straight up to Trongate, but Bridgegate or Briggait looped off to join Saltmarket Street. The schoolroom had only one table with two stools and a window so tiny that even when the pupils crowded close against the wall it was difficult to catch enough light to help them puzzle through their Catechism. Most of the time they lay on their bellies on the muddy floor or, taking advantage of the dominie's temporary absence, fought viciously with fists and feet. Often the fights were caused by the other boys tormenting Gav for his Jacobite sympathies. They pulled his curls and called him a traitor because his hair was red like the Highlanders'. He in turn punched their faces and called them Lowland Whig pigs. He had never seen the Highlands, but its wild grandeur had been described often enough by his mother and he felt proud of her origins, proud of his giant grandfather with his bushy red beard, huge double-edged sword and round targe with spike sticking out from its centre.

'A fine figure of a man,' his mother always said. 'One day, Gav, you'll be big and strong and brave like that.'

He was brave now, he kept telling her. He had thrashed every boy in the school and was only bloodied and beaten himself when set upon by all the other boys together. Even then he went down sturdily fighting and he had never been known to cry. Of course he did have a few secret fears, but these he never admitted not even to himself. There was Blind Jinky and Spider and there were the debauched and blaspheming harlots. He never felt happy about seeing the lepers either. The leper hospital was near the village of Gorbals across the other side of the bridge. At certain times the lepers could be seen like grey ghosts in their long hooded cloaks in which their lowered faces and their hands were partly hidden. The noise of the clappers that they were forced by law to carry to give warning of their approach struck terror into Gav's heart.

He heard their mournful repetitive sound now as he made to leave the school, and hesitated in the doorway, fighting to keep a grip of his fast-disappearing courage.

'Gav, take my hand and let's run as quick as we can,' Regina said. 'I'm frightened.'

'Och, I'm not frightened,' Gav scoffed, and instead of accepting the comfort of her proffered hand he stuffed his fists into the pockets of his jacket and swaggered out.

Now, moving away from the light of the dominie's candle, he

was swallowed into the shadows of the houses. High above, the moon slipped slowly in and out of clouds. Blackness stealthily lifted from the city and left a grey shroud drifting across the church steeple, the crow-stepped gables, the thatched roofs. Blackness again, closing smoothly over like a velvet curtain. From the river and the water came the noise of the lepers, the bridge lending it an eerie echo.

'Don't go away without me, Gav.'

'Och, stop your whining. I'm here.'

'We'd better go straight home.'

'I wonder what time it is?'

'I don't know. Where are you, Gav?'

'I'm here.'

'Keep in to the side of the houses in case a horse comes galloping along and knocks you down.'

His heart quailed at the thought of huge horses bursting suddenly from the blackness with wild eyes and foaming mouths, their iron hooves flattening him into the ground.

'Don't be daft. There's no horses here.'

'When we get to the Trongate then.'

'What's there except a few silly sedan-chairs?'

'Sometimes there's horses.'

'I don't care. I'm not frightened of horses.'

'Gav. Give me your hand.'

'No.'

'I'm frightened I might lose you.'

'Hold on to my jacket if you must.'

She clutched immediately at the material flapping out behind him.

'Don't chug at me,' he growled. 'You're always chugging at me.'

'No, I'm not.'

'Yes, you are.'

'No, I'm not.'

'Yes, you are. You are so!' Despite his aggressive irritable tone, he was grateful for the contact with his sister and comforted by the familiar sound of her voice.

Trongate Street was aflicker with lanterns and shadowy

39

figures. Somewhere two dogs barked excitedly. As they passed the Tolbooth they heard someone groaning and moaning like one of the doomed that the minister spoke of, who went down to hell wailing and weeping, roaring and yelling in everlasting despair.

'Oh, Gav, hurry,' Regina whispered, and it took him all his will-power to be thrawn enough to slow his pace instead of quickening it.

Past the Cross, along the Gallowgate. The difficult journey took a long time to negotiate and played havoc with their bare feet, while a wind like a knife hacked and flapped at their clothes.

'We'll run,' Gav conceded, 'when we come to Tannery Wynd, all right?'

'All right.'

His heart began to beat faster when he approached the narrow winding lane that led off Gallowgate Street. He could hear mad sounds from the houses. Again he was reminded of the minister's words, drummed into horrified ears for long hours twice and three times every Sunday and often during weekdays as well. 'And there shall be the roaring and screeching and yelling of devils in such hideous manner that thou wilt be ready to run stark mad for anguish and torment.'

'Run,' Regina said. 'Run.'

Eyes popping, mouths gasping in the putrid stench, they flew along the lane and battered themselves thankfully against the door of their house.

It did not open.

Shivering they waited. Still it did not open. They were too shocked to break their private pool of silence, and in silence they waited again.

Chapter 4

'She's not in,' Gav said incredulously. 'Mammy's not there!'

'Wheesht, they might hear us. Oh, Gav, what are we going to do?'

'She must still be at the Ramsays'.'

'Or the Halyburtons'.'

'Does she work for other folk as well?'

'I don't know.'

'I suppose . . .' Gav's voice faltered, 'I suppose we'll have to wait for her.'

'Maybe if I helped you up, you could climb in the window, Gav.'

'I'm too fat. I'd get stuck.'

'Try. Oh, please try. Quickly, before anyone hears us. Before anyone comes.'

Sounds multiplied and mushroomed all around them. From across the lane and down the lane and from round each corner it mixed towards them in different shapes and sizes. Wails of babies, tired threads trailing in the air. A drunken song, a merry bouncing ball deflating and dribbling sadly away. Quarrelling, sharp daggers recklessly flung. The dog Spider growling and becoming aware.

The window was unsashed and covered with a stretch of rabbit's skin instead of glass. Gav punched and pulled it aside while Regina clung grimly to his legs and staggered under the weight of him. He heaved himself up and jerked his head and shoulders forward. Then he began breathlessly wriggling and kicking.

'I can't. I can't. Regina, let me down. I told you it was too wee.'

The scraping and tapping of Blind Jinky's stick quickened their panic. His door creaked open, Spider catapulted out, eyes like burning coals in the dark.

41

Gav and Regina flew back along Tannery Wynd, oblivious of the icy earth and stones slashing their feet. They reached the comparative safety of Gallowgate Street, sobbing in distress.

'Don't cry, Gav,' Regina managed eventually. 'We can wait in one of the closes or up one of the stairs.'

'I'm not greetin',' Gav said brokenly. 'I'm not a stupid bubbly, greetin' face like you.'

'If we walk along to the Trongate we'll maybe meet her.'

'All right.' He wiped his nose and eyes with the back of his sleeve. 'I'm hungry.'

'So am I. But we'll get our supper when Mammy comes.'

Moonlight picked out the high crowned spire of the Tolbooth and its wall topped with ornamental battlements. A horse, tethered to one of the posts in front of the plainstanes, pawed the ground and snorted out clouds of steam. Men in voluminous cloaks spilled from the Exchange Tavern and Coffee House.

Awestruck, Gav and Regina watched them, but soon their attention was pulled round to a sedan-chair rocking on its two poles, lantern swinging and sending waves of yellow light splashing up the darkness. It was carried by two frockcoated men, one in front and one at the back. As it passed, the children cowered away from its light, but not before they caught a glimpse of the blue silk curtains draped at its windows and the fine lady with the powdered wig and golden gown who sat inside.

Somewhere from above their heads a servant girl's voice bawled out: 'Caddie! Caddie!'

Then a shadowy man wearing a Kilmarnock bonnet, shoulders hunched in tattered coat, came jogging along with his hand cupping his ear and his face anxiously upturned.

'Whaur are ye?'

'Two up, on the right.'

'What do you want?'

'A sedan-chair for my lady.'

'Hang on then, I'll no' be a meenit.'

He scuttled away to find a chair and bearers, sweeping the children aside as he passed. They stumbled on their sore feet and thumped to the ground, bruising legs, elbows and hands. Then a terrifying sound assailed their ears. Bearing down on them rattled a carriage drawn by six prancing horses. They scrambled up and out of its path just in time.

'We'd be safer in one of the closes or up one of the stairs,' Regina said. 'We'll wait for a while and then we'll go back and Mammy'll be in.'

'All right.' Gav tried to sound nonchalant but failed. He even allowed Regina to grasp his hand and hold it tightly as they edged along.

'What close will we wait in?'

Regina rubbed a fist hard against her eye. She had never in her twelve years been out so late before. It was as if she and Gav had wandered alone into a different world, a world in which they knew no one, where no place was familiar and where no one knew them.

'In here. She slid round the wall of the first close they came to. The entrance gave way to a small yard like a cul-de-sac crowded on every side by the backs of high buildings. The moon's pale light revealed that some of the buildings were entered by outside wooden stairs. Others by stairs made of broken stone slabs jutting out at different lengths from underneath a wooden banister. Others had brick towers with turnpike stairs inside. Rubbish littered the ground and every now and then they noticed the brown humped bodies and long tails of rats.

Trongate Street was still visible through the close-mouth. Lanterns bobbed past. Voices ebbed and flowed.

Regina hesitated in bewilderment. A nerve began to twitch in her face. She rubbed at it.

'We'll see Mammy coming from here.'

She tried to comfort Gav, who was shivering despite his too big jacket and hat. He made no answer and they hung together in silence until the Tolbooth clock struck ten. Then suddenly they were startled by a great noise of windows opening and voices chanting:

'Mind yer heid!'

Before they could run and take shelter an avalanche of fulzie rained down on their heads from the skies; the stinking contents of chamber-pots, rotten food, vomit, putrid water and rubbish of every kind.

'Och, my good clothes.' Regina began to weep. 'And Mammy washed them not that long ago.'

Gav pulled off his hat and shook it angrily. 'Bubblin' and greetin's not going to make them any cleaner.' He squashed his hat back on again. 'And we'll freeze to death standing here. We'll have to go and wait in a stairway.'

'All right,' she agreed, delicately drying her eyes with a clean corner of her cape as she followed his sturdy figure across to one of the towers. It was pitch black inside.

'Shall we go further up?'

'If you want.'

But they only found the courage to penetrate the darkness a few steps before sliding down the wall into a squatting position.

'I'm hungry,' Gav said.

'So am I.'

'I'm tired too.'

'So am I.'

They tried to keep their eyes open, but the darkness weighed heavy on them and gradually they relaxed against one another and sleep crept over them.

It seemed that she had been asleep for only a few minutes, yet when Regina awoke everything felt different. She knew that she and her brother were no longer alone. All around them breathing sounds were building into a crescendo, funnelling and echoing upwards. Long smooth breaths, light tripping breaths, uneven stumbling breaths, puttering, snorting, snoring breaths were sawing the air and jostling for space.

'Gav,' she whispered.

'Eh?'

'Are you awake?'

'I think so.'

'Listen.'

Carefully they felt for each other's hands. Then, trembling with apprehension, they rose and made their first tentative step. But their feet came into contact with curled-up bodies and one jerked awake and pounced on Gav. He struggled to free himself.

'Leave me alone.'

'Leave him alone,' Regina echoed. 'We're going home to our mammy.'

'You're a bloody lee-ar.'

'Don't you call my sister a liar.'

'A bloody lee-ar.' The man's other hand clutched at Regina. 'Why are you sleeping here if you've got a mammy?'

Before she could answer he had dragged them both over the tops of the other sleepers and outside.

'Are you hired to anyone for begging?'

Gav punched and kicked as viciously as he was able. 'Our mammy works and we go to school. We've never been beggars.'

The man hoisted both of them up by the throat, pushed his face close, then in a low menacing voice said, 'Well, ye are noo!'

Ramsay was glad that his two ships the *Mary Heron*, named after his late wife, and *The Glasgow Lass* were somewhere between Glasgow and Virginia. They might now be in danger from the perils of the sea and from Spanish privateers and pirates operating from the Caribbean, but at least they escaped the plundering hands of the Highland rebels. In their holds, as well as all the produce of Glasgow, were serges from Stirling, stuffs from Musselburgh, stockings from Aberdeen, shalloons and blankets from Edinburgh.

He was proud of his three-masted 'snows' with their fore and main masts square-rigged, and with boom and gaff of the fore-and-aft trysail attached to the stout mizzen mast. This reduced the strain on the main mast and made for a less leaky boat. Snows were grand boats for standing up to rough Atlantic weather and they could travel at a goodly pace. They certainly carried his cargoes with more speed, safety and success to and from Virginia than any vessel owned by a London or Bristol merchant. Admittedly there was the more direct north-west route from Glasgow and the English ships had to brace the Channel which was often packed with foreign privateers. Then, of course England was always fighting the French, whereas Glasgow had won contracts to supply with tobacco the monopoly group called the United General Farms of France.

Business had been steadily prospering for some time and

would have continued in its healthy state had it not been for the damned Pretender. On his way down to England he had sent a messenger to Glasgow to demand a huge sum of money on pain of execution, threatening too that if Glasgow did not pay, the Highland army would invade the city. They had avoided that calamity by paying up and nearly bankrupting themselves. Now only God knew what would happen.

He was on his way with his family to a special church service to ask His help and protection against the enemy. With one hand he thumped his heavy gold-topped cane on the ground as he walked, the other he cupped at his back, fingers stretching and bunching. His head and chin thrust forward and the curls of his long black wig trailed down over the front of his shoulders. Beside him strolled his son Douglas, resplendent in white tie wig, frothy lace cravat and shimmering pink cape. One of his hands was hidden in a fur muff, the other fluttered a lacy hanky. It would be good thing if Griselle Halyburton accepted Douglas. Griselle would maybe make a man of him. The Halyburtons were good merchant stock. They knew how to make a sovereign and how to hang on to it. Douglas was a weakling. He was absolutely besotted with the girl for a start.

'I'll do something desperate if Griselle refuses me, I'll be so cast down,' he kept repeating.

'As long as you don't do anything desperate with my money, Douglas,' he told him.

His daughter walked beside him too, looking as perjink as ever with her yellow hair swept high over its padding and bobbing with bunches of curls on top and fluttering with feathers. She was wearing a long-waisted blue satin dress with what seemed miles of frills going down and across and all around it. She took up half the road with the width of her hoops. Her whole appearance was far too frivolous to be going on her way to church, and especially on such a solemn occasion.

'Can you no' even dress yourself right?'

'Don't I look splendidly beautiful, Papa?' Her eyes sparkled up at him. 'Come now, be honest. You know you're mightily proud of me.'

'I know that pride is a mortal sin.'

'Fiddlesticks! You're such an old misery. Even the sun's managing to shine and it's the middle of winter. Be happy.'

'Be happy?' her father echoed. 'Oh, aye, we've plenty to be happy about. There's a whole army of thieving Highlandmen outside the town for a start.'

'Irishmen as well, I've heard. Wild Geese, they call them. Soldiers of fortune.' Handsome gentlemen too no doubt, she thought with a flutter.

'Oh, aye! That's sure to be a great help. It's a great source of joy and jubilation to us a' to know there's hordes of Irish mercenaries oot there.'

Her laughter cascaded all around. 'Papa, Papa!'

'Enough of your wicked levity! We're entering God's house.'

The Tron Church stood west from the Cross and behind the dwellings which immediately fronted the street. Entry to it was under a wide arch. It had been founded in 1484, fell into ruin and then repaired in 1592, and its spire, 126 feet in height, stood between it and the street. It had a clock, two bells, a battlement and windows in the pointed-arch style.

Inside was dark and cold and stank of old bones dug up and left to make room for new burials. Most people had to stand crowded together in the middle of the church, kicking the stinking bones aside while complaining about the disgrace of it. The aristocracy and the lairds and the Virginia merchants were spared the annoyance. They and their families had seats raised on platforms round each side. High above everyone loomed the pulpit and the long face of the Reverend Blackadder. His hands grasped the edge like eagle's claws and he pushed his shoulders high and bent forward.

'. . . and our enemies shall be damned. And as to the curse under which they shall be shut up in hell, a black cloud will open upon them and a terrible thunderbolt strike them and God's voice will cry from the throne: "Depart from me, ye cursed!" There are no offers of Christ for you, no pardon, no peace, no wells of salvation in the pit of your destruction . . .'

Ramsay had never heard him preach so well. The man worked up such righteous zeal that at times he was howling and weeping and most of the congregation were moaning and wringing their hands along with him. There were always some sinners that he could not reach, of course, and he never failed to notice them. He could suddenly stop in the middle of an impassioned piece of oratory, point a bony finger in the culprit's direction and accuse.

'Jeems Burke, I'll no' countenance sleeping in the presence o' the word o' the Lord.' Or, in a more sarcastic tone, 'Bailie Tamson, will you stop your snoring. You'll waken the Provost!'

The Reverend Blackadder walked in the way of the Lord, he had a good Scotch tongue in his head and he feared no man. What better husband for Annabella could be found anywhere in Glasgow? Who else was better fitted to keep her on the straight and narrow path of righteousness? One day she would thank him for saving her from a life of sin. That was what she was heading for if something was not done, and soon. He prayed for God to forgive him for being too lax with her in the past. 'Lord God, forgive me for abandoning Annabella in her tender youth into the hands of my servant Chrissie Kinkaid, knowing that although she was a good servant, and saw to me after my wife died, knowing also that she was a wicked and immoral woman. Oh, in Thy Infinite Mercy, save our Annabella from the pit.'

At least he had tried, when business permitted, to instil into Annabella religious instruction. He had also done his best to make sure she was treated with strictness at school. He remembered taking her on the first day and warning the dominie, 'I've brought you our Annabella; see ye thrash her weel.' But nothing seemed to daunt the girl. She grew worse instead of better. Even now, sitting in God's house, she was sporting her fan and tipping her head this way and that, flaunting herself as if she were in a dancing salon and hoping that some fop would ask her to jig or minuet.

'Annabella, can you no' hear the preacher?'

'How could I not hear him, Papa? I swear one day the man will take a stroke.'

'Mind your tongue.'

He resolved to waste no more time and when they left the church he stopped to have a word with the Reverend Blackadder at the door.

'We would be verra pleased, Blackadder, if you would come and sup with us tonight.'

'Uh-huh, and there's Mistress Annabella. Weel, I'll come if God spares me.'

'If you're dead, sir,' Annabella flung at him as she swept past, 'we'll not expect you.'

Ramsay strode after her.

'You'll be lucky if he'll have you after all your snash.'

'Papa, you can't really, honestly, truly see that horrible black crow as a husband for me?'

'In my day you would have been flogged to death for making a fool of the minister. And so it should be yet. That's what's wrong with young folks now. They're treated far too soft.'

She sighed in exasperation.

'I wish somebody would do something, or something exciting would happen. I've never known such a prodigiously boring time in all my life. It's the day before Christmas and no one has arranged one assembly or party or anything. And there's going to be the same deficiency at New Year. It's fearfully hard to bear, Papa.'

Suddenly her brother gave one of his high-pitched excited snickers.

'Isn't she the limit, Papa? One has to be amused.'

'No,' his father growled. 'One has *not* to be amused. If you can't talk sense, sir—hold your tongue!'

The afternoon stretched before Annabella like death itself. And an evening in the company of the Reverend Blackadder promised to be no more cheerful.

She sighed when they arrived back in the house. The best she could do was to busy herself with a little embroidery while her father sat muttering over the Bible, and Douglas endlessly polished his nails. After a time she went through to the kitchen, hoping for some gossip with Nancy. But the maid never could thole being watched while she cooked and she was in the midst of preparing a special supper because Mr Blackadder was coming.

'Hm! That smells good,' Annabella said, taking a peep into the pot hanging on the swee above the fire.

Nancy glowered and said nothing.

'You're an ill-mannered bitch,' Annabella remarked, swishing aimlessly around the kitchen. 'Did you know that?'

Still Nancy did not speak, but her resentment was so strong it could almost be seen as well as felt.

Annabella selected a sweetmeat from a plate, popped it into her mouth, then daintily licked her fingers.

'That table's filthy. See that it's washed today.' As she sauntered past the dresser she kicked at a woollen plaid. This was what covered Nancy during draughty winter's nights while she slept on the kitchen floor. 'And get this tidied away at once.'

Nancy's hatred followed her like a dagger twisting in her back as she left the room and returned to where her father was still poring over the Bible. Douglas had gone.

'Shall I light a candle, Papa?'

'Is there something wrong with your eyes, mistress?' He tried to squash her with a look not unlike Nancy's. But Annabella was not so easily suppressed.

'No, Papa, but there will be something wrong with yours if you persist in reading in such poor light.'

'Aye, it's your tongue that's your trouble.'

She laughed and went over to gaze out of the window, determined not to be cast down by her father's sarcastic tone or the gathering gloom or the fact that Mr Blackadder would soon be arriving.

Letitia Halyburton was coldly furious. She had always been a conscientious and thrifty housewife. Never as much as an oatcake had ever gone missing before. She kept the keys of the food cupboard and the linen kist hanging on a chain round her waist along with her snuffbox and perfume bottle. Her sharp eye kept constant watch on her daughters as well as the servants. No one was allowed to waste anything and a meticulous household account was kept. To lose or have stolen nearly half of all the linen she possessed was unthinkable. She could not, she would not, accept such a calamity.

Summoning the servants to her room, she sat rigid-backed, tapping her closed fan against her palm, too angry to speak.

'Weel, ma'am,' Tam said at last. 'What ails ye?'

'Aye, well may you ask.' Her words squeezed through tight lips and her fan increased its rhythm.

'Weel, then?'

'What about my good linen?'

'What about it?'

'You ken fine.'

Kate squinted up through leathery wrinkles.

'It's your ain fault. You should have made her do it.' She jerked a thumb towards young Nell.

Nell murmured under her breath: 'You know I'm always willing and able to do anything I can to help, ma'am.'

'Liar, liar!' Kate screeched out. 'You couldn't wash a puddock's bum.'

'This is not getting me my fine linen.'

Kate simmered down again. 'Do you think one o' them Highlanders could have run away with Jessie?'

Tam shook his head.

'He wouldn't run very far with a one-legged auld witch like her. Naw, I shouldn't think they're that hard stuck for doxies.'

'Tuts,' Letitia said irritably. 'They can't be anywhere near Woodside. That's only about a mile out of town. Tam, you go down to her house this very minute and see if she's there.'

'Why can't the lassie go? Why must I trail away doon there when I'm busy setting up the table for the denner?'

'Stop your arguing, man.'

'Aye,' cackled Kate. 'He's like an auld witch himself.'

'I'm sick and tired of your snash as well, Kate, I've a good mind to terminate both your employment.'

'No, no, ma'am.' Tam shook a finger for emphasis. 'I'm no' having that. If you don't know a good servant, I know a good place.'

'And I've been with you since we were both wee bairns,' Kate said. 'And I'll be with you till I die.'

'Tuts, why am I plagued with such devils o' servants? I can't send young Nell to Tannery Wynd, Tam. There's harlots and all kinds of wicked creatures down there. I should have known better than to trust somebody from such a place with my fine linen.'

'Just the right place for her,' Kate said. 'She's a wicked, sly, lazy besom.'

'That may be so,' Tam conceded grudgingly, 'but the mistress is right enough.'

'And I can't send Nell out to Woodside, either,' Letitia said. 'I need her here to do my hair. So, Kate, you'll have to go and have a search around.'

Kate clenched her fists and shook them in the air.

'I've done your hair all my life. That sly wicked besom's trying to steal you away from me.'

'What nonsense! Go away and do as you you're told. Nell, you stay. I want my hair dressed before the gudeman comes home.'

Kate shuffled out muttering oaths under her breath. Once through in the kitchen, she draped her plaid over her mutch and down to cover her grotesque hunchback. Then she pinned it across her chest and repeated to Tam:

'That wicked besom's trying to steal the mistress away from me.'

'Ach, woman,' Tam said, 'you're just getting too old for the job.'

'Too old?' Kate echoed incredulously. 'You dreepy-nosed dunnerheed. I'm only a handful o' years older than yourself.'

'Away and do as you are telt.'

'Away yourself.'

Mumbling and muttering, they both left the house to go their separate ways. Tam turned left towards the Cross and Gallowgate Street. Kate took the opposite direction and was soon past the Shawfield Mansion and had turned up the winding path that led through empty countryside to Woodside.

She talked to herself most of the way. Or carried on imaginary conversations with Nell.

Her face twisted in mimicry. ' "You know I'm always willing and able to do anything I can to help, ma'am!" Sly, wicked besom. I'll get her out of there yet. Think you'll get rid of me, do you? Think you'll steal my good job and my good home and my good mistress, do you? Well, just you wait, my lass. Just you

52

wait. We'll scc. I'll get rid of you first. Aye, I will. I will. I'll get rid of you first.'

Suddenly she stopped. The thought of Nell Nesbit's hands brushing and fondling Mistress Letitia's hair was unendurable. And fears of what else she might be whispering in the mistress's ear built up to a terrible crescendo of distress until the insecurity of not knowing what harm Nell might be causing in her absence proved too much for Kate. She turned and hurried back to town again without having reached the woods.

But she had seen them in the distance. The burn where Jessie did the washing sparkled in the winter's sun. The fields ruffled in the wind. But of Jessie there was definitely not a sign.

'I looked and looked,' she told Letitia afterwards, 'and there was neither hunt nor hare of her. Or your linen.'

'I knew it!' Letitia said. 'They're all rogues and vagabonds from Tannery Wynd. I told Adam Ramsay. This is his fault and I'll never forgive him. He recommended Jessie Chisholm. Almost begged me indeed to give her employment.'

Kate nodded sagely.

'He's always been a bit queer since the burning of Jessie's mother. His sister was to blame, remember. They're a family worth a' watching. Take your auld Kate's advice, mistress. Think twice before letting his Douglas wed our Griselle.'

Chapter 5

Most of the man's ear had been hacked off, and a swelling under one eye like a giant egg blocked out sight. He cocked his head and with the other eye peered at Gav and Regina who were viewing him with undisguised horror.

'You see that, do you?' He pointed at the pieces of torn flesh where the ear had once been. 'That's what'll happen to you if you don't do as Quin tells you. Quin cut it off himself. The hangman nailed Quin by the lug and gave him a knife and told him if he wanted to get free he'd have to cut his own lug off and he did.' He made wild slashing motions and the children shrank back. He pounced on them and this time caught one of their ears in each hand and twisted it until they howled with pain. 'Quin still has that big knife in his coat. Which of your lugs will he hack off first, eh?'

'No, please don't,' Regina squealed. 'We'll do as you say, won't we Gav? We promise.'

'You'd better. Quin's got Auld Nick to help him, and if Quin can't catch you, he will, eh? He was talking to Quin the other day. He came in the guise of an auld man with splits in his shoes to fit his hoofs and "Quin," says he, "Quin, I'm giving you verra special powers. I'm giving you a magic eye."' He jerked his head to one side and rolled his eye nearer, first to Gav and then to Regina. 'See it, eh? "Quin," says the devil, "Quin, you're a verra lucky man. With that magic eye you'll be able to see into any place—even when your body's no' able to go." What do you think o' that, eh?'

The children said nothing.

'Have you eaten, eh?'

With difficulty they moved their heads.

'Quin's got a dod o' salmon.' He let go of their ears, plunged inside his coat and came out with two filthy hands in which were squashed a mixture of cooked fish, dust, threads and hairs. He thrust one hand towards them. They stared at it in disgust.

'Come on, come on,' he urged. 'Quin's no' got all day.'

'Mammy makes us porridge,' Gav said.

'She can't any more, eh?'

'Why not?'

'She's away with Auld Nick. Auld Nick turned her into a black hen, tucked her under his arm and trippit away with her.'

Gav's lips trembled.

'Right,' said the man. 'Are ye going to eat or are ye no'?' Slowly Gav and Regina picked at the proffered food and stuffed it into their mouths.

'Now,' said the man. 'Time to go, eh?'

'Go where?' asked Regina.

'Everywhere,' said the man. 'And mind, Quin's yer faither.'

'We haven't got a father,' Gav protested. 'We've never had a father.'

'Well, ye have noo.'

'I'm thirsty,' Regina said.

'Quin's thirsty. That's where we'll make for first, eh?'

He prodded and hustled them out of the close and into Trongate Street. Watery light spread over tenement buildings. The spires of the Tolbooth on one side of the road and the Tron Church on the other pierced silver clouds. High on its pedestal, the pawing horse bearing the victorious King William sweated ice. The plainstanes were empty, but along the road from all directions came barefooted serving girls with stoups and jugs to fill at the public draw-wells. Along trundled a cart heaped with the yellow sand that housewives sprinkled on their kitchen floors and stairs. Pulling the cart was an old horse with its head drooping low and sitting among the sand a man was sadly chanting:

'Ye-sa! Ye-sa!'

Hustling past were the sutie men with their faces blackened by going down chimneys head first. The town cowherd, blaring his horn, drove cattle towards the green pastures of the Cowcaddens. A man in a blue bonnet came riding a black horse with his gudewife sitting side-saddle behind him. And Moothy McMurdo swaggered by ringing his bell.

'Pin back your lugs, pin back your lugs!
A Parcel o' juicy Lisbon lemons
Has arrived in the shop of Johnny Spuds!
There is likewise to come here
A variety of stoneware
And fine boiling green peas
Best mustard and English cheese.'

Quin and the children took a drink at the well.

'Oh-ho!' Quin gave a little dance as he spied the hangman emerge from the Tolbooth building, pulling behind him a woman with long tousy hair. 'Oh-ho—now we'll see some fun, eh?' He hustled the children nearer. Already other people were gathering around to watch with interest. Hangy Spittal tied the woman to the back of a cart waiting in front of the Tolbooth for the purpose.

Hangy's uniform consisted of a long blue coat with yellow buttons and with collar, cuffs and other facings in scarlet and a cocked hat with white edging to match his white stockings. He had buckles on his shoes and at his knees, and frills from his wrists reached down over the knuckles of his fingers. The uniform looked splendid, but the man inside it was a miserable specimen, lank and shrivelled with a small head and a wizened countenance from which hung lips that continually dripped spittle.

A rabble of people had now collected and Quin and the children were roughly punched and squeezed and jostled about.

Suddenly recognition dawned on Regina.

'Gav,' she said, 'that's one of the women who lives upstairs from us.' She felt uneasy and disturbed. The woman looked helpless. With her arms stretched out and her wrists tied and her head twisted awkwardly to one side she was not in the least menacing or frightening.

Inside the rabble and forming a circle round the prisoner were the town's officers in full dress and armed with halberts. The town's drummer appeared too. Then on tuck of drum a gasp of excitement swirled about as the hangman began to tear at the woman's white shirt until she was naked to the waist with milky breasts hanging soft and vulnerable. The drumming swelled to crescendo. The hangman lifted his cat-o-nine-tails and before the children's horrified gaze proceeded to lash the woman until blood spurted from her back. Regina was standing so close she could look into her eyes and they contained such anguish and appeal it made the little girl weep and wail at her own inadequacy.

'What's wrong with you, eh?' Quin asked in surprise.

Gav stretched a protective arm round his sister.

'We know that woman.'

'So you know harlots, eh? Quin knows a few as well. Follow them around the streets, will we? They'll whip her along the Gallowgate down the Saltmarket and back here again. Or to business right away, is it? Eh?'

He cocked his head, making his greasy hair fly about.

'Right, come on, then. There's no money here. It's down to the bridge, eh? There's a toll down there and folks are having to open their pouches. After that Quin has two good stands up the High Street. First at the Cathedral and then at the College.' He winked his only eye, making his face look like a speckled stone with sharp edges and round bulges in strange places.

'Maybe we'll manage to do a wee bit of pickering. Get a pouch or two for ourselves, eh?'

'Is that the reason they nailed you to the pillory?' Gav asked.

Quin nodded enthusiastically. 'Quin wants to hang on to his other lug. That's why he needs help.'

'I'm not going to steal.' Gav glowered at him. 'And my sister's not going to steal either.'

'Maybe Auld Nick can persuade you. Sometimes he comes as a great bee and buzzes round Quin. Other times he's a black dog. Oh-ho!' His eye immediately perceived Gav's look of fear. 'You've seen him, eh?'

'We know a dog called Spider.'

'The verra one. The verra one! Down to the bridge before he comes, eh?'

Dragging the children with him, he jogged along, bouncing from one foot to the other, his hair and his coat-tails flapping.

The noise alerted Jessie again. It *was* footsteps. Immediately she renewed her cries and was confused as well as relieved when the branches above her rustled open and two or three faces peered down. Then a voice called in the Gaelic:

'Have you had an accident, old woman?'

'I've been here a long, long time.'

'Will you pe a witch or a wood fairy, I'm wondering?'

'I was doing the washing and I fell down this pit. I was doing the washing for my lady.'

'Will you just pe a poor washerwoman, then?'

'I want to go home.'

'And where will your home pe?'

'Up the mountain from the Black Glen.'

'Ach,' the man said, 'fetch a rope, Tougal. Isn't she one of us?'

They whisked her up as swiftly and as easily as if she had been a feather in the wind.

Once back in the woods, she saw that the trees and bushes were moving with people. Surprised, she hopped around, leaning on her crutch and stamping this way and that. Huge men with tangled hair and beards like bushes gripped giant swords and shields with spikes sticking out. There were women camp-followers and doxies dressed in a hotchpotch of different clothes: a soldier's red jacket, a kilt, a beggar's blue coat, tartan trews, yellow breeches, tattered shirts and shawls, cocked hats and tam-o'-shanters. All of them, men and women, were filthy, their hair dark and matted, and skin reddened with long exposure to the elements.

'Flora!' one of the rescuers shouted, 'you will pe taking care of the washerwoman.'

He looked like her father. A strong erect man with hair like fire. She said to him. 'Let me go with you. You can't go away without me again.'

'Ach, well,' his voice gentled, 'you will not pe liking Glasgow. Such a place of tirty traitors there never was the like. Flora will keep you safe here until we return.'

'I want to go home. Back to the mountains.'

'Ach, now, is that not where we will all pe going? Just you pe resting here for a wee while.'

She allowed herself to be led away by the woman in the red coat that had once belonged to an English soldier.

58

'I've a drop porridge on the fire. You can share it because they'll bring us plenty food when they get back from Glasgow.'

Jessie felt sad at the mention of Glasgow. She could not think why. Yet the sadness grew, became unbearable, came rolling towards her like a black snowball growing bigger and bigger. She whimpered and cursed and skittered around.

'Where's my washing? Who's stolen it? Bloody thieves and vagabonds. You'll have me locked in the Tolbooth. What have you done with my lady's fine linen?'

'Hold your wheesht!' Flora said. 'Or I'll get a bloody sword and cut your other leg off.'

'They'll lock me away in the Tolbooth.'

'No, they'll not. Here, sup your porridge.'

With difficulty Jessie manoeuvred herself on to the ground and did as she was told. But in between sups she nodded her frizzy head and muttered to herself: 'I laid it out on the field beside the burn, mistress. Aye, that's what I did. Bonny and bright it was. White against the green.'

The wood fire in front of which she was squatting crackled and belched black smoke. Hunched low over the porridge bowl she ignored it, but red fingers of light reflected in her eyes and trembled over her face accentuating its hollows.

Flora said: 'I saw no linen by the burn. You're havering, woman.' She was eating a small bird, tearing at its flesh with her teeth. Every now and again she stopped to wipe her mouth with the back of her sleeve or to slide her hand inside her coat and absent-mindedly scratch herself.

'I spread it out and the wind dried it.'

'It was your own fault for wandering away. You should have stayed and watched it. What made you come into the woods?'

Jessie shook her head. 'I don't know.'

'The fall's taken your mind.'

'There were frogs and toads and beetles loupin' all over me the whole night. They scuttled down my neck.' She shuddered and twitched about. 'Crawling inside my clothes the whole night they were. I screamed at them and flung myself this way and that, but they just kept on loupin' and scuttling and crawling.'

59

The porridge finished, she put down the bowl and peered about. It was beginning to get dark again and a cold wind was blowing clouds across the moon. Tall trees swayed and danced like long-fingered witches. Everywhere she looked were crowds of men in tartan, some standing, some sitting, some lying sleeping rolled in plaids. There were hundreds and hundreds of them. She had never seen so many Highlanders all together before. Then there came the sound of the pipes and she spied a piper swaggering along. Behind him there strutted a youth who was barely more than a child. Something about his freckled face and aggressive air disturbed Jessie. She struggled up, bewildered and not knowing what to do. Then suddenly like a dagger plunging in her breast came the memory of Gav and Regina.

'My bairns!'

Flora got up, wiping her hands down the front of her coat.

'Stop your noise, madwoman.'

'I must hurry away.'

'Where the hell do you think you're hurrying to?'

'To Glasgow.'

'Not before the Highland army, you're not.'

Jessie tried to hop in one direction and then in another, but everywhere she turned, Flora laughing, pranced round to bar her path.

'Out of my way, you dirty harlot.'

'Dirty harlot, is it? You ugly one-legged old crone. If you don't sit down I'll knock you down.'

Jessie kept a grip on her crutch, but her free hand shot out and caught Flora by the throat and with strength born of desperation, and years of wringing heavy washing, she crashed the younger woman's head against a tree. Then she bounded away as fast as she could, but Flora was only dazed for a second or two before recovering her wits and lurching after her.

'You ungrateful old cow!' She grabbed Jessie's frizzy hair and hauled her backwards, knocking her off balance and thumping her to the ground. Before Jessie could do anything to defend herself she grabbed her crutch and battered her over the head with it. She might have killed her had it not been for one of the men who came striding over and flung the crutch into the thicket.

Through a red haze of blood Jessie watched Flora return to squat by the fire. She felt ill and it reminded her of the time she lay ill in Tannery Wynd with the smallpox. One of the drunken soldiers who had come to visit the harlots upstairs had wandered into her house instead and despite her screams and struggles had managed to rape her. She chuckled to herself now, for he had later got the pox himself and died of it. That had been many years ago, perhaps twelve or thirteen.

'What are you snickering at, madwoman?' Flora called out.

Jessie laughed again. Then lying on her side with blood trickling over her eyes she began to automatically sing a song that was very familiar to her. She had often crooned it to Regina as they lay together in the hole-in-the-wall bed. But she had no recollection of that now.

> 'Homeward ye're travellin'
> In the soft hill-rain,
> The day long by
> That ye wearied o' the glen
> No ring upon yer hand,
> No kiss upon yer mou',
> Quiet noo.
>
> Cold was the sky above ye,
> The road baith rough and steep.
> No further shall ye wander
> Nor greet yersel' tae sleep,
> My ain wild lass,
> My bonnie hurtit doo,
> Quiet, quiet noo.'

'Times are no' what they used to be, no.' There was a stiffness about the minister, as if his arms were wooden and screwed high in his shoulders.

'Will you say a few words over the dram, minister?'

Ramsay and the minister, who always kept their hats on in the house, now respectfully removed them and held them against their chests while the Reverend Blackadder cried out with feeling.

'Oh Lord, Lord, bless this whisky and make us duly grateful for its warmth and health-giving properties and the fellowship it brings between man and man. Amen. Amen.'

They drank down the whisky, smacked their lips, then replaced their hats. The minister continued:

'Only the other day I heard about farmer folk talking about corns and markets in the kirkyard. On the Sabbath. Oh, the devil is busy nowadays. It's sad times we're living in, Ramsay.'

Annabella smoothed a hand up her hair and gave it a little pat. 'Talking about corns and markets? Gracious heaven, what's so wicked about that?'

Her father said: 'You see what I mean, Blackadder. Another wee dram?'

'God bless you, merchant.'

Ramsay signalled to Big John, who lumbered over to splash the glasses full again. The minister raised his:

'And may you always prosper. Mistress Annabella, did you not know that even asking, listening to, or telling news on the Holy Day is sinful?'

'Indeed I did not, sir. I am cruelly confused.'

'But God is good. Just fill up my glass again, lad. God is generous. He has in His goodness given us a variety of delights for the Sabbath, so that if we weary of one, another may be our recreation.'

'Delights?' Annabella frisked in her chair, flounced out her gown and sparkled mischievously at the minister over the top of her fan. 'Delights, sir?'

'Indeed, indeed. If you weary of listening to preaching, then you may recreate yourself in prayer. If you weary of that, recreate yourself with singing God's praises. If you weary of that, recreate yourself with meditating.'

'And what delights would you have me meditate upon, I wonder?'

'Oh, Mistress Annabella. Yes, another wee drop would go down very well. Oh, Mistress Annabella. Many are the delights of fruitful meditation. In the morning, as you put on your robes, think of the soul's nakedness.'

She gave a little gasp and fluttered her fan.

'Nakedness, minister?'

'. . . and need of the robes of righteousness. And when you comb your head, think of your sins, which are more than the hairs thereon. Then . . .' He plumped his palms on the table and his shoulders pushed up to his ears as he leaned forward. 'Then, at night when you see yourself stripped of clothing . . .'

'Minister!'

'Think, Mistress Annabella, think! . . .'

'Indeed I am thinking, sir.'

'Naked came I into the world . . .'

'Naked? Sir, sir, you are disconcerting me!'

'And naked shall I return. And when you lie down in bed.'

'And when I lie down in bed?'

'And cover yourself with blankets, let it remind you of your lying in the cold grave and being covered with earth. Thank you, Ramsay, I will take a drap more.'

He relaxed back and watched his glass becoming golden coloured with warm appreciative eyes.

'Many and varied are the Good Lord's delights. Och, yes.'

Annabella began to feel unbearably restless. Her eyes sped over the room while all the time she agitated furiously with her fan. She wished the long-visaged melancholy idiot would leave so that she could get to her bed. But she knew that once there it would not be the grave and the cold earth she would be thinking about. 'God help me!' she shot up a fervent prayer. 'Send me a handsome, daring, passionate, devilish darling of a man.'

But the Reverend Blackadder was in no hurry to leave and it was a long time and many glasses of whisky later before his goodbyes were said. He was very drunk as usual and Big John had to hoist him over his broad shoulder and carry him home. His capacity for drink was the subject of much admiration among his flock.

'Aye,' they said. 'There's no much wrong with a man who can take a good dram.'

The minister held on to his hat.

'Goodnight to you, merchant.'

'Goodnight to you, minister.'

'And a verra good night to you, Mistress Annabella.'
She flounced into a low curtsy, holding her skirts wide.
'Minister.'
Afterwards her father said: 'The verra man for you.'
'Papa!' she groaned.
'The verra man.'
'I don't understand you. Really I don't. I might get somebody with money.'
'Aye, aye. But money's no what you need the most, Annabella.'
She laughed. 'On that we can agree, Papa. But the minister's not got anything I either need or want.'
'He's a fine honest man of God.'
'Maybe, Papa. Maybe.'
'No maybe's about it.'
'To tell the honest truth, Papa, I don't care what he is.'
'Well, you'd better start caring, for he's asked to wed you.'
She stamped her foot. 'It's monstrous and damnable.'
'Mind your wicked tongue. It's the minister you need to put the fear of God in you.'
'I will not ever, ever marry that odious creature. I will not, sir.'
'Aye, weel, you've got a few days' grace. It would not be verra ladylike to jump at him.'
'Jump at him? The very idea. Papa, am I not the most beautiful woman in Glasgow and the most spirited?'
'A spirited horse has to be broken.'
'Oh, pooh! A spirited horse is marvellously exciting.'
'Compose yourself, woman. It's time for our prayers. Away and tell your brother and the servants.'
Annabella swept past him and manoeuvred her hoops sideways out of the door. She was heartily sick of prayers.
'Douglas, are you there?' she called in the direction of the other bedroom. 'Time for the reading.'
He appeared holding his candle and she immediately detected a languor about him.
'What ails you?' she asked.
'Not what ails me, sister. What ails my Griselle.'
'What ails her then?'
'That I do not know. Perhaps it's only my sensitive imagination

64

but I fear her affections have cooled a little. I must waste no time in pressing my case. She must marry me post-haste. I cannot bear to be flustered like this any longer.'

'I wish you happiness. But was Griselle ever warm, Douglas? I cannot imagine it. She is surely a cold calculating fish like her mother.'

'How dare you miscall a lady, you ignorant strumpet.'

'How dare *you* miscall a lady, sir,' Annabella said, and snuffed out his candle with a quick rap of her fan, leaving them both in darkness.

Then Douglas took pleasure in informing her:

'Papa's promised you to the minister.'

A foreboding like a black cloud of fear came drifting towards her. It made her heart quail and her mouth go dry. Never before had she allowed herself to think of marriage to the Reverend Blackadder as something that could actually happen. It took all her courage and spirit to prevent herself from floundering under her father's gloomy talk. All her life she had been subjected to the bleak and depressing philosophy that everything gay or beautiful or enjoyable must be wicked and punished with the utmost severity. She could not believe this to be right and had often risked the pillory or worse herself by marching up to culprits being punished for some moral misdemeanour and helping them. Many a sustaining sup of whisky she had held to grateful mouths. Many times, to her father's horror and fury, had she stood in front of the stocks and bawled abuse at the citizens in an attempt to shame them for pelting victims for no other reason than for kissing on a Sunday or actually laughing on that day.

Oh, sins of sins—loving and laughing on the Sabbath! She felt more like weeping than laughing now. But she swallowed down her tears, then tossing back her head and holding herself with nonchalant dignity, she swept past her brother saying:

'Pox on the bloody minister!'

Chapter 6

'Quin,' said Quin, 'is verra pleased. Quin has never needed the help of Auld Nick the whole day. Not as a green ghost, nor a giant bee, nor even a black dog called Spider.'

'Will you let us go now?' Gav asked.

'Go? Go?' Quin danced from one foot to the other and cocked his head. 'Go where?'

'Home.'

'Where's home?'

'Tannery Wynd.'

'You're telling lies to Quin again.'

Regina dragged herself out of her lethargy. She was exhausted with standing around and wandering about all day. She longed for her mother. She longed to cling close to her mother's skirts and feel safe. She longed to sink into sleep under her mother's warm plaid.

'No, he isn't. We do live in Tannery Wynd.'

Quin scratched his head and blinked his eye.

'You were sleeping on the stairs for a wee change, eh?'

'We went to the door yesterday.' Regina palmed away tears that unexpectedly overflowed. 'And our mammy wasn't in.'

'Quin had a mammy once. Quin had a father as well. What do you think of that, eh?'

The children were suitably impressed.

'Where are they now?' Gav asked.

'With Auld Nick. That's what the minister told me after they were hangit. "They've gone to the devil, Quin," he says. "They've gone to hell. They've sunk into the pit." "But, ach, Quin," says Auld Nick, says he, "you deal fair with me and I'll deal fair with them!" '

Regina said, 'Come with us and we'll show you where we live.'

'Yes,' Gav nodded excitedly. 'Come on, Quin. Mammy'll

give you porridge, too.'

Quin rubbed his torn ear and made his hair straggle about. 'Quin doesn't know what Auld Nick will do about this.'

'We'll run quick down Tannery Wynd so he won't catch us. Regina and me always do that, don't we, Regina?'

'Yes, and Mammy will let us in and we'll be all right, you'll see.'

'Quin's remembered something.'

'What?'

'It's Christmas Eve.'

'Does that mean we can go?'

'You stay with Quin. Quin'll go.'

The children laughed and wept with relief and jumped up and down and clapped their hands. Quin laughed too and cocked his misshapen face to one side and watched them, thumping his hands together as if he were marking time to a merry dance.

'Come on then,' Gav urged. 'It won't take long from here.'

Past the Tolbooth they went, scampering and skipping, Regina's green cloak and long auburn hair swirling about. Gav kept disappearing into his man-sized jacket and hat. Quin's shoulders jerked up and down and his coat-tails whisked from side to side. Past the Cross and along Gallowgate Street. Then Tannery Wynd at last. They stopped to get their breath for a minute and then were just about to break into a run when they heard a moaning sound coming from just inside the lane. A pale moon revealed a woman on her hands and knees crawling along beside one of the dunghills.

'It's the woman the hangman was whipping,' Regina said.

'Come on, Regina,' Gav pleaded. 'I want to go home.'

'Quin's seen a few harlots whipped,' Quin said.

Regina bit her lip. Distress mounted inside her at the sight of the woman until she could hardly bear the pain of looking at her. Yet she could not tear her eyes away.

'Shouldn't we help her?'

'She wouldn't help us,' Gav protested. 'She's never helped us.'

Quin said: 'Never did Quin any good either.'

'Come on, Regina.'

They broke into a run and Regina ran along with them but

stopped and impulsively hurried back after only a few seconds. She bent down and caught the woman by the arm.

'Can you walk if I help you?' She struggled to hoist her up, at the same time trying to be as gentle as possible. 'Here, lean on me. You'll be all right once you get home.'

The tousled head screwed round. 'You're the washerwoman's lassie.'

'Regina Chisholm.'

'I'm Jeannie.'

'We won't be long. Just keep leaning on me.'

'Regina. My, that's a bonny name. You're a bonny big lassie.'

'I'm not very big for my age.'

'What age are you, pet?'

'Twelve.'

'My, oh, my.' She winced with pain and Regina winced in sympathy.

'Are you all right? We're nearly there.'

She could hear Gav battering on the door and shouting: 'Mammy! Mammy!'

When she reached the house Gav called to her broken-heartedly:

'Regina. She's not in again.'

Regina felt frightened and the closeness of the other woman did nothing to comfort her.

'Quin is a dab hand at opening doors,' Quin said. 'What do you think of that, eh? What if Quin could open this door?'

'Could you?' Gav's voice cheered a little. 'Well, go on. Try!'

Regina said to Jeannie: 'Do you think you could get up the stairs by yourself?' She had no desire to go any further. Jeannie was helpless with pain but upstairs Regina knew there would be two other women both hale and hearty and perhaps a crowd of men as well.

'Has your mammy gone away and left you, pet?' Jeannie avoided Regina's eyes.

'I don't know.'

'Never mind, come on up to me and I'll give you a nice sup of ale.'

'A nice sup of ale?' Quin said. 'Quin would enjoy that.'

Gav pulled impatiently at Quin's sleeve. 'Open the door before Spider comes and bites us. He's always biting me.'

Jeannie got down on her hands and knees on the stairs and started to climb slowly and painfully.

'You're all welcome, I'm sure. I'm just away up and pour some ale ready.'

Quin fumbled with the lock on the door, and heaved his shoulder against it until it burst open.

'What did Quin tell you?'

He did a triumphant little dance before following Regina and Gav inside. Regina fastened the door again. The room was in darkness except for a feeble patch of moonlight that the window allowed to filter in. Her heart began to race and stumble about. She could hardly breathe.

Quin looked like a creature from hell with the moon ghosting his torn flesh and huge bump instead of an eye.

'Oh-ho,' he said. 'Now for some fun, eh?'

Jessie had been sleeping and now early-morning light sparkling through the trees like a river upside down made her stir. Her face and eyes were sticky with dried blood from the cut on her head and she rubbed at herself and looked around for her crutch. Spying it eventually among some bushes, she crawled and hauled herself towards it.

Flora had wakened too and was yawning and scratching herself.

Jessie said: 'Where are all the Highlanders?' She thought perhaps she had been dreaming that the woods had been packed with Highlanders the night before.

'Away to Glasgow.'

'All of them?'

'All that you saw. There's plenty others with the Prince. They're waiting until tomorrow or the next day, I've heard.'

She flung back her head and enjoyed a burst of laughter.

'It's Christmas Day today. That'll give these lowland traitor scum a Christmas they'll remember. Where do you think you're going?' Her tone sharpened as Jessie made to limp away.

'To the burn to splash water on myself. I must have fallen and hurt my head.'

'All right, but remember, I can see the burn from here and I'll be after you if you try to go any further.'

'Why should I want to go any further?'

'Oh, go away and don't irritate me, madwoman.'

Dead leaves rustled and scraped as Jessie hurried along. She felt cold and stiff and her head throbbed. Reaching the burn, she twisted herself down and shivering, cupped the icy water in her hands. It stung her face and sent a dagger of pain across the cut on her forehead. She whimpered and wiped herself dry with the end of her plaid. She kept thinking of Mrs Halyburton.

'I laid it on that field alongside here, mistress. So bonny and white it looked.'

Mrs Halyburton was thinking of her too. The Halyburton family were having breakfast at the table in the main bedroom. Letitia was in undress in a chocolate-coloured sack gown with long tight sleeves, at the wrists of each of which was a small frill of white. The neck plunged into a low 'V' reaching her waist, but a frill of the same white material modestly covered the cleavage of her breasts, and though the dress fitted neatly at her waist at the front, at the back it hung in loose voluminous folds from her shoulders to the ground.

On the table was fish and eggs for eating, and broth for drink, but she did not feel like touching anything. Instead she encouraged the gudeman, 'Willie, have some more fish. You must keep up your strength.'

Her husband, looking as big and strong as an elephant, boomed:

'What's wrong that you're no' eating yourself, Letitia?'

'Tuts, I'm that vexed. I dare swear we'll never see that thieving washerwoman or my fine linen again.'

William Halyburton had not yet donned his wig and his shaved head was covered by a red night cap. He was wearing a dressing-gown of the same colour as his purple-veined nose.

'Weel, weel, don't fash yourself, wife. I'll soon get you some more linen.'

'Good money wasted.' Letitia's face hardened with regret. 'I can't stand good money to be wasted. Mistress Griselle and

70

Mistress Phemy, do you hear that?'

'Yes, Mother.'

'Yes, Mother.'

'Weel, weel, Letitia, they never wasted anything.' Turning to his daughters he beamed and asked, 'And how is my wee bit lady and my wee lintie today?'

Griselle had her mother's raven locks and stiff formal manner, but she had not her mother's sallow complexion. Her skin was creamy and her cheeks a pretty pink.

'Very well, Father,' she replied politely.

Phemy grinned. She had a pocked face and bright mischievous eyes. Her father called her his wee lintie because she not only could sing as sweetly as any bird but also had quick bird-like movements. She was always busy doing something, sewing, spinning, cooking, cleaning, or getting ready for 'cummers' or for going to a dance or assembly, or running upstairs to see Murn, the ailing Lady Glendinny.

'I told Mother I'd soon find Jessie and the washing. I'd just run around and search and search until I found them and wouldn't mind a bit. It would give me something to do. But Mother won't let me.'

'Quite right, too. A sensible woman, your mother. You do as she bids you.'

'Yes, Father.'

'This is no time for young lassies to be wandering about.'

'Why, Father?'

'We've had word the rebels are closing in. I'm going to meet the magistrates and some other folk in the clerk's chamber later this forenoon. Not that there's much the magistrates or anybody else can do. If they're coming, they're coming.'

'Tuts,' gasped Letitia irritably. 'These days it's just one irritation after another!'

What Annabella Ramsay felt was much stronger than irritation. She was saying to the maid Nancy:

'Misfortunes appear to be overwhelming me, Nancy.'

'You mean the minister?'

Laughter fizzled up despite her despair. She put her hand over her mouth and made a desperate effort to suppress her giggles.

71

She did not know why she laughed unless from hysterical desperation.

'Damnation, this is no laughing matter.' She managed to straighten her face. 'It's a hateful calamity.'

'I must admit, mistress, I can't see you settling down with the minister.'

The spoiled brat couldn't settle down with anyone, Nancy thought.

'You've got to help me, Nancy.'

'How?'

Annabella stamped her foot. 'I don't know how.'

Nancy shrugged.

'Oh, hell and damnation!' Annabella flapped her arms as if she was going to fly away. 'I could scream.' She began rapidly pacing the bedroom, her peacock-blue velvet gown and her yellow hair bobbing and swishing around. In the tiny room, with its dark brown ceiling, walls and floor, she was like an exotic flower captured in a box.

Excitement brought colour to her cheeks.

'We could run away. We could dress as young men.'

Nancy raised an eyebrow. 'We?'

'Yes, we!' Annabella snapped. Then despite herself her face crumpled. 'You wouldn't desert me. I know I've been ill-humoured of late but so would you if you thought you had to marry the minister. Oh, Nancy, you cannot wish me to stay and suffer such a fate. Nor can you leave your mistress with no one to look after her. I cannot believe it.'

Nancy sighed and rolled her eyes and Annabella's excitement fluttered back.

'We could take some of Douglas's clothes. And Papa's pistols and horses.'

'Steal.'

'Borrow.'

'We could get nailed to the pillory or put in the stocks and whipped through the streets.'

'Nobody would dare lay a finger on me.'

'What about me?'

Annabella fluttered her hands. 'Heavens, you're always such

72

a dreary spoilsport. Stop worrying.'

'Oh, aye,' Nancy's mouth twisted with sarcasm. 'I've nothing to worry about, of course.'

'You sound just like Papa.'

'And where do you plan we should go?'

'Anywhere away from this boring sanctimonious place.'

'The master would grieve for you.'

'Fiddlesticks and poppycock! Big John would grieve for you, but Papa's far too busy selling Virginia tobacco.'

'I'm not interested in Big John.'

Annabella's eyes sparkled with amusement.

'Oh, I know that. You have wondrous dreams of capturing a gentleman.'

Nancy stared at her. Why not? she thought. Why not?

'You can't stop me dreaming.'

Annabella threw up her hands. 'Heaven forbid.' Then she gasped. 'What are you doing?'

'I'm going to do what I came in to do—wash the floor.'

She flung a cloth heavy with soapy water on to the floor, then stood on it and began to shuffle the cloth about, hands on swaying hips.

'God dammit! How can you think of a floor at a time like this?'

'I'm not thinking of floors, mistress.'

'Well, if you're dreaming of a marvellously handsome gentleman just now, I forbid it. Think of me!'

Nancy slid her a sarcastic look.

'Oh, yes?'

'Yes, damn you.' Furiously trying to prevent herself from weeping Annabella suddenly raced across and grabbed Nancy's hair. 'And I'll have none of your bloody sauce either.'

Nancy gave a half howl, half growl like an animal and made a grab at Annabella's curls, but Annabella gave a mighty heave, swung Nancy round by the hair and clean off her feet. She landed in a pool of soapy water, but immediately scrambled up again, at the same time swooping up the filthy floorcloth and rushing at Annabella, slapping her viciously this way and that with the cloth, splattering her with filth. Annabella clawed and kicked and screamed.

'Damn bloody, black-hearted, fornicating, fiendish, filthy fulzie.' She managed to get a grip of the cloth, jerk it out of Nancy's hands and swing her such a blow across the face that again the maid stumbled and fell. This time Annabella leapt on top of her, sat astride her and wildly belaboured the girl with her fists until Ramsay burst into the room and hauled her off.

'Annabella, are ye no' ashamed?'

He was genuinely shocked. 'What kind of way's this to behave? God forgive you.' His jaw hardened and pushed forward. 'You get your Catechism and copy it out and I'll question you on it later. I've to go to an important meeting in the clerk's chambers across the road.' He glanced at her. 'You're a sorry sight, mistress. I'll be glad when the minister's got the worry of you.'

Annabella's hair was tangled, her face was spotted and streaked with mud. Her dress was filthy too and hanging half off her shoulders and breasts. She stamped her foot.

'To hell with Blackadder.'

Ramsay's hand shot out and slapped her so hard across the face it left a scarlet weal. Her lips trembled, but she tossed her head high and refused to weep.

Nancy moved across the room swiftly and smoothly like a cat. She put an arm around Annabella's shoulders and slid a malevolent look in Ramsay's direction.

'Can you no' pick on somebody your ain size?'

'Lord! Lord!' Ramsay roared an angry protest heavenwards. 'Are my sins so vile I must be punished with such thrawn and devilish women? Especially now when my enemies are at the verra gates of Glasgow.'

They managed after a long fight with the tinder-box to light a fire so that they could make some porridge. Afterwards Quin had tried to persuade them to go upstairs with him to visit Jeannie. But they had refused on the pretext of being tired. It was not really a lie because they were so exhausted they could barely stand up. All they wanted to do was crawl into the hole-in-the-wall bed and stay there until morning. Quin agreed eventually.

Then as soon as they heard his feet thump up the stairs Regina ran over to the door and drew the big bolts.

'He won't get back in now,' she comforted Gav. 'Nobody will get in. They'll all get drunk and sleep until late tomorrow anyway.'

They crawled into the hole-in-the-wall bed and shut the bed-doors.

'Where's Mammy?' Gav asked in a small voice.

'Maybe they've kept her at work,' Regina said, not really believing it. Right away Gav's voice loudened with hope.

'That's where she is. She's at Maister Ramsay's or Maister Halyburton's house. We'll go and see her tomorrow, won't we, Regina?'

'Yes, all right.'

A feeling was growing inside her that something terrible had happened to their mother and that they would never see her again.

In the total darkness of the hole-in-the-wall bed she bit her lip and rubbed her fingers against her eyes to keep her tears in check so that she would not frighten or upset her brother.

If they were going to be alone from now on, what could they do, how would they live? Once they left the house again they would not be able to bolt the door and Quin could gain entry. Yet they could not stay bolted in the house for ever. The supply of oatmeal was nearly finished and there was no more peat or wood or coal for the fire. Perhaps staying with Quin was the only way to survive. But her fear of him had intensified since he had tried to cajole her to go with him upstairs. Her mother had always warned her about going near the place or having anything at all to do with the harlots. Already she regretted helping Jeannie. She felt apprehensive and uneasy. Despite the woman's gentle and kindly tone of the previous night, she mistrusted her.

Every now and again the insecurity of her present situation was too much for Regina's mind to cope with and she rejected it. It was all a nightmare. She often had nightmares. She would imagine that she was alone in the world and a prey to all sorts of hideous people and she was completely helpless not knowing what to do or how to protect herself. She would wake up shivering and shaking with terror, not even sure of where she was any more. Then after a long time lying rigid in the darkness she would pluck up enough courage to stretch out a tentative hand to touch her mother. She reached out now but there was no one there.

Suddenly panic attacked her like all the fiends in hell. She began to moan and squeal, louder and louder and quicker and quicker.

Gav woke up.

'Regina? Regina, what's wrong?'

'I'm . . . I'm. . . frighten . . . frightened.'

'Be quiet! They'll hear you.'

But she could not be quiet.

'Stop it! Stop it!' Gav clutched at her. His hands found her mouth and squashed with all his strength on top of it.

'Bubbling and bawling's not going to help us. You'll only make everything worse. You're always the same. You've always been a coward and a bubbly jock.'

Gradually her hysteria dwindled away and left her sighing big shuddering sighs of sadness and exhaustion. He let go of her mouth and she managed to say, 'I'm not a coward.'

'You are so.'

'I am not.'

'You are so. You are so!'

'Och, be quiet and go to sleep.'

'I was sleeping. You woke me up. You're always waking me up. You go to sleep!'

They fell into silence and soon were both completely relaxed and breathing deeply and rhythmically as exhaustion got the better of them. In his eagerness to go and find his mother it was Gav who awoke first. He flung open the bed-doors, then gave Regina a shake before clambering out of bed.

'It's morning, Regina. I heard the bells. Come on, hurry. I want to go to Mammy.'

A nerve twitched at the side of one of Regina's eyes, twitched and fluttered and wouldn't stop, no matter how hard she knuckled them.

'Maybe she won't be there.'

'Och, come on.'

'I'm coming.'

They both used the chamber-pot then, while Gav searched for some oatcakes to eat, Regina slipped out to empty the pot on the dunghill. Back inside the house, she greedily ate one of the bannocks Gav had found and they both drank the last of their mother's ale.

'Where will we go first?' Gav asked.

'I suppose Maister Ramsay's the nearest.'

'Are you ready then?'

Unhappily Regina nodded.

'If we go we'll not get back in by ourselves.'

'Mammy's got the key.'

'You don't understand.'

'Oh, come on.'

As quickly as possible they tiptoed from the house, carefully closing the door behind them. Then they sprinted towards Gallowgate Street and then along to the Cross.

'That's their windows up there at the corner, see! They call that the lantern storey because that bit sticking out is shaped like a lantern,' Regina said. 'Their other windows are on Trongate Street but their close is along here on Saltmarket Street. I remember Mammy telling me.'

They turned down Saltmarket Street and went in the close, round by the back and up the turnpike stair. On reaching the Ramsays' door, they were startled when it flew open before they had a chance to knock. In the doorway stood a man with bushy brows and hooded eyes under a long black wig and three-cornered hat. He wore a scarlet cloak and black breeches and in his hand he held a gold-topped stick. He suddenly bawled out:

'Who the hell are you? What do you want?'

Regina was struck dumb with fear, but Gav managed to find his voice.

'I'm Gav Chisholm. I'm looking for my mammy.'

'Well, she's no' here. She never turned up at the Halyburtons' either. I've more important things to concern me just now. Get out of my way.'

He brushed them aside and thundered down the stairs. In a minute or two and in silence Regina and Gav followed him. They wandered up to the Cross and along Trongate Street, silently, listlessly, then suddenly Gav shouted:

'Regina, look! Look!'

It was the vanguard of the Highland army.

Chapter 7

Handsome grey stone tenements, some small, some tall, but all with imposing arches and pillars underneath, undulated into the distance as far as the eye could see. From the distance and swelling the broad dirt road between the buildings came a riot of colour.

Clopping along in front were horses carrying French, Irish and Highland officers. The men bobbed up and down, Highlanders in scarlet and green and blue tartan kilts, and trews and jackets with epaulets and large cuffs and plaids draped over one shoulder and targes over one arm. Men with round flat bonnets and white cockades and silver-buckled shoes. Frenchmen with thigh-length boots and three-cornered hats, long grey coats and blue breeches. Irishmen with jackboots, grey coats and breeches of emerald green.

There was also Lord Elcho's Highland gentlemen on horseback looking very splendid in their blue coats and red vests and cuffs. And Lord Murray's troop of young hussars in plaid waistcoats and large fur caps.

As the noise and clatter of the horses swelled louder and louder Regina tugged at Gav's arm.

'Stand in a close out of the way or we'll get trampled.'

They sprinted down Trongate Street and into the first close they came to. Then they peeped out to view the spectacle again. The horsemen and the mass of men following behind on foot were fast approaching the Cross.

Regina pulled Gav further into the shadow of the close wall as they came nearer. She was violently trembling.

The horses clattered to a halt outside the Tolbooth and two of the officers dismounted and climbed the outside stairs of the building. One of them carried a standard. He thrust it high and roared out:

'I, John Hay of Restalrig, in the name of our rightful sovereign,

King James, do proclaim his son, Charles Edward, Regent of Scotland.'

Inside, in the council chamber the Provost Andrew Cochrane, the town clerk, the magistrates and tobacco lords waited in silence. The council chamber had a high ceiling, an antique ornamental ceiling piece and around the walls hung many portraits. The Glasgow men sat at an oval table made of polished mahogany. Hay entered first and immediately rounded on them, accusing them of being rebels and traitors.

'An English army we can understand, sir. They are regular fighting men. They are doing their job. They are obeying orders like the men in King George's Highland regiments are obeying orders. We can understand that. Yes, even the Campbells we understand. But you, sir, you Glasgow scum, you money-grubbing tradesmen, you took it upon yourself to form a militia for the sole purpose of destroying your fellow countrymen and your prince.'

'Our allegiance, sir, is to King George,' Ramsay said, 'not to any Pretender.'

'Wheesht, Ramsay,' Halyburton warned. 'Do you want to get yourself shot?'

'It's scum like you that the Prince is resolved to make an example of, to strike terror into other places.'

'I fear only God, sir.'

'Then God help you!'

The Provost held up a restraining hand. 'Now, now, Mr Hay, let us talk in a reasonable and civilised manner. You call us tradesmen. Well, we are merchants, that is true, but surely that is no reason for us to be either ashamed or abused.'

'You marched a battalion to Stirling to fight against the son of your rightful sovereign King James.'

'The battalion is a matter of fact, Mr Hay, and we are not denying it. But who our rightful sovereign is, is a matter of opinion.'

Ramsay stuck out his jaw.

'We are Whigs and Presbyterians, sir. Why should we follow a man who would prevent us worshipping in the way we want? And we are intelligent men. Why should we support a man who would ruin the business and prosperity not only of Glasgow but of the whole of Scotland?'

'So it is as I say,' Hay sneered. 'You are a money-grubbing traitor, sir. You would be dependent on England. You would grovel to the English, the enemy of us all.'

'The English are my business competitors, not my enemy. And I grovel to no man, sir. I am a better businessman by far than any English merchant and I have proved it. I do not need to prove that I am braver and fiercer in the field.'

'You Lowland scum. You talk of bravery and fierceness in the field in the presence of Highlanders? There is no man anywhere in the world who can match a Highlander for daring and courage. We are fighters born and bred, sir.'

'And we are intelligent men!'

Hay drew his pistol and held it close to Ramsay's face.

'I am tempted, merchant, to deny my prince the pleasure of dealing with you.'

His companion, a handsome man with dark lustrous eyes, stepped forward.

'Stay your arm, man. This is not what we came for.' He turned to the Provost. 'I am Cameron of Lochiel. Some of our men are outside and we must see them properly housed and fed. This I hope your townspeople will do with good grace. If they do they have nothing to fear. No harm will come to them. Our men have always behaved well to the populace.'

Hay replaced his pistol.

'Who owns the mansion house we passed as we came into town?'

'I do,' said John Glassford.

'Then, sir, you will have the honour of giving hospitality to Charles, Prince of Wales and Regent of Scotland, England, France and Ireland and the dominions thereunto belonging, and to some of his gentlemen.'

'Oh, aye.' Glassford was unimpressed. 'And who's going to pay for all this?'

Before Hay could retort, Lochiel said quietly:

'You will not be required to pay one bawbee for a crumb that goes over the Prince's throat, sir.'

'Oh, aye.'

'Another column of the army will arrive tonight. Another tomorrow. On Friday the Prince will arrive at the head of the clans.'

'Weel, weel.' Halyburton shook his head. 'It beats me where you're going to put them all.'

'Those who cannot pack into houses will camp in the streets. But each house will have to take at least ten or twenty. And, merchants, that includes your houses.'

'Weel, weel. If that's what has to be. But I tremble to think what my gudewife will have to say about a crowd like that in her house.'

'Tremble away, sir. Tremble away.'

Lochiel put a hand on Hay's arm.

'We've said our piece. The men are waiting outside.' Then he turned to the Provost and gave a slight bow. 'Lord Provost.'

The Provost gravely returned the compliment. 'Sir.'

Hay called out before leaving:

'We will be in contact again, merchants. Do not imagine we are finished with you.'

Gav and Regina saw them return outside and remount their horses. Then suddenly there was a cry of 'Free quarters!' and the tightly packed mob of men and the mounted officers began to disperse in all directions. Down Trongate Street they swarmed and up High Street, along Gallowgate Street and down Saltmarket Street, along wynds and in closes.

A crowd came hurrying in the close where Gav and Regina were hiding. They froze with terror, but the men pushed past them without as much as a second glance.

Some of the officers hesitated at the Cross, their horses rearing up in different directions. Then some of them cantered along Trongate Street. Others made for the Saltmarket. A crowd of them turned in the first close.

Big John was standing guard on Ramsay's stables at the back of the building near the turnpike stair. He glowered and refused to budge when the officers appeared and ordered him to take care of their horses.

'Rebut!' A tall Frenchman sprang from his horse and came

82

striding towards the servant with sword brandished out in front of him. 'You do not know what this means, Ecossais? It means scum.'

Big John spat defiantly, missing the Frenchman by only a few inches. Immediately the officer leapt forward and held his sword against Big John's throat and from the surrounding kitchen windows, screams of terror and protest arose.

Nancy Kinkaid left her window and went to tell Annabella what was happening. In a matter of minutes Annabella had flown down the stairs, flounced out, pink-faced and blonde curls bouncing, and shouted at the officer.

'How dare you, sir? This man is my servant. Leave him be at once or I shall box your ears.'

The man looked round in surprise, then amusement, and appreciation glimmered in his face.

'Ah, mademoiselle.' He quickly replaced his sword and flung up his hands. 'Who could resist such beauty? I capitulate gladly. Whom have I the pleasure of addressing?'

Annabella was still hot and ruffled, but her usual pertness came to her rescue. She tipped up her chin and flickered him a coquettish glance.

'Sir, I cannot think that it is any of your business who I am.'

'Ah, but indeed it is, mademoiselle. I shall be living in your house during the whole of my stay in Glasgow.'

'Indeed, sir. By whose authority?'

'By the authority of His Royal Highness Prince Charles.'

'You mean the Pretender?'

'*Mon dieu!* You have courage as well as beauty. But take care.'

'Fiddlesticks! I never take care. To be cautious is to be a bore.'

His smile came slowly, dimpling his cheeks and reflecting in his eyes. With formal exaggerated flapping and swooping of arms he made a low bow.

'Jean-Paul Lavelle at your service, mademoiselle.'

She frisked her skirts wide as she curtsied, then gracefully undulated an arm and a hand towards him.

'Annabella Ramsay.'

'*Enchanté, mademoiselle.*'

He kissed the back of her fingers, then holding them he raised her upwards and closer as he repeated, '*Enchanté*.'

She swooped away from him and did a little pirouette around the grinning crowd of officers.

'Gracious heavens, how can I feed and bed so many? It is a monstrous imposition. I cannot think what my papa will say.' But she could barely contain her delighted giggles as, clutching her skirts high to protect them from the filthy ground, she dashed back towards the house.

Gav and Regina did not know what to do. The day stretched before them fraught with dangers and privations. They ventured out of the close and aimlessly crossed the road. In front of the Tolbooth they stood reading the motto on the front:

THIS HOUSE HATES	LOVES	PUNISHES	PRESERVES	HONOURS
INIQUITY	PEACE	CRIME	THE LAWS	THE UPRIGHT

Then, being careful not to put foot on the plainstanes, they wandered along, stopping for a time to gaze up at the statue of King William and his horse. Behind the statue, the Town Hall and Exchange building afforded some interest because above each archway was a grotesque carved face or mask.

Now that the soldiers had dispersed, Trongate Street was almost empty. There were no tobacco lords talking business in little groups near the stairs of the Tolbooth or standing around the piazzas under the Town Hall. There was only a man with a barrow disappearing down one side of the street and a caddie bent underneath a keg of herrings slowly advancing along the other. From the distance came the two-horse fly on its return from Greenock. And proceeding in an opposite direction was the carriage of one of the neighbouring county gentlemen with his livery servant behind.

Echoing from one of the side streets came Moothy McMurdo's bell followed by his lusty voice:

'All the shops are shut today
The toon has been invaded.

84

The Highland army's come to stay
And before this day has faded
Another mob are due.
There's nothing you can do
Except get fu'.

He appeared from Candleriggs Street and stopped at the guard house which was at its corner.

'It's going to get worset
Until your hooses are bustet;
For there's thousands mair coming tomorrow,
On Friday as well,
I'm sorry to tell,
Will bring us the cause of our sorrow.'

Gav said: 'Maybe there's crowds of them in our house.'
Regina sighed.
'I expect so.'
'There won't be room for us anywhere.' Regina rubbed at a flickering nerve at the side of her eye. 'We'll have to think of how we're going to get food.'
They stood in silence for a while, gazing helplessly down Trongate Street at the disappearing figure of the bellman. Eventually Regina said:
'I suppose the only way is to beg like we did yesterday.'
'I don't like begging.'
'I don't either, but how else can we get anything?'
'There was still some bannocks left in the house.'
Regina shook her head. 'I'm not going back there. I don't like that Jeannie. Anyway there'll be crowds of Highlanders.'
'I'm not afraid of the Highlanders. I'll tell them that I'm a Highlander too.'
'I wonder . . .' Regina nibbled at her lip. 'I wonder if I could do Maister Ramsay and Mistress Halyburton's washing like Mammy did.'
'Ask.' Gav jumped up and down with eagerness. 'They paid Mammy money. Maybe they'd pay you too. Then we could buy lots of food.'
'All right. Let's try Mistress Halyburton first this time.'

Energised by this new hope, the children hurried down Trongate Street until they came to Locheid's Land. Once at the back of the building, Regina said:

'You wait there in case they think that having a little brother is a nuisance and don't give me the job. Then what will we do?'

'I'm not a nuisance,' Gav indignantly protested.

'I know you're not, but Mistress Halyburton is a terrible targe. I remember Mammy saying that. She might think you'd get in the way or something.'

'Oh, all right.'

'I'll try not to be long. Hide in the stairs until I come back down again.'

Unhappily Gav nodded. Then he crouched down in one of the shadowy corners and almost disappeared inside his outsize jacket. Impulsively Regina bent down and kissed his freckled face.

'We'll be all right.'

Then she ran quickly up the stairs. Arriving at the Halyburtons' house, her courage suddenly deserted her. She could not bring herself to tirl the door-pin. But the thought of the terrible situation she and Gav were in brought desperation to her aid. Before she could change her mind she grabbed the iron tirling pin. It made the rasping sound that had given tirling pins the nickname of 'craws' or 'crows'.

Almost immediately the door jerked open to reveal a small hunchback with bald patches in her hair and narrow slits for eyes.

'I know you!' she accused. 'You're Jessie Chisholm's lassie. Come here!' She grabbed Regina by the front of her dress, hauled her into the house and shut the door. 'Mistress Letitia!' she screeched. 'Mistress Letitia!'

Regina gazed around trembling with fear. A door lay open into what looked like a dining-room and it was full of Highlanders.

From another room Mrs Halyburton appeared like a warship in full sail. She was rigid-backed under her high powdered wig and dangling earrings, and her yellow quilted petticoat and green hooped skirt did nothing to improve her sallow complexion.

Eyes wicked with fury, lips a narrow line, her hands clutched at her waist hoisting up her bosom.

'What is it now, Kate?'

'It's Jessie's lassie.'

Without hesitation Letitia shot out a hand and cuffed Regina on the head and face.

'Steal my fine linen, would you?'

'I didn't! I didn't!' Regina sobbed.

She cuffed her again.

'Well, where is it? And where's your mother?'

'I don't know. She never came home and I don't know what to do. I've no money and I was hoping you'd give me work. I'd work very hard. I promise.'

'Your mother promised to hurry straight back with my linen. But did she? No, she did not.'

Kate punched Regina's back, making her stagger off balance.

'The nerve of it! Coming to oor door like that.'

Letitia said: 'The pillory's the place for her and her thieving mother.'

Regina's sobs heightened to wails of terror.

'Oh, please, please. I didn't steal anything and I don't know where my mammy is, but if I find out I'll tell you. I promise. I promise!'

'You'd better,' said Letitia, cuffing her again. 'If you don't keep that promise it's the pillory for you or the stake, like your wicked old witch of a granny. Now get out of my sight.'

The door was opened and Regina hurled outside to land on her back on the floor. She cowered there too terrified to move until the door crashed shut and there was silence. Boxes lay about the landing among mountains of dirty newspapers. Somewhere a rat rustled. Regina struggled up, rubbing at her eyes. She felt heartbroken at having to go and disappoint Gav by confessing her failure and she tried, as she made her way slowly downstairs, to think of some other solution to their problems. But everything had swelled to such terrifying proportions that her mind kept fuzzing as if it were filled with balls of wool. Then when she reached the foot of the stairs Gav was not there.

'Gav?'

She ran outside, this way and that, round in a circle then back to the stairs. She began to sob.

'Gav, where are you? Don't play games. I'm frightened.'

She climbed up to the top of the stairs and ran back down and out to the back close. She flew up and down all the other stairways in the yard all the time, calling his name. Then through the narrow entry alongside the warehouse under the arch and out on to Trongate Street. Still there was neither sight nor sound of him. She ran down Candleriggs Street and back to Trongate Street and then stopped. Her heart seemed to have multiplied a thousandfold and was drumming mercilessly in every part of her. She could hardly breathe.

Unable to cope with the idea that she could be alone or that any harm had come to her brother she made up her mind that he must have felt hungry and gone to Tannery Wynd to fetch the bannocks he had spoken of.

'I'll box your ears for you when I catch you,' she muttered to herself. 'You'll howl and bubble and greet today, all right.'

She wondered if she ought to go back to the Halyburtons' stairway and wait for him or if she ought to walk towards the Cross and meet him halfway. She decided to start walking. In a secret chamber of her mind the thought that Gav was being held prisoner at the house grew like an ominous shadow and blurred her vision everywhere she looked. At the Cross she loitered, every now and again rubbing one bare foot against her leg, or a clenched fist into her eyes.

Rain had begun to smir across the city and the sun which had earlier dappled the buildings now retreated behind black clouds. Regina shivered and drew her cape tighter round her. She peered down Saltmarket Street and up High Street. It was like a Sabbath day. No one was walking the streets and an almost complete silence prevailed. Reluctantly she started walking again, this time past the Cross and along Gallowgate Street. She hesitated once more when she reached Tannery Wynd. Oh, she would box his ears for him like he had never had them boxed before. It was not fair of him to torment her like this. She quickened her pace along the narrow lane, flicking nervous glances in all directions in case Spider was watching in one of the doorways or behind one of the dunghills to bite her. But she reached the cottage unharmed and pushed at the door. It opened to reveal a crowd of French and Irish soldiers. There was a shout when they saw her and before she could turn and make her escape one of them grabbed her and pulled her inside.

'Let go of me. Let go of me!' Regina screamed and kicked and struggled as hard as she could, but the man just laughed and called out something in French.

The doors of the hole-in-the-wall bed had opened to reveal Jeannie and another soldier. Both were naked.

'Oh, there you are, pet.'

Jeannie pushed the naked soldier aside, and slithered from the bed, pulling on her skirt.

'I wondered where you'd gone. I worried and worried.'

'Where's my wee brother?'

'He disappeared as well, pet, and that robber Quin. You don't want anything to do with a man like that, pet. He robs a poor lassic instead of helping her with a wee bit money.'

'I'll have to go and look for my wee brother.'

'Och, there's plenty of time, pet. Tell me something. Have you got any money?'

'No.'

'And now that your mammy's gone you'll need some to buy food. Is that right, pet?'

'Yes.'

'Well, pet, this big soldier man's got money. So if you just be nice to him and let him do what he wants he'll give you all that you need.'

Suddenly one of the other men lurched forward.

'It's an Irishman she'll be having first, not a French fop.'

Another pushed him aside.

'Quite right, Michael—*this* Irishman!'

Others staggered towards Regina with drunken leering faces and loose mouths and hands outstretched. Suddenly the Frenchman who had a grip of her pulled out a pistol and aimed it at the rest.

'*Après moi!*' he snarled at them before hoisting Regina up with his other hand and tossing her into the bed. Then he climbed in and shut the wooden doors. Darkness enclosed her and she withered back against the wall, able only to squeeze out small animal noises.

Chapter 8

It was the 'four hours', the time when Glasgow ladies entertained their 'cummers' or afternoon visitors.

Annabella handed round the delicate teacups to the French officers. The dishes had come all the way from China and she was extremely proud of them. Like all the other ladies who owned teacups and saucers, she did not allow the servants to touch them but carefully washed the china herself after her guests had departed and packed them away in a chest.

'The minister and others tell me that tea is a wicked drug,' she said. 'And as I do not wish to do you any harm, gentlemen, I suggest you take a little whisky in it to correct the bad effects. Will you translate for the benefit of your friends, Monsieur Lavelle?'

'It is not necessary. They understand most of what is said although they cannot speak the language.'

The whisky bottle was passed around, then the mixture tasted with sighs of appreciation.

'Pray continue, monsieur,' Annabella encouraged. 'I am prodigiously entertained by your adventures on the way to England.'

'*Merci, mademoiselle. Maintenant*, where were we? Ah, yes, Edinburgh. Dragoons came to intercept us at Coltbridge. Dragoons and a few students ventured outside Edinburgh's walls. The rest of the timid citizens had slunk into the lanes and houses. The dragoons lined up, but as soon as a few Jacobite gentlemen rode towards them and fired their pistols the horsemen took to flight and did not cease their ignoble retreat till many miles distant.'

'Laud's sakes!' Annabella exclaimed. 'Such a thing could never have happened in Glasgow.'

'The citizens of Edinburgh, they trembled, mademoiselle, and eagerly surrendered. And next day as Prince Charles Edward

91

came on horseback towards Holyrood Palace the crowds to see him were huge, some trying to kiss his clothes or touch his hand.'

'The gentleman must be uncommonly attractive.'

Lavelle nonchalantly raised his shoulders.

'He is a slender young fellow, almost five feet ten or six feet high. He has a long face and large eyes and reddish hair. He is dignified and gracious but he has changed a lot since we marched into England. Then he was most elated and mixed freely and spoke much to the men. Even attempting words and phrases in Gaelic. But he has never recovered from the acuteness of his disappointment at not marching in and capturing the city of London. He was most set on reaching St James's Palace. All day he argued with the chiefs, I remember, and especially with Lord George Murray. My Lord Murray kept reminding the Prince that they had barely five thousand men and although so far they had outmanoeuvred the King's armies, nevertheless upwards of thirty thousand men were fast closing in on them. And of course the populace was hostile as well.' Lavelle sighed. 'But nothing would sway the Prince from his resolve. He believes his clansmen are absolutely invincible, mademoiselle. He believes too in the divine right of his cause and to boot he is a very stubborn fellow. I remember him crying out, "I would rather be twenty feet under the earth than turn back now, gentlemen".' Lavelle shrugged again. 'But Lord Murray is stubborn too and he and all the chiefs outvoted the Prince. I do not know who was right but the clansmen were very angry. The Prince has great charm and the men would have followed him even into London.'

'No doubt he used his charm to great advantage with the Edinburgh ladies,' Annabella said.

'Ah, Edinburgh! What a splendid ball there was at Holyrood Palace. What a scene! All the rank and fashion of the town and all the Jacobite nobility were there. But that was nothing compared to the enthusiasm of the populace when we returned after the battle of Prestonpans. That was where Sir John Cope's men ran like rabbits.' He laughed loudly. 'I cannot blame them. Those Scottish pipes droning weird, wild, agonizing strains are enough to make any man wish to run.'

Annabella rapped him playfully on the knee with her long

fan.

'I am tempted, sir, not to believe one single word you tell me.'

'Ah, sincerely, mademoiselle. In a very few minutes the whole army, with horse and foot, were put to flight. And not one of us had to load our pieces again and not one bayonet was stained with blood. And when, two days later, we returned to Edinburgh the acclamations of the populace were vociferous. Even in the church the minister prayed . . .' The Frenchman clasped his hands together and mimicked a supplicating tone. 'As to this young person who has come among us seeking an earthly crown, so then in Thy mercy send him a Heavenly one.'

Annabella giggled.

'You are a disrespectful, impertinent rascal, monsieur, but mightily entertaining. Tell me about the festivities.'

'They cajoled the Prince. They sang to him, drank to him, danced to him. Ah, what festivities and parades and dances there were in Edinburgh. But the strange thing was, mademoiselle, that while rousing romantic sentiment and enthusiasm in others the Prince displayed little himself. "They are my beauties," he said pointing to a huge bearded Highland sentinel, when reproached with indifference to his fair admirers.'

Annabella rolled her eyes.

'Gracious heaven! What kind of man is this?'

'A brave man, mademoiselle. A man with surprising physical endurance. If you had seen him at his best on the march down through England, stoutly walking the rough roads, in lashing wind and wet and cold, sharing the poor fare of the Highlanders, yet always in good humour and full of inspiring confidence, you could not but admire him. In his Highland garb he marched at the head of his column, while he put old Lord Pitsligo in his carriage. He lay down to sleep every night without undressing and by four o'clock in the morning he was up once more.'

'I am impressed.'

'Then when he rides into Glasgow I hope you will be out on the street fluttering your handkerchief and raising huzzas of welcome, mademoiselle.'

'I fear I must dash your hopes, sir, because indeed I will not put one foot outside.'

'But . . .'

She eyed him with provocative amusement.

'I might notice your prince from my window. If I am not too busy doing something else.'

'*Your* prince, mademoiselle! I am a Frenchman, a loyal subject of King Louis.'

'A Popish prince cannot have the allegiance of a Glasgow Presbyterian, sir. You will soon find that Glasgow is a mightily different city from Edinburgh.' She swooped open her fan. 'Glasgow is a solemn, sanctimonious Presbyterian bore of a place.'

The men roared with laughter and Lavelle said:

'*Non, non!* I cannot believe you. How could any place be boring, mademoiselle, when you are here?'

'Gracious heaven, even I am weighed down at times. I ache to be far away from here. I long for exciting adventures and diversions and for the lively, interesting company of charming people who know how to enjoy life.' She fluttered her lashes at him and added: 'Like yourself!'

The other officers raised noisy whoops and nudged Lavelle and spoke in rapid French interspersed with ripples of laughter.

Annabella sipped her tea with dignified unconcern.

'Believe me, gentlemen, if you had suffered a Glasgow Sunday you would not be in the least surprised at my words. Silence is like a suffocating blanket over the place. Not even a dog dare bark and the inquisitors, or bum-baillies as they're sometimes called, poke and pry round every corner and into every house. I tell you the truth, sirs, they have you before the Kirk Sessions for combing your hair. And losh and lovandie!' She rolled her eyes and flung up her hands. 'For humming a merry tune they say you are kowtowing with the devil and are destined to burn for ever and ever in the pit!'

'I think at heart you are no Presbyterian, mademoiselle.'

'At heart, monsieur, I am just a woman.'

Lavelle tossed kisses from his fingertips. 'A beautiful woman. An enchanting woman. A woman of spirit.'

'Of course!'

Lavelle laughed and shook his head.

94

Gav had been squatting in the corner of the stairs where Regina left him when he heard a piper tune up. He wondered if this meant that more Highlanders were marching into town. Curiosity eventually overcame him and he slipped through the archway to the front of Locheid's Land. Cautiously he peeped out. All that could be seen was a lone piper, a ragged Highlander playing a lament to himself across the road. Gav glowered at the man's pathetic and unkempt appearance; the matted hair, the scarred and naked body covered only by a filthy plaid looped up between his legs, the bare feet swollen and misshapen with mud and dung. It was such a different picture from the Highlanders his mother had always described, he felt cheated and bitter. Stuffing his hands deep in his pockets he dug moodily at the ground with his heel. Then suddenly he was startled into awareness by a hand grabbing him by the lapels and a one-eyed lumpy face framed with hair like strands of wet wool.

'Auld Nick was verra angry at Quin. "Quin," says he, "Quin, you shouldn't trust folks like that. That was verra foolish of you to go upstairs and leave them childers by themselves." '

'Let go of me!' Gav punched and kicked as hard as he could. 'I'm not going to beg for you every day. Beg for yourself!' With a determined wriggle he managed to free himself and race across the road and down King Street.

King Street ran parallel with and between Saltmarket and Stockwell Street but the King Street tenements were of different heights. Some were only tiny thatched hovels and most of the buildings were divided by large stretches of waste ground. Gav had no sooner entered the street when he regretted his rash choice of direction. The waste ground afforded him no cover and he was forced to continue his flight. King Street led into Briggait, but instead of going right down on to the bridge he cut off at the narrow lane called the Goose Dubs which brought him on to Stockwell Street. There he stopped for breath and dared to glance back. Much to his relief it was as he hoped, he had proved himself faster on his feet than Quin who was nowhere to be seen. Indeed that was the strange thing. Nobody was to be seen. Choking for breath, Gav wiped at his face with the sleeve of his jacket. He felt uneasy, as if he and Quin were the only people left in the world and now even Quin had gone.

He tugged his hat defiantly down over his springy curls and marched up Stockwell Street. Turning back at Trongate Street at last, he squinted round the corner to see if there were any signs of Regina. There was no one at Locheid's Land. She was taking an awful long time at Mistress Halyburton's. But, of course, she might be waiting for him at the back on the stairs where she had left him. He wondered if it was wise to risk walking along the deserted Trongate to Locheid's Land. Yet what else could he do? He sniffed, rubbed his nose with his sleeve and marched round the corner and across the road. He was nearing Candleriggs when suddenly Quin leapt out from behind one of the pillars of the Guard House.

'Quin's legs are no' as fast as yours, eh? But he's wily.'

'I've to meet my sister. She's waiting for me in Locheid's Land. So let go of me.'

'Locheid's Land, eh? No' half a dozen steps along the road. Quin's coming.'

He cantered along, keeping a firm grip of Gav's ear and making the child run and stumble alongside him. In the back close he said:

'Weel, where's the lassie, eh?' He gave a vicious twist at the ear, making Gav howl in pain. 'Tell Quin.'

'She was upstairs at Mistress Halyburton's asking for work. She must still be there.'

'Oh-ho, Quin knows auld Kate. Auld Tam Bogle as well. Upstairs.'

He pushed and pulled and twisted at Gav until they had reached the Halyburtons' door. Gav's lips were trembling and he bit at them in an effort to stop himself from bursting into tears.

The bent iron door-pin rasped round and round until the door opened and revealed an old crone with a hump on her back that twisted her forward and to one side. She had a long nose with a black wart on the end that nearly met her chin.

'The cheek of some folks,' she screeched on spying Quin. 'We'll no' have begging at oor door.'

'Quin's no' begging, Kate.'

'What do you want then?'

'Quin's just anxious to find a lost friend. A wee childer by the name of Regina.'

'Oh, I might have known she was a friend o' yours. The mistress kicked her down the stairs on her backside a long while ago. And I'll put my foot up your bum in a minute for pestering respectable folk.'

'Quin's away. Quin's away.'

Down the stair he jogged until they reached Trongate Street again.

'Weel!' he said. 'She's no' there noo!'

'I . . . I don't understand.' Gav's voice shook despite his efforts to sound brave. 'I thought she would have waited for me.'

'It's Auld Nick,' said Quin, scratching his head. 'He's a right auld devil, eh? First he whisks your mammy away and now he's whippit your sister. He'll nab you yet if you're no' careful.'

Gav's eyes widened with anxiety.

'Stay with Quin. Quin'll find her, eh?'

'Could you?'

'Quin's in league with Auld Nick. "Quin," Auld Nick says, says he, "Quin, you play fair with me and I'll play fair with you. Many's the time Auld Nick's helped Quin." '

'Could you get her back?'

Quin released his grip.

'You'll stay with Quin, eh?'

Gav nodded, then repeated hopefully:

'Could you get her back now?'

Quin poked an exploratory finger in the hole that had once been his ear.

'Witches or fairies, Quin wonders.'

'What do you mean?'

'Auld Nick farms them oot. All sorts of creatures keep childers for him. It'll take Quin a wee while.'

Men were beginning to emerge from the taverns and at the sight of them spilling on to the street Quin did a gleeful little dance.

'Make for the Exchange, lad. That's where we'll find the most

97

sillar.'

Off he jogged with elbows bent and fists clenched.

Moothy McMurdo was strolling from the other direction swinging his bell.

> 'Windie Hodge sells burial crapes ready made,
> And his wife's niece who's verra pretty,
> And recently arrived from the capital city
> Dresses corpses at a verra cheap rate.'

Rain was melting Trongate Street into a grey blur as servants led horses out from stables and men mounted up with wide swirling of capes. Others who lived only a few steps from the tavern, like Adam Ramsay, strode away with head down and feet splashing in the deep ruts of the road that was fast becoming a quagmire. Others again, too full of ale and whisky for rain to dampen their spirits, stood swaying and talking in groups under the archways or out in the open.

It was still afternoon and normally these men would have been in their shops, or warerooms, or counting houses, or colleges. There were many professors to be seen among them. Professor Simson, the absent-minded mathematician who always counted out loud to himself each pace he took between the college and the tavern and back or to and from anywhere else he happened to be going. There was Hume the philosopher and historian, and Adam Smith the political philosopher, with his cane over his shoulder like a musket. There were the Foulis brothers, the printers, James Watt the engineer and Robert Adam the architect.

On reaching the first group, Quin suddenly drooped in a lethargic fashion, doubled over and leaned pathetically on Gav's shoulder. Gav took off his hat and held it out and Quin cocked his face to one side so that his egg-shaped protuberance and his ragged flesh could best be seen.

Ramsay pushed roughly past them. He was in a vile mood. Business was completely held up. He had not been in his counting house all day. Even the churches had closed their doors. Life in the town was hanging fire, ranks had closed, people waited with stubborn dourness. The Pretender and his followers would find no welcome in Glasgow and Ramsay hoped they would not as a result stay long. The quicker business was back to normal the better. He could hardly believe his ears when he arrived at his house and heard sounds of gaiety and laughter. He stormed into Annabella's bedroom and found her surrounded by French officers. The tea-things were still lying on the table and so was an empty bottle of whisky. Annabella's face was like a rose in full bloom and her eyes sparkled like blue stars. She was resplendent in a cherry satin hoop over a crimson velvet petticoat trimmed with silver and gold and she had cherry and white ribbons in her hair.

'Papa! Papa!' she cried out as soon as she saw him. 'I'm having a wondrously happy time!'

'Deevil choke you, Annabella!'

'Papa, don't be such a misery and spoil it all. These gentlemen have been miraculously entertaining.'

Ramsay turned on the officers.

'Get out!'

Lavelle shrugged. 'We are billeted here, monsieur. Whether you like it or not we stay in your house until his Royal Highness Prince Charles Edward decides that we should leave it.'

'In my house maybe, sir. But not in my daughter's bedroom.'

'But it is a custom of the country, is it not, that you entertain in the main bedroom?'

'Aye, that's verra true, but it doesn't apply to French sodgers. You'll eat, drink and sleep in the kitchen, in the lobby, or in *my* bedroom, sir.'

'Or, monsieur?'

Ramsay jerked a pistol from under his cloak.

'Or, I'll blow your bloody head off.'

Lavelle grinned. '*Touché.*'

Turning to Annabella, he made elegant ever-growing circles with his outstretched fingers and bowed gracefully and low.

'Mademoiselle Annabella.'

With one hand Annabella flourished her fan, the other she stretched sideways over her hoop as she sank slowly into a curtsy.

'Monsieur Lavelle.'

After the bedroom door closed behind them Ramsay groaned.

'Annabella, Annabella!'

'Oh, Papa. They have done me no harm and I was only being civil.'

'They are our enemies.'

'The French? But Papa, you cruelly confuse me. Have we not entertained French merchants?'

'That is different and fine you know it, mistress.'

'But, Papa . . .'

'Hold your tongue.'

He could well have done without gathering the servants together and going to the bother of giving a reading and reciting prayers but he felt duty bound to do so. These past few days he had laboured under a lowness of spirit and uneasiness of mind arising from various causes outward and inward. He suffered an indisposition of body as well as of mind and he looked on it as the fruit of evil and the punishment of sins which the Lord knew he had committed.

'Oh Lord,' he thought, 'wean my heart away from a present world and produce in me the peaceable fruits of righteousness.'

'Where's Douglas?' he asked.

Annabella rolled her eyes. 'Need you ask, Papa?'

'Aye, it's time he was wed as well, I'm thinking. Well, go and fetch Nancy and Big John.' Then as she was swooping towards the door, he added: 'I don't suppose you've heard what's happened to Jessie?'

'No, Papa.'

'Aye, you'd be too busy thinking about your French sodgers to bother about the likes of Jessie.'

'Indeed, sir, it fluttered me a trifle when she did not come to collect any washing these past two days and Nancy flew into a pretty passion when I told her that she would have to attend to it until other arrangements could be made.'

'Aye, aye.' He sighed. 'Away and tell them to come.'

He flung off his cloak and thumped down on a seat at the bedside table. He stared at the Bible which was always kept there in the vain hope that it might encourage Annabella to peruse it.

'O Lord, cause Thy face to shine on me again and I shall be safe.'

Outside in the lobby some of the officers were squatting and lounging on the floor. Others were through in the kitchen trying to flirt with Nancy. Annabella entered just in time to save one of them from Big John's fists. She picked up a pewter plate and flung it at the servant cutting him on the brow.

'He has a pistol, you fool,' she said. 'Do you want to get yourself shot? And stop bleeding all over the place. Come, Papa is waiting for you and Nancy.'

Lavelle was straddling a chair at the other side of the room. He beckoned with a finger for her to approach him. She tossed her head but did not budge from where she stood near the door.

'If you wish to speak to me, sir, you may rise.' She jabbed a finger at a point immediately in front of her. 'And come over here!'

Trying to conceal a smile, he rose and bowed.

'I only wished to remark, mademoiselle, that it did not seem proper that I as a senior officer should have such cramped quarters.'

She raised an eyebrow. 'While I have a whole room to myself?'

'And a comfortable bed.'

'Oh, sir, how ungallant! You surprise me. So it is only the comfort of my bed you are after.'

'You are the comfort of the bed, mademoiselle.'

'No, no, monsieur, I am much more than a comfort!'

Just then a bawl issued from the bedroom: 'Annabella, are you at it again?'

Lavelle said quickly: 'If I visited you later, what would you say?'

She slid him a roguish look before flouncing away.

'How little you know me, sir. I never chatter in bed.'

Ramsay was waiting with jaw jammed forward and fingers drumming the table.

'Oh, aye. You've decided to join us, after all, have you? Well, maybe now that you're ready we can all get the benefit of God's word.

'James, Chapter 4: "From whence come wars and fightings among you? Come they not hence, even of your lusts that war in your members? Ye lust, and have not . . ." '

His voice loudened until it broke into a desperate roar:

'Submit yourself therefore to God. Raise the devil, and he will flee from you!'

Chapter 9

'Are you all sticky, pet?' Jeannie bent over Regina. 'Here's a wet cloth. Wipe yourself with that like a good wee lassie.'

Regina was upstairs in the harlots' house cowering on the floor in a corner. The skirt of her petticoat was soaked with blood. She gazed up at Jeannie from the shadows, eyes enormous.

'Duck her in the river,' one of the other women said. 'That'll liven her up.'

Jeannie smiled. She had a heart-shaped face that had once been pretty but some of her teeth were missing and her eyes had sunk deep into black crêpe hollows.

'Don't mind Muckle Mary, pet. Her gob's as big as everything else.'

Muckle Mary's flesh bulged out and suspended over the chair she was sitting on, rolled over the table she was leaning on and threatened to engulf the clay pipe she was smoking. Opening her mouth like a whale coming up for air, she kept a grip on the pipe with one bunched fist and said:

'The sodgers don't complain.'

The third woman in the room tittered.

'She can take three f . . . sodgers on at once, can't you, Mary?'

'That's Leezie,' said Jeannie. 'An awful nice lassie. She'll give you a wee sup of her whisky, pet, and you'll be singing like a lintie in no time.'

'Christ!' Leezie exclaimed. 'You're bloody generous with my whisky. What the hell's wrong with your own?'

'Wasn't it me that got her and isn't she going to be a help to us all? Aren't you, pet? You're going to be a good wee lassie, sure you are?'

She smiled again. Regina looked away. Her eyes sought a place on the floor directly in front of her. She riveted her gaze on the spot. The wooden floorboard had once been warm brown, but was now cold black with only a faint port wine stain coaxed out by the sun's rays. Once it had been smooth, but now it looked as if miniature wheels had scored it a thousand times, coarsening its surface, rutting it, rotting it. A beetle like a black mirror laboriously seesawed.

'Wipe yourself, pet,' Jeannie repeated.

Leezie came over with the whisky and forced it against Regina's lips. As she bent over her, Regina could see down Leezie's shirt a suppurating sore on one of her breasts.

'Come on, you red-headed wee cow. Do as you're telt or we'll fling you down to the sodgers again the way you are.'

'She's got bonny long hair,' Jeannie said. 'Haven't you, pet?'

The two women were blocking out the sun. It was dark and cold.

'And such a nice creamy skin. No' a spot on it. And such fine green eyes. Och, you're a bonny wee lassie, pet.'

Some of the whisky trickled over Regina's face. The rest found its way down her throat. She wiped her legs with the wet cloth without looking.

'Take off your petticoat and give the skirt of it a rub in this bowl of water. It'll soon dry at the fire.'

Like a feeble old woman Regina peeled off the striped woollen petticoat and left herself naked.

Leezie laughed.

'Hey, Mary, would you take a keek at this. You call me skinny?'

Muckle Mary had a husky low-pitched voice like a man.

'It'll no' be three at a time for her.'

'Never mind, pet,' said Jeannie. 'You're still growing.'

'Hurry up.' Leezie gave Regina a punch. 'Do what you're telt.'

Regina fumbled the skirt about in the bowl until the water dirtied into dark red. Then Jeannie took the petticoat and hung it close to the fire. She came back over.

'Here's your nice green cape, pet. But its no' a nice bright green like your eyes. What bonny eyes you have, pet.'

Regina allowed the cape to be draped over the front of her.

Across the other side of the room on one of the rafters a rat was sitting up on its haunches like a dog begging. It had a tiny pointed mouth and tiny pointed paws. Its black tail hung down and swayed slowly to and fro like a pendulum. There was a hole in the thatching of the roof. The sun was fading away, leaving the sky slate-coloured. The sky was a jagged patch in the rat-brown thatching of the roof.

'The Highlanders didn't look as if they'd have two bawbees to rub together.'

'Christ, Mary, what are you worrying about. There's thousands more men coming today. And thousands more on Friday. There's bound to be plenty money among all that lot.'

Muckle Mary's laughter came slowly as if it could barely heave up through all her flesh.

'I'll fight the pair of you for Prince Charlie.'

'The three of us she means, doesn't she, pet?' Jeannie's face creased in Regina's direction. 'Och, now, wouldn't a prince be awful nice.'

'We'll no' get f . . . near him.'

'Och, well, I was forgetting anyway. He's a Pape, and we don't want anything to do with dirty Papes, sure we don't, pet?'

Leezie rolled her eyes. 'Christ, what the bloody hell do you think the whole Highland army is?'

'Och, don't listen to her, pet. Don't you worry your bonny wee head. The Highland army's maybe "piscies" but they're no' Papes.'

'They say the Prince is bonny.'

'Christ, what does it bloody matter if he's cockeyed or bandy-legged. He's no' going to look at the likes of you.'

'What's wrong with the likes of me?' Mary rumbled. 'How would you like a kick up the arse?'

Steam was rising from the striped wool. A hen splay toed its way daintily across the floor. Leezie kicked it aside as she strolled towards the table. It squawked in furious indignation and ruffled its feathers, making itself swell to twice its size.

'I'd rather have a bloody drink.' She flopped down and raised the whisky bottle to her mouth.

Jeannie went over and did the same and soon they were all carousing and singing.

'Who learned you to dance,
Babity Bowster, Babity Bowster?
Who learned you to dance,
Babity Bowster, brawly?

My minny learned me to dance,
Babity Bowster, Babity Bowster,
My minny learned me to dance,
Babity Bowster, brawly.'

They did not notice Regina sliding over towards the fire to get her petticoat and slithering back again to put it on.

Light blurred and faded with the harlots' voices. The fire died under trickles of black smoke. The rats descended from the rafters in single file like soldiers.

Slowly Regina eased herself nearer the door. On reaching it she stretched up her hand and found the latch. Without a sound the door opened. On all fours she crawled from the room on to the wooden landing. Downstairs, men were laughing and talking. She could not get up. Standing up would make her noticeable, vulnerable. She half slithered, half crawled down the stairs and along the lane like a snake writhing around between the dunghills. Not until she reached Gallowgate Street could she believe that she had truly escaped. She remained crouched on the mud for a few minutes before rising. Then she moved cautiously in the direction of the Cross. Never before had she looked forward to darkness. She willed it to come, to change the dusky shadow to black, to obliterate her. Once darkness had meant fear. Now it was velvet to draw round her and cover her face.

The musical bells of the Tolbooth clock chimed their merry, incongruous tune.

She hesitated, not knowing which way to turn. The close where she had spent the first night away from home was only a few minutes along Trongate Street. At least she knew that place and drawn by this thread of familiarity she made her way head down towards it. Through the archway into the back close, over to the tower.

'Regina, is that you?' a voice suddenly cried out from the shadows. 'Is it really you?' A small figure dwarfed by a big hat and jacket leapt up and down with joyful excitement then came hopping and skipping towards her. 'Regina! Regina!'

She sprang on him tearing wildly with her nails, eyes protruding, teeth bared, making him scream with surprise and pain.

'Regina, it's me Gav. Regina!'

Blood rapidly criss-crossed his face like cracks on glass.

'You left me, you bastard.' Regina said brokenly. 'You went away and left me. You bastard.'

'Well, he's here noo!' Quin grabbed her by the hair and jerked her back.

Gav was choking and sobbing.

'I didn't! I didn't mean to. I didn't. Quin came and I ran from him. When I got back you'd gone.'

'You bastard.'

'Quin's no verra pleased.'

'Why should I care?'

Quin gave a twist to her hair and she yelped with pain.

'Gav and Quin have been working all day by themselves.'

'And you've been keeping all the money.'

'Quin's fed the childer. Quin knows where to get food.' He let go of her hair. 'Quin's got bannocks.'

'He stole them,' Gav said, wiping his eyes and his bloodstained face, his breath still lurching and hiccoughing. 'He tried to make me steal but I wouldn't.'

'If you hadn't got Quin,' Quin said, 'you would have to steal, eh?'

'Why would I?'

'Oh-ho. Quin can see you're no' very clever.'

'I am so. I was getting Latin at school.'

Quin cocked his head and doubled forward until his face was level with Gav's.

'Quin's cleverer than you.'

'You can't read or write. Even Regina can read and write, can't you, Regina?'

Regina could not bear to look at either of them. She hated them for talking about ordinary things as if nothing had happened when she had died so many deaths inside.

107

Quin waggled a finger.

'Quin can't eat reading or writing and neither can you. Is it clever to starve, eh? Is that what clever Gav wants to do?'

Regina replied for him, with much bitterness and without raising her eyes.

'No, it's not. And clever Regina for one is not going to.'

Glasgow had become a tartan city. In every house the eye could not escape the different coloured checked material. It bent over cooking pots in kitchens. It lay about floors. It draped against walls. It blocked windows. It bunched in dark corners. It rippled on stairs. It spilled out on to streets. Yet many soldiers had deserted. To the Highlander, however, desertion was merely a temporary visit home to deliver loot to help his family survive or to plant seed or do other necessary chores for their well-being. He always tried his best to return in time for the next battle. Although in the first place he was likely to have been pressed into service by his chief. Cameron of Lochiel, for instance, sent his tacksmen round all his clansmen warning them that if they did not follow him all their barns would be burned and their cattle killed.

The procuring of loot in Glasgow was not such a simple business however. Glaswegians did not part easily with their goods.

One barefooted Highlander proved this to his cost. A Glasgow workman was walking along Saltmarket Street wearing an especially good pair of shoes and the Highlander stopped the man and indicated that he wanted them. The workman indignantly refused. The Highlander bent down to pull the shoes off the man's feet and the outraged owner of the shoes promptly cracked him over the head with a hammer and killed him.

For the most part the Highland army, or at least the part of it that had arrived by Thursday night, kept to themselves, only spoke to each other, cooked their own oatmeal and had as little to do with Glaswegians as they could.

Highland officers drank their whisky alone or together in the Old Coffee House Land Tavern or in the Exchange Coffee

House, while groups of Glasgow merchants sat in different rooms and drank theirs.

From various streets came the wail of the pipes sounding lost and nostalgic as if they were longing for the mountains and glens where they belonged. Men lounged in the road in the shadows of buildings with their plaids wrapped round them like cloaks.

Huge men like grizzly bears were eating and sleeping in Letitia Halyburton's dining-room and no matter how she raged at them she could not shift them out. She hung on to the key of her larder like grim death and refused to part with one grain of oatmeal.

Her husband was worried.

'For your own safety, Letitia, you'd be wiser to let them have something. Anyway, they look famished and there's plenty in the house. We'll surely no' miss a bannock or two.'

'A bannock or two? Man, there's about twenty barbarians ben there. I ken my duty and it's no' to barbarians.' She clasped her hands in front of her waist and hoisted herself erect. 'They'll get nothing from me but the sharp edge of my tongue.'

Nevertheless her daughter Phemy managed unknown to her mother to secrete supplies to the unwelcome guests who could not thank her because they spoke nothing but the Gaelic.

Griselle was angry when she found out what Phemy had done.

'I've a good mind to tell Mother. Apart from giving them food when Mother said not to, it's behaving like a traitor.'

Phemy laughed.

'They think we're traitors anyway.'

'What does it matter what they think? We are loyal subjects of King George.'

'Yes, and I'm no less loyal for giving a few handfuls of oatmeal to some starving men.'

'*Our* oatmeal. Really, Phemy, I can't understand you at times. Why even think of such shabby creatures? You'll never capture a husband with money if you don't organise yourself better and show more self-discipline and single-mindedness. Don't you think so, Father?' she added, turning to William Halyburton.

109

'Aye, my wee lintie, you're too kind-hearted for your own good. Some useless blackguard without a bawbee to his name is liable to come along and take advantage of you if we're no' careful.'

This had been a worry niggling at his mind a lot recently and the fact that Phemy was no beauty with her pockmarked face and wispy hair increased rather than alleviated his worries. Any young rascal after Phemy would be after the Halyburton money.

Later that evening he confided his concern about Phemy to his old friends upstairs, the Earl of Glendinny. The Earl patted his arm reassuringly.

'Just bide a wee! Patience, Willie. The wife's no' keeping well at all these days.'

Halyburton took the hint and felt very relieved. It had never occurred to him that Phemy could one day be matched with Glendinny. Admittedly the Earl was a wheen of years older than Phemy and he was no beauty either. But he was a sensible man and he had a good trade in tobacco with three sturdy ships sailing to and from Virginia.

Further along Trongate Street, Ramsay was equally concerned about his daughter and he too felt compelled to confide his worries in a friend.

'Aye, minister, it's a fact as you well know that our Annabella has beauty, but beauty is a terrible snare.'

'Oh, terrible, terrible!' Blackadder solemnly agreed.

'It's good of you to promise to take her on.'

'Uh-huh, och, weel, the lassie's no' beyond redemption.'

'Aye, at least she's got courage and that's more than I can say for my son.'

'I'll put up a prayer for them both, merchant.'

He took off his hat, clasped it against his chest and closed his eyes. Ramsay did the same.

'Oh Lord, Lord,' Blackadder cried heavenwards, 'have mercy on Annabella. You ken fine what a wild and wayward wench she is and how she thinks no more of committin' sin than a dog does lickin' a dish. Put Thy hook in her nose and Thy bridle in her mooth and bring her back to Thee with a jerk that she'll no' forget for the rest o' her days.

110

'And we pray Thee no' to forget Douglas. We would be verra grateful indeed, O Lord, if Thou saw fit to put a wee bit spunk in the lad and no' have him prancing aboot like a bunch o' flowers and scunnering his faither.'

Ramsay prayed too that the present troubles and tribulations of the city would soon be over and life could return to normal. It was impossible to arrange a marriage and have a wedding feast while every place was crammed to overflowing with enemies. So far nothing worse than the inconvenience of having hordes of men billeted in folks' houses had occurred, but the Pretender and the clans had yet to arrive and something was bound to happen. They were not coming to Glasgow simply to spend a few days loitering about and sampling Glasgow oatmeal.

Tomorrow they would swell the already seething city. Tomorrow the citizens of Glasgow would have a hard job trying to avoid being trampled underfoot.

Chapter 10

On Friday, 27th December 1745, not one Glaswegian went out on the streets and Prince Charles Edward Stuart entered a silent city.

He rode on a silver-grey charger over which his voluminous blue velvet cape was draped. Underneath the cape which hung loosely over his shoulders was a jacket of fine silk tartan. He wore a sword and pistols, crimson velvet breeches and thigh-length boots and on top of his powdered tie-wig he wore a three-cornered hat.

Behind him rode chiefs and chieftains and duine wassails, or 'gentlemen of the clans', and behind them marched the clansmen.

Annabella was gazing from her window of the lantern storey in the Old Coffee House Land and she cried out to Ramsay:

'Oh, Papa, he is indeed marvellously handsome. Such eyes and princely beauty!'

'Compose yourself, woman, and come away from there.'

'Papa, Papa, does your curiosity not overcome you? It is not every day we have the opportunity of feasting our eyes on a real live prince.'

'A Pretender.'

'Or even a Pretender. Oh, losh and lovenendie, what a colourful scene it is. Other handsome men on horses, oh, such handsome men, Papa, are carrying huge standards, long poles with enormous coloured flags and banners billowing out and tassels bobbing and swaying.'

'Annabella, all I want to know is when the rebel upstart has disappeared into the Shawfield Mansion so that I can go to the tavern and meet my friends.'

'Look at the men!' Annabella gasped. 'Why, they're . . . They're like monsters.'

Their hair and beards were so long and thick and uncombed hardly even their eyes could be seen. They were all crowding, jostling, shuffling along barefooted and bareheaded. They wore nothing but a plaid. Some had the lower part of it belted round their waist as a kilt and the upper part covering their shoulders like a cloak. Others just had the long piece of material looped up between their legs and round their waists with the end flung over one shoulder. Their skins were filthy and weather-beaten, almost black. Some carried huge rusty swords. Others had only scythe blades fixed to poles. Some had old Lochaber axes. There were others too in tattered grey coats and breeches of either blue or green. They had guns.

Annabella clapped her hands and did a little jig of joy.

'It's so exciting!'

'Will you come away from there and no' disgrace me?' her father shouted irritably.

She paid not the slightest attention. It was not only the spectacle she was watching that she found distracting. Joy had descended on her like rose petals from heaven. She had always made the most of every moment of each day to the best of her ability but only now could she appreciate the ecstasy her life had lacked. The efforts of previous lovers, ardent though they were, seemed gauche and clumsy and without the slightest romantic feeling compared with Jean-Paul Lavelle. She had admitted him to her room in the middle of the night and he had been so charming, so delightful, so passionate she felt delirious at the thought of him. His face swam continuously at the back of her mind. His touch remained to tantalize her. His voice still whispered close to her ear and kept a need of him gnawing inside her like hunger. Yet it was not just a physical need. At least not in the sense that she had needed men before. She felt caught in a beautiful web that she had no desire to be free of. He was out of the house at the moment, she knew not where yet an invisible thread still attached her to him. She dared not think of a time when that thread would be broken. She refused to countenance any separation. Jean-Paul Lavelle must stay in Glasgow with her for ever and ever.

'The Pretender is out of sight now, Papa.'

'Aye, weel, that's John Glassford stuck with him. And I hear that when they can't pack any more clansmen into the houses, they're going to camp the men down in St Andrew's Kirk.'

'The church that's being built off Saltmarket Street at the back of the Weel Close?'

'The verra one.'

'But that won't be any shelter in cold damp weather like this. The walls aren't even finished. There isn't a roof on it yet.'

'They can lay themselves down in the middle of the Clyde and get drowned for all I care.'

She laughed and flounced away from the window.

'Papa, Papa!'

She felt like dancing round and round. Happiness overflowed from her, could not be contained. She did dance round and round. Ramsay groaned.

'Have you taken leave of your senses?'

'Must I be either mad or wicked to be happy, Papa? I don't see why. I don't even see why I must wear a long miserable face on a Sunday.'

'The Sabbath is a serious business. It's no' a time for flipperty-gibberty.'

'Oh, fiddlesticks!'

Ramsay's eyes caught fire and he roared out:

'Annabella, I'll no' have you despising and profaning the Lord's day.'

'No, Papa.'

'It's a good bleeding you need, mistress. I'm away to the tavern. You behave yourself till I get back. Read your Catechism.'

'Yes, Papa.' She sang out the words and he stalked away with an angry smouldering face. As soon as he had left the house she skipped back to the window again.

The street was seething with Highlanders, and not just Trongate Street. There were three windows, one on each side of the lantern-shaped corner of Annabella's room, and from one she could view Trongate Street, but she could also see across to High Street and down Saltmarket Street as well. Everywhere she looked were men in tartan, some on the move, others just stood in groups, their targes strapped to their arms. Some rode horses that were rearing up and splashing around. The ground was still muddy from the rain of the night before and deep ruts and holes

114

had filled with water. Her father, wearing his black top boots, came striding across Trongate Street towards the Exchange Tavern. His cloak billowed out behind him and water leapt away from either side of his feet. He stopped to speak to a group of other men in cloaks and three-cornered hats who were standing in front of the Tolbooth stairs and there was much glowering and shaking of heads before they all disappeared inside the Tavern and Coffee House.

A smattering of grey coats caught her eye and made her heart beat a little faster and then her heart swooped like an eagle in her chest when she spied Lavelle perfectly relaxed yet dignified on a black horse. Never in her life had she known such an enchanting man. She had met good-looking men before, but somehow he was different. Indeed, it was questionable if he could be described as handsome. He had broad cheekbones and a wide mobile mouth with such a twisted shape that she could never be quite certain whether it was expressing sarcasm, tenderness or amusement. He had thoughtful, yet laughing eyes, and the relaxed sinewy body of a jungle cat.

'Mistress Annabella,' Nancy said from the door. 'The maister was asking about Jessie.'

'Jessie? Oh, Jessie! What about Jessie?'

'What about me doing the washing? I've enough to do without that.'

'Hell and damnation!' Annabella swirled her skirts round from the window. 'What do I care about you and your ridiculous washing?'

'The maister said I've to go and ask my mother if she's heard anything. My mother knows Jessie. I'm just telling you I'm going.'

'Well, don't be an age in case I want a drink of chocolate or something.'

'Oh, aye.' Nancy slid her a look before leaving. 'I'll flee there and back.'

Annabella shouted after her:

'Impertinent black-headed crow! Filthy strumpet! Don't you dare bring back any bugs or lice from your minny's hovel.'

A few minutes later Lavelle entered and it was as much as

115

Annabella could do to restrain herself from rushing across the room and prostrating herself before him. Instead she bobbed into a cheeky curtsy.

'Monsieur.'

He bowed with an easy flip of arms and hands.

'Mademoiselle.' Then he remarked: 'Your maid passed me on the stairs. She's a good-looking wench. I have never seen eyes of that strange violet colour before.'

'Ah, you disappoint me, sir. I thought you a gentleman of good taste and breeding.'

'I trust I am, mademoiselle.'

'Yet, you indicate a taste for common serving wenches?'

'I indicated only that she was not common.'

'Her mother is a slut and a whore. Her brothers are monstrous, filthy fulzie men and they are all daft in the head.'

He laughed. 'Ah, you Scottish! I will never understand you. You are all so . . . so . . . afraid . . .'

Before he could finish his sentence Annabella stamped her foot in rage.

'Afraid, sir, afraid? How dare you, you ignorant French dog. That is one thing we most certainly are not, sir!'

He bunched his fingertips to his lips and tossed her a kiss.

'*Mon dieu*, you are beautiful when you are angry. And perhaps what I meant to say does not apply to you.'

'Well, monsieur. What do you mean to say?'

He shrugged.

'It is hard to explain, but most Scottish people seem to have passion driven inwards. They do not enjoy showing or admitting their true feelings. They are afraid of betraying weakness, mademoiselle!'

'Fiddlesticks and poppycock! In this country we know our own worth and we say what we mean, and to hell with anybody else, sir.'

'You speak ill of your servant.'

'I speak as I wish!'

'Yet it is obvious in this country, and especially in the Lowlands, between master and mistress and servant an astoundingly different relationship exists. I have never witnessed

116

it anywhere else and find it both confusing and amusing.'

'Oh, do you indeed.'

'You see, mademoiselle, you know your own worth, that is true. But so do your servants!'

Laughter came to sparkle her gaze.

'And how do I compare with an uncommon serving-wench with beautiful violet eyes, monsieur?'

'Ah, mademoiselle, your beauty is beyond compare. You are perfectly delicious, enchanting and adorable.'

'And did I not convey to you my true feelings last night?'

'Mademoiselle!' He threw her another kiss.

'I defy you to say that I betrayed weakness in so doing.'

'*Non, non, ma petite,*' he said, coming over and taking her in his arms. 'You showed only passion.'

'No, you are wrong again. How mightily unperceptive you are, sir. Have you discerned nothing more than passion?'

'Are you trying to tell me that you love me?'

'You talk, sir, as if you did not express these very sentiments to me last night.'

He did not say anything and she was disappointed he did not reassure her with a declaration of love. Instead he slipped a hand down the front of her petticoat and eased out one of her breasts. She was wearing a stiff corset from her waist up to under her arms which was designed to push her breasts high until they bulged over the top with all but the nipples showing.

Tenderly Lavelle kissed the breast now nestling on top of the green frilled taffeta like a pink rose. Then his lips wandered over her throat as she became more and more breathless and flushed. Before many minutes were passed their mouths were open against each other and she was fumbling frantically with the buttons of his breeches. Then suddenly the tirling of the door startled them and they drew apart to listen to Big John's heavy feet in the lobby. Then a familiar sniping voice enquired:

'Your mistress is at hame, I hope?'

'Hell and damnation!' Annabella cried. 'It's Letitia Halyburton. Quick, hide under my hoops.' She bunched her skirts high and Lavelle crouched close to her legs before she dropped the shimmering taffeta down again. Then, not without

117

some harassment and difficulty, she tucked her bosom back into her stays and just in time composed a bright smile on her face, and when Letitia swept in she curtsied elegantly but carefully.

'Madam.'

Letitia gave a brief nod. 'Mistress Annabella.'

'Can I ask the servant to bring tea? Or would whisky or claret be more to your liking?'

'No, I'm no' stopping. Griselle and Phemy are waiting for me outside. I just wanted to ask in the passing if your father's found out anything about Jessie. He said he was going to do a bit o' spierin'.'

'Nancy is away this very minute enquiring at her mother's.'

'I don't suppose you've found anybody to replace her yet?'

'No, indeed I have not and it is a monstrous inconvenience.'

'Aye, weel, Jessie's lassie had the cheek to come offering her services to me but I sent her away with a flea in her ear.'

'Gracious heavens, I wish you'd sent her to me, ma'am.'

'You would employ her?'

'Indeed I would.'

'More fool you. I'm away. Tell your faither to let me know immediately he learns anything.'

Annabella curtsied again and Mrs Halyburton swished away. Then as soon as the outside door banged shut Annabella began leaping and prancing about and screaming with laughter until Lavelle, laughing too, was on top of her.

Her earlier moment of unease when he had not told her that he loved her was forgotten. She adored him and the uninhibited generosity of her passion tossed all caution to the winds.

The rain returned suddenly, as if clouds had exploded at exactly the same time and poured all the rain in the world down on Glasgow. Wind came too and gathered strength from faint soughing and sighing to whining and whistling, to blustering and battering, to screeching and snatching at roofs and chimney pots and hats and wigs and whirling and skirling them up to fly about like witches in the air. Men struggled with and leaned against the gale, their cloaks like bats' wings. Ladies flustered and panicked and lost control of their hoops and showed striped stockings and scarlet garters and were sent flurrying home like ships tossed from side to side on a stormy sea.

It sent Quin's hair standing on end like a crown of spikes and his coat-tails flying. He jogged along as best he could gripping a child in each hand. Gav clung on to his hat and Regina fought to keep her cape from swirling away.

'Auld Nick's angry at somebody,' Quin puffed. 'Quin hopes it's no' Quin. Right, this close'll do, eh?'

It was known as Fiddler's Close and its entry was on High Street. Many of the buildings had overhanging thatched roofs and were semi-wooden erections of various shapes and sizes, all huddled together and all with crow-stepped gables and outside stairs.

'There's no shelter here,' Regina shouted against the noise of the storm. 'You shouldn't have brought us.'

'Further on and round. Quin knows.'

And sure enough they came to a building taller than the rest and with a turnpike stair at the back. Thankfully they plunged into it for protection.

Gav and Regina were violently shivering.

'I didn't know there was any place here,' Regina said.

'Weel, ye know noo!'

'Do you really think it's the devil being angry?' Gav asked.

'Maybe no'. Maybe there's just nobody in charge o' the dead up the road at the graveyard. Maybe Auld Nick's just having it all his own way.'

'How do you mean, in charge of the dead?' Regina asked. 'Do you mean the beadle?'

'Thon wee bauchle? He couldn't take charge o' himself.'

'Who then?'

Quin cocked his head down at them and strands of wet hair hung over the bump on his face like prison bars.

'The speerit o' the last person buried.'

'The spirit?'

'That's what Quin said. The speerit o' the last person buried has to keep watch over the graves, till the speerit o' the next one buried takes his place.'

Gav said: 'I don't like graveyards.'

119

'Is that where they buried your mother and father?' Regina asked. 'In the graveyard up the road?'

Her legs and striped petticoat and cape were covered with mud and soaking wet. Her face was mud-streaked too and glistened with rain.

Quin poked a finger in his torn ear and rubbed it. Then he scratched his head.

'They buried them all on their own out past the Gallow Moor at the crossroads. Quin whiles trots out there to keep them company. Auld Nick's pleased as punch then, eh? "Quin," he says, "Quin," says he, "you're welcome to come here and have a wee blether with your mither and faither anytime. Anytime at all, lad!"'

The wind found its way into the stair tower and tugged their clothes about and made them shiver worse than ever.

'Quin knows. A bit at a time,' Quin said.

'What do you mean?' Gav asked.

'Quin and the childers could make their way to Tannery Wynd. A bit at a time. Shelter in houses is better than closes.'

'No.' Panic immediately alerted Regina. 'I'm not going back there.'

'Why not?' Gav asked indignantly. 'It's our house. Even if there are Highlanders there, they won't hurt us. We've seen them everywhere all day and they've never hurt us, have they? I'm not afraid of them. Anyway, Mammy's maybe come back.'

'There's others.' Regina rubbed a fist hard against her eyes. 'I hate them.'

'What others?'

'Quin knows. The lassie means the Frenchies. Quin's no' keen on them either. Auld Nick can't understand their jabber. And they've got pistols.'

'Why should the Frenchies want to pistol us?' Gav scoffed.

'Oh-ho! Why is a wee key to a big door, eh?'

'I wish I could get a gun,' Regina said. 'I'd pistol them. I will one day. One day I'll pistol them.'

'Oh-ho! One day you're for Hangy Spittal.'

He caught at his throat and mimicked being choked. Then he

120

said cheerily:

'Quin will be blethering to you as well as his mither and faither out past the Gallow Moor. Och, you'll be rare company for them!'

'Regina, they must be Jacobites the same as the Highlanders. They won't do us any harm if we explain we're Jacobites too.'

'I'm not a Jacobite. I'm not. I hate them.'

Gav angrily tugged at his hat.

'But we are so. Grandfather Chisholm was a Highlander.'

'There's Highland regiments fighting on the other side for the Campbell, Duke of Argyll. Everybody knows that.'

'But Grandfather Chisholm had a white cockade in his bonnet and was for King James. Mammy told us.'

'I don't care what Mammy told us. A lot of bloody good she is.'

Gav's voice stretched up an octave.

'You're wicked!'

'I am not,' she shouted brokenly, and flung herself at him, fists flying. 'I hate her, and I hate you!'

Quin grabbed her by the hair and jerked her roughly back, making her burst into tears of frustration and pain.

'Quin's no verra pleased at you again.'

'I hate you as well.'

'Gav,' said Quin. 'Quin thinks he should give this childer to the Frenchies.'

Regina's sobs careered into hysteria. She lost control of her mind. It exploded, splintered, cavorted about in terrifying insanity.

'I'm not going back there. I'm never going back there!'

Quin's free hand clamped over her mouth and muffled her screams. He cocked his head at Gav.

'Maybe no', eh?'

Gav sighed. 'I suppose not. Not when she's such a terrible coward.'

Regina's hysteria subsided but she was unable to gather together the wayward fears inside her head. Quin withdrew his hands. Then both he and Gav solemnly studied her. She rubbed at her eyes and spoke inwards to herself.

121

'I hate them.'

'Quin thinks,' said Quin, 'Auld Nick's found a new friend.'

Chapter 11

'I knew it!' Ramsay paced the floor of the council chamber, hands thumping behind his back, head thrust aggressively forward. 'I said the blackguards were out to ruin us.'

'Wheest, Ramsay,' warned Halyburton.

John Hay of Restalrig lounged back in his chair.

'Think yourself fortunate, merchant, that you still have your life. It is His Royal Highness' pleasure that you should provide his army with twelve thousand linen shirts, six thousand pairs of shoes, six thousand pairs of hose, six thousand cloth short coats and six thousand blue bonnets. And provide them you must.'

Provost Cochrane's pale sensitive face turned to Cameron of Lochiel. 'Sir, I beg of you to do your utmost to persuade your prince to reconsider. This will bankrupt us all. It will be the ruination of the city. We have not yet recovered from the five thousand pounds in cash and five hundred pounds of goods extorted from us only four months ago.'

Lochiel shrugged his broad shoulders.

'I can sympathise with your predicament, Provost, but Quartermaster Hay has fixed the Prince in his resolution of adhering to these demands and it is not possible for me to change the matter.'

Ramsay glowered round at Hay.

'I refuse. I absolutely refuse, sir.'

'Now, now, Ramsay,' Halyburton said. 'This is not getting us anywhere.'

'Except to hell,' Hay informed him. 'The Prince said you are rebels, merchant, and must perform all this on pain of military execution.'

Lochiel addressed the Provost again.

'I believe what has contributed to the Prince's attitude, Lord Provost, is the stubbornness of your inhabitants. He has appeared publicly in your streets without acclamations or one huzza; no ringing of bells, or smallest respect or acknowledgement paid him by the meanest inhabitant.'

Provost Cochrane gave a slight bow of his head in agreement.

'True, sir. And it is not possible for me to change that matter.'

Ramsay shouted: 'And I suppose this is over and above the cost of free quarters for your whole army, foot and horse.'

'I and some of the Prince's Irish advisers have much more in mind,' Hay said. 'Glasgow has always been a breeding ground for rebels, sir, and deserves to be burned to the ground.'

Lochiel looked grave.

'That is a matter I will have a say in. There will be no sacking or burning done in my name or in the name of my men.' He turned again to the Provost. 'Provost, you say you cannot change the way the Prince is being received. I suggest you and your colleagues think again on that. It might very well be if some of you gentlemen address him there could be an abatement.'

'I personally decline to do that, sir. I cannot speak for the magistrates and other principal burgesses.'

Ramsay thumped his fist on the table.

'Of course you can, Cochrane. There's no' a man in Glasgow going to truckle to an upstart Pretender!'

'Then you all die, merchants!'

Hay's chair clattered backwards as he lunged towards Ramsay, but Lochiel swiftly stepped between them. He was a bigger man than either Ramsay or Hay, as well as having muscles of iron. He had an authoritative eye that could not be ignored.

'No, Hay, they don't die.' Despite the quietness of his voice it held strength. 'They meet the bill for free quarters and they kit out the Highland army. That is harsh enough.'

Gradually Hay relaxed. Then he gave a burst of laughter.

'Maybe you're right, Lochiel. It occurs to me that to a Glasgow merchant, parting with his money is a fate worse than death.' He turned to the Provost. 'We leave you, sir, to arrange the supply of the said goods with all due speed.'

After they'd gone the Provost said:

'We'll have to call a meeting of the inhabitants. There's no time to lose. Hay has a mind to plunder and burn the city and he might manage it yet. Get hold of the bellman and instruct him to tell the folk to gather in the New Hall right away.'

Ramsay banged the table again.

'A bloody disgrace!'

Halyburton heaved a sigh that stretched and lifted his huge chest.

'What can we do, Ramsay? We might as well cough up. You ken fine if we don't give what they ask, they'll just take it and probably more.'

'I don't care if they burn my house to the ground. I don't care what they do, Willie. They're no getting one bawbee out of me.'

'I appreciate your feelings, Ramsay,' said the Provost. 'But think a wee. If you don't give your share it only means that one of the other merchants has to give more. You punish your friends, sir, not your enemies.'

'Aye, well, if you put it that way, Provost,' Ramsay growled, 'I suppose I've no' much choice. But the rest of the merchants are no' going to like it any more than me.'

Halyburton slapped his fleshy hands on the table and hoisted himself up. 'I'm away for me denner. I'll see you in the New Hall in a wee while.'

The others nodded.

Ramsay got up too.

'I'll get you out, Willie.'

In silence they left the room and did not speak until after they had descended the stairs in front of the Tolbooth and were on the plainstanes, the wind and rain tugging at their cloaks.

'It's going to be some job organising all these supplies in the couple of days they seem to expect,' Ramsay said. 'Quite apart from the money.'

'One hell of a job,' Halyburton agreed.

'If we can do this, Willie, we can do anything.'

'Weel, that's one way of looking at it.'

Ramsay held grimly on to his three-cornered hat as the gale-force wind fought to divest him of it.

'Come across and take pot luck with me,' he shouted against the noise of the wind.

'No, I'd better go home and tell the gudewife what's

happening.' Halyburton's ruddy face became purple with cold, but he stolidly ignored the discomfort. 'She's vexed enough as it is with this business about Jessie. She tells me you've been spiering around.'

'No' with any luck so far. Nancy's mother saw her last on the Green with our washing. If she was back later with yours, nobody saw her.'

'Och, but she never went to the Green with ours. Letitia likes ours done out at the Woodside Burn.'

'There's your answer then. She's lying out there somewhere. Crippled as she is, it would be easy enough for her to fall and hurt herself.'

'No, Letitia sent Kate to look. She saw nothing. Letitia's been that vexed there's just no consoling her.'

'Aye, weel, we've more urgent and important matters to attend to just now, Willie. But afterwards, if God spares us, I mean to get to the bottom of this. Nobody disappears into thin air. And she's left children roaming about, it seems.'

'It's a mystery, right enough. I'll be seeing you in the New Hall, then?'

'Aye.'

Ramsay nodded and still hanging on to his hat he crossed the road towards the Saltmarket. On the way he stopped and cursed vehemently as horses ridden by French and Irish officers galloped past, spraying muddy water over his already saturated breeches and cloak.

Moothy McMurdo's voice and bell were fighting to be heard above the hysteria of the wind.

'An urgent message from the Provost to one and all,
Hurry at once to a meeting in The New Hall.
It's a matter of life and death he says,
We've got to supply the rebels with claes.'

All night the storm raged and it was no better when the Sabbath day dawned. But the people struggled to church and stood or sat in their dripping wet clothes and strained their ears to hear the minister above the racket of the elements.

'O Lord, Lord!' Blackadder bawled at the top of his voice.

'You ken fine we're being sore tried what with one thing and another. Have mercy on poor Glasgow folk, we petition Thee. Deliver us oot o' the greedy graspin' hands o' our enemies. Thou knowest that they are not worthy even to keep a door in Thy house. Cut them down, Lord, tear them up by root and branch, cast oot the wild, rotten stump. Thresh them with the flail o' Thy wrath and toss them down to hell.

'And, Lord, I wish Ye wouldn't pile on oor agony by sending a' this wind and rain. An oughin' soughin' winnin' wind we'd be content with, but O Lord, Lord, none o' Your rantin' tantin' tearin' winds. We pray Thee for the Redeemer's sake that the floodgates of heaven might be shut for a season.'

Just then a fierce gust of wind exploded through the roof window of the church and scattered broken glass downwards.

'Oh,' Blackadder cast up his eyes despairingly. 'O Lord, this is perfectly ridiculous!'

Annabella was not listening to either the wind or the Reverend Blackadder. In mind and spirit she was with Lavelle. He had informed her that the Highland chiefs were planning to hold a ball in honour of the Prince.

'I would be enchanted, mademoiselle, if you would attend. I would be proud to lead a lady of such grace and beauty in a minuet.'

She laughed.

'I fear, sir, that at a Highland ball the dancing will be of a type much wilder and less dignified than a minuet. Even at our normal Glasgow assemblies the dancing is most vigorous. A Scotsman, sir, comes into an assembly room as he would a field of exercise and dances until he is exhausted, and in most instances without ever looking at his partner.'

'*Mon dieu*, I cannot believe it. No gentleman could be so uncouth and ungallant to his lady.'

'Ah, but you do not understand, monsieur. The ladies are equally vigorous. Even elderly and portly dames bounce off their feet and frisk and fly about the room.'

'I will insist on a minuet. Do say you will come, Mademoiselle Annabella. The Prince is so sad and dejected. In Glasgow he dresses more elegantly and carefully than he has done at any

127

other town and he tries so hard to be at his most charming. All to no avail. He has held court, but, oh, such a melancholy affair it was, with only one or two ladies arriving to be presented.'

Annabella rolled her eyes. 'Probably Clementine Walkinshaw and Margaret Oswald.'

'You know them?'

'Mistress Margaret's brothers are tobacco merchants and shipowners like my papa. They have the *Martha*, the *Amity* and the *Speedwell*. They built that grand tenement round in Stockwell Street called Oswald's Land. But I cannot imagine my papa allowing me to go near the Prince, either to be presented or to attend a ball.'

But, oh, how she adored the idea of getting all dressed up and going to the affair and looking miraculously beautiful and having so many handsome men dancing attendance. She considered if it would be worth while trying to cajole and persuade Ramsay. She slid a tentative gaze at him, but he looked so dour and stern, leaning forward concentrating on hearing every word of Reverend Blackadder's sermon, that she quickly abandoned the notion. Then a more promising and exciting idea occurred to her. Why should Lavelle not force her to go—at pistol-point if necessary? Delight surged up and brought warm colour to her cheeks despite the desperate cold in the church.

The minister was struggling to give his sermon but was finding himself compelled to make interruptions in order to chastise some irritating members of the congregation.

'And the Lord said unto Moses—will ye shut that door, Tam Broon? Do you want me to get ma death o' cauld? There's such a draught blowing up here, I'm near flying oot the poolpit.

'And the Lord said unto Moses—put oot that dog; who is it that brings dogs into the kirk, yaff, yaffin'? Don't let me see you bring your dogs in here again or I'll help you and them both oot with my foot up your backsides. And the Lord said unto Moses . . .'

She could hardly wait until the sermon was over and she could return home to tell Jean-Paul of her plan. She would wear her blue satin gown trimmed with gold and silver and she would sport the largest hoops in Glasgow and the longest fan and she would order Nancy to dress and powder her hair as she had never dressed it or powdered it before.

'Dozing again, mistress?' Ramsay prodded her arm with his cane. 'Are you no' aware that the service is finished.'

Douglas, who was sitting at his father's other side, tittered then quickly sought to stifle his hilarity in a lace-edged handkerchief. He was wearing a pigtail fastened to his wig with a large satin bow.

'Dear sister, are you dreaming of when you will be married to the good preacher?'

'Indeed I am not, sir, that would be a nightmare. My thoughts were straying along much pleasanter paths.'

Ramsay shook his head. 'And you've the nerve to admit it.'

Douglas giggled.

'Do you not remember, Papa, the last time we were in the Ramshaw Church the minister's wife fell asleep and had to be publicly reprimanded? It was very comical.'

'It was no' comical at all, Douglas. It was a bloody disgrace.'

Annabella fluttered her hands and eyes in mock shock.

'Papa, Papa! Such wicked language, and in God's house! I am mightily shocked.'

'You're a leear, mistress. It would take a lot more than that to shock you and you're enough to drive any man to cursing and swearing. Move yourself. It's time we were away.'

The service had lasted six long hours and Annabella was only too glad to make her escape. Outside the rain had stopped and the wind had lost its fury but Trongate Street was still a muddy sea. Nancy was waiting by the door and on catching a glimpse of Annabella approaching she shouted out to a caddie that a sedan-chair was wanted. In a matter of minutes two men splashed along carrying a chair which they brought right under the archway and Annabella manoeuvred herself gracefully inside it. Big John brought the horses for Ramsay and Douglas and they mounted and cantered away leaving the servants and the sedan-chair men to splash and stumble along as best they could.

Already Annabella was busy making plans and preparations for the next evening's ball and as soon as she arrived home she started putting them into practice. With Nancy's help she concocted a hair wash of honey-water, tincture of ambergris, tincture of musk, with some spirits of wine and all shaken well together. Then, with much giggling and squealing, Nancy helped her wash her long hair.

No Scottish lady worth her salt ever painted her face as Englishwomen did, but a cold cream patted on occasionally at night protected the skins from the harshness of the Scottish climate. Annabella had a good cream she had composed of oil of sweet almonds, white wax and spermaceti. She melted these ingredients in an earthen pipkin and when the mixture was smooth and cold she moistened it with orange-flower-water or rose-water. It was kept in a gallipot covered with leather and she had it brought out ready for use.

Fortunately Lavelle and his fellow officers were out for the evening and so she could proceed with all her beauty plans unembarrassed and undisturbed by them.

'Vanity! Vanity!' Ramsay accused. 'It'll be the death of you yet, mistress. And if the inquisitors catch you, you'll be up before the Kirk Session.'

Annabella laughed. 'A fate worse than death.'

'You are a verra wicked woman, Annabella. I've warned you before about profaning the Sabbath.'

'Oh, Papa, what a misery you are. Why shouldn't I look after my bonny hair? And my skin that's as smooth and fair and as delicious as peaches and cream?'

'Annabella!'

'But it is the truth, Papa. I am beautiful. Why shouldn't I be? And why should you pretend that you are not prodigiously proud of me? Perhaps it is as Monsieur Lavelle says. We Scottish folk twist and distrust and hide our feelings because we're afraid of them.'

'Afraid?' Ramsay roared. 'I'll soon show him who's afraid.'

'No, no, Papa. You don't understand. I didn't either at first, for, oh, he is so clever.'

'He's just a sodger like other sodgers. It doesn't take many bloody brains to be a sodger.'

'He meant, Papa, that we do not like to show weakness. He

did not mean to be insulting. Indeed he is an uncommonly gallant and charming man.'

Ramsay eyed her suspiciously.

'You keep well away from him, mistress. I'm warning you. Sodgers mean nothing but trouble.'

'Oh, fiddlesticks!' she said.

It was the storm that decided the doxies and camp-followers.

Flora said: 'I've had enough of this, I'm going into the town for decent shelter.'

And so she and the rest of the women set off for Glasgow. They were a motley crew dressed in all their various pieces of clothing most of which had been taken from dead English soldiers.

Tall women, small women, fat women, thin women; women with long lank hair, women with round unkempt bushes of hair. Women with long skirts trailing in the mud, women with short ragged skirts barely covering their thighs, women with men's tight breeches. Women tired-looking in soldiers' heavy greatcoats, women cold-looking in loose open-necked shirts. Women with pinched, anxious faces.

Jessie limped as fast as she could to keep up with the crowd, but her crutch kept sinking deep into the mire and each time she had a breathless struggle to retrieve it. Soon she was left far behind, but continued the journey with desperate concentration. Every now and again, exhausted by her efforts, she stopped to rest and look around. The countryside was bleak with muddy fields and prickly acres of gorse and broom, but in the distance she could see the town tightly packed in a valley and surrounded by a collar of hills. The picture of it was not strange to her and she approached it with a mounting excitement that try as she would she could not comprehend. She went down the Cracklin House Brae towards Candleriggs Street. This hill was so named because the 'cracklins' or refuse from the tallow from the candlemakers was used for feeding dogs.

She found herself in the Black Cow Loan with its stone walls and hedges and mountains of filth caused by the fulzie men often emptying their carts there. The workers in Candleriggs Street

131

also used this country road and the long grass behind the wall as a depository for urinal and other excretions.

Candleriggs Street was a busy, lively place. There was the Wester Sugar Work and the Soap Work and the Bowling Green and some two-storeyed houses. The Bowling Green was bounded by an eight-foot-high wall on Candleriggs Street and round into Bell's Wynd. In front of the Candleriggs wall there was a stagnant ditch full of tadpoles. Jessie shrank back from it, yet felt compelled to stop and watch children wade into the ditch and come out again giggling and pointing in delight to each other's bare legs which were now black with mud and looked as if they were wearing shiny top boots. The children disturbed her deeply, yet she could not think why.

Continuing on her way, she shook her frizzy head and muttered to herself. Then when she came to Trongate Street she stopped again, her heart beginning to thump and make her all the more breathless. Slowly now she made her way eastwards towards the Cross, but it was not until she passed the Cross and saw the long stretch of Gallowgate Street that memory began to heave open the doors of her mind. She shrank from the pain of discovery, moaning out louder and louder as she hirpled along. By the time she turned down Tannery Wynd she was weeping broken-heartedly, something she had never done since she was a child. The door of the house lay open and she went inside. It was full of soldiers, but not wearing the tartan. The men had blue breeches and green breeches and long grey jackets.

'What do you want, cripple?' one of them asked.

'This is my house,' Jessie managed hoarsely. 'What have you done with my bairns?'

'What bairns?'

'A wee laddie called Gav and a wee lass called Regina.'

'Sure and we don't know anything about the boy but the whores upstairs had a girl.'

Jessie's eyes protruded.

'Not my Regina. She's just a wee lassie. A wee lassie with long red hair.'

'That's the one. You'd better ask them.'

She could hardly drag herself away. It was as if her spirit

could not suffer any more and had fled, leaving her body limp like a rag doll. Anguish fuddled her mind and she kept trying to speak to herself as she climbed the harlots' stairs, but her lips stretched feebly and her head wobbled loose and no coherent words would come.

Jeannie opened the door.

'Oh, it's you, Jessie. Where have you been, pet? My, my, there's been folk spierin' all over the place after you. I hear they're wanting you for stealing some woman's washing.'

Jessie's head wobbled all the more and saliva dribbled from one corner of her mouth.

The harlot continued: 'The further and faster you get away from here the better, pet. I wouldn't like to see a poor soul like you get hanged or banished to Virginia. See, if they banish you to them wicked plantations, they say you're a slave for ever after. Better to be hanged, pet.'

Jessie gazed in dumb bewilderment at her.

'If you're looking for your bairns, pet—they're no' here. I've never seen them a while. If they're with anybody it'll be that one-eyed, wicked rascal, Quin. You'd better away and look for him, pet. On you go now, but watch yourself and no let Hangy Spittal catch you and fling you in the Tolbooth.'

Jessie's crutch thumped awkwardly back down the stairs and then along the lane and at the same time Quin and Gav and Regina were trotting along the Gallowgate within calling distance.

'Quin's faither and mither's going to be verra pleased at having extra folk come to blether with them today.'

'But, Quin,' Gav sounded worried, 'how can they talk back to you if they're buried?'

'Did Quin say they spoke to him, eh?'

'Well . . .'

'Quin's faither and mither are happet well doon but they can always hear Quin although Quin can never hear them.'

'How do you know?'

'Auld Nick telt Quin. "Quin," he says, says he, "Quin, you'll never be parted from your mither and faither as long as my name's Auld Nick." Quin's mither and faither knew Quin didn't like to be left on his own. Quin remembers them crying out to the hangman, "Who's going to look after oor Quin?" and the hangman, he says, says he, "The devil looks efter his own!" '

Regina said worriedly, 'You're not going to take me down Tannery Wynd, are you? Promise me you're not going to go down there.'

'Och,' Gav gasped with impatience. 'We're fed up promising that.'

'Here's Tannery Wynd now,' Quin said. 'Give Quin your hand.'

Trembling, she did as he suggested and just as they approached the entrance to the lane he gave a leap and a skitter and then sped like a hare along the Gallowgate with the children flying off their feet on either side of him. After his initial surprise Gav began to laugh. Regina laughed too in a high-pitched hysterical wail at Quin's reckless speed until tears of hilarity were streaming down both their faces and they were choking and pleading with him to halt.

At last he stopped. 'This is the road to Edinburgh,' he said.

Gav wiped away his tears with the sleeve of his jacket.

'I never knew that.'

Quin doubled over and cocked his head making his hair fly about.

'Well, you know noo.'

Chapter 12

It had not been as easy as she thought to get to the ball, even at pistol-point. The pistol, in fact, had not helped at all and Lavelle had said gently:

'Mademoiselle, did I not warn you?"

Her father had showed quite astonishing courage and devotion to her well-being, or of what he considered to be her well-being, and had paid not the slightest deference to the pistol.

'Shoot me if you will, sir,' he had roared, placing himself between her and Lavelle. 'Only over my dead body will you be able to abduct my daughter!'

'Oh, Papa, Papa!' She eventually stamped her foot in a fury of frustration and impatience. 'Get out of my way. I *want* to go to the ball! I absolutely refuse, sir, to spend this evening in any other fashion.'

There had been a frightful scene while her father had called God's wrath down upon her head and she had thrown herself about screaming and kicking and cursing until he had been glad to silence her in case she took a fit or went too far in one way or another.

'Not another wicked blaspheming word, Annabella,' he groaned, 'or you'll be beyond redemption and we'll never be able to rescue you from the devil's clutches.'

'I can go, Papa?' Immediately she brightened into her mischievous charming self again. 'Oh, Papa, Papa. I am enormously relieved to have secured your permission.' And she had the temerity to rush at him and give him a quick kiss before flying from the room in a shimmering froth of blue.

So deliriously happy was she that she barely remembered how she got to her destination and when she did she swept in like a ship in full sail with her enormous swaying hoops glistening with gold and silver embroidery and her arms and fingers and ears asparkle with jewellery and her hair powdered and padded to a stupendous height and reflecting the candlelight in the loops of beads that bounced from side to side as she walked or moved her head.

In a way it was both disconcerting and disappointing to discover that only two or three ladies in the whole of the city had accepted the chiefs' invitations. It would have been interesting to see lots of other gowns and fashions and she would have enjoyed the stimulation and challenge of competition. Of course, there could hardly be much proper dancing, certainly not Highland dancing of the type she expected, when there were so many men with so few partners. On the other hand, it was thrilling to have such a lot of attention lavished upon her and so many admiring eyes following her every move. The chiefs looked magnificent in their tartans. Some, like the dark-haired handsome Lochiel, were clean-shaven and wore skintight trews and jackets of green or blue or black cloth adorned with silver or gold epaulets and cuff buttons. Hefty plaids were wrapped around their bodies bandolier fashion, with the end slung over their left shoulder and fastened across the breast by a large silver or gold bodkin or circular brooch enriched with precious stones and engraved with mottoes or armorial bearings. A large purse of goats' or badgers' skins answering the purpose of a pocket and ornamented with a silver or gold mouthpiece and many tassels hung from the front of their belts.

A dirk in a sheath and a pair of pistols also adorned the belts. Some men were bearded. Some wore the kilt. But all were bigger men than Annabella was used to seeing in Glasgow and they had a ruggedness yet a magnificent dignity about them.

The Prince had the same sturdy dignity, with straight back and head held high. He had a long-shaped face and nose with flaring nostrils and piercing blue eyes. Resplendent in an English court coat of gold silk brocade with silver embroidery, he wore the ribbon star and other insignia of the Order of the Garter.

When Lavelle presented her she dropped into a low curtsy with much graceful undulating of arms and the Prince raised her up and kissed her hand. Then he drew nearer and pressed a kiss on her forehead. He bestowed the same honour on Clementine Walkinshaw and Margaret Oswald and it was said afterwards that Margaret never recovered from the royal kiss.

A meal was served and the ladies allowed to sit on either side of the Prince at the top of the table. The room was lit by many candelabra and although there was such a dearth of gowns, the tartans and jewellery of the chiefs made up a vivid colourful scene. The table was heavy with pigs that had been spit-roasted and the heads cut off and served on a dish with the jaws, and ears round the dish. A sauce had been made of the brains chopped small and put in melted butter with gravy and chopped boiled eggs and poured round the meat. There was also poultry, fish, oysters, geese, woodcocks, partridges and ducks. There were even adventurous dishes like cows' palates and udders and cocks' combs. Tongues and udders had been boiled together with almonds, currants and raisins, seasoned with grated lemon-peel, cinnamon and nutmeg and garnished with fried parsley, and sliced lemons. Ragout of ox palates and eyes were cooked with butter, herbs and lemon juice and served with forcemeat balls, oysters and white wine. There were also boiled sheep's heads which Lavelle thought were disgusting.

'I cannot understand why this is one of the favourite dishes of Scotland, mademoiselle,' he said. 'All I associate it with is mouthfuls of partially singed wool. Ugh, quite revolting!'

'Then the heads you have tasted have not been properly prepared,' she told him. 'The proper way is to hold it over the fire and scrape off the wool as it is singed and then finish off by scrubbing it with a hot iron until no trace of wool is left.'

'It still revolts me!'

'I hear, sir,' she eyed him pertly, 'that you are very partial to a puddock?'

'A puddock?'

'A frog. *La grenouille.*'

'*Ah, oui! Délicieuse!*'

All during the meal the Prince spoke little and he looked downcast, but Annabella managed at one point to make him smile. They had been talking about language differences and Annabella had remarked that surely the Prince could not be expected to fully understand the Scottish tongue when he had been absent so long from it. The Prince answered her that there was nothing she could say that he would not understand.

'Then, sir, would you rax me a spaul o' that bubbly jock?' She allowed only a moment's hesitation before adding, 'Forgive me, I see by the intelligence in your face that you are perfectly aware that I have asked you to reach me a leg of that turkey.'

The Prince smiled and touched her hand. 'You are as charming as you are beautiful.'

After the meal and much drinking of wine the usual rounds of toasts began, but they were proposed in the Highland fashion, which Annabella found terrifically exciting. The other ladies, however, were not a little alarmed when the chiefs suddenly leapt up on to the chairs and with one foot on a chair and one on the table they drank the toasts with Gaelic shrieks which were awful to hear. Even Annabella's heart fluttered at the noise and wildness of the scene as one roar followed another.

'*Se!*'

'*Nish! Nish!*'

'*Sud ris! Sud ris!*'

'*Nish! Nish!*'

'*Thig ris! Thig ris!*'

'*A on nair eile!*'

Eventually it was announced that although the ball regretfully could not continue as planned, there would be some dancing to the minuet. None of the chiefs took part, but stood or sat in morose or disdainful groups. Only the Prince and the French officers rose to the occasion and joined the slow, stately dance with the ladies to the tune of the fiddle and the spinet. As Annabella floated gracefully along, arms outstretched and head held high, it seemed to her that she was in a beautiful dream. Never before in her life had she experienced such perfect happiness and she refused to countenance a world in which she would never know such joy again.

Halfway along Tannery Wynd Jessie realised that if she were caught and either hanged or deported it would be of no help at all to Gav or Regina. Care had to be taken. Great care. She had to have time to think, to clear her mind, to gather her wits, to pull together her scattered nerves, to seek physical as well as mental strength. She stopped in her tracks, not knowing how to do any of these things, yet knowing that do them she must. Turning eventually, she made her way back down the lane, but this time she passed the house and went round by the back of the Tann Yard. Then she followed the course of the Molendinar Burn until she reached the College Garden. Leaving the burn there, she turned left past the weavers' factory and along the Old Vennell until she came out at the middle of the High Street just down from the College Church. Opposite the church was the Grammar School and the School Wynd. Hurriedly she crossed the street and along the School Wynd which at last brought her to the Back Cow Loan and the Cracklin House Brae. She climbed the Brae and now she could see in the distance beyond the acres of gorse, the Woodside fields and Burn, and beside them the dark huddle of trees. She did not want to go back there on her own. Yet she was known to too many people in the town, the hangman included. She gazed back down at the city. Somewhere in one of those narrow back streets, somewhere in one of those tall tenements or thatched hovels, were her children. She began to moan and wail and weep and thump her crutch around until suddenly she heard a man's voice. It was the town's cowherd.

'What's wrong, woman?' he called out. 'Something paining you? Have you gone demented?'

Her head violently wobbling, she scuttled away towards Woodside. And as she made a northerly direction, Gav and Regina and Quin reached their easterly destination. It was a lonely crossroads between the High Gallow Moor and the Low Gallow Moor. But where a narrow road crossed the main one there was a toll house.

'Quin can tell you the name of this other road,' he said, indicating the narrow track with his thumb.

Gav asked: 'What's it called, then?'

Quin nodded knowingly.

'Witch Loan.'

Regina's face pinched in with anxiety. 'Are there witches here?'

'Does a witch live in that house?' Gav said.

'At the dead of night,' Quin said, 'all the witches gather here to have a coven and cast spells and get orders from Auld Nick.'

'I don't like witches,' Gav said.

'Wheesht!' Quin waggled a finger in front of his swollen face. 'Auld Nick might hear you.' Then suddenly he danced from one foot to another and cocked his head this way and that, making his hair and his coat-tails frisk about.

'Mither, Faither, Quin's brought wee childers to see you. You liked childers, remember? You were awfi fond o' wee Quin.'

'You're not wee now,' Regina said.

'Och, Quin's mither and faither will still like Quin. They said Quin wasn't to worry. They'd always be with him, they said. Quin's mither and faither liked songs.' He capered round and round and ding-donged.

'I had a wee cock, and I loved it well. Come on, childers—dance and sing with Quin.'

Giggling, the children began to jump and skip and dance clumsily around with him.

> 'I had a wee cock, and I loved it well.
> I fed my cock on yonder hill;
> My cock, lily-cock, lily-cock, coo;
> Everyone loves their cock, why should I not love
>   my cock too?
>
> I had a wee hen, and I loved it well;
> I fed my hen on yonder hill;
> My hen, chuckie-chuckie,
> My cock, lily-cock, lily-cock, coo . . .'

Gav and Regina had to stop because they were breathless with trying to dance and sing and laugh all at the same time.

But Quin went on, his song in cumulative fashion including other beasts:

> '. . . My duck, wheetie, wheetie.
> . . . My dog, bouffie, bouffie.
> . . . My pig, squeakie, squeakie . . .'

By the time his singing and skittering about had stopped, the children were red-faced and weak with hilarity. They wiped their eyes with their sleeves.

'Oh-ho!' said Quin. 'Quin's mither and faither enjoy that!'

'So did we,' Gav managed. 'Do you know any more?'

Quin bowed low.

> 'How many miles to Babylon?
> —Three score and ten.
> Will we be there by candlelight?
> Yes and back again.
> Open your gates and let us through!
> Not without a beck and a boo.
> There's your beck, and there's your boo;
> Open the gates and let us go through.'

'Did your mother and father teach them to you?' Regina asked.

'Quin's mither and faither were always singing.'

Gav sighed. 'Our mammy used to sing songs to us too but they were mostly in the Gaelic. I couldn't understand them, but I liked them just the same. Our mammy was a good singer.' He sniffed and rubbed at his nose. 'I wonder why she went away and left us?'

'Mither and Faither!' Quin pealed out. 'This wee childer would be obliged if you'd find oot aboot his mither. He hasn't got a faither.'

Gav said: 'They don't even know her name.'

'Oh-ho, that's true. Weel, what is her name, eh?'

'Jessie Chisholm. And she has frizzy grey hair and walks with a crutch because she's only one leg.'

'Mither and Faither, did you hear that, eh? Gav's lost a one-legged mither called Jessie Chisholm,' Bouncing back to Gav again, he said: 'Weel, they know noo!' Just then his attention riveted on something over and beyond Gav's head. 'Oh-ho! What does Quin see?'

Nervously Gav and Regina followed the direction of his gaze. Along Witch Lane approached an ugly-looking group of men and women in rags and with dark weatherbeaten skins and matted hair.

'Egyptian sorners,' Quin said. 'Quin's no' keen on them.'

'What's sorners?' Gav queried nervously.

'Beggars.'

'Like us?'

'Quin's no' terrored folk or killed folk to get bread. Quin's no' kidnapped childers.'

'I'm frightened,' Regina whispered.

'Mind,' said Quin, 'Quin's yer faither.'

The group drew near. They were filthy and coarsened by years of having to survive in the open. Banished from one town, in most cases for some trifling offence but having no church references as a result, they were denied work and hounded from every other community. Some banded themselves together in large groups, armed themselves with stolen dirks and muskets and plundered people on their lonely paths homeward from fairs or markets with their purchases. They pilfered fowls from isolated farm and moorland cottages and often kidnapped young people and children. It was sorners who kidnapped the eminent grammarian Thomas Ruddiman when he was trudging as a lad to Aberdeen University and stole from the student the little money he had saved for his 'upkeep' in the college and even the hard-worked-for clothes off his back. It was sorners who kidnapped Adam Smith when he was a child and nearly deprived the country of one of its most brilliant citizens and the world of its most original political economist. But the group approaching Gav and Regina only consisted of three men and two women.

'Oh-ho, oh-ho there!' Quin called out before the sorners reached the crossroads. 'Quin and his childers bids a verra good-day to you. And so does his brithers in the toll house. Are you bound for Glasgow? Quin's for there with his brithers. Quin's brithers have pistols. But Quin's got a rare knife.' He jerked a knife from inside his coat and did a little dance, slashing the air all around with it. 'Oh-ho! Quin's a dab hand with a knife, eh?'

The sorners glowered and muttered to one another as they turned along the road towards Edinburgh.

Quin and the children peered after them in silence until they had shrunk to doll's size on the wide moorland horizon. Then suddenly Quin grabbed the children and whirled them around in a circle.

> 'Here we go round the mulberry-bush,
> The mulberry-bush, the mulberry-bush,
> Here we go round the mulberry-bush,
> And round the merry-ma-tanzie!'

Then, still gripping them by the hand, he trotted away towards the Gallowgate, calling out:

'Quin'll be back to see his mither and faither. Quin'll be back to cheer them up some other time, eh?'

By the time they had reached Glasgow Cross, Regina felt tired as well as hungry and the pain of her recently inflicted injuries gnawed and burned and dragged down inside her, adding to her fatigue. She longed for how life had been before. School then home to a seat by a warm fire and a bowl of porridge or sowans or kale. Then, after exchanging news of the day, their mother might tell them stories or sing songs. At last the three of them would climb into the hole-in-the-wall bed, shut the doors and cuddle close to one another under their mother's plaid. But she nursed no hope of ever recapturing that life. A bitter fatalism had entered her soul. She felt bitter against her mother and still, in her heart, bitter against Gav. One day after another came as a desperate animal struggle for survival. And the worst animals were men. They fought each other, tortured each other, killed each other, stole from each other. And French soldiers were the worst animals of all. Often, especially when she was tired and depressed in spirits, her mind twisted into vengeful thoughts and plans of how one day she would kill them. Sometimes she imagined herself with a pistol shooting them and with a knife slashing them into pieces of butcher meat. Other times she saw them tied to the stake and burned and she lit the faggots herself and made sure they burned slowly. Or she visualised the hangman forcing their legs into the boot and she savoured the sound of his mallet dong-donging the flesh and bone into pulp. Hatred completely possessed her and nothing could give relief or exorcise the memory of the terror, the weight, the pain, the smell of the animal men.

At the Cross, Moothy MacMurdo was heaving his bell about and crying:

> 'In Glasgow Green tomorrow it's said
> The Highlanders are giving a big parade,
> In the part of the Green called the Flesher's Haugh,
> There will be such a sight as you never saw,
> With new kilts and bonnets and shoes from us a',
> Will it be any wonder the sodgers look braw?'

'Oh-ho!' said Quin. 'Now for some fun, eh?'

Chapter 13

The orders from the Prince to the Town Clerk read:

> Charles, Prince of Wales, and Regent of Scotland, England, France and Ireland and the dominions thereunto belonging, to Zacharias Murdoch:
>
> These are hereby ordering you to deliver into our Secretary's office, within one hour after receipt hereof, the Impost Books of the Town of Glasgow and Suburbs thereof. This order you are to obey, under the pain of military execution to be used against your goods and effects. Given at Glasgow, the thirty-first day of December, 1745.
>
> By his Highness's Command,
Signed: J. Murray
(Secretary)

'They're making sure they squeeze everything they can from us, Provost,' Ramsay said.

Cochrane replied: 'I'll not let the matter rest here, Ramsay. Even if I've to go to London and petition the King, I'll see that the folk of Glasgow are compensated for this injustice.'

'I hear they asked for a list of us who subscribed to the raising of the battalion and you refused, except to say that you were top of the list yourself. You're a brave man, Cochrane.'

'Och, you've a goodly share of spunk yourself.'

'It's no' my person I worry about, Provost. It's my business.'

The Provost sighed.

'I know how you feel. I can't see how the town can survive all this.'

They were sitting in the Exchange Tavern and they could hear the murmurings of the crowd outside. Ramsay jerked his head towards the door.

'Folk have turned out to see our braw coats and kilts and

bonnets and brogues.'

'Squire Hay is threatening to take two of us as hostages until we supply the full order of goods they demanded.'

Ramsay sighed. 'What do they think we are, bloody magicians? We've managed most of what they asked.'

The Provost shrugged and Ramsay went on:

'What's angering them, Provost, is the lack of Glasgow men to support them. I hear the only recruit they've managed to drum up is a drunken shoemaker who was due to be banished anyway.'

'I suppose the Pretender's hoping to impress us so much with this parade and review on the Green that we'll all be running to join his banner.'

'I'll see him run first.'

From the distance grew the sound of pipes and drums and outside in Trongate Street people jostled and jumped to see over each other's heads. Frost had hardened the ground and sunshine sparkled the ashlar stone of the Tolbooth and the pillared arcades and tenement buildings above them.

The pipers came into view first and the skirl of the bagpipes filled the air louder and louder, the excitement of them quickening with the stirring sound of the French drummers. Along the pipers marched, kilts swinging. The drummers followed, rattling smartly at every step.

People mobbed the street and crowded in from either side. There were workmen in blue bonnets, hodden grey jackets and breeches. There were young serving maids in striped dresses, white frilly caps and bare legs and feet. There were old servants in linen skirts and mutch and plaids draped over their heads and hanging down to cover their knees. There were tradesmen in brown short-coats and bonnets and breeches and buckled shoes. There were gentlemen of fashion in embroidered coats, wired at the hem to stick out. Coats with huge buttons and with cuffs to their elbows, and frilly neckcloths and three-cornered hats and breeches with small buckles and shoes with buckles so enormous that nothing of their feet was visible. There were ladies in 'high dress' with wigs ornamented with beads and brooches and ribbons and miniature ships; and ladies in long waisted dresses with side panniers and black silk and velvet cloaks called capuchins, or with a silk plaid draped over their heads and shoulders. There were children dressed like exact miniatures of their wealthy parents. There were the ragged children of the poor. There were the licensed beggars or gaberlunzies in their long blue coats and there were the other vagrants and destitutes like Quin. There were the maimed, the misshapen, the grotesque and the crippled. There were dogs barking and jumping with eagerness to see what was going on.

The crowd ran before the pipes and drums. They squashed into the sides of the buildings to let the galloping horses and marching army pass, not making a murmur as they were pushed and crushed and jostled.

The Prince, straight-backed with head held high, rode a proud grey charger that was resplendent with gold braid and many gold and silver and blue tassels. The Prince led the army along Trongate Street and then veered right and cantered down the Saltmarket.

Everywhere mobs of people were forced to separate and squeeze to each side or run on in front, but nowhere did there issue any sound from them. Although there was an excitement fevering the air stirred by the pipes and drums and the colourful spectacle, it was a silent excitement. No one gave vent to it in any cheering whatsoever. Indeed, it was only the quick action and prudence of a bystander that prevented a man who happened to be standing next to him from pistolling the Prince.

From Saltmarket Street Charles Edward Stuart entered the Low Green, then the High Green and then the part of the Green called Flesher's Haugh. There he dismounted and stood under a thorn-tree to review his troops.

Gav and Regina were so close to him they could have reached out and touched him with their hands.

'He looks awful sad,' Gav said.

Quin shrugged.

'He hasn't lost a battle but he knows he's beat.'

'What do you mean?'

But before Quin could attempt a reply, Regina cut in:

'I don't think he's bonny. He's got a long face and long nose

147

and a bitter wee mouth.'

'Och,' said Gav. 'You just hate everybody.'

'I didn't say I hated him. I just described how he looked.'

'He looks like a prince.'

'What's a prince supposed to look like?' Regina asked irritably. 'Is he supposed to have a long stupid face?'

'You're terrible!' Gav gasped. 'If he hears you he'll have you shot.'

'I don't care,' said Regina.

'Well, Quin cares about being shot. Quin didn't like having his lug cut off and he wouldn't like being shot either.'

'He must be brave,' Gav said. 'He looks brave.'

Regina's mouth twisted.

'Och, you'd believe anything. How do you mean he must be brave? Easy enough to be brave with a sword and pistols in your belt and a whole army to defend you.'

'Weel, now.' Quin cocked his head and rubbed his ear. 'He does have a brave and princely look about him, even although he has a downcast eye. Yet he's no' all that bonny, Quin admits. No' unless you're partial to long faces and bitter wee mooths. But then, Quin knows a lassie who's getting a right bitter wee mooth herself. And it's no verra bonny either.'

'What a difference in the men,' Gav said, 'since they've got all cleaned up and dressed in new clothes.'

The parade had begun and each regiment, with pipes playing and drums drumming and colours held aloft and billowing in the wind, passed where the Prince was standing.

There were the dragoons, the infantrymen, the Irish picquets, the Hussars, the Life Guards, and the many clans under their lords and chiefs, and all carried themselves proudly like a triumphant army.

'I think I'll join them,' said Gav.

'No, you'll no',' said Quin.

'Why not?'

'Quin knows they haven't got a kilt that's wee enough for a childer like you.'

'Some are wearing the trews and the Frenchies and the Irish wear breeches.'

'If you joined the Frenchies I'd never speak to you ever again,' Regina said. 'I'd hate you and I'd hope you'd be killed.'

'Quin's no' verra pleased at you.'

'She's wicked, isn't she, Quin? You wouldn't want to see me killed, would you?'

Quin violently shook his head, making his hair spike out. 'Quin doesn't like being on his own. Quin's partial to a bit o' live company.'

'You're too wee anyway,' Regina said. 'They wouldn't want you.'

'Oh-ho! Good gear goes into wee book, eh? Eh, Gav?'

Gav tugged his hat down over his curls. 'I'm a good fighter. I used to fight everybody at school.'

Quin laughed and cocked his head this way and that and danced from one foot to the other with his fists flaying the air until Gav and Regina had to laugh too. Especially when the people crushing around for a better view of the parade and of the Prince nearly knocked Quin off his feet. As he staggered and was squashed and jostled about, the children detected his long fingers picking pockets as quick as lightning. They put their hands to their mouths in fear and horror, yet they could not stop giggling. Quin dusted himself down and said:

'Quin's no' verra pleased. It's a terrible crowd here. Verra rough and common, eh?'

The cavalry were clattering past and the children's attention was drawn back to the magnificent panorama. Eventually the Prince mounted his charger and led the army away, still without one murmur of acclaim from the thousands of spectators. Back up the Saltmarket, round to the left at the Cross and along Trongate Street swept the colourful procession, with people shrinking and separating to make a path for it, then surging close together in its wake.

Annabella was flushed with animation, all eagerness to rush after the parade with everyone else so that she might get another glimpse of Lavelle, but her companions, Griselle and Phemy, dissuaded her. Griselle cried out:

'For pity's sake, Annabella. I feel quite faint with all this crushing and rushing. Would you leave me in my distress?'

Phemy vigorously flapped her fan in front of Griselle's face to give her air and then took benefit of it herself.

'Such excitement! I hope the servants are all right.'

'Oh, they'll be having a good time, never fear!' Annabella laughed.

Griselle's lips tightened like her mother's. 'If I thought they had purposely disappeared, I'd have a thing or two to say to them.'

Annabella's eyes strayed impatiently around.

'I've no doubt, Grizzie, you'll spend a prodigious time spiering when you do get your tongue on them.'

'And why not?'

'Why not indeed! Oh, do come, move, do something, the pair of you. You imprison me in a fever of restlessness.'

Griselle rolled her eyes.

'Annabella, you've seen everything there is to see and it's not ladylike that you shouldn't at least have a headache after being crushed in such a rough mob and being prey to such excitement.'

'Oh, fiddlesticks! I feel . . .'

'Would you look over there!' Griselle interrupted.

'Where?'

'With that horrid rascal Quin.'

'Those two little red-headed tramps?'

'They're Jessie Chisholm's children, aren't they?' Phemy said. 'I remember thinking how funny the little boy looked in that big jacket and hat. But underneath all that dirt the girl's very pretty.'

'Oh, nonsense, sister. She has horrid red hair.'

'I don't think it's horrid. Not if it were washed and brushed and her eyes are like little emeralds and, oh, what a lovely skin.'

'Just because it's not pocked like your own? Do be quiet, Phemy. Your silly chatter doesn't help my headache.'

'I want to employ her,' Annabella said.

'You must be mad,' Griselle gasped. 'Her mother's a thief and so is that ruffian Quin.'

'I don't want to employ him. Just the girl.'

'I refuse to go near that dreadful creature. He's liable to kidnap us or steal our purses. Phemy, I knew we shouldn't have come with Annabella. She always flutters us.'

'Gracious heaven, stay here and I'll go and speak to her myself.'

As she swept away Griselle called after her: 'If you give her any of your linen, that's the last you'll see of it!'

Quin had dawdled behind the crowd to examine what he had picked from various pockets and he was so disconcerted to see a fine lady suddenly bearing down on him flapping her fan in what seemed an angry manner that he dropped several articles.

'Mind,' he said to the children. 'Quin's yer father.'

Annabella rustled to a halt in front of him.

'Quin, I have heard that you are a monstrous rascal and a thief and that it will be the gallows for you soon.'

Quin rubbed at his ear and hopped from one foot to the other in extreme agitation.

'No' me, mistress. Auld Nick wouldn't let Quin choke on the gallows. Quin's too good a freend for that.'

'Yes, it'll be the gallows for you, all right,' Annabella said. 'You've kidnapped these children.'

Gav glowered at her.

'He has not. It's Egyptian sorners who kidnap children.'

Quin nodded enthusiastically.

Annabella swung on Regina. 'You, girl! Do you know who I am?'

Regina rubbed a fist against her eye, then her mouth.

'Are you . . . Are you . . .?'

'Speak up!' Annabella rapped the child's fist with her fan. 'And stop rubbing at your face in that ridiculous manner. I asked you a question. Look me straight in the eye and answer it.'

'Mistress Ramsay?'

'I am indeed. And I am monstrously inconvenienced by the want of a washerwoman. That is why I wish to employ you. But you must do the job well or I shall box your ears. Do you hear what I say?'

Regina's fist crept up to her face again.

'Yes.'

'Address me as "mistress".'

Another rap from the fan shrivelled Regina's hand down.

'Yes, mistress.'

'I will pay you a fair price for your labours but only after you have proved to me that you have laboured well. Come to my house tomorrow to collect the washing.'

'Yes, mistress.'

Annabella switched her attention back to Quin.

'And if she doesn't come, I'll know what rogue and vagabond to blame and I won't rest in peace until I've his other ear cut off and him dangling from the scaffold.'

And with that she swished off again with her head in the air.

Quin said: 'Quin's no' verra keen on her.'

He cocked his head at Regina. 'It'll serve her right if you steal her washing.'

'I'm not a thief and you're not going to make me.'

'Oh-ho, no need to be like that with Quin. Auld Nick says to Quin, "Quin," says he, "I think Jessie Chisholm stole some washing."'

'She did not. Something must have happened to her. These horrible Frenchies have done something to Mammy. Maybe they've killed her.'

'Don't say that about Mammy.' Gav's voice trembled. 'Mammy's not dead.'

'Well, why hasn't she come back?'

'I don't know. But Quin's going to find her. He promised. Didn't you, Quin?'

Quin waggled his finger. 'Oh-ho! Quin's the clever one, eh?'

The crowds had disappeared from the Green and only a few ladies and gentlemen remained to enjoy a leisurely stroll. Towards the east, along the brow of the Flesher's Haugh, there were belts and clumps of trees among which were fine specimens of elm, and beech, and saugh and ash. In summer this part of the Green was particularly beautiful, with the various shades of the trees and the spreading lawns and gently sloping banks spangled with daisies and dandelion and buttercup. But even now, with the wintry sun silvering the grass and sparkling the river, it was a very pleasant place.

Annabella stepped out briskly, showing flashes of yellow and black striped stockings as she went. Her hood slipped back and her cloak fluttered open to reveal her yellow panniered gown. She wore black lace mittens and a muff and she sang gaily to herself, completely ignoring Griselle and Phemy hurrying and protesting on either side of her until Griselle said:

'And I think your liaison with Monsieur Lavelle both disgusting and disloyal.'

'Jean-Paul is marvellously handsome and he makes love like an angel and you are frightfully jealous. Come now, admit it.'

'Jealous of you?'

'You needn't be, Grizzie.' Annabella laughed. 'There's plenty of French officers to go round. Come home with me now and I'll introduce you to some and even give you the use of my bed.'

'It's disgusting.'

'On the contrary, it's perfectly delicious and delightful. But you cannot have Monsieur Lavelle. He is for me and me alone and, oh, how I adore him.'

'Annabella,' Phemy said, 'you really should try to restrain your feelings.'

'Why, for heaven's sake?'

'Because you're going to get hurt if you're not careful. I don't want to see you hurt and unhappy.'

'Dear little Phemy, why should I get hurt? How could I be unhappy? I refuse to be unhappy.'

'Monsieur Lavelle will not be here for ever. I hear, in fact, that the army will be leaving almost immediately.'

'Nonsense, that cannot be.'

'But, Annabella, they only wanted rested and re-clothed. Why should Monsieur Lavelle stay here?'

'Because I am here, of course!'

Griselle laughed. 'You are the limit, Annabella. Monsieur Lavelle cannot take his orders from you. Would you have him shot as a deserter?'

'Losh sakes, the Highlanders are always deserting and they don't get shot.'

'But, Annabella, Highlanders are different. Monsieur Lavelle is not a Highlander. He is an officer and a gentleman of King Louis' army.'

'Well, Phemy, I can tell you here and now that neither Prince

Charles Edward Stuart nor King Louis are going to separate me from my adorable, fascinating, passionate, gentle Jean-Paul.'

Griselle shook her head. 'Tuts, Annabella, saying things and wanting things doesn't make them happen.'

'You're right, sister, I fear poor Annabella is going to be hurt and distressed.'

Annabella tossed her head. 'Poor Annabella, indeed! I'll have you know that when I say things and want things, they *do* happen!'

'But, Annabella . . .'

'If Jean-Paul must go, then I must go too, for I tell you I absolutely refuse to be separated from him.'

'Annabella!' Both Phemy and Griselle were genuinely shocked and distressed. Phemy cried out:

'You cannot mean you would leave the safety and comfort of your home and the protection of your papa and expose yourself to the dangers of travelling with the rebel army.'

'Danger is the spice of life! To be comfortable can be prodigiously boring.'

'Tuts, Annabella,' said Griselle. 'It is one thing to have a discreet liaison but quite another to be a common camp-follower.'

'If we were not now in the middle of Saltmarket Street, Griselle, I would knock you down and give your face an uncommonly good punching.'

'Annabella!'

'Do come discreetly home with me. Do not deny me such enormous pleasure.'

'You are quite incorrigible,' Griselle said.

Phemy's small pocked face creased with concern. 'Think, oh, do stop and think, Annabella.'

'No, to feel is so much more exciting, Phemy, and to put one's feelings into action is a bewitching adventure.'

They had reached Annabella's close in the Saltmarket and she repeated her invitation.

'Come upstairs and have tea with me. I have made some delicious sweetmeats.'

Griselle shook her head. 'No, you have us so fluttered,

Annabella, we just want to go home and lie down until we recover.'

'And what will the minister say?' Phemy cried. 'Och, poor Mr Blackadder!'

'To hell and damnation with Mr Blackadder!'

'Annabella!'

'And I warn both of you. If you tell your mama and your mama tells my papa and my papa tries to prevent me doing as I wish in this matter, I will pistol all of you before I'll be thwarted.'

'Annabella!' the sisters wailed. 'How can you be so wicked?'

'With prodigious ease,' said Annabella. 'And don't you forget it.'

And with that she swished into the close, her curls bouncing and tossing.

Across the other side of the street, Quin and Regina and Gav watched her disappear and then Griselle and Phemy fan themselves and roll their eyes and clutch their bosoms in obvious distress before hurrying towards the Cross and then round on to Trongate Street.

'Oh-ho!' said Quin. 'There's another one for Auld Nick.'

'Wasn't it a relation of hers that got our granny killed?' Gav said.

'Our granny,' Regina explained, 'was burned because Prissie Ramsay said she was a witch.'

Anxiety grafted over Gav's face. 'Do you think our granny was a witch?'

'I don't know.'

'They hanged Quin's mither and faither.'

'Was that because of Prissie Ramsay too?' Gav asked.

'Quin's wondering. Quin's wondering.'

'I don't like Prissie Ramsay.'

'Och, she's dead long ago,' Regina said. 'Mammy said the devil took her away.'

'Weel, it looks to Quin as if Auld Nick's left another Mistress Ramsay in her place. She's worth a watching that one. Quin knows a wee childer who'd better take care.'

'Maybe you shouldn't go tomorrow, Regina. Maybe it was

155

her that made our mammy disappear. Maybe she'll make you disappear too. Don't go, Regina.'

Worriedly Regina screwed her fist into her cheek.

'But we need the money I could earn. And you heard what she said she'd do to Quin. We don't want Quin cut to bits and choked to death, do we?'

Both Gav and Quin shook their heads.

Chapter 14

The doors of the hole-in-the-wall bed lay open. The candelabra burned low. The flames of the candles, like yellow pendants, softened into amber against the darkness. Flickering light from the fire added to the warmth and spilled out shadows like port wine. The air was thick with the scent of musk, liberally sprinkled to counteract the stink of fulzie from outside. Mixed with the musk, close to Annabella's nostrils, was the smell of sweat from Jean-Paul. She lay half on top of him, her lips moving over his moist skin. He had one arm around her naked body and his eyes were closed. He said,

'*Ma petite*, you will never persuade me. I cannot allow you to risk your life in such a venture. You are far too precious.'

'Then I will come without your permission.'

'Annabella, I will not be able to look to your safety and well-being. I am an officer in charge of a company of men. I have my duty to them. I have also to obey the orders of the Prince. Women have to fend for themselves on such expeditions and it is not easy.'

'Do you know so little of me, Jean-Paul? Do you think I am some feeble milksop ready to swoon away at the first sign of difficulty? I am a woman of spirit and daring, sir.'

'And a damned determined one too. You do not understand the difficulties. You cannot comprehend the hardships.'

'I would willingly suffer every difficulty and hardship in the world for you. You cannot stop me, for I insist.'

Lavelle sighed.

'Annabella, how can I make you see? How can I dissuade you?'

'You cannot.'

'But your life will be in danger.'

'I am not afraid of danger but I will go suitably protected with Papa's pistols and I will take servants too.'

157

She grinned mischievously at him. 'You will be glad of me many times, I dare say. Think of the comfort I can bring you.'

'This is no laughing matter. It is impossible I tell you.' There was an edge to his voice but she softened it with kisses.

'Damn you,' he said eventually. 'You beautiful, impossible, Presbyterian witch. Do you not even care that I am a Catholic?'

'Ah, yes, it is very foolish indeed for a Scottish Presbyterian Whig to risk her life for a French Catholic Jacobite.'

'Well?'

'Well, love makes fools of us all. But I still say it's worth it. Make love to me again and then try and tell me it's not worth it.'

He groaned and shook his head but his other arm went round her neck and drew her face close. And while they kissed and made love and then slept soundly in Annabella's warm musk-scented bed, outside Quin and Gav and Regina and many other homeless people and orphans huddled together in the clay-cold stair. Regina was exhausted beyond tears but so benumbed with cold she could not close her eyes. Under her eyelids were sheets of ice. Ice spiked through her veins, threatening to crack her spine and pierce her heart. She believed only one thing kept her from freezing to death. Bitterness had settled over her like a black cloud but it had a fire of hatred at its centre.

In her house, in her bed in Tannery Wynd, Frenchies were sleeping in warmth and comfort. She hated them. She thought of them. She imagined them. She remembered them. She churned herself with a head-thumping, chest-tightening madness. Sleep calmed her down, but the hating and the terror never stopped. She kept jerking, scrambling awake in a confusion of moans and squeals. Only when she heard Quin's or Gav's voice could she be sure it was not the Frenchies lying beside her in the dark.

Hatred writhed out from its octopus centre to grab at everyone and everything connected with it. She despised the Jacobite cause. Why had the Pretender Prince come from across the water to stir up so much trouble and cause the deaths and suffering of so many people? Everyone had been all right before he arrived. Now everything was all mixed up. There was a terrible civil war. Scotsmen were against Scotsmen. She hated

158

the Irish, who were the same as the Frenchies in their French uniforms. Why could they not just stay in their own country? Why had they to fight for France and then for Prince Charlie? Why were they in her house?

She was still hammering herself with bitter questions when morning came and people began to creak and crack their frozen bones all around her.

'Oh-ho,' said Quin, rubbing his hands as best he could. 'Quin and his childers are lucky to be alive this morning, eh?'

Gav whimpered from deep inside his jacket.

'I'm awful cold.'

'Give Quin your paws.'

With difficulty Gav pushed out his hands and Quin smacked them between his and rubbed them briskly.

'If I go early to Mistress Ramsay's, maybe I'll get something to eat,' Regina said.

'Ye'll no' forget to put a wee share in your pocket for Quin and Gav, eh?'

'If I can.' She went into a spasm of shivering. 'Maybe they'll let me have a heat at their fire.'

Gav said: 'You're lucky. I wish I could do washing and get a heat at a fire.'

'When all the Frenchies go away we'll get our house back and I'll make lots of money and we'll have a warm fire.'

Gav brightened.

'And porridge?'

'And ale?' said Quin, nodding enthusiastically in anticipation.

'And milk. We'll never be cold and hungry again. I promise.' She struggled stiffly to her feet. 'I'll see you both on the Green later. If I'm not at the Green, I'll be here.'

To get up the stairs she had to squash past and climb over the top of a tightly packed mob and by the time she arrived at the Ramsays' door she was beginning to feel apprehensive. This would be the first time she had done washing. She had seen serving-maids and washerwomen in the Green and noticed that they tackled the job in a completely different way from her mother but that was as far as her experience went. Her mother had set great store by education and so Gav and she had spent most of their time at school learning to read and write. Gav had also been learning Latin because at the college the lectures were all given in that language. Their mother had nursed a grand dream of Gav going to college and he might have gone quite soon because he was very clever at his lessons. But the Pretender and his Frenchies had come and spoiled that too. It was they, she felt sure, who were responsible for her mother's disappearance. They had ruined all their lives. They had ruined the whole country.

Inside the house darkness faded and left the low-ceilinged rooms shrouded in a veil of grey. Annabella was already up and Lavelle had slipped from her room through to the kitchen. Some of his colleagues who had been sleeping on the lobby floor were stretching and stirring. Others were appearing from Ramsay's bedroom. Nancy, who slept in the kitchen on the floor in front of the fire, had been ordered by Ramsay to move into Annabella's room. Annabella, however, had told her later that she was to do no such thing. So, unknown to Ramsay, Nancy continued to sleep in the kitchen with Big John curled up like a dog in the hall guarding the door. Now she was preparing breakfast. It was later than usual because, since the rebels had entered the town, business had come to a standstill and everybody's routines were disorganised. The fire crackled and smoke and flames curled round the black cauldron like red claws. Clouds of steam floated up from the porridge. Its nutty smell thickened the air and mixed with the pungent odour of herrings, the yeasty aroma of ale and the stench of fulzie. She did not look round as the French officers came crushing into the kitchen to sit on stools and table and floor. After attending to the cauldron hanging over the fire on its chain, she turned to haughtily push aside the men who were taking up space on the table. They laughed and eyed her appreciatively, taking in her black mane of hair, her sulky violet eyes and provocatively swaying figure. They talked rapid French and guffawed again, but still she paid them not the slightest attention. Yet when the outside door tirled and she went to answer it there was a studied grace about her movements.

On the doorstep stood an anxious-looking girl with a mud-caked face, matted hair and filthy legs and feet.

'Mistress Ramsay told me to come for the washing,' she mumbled, lowering her eyes, then stealthily rubbing them.

Nancy opened the door wide to allow Regina to enter. Then she was just about to lead the girl through to the kitchen when Annabella radiated from the bedroom in a blue dress flowered all over with pink rosebuds.

'Gracious heaven, Nancy, she cannot be allowed to touch our washing until she's washed herself. Is there any water left in the kitchen?'

'Enough.'

'What is your name?' Annabella asked.

'Regina.'

'Very well, Regina, go with Nancy and try to rid yourself of that noisome filth.'

But before she reached the kitchen the door opened, revealing the crowd of soldiers. Lavelle emerged first and immediately Regina screamed. She whirled round, clawing at the air in a panic to escape. Both Nancy and Annabella caught hold of her and shouted at her to be quiet and that no harm would come to her. Lavelle also attempted to pacify her without success and Douglas fluttered out, holding his head and begging for the clamour to cease. But it was not until Ramsay strode from his room and slapped her soundly on the face that the screaming abruptly stopped. Her head shrank down and her fists screwed hard against her eyes.

'Now tell me, pray,' Ramsay commanded Regina, 'what all this commotion is about?'

'I'm afraid of the Frenchies.'

'You've no need. No Frenchman would dare to lay a finger on you in my house. That I promise you. You're Regina, Jessie's lassie. Am I right?'

'Yes, maister.'

'No word of your mother, yet?'

She shook her head, still without raising it.

'Aye, weel, I'm still spierin' around. Something will maybe turn up.' Switching his attention to Annabella, he sharpened his voice. 'Is my breakfast no' ready yet, mistress?'

'Yes, Papa. On you go through. I was just going to tell Nancy

161

to bring it.' Then after her father had gone through to her bedroom, where all the meals were served, Annabella swung on Regina. 'You wretched girl, do you not know that Monsieur Lavelle is an officer and a gentleman? Why should he wish to soil his fingers by touching you? How dare you stir up such a provoking hullabaloo!'

Lavelle favoured Regina with one of his twisted smiles.

'*Ma petite*, I'm sorry if I frightened you. But you are quite safe, I do assure you.' He turned, spoke to his men in French, and then continued in English to Regina. 'There, I have commanded the others. You have no need to worry.'

Annabella tossed her hair.

'You are far too kind, sir.' She gave Regina's shoulder a push. 'Do as you're told, and not another moment's delay.' She flapped a hand. 'Nancy, see to her, and for pity's sake hurry with Papa's breakfast.'

Nancy prodded Regina into the kitchen and left Lavelle and Annabella gazing into one another's eyes in the shadowy lobby. He murmured softly so that her father or brother could not hear.

'*Ma belle Annabella*.' His fingers lightly caressed her arm.

She sighed. 'I wish you could make love to me.'

'But I am making love to you.'

'Annabella!' Ramsay roared from the bedroom. 'What kind of house is this that a gudeman has to ask twice for his breakfast?'

'Coming, Papa!' she called, stealing a quick kiss from Lavelle as she passed into the kitchen.

'Nancy, have you fallen asleep? Do you not hear Papa calling? What is the meaning of this ridiculous delay and where is Big John?'

'He's down seeing to the horses. And the delay's caused by French sodgers but not by me entertaining them. I leave that to you, mistress.'

But Annabella was too happy to be provoked.

'I know you're uncommonly jealous and I don't care a fig.'

Nancy raised an eyebrow.

'Of foreigners? No, it's a man of my own country I want.'

'A gentleman, of course.'

162

Nancy shrugged and looked away, afraid that Annabella would see the need and the longing in her face. More than anything else in the world she wanted to capture the love of a real gentleman. Someone who could free her from bondage and give her the life she felt she deserved.

'Oh, Nancy, Nancy,' Annabella laughed. 'Give me the porridge bowls. I'll take them through. You bring the herring.'

After Annabella had skimmed away, Nancy gave Regina a bowl of water and a cloth.

'Clean your face and hands. You can wash your feet and legs when you're down at the Green.'

Regina was glad to hide her face in the cloth, but as soon as she detected Nancy leaving the kitchen she hastened to follow close behind, much to Nancy's annoyance.

'I've more than enough to bother me with crowds of Frenchmen under my feet without having you as well.'

'I'm afraid.'

'Did you not hear what the maister told you?'

Miserably Regina nodded. 'I can't help it.'

Nancy rolled her eyes and continued into Annabella's bedroom with the dish of herring she was carrying. Regina still stuck to her heels.

'Gracious heaven, Nancy,' Annabella said, 'why are you bringing the little tramp in here? She has a monstrous stink.'

'I didn't bring her. She's following me around like a dog.'

Annabella fluttered her hand in Regina's direction.

'You are not a dog. Hold up your head. Do not skulk about in this preposterous manner.'

Nancy plumped the dish on the table, then grabbed Regina by the ear.

'Come on.'

Through in the kitchen she presented the child with a big wooden tub packed with linen. She flung a lump of soap in it.

'Right, down to the Green with you.'

The tub was bigger than Regina and it was with considerable difficulty that she managed to stagger outside with it. As soon as Nancy banged the door shut behind her, she dropped the tub, dragged it across the landing, them bumped it down the spiral stairs. She hoped that Quin and Gav were still on the stairs so that they could help her along, but they, with the other vagrants, had disappeared in search of something to eat. As a result, she was forced to fight with the tub all the way along the bumpy, rutted roads to the Green. After much determined effort she managed it.

The Green was crackling with fires, steaming with tubs of hot water and thronged with hundreds of maidservants and washerwomen. Rosy fingers were busy rubbing and rinsing linen in the river or at the fountains. Pink feet were energetically trampling it in foaming tubs. Petticoats were hitched up, knees bounced high, voices were raised in chatter, in laughter and in singing and shouting. And all around the edges of the Green men strolled past watching. Some travellers and foreigners who had never witnessed such a scene in their own country, were amazed, delighted and not a little shocked at the immodest show of legs and thighs. But their appreciative gasps only caused the women to kick and prance and hitch their petticoats even higher.

Regina felt harassed and overwhelmed by it all and did not know how to start, but one buxom, scarlet-faced woman, on spying her wretched hesitation, came bounding over as if she were going to whisk her into a dance.

'Come on, wee lass. I'll help you get water.'

Up flew Regina's tub with Regina hanging on and running alongside it. Down cascaded the water. Up frothed the soap. In splashed the linen. Then before Regina could struggle or cry out in protest the woman sprang her up and plunged her down into the tub. Within seconds, Regina had stumbled and slithered and fallen on her back and was screaming in panic and gulping in hot soapy water, while all around her laughter screeched to a crescendo.

'Move over, wee lass.' The woman leapt into the tub beside her and heaved Regina up. 'Now grab me round the waist with one arm and I'll hold an arm round your shoulders. When we trample in pairs we hold each other round the shoulders but you're too wee to hold mine. So round the waist it is.'

Regina was still coughing and spluttering but she did as she was told.

'Now,' said the woman. 'Bunch up your petticoats with your free hand, raise your chin and start high-stepping. One-two-three!'

She gave a sudden screech as she began wildly prancing and splashing, big thighs and full breasts bouncing. Regina could not help laughing at the same time as choking and stumbling. Eventually she managed to fit into the woman's rhythm. Round and round they went, the woman lustily singing and Regina laughing. Forwards and backwards, backwards and forwards like heathens in some primitive tribal dance. All around them women were trampling in their tubs with the same merry abandon, and steam was forming a cloud canopy in the icy air. Then, the trampling finished, Regina's companion skipped on to the grass, taking Regina with her.

'Now out with the linen,' she ordered cheerfully. 'And into the river with the water and then to the rinsing.'

The River Clyde at this part of the Green was frothing like the tubs, yet the water was cold and sparkling underneath and the washing was dipped and squeezed and came out fresh and clean. The woman grabbed each piece of cloth and twisted the water from it, strong arms bulging with the effort. Regina tried to do the same, but was such a puny failure that the woman had to keep snatching the linen from her and wringing it again.

'Try imagining it's somebody you'd like to choke,' the woman suggested cheerily, then roared with laughter when Regina's whole appearance changed to one of utter concentration. Her thin hands and arms strained until blue veins swelled and the muscles of her face contracted and bulged her eyes and drew back her lips to reveal teeth gritted tightly.

The washing was soon spread out with everyone else's on the part of the Green called the bleachfields and left to whiten and dry.

'Leave it for a while,' said the woman. 'All day and all night if you like and then take it back to finish it off in front of your mistress's fire.' And with that she gave Regina a wave and bounded away.

Regina was afraid to go and leave the linen in case someone stole it. Despite the fact that people had been deported as slaves to the Virginia plantations for stealing a piece of linen from the bleachfields, thieving still went on.

Now for the first time in hours she realised that she was soaking wet and cold. Also she had had nothing to eat all day. Pangs of hunger added to her miseries as she crouched down on the grass beside the washing and hugged her knees and tried to stop shivering. She seemed to have suffered an endless anguish of time there in the biting wind before, to her relief, she saw Quin and Gav approaching. Never before had she felt so glad to see anyone. She longed to run and welcome the two familiar figures, the tall lanky one with the flying hair and coat-tails and the grotesque face, and the little one like a dwarf in his too big clothes. But she was too stiff to do more than struggle to her feet.

'Quin's brought apples,' Quin said.

She grabbed one and sank her teeth into it like an animal, only stopping after a few huge bites to mumble with her mouth full:

'Have you got anything else?'

Quin held up a finger before plunging his hand inside his coat. Then with the panache of a magician he whisked out a whole cooked chicken.

'Ooh!' Regina's eyes stretched wide. 'Where did you get that?'

'He stole it,' Gav said. 'He's a terrible thief. I've warned him he's going to get his other ear cut off. But he doesn't listen.'

'Quin listens all right. But listening's no' eating and Quin gets hungry same as you.'

Regina finished eating the apple, core and all, in a matter of seconds, and then, along with Quin and Gav, she tore into the chicken. Afterwards, cleaning her greasy hands on her cloak and petticoat, she sighed.

'Oh, that was good.'

Quin laughed and did a little dance.

'Quin's the clever one, eh?'

'Where have you been all day?' Regina asked, wiping her mouth with the back of her hand. Quin broke into perky singing.

> 'Poussie, poussie baudrons,
> Where have ye been?

—O, I've been to London,
Seein' the Queen.'

The children began to giggle as he waggled his head and tripped on.

'Poussie, poussie baudrons,
What got ye there?
I got a good, fat mousikie,
Runnin' up the stair.

Poussie, poussie baudrons,
What did ye do with it?
—I put it in my meal-poke,
To eat with my bread.'

Regina tittered into her cupped hands, but Gav laughed with mouth open and eyes all the time shining expectantly up at Quin. Quin hoisted one finger again. Then, after plunging and fumbling both hands in his pockets, he hid his clenched fists behind his back and sang out.

'Neive—neive—nick-nack,
Which hand will ye tak'?
Tak' the right, tak' the wrang,
And I'll beguile ye if I can.'

The children both dived at him, grabbed a hand each, and giggling and squealing fought to prise open Quin's fingers. At last, after much merriment and dancing up and down and whirling all around, Quin snapped open his fingers to reveal a sugary sweetmeat in each hand, half-melted and sticking to his palms. Gav and Regina quickly popped the confection into their mouths and Quin licked his palms and smacked his lips.

'Oh-ho, Quin's been the clever one today, all right, eh?'

Dusk was gathering round them and making the washing on the bleachfields look like shrouds. It only took a little imagination to see the white cloths rising up in the gloom to encircle them in some macabre dance.

'Come on,' said Gav. 'It'll soon be dark and we won't be able to see our way back.'

Regina began gathering up the washing and packing it into the tub and before she could ask for his help Quin hoisted it on to his head and jogged away with the children running and skipping on either side of him. They made their way alongside the river through the Low Green. The entries to the Low Green by the Saltmarket and the Old Bridge were narrow, irregular and dirty because of their nearness to the slaughterhouse and much used by cattle and fleshers' dogs. The Molendinar and Camlachie burns ran through the streets in an uncovered state, crossing the part of the Low Green next to the slaughterhouse called Skinner's Green and the Saw Mill in an oblique direction. At the bottom of the Low Green were offensive pits used by skinners and tanners. The slaughterhouse spread over a large and irregular surface on the banks of the river and was bounded by crooked lanes on the north and north-east and there was no other entry to the Green from the west. The dung from the slaughterhouse and the intestines from slaughtered animals were collected in heaps and allowed to remain for months until putrefaction took place, much to the annoyance of the neighbourhood.

Gav screwed up his nose and shuddered as he passed.

'Ugh, what a horrible stinky place.'

'Quin remembers before there was a slaughterhouse. This is a new place, this slaughterhouse. It's only been here about a year. Before that the butchers used to kill the beasts up the High Street or at the Cross or wherever they could catch them. Oh-ho, then there was the awfulest hacking and squealing and bleeding on the streets you ever did see.'

'I didn't know that.'

'Weel, ye know noo!'

'We used to be at school all day.'

'Quin's never been at school but Quin knows a thing or two, eh?'

They turned up Saltmarket Street at last, reached the Ramsays' close and stair, and Quin did not slacken his jaunty jog-trot until they were all crowding on to the landing. He dropped the tub down.

'Tirl the door and in you go with it now. It's time Gav and

Quin were making sure of a place on the stairs.' Before jogging away, he turned waggling a finger. 'When you get your money, mind, Quin's yer faither!'

As soon as they disappeared Regina remembered the Frenchies and began to tremble. Hatred of them for always spoiling everything and for causing her to suffer such terrors burned through her like bile and made her want to vomit. She felt so ill she could hardly raise her hand and find the door-pin. The rasping noise sounded ominous in the gathering darkness and made her shivering become so violent, even her brain rattled around in her head. It took all her will to remain standing. The door creaked open to reveal Nancy holding a candle. The flame fell backwards in the draught from the door and its capering light pointed out grey coats and blue breeches and tie-wigs all over the lobby.

Regina withered back, her fist rolling hard against her mouth.

'Oh, come on,' Nancy said impatiently. 'How many times must I tell you? They won't do you any harm. Bring the tub inside.'

Regina struggled with the tub and finally managed to raise it and follow Nancy through to the kitchen. Nancy put the candle on the table and its circle of light blurred into the glow from the fire. After depositing the tub in a corner, Regina sidled cautiously over to the fire and warmed her hands.

Nancy said: 'I don't suppose anybody would mind if you slept here. You'll have the ironing to do tomorrow and you might as well get an early start.'

Regina's eyes strayed towards the door and Nancy went on.

'Oh, don't worry, they stay out there and Big John makes sure they do. It'll only be you and me in the kitchen.'

It seemed too good to be true. A place to sleep beside a fire. Regina made to curl down on the floor but Nancy said: 'Not yet. Come on through to the mistress's room. The maister's still to give the reading.'

Through the lobby again and into the bedroom with the lantern-shaped corner with its three windows.

The maister was sitting at the head of a table in the centre of which a silver candelabra gave graceful light. A Bible lay open in front of him. On one side lounged his son Douglas, wearing a frilly shirt and long pink waistcoat. On the other side, straight-backed and restless-looking was Mistress Annabella in her flowered gown and her hair in ribbons and ringlets. Over in one wall a fire burned bright.

'She did the washing so well I said she could sleep by the kitchen fire,' Nancy said.

'Aye, weel,' said Ramsay. 'Sit doon and listen to the word o' the Lord.'

Both Nancy and Regina drew in stools and sat with the others at the table. She envied the comfort and warmth of the place.

Mammy had said that Maister Ramsay was rich. 'One day,' thought Regina, 'I'm going to be rich.' She had not the slightest idea when or how this feat could be accomplished, but be accomplished it would. The roots of her hatred hugged round this certainty, intertwined with it deep inside her secret self, and gave satisfaction to her bitterness.

The maister was saying:

'. . . Therefore will I number you to the sword, and ye shall all bow down to the slaughter . . .'

Regina smiled.

Chapter 15

Each night Jessie limped back into town after dark to ask if the harlots had seen or heard anything of the children or the beggar Quin. But they knew nothing. Then she slunk round streets and lanes and closes, but the only thing she learned was that the army were moving out on Friday morning. One of the camp-followers told her: 'So be ready early if you're coming.' The woman advised: 'You can maybe get a seat on one of the supply carts.'

'But I've lost my bairns. I can't go without them.'

'Better to search during the day than at night.'

'But the hangman's after me for stealing some linen.'

'Too bad.' The woman shrugged. 'That's what you get for thieving.'

'I didn't steal it. I don't know where it went.'

'Do you think they'd believe you if you told them?'

Jessie's head wobbled about in worried silence for a minute or two.

'I never thought of that. I wonder if I dare go and see Mistress Halyburton.'

'What's she like?'

'She told me if I didn't hurry back with her fine linen she'd get Hangy Spittal to throw me in the Tolbooth.'

The woman laughed. 'I wouldn't risk it if I were you.'

After another silence Jessie murmured weakly: 'But she might know something about my bairns.'

'You'll no' be much good to your bairns or see them for long if the hangman gets you.'

Jessie slowly limped off into the dark. There was no use going to the Halyburtons' house until daylight if she were going at all. One thing was certain, Mistress Halyburton's temper would not be improved by being awakened from her bed in the middle of the night. Better to hide somewhere and try and think what to do and if she did decide to go to Locheid's Land then she could do so once daylight came. Perhaps it would be even wiser to wait until the army had gone. If there had been soldiers in the Halyburtons' house that would not have sweetened Mistress Halyburton's mood either. Jessie found a sheltered spot beneath a wall and behind some bushes in the Back Cow Loan. Easing herself down, she enveloped herself in her plaid, muffling it up and over her face and her frizzy head. Yet still the icy air reached her bones and made breathing painful. Her mind turned to stone and she nursed herself in distress. The rhythmic rocking motion reminded her of her mother.

The Highland cottage had thick walls and a hot fire and her mother sat nursing her on her knee on the rocking chair. There was no sound but the wailing of the wind, made far off by her mother's harn shirt and the warmth from her body. The chair rocked lazily, sleepily. Jessie rocked herself, desperate to hold tight to the illusion. Her mother's body was comforting and soft, her arms secure and strong. Her face as she gazed down through her spectacles had a rosy glow and her eyes were melting with love for her. Her mother was a good honest woman. She had never done anyone any harm. A shuddering sigh racked Jessie. She struggled to blot out other pictures, knowing that she could not bear them, feeling instinctively that she must fight to keep herself sane if she were ever to have a chance of finding her children.

She shook her head and wailed and cursed at the other pictures and sounds that kept flashing in front of her.

Prissie Ramsay's beautiful perky face. The way she tossed her head. Her laughing eyes that could change like the sea. The words that poured from her mouth. The way she pointed her finger . . . 'That's the woman. Yes, she was one of them. I was coming home by the Low Green when the devil suddenly appeared in the form of a bull with its intestines hanging out and he told me that he had several witches in the town who were helping him in his work. They were holding a coven with him that night and he would like me to join them. I said Christ's name as my protection and recited the Lord's Prayer and refused to have anything to do with his evil work. I ran quickly away, but I hid behind a bush so that I could discover who the witches might be and what their wicked plans were. One by one they came and each was given their job to do.' Dramatically the finger pointed. 'She was to bring back the plague!'

Jessie's moans and wails became louder and were snatched up by the wind and tossed to and fro in the empty lane.

They had sent for the witch-pricker and he had stripped and bound her mother with cords. Then he had thrust needles everywhere into her body until she had been exhausted by an agony too terrible for screams. Her silence, the witch-pricker said, proved that he had found the devil's mark and she was guilty.

But still her mother had refused to confess. 'I'll make her talk through the child,' the hangman said, and pounced on her and held her as he crushed her leg into the boot. Before her mother could gather strength or wits to say anything the mallet had pulped the flesh and bone. Jessie remembered the pain of it, but it was as nothing compared to the agony of remembering her mother. Her head wobbled about trying to shake away remembrance.

'Oh, Jessie, Jessie,' the voice called from the past and Jessie answered it.

'Mither!'

All night long she nursed herself and repeated the word until at last daylight picked her out like a bundle of rags behind the bushes. And the cowherd came blowing his horn. And the college bells rang and the Tolbooth bells sang their musical song.

All the excitement and extra work of the soldiers billeted in her house had been too much for the ailing Lady Glendinny. She had retired to bed and despite Phemy Halyburton's tender ministrations had speedily become weaker until it was obvious to everyone, including herself, that she was dying. The Earl sat patiently by her bedside and she took him by the hand.

'Weel, gudeman, we're going to part.'

'Aye, Murn.'

'Have I been a good wife to you?'

'Middling. Middling,' said the Earl, not disposed to commit

himself.

'Now, I want you to promise me something,' Murn said.

'Aye, and what's that?'

'Promise you'll bury me in the auld kirkyard at Ayr. It's such a bonny country place. I couldn't rest in peace in the midst o' all the noise and bustle o' Glasgow.'

'Weel, weel, Murn,' soothed the Earl, patting her hand. 'I'll just put you in a Glasgow kirkyard first and if you don't lie quiet there I'll try you in the other. Would you like me to fetch Phemy now to give you a wee strengthening sup o' something?'

Murn sighed. 'I'll be glad o' a sup but it's no' likely to do muckle strengthening.'

'Whatever's the Lord's will,' the Earl said, rising.

'Amen,' said Murn.

Downstairs William and Letitia Halyburton, like himself, were relieved that the soldiers had left their house if not the town as yet. But Phemy and Griselle seemed extremely agitated.

'Tuts,' said Letitia. 'You, Mistress Phemy, and you, Mistress Griselle, seem more perturbed by the rebels' departure than by their arrival. You surely were not catched by them.'

'No, Mother.'

'Of course not, Mother.'

'Then why, pray, are you in such a tither?'

'We are concerned about Annabella,' said Phemy. 'She is so catched by Monsieur Lavelle.'

Glendinny shook his head.

'There never was a kinder heart than Phemy's, Letitia.' Then turning to Phemy he added: 'Lass, would you run up with a sup of something strengthening for Murn. It'll no' do much good, for she's slipping fast away, but it would please me.'

Letitia said: 'Heat some honey and whisky, Mistress Phemy, and add a little meal and butter.'

'Yes, Mother.'

'Weel, that sounds a lot more sensible than what Dr Kilgour prescribed. It fair scunnered oor Murn. He said to cook toads alive and then mash them doon and drink the brew. She near puked her heart up after drinking a dishful.'

'Tuts! Doctors! A waste of good money!'

174

'You're quite right, Letitia.'

'My gudewife,' boomed Willie Halyburton, 'is a very sensible woman.'

'Aye.' The Earl nodded. 'And I'm sure Mistress Phemy's the same.'

Halyburton said: 'Isn't it terrible what the rebels are going off with? As if they hadn't taken enough from us already. Now it's all our arms, powder and balls and they've taken the printing press as well, a fount of types, printing paper and three workmen.'

'Aye, no' forgetting our ain colleagues, Willie. Poor George Carmichael and Archibald Coats. It's terrible times we're living in. And they've burned and plundered the village of Lesmahagow I hear—especially the clergyman's house. It was under that reverend gentleman's direction that the village folk attacked and made prisoner Macdonald of Kinlochmoidant. Apparently he was traversing the county unattended. The Prince had sent him on some mission to the Western Isles.'

'They would have burned and plundered Glasgow as well, Glendinny, had it not been for Cameron of Lochiel.'

'True, there's always something to thank God for. No doubt all the churches will have special services of praise and thanksgiving for our safe delivery.'

'Och, aye. Aye. Will you have a dram, Glendinny?'

'I'll no' say no.'

'Gudewife!' roared Halyburton, as if she were in the next room instead of at his elbow. 'We'll have a dram.'

'Then I'd better hash back upstairs to Murn. We've been together for many a long year and I'm partial to saying a warm goodbye to friends when they tak' their leave.'

Halyburton raised his glass, now dutifully filled by his gudewife.

'To the Lady Glendinny. May she have a safe journey to the other side.'

'To oor Murn.' The Earl gulped over his whisky, smacked his lips in appreciation and rose to take his leave.

'You'll be wanting a woman's help with the funeral,' Letitia said. 'A man's no good at organising such things on his own.'

'Weel, weel, Letitia, I suppose you're right again.'

'I'll come upstairs with you and find out what's wanted.'

On the way up the narrow tower she walked with dignity, holding up her skirts to protect them from the filth, and on reaching Lady Glendinny's bedroom she signalled Phemy to quit the room and settled herself on a chair close to Lady Glendinny's head. Lady Glendinny's long waxy face could only be distinguished from the pillow by the dark hollows of her eyes and mouth lying open.

Letitia nodded.

'I see you're still with us, Murn.'

'Aye,' said Murn, but feebly, unable to lift her sagging chin.

'I was wondering about the funeral arrangements. Was there anything special you wanted in the way of food or would you rather just leave it to me?'

'I dare say you'll manage fine, Letty.'

'And would you like brandy and claret?'

Murn's eyes widened.

'Whisky.'

'Tuts, woman, I meant as well as the whisky.'

Murn relaxed again.

'Aye.'

'And would you have us in mittens or muffs?'

Murn's lips closed, then sagged open again.

'Muffs,' said Letitia. 'Very well. High dress, of course. Don't worry, Murn, we'll do you proud. Oh, and when you get to the other side you find old Jock Currie and just you tell him how lucky he's been to miss all this terrible business with the rebels. Tell him even their horses have been eating off us and we're all but bankrupt.'

'Letty, the way I feel noo,' Murn whispered, 'I can't see myself tramping all over heaven looking for auld Jock Currie.'

'Tuts, you'll be fine once you get there. Could you do with another sup to help you on your way?'

'Aye.'

'Very well, I'll send Phemy back in. Now you're no' to worry, Murn. Phemy'll look after the gudeman once you've gone.'

She swished away, hands clasped neatly under her bosom, and to Phemy who was waiting outside she commanded:

176

'Mistress Phemy, Lady Glendinny fancies another sup before joining her Maker. Hurry through.'

Then she swept downstairs to begin preparing the funeral food.

Lavelle had to leave early to report to the Prince and to attend to the mustering of his company, but before he left with his fellow officers he tried once more to reason with Annabella.

'Mademoiselle, it is madness.'

She laughed. 'I agree, sir. It is a mad, exciting, fascinating adventure and I cannot wait to get started.'

'You will regret it.'

'Regret being with you? Impossible!'

'But you cannot be with me all the time. I would not be so keenly concerned for your safety if you could.'

'There will be precious moments. There will be nights when I will lie in your arms. That will be worth any inconvenience.'

He sighed. 'Inconvenience? *O, Mon Dieu!*'

'Gracious heavens, if you're going, go. You will depress me with your long face. I will look to myself, never fear. And I'll have the servants.'

'Your fierce papa is not going to be happy about losing his daughter, his servants, his horses and his pistols. Ah, mademoiselle, such courage. One has to admire it.'

'Oh, I'll leave him Big John. I'll take Nancy. The little tramp Regina might be useful too. Nancy speaks well of her.' Suddenly she swooped her arms sideways and dropped into a low curtsy. '*Au revoir, Monsieur Capitaine Lavelle.*' Her eyes twinkled up at him. '*Bon voyage!*'

He made elegant circles in front of him with his hands, then bowed and backed towards the door.

'*Mademoiselle Ramsay. Enchanté!*'

After he had gone, Annabella skipped through to the kitchen window to watch Big John lead the horses from the stable. Lavelle and the other officers mounted up, but she had only eyes for Lavelle, looking very grand in his cocked hat and jackboots and his sword by his side. Immediately he was seated in his usual relaxed loose-limbed manner she raced through to the bedroom again to watch for him to come cantering from the close in Saltmarket, round the Cross and along Trongate Street. After he had disappeared from view she called on Nancy and when the servant appeared she clapped her hands in excitement.

'I'm ready now, Nancy, are you?'

'Mistress, one thing I'm not ready for and that's my grave.'

'Gracious heavens, what cowardly talk is this? We're setting out on an adventure. You ought to be uncommonly delighted.'

She was the absolute limit, Nancy thought. What the hell was there to be delighted about?

'Well, I'm not.'

'Hell and damnation, Nancy, don't provoke me. If we don't get away soon Papa will be back from the tavern and Big John will have returned from the errand I sent him on. Where is Regina? Have you told her she's going?'

Nancy shook her head. 'I was teaching her how to do the ironing yesterday and again this morning. She's slow but she's determined.'

'Oh, to hell with the ironing. You said she'd make a good servant and I need good servants, so tell her to put on her cloak, we're setting out on a mighty important journey.'

'We?'

Annabella stamped her foot. 'Yes, we. But if you absolutely refuse to accompany me then I'll go on my own and to the devil with you all.' Her voice broke. 'But I never dreamed you, you of all people, Nancy, would desert me and let me down.'

Nancy rolled her eyes. 'Och, all right.'

Immediately Annabella brightened and jumped up and down and clapped her hands.

'Oh, Nancy, what fun, what fun!'

'I'll go and put the bags on the horses but I still think you're taking far too much. What do you need with stays, ornaments, comfit-boxes, fans, purses, patch-boxes . . .'

'Fiddlesticks, I know what I need. Get the girl to help you, and hurry. Hurry!'

She did a pirouette around the room, then snatched up her cloak and whirled it around her shoulders. Underneath the blue cloak she wore a crimson velvet gown with small panniers because it was morning. In her luggage she had packed a bell-hoop, which was a sort of petticoat, shaped like a bell and made with cane for framework. This was not quite full dress and could only be worn in the afternoon. For full-dress or high-dress she had a full-size hoop which she was sure was the most wide in the whole of Scotland. She had packed her green silk, her purple satin, her flowered silk, her scarlet taffeta, her yellow voile. To wear with them she had silk stockings and buckled shoes, and green and blue and scarlet ribbons for her hair, and the same colours for garters all with gold and silver tassels. And, of course, she had her long cherry and white striped plaid which was very elegant and useful.

She gave a last admiring stare in her pier glass. How beautiful she looked with her rose-petal cheeks and lapis-lazuli eyes and her hair padded high and curled and powdered and ornamented with beads. How neat she looked in her long-bodiced dress. She gave a sigh of satisfaction, then blowing herself a goodbye kiss she sallied forth.

Downstairs in the back close Nancy had the horses ready. Beside her stood a bewildered-looking Regina. Annabella leapt up unaided on to her horse. Nancy mounted and hauled Regina up to sit behind her. Then Annabella kicked her horse's flanks, gave a yell of encouragement, and they went galloping off into the Saltmarket, then along the Trongate they sped with people flurrying and jumping away from their path.

Chapter 16

'Brothers and sisters, hear what I say,
There's a sister departed this verra day,
The guid Lady Glendinny has gone to her rest,
We'll miss her, of course, but the Lord knows best.

Her lyke-wake's tonight,
And her burying's tomorrow,
I'm sure you'll all share in the guid Earl's sorrow,
So come to Locheid's Land,
At the hour of three,
And join wi' him in the drinking spree.'

Moothy McMurdo went round every street ringing his bell as if he were taking the leading part in some glorious festival. He was carefree and brimming over with energy because the rebel army had quitted the town. More than once he had been manhandled and threatened because of his plain-spoken announcements and his stubborn habit of bawling out references to 'The Pretender' instead of to 'The Prince'. This undignified and rough treatment had shocked him. He was a man whose fitness for his job had never been questioned. Now he sang out:

'Another lady's departed but in a different way,
And where she is exactly is difficult to say,
Mistress Annabella Ramsay has her faither worried,
And all her freends are awfi' flurried.
She's galloped off into danger and strife,
And the meenister's frettin' for he's lost a wife.
Did ever ye hear such a stramash in your life,
And she's taken twa servants with her tae,
And her faither's horses I dare say.'

Gav and Quin were coming down the High Street when they heard McMurdo and Gav tugged at Quin's sleeve in distress.

'Quin, Quin!'

'Oh-ho, oh-ho!' Quin cocked his head and scratched his torn ear. 'Now for some fun, eh?'

'Does that mean she's galloped off with Regina?'

'Could be, Gav. Could verra well be. Auld Nick said to Quin, "Quin," he says, says he, "that Mistress Annabella's a devil o' a woman." '

Gav's lips trembled.

'She's wicked all right if she's stolen Regina. First my mammy and now my sister. I never knew anybody could be as wicked as that.'

'Weel, ye know noo.'

'And you said you'd find my mammy and you haven't and now Regina's gone.'

'Patience, laddie, patience. If Quin said he'd find your mammy, he will.'

'I'm going up to that house to see for myself.'

'See what, eh?'

'I'm going to get to know from Maister Ramsay where Regina is.'

'All you're liable to get is a punch in the ear. Quin knows that maister. He can be a devil when he's angry and he'll be fine and angry just now, eh?'

'I don't care. I'm not frightened of him.' Gav stamped towards Ramsay's close in the Saltmarket with fists clenched tightly under long sleeves. 'He shouldn't have let Mistress Annabella kidnap my sister if he's the maister.'

'Oh-ho, it's no' called kidnapping when they kind o' folk do it to your kind o' folk.'

'Why not?' Gav stared up at Quin in astonishment.

'Because they've got money, eh? Auld Nick always says, "Quin," he says, says he, "money changes the complexion o' things." And what's more, it's grand protection. Gather as much as you can around you, lad.'

Gav marched into the close and up the stair, with Quin jogging along beside him, still chattering.

'So until Gav and Quin have a wee bit sillar they're no' really in a position to go spiering a rich man like Maister Ramsay, eh?

And Maister Ramsay's no' going to waste his time talking to the likes o' Gav and Quin.'

Gav reached up and tirled the door-pin. His face was grey under freckles which had faded to a jaundiced hue. Quin's head fell to one side to display his grotesque swollen face and he doubled forward and leaned a hand down on Gav's shoulder in the way that he did when they were begging. They waited like this for the door to open. When it did, Big John glowered down at them.

'Away with you. You'll get nothing here.'

Gav spoke up.

'He doesn't want anything. I want to speak to Maister Ramsay.'

'Oh, do you, you cheeky wee devil? Weel, he's no' here. He's at his counting-house doon at the Briggait.'

With that, Big John banged the door in their faces.

'Come on, Quin,' said Gav.

'You're no' going to brave the Briggait, eh?'

'What's an old counting-house to be afraid of?'

'Oh-ho, now for some fun, eh?'

Quin scuttled along beside Gav, down Saltmarket Street until they came to the narrow Briggait which cut off Saltmarket before it reached the Green. Briggait Street looped round to join the foot of Stockwell Street and the river at the Great Bridge. One of the oldest tenements in the city occupied the whole frontage between the New and Back Wynds of Briggait Street and it had four crow-step gables to the street and moulded chimney-stalks. In the area there were also the town houses of many old merchant families, like the Campbells of Blythswood. There was the residence of Douglas of Mains and Her Grace the Duchess of Douglas; of the Campbells of Silvercraigs (in whose house Oliver Cromwell had lodged); of Crawford of Crawfordsburn, of the Honourable John Aird, of Bailies Robert and George Bogle, of the Reverend Mr Blackadder, of Provost Cochrane, of the Dean of Guild Bogle, and also of Sir Robert Pollock of Pollock.

But the most imposing of all the buildings in Briggait Street was the Merchants' Hall, at whose meetings the Dean of Guild took precedence over the Provost and who, according to the Letter of Guildry, 'shall always be a Merchant and a Merchant Sailor and Merchant Venturer . . .' The Merchants' Hall had a curious steeple which boasted three battlements one on top of the other and a clock of molten brass. On top of the steeple there was a spire which was mounted with a ship of finely gilded copper instead of a weathercock.

Gav barely gave it a glance, he was so intent on his search for Merchant Ramsay's counting-house. Quin knew where it was but was refusing to co-operate in the hope of deterring Gav. In fact, when Gav did find the place, Quin leapt in front of him in great agitation and spread out his arms.

'Gav, Gav! Quin canna let you go in. They'll fling you in the Tolbooth and you'll no' like it. Quin knows. Quin's been there.'

But Gav suddenly darted beneath his arm and Quin was left doing a distracted dance, hair and coat-tails flying, before deciding in desperation to dash in after him.

Inside the counting-house there was, as he expected, a terrible stramash. Counting-house clerks were shouting indignantly and furiously struggling to restrain a kicking, punching, biting Gav. Joining in the shouting and struggling, Quin added to the noise and confusion and then Ramsay burst out from another room and bawled above everybody else. 'What the deevil's going on?'

Everybody, including Gav and Quin, tried to tell him and he roared at them again.

'Will ye all hold your tongues?' And when he got silence at last he said to Gav: 'You, sir, have I no' seen you somewhere before?'

'First my mammy and now my sister. It's wicked, that's what it is, and it doesn't make any difference if you've got money or not.'

Ramsay eyed him for a minute.

'Aye, you've got spunk if you've nothing else.'

'Where's my sister Regina?'

'She'll be with oor Annabella, no doubt.'

'Kidnapped!' Gav shouted and began struggling again. 'And kidnapping by a mistress is just as bad as kidnapping by

Egyptian sorners. You can't fool me.' His voice broke. 'I can read and write and count and speak Latin.'

And before anyone could do anything he wriggled free and raced out of the building with Quin skittering excitedly after him.

Ramsay called out, but too late, and he returned thoughtfully to his room, ignoring the profuse apologies of his clerks.

Outside Gav and Quin cut through the Goose Dubs and up Stockwell Street and did not stop running until, gasping for breath, they reached the Trongate. Quin clutched at his chest in choking harassment.

'Quin's never been in such a terrible stramash for years.'

'I hate them Ramsays,' said Gav.

'Hating tobacco merchants is no' going to do Gav or Quin any good. Tobacco merchants run this toon.'

'I don't care.'

'You're a terrible childer. What's Quin to do with you, eh?'

They walked along Trongate Street in silence for a few minutes, then Quin said: 'They've ships as well.'

'Who?'

'The tobacco merchants. Quin knows where the ships are.'

'At the Broomielaw?'

'Quin's cleverer than you, eh? Quin knows only wee cobbles can come up to the Broomielaw. There's no' enough water there for big sailing ships.'

'Where are the big ships, then?' Gav's interest made him forget his distress.

'They built a port—about eighteen miles from the toon. And because it's Glasgow's port they called it Port Glasgow.'

'I've never seen big ships.'

'Oh-ho! Quin's the clever one, eh? Quin can show you.'

Jessie climbed the Cracklin House Brae and hid among the broom. She listened to the town stirring and going about its business. There were bells and street cries, and the clappers of the lepers. There was the rumble and creaking of carriage wheels and the clip-clopping and whinnying of horses. She smelled the sickly odour of the sugar works, and the sour stench from the mutton market. They came mixing up with the pleasant aroma of the orchard garden and the herb market. Occasionally she peered out and caught glimpses of cadgers leading their pack-horses, some with creels, some with sacks, some with panniers loaded with fish or salt or eggs or poultry or crockery-ware. There were different-coloured sedan-chairs being carried along. There were gentlemen riding on horseback. Barefooted servant maids and water caddies waited at wells. Then suddenly from everywhere Highlanders appeared until the whole of Glasgow was blanketed with tartan. The wail and skirl of the bagpipes filled the air. Kettledrums rattled. Gradually the tartan faded away and disappeared.

Still Jessie waited. She did not know what to do. The longing for her children and her anxiety about them was a pain tugging at her with ever-increasing urgency. Yet to suddenly appear before Mistress Halyburton after all this time, and without the fine linen she had been entrusted with, was a terrifying thought. Mistress Halyburton's wrath was something worth fearing and she was a woman of her word. If she said she would get you flung in the Tolbooth, get you flung in the Tolbooth she would.

Then a new thought struck Jessie and she clung to it hopefully. Maybe Mistress Halyburton had found her linen by now. There was always the chance that she had sent one of her servants to look for it and they had gathered it up while she was lying helpless in the pit. The more she thought of this, the more elated and certain she became. Of course, that must have been what happened. Mistress Halyburton would be bound to make some efforts to find her linen. Jessie struggled up, half laughing, half crying with relief. Every bone in her body felt as stiff and as brittle as an icicle and she was unable to hurry as she would have liked. Instead, her journey down the Cracklin House Brae into the Back Cow Loan, along Candleriggs Street and into the Trongate was a series of fits and starts. She entered the archway that led to the backclose and the Halyburtons' stairway, her heart racing in her chest as if it were going to explode and by the time she had hauled herself up the stairs, she no longer knew what she was doing or why. The door-pin rasped round and round and reminded her of hoarse black crows.

Birds sang early in the morning outside the cottage. Birds soared up the mountainside and wheeled in the glen. Birds cawing, croaking, chirping, cheeping, chirruping in happy chorus. Her mother had been content to welcome each dawn.

'Aye, Jessie.' She smiled. 'Another day.'

Her father had a smile for her as well. He ruffled his big hand through her hair.

'There you are, lass. Up with the birds as usual. But you're your daddy's own wee bird.'

Jessie was smiling at her father when the door opened and she found herself face to face with Mistress Halyburton who happened to be passing in the lobby. At first Letitia could not believe her eyes, then fury fouled up her tongue and prevented her from speaking.

Jessie said: 'Have you got the linen, mistress?'

Letitia suddenly grabbed Jessie by the hair and hauled her into the house.

'You impudent, thieving witch! You've the audacity to come back here asking for more of my good linen. You'd have it all, you'd steal every last thread from me.'

'I put it out on the grass by the burn to dry,' Jessie wailed. 'And when I got back it wasn't there. I didn't steal it. I'm a respectable woman. I'm no' a thief.'

'Respectable? Respectable?' Letitia's voice screeched high. 'With two illegitimate brats? You're a liar, Jessie Chisholm, and lying's punishable by law as well as thieving. And the nerve of you to come back here after all this time. As sure as my name's Letitia Halyburton I'll see you hang for this. Tam! Kate!' she called but both servants were already at her elbow. 'Would you look at this?'

Kate screwed up her leathery face until the wart on her nose touched her chin. She shoved it close to Jessie who could not shrink back because Mistress Halyburton still held her hair in an iron grasp.

'Steal frae my mistress, would ye?' She spat in Jessie's face.

'No, no,' Jessie whimpered. 'No, I didn't.'

Letitia said: 'Fetch my cloak, Tam. We'll march her along to the Tolbooth.'

'No, no. No' the Tolbooth. I have to find my bairns.'

'Your bairns are away with the Highland army,' Kate told her maliciously. 'You'll never see them again.'

Jessie began to struggle. 'For pity's sake let me go, mistress. I'll have to go after my bairns.'

'You should have thought of your bastards before you started your wicked thieving.' Letitia gave Jessie's head a jerk and she cried out in pain.

'I laid it out to dry by the Woodside burn.'

'Oh, come on.' Letitia hauled her out of the house with Kate running after her, fastening the cape round her shoulders. 'Tam, you stay here. Kate and I will manage fine. Here, Kate, you keep a grip of her going down the stairs while I attend to my skirts.'

She was wearing a plum-coloured sackdress with a long train which she had to hitch over one arm to protect it from the dirt. Outside she said:

'You're doing fine, Kate. Just hold fast to her and follow me.'

'Wicked thieving witch,' Kate said, twisting at Jessie's arm. 'They should burn you like your mother.'

'I fell down the pit. And when I got back out it wasn't there.'

'Well, where is it then?'

'I don't know. Somebody must have stolen it.'

'Aye, we know what wicked auld witch stole it, all right.'

As they hurried along Trongate Street, people stopped to stare and some ragged children skipped excitedly after them. A cold wind was tugging at Mistress Halyburton's cloak and rain sprayed down to rapidly fill up the ruts and holes in the road. Letitia in her hurry had forgotten to put on her pattens and her silk shoes were getting ruined, a fact that did nothing to improve her temper. By the time they reached the Tolbooth, Jessie was in physical as well as mental distress. Her crutch was stabbing into her armpit with each hurried step and the rain was soaking her hair and running down her neck, making the wind doubly chilling.

The Tolbooth, which had been built in 1626, consisted of the ground floor and five floors above; the windows of the rooms where prisoners were confined were strongly barricaded by massive iron stanchions. The ground floor was where the town

187

clerk had his offices and entry was below the outside stair. Entry to the prison wards was by a narrow turnpike stair in the steeple. During the day the outer door of this entry was only a half-door wicket, guarded by a janitor who kept his seat constantly in the passage and amused himself by looking over the half-door at what was passing on the street. Besides this outside wicket-door there was a strong inside door, securing the entry up the narrow staircase to the prison wards. Also near to the outside door there was a sentry-box and a soldier was always on guard there.

Mistress Halyburton marched straight to the janitor.

'I have a prisoner for you. A wicked, thieving witch of a woman. Guard her weel until I get one of the bailies to deal with her.'

Jessie wept.

'Mistress, mistress. You've had bairns yourself.'

'The impudence of her.' Letitia grabbed Jessie and hurled her at the wicket-door and, losing her balance, Jessie crashed on to the road at the janitor's feet. She could not believe that she was going to be imprisoned and unable ever to see Regina or Gav again. She refused to give them up. With the help of her crutch she struggled to rise. Then she tried to limp away, only to be hurled back against the door again. This time the janitor got a grip of her.

'Come on. Inside with you.'

Jessie began to scream.

'Gavie! Regina! Gavie! Regina!' she screeched over and over again, her voice trailing fainter and fainter up the dark spiral stair.

Bailie Steenie was a plain man, not renowned for brains nor education. He knew very little, if anything, about the law, but dispersed his magisterial duties as best and as speedily as he was able. He had been heard to say: 'A statute? What's a statute? Words, just words. Have I to be tied down by mere words? No, no—I feel my law—here.'

And he struck a fist against his heart.

Drinking in his estimation was a positive virtue and in a recent case, when he learned that a man charged with stabbing another had been drunk at the time, he was shocked enough to cry out:

'Good Lord, if he will do this when he's drunk, what will he not do when he's sober?'

Now first thing in the morning a boy was brought before him charged with stealing a handkerchief. The indictment having been read, the bailie addressed the boy.

'I've no doubt you did this deed, because I had a handkerchief stolen oot o' my ain pocket this verra week. So I'm sending you to jail for sixty days.'

The assessor rose up as if in pain. 'Yer honour, ye canna do that.'

'What for no'?'

'The case has not yet been proved.'

'Och, weel, I'll just give you thirty days.'

Up creaked the assessor again, this time with closed eyes. 'Yer honour!'

'Weel, my lad,' said Bailie Steenie, reluctantly disposing of the case. 'The evidence seems a wee bit jimp this time, so I'll let you off. But you'd better no' do it again!'

The next accused was Jessie Chisholm.

'This is much more serious than pickering a handky.' The bailie peered reprovingly at Jessie from over the top of his spectacles. 'You've stolen a' Mistress Halyburton's linen. Good expensive stuff. And after her trusting you with it. I don't know what the world's coming to.' He eyed the assessor, squashing him down before he arose. 'She had it and you're no' going to tell me any different. I've put up with enough of your law for one afternoon. She had it in her possession and therefore was responsible for it.' He turned his attention back to Jessie. 'Now, deported or hangit, which is it to be?'

Jessie stared back at him in anguish.

'I want to go to my bairns.'

'Where are your bairns?'

'With the Highland army.'

'Rebels, are ye? Ye'd a' hang if I had my way. Every traitorous one o' ye. This toon's near ruined because o' a' you rebels.'

The assessor closed his eyes again, but did not bother getting up.

'Yer honour, she's no' on trial for being a Highland rebel.'

'Aye, weel, that may be so, but she'd no' last long ower in Virginia, crippled as she is. It'll be a kindness to hang her.'

'Yer honour!'

'Tell the hangman to get the gallows ready.'

'Oh, verra well.'

Jessie just stood leaning on her crutch, looking bewildered.

'Away ye go to your rest, woman,' said the bailie, refreshing himself with a glass of brandy from the decanter on the bench. 'And may the Lord have mercy on your soul. Next case.'

Quin and Gav were admiring the ships at Port Glasgow. The wind was whipping the waves into 'white horses' and sending spray flying over the bows. They could see the Gareloch and the widening firth and the mountains all around. Port Glasgow consisted of a straggle of buildings curving along the edge of the water, houses, sheds and bonded warehouses where the tobacco was kept until tax was paid on it. A jetty stuck out like a long finger and on either side and around it some of the Virginia Fleet was at anchor. There was the *Thetis,* the *Advice* and the *Grizie,* and William Halyburton's ships, the *Letty* and the *Lintie.* They all had tall masts and spars and low hulls and were square-rigged.

Gav was very impressed. 'I'd love to sail to Virginia in one of those ships.'

'Quin knows a few stories about them. They're lucky if they get there. Quin's heard it can be verra windy. Quin's heard ships can be blowed all to bits. And even if folks do get there a' in one piece, it's just to die of the scurvy or starve to death.'

'Don't they take enough food with them?'

'Salt pork and biscuits full o' weevils. Quin knows you wouldn't like being a sailor, Gav. It's time Quin and Gav were trotting back to the toon.'

Reluctantly Gav followed Quin away from the harbour. The sturdy three-masted ships fascinated him and he would have enjoyed inspecting the inside of one.

Quin called back to him: 'Are you going to wait until it's dark, eh? And you no' with a lanthorn or a candle to your name?'

190

Gav made up to Quin but had to run to keep alongside him. 'What's all the hurry?' he asked breathlessly.

'Och, Quin's no' verra keen on this place. The toon's the place for Quin.'

It had begun to rain and the road, which was hardly more than a track speckled with loose stones, became sticky with mud and blackened their feet. At one point they heard the sound of galloping and had to jump to one side among the prickly gorse to allow the horseman to splash and clatter past. Mud smacked all over them and some stones whipped up and cut their legs. Gav's freckled face screwed up against the pain and Quin said:

'Quin and Gav will soon be back in the toon and Quin'll wash Gav's sore legs in good Glasgow water.'

At long last they saw the Great Bridge with its eight arches crossing the River Clyde. At that point near the bridge it was so shallow horses and carts splashed through the ford rather than climb the steep, worn roadway of the bridge. Above the glistening roof-tops of the town Gav could pick out the Cathedral up on the left, then more towards the river there was the towering spire of the University, the Ramshaw Church, Hutcheson's Hospital, the Tolbooth, the Tron Church and the Guildhall with a wintry sun sparkling the gilded ship that formed its weathervane. On the other side of the river was the pretty country village of Gorbals and on the river they could see the white sails of little boats.

They squelched across some fields and came out on the country lane that led past the Shawfield Mansion and along Trongate Street.

A crowd had gathered in front of the Tolbooth and the gallows had been erected on the platform on top of the outside stair. Men, women and children crushed around, laughing and chattering expectantly. Street pedlars cried their wares. The town's drummer banged with great gusto.

'Oh-ho,' said Quin. 'There's going to be a hanging. Now for some fun, eh?'

'My legs are still bleeding.' Gav came limping after Quin as best he could.

'There's the cure,' said Quin, pointing to a well across from

191

King William's statue. 'Quin'll soon stop the blood seeping oot. Once Quin gets this water on you, your blood'll turn to icicles and no' be able to move.'

Gav yelped as the water gushed over his leg, but Quin was not paying much attention. He had caught sight of the cripple woman hobbling up the stairs of the Tolbooth leaning on her crutch with one arm and on the banister with the other.

For a minute or two he jumped about in agitation in an effort to screen Gav's view. Then eventually he bent over the child and hissed in a confidential tone: 'Gav, get ready to flee like the wind. Here's thon black dog called Spider coming to chow that leg o' yours right off.'

Back down Trongate Street they both raced, the pain of Gav's legs forgotten. Round King Street on to Bridge Street and then down by the slaughterhouse on to the Low Green. Quin stopped and leaned on Gav, at the same time clutching his chest and choking for breath.

'Oh-ho, that was a close one, eh? Auld Nick nearly had you that time, Gavie, m'lad.'

'Is he away now?' Gav gazed anxiously around.

'Of course. Of course. You're far too good a sprinter for Spider. He's trotted away hame to Tannery Wynd.'

'Can we go back to the well then?'

'Eh . . . no, Quin's got a better idea. There's a fine spring along there by the bleachfields. Come on.'

On passing the bleachfields, Quin whipped up a linen sheet and stuffed it under his coat, making Gav nearly weep with agitation.

'Quin, they could send you to the plantations or hang you. Mammy's told me about lots of people being deported or hanged for stealing from the bleachfields. Put it back. Oh, put it back, please, Quin.'

'It was just lying there, Gav, serving no end or purpose, and Quin has a verra good purpose for it. Now you stay here and wash your legs and then meet Quin at the Cross in a wee while. Quin has a wee bit business to attend to.'

And before Gav could make any more objections Quin jogged away.

By the time he reached the Tolbooth, the crowd was dispersing and Jessie was swaying high in the gallows, one-legged and with frizzy head twisted to one side. Her eyes were open and her body was twitching. Quin made straight for Hangy Spittal.

'Maister Spittal,' he said deferentially, 'Quin would be verra obliged if you gave him that body to bury. It's the mither of a friend o' his. You've seen him with Quin. A wee red-haired, freckly-faced childer.'

Hangy Spittal's wizened face seemed too small in proportion to his blue coat with its big red collar.

'How do I know you're no' one o' them wicked resurr-ectionists?' he wheezed.

'What if Quin was?'

The hangman hesitated and glanced around.

'Then I'd maybe give you the body for a price.'

Quin plunged his hands into his pockets and produced a few merks.

'That's all Quin's got.'

The hangman carefully plucked the money from Quin's palms.

'Done!'

Jessie was dropped to the ground and Quin whipped out the sheet from under his coat and smartly covered her body with it.

'Quin's to wait on the wee childer. He'll be here in a minute.'

Sure enough in a very short time Gav appeared from Saltmarket Street and Quin dashed across the road to meet him.

'Gav, Quin's kept his promise. Quin's found your mammy.'

Gav gazed up at Quin, his face radiating joy as if a beacon had been lit inside him.

'But wait a wee,' said Quin. 'Wait a wee. She's been hangit.'

The beacon's bright flame flickered, then extinguished.

'Hanged?'

'That's what Quin said.'

'Mammy's dead?'

'Quin's never known anyone hangit and no' deed.'

Gav's head drooped low. A storm of grief was gusting about in his chest, heaving it up, tightening it, paining him. Jerkily he struggled to breathe and to swallow.

'Come on,' Quin said. 'Quin and Gav's got work to do. There's a mither to be buried.'

He hurried back to where Jessie was lying. Gav came slowly after him to stand gazing down at the sheet with a pale stricken face. His mouth moved but no words came.

Quin said: 'You stay with your mammy until Quin gets a wee loan of a shovel oot the Tolbooth.'

Into the Tolbooth he went and out again with the shovel to find Gav still standing as if still fighting to drag words up from his chest. He pushed the shovel under Gav's arm.

'You carry the shovel and Quin'll carry the mither.'

He hoisted the body over his shoulder and scampered away with Jessie's arms dangling and jerking and swinging behind him. Gav caught one of the hands and held on to it, struggling at the same time with the shovel which was as big as himself.

All the way along the Gallowgate he desperately held on, past the houses and on to the lonely road to Edinburgh. At the crossroads they stopped and Quin laid Jessie down, with Gav still clutching at her hand.

Quin cocked his head to one side and scratched his ear.

'Aye, weel, you're maybe a bit wee for the digging. Quin'll do it. He's done it before. You just have a seat beside your mammy.'

Huddled as close as he could to Jessie, Gav thought of the times when he'd sat on her knee and she had rocked him and sung to him. Her arms had been strong and her hands warm and comforting as she patted and fondled him in time with her song. Tears spurted from his eyes and his lips quivered.

Ignoring him, Quin set about digging the grave and when he was finished he said:

'Quin'll wrap her up nice and snug and jist drap her in.'

Through a flood of tears Gav shook his head. After a struggle he managed to steady his voice enough to make his words decipherable.

'When folks get buried at the church something's always said.'

Quin scratched his ear. 'Quin's never been to church.'

'Well, I have,' Gav managed. 'I've been to church and I've been to school and I know something should be said for my

194

mammy.'

'What sort o' things are said, eh?'

Gav shook his head again and rubbed at his flushed and swollen face with the back of his sleeve.

'I can't remember.'

'Weel, Quin and Gav'll just have to drap the mither withoot saying anything.'

Quin snatched the sheet from over the top of Jessie and began wrapping it tightly round her body. Seeing her face, Gav's weeping raged louder and he cuddled and nursed it against himself.

'Quin's mither's doon there and Quin's no' greetin'.'

Eventually he managed to prise the body away from Gav's arms. Then he slithered down into the grave with it, arranging it neatly at the bottom, and scrambled back up again. He was just about to throw the first spadeful of earth when Gav protested louder than ever.

'No! Something must be said. We must say something for Mammy.'

'But, Gavie, Quin doesn't know what to say.'

Hiccoughing with grief, Gav wiped his eyes with the back of his sleeve.

'I think I remember the Lord's Prayer.'

'Oh-ho, you're the clever one, right enough. Weel, you start and Quin'll follow as best he can.'

He leaned forward on Gav's shoulder and cocked his head.

Gav's lips were trembling violently but somehow he managed.

'Our Father . . .'

'Oor Faither . . .'

'Which art in heaven . . .'

'Which art in heeven . . .'

Chapter 17

The Prince, as usual, led the minuet. He and some of his officers were staying at Bannockburn House, the castle of Chevalier Sir Hugh Paterson. Also at the castle was Annabella Ramsay and Sir Hugh's niece Clementine Walkinshaw. Sir Hugh was an enthusiastic Jacobite and his hospitality was lavish. Nothing had been too good for the Prince. He had been wined and dined. He had been entertained by a fiddler and by Miss Walkinshaw on the spinet. Annabella sang an amusing but bawdy song at which they all laughed heartily, except the Prince, but even his mouth twitched up at the edges and his eyes glimmered in appreciation. Miss Walkinshaw hid her face modestly behind her fan, but she emerged to partner the Prince in the minuet and they both seemed to enjoy the dance.

It was while they were at Bannockburn House that they were visited by Sir John Douglas, MP, with a message from the English Jacobites. He told the Prince:

'Your Royal Highness, ten thousand pounds has been collected for you in London.'

Sheridan, the old Irishman who had been the Prince's tutor and his constant companion, growled, 'Since they have collected money, why the devil did they not send it?'

The army could have done with some money. They also were badly in need of stores. Some of the Highlanders under the Prince were now quartered in the neighbourhood of Bannockburn. The rest of the army, commanded by Lord George Murray, made up of five clan regiments and part of the cavalry, had at first been stationed nine miles further eastwards at Falkirk. Murray, the Prince's Lieutenant General, knew that Huske of the King's or Royal Army and second-in-command to General 'Hangman' Hawley, had left Edinburgh and was marching westwards with five regular battalions, the Glasgow militia and Hamilton's and Ligonier's dragoons. Murray had also heard that supplies for the royal troops were being collected at Linlithgow and he resolved to carry away as much as possible. He had set out with his division from Falkirk and reaching Linlithgow sent forward the horse under Lord Elcho to patrol the area. Elcho reported that a very large body of horse and foot were advancing and Lord George waited at the bridge over the Avin, planning to attack the enemy when half of them passed the bridge. However, none of them passed it. Instead, some dragoons who were in front of the regulars drew up close to the bridge and abusive language was hurled between both sides. Then Lord George, deciding that it was better not to have a fight when a general action was impending, withdrew to Falkirk and next day received his order to rejoin the Prince at Bannockburn. But a body of horse was ordered to patrol all that night as near Falkirk as they could. Next day sixteen of that party sent word to the Prince that all the foot of Hawley's army had arrived at Falkirk, also one thousand Highlanders under the command of Colonel Campbell.

Murray advised the Prince that, instead of waiting to be attacked, the Highland army should take the offensive. Knowing the Highlanders' preference for high ground, he suggested as their objective the hill of Falkirk. This ridge rose steeply to the south-west of the town about a mile from General Hawley's camp. The plan was, first of all, to distract attention from the main body of the Highland army. Lord John Drummond, with his own regiment, the Irish picquets and all the cavalry, should take the main road from Bannockburn to Falkirk. This passed the remains of the old Caledonian Forest at the north and from there his force could be clearly seen from the enemy's camp. At the same time, marching by side roads and across fields, it was hoped the main body would be able to advance unnoticed until they reached the ford over the River Carron about two miles from Falkirk.

The Prince and his officers took their leave of Bannockburn House and started on the march between twelve and one o'clock, followed on horseback by their host and Miss Walkinshaw and Annabella and some servants, who were all anxious to have a good view of the battle. The army advanced in two parallel columns, the left-hand column under Lord George Murray was headed by the three Clan Donald regiments. Led by the Atholl Brigade, the right-hand column was commanded by the Prince. The numbers that made up the Highland army were less than Hawley's, because a detachment of the Highland army had been left, under the Duke of Perth, to cover the siege of Stirling Castle.

General Hawley, who did not believe the Highlanders would dare to attack, was wining and dining at Callender House and did not even think it necessary to send out cavalry patrols to collect information. Nevertheless, about eleven o'clock some of his soldiers noticed a body of horse and foot moving about to the north of the Caledonian Forest with their colours. This was standard and the royal army stood to arms. But they were soon ordered to stand down again and they went in search of food to cook for their dinner. This was not easy to find and by the time they found it and cooked it and began eating it, it was nearly one o'clock. They had barely finished when a countryman came rushing into the camp shouting:

'Gentlemen, what are you about? The Highlanders will be immediately upon you.'

Two officers hastily climbed a tree and by means of their telescopes verified that the main body of the Highland army was approaching to the south of the woods. Their commanding officer immediately galloped off to report to Hawley at Callender House, but so convinced was Hawley that there could be no attack, he did not return to the camp. He gave orders that the men were to put on their equipment but that there was no need for them to stand to arms.

As it happened, the Highland march had nearly been abandoned. Captain O'Sullivan rode up to Lord George Murray and told him he had been talking to the Prince and advised him that it would be too dangerous to pass the river in sight of the enemy and it would be better to wait until night.

Murray said: 'You surprise me, O'Sullivan. Don't you realize we could all be past the water in less than a quarter of an hour and the place we've to pass is a full two miles from the enemy?'

A little later the Prince rode angrily up to Murray accompanied by Brigadier Stapleton, the commander of the Irish picquets, O'Sullivan and some other Irish officers. They all remonstrated with Lord George, but he kept on the march, at the same time pointing out:

'It's impossible for the men to lie out all night at this time of year. I know them. They would just disperse and look for shelter. Either we continue to advance or we return to our quarters, for it's threatening a very bad night.'

Murray was a sturdy, good-looking man with a determined mouth, intelligent eyes and quick, impatient movements. He had been the one who, as well as engineering all the Highland army's successes, had also advised their retreat from Derby. The Prince had never forgiven him for what he termed this treachery. He believed that Murray had betrayed both him and the Highland army. None of Murray's brilliant tactics on the field or his unswerving loyalty to the cause could change the Prince in this conviction. From the moment they began the retreat, he listened with trust only to his Irish officers.

Now he glared furiously at Lord George and was about to call after him when Stapleton said:

'Perhaps on this occasion, Your Royal Highness, there's something in what Lord Murray says. If the enemy isn't sufficiently near to dispute our crossing the river, then there isn't any danger.'

So it was between one and two o'clock that a party of volunteers rode into Hawley's camp 'upon the spur', bringing the news that the Highlanders were fording the river with the obvious intention of making for the high ground on Falkirk Moor. Immediately the drums were ordered to beat to arms and a messenger was hurriedly sent off to Callender House.

Hawley arrived at the gallop without his hat and ordered the cavalry forward, followed by the foot and artillery in the hope of stopping the Highlanders reaching the summit. From its lower slopes on the outskirts of the town, the hill rose steeply to a large moorland plateau of scrub and heather and the side of the hill was cut by a deep ravine.

As Lord George Murray had said—a storm was on its way. The sky darkened and a gale-force wind came howling from the south-west. He made sure it was behind the Highland army on its forming line by making a wide circuit after crossing the Carron and marching very quickly up the hillside. The dragoons hurried up from the opposite direction and it was not until the two sides had almost reached the summit that they came in sight of each other. When, earlier that morning, the Jacobite order of battle had been arranged, Lord George Murray had twice reminded the Prince:

'Your Royal Highness should appoint the officers that are to command and where.'

But this had not been done and even he had not received any particular charge, other than a vague order to lead the front-line troops. He inferred by this that he was to command the right wing. It was later discovered that no one was officially in charge of the left wing and Lord John Drummond, who was not there when the battle began, had eventually taken over the position of his own accord.

But while the Highland army was forming, the Prince sent O'Sullivan to arrange the front line and as usual he proceeded to criticise Lord George, who stonily ignored him.

The storm which had been threatening now broke and rain lashed down in torrents.

Annabella and the others from Bannockburn House, and also some farmers from the surrounding district and some townspeople from Falkirk, gathered under a clump of trees. Annabella was afever with excitement. Her cheeks burned and her eyes were wide and expectant. Clementine Walkinshaw was upset by the sudden downpour.

'Our heads will be ruined,' she wailed.

'Oh, put your hood up,' Annabella said impatiently. 'Anyway, rain is uncommonly good for the complexion. Oh, Mistress Walkinshaw, look at the men forming up. Isn't it exciting?'

She could see the Glasgow Regiment well in the rear of the dragoons near some cottages. They had been considered insufficiently trained to be given a place in the line.

It was nearly four o'clock by the time both armies were formed and Hawley sent orders to Colonel Ligonier to begin the attack. The Colonel did not share the General's faith in the superiority of cavalry over Highlanders. However, the three regiments advanced on the Highland right, coming at full trot and in good order. Lord George Murray waited. The horses charged closer and closer. Annabella and Clementine and the other woman watching covered their mouths to stifle their screams. It looked as if the Highlanders were just going to stand motionless until they were pounded into the mud by the horses' hooves. Not until the charging cavalry came within a few yards did Murray raise his musket as the signal to fire. Delivered at such close range, the Highlanders' fire was devastating and about eighty dragoons fell dead on the spot. The rest all turned and fled, with the exception of one small party of Ligonier's men who stood their ground, but to their horror and to the horror of those watching, who had never seen the Highlanders' method of fighting, the Highlanders flung themselves under the horses and thrust their dirks into the animals bellies, hacking them open until their bowels trailed out. Horses screamed and men screamed along with them as they were dragged down by their clothes and stabbed.

After the cavalry had been repulsed, Lord George Murray ordered the three MacDonald regiments to stand their ground, but he could not restrain Glengarry's and Clanranald's men. Brandishing their swords and screeching at the tops of their voices, they rushed off in pursuit of the runaway dragoons.

In blind panic, the troopers galloped into the fifteen thousand strong Glasgow Regiment, riding over them and killing those who did not manage to race out of their path in time. It was the same panic that made two of the other royal regiments break away and plunge into their own left wing, scattering men in all directions.

The Glasgow militia re-formed and stood their ground in the face of the fast-approaching Highlanders, who fell upon them and gave them no quarter.

Dougal Grahame, the packman poet, who was also watching the battle, wrote of the scene:

> 'On red coats they some pity had,
> But 'gainst the Militia were raging mad.'

Annabella felt real distress for the first time. They were her townspeople and she felt for their brave stubborn spirit. Then in the confusion of her concern it occurred to her that the Highlanders were her countrymen too and, that, as well as the English in the battle, Scots were fighting Scots. Scotland was in fact involved in a bitter civil war.

War had never been a reality to her before. She had heard exciting stories from men who had taken part in the fighting or from ladies and gentlemen who had been spectators, but this was the first time she herself had been present at a battle. Certainly it was exciting and she had not the slightest regret at being there. Nor was she afraid. Yet her emotional confusion remained.

Regina was sitting behind Nancy on one of Ramsay's horses. She said bitterly:

'It's disgusting. They're like animals. The Highlanders are as bad as the Frenchies.'

'Wheesht!' Nancy said. 'Do you want to get yourself shot?'

Annabella called over to her: 'I'll shoot you myself if you don't guard your impudent tongue.'

Through her telescope she could see in one direction the two MacDonald regiments, some of them still pursuing the dragoons, others plundering the dead and others hacking down the Glasgow militia. She saw one plump Glasgow shopkeeper being attacked by six Highlanders and for some time defending himself with his half-pike. He appeared to kill two, but a seventh coming up fired a pistol into his groin and as he fell another of the Highlanders slashed him across the eyes and mouth with his sword.

After the rout of the dragoons, on the left wing the Highlanders faced the royal foot. The front-line Highland regiment having expended their fire on the dragoons, now found themselves unable to reply to that of the royal foot. Because of the heavy rain, and because the Highlanders did not use cartridges, reloading was impossible. So with what O'Sullivan called, 'one of the boldest and finest actions any troops in the world could be capable of', they flung down their muskets and charged forward sword in hand and shrieking out battle-cries as they hurled themselves at the enemies' guns. The front rank broke against the onslaught and many of the second-line regiments followed hard on their heels. Hawley's left-wing troops, already disordered by the dragoons, gave only a weak and ineffective fire. Four of his six front-line regiments, Wolfe's, Cholmondeley's, Putteney's and the Royal, turned and ran and they were immediately followed by the whole of the second line. The disorder and confusion increased and General Hawley rode back down the hill. But although Hawley had obviously lost control of the situation, his second-in-command, Huske, kept his head.

Protected by the ravine in front of them, three regiments under Huske stood their ground and poured heavy fire on the flank of the pursuing clansmen, which threw them in great disorder. To add to this confusion, Colonel Roy Stewart, afraid that the Highlanders were racing into an ambush, called on them to stop. The cry flew from rank to rank and some of the men stood still. Others, uncertain of what to do, returned to the ground on which they had formed. Some even left the field and hurried back to Bannockburn and Stirling where they spread the word that the Highland army had been defeated.

Out of sight on the ridge above, Lord George Murray and what remained with him of the MacDonalds were joined by the Atholl Brigade whose three battalions were the only ones who had kept their ranks. They advanced down the hill in good order. The enemy could be seen running off in forties and fifties to the right and left to get into Falkirk and Murray was determined to follow and attack them.

At the other side what was left of the dragoons had rallied and were galloping up the hill at the rear of the Jacobite position, with the apparent objective of capturing the Prince, but the Irish picquets were immediately moved forward from the reserve and at the sight of their advance the dragoons fell back on their three right-wing regiments. Forming a rearguard, the dragoons retreated with them towards Falkirk.

Lord George Murray halted at the foot of the hill. He had only about six or seven hundred men with him, the others being scattered on the face of the hill, but he was soon joined by Lord John Drummond and the Prince. It was getting dark and the urgent question now was where the Highland army would be quartered for the night. Most of the officers were for retreating towards Dunnipace and around that area where the men might be at least covered from the heavy rain, but Murray disagreed.

'No, I say we must waste no time in marching into Falkirk. We mustn't give the enemy the least time to line the houses or clean their guns. Like Count Mercy at the Battle of Parma, gentlemen, I say, I will either be in the town or in paradise.'

It was agreed eventually that they would attempt the town, but the Prince was advised to stay at some house in the face of the hill until Lord George Murray sent him word of success.

As it happened, this did not take long because it was discovered that the royal army was already hurrying away from Falkirk in full retreat. It was fortunate that this had happened because by the time Murray reached Falkirk, most of the Highland army were widely dispersed. Only fifteen hundred men came into the town that night and he was hard put to it to find enough guards for the place. Many of the Highlanders were too busy pillaging the dead and ransacking the deserted royal camp. Still larger numbers had returned to their old quarters near Bannockburn, knowing nothing of the outcome of the battle.

Like Prestonpans, the Battle of Falkirk lasted a very short time and Annabella reckoned that not more than twenty minutes had elapsed between the firing of the first shot and the retreat of the royal army.

Next day she cantered out to survey what was left of the scene, with Nancy and Regina following close behind her.

The Prince had given orders to the Highlanders to bury all the dead, the English dead as well as their own, and crowds of tartan-clad men were busily digging a pit.

The dead had been stripped of everything by the Highlanders and by women camp-followers and by local boys and beggars. Their naked bodies now lay on the hillside like a flock of sheep. Soon the Highlanders began tossing them into the pit and as Annabella passed she noticed that some of the bodies were in fact still moving and groaning. She called out immediately:

'Stay your hand, sir! These men are alive.'

One of the Highlanders drew his dirk and began stabbing the bodies, calling back to her as he did so:

'Ton't worry, mistress. They pe tead now.'

Another said to a groaning, struggling man as he forced him into the pit: 'Och, will you pe lying down for the Prince like a tecent fellow.'

'Animals,' said Regina. 'Bloody animals.'

'Oh, be quiet, girl,' Annabella said. 'This is war. What do you expect?'

She was no longer sure what she herself expected. There was now uncertainty and anxiety at the central core of her excitement. The uncertainty and anxiety kept beating in and out like a heart and pushing all her pleasurable feelings further and further towards a superficial circumference. She tried to ignore this discomfort at the root of herself. She held fast to her bright, brave appearance and mischievous, impudent stare and when she met Lavelle again at Bannockburn House he could detect no change in her. He shook his head.

'Mademoiselle, you continue to astonish me. You do not seem in the least put out by the recent activities.'

'Not in the least, sir,' she agreed. 'But did I not tell you that I was a woman of prodigious spirit?'

He laughed.

'You did indeed. Maybe you will survive this "adventure", as you call it, better than any of us.'

'Well?' She raised an eyebrow. 'Tell me! What happens now? Where are we headed?'

Lavelle shrugged.

'Some of the officers were for going after Hawley's army or even marching to London. Others voted for the siege of Stirling Castle and Stirling Castle won.' He looked worried. 'I personally feel that we should not allow Hawley any breathing space. I cannot see of what importance this petty fort at Stirling can be to us. However . . .' He shrugged again.

'Jean-Paul, the only way that I can be disturbed is to see you so unhappy.'

His face immediately crinkled into one of his most charming smiles.

'*Mais non*, I flatter myself, mademoiselle, that I can disturb you in another way that is delightful.'

She laughed.

'Prove it, sir. Prove it here and now.'

They were sitting in one of the public rooms of Bannockburn House under a magnificent seventeenth-century ceiling. It was very late, but the room was still bright with many silver candelabra.

His wide mouth twisted up at one side.

'You are a witch. I cannot match your courage.'

'Huh!' Annabella impatiently flapped her fan. 'You are afraid your precious prince might stumble upon us fornicating on the carpet. Mark my words, sir, he is at this very moment riding high on the prodigiously ambitious and conniving Miss Walkinshaw.'

'A witch!' Lavelle repeated, eyes narrowing and glimmering with amusement. 'But I have a duty to attend to before retiring. I did warn you, mademoiselle, that duty came first.'

They both rose. He bowed as he backed through the door while she curtsied slowly and elegantly.

Before leaving the room he murmured: 'May I see you later?'

'You may try, sir,' Annabella said.

She felt secretly hurt, yet her common sense told her that what Lavelle said was perfectly true. He had warned her and she still agreed with him that his duty must come first. She admired his strength of character and his conscientiousness. At the same time, she recognised her unexpected vulnerability and was disturbed again. Her heart was saying, 'I hate to be separated from you even for a few minutes. To hell with your bloody duty. Put me first!'

Lurking at the back of her mind was the new knowledge born of the realities she was now aware of, that her Jean-Paul Lavelle could be hurt or even killed. He could be separated from her for ever. Firmly she crushed the thought. She refused to fall prey to cowardly fears and debilitating emotions. With head held high, she swished from the room and along the corridors to the bedroom that had been allocated to her.

On her way, she came upon Clementine Walkinshaw, who

was just about to enter the Prince's bedroom.

Annabella said: 'Nobody better to show him what houghma-gandie means than you, Miss Walkinshaw.'

Then, with a rustle of skirts, she swept past.

Once in her own bedroom she could not settle. She paced the floor, the enormous hoops of her frilled blue satin gown swinging and seesawing.

Then she stopped abruptly and stared at herself in the pier glass.

'Hell and damnation!' she said, 'you really do love that man!'

Chapter 18

After the rebel army left the town, Glasgow had returned to more or less normal. Griselle Halyburton married Douglas Ramsay. John Glassford's tobacco fleet had returned from Virginia. Survivors of the Glasgow militia had been honourably discharged and come home. They were no longer needed because now the Duke of Cumberland and most of his army had arrived at Edinburgh to take over command from Hawley. Since Falkirk, the royal army had been joined by the artillery train from Newcastle with a complement of regular gunners. Cavalry reinforcements had also arrived and others were on their way.

Lord George Murray and the chiefs of the clan regiments stationed at Falkirk presented the Prince with an address. It said that the Highland army, owing to desertion, was in no fit state to meet Cumberland's forces. They advised that an immediate retreat to the Highlands should be made and winter spent reducing the government's forts. An army of ten thousand men could be assembled in the spring. It continued:

'The greatest difficulty that occurs to us is the saving of the artillery, particularly the heavy cannon; but better some of these were thrown into the River Forth as that your Royal Highness, besides the danger to your own person, should risk the flower of your army . . .'

Charles argued indignantly in reply.

'A retreat, gentlemen, will result in nothing but ruin and destruction and will raise the morale of the enemy and proportionately lower that of the Highland army. It will destroy all hopes of further foreign aid, and in particular any prospects of a large-scale French landing. Not only will it result in the loss of the heavy cannon, but by retreating, the Highland army will throw away all the advantages it has previously gained. In any case, the enemy is no more formidable than it has been earlier and is still smarting from its defeat.'

But Lord George and the chiefs were concerned at what was happening at the siege of Stirling. With nothing to do, the Highlanders were sauntering about all the villages in the neighbourhood of their quarters and an ever-growing number of them were absent from their colours.

Finding that his arguments failed to win the chiefs over, the Prince recorded them in a letter which contained no recrimination but disclaimed all personal responsibility for the retreat.

It was agreed that the army would rendezvous near St Ninian's at nine o'clock in the morning of February 2nd, where a rearguard would be chosen to be commanded by Lord George Murray. But, according to Murray, someone altered his order and before daybreak the Highlanders began streaming westwards instead towards the Fords of Frew. It was said:

'Never was there a retreat resembling so much a flight, for there was nowhere one thousand men together, and in great confusion, leaving carts and cannon upon the road behind them.'

It was with astonishment and anger that Lord George arrived at the rendezvous to find that not one man was in sight. He had no alternative then but to take the road to Frew.

The Highland army crossed the Forth with Annabella and some wives of the chiefs and other women splashing behind them on horseback. Then the army headed towards Inverness. Horse and the low-country regiments, under Murray, marched along the more dangerous coast road, a route he offered to take after others had refused it. The Prince with the clans took the Highland road. On the day the divisions went their separate ways, Cumberland and the royal army, following in pursuit, left Stirling and on the 6th of February they reached Perth.

News kept seeping back to Glasgow by means of official riders and also with ordinary travellers arriving by horse or coach, or with packmen coming in from the country to sell their wares. Gypsies and sorners too added to the town's store of news and gossip which was conscientiously passed on in lusty voice by McMurdo the bellman. But despite the exciting news of what was going on outside of Glasgow there were other

209

important things happening of more immediate interest and concern. Business was getting back to normal. Shops, warerooms and counting-houses were open again and supplies were pouring in.

McMurdo shouting around the streets the announcement that new table delicacies or toilet preparations had arrived by ship caused just as much stir and commotion as the latest move of the Highland army or of Cumberland's troops.

'The best eating oil, cucumbers, capers,
Oh what a ploy,
Olives, anchovies, Indian Soy,
Barberries, vermicelli, everything to please,
Fine salt loaves, split and whole peas.

London pomat, true French hungary water,
Things tae beautify yersel' and yer daughter,
There's plain and there's scented hair powder,
There's things needed—even by fops,
There's steel wig-machines, powder-machines,
There's razors, hones and razor strops.'

There were other business-type announcements too.

'If any young lads who can read and write,
Who are strong and healthy, virtuous and bright,
Want a life of adventure in a far off land,
Listen tae me, for the news is at hand,
The Glasgow Lass and the *Mary Heron* are snows,
Sturdy ships as everyone knows;
Kilfuddy and Daidles are their captains true,
And from Port Glasgow with cargo and crew,
To James River, Virginia they're waiting to go,
But canna leave yet and how is that so,
Because they need lads and they're waiting with patience,
For indentured servants to work the plantations.
So if a plantation job to you would be great,
And if you're a lad who can write and read,
Skelp away doon with a' your speed,
To Maister Ramsay, the merchant, Briggait.'

The facts of this announcement were not quite true because the ships had not yet unloaded their cargo of tobacco, far less

210

taken on the goods that had to be shipped back across to Virginia. There were some repairs to be made to the vessels because they had run into bad weather on the journey and the storms had played havoc with both sail and timber. But it was the return cargo, or rather the lack of it, that threatened to cause the longest delay. The enormous amount of goods and money that had been supplied to the Highland army had crippled the tradespeople and it would be some time before they could recover sufficiently to supply what was required for the Virginia trade. But it was true that indentured servants were urgently needed and it was thought wise to start right away to try and get boys, and girls too if possible, to sign up.

Slave labour was employed on the plantations not because it was cheap, because it was not, but for the most part it was the only labour force available. But unless the Negroes were plantation born and trained, they were clumsy and slow.

As soon as it began to rain everyone had to rush to the tobacco beds where the delicate tobacco seedlings had already been planted. Careless handling could destroy the seed, yet the workers had, at feverish speed, to lift the small tobacco plants and transplant them to the raised tobacco beds or hills nearby. The plants could only be moved when it rained and sudden spells of frenzied activity were typical of a plantation and the reason why so many workers were needed.

The only Glasgow tobacco lord who owned a plantation and was therefore a planter as well as merchant and sea adventurer was Andrew Buchanan. He employed slave labour. Others dealt in the slave trade, buying and selling slaves, but Ramsay dealt only in indentured servants. This was not because of any principles involved. He never gave a thought to slave trading and only dealt in white servants from Glasgow because for him it was better business to do so. His ships took them out to masters in Virginia and he also employed them in his company stores and offices.

He and his colleagues had managed to get a hold on the tobacco supplies of Virginia so that they were the only people who could supply it in bulk to the French. The main reason for this lay in the chains of small stores they had set up in the interior. All the Glasgow tobacco lords had started trading stores to serve the many small plantation owners.

The idea was that the store offered credit to its customers and paid for the planters' tobacco crops in money, goods or a mixture of both. But owing to a shortage of coin in the country, the Virginians rarely had any money and this meant that the planters could not do their shopping anywhere except at the tobacco company's store where they were allowed to buy goods up to the limit of their tobacco produce.

Every store displayed its goods under two different price tags, 'cash price' and a higher 'goods price'. Those who paid in money or tobacco were allowed goods at the cash price. Those who wanted credit, however, or were paying off old debts, had to pay the higher goods price. Once a planter got into debt it was, as a result, difficult for him to pay it off. He had to keep paying for all the things he bought at the higher price, so his debts kept increasing. Most of the Virginians were heavily in debt and their next year's crop of tobacco already mortgaged to the store.

Goods valued in Britain at one hundred pounds were selling in Virginia at one hundred and seventy-five pounds, so even if they sold tobacco at a loss, men like Ramsay would make huge profits from their retail stores.

After learning that Gav could read and write, Ramsay immediately thought of his possibilities as an indentured servant, although he realised that the boy was very young. He was prepared, however, to send him to the Grammar School for a short time because the school taught bookkeeping, which would be a valuable asset. And, of course, the school only cost about four shillings a quarter, plus the voluntary Candlemas offering.

He called his clerks into his Briggait office room. After allowing them to stand in suspense for a while until he finished attending to some papers on his desk, he glowered up at them.

'Mind thon red-headed wee rascal? I want him nabbed and brought here!'

He tried to tell himself that there was no more to his thoughts on Gav than business. Yet, forever nudging at the back of his mind and causing him discomfort, was the unfortunate connection between the Chisholm family and his own. Always when he had looked at Jessie he had been reminded of her mother and, in turn, reminded of his sister Prissie.

When they had been very young he and Prissie had got on well together. He had been three years older than her and although they had argued and fought like any other brother and sister, he had been secretly fond of her. He had admired her too. He remembered her vivid imagination and the way her eyes used to widen as she chattered on to him about the most outrageous and fanciful things she had seen or done. Prissie was a marvellous storyteller and kept him enthralled many times. Or made him roar with laughter. It was not until she came into her teens that she was the cause of any worry. It was then her recreations changed from playing ball or hide-and-seek to stranger pastimes like the ritual of the faggot. This was supposed to, according to Prissie, bring about the punishment of someone who had wronged her. The first time it had been her teacher Dominie Bain. She had thrust incense and alum into a faggot and while it burned she chanted:

'Faggot, I burn thee, but it is the heart, the body and the soul, the blood, the mind, the power of action and the spirit of Dominie Bain which shall burn also. By the power of the earth, the heavens, the rainbow, the twelve lines, by the might of Mars and Mercury and all the planets, may he be unable to rest in peace, to the marrow of his bones. In the name of all demons, depart, faggot, and consume the body, the soul, the power of action and the mind of Dominie Bain so that he may neither stand still, nor talk to any person, nor rest, nor mount a horse, nor cross a river, nor drink, nor eat, until the time when my desire and my will upon him be accomplished. *Quanto, gino, garoco!*'

Only a few weeks afterwards Dominie Bain had gone swimming in the river down by the Flesher's Haugh and been drowned. Prissie said it happened because of the faggot ritual. She was elated. He was deeply shocked.

Other rituals had followed at which she had sacrificed puppies and kittens. Then eventually she had begun taking strange fits during which she jerked and moaned and frothed at the mouth. From her mouth also poured cinders and eggshells, feathers and other objects, and despite the fact that he had once caught her gobbling a piece of soap just before one of these fits, he never could be quite sure if the other things were part of a frightening trick Prissie was playing or if the phenomenon was genuine. Prissie moaned and wailed in what certainly appeared genuine distress and told everyone that the devil had come to her in a vision and told her who were his devotees in the town. She now knew the Glasgow witches.

Ministers and lairds and lords and lawyers had come to see her and gone away completely convinced. And so Prissie had begun to point the finger.

Jessie Chisholm's mother had been the seventeenth victim. He remembered her very well. She had been a sweet and gentle countrywoman and Jessie had been a bonny, loving child.

He had watched the woman burn as he had watched all the others, but this time he knew this burning had to be the last. Prissie had been there too, her face glowing and her eyes wild. They had walked home together. He was silent and she chattered all the time. Once home he had shut the door and followed her into her room. They were alone in the house.

He said: 'Oh, Prissie, lass. I canna let you go on.'

She looked surprised. 'What do you mean?'

'Forgive me,' he said. And before she could recover from her astonishment his hands were round her throat. His fingers pressed tighter and tighter and all the time her eyes stared into his. He would never forget them. Such shocked, accusing eyes.

Prissie had always been fond of him. She had trusted him completely.

He had never quite lost track of Jessie Chisholm. He knew the child had to have a leg amputated as a result of the torture she had suffered. He knew she was homeless and sleeping on the streets and stairs. It was not until quite a few years had passed, however, that he was able to do anything for her. He put in a good word for her to the Halyburtons and as a result she got work there and he also employed her himself.

Yet nothing could assuage the guilt that plagued him. He tried to crush it out with hard work and conscientiously built up his business. After his wife died he sought comfort in illicit sex with his servant Chrissie Kinkaid, but all that did was to produce more guilt, and a daughter. Often he wondered if Annabella and Nancy knew they were half-sisters.

Thinking of Annabella was like twisting a dagger in his heart. Every day he prayed over and over again that God would forgive her wild and wicked ways and lead her safely home, but there was no hope in his heart. The devil had long ago reached out from Prissie and entered Annabella. Only death would stop the girl now.

Death was in the minds of the Halyburton family too. They had all gone to watch the execution of Jessie Chisholm in order to see justice done. Phemy had felt flustered for quite a time afterwards. She never could enjoy hangings.

'Poor Jessie!' she said. 'I hope she didn't suffer.'

'Tuts, Mistress Phemy,' her mother scolded. 'What's punishment without pain?'

Then there had been the Lady Glendinny's death and funeral. The funeral had been a great occasion and Letitia was confident that if her old friend Murn was looking down from heaven she must have been very pleased. There had been brandy and ale and whisky in abundance. With her own hands she had cooked parn pies, and larks and partridges and pullets and a pyramid of syllabubs and orange cream and sweetmeats wet and dry.

And there had been plenty of ribs and scraps to throw to the dozens of beggars and sorners who crowded the stairs and hopefully followed the funeral procession.

But now Letitia's thoughts were busying themselves with other plans. One day soon Phemy would take Murn's place as the Earl's wife and a trousseau must be gathered. Phemy had not been ecstatic about the choice of husband at first, but she had given in with good grace.

'You're no beauty, Mistress Phemy,' Letitia reminded her. 'Think yourself verra fortunate a gudeman's willing to have you.'

Soon Griselle, who was of course now a married lady herself and in an 'interesting condition', and Letitia were enjoying themselves helping Phemy with her shopping. They bought wrapping gowns, and powder-gowns and hoops and skirts and petticoats and garters, and ruffles and night-clothes and aprons, all trimmed with lace.

It was on one of these shopping expeditions to the warerooms of John Bogle and then to some booths in the Gallowgate that Phemy spied some of the linen that Jessie was supposed to have stolen.

On questioning the shopkeeper, it was discovered that he had bought it from a packman who had been passing through the town on his way to Edinburgh. The packman had sworn he had come by it honestly, saying that it had been given to him by a distraught widower who was anxious to get rid of his domestic goods and leave the house of grief where his young wife had died in tragic circumstances.

'Wicked lies,' wailed Phemy. 'The packman's the one who stole your linen, Mother. It wasn't poor Jessie after all.'

'Aye, weel, I'm glad to hear it,' said Letitia primly. 'It's a bad day when servants canna be trusted.'

'Will you tell the bellman? It's only fair to see that her name is cleared, is it not?'

'Indeed, Mistress Phemy. You've no need to ask. I've always been a verra fair-minded woman.'

And so the bellman bawled through the streets that Jessie Chisholm recently hangit for stealing linen had not in fact stolen anything at all.

Gav listened, his face grey with anger.

'I knew my mammy wasn't a thief. I hate them for murdering her.'

Quin said: 'Oh-ho, murder, is it?'

'They murdered her.' Gav fought to keep his lips from trembling. 'I hate them.'

'Quin keeps telling you, Gav, it's different for folks with money.'

Gav's jaw set and he glowered at Quin.

'Murder's murder! I don't care how much money these bloody tobacco merchants or their bloody families have.'

Quin rubbed his ear.

'Oh-ho, that's dangerous talk, Gavie. Dangerous talk. Could

you no' just hate another wee beggar like yoursel', eh?'

But before Gav could answer both he and Quin were startled by a sudden shout that echoed recklessly down the street.

'Catch that wee red-headed rascal. He's wanted by Merchant Ramsay!'

Without waiting to see who set up the cry, Quin and Gav gusted round the nearest corner like the wind. Then in and out through the maze of back closes they raced until the voices faded away further and further behind them.

'Phew!' puffed Quin eventually. 'Quin's no' as young as he used to be, eh!'

'It's all right. We've lost them.'

Gav felt suddenly spent. But it was more the intensity of his emotions than from his physical exertion. Thoughts about his mother had stirred memories of Regina. He missed her acutely and worried about her all the time. He longed for some assurance that she was safe.

At that very moment Regina was thinking much the same about him and her emotions kept tugging at her and tiring her too. Life was becoming more and more frightening and bewildering. From her own eavesdropping and that of other servants she picked up a continuous flow of confusing gossip and information. Nancy, especially, knew a great deal that was going on because she had, it seemed, bewitched one of the chieftains. She was equally catched by him because often late at night she would whisper to Regina:

'You see to the mistress if she calls before morning. I'm away to lie with my big handsome Highlander.'

Regina did not mind so much if she was left to sleep on the floor inside Annabella's bedroom. But if Lavelle was there, and he usually was, she had to sleep outside in the corridor. Only she never slept because she was so terrified that some of the other Frenchies or Irishmen might suddenly appear and grab her. And each time Lavelle came she hated him all the more. She hated the whole Jacobite army for causing the danger and insecurity of her existence. She did not know where they were going or what they were doing except that they were retreating. Yet why they should be retreating she could not fathom because it seemed they were still winning every battle.

After struggling through heavy snow, the Prince and Lord Murray's divisions had reunited at Inverness. They had taken Fort George, Fort Augustus and Fort William. A raid on government outposts in Atholl was brilliantly successful and later, when on the point of taking Blair Castle which was occupied by government forces, Lord George Murray was recalled by Sir Thomas Sheridan. Murray suspected that it had been Sheridan or O'Sullivan who was also responsible for changing the orders about the rendezvous of the troops.

The Prince was now spending most of his time shooting, fishing and dancing. He had either recovered his original optimism or he was putting on a very good front of nonchalance, or he had just lost all interest in everyday military matters. The chiefs were inclined to the belief that his favoured circle of Irish advisers were so flattering him and so softening and distorting every harsh fact that the Prince was becoming more and more divorced from the realities of the situation. That the Irish mercenaries, or 'gentlemen of fortune' as they preferred being called, or 'wild geese' as they were nicknamed, were the Prince's favourites and that he felt gratitude towards them there could be no doubt. He was continually anxious to know if he had rewarded them with suitable commissions and honours. The Irishmen seemed to blend more smoothly and easily with the type of men and the life Charles Edward had been used to. They were, for a start, of the same religion as himself. They were gay, charming, honey-spoken yet volatile, and they, like the Prince, were genuinely shocked and deeply disturbed by the way in which the Scottish chiefs could argue with, contradict and even disobey royal wishes and commands. Believing as they did in the Divine Right of Kings (as also did the chiefs, it had to be admitted) it was inconceivable that such behaviour could stem from anything except villainous treachery. And to support their case they could point to Highlanders like old Simon Fraser, wily Lord Lovat, 'the fox of the Forty-Five', who acted as a government man and was feeding information down to London, yet keeping a foot in both camps by sending his son to lead his clan of Frasers for the old cause. It was also remembered that although Lord

George Murray had as so many young men fought for King James in the 1715 rebellion, he had afterwards asked for and received a pardon from the English government.

But whatever the Prince's reasons for favouring the Irish, the fact remained that his Irish advisers began issuing orders without consulting the Prince. This was causing great confusion to everyone. Every effort made by the Scottish chiefs and nobles to organise their army was liable to be countermanded. With the command split, the rank-and-file were encouraged to ignore orders and began to deteriorate into a rabble. They were becoming more and more dispersed. The Prince's war-chest was empty and his men were without pay or meals. They had, as a result, to go foraging for food and could not be easily assembled when the need arose. But the Prince was not able to face these facts and this inability was steadily widening the breach between him and his long-suffering commander, Lord George Murray.

There were angry murmurs among all the chiefs about the Prince's growing habit of surrounding himself with Irishmen. As loyal and courageous as the Highland chiefs in battle, they might well be, although O'Sullivan had a nervous disorder and when he was upset he would retire to bed for frequent bleedings. In Lord George's opinion he was an idiot who fought wars in his nightcap. But the ability of the Irishmen to advise in military matters had over and over again proved them not only wrong-headed but in O'Sullivan's case muddle-headed and completely ignorant of the character of the Highlander.

Nancy told Annabella: 'The chiefs are still loyal to their prince but they are beginning to feel badly used. They did not give up all their land and everything they owned to be ordered about like common soldiers by Irish mercenaries. Or indeed treated by the Prince as being no different from ordinary soldiers. They are given no respect for their titles and position, while at the same time His Royal Highness heaps honours on his Irish favourites.'

But Annabella was not much interested in either political or military matters. She just laughed and said:

'So, Nancy, you have captured your gentleman at last, and a fellow countryman just as you said. You are an uncommonly determined wench. And he is a fine big strapping fellow. I have never made love with a bearded man. Maybe I'll have to try with him.'

Nancy's eyes flashed a warning. 'I will kill anyone who lays a finger on him.'

Annabella laughed again.

'Have no fear, Nancy. You may keep your big bearded Highlander. I am perfectly content with my handsome, clean-shaven Frenchman.'

'You're more than content, mistress,' Nancy said. 'I can see that, and now I know how you feel.'

'Do you?' Annabella avoided Nancy's eyes and Regina noticed a level of emotion that she had not suspected Mistress Annabella capable of. 'Oh, Nancy, Nancy,' Annabella said.

Chapter 19

It was time for 'the occasion' of open-air communion, and Ramsay guided his horse with ill-concealed impatience through the hundreds of people crowding along the road and overflowing into the fields on either side. Nearby an old laird with his gudewife riding side-saddle behind him called out:

'Aye, it would fit them better to put a jerk on and march along smartly instead of dallying and giggling and capering about and holding up the horses.'

But even some folk on horseback were in no hurry, Ramsay noticed; folk like his son Douglas in laced three-cornered hats, gay-coloured gilt-braided coats, and jackboots, and their ladies in silken plaids of scarlet, yellow, purple and orange making the countryside seem alive with flowers.

Then suddenly a ripple of excitement quickened everyone's pace. Through a shimmering curtain of trees, flashes of white could be detected. These were the white cloths that covered the communion tables in the field where the occasion was being held. Old women in mutches and ploughmen, bent with a lifetime's hard labour, earnestly concentrated in bustling forward as fast as rheumaticky limbs could carry them. Young women, pink with excitement, pushed and wriggled towards the front, and children skipped away and became separated from parents.

As soon as Ramsay reached the communion field he dismounted and secured his horse. Then he strode along, palms thumping behind his back towards the wooded erections like sentry-boxes that were called 'tents'. It was in these tents that the ministers, dressed in their bob-wigs and blue or grey coats and cravats, gave long 'action' services before handing out the elements. An enthusiastic minister like the Reverend Blackadder was referred to as 'an affectionate weeping preacher'. He could enrapture the crowds so much that, moved by his strenuous roaring, ranting voice, they burst into tears and sighs and groans.

Then before the people lined up for communion the Reverend Blackadder 'fenced' the tables, debarring from them all unclean and unworthy persons. In his fencing address he reminded them of St Paul's words: 'Whoso eateth and drinketh unworthily, eateth and drinketh damnation to himself.' Then he went on to enumerate in detail the various sins which rendered people unfit to take part in the 'sealing ordinances'. He rolled his eyes heavenwards and cried out:

'I order away a' you wicked Sabbath breakers and profane swearers and a' that put on gaudy and vain attire. I debar a' that tell lies, and a' you folk that keep coming oot wi' minced oaths such as "losh", "gosh", "teth", or "loventy".' His eyes then took on a fierce and terrible glare as they searched the crowd for those who might dare to take the communion unworthily. 'Will ye seal this damnation? Will ye make it sure that ye shall be damned? Will ye drive the last nail in your damnation? Rather put a knife to yer throat than approach these tables for ye will eat and drink eternal vengeance. I'm warning you a'.' He stabbed a long finger at this one and that one and the crowd shrank back. 'You and you and you, to approach these tables unworthily is to break the commandment—Thou shalt not murder. It is a soul-murthering sin to eat and drink your own damnation. It is a relation-murthering sin; for yer wives and yer bairns bear the mark of yer unworthy communicating. Oh, dreadful! Dreadful! Ye will be the worse o' communion and your salvation more difficult and you seven times worse a bairn o' the devil than before.'

The people were put in a fearful quandary because although the Reverend Blackadder told them they were running terrible risks if they approached the tables, yet he also warned them that it was as guilty to withdraw.

'Dare ye bide awa'? Dare ye take the Lord's anger upon yersels? Dare ye affront yer Redeemer, spite His supper and frustrate the Grace o' God?'

They knew also that they ran the risk of being fined and of standing in the pillory for a Sunday.

Ramsay always suffered much painful soul-searching before

eventually deciding to take communion. He was a man deeply sensitive to spiritual emotion yet full of sensuality. He was not only moved by the fencing sermons but also disturbed by the sight of many men and women in the outer circle of the crowd lying together in the long grass. Some sleeping and snoring, others whispering and caressing. He believed them to be sinners and he prayed that one of the elders or bum-bailies would catch them and have them up on the cutty stool or worse the very next Sunday. Yet his sensuous longings flared up with his religious passion and he had to struggle with himself as he concentrated on pushing nearer to the tent.

The minister was sweating, bawling, jumping and beating his desk. Some of the crowd were sobbing, others laughing. Others were fainting in the stifling heat or wrestling to free themselves from the crush. At one moment people seemed devout and serious, the next minute they were cursing their neighbours for squeezing or treading on them. Girls were groaning and weeping while young men, unnoticed, slipped a hand from round their shoulders to down inside their gowns. Others were making assignations to go home together later at night or to meet at ale-houses.

Then in the middle of the service came a clap of thunder and another and another, and the sky grew dark with clouds that leapt on fire with sizzling yellow flashes. The Reverend Blackadder clasped his hands and held them high, calling heavenwards as people drew their cloaks about them.

'Yer great glory, Lord, thundereth doon among us. O Lord, Lord, give us, yer ain folk, strength and peace.'

Later in a local tavern Ramsay drank whisky and ate bread and cheese with the minister. All around them women were supping ale or whisky or brandy and gossiping about what other women were wearing or whom they were going home with later. Men were imbibing deeply while they discussed the sermons. Other groups of young men and women huddled together, giggling and whispering and laughing. An old woman sat in a corner with a round of cheese in her lap that she was cutting with great care and concentration.

Blackadder gave a blessing to each glass of whisky before

downing it.

'Bless this guid whisky, O Lord! A pity the weather broke doon, Ramsay. Still it's clearing again.'

'Aye, it should be all right for this afternoon.'

'No word from Annabella, I suppose?'

Ramsay shrugged.

'Cumberland's chasing the Highland army. Only the Lord knows what'll happen when he catches up with them. As for Annabella . . .' He shook his head and the minister sighed in sympathy, then rolled his eyes upwards.

'O Lord, Lord, let not this rod be lost on Maister Ramsay. Aye, another wee drop would go down verra nicely. God bless this dram.'

Ramsay studied his glass, moved it round and round in his hands.

'I think she's deed, minister.'

'Och, merchant, dinna despair. Thon lassie's got more o' her fair share o' spunk and speerit. She'll no lie down and dee if she can help it. No, no, oor Annabella'll live to cause a lot more trouble and worry, Ramsay. I'm convinced o' it.'

'Aye, maybe you're right. Even as a wee lassie there was no telling what she'd do. I mind once at school the dominie tried to give her a thrashing and she stood her ground and warned him that if he laid a finger on her she'd see that he never got any Candlemas offering nor ever a bawbee at any time from me. Damned lies and impertinence, Blackadder, but for a wee thing hardly more than a babe . . .'

'Och, Ramsay, I ken fine yer fond o' the lass, despite a' her wicked ways; and, may the good Lord forgive me, so am I. Verra weel, if you insist, I will have another dram. O blessed Redeemer, we thank thee for this speerit, this gracious, golden gift of whisky, Amen.'

After the 'occasion' people returning home along country lanes and over fields took their time on foot or on horseback. But once back in Glasgow they made straight for inside their homes without wasting any time in case they would be arrested for Sunday strolling or vagrancy. Yet even indoors no one was free from inquisitional intrusion. The seizers might enter any house and pry into any room. Patrols of elders, deacons, beadles and officers solemnly paced the deserted streets, eagerly peering in every door and window, craning their necks up every close and lane. Glasgow folk who during weekdays were bouncing with noise and merriment shrank into the obscurity of shadows and kept hushed silence. The Glasgow streets were still and empty and no lamps or lanterns were lighted.

Acts of Parliament, resolution of town councils and decision of sheriffs all supported the Church. Fines were imposed for idly gazing out of windows, carrying a pail of water to a house, for powdering a wig, for trimming a beard, for whistling, for combing hair, or for looking into a pier glass. To be in the house during a sermon was a sin and a crime, to drive a cow along the road, to bake bread, sell milk, carry parcels, to wash clothes, to shave others or be shaved, to engage in worldly conversation. Nearly everything in fact, except Bible-reading, catechising, psalm-singing and praying was under penalty. And to those like Annabella who expressed feelings that the Sabbath was tedious and burdensome the question was asked: 'How, then, do you expect to be able to support the eternal Sabbath of Heaven?'

This state of affairs was particularly harassing and restricting to the vagrant community who had to spend the whole day from morning till night cramped together without food or water on the dark tenement stairs. If they ventured forth they risked immediate arrest and punishment.

Gav got to a point when his thirst and restlessness became so great he could not any longer bear the stench and the crush of the stair where he and Quin were sheltering.

'I'm going to the well for a drink,' he told Quin, and made to struggle away. Quin grabbed hold of his jacket.

'Gavie, Gavie, Quin canna let you go. Quin doesn't want to see you arrested.'

'I can run fast. I'll be all right.'

'Quin canna let you go.'

'Why not?'

'Quin's never seen anyone like Gav for getting into trouble and making folk chase him. Quin's getting fair puffed with getting chased so much. The whole o' Glasgow seems after Gav.'

'Well, you wait here. I won't be long. I'll run like a hare and they'll never catch me. Anyway, it's dark now. They won't even see me.'

'Oh-ho, true enough, Gav, true enough. Weel, if there's no so much chance o' chasing and racing you can go and Quin'll trot alongside you. Quin's needing a drink as well, eh?'

Although it was very dark, they moved with studied silence and care. At the well they drank deeply and gratefully and were just about to slip back to their shelter in the stairway when two inquisitors grabbed them by the back of the neck and despite their desperate struggles dragged them off to the Tolbooth. Once there, they were peered at under the light of the janitor's lantern and then separated. Quin was dragged upstairs and Gav hauled out, across the road down the Saltmarket and up the stairs to where Ramsay lived.

Big John opened the door and ushered them in. Ramsay was sitting reading his Bible. He looked up when they entered.

The inquisitor said: 'Is this the lad you've been after, Ramsay?'

'Aye, the verra one.'

'We caught him and another beggar 'vaging doon by the well.'

'I'm obliged to you, sir. Just leave him with me. I've a use for him. You'll have a dram before you go?'

'Weel, just to help me continue with the work o' the Lord.'

'Aye, here ye are then.'

They both muttered, 'God bless this whisky.' Then after drinking it down they smacked their lips and Ramsay said:

'Big John, show oor freend to the door then come back and keep a verra wary eye on this lad here.'

Gav was standing looking cautiously around, trying to assess his chances of escape.

'Now, lad,' Ramsay addressed him. 'I want to talk to you. There's nothing for you to fear. I want in fact to do you a favour. You seem a right clever one if all you claim is true, and it seems to me a pity to see such cleverness going to waste. You say you can read and write and count and speak Latin.'

Gav eyed him suspiciously, yet not without interest.

'Yes, it is true. I was the cleverest at school. Next to me was my sister Regina. She was clever too.' His voice weakened. 'I wish I knew if she was all right.'

Ramsay sighed.

'I know verra well how you feel. I've many an anxious thought aboot oor Annabella.' He suddenly cleared his throat and glowered sternly at Gav. 'But gossiping about lassies is not what I had you brought here for. The reason I had you brought here is business. Would you like to have a sail in one o' my ships?'

Gav's face immediately brightened with delight and disbelief and Ramsay hastened to add: 'Oh, not for pleasure, lad. Not for pleasure. I need indentured servants for Virginia. You'd get new clothing, your passage free and bed, board, washing and lodging as customary over there. And you can get 50 acres of land when your indenture is finished. But you'd have to work hard.'

'I can work. I'm strong and healthy.'

'Aye, but to work for me you need more than that. You need brains, lad, and a knowledge o' bookkeeping. Then y'see there's a chance that one day you might be one o' my managers out there. Now that's an important position, Gav. That's what you're called, I believe. Gav Chisholm?'

'That's right, maister.'

'Weel, Gav. What do you think yersel'?'

Gav thought for a moment, his face attempting to assume the same stern expression as Ramsay's. Eventually he said:

'I'm no liar, Maister Ramsay. I said I was clever and I am. But I don't know your bookkeeping. That's not to say that I couldn't learn though.'

'Good for you, Gav. I was hoping you'd say that. Now what think you of this idea? My ships are due back verra soon. Meantime you could go to the Grammar School and be taught bookkeeping. At night you could sleep in the lobby out there with Big John.'

'How about my food?' Gav asked.

'You drive a hard bargain, lad. But that's the verra thing a good manager needs to be able to do. Aye, you'll be fine and you'll get fed all right while you're here.'

'Then it is agreed, maister.' Gav stuck out his hand. 'There's my hand on it.'

Ramsay's heavy jaw gave only the slightest twitch as he accepted the filthy paw and solemnly shook it.

'It is indeed, sir, but it is usual procedure to sign papers as well. You'll go down to my counting-house in the Briggait tomorrow before you go to the school. And, oh, aye, I believe they're a bit disorganised with being shut for a while because of all the upset with the rebel army. So their Candlemas offering was postponed until now.' He prodded his fingers into his pocket and came out with a half-guinea which he flourished towards Gav. 'Now, Gav, here's your first test. Let's see if you can be honest.'

Gav's eyes stretched enormous. Never in his life had he seen so much money. He could not believe that Ramsay was trusting him with such an enormous sum. He felt bewildered and flattered and deeply moved. He felt not only admiration but a sudden rush of affection for the man.

'I take this half-guinea tomorrow to the Grammar School up the High Street and at some sort of ceremony I give it to the dominie there.' He tried to sound brisk and business-like.

'That's the verra idea.'

'Well, that is exactly what I will do, sir. I shall not let you down.'

'Aye, weel, away with Big John to the kitchen now and sample some o' that food ye were so anxious aboot. Then come back here,' he tapped the Bible, 'for the reading.'

Gav could hardly credit his good fortune and the only thing that spoilt his great joy was the thought of Quin imprisoned in the Tolbooth. Perhaps once he had proved himself to Mr Ramsay he could help Quin in some way. Perhaps he could persuade Mr Ramsay to let Quin go to Virginia too. But while Quin was in the Tolbooth he supposed there was nothing much anybody could do. He resolved to talk things over with Quin the moment he emerged from the prison. Meantime, he could not help feeling happy. He did not really believe he was going to the Grammar School until he actually arrived there early next morning.

It was an old tenement building that had been bought from the various tenants who had once lived in its separate rooms. On the bottom floor there was a long lobby and to the left 'The Keeper's Lodge'. To the right was the Great Hall where everyone assembled for prayers and four venerable masters with their black gowns sat in their respective pulpits until prayers were over. Upstairs were two low-ceilinged classrooms and upstairs again there were two more rooms.

In the same way as students were classified at the University, so were the Grammar School scholars dubbed—1, Cocks; 2, Hens; 3, Earocks; 4, Chickens.

First of all Gav paid for the term the four shillings that Ramsay had given him that morning. Then, as an accepted scholar, he joined the others in the Great Hall, not for prayers but for the ceremony of the offering.

The headmaster sat in his pulpit desk, his stern air of authority gone, his face barely concealing his eager expectancy.

Then the roll was called and each boy marched up to the desk and handed over his offering, which usually varied from sixpence from poor boys up to half a guinea from the sons of wealthy parents.

If a boy gave only sixpence, however, it was received in complete silence and the child had to return crestfallen to his seat, head down in an attempt to hide his humiliation. If the gift was two shillings and sixpence the master followed by the whole class shouted out '*Vivat!*'(Let him live!) And then they gave one ruff or stamp with their feet.

If the boy presented up five shillings the master roared out: '*Floreat!*'(Let him flourish!)

And two ruffs were given.

The shouting and stamping kept adding to Gav's mounting excitement. His name was the last on the roll and the master called it out, not expecting him to produce anything when he had only just arrived. But up Gav marched and proudly presented the half-guinea.

The master was delighted.

'*Gloriat! Gloriat!*' (Let him be glorious!) he shouted. And the applause and the thunder of the feet was deafening as Gav returned to his seat.

Never in his life had he felt so wildly happy. This was what life was all about. This was really living. Money was the thing. Money was the key. Money was the magic wand that changed the whole quality and complexion of everything.

How right Quin had been. He had never understood what Quin meant about money until now. Yet did Quin really know himself? Had Quin ever experienced anything like this? This heady pride, this smell of success, this taste of what could be. Poor Quin could not even read or write and he had never been anything else but a thief and a beggar. Was he capable of anything else? Surely if he had been capable he would not have chosen to live as he did. Already Gav viewed his recent hardships with horror and dismay. Never again if he could help it would he live like Quin; freezing almost to death in draughty closes, wandering about all day getting soaked to the skin, or cuffed or chased; being hungry and tired and wretched and with everyone despising you and all the time being in danger of suffering the pillory or worse. He saw a vision of many pinched, suffering and hopeless faces, young and old round every shadowy corner and in every close. He had been one of them. But never again. No, not for him. Now he had the chance of a lifetime and by God he would grasp it with both hands.

Every day he flung himself into his studies and every night he learned his Catechism and studied again.

'Aye, Gav, you're a good lad,' Ramsay told him eventually. 'I'm no' disappointed in you. And because of that you won't be going to school today. You'll come with me and Big John to Mistress Halyburton's wedding. The Halyburtons' servants will be needing all the help they can get today.'

'I'll lend a hand, sir.'

'Aye, I know ye will, Gav. Weel, get yourself ready. Big John's waiting for us down at the stables. Have you ever ridden a horse by the way?'

'Regina and I rode horses bareback when they were in the fields.' He flushed. 'I know we shouldn't have because they didn't belong to us but we didn't do them any harm or steal them away.'

'Och, I used to do the same myself. I remember me and my sister . . .' His face darkened. 'Don't just stand there, sir. I told you to go down to the stables.'

'Yes, maister.'

Gav hurried away to find Big John leading Ramsay's horse out to the yard. In a minute or two Ramsay came striding out, mounted the animal and galloped off without a word. Gav and Big John followed on foot. The first destination was Tron Church where the wedding service was to take place. They had only been standing a few minutes in the crush of folk in the middle of the church when Phemy entered looking like an ugly-faced bird with glorious plumage. She was wearing a silver satin dress with huge hoops and sewed all over it from top to bottom, back and front, neck and sleeves, were 'favours' of different-coloured ribbons. The Earl of Glendinny looked very grand, too, in a cutaway coat of shining peach damask embroidered with tiny blue, purple and green flowers, and breeches to match.

After the ceremony the guests suddenly rushed at the bride and in a matter of moments they had ripped every single favour from the dress. The next ceremony was the garter, and the bridegroom's man tried to pull it off her leg but she managed to drop it through her petticoat on to the floor. And all the time there was much screaming and laughing and hilarity. Afterwards Ramsay walked with Gav and Big John, with Big John leading the horse, across the road to the reception at the Halyburtons' house. Ramsay strode along with hands thumping behind his back.

'It's a bloody disgrace,' he growled. 'High time it was stopped—all that sinful laughing and levity in God's House.'

The laughter and gaiety was spilling out all around them and splashing recklessly, heedlessly across to the Halyburtons'. Up the stair it echoed, to cascade into every room in the house with a rainbow of colour.

The fiddlers were already scraping away as fast as they could, but before any dancing began the guests energetically attacked the food Letitia had provided. A long table was packed from end to end. A huge platter held a hind quarter of boiled mutton with cauliflower, turnips and carrots. There was roast beef. There were geese and ducks and pigs. There were oysters; and, of course, there was the bride's pie made with calves' feet, suet, apples, raisins, currants, peel, cinnamon, nutmeg and mace, well moistened with a glass of Madeira and one of brandy and baked in puff paste. Somewhere concealed in the crust was a gold ring, as was the custom, and the pie was decorated with cupids, turtles, torches, flames and darts.

Gav was overwhelmed by the magnificence of it all. Everything, every sound, every touch, every smell, every taste, every sensation, he relished to the full, and he vowed yet again and even more passionately that from now on this was the life for him.

He had enquired a couple of times about Quin and been told that his case had not been dealt with yet but that it would be soon. He had no idea what he was going to say to Quin or what he was going to do about him. He had no wish to hurt him, but there could be no question of resuming their old life together. None at all. He did not want anything more to do with Quin. A person like Quin could have no place in his new life. Yet at the same time he could not stop worrying. He wished he did not have to make a decision about him or speak to him again. He realised he did not need to, but knew that to avoid the confrontation would be cowardly and he was not a coward. If he had something to say to a man, he would say it to his face. He went yet again to the Tolbooth and learned with a mixture of real regret that Quin, because he had been convicted and punished several times before as a thief, had this time been banished from the town.

But no doubt he would trot off to Edinburgh or some other place and be perfectly happy in his own strange and terrible way. So, sadly, yet thankfully, Gav put Quin out of his thoughts.

But Quin had Gav very much on his mind and was determined to find out where he was and what had become of him. He was only too well aware that hanging was the punishment for anyone who returned to the town after being banished but he was so agitated about Gav he could not do anything else but risk the terrifying consequences.

He wandered about the wynds and closes in bewilderment, all the time talking to himself.

'Quin's lost his childer. Quin's lost wee Gavie.'

He rubbed his torn ear and scratched his head and couldn't understand it.

Chapter 20

It was O'Sullivan who chose the battlefield of Drumossie Muir for the vital confrontation with the Duke of Cumberland. The Prince who was staying at nearby Culloden House, approved the choice. But all along the chiefs and General Murray favoured the method of a long war of attrition against Cumberland, gradually wearing him down in strength and confidence. They believed in striking only when and where it favoured the Highlanders and never committing the whole Highland army in one sweep. There was no doubt that this was the wisest policy. But the Prince was young and headstrong and impatient. Most of his Irish friends were the same. O'Sullivan, in particular, considered himself quite worn out by the stresses and strains he had undergone since coming to Scotland and wanted to be done with this without further delay. Along with the Prince he concocted another plan to be put into practice immediately. They knew that Cumberland's birthday was on 15th April, and reports had reached them at Culloden that there were celebrations among the government troops. The Prince and O'Sullivan wanted a surprise dawn attack on Cumberland's camp at Balbair.

Most of the chiefs refused to consider the plea until reinforcements arrived. But the Prince was optimistic as usual, with never a thought of defeat. Lord George agreed with the chiefs' objections. But he had just come from inspecting Drumossie Muir and had been appalled at the boggy state of the ground and the vast flat openness of it. No worse place in the whole of Britain could have been chosen for Highlanders to fight on. It was only because the plea for a dawn attack was the lesser of two evils that he eventually agreed to it. The Prince was so delighted he flung an arm around Murray's neck and said:

'This will crown it all! You'll restore the King by it! You'll have all the honour and glory of it! It is your work . . .'

Lord George took off his bonnet, bowed coldly and said nothing. He knew that the odds were stacked against the Highland army because over a third of it had not yet returned from foraging. Officers rode off to try and round up the men, but were told by them:

'We are starving. Shoot us if you like but we will not return until we get meat.'

On hearing this the Prince was not in the least perturbed.

'Whenever the march begins the men will be all hearty and those who have gone off will turn and follow.'

Less than four and a half thousand clansmen were finally available to march against an army of over eighteen thousand strong who were well fed, well rested and in good spirits. But the Prince's Irish favourites assured him that Cumberland's army would be 'utterly dispirited and never be able to stand an attack'. The Prince enthusiastically agreed and said that even if he had only one thousand clansmen he would still march that night.

Lord George led the front column at his usual brisk pace and soon far outdistanced the heavily equipped French troops in the rear. The Prince was in the middle of the column and had to send a messenger forward asking Murray to slacken his pace. Soon the men had to go in single file because of trackless paths, marshes and quagmires, and became bogged down. Sometimes they sank waist-deep and horses and men had to violently struggle all the time to extricate themselves.

Halfway to Balbair, Murray sent back Colonel Kerr to warn the officers not to raise the alarm by using their firearms.

'Attack the tents sword in hand,' he commanded. 'Strike and push vigorously wherever a bulge appears in the canvas.' At the same time he also sent a message to the Prince asking him to form the centre and rear of the second column as they came up so as to make sure the attack was made simultaneously and without confusion. In reply he was astounded to receive the order that he was to attack without waiting on the rest of the troops to arrive. Murray had started off with less than two thousand men under his command and a great many of this number had now fallen out, collapsing for want of food. He therefore sent back word with Cameron of Lochiel that it was useless to continue as there was no possibility of his being strong enough to attack. The Prince, however, was convinced that the army was stronger than it had ever been and sent Lochiel back to Murray with positive orders to continue.

Lord George was joined by some other officers, who confirmed that there was still a gap in the line of over half a mile and it would be impossible for the rear to catch up with them. As a result, Murray ordered the troops to halt. O'Sullivan galloped up then, shouting:

'What is this, gentlemen? Do you not know that it is the Prince's wish that the march should be continued?'

Before Murray could answer, Lochiel burst out in disgust:

'The delay on the part of the rear is inexcusable, sir. Murray is perfectly justified. Indeed, he has no alternative.'

Then one of the Atholl Brigade officers broke out violently:

'Those that are so much for fighting, why don't they come up with us?'

Just then, John Hay, the Prince's secretary, did so, but his angry arguments were equally ineffective. Lord George ignored him. Drums were already beating in the distant camp, which told him all too clearly that Cumberland's men were on the alert. He said to his Highland officers:

'The day is coming, gentlemen, and I have taken my decision. Guide your men back down the road.'

The Duke of Perth and Lord John Drummond rode back to order the second column to face about, but an infuriated O'Sullivan and John Hay galloped back ahead of them to warn the Prince.

'Your Royal Highness, unless you come to the front and order his Lordship to go on, nothing will be done.'

Charles immediately spurred his horse forward through the darkness and on coming upon the retreating men of the second column he demanded:

'Where the devil are the men going?'

And when he was told that they had been ordered by the Duke of Perth to return to Culloden House he broke out excitedly:

'Where is the Duke? Call him here. I am betrayed! What need

have I to give orders when my orders are disobeyed?'

But the Duke and O'Sullivan had lost their way in the darkness. Nor could Lord George be found. Distracted aides-de-camp rode about demanding:

'For God's sake, what has become of His Lordship? The Prince is in the utmost perplexity for want of him.'

Eventually the Duke of Perth presented himself and the Prince demanded:

'What do you mean by ordering the men to turn about?'

The Duke replied:

'Your Royal Highness, Lord Murray turned back with the first column three-quarters of an hour ago.'

'Good God!' Charles cried out. 'What can be the matter? What does this mean? We were in equal numbers and could have blown them to the devil. Pray, Perth, can't you call them back yet? Perhaps he has not gone too far?'

But the chief was firm.

'It is now daylight, Your Royal Highness. Far better to march back than go and attack the Duke who would be prepared.'

The Prince did his best to hide his disappointment and to encourage his followers.

'There's no help for it, my lads, march back. We shall meet them later and behave like brave fellows.'

On the way to Culloden he confided in his Irish officers that he suspected Lord George of being responsible for the failure. As usual they did nothing to allay his suspicions and by the time he had reached Culloden House he was convinced that Murray had deliberately wrecked the plan.

About six o'clock in the morning of Wednesday, 16th of April, the Jacobite army returned to Culloden, and although the first column had a greater distance to march, they arrived before the others. Everybody could think of nothing but sleep. The officers threw themselves on beds, floors, even on tables to snatch some rest. The Prince arrived last. On the way he had become aware for the first time that the men were hungry enough to desert and in case he would be left with no army he decided to gallop on to Inverness in order to have the meal stored there immediately dispatched to Culloden. But on hearing this the Duke of Perth rode anxiously after him to warn him that his impulsive departure might be misconstrued by the men as abandonment. He suggested that instead the Fitzjames' Horse should be sent to fetch food from Inverness. The Prince was persuaded back to Culloden House and on arriving tired and irritable the first person he encountered was an equally exhausted Murray. Immediately the Prince was roused to temper and shouted publicly at him:

'In future, my Lord Murray, no one will command my army but myself.'

He was so agitated that he later asked some Irish officers to watch Lord George's motions, particularly in case of a battle and they promised to shoot the General if they should find he intended in any way to betray him.

In the early hours he also gave an interview to the Marquis d'Eguilles, who wrote in a letter to King Louis:

'I requested a quarter of an hour's private audience. There I threw myself at his feet. In vain I represented to him that he was still without half his army; that the great part of those who had returned had no longer their targes—a kind of defensive armour without which they were unable to fight to advantage; that they were all worn out with fatigue by a long march made on the previous night and for two days many of them had not eaten at all for want of bread.

'In the end, finding him immovable in the resolve he had taken to fight at any cost, I made my desire to yield to my duty. I left him for the first time. I retired in haste to Inverness, there to burn all my papers and there to think over the means of preserving your Majesty that portion of the (French) troops which might survive the action.' He went on to tell the King how he had advised the Prince to fall back and put the river between himself and his enemies and to give his army rest. 'But Charles, proud and haughty as he was, badly advised, perhaps even betrayed, forgetting at this moment every other object, could not bring himself to decline battle even for a single day.'

That morning the chiefs and Murray also strongly declared themselves against fighting that day and all pleaded with him to fall back to the hilly ground beyond the Nairn until Charles exclaimed angrily:

'God damn it! Are my orders still disobeyed? Fight where you will, gentlemen, the day is not ours.'

But Walter Stapleton, commander of the Irish picquets, brought about the Prince's wish to engage the English army on the field of Culloden. He sneered at the chiefs:

'The Scots are always good troops till things come to a crisis.'

As usual Lochiel and the other Highland chiefs could not bear anything that affected their pride. To them there was only one answer to this. They would go down in glory fighting against odds on unfavourable ground. Lochiel said:

'I do not believe there is a Highlander in the army who would not run up the mouth of a cannon in order to refute this odious and undeserved aspersion.'

At last the Prince lay down without taking off his boots to try and snatch some sleep. First, though, he gave the order that the men should have a good meal as soon as supplies arrived from Inverness and also all cattle there and at Culloden had to be slaughtered for this purpose.

But Cumberland having been informed of the abortive night march, had no intention of allowing the Highlanders any time to recover from it. Before the Prince had time for one hour's rest, and before even the officers had eaten anything, a Jacobite cavalry patrol clattered in with the warning that Cumberland's horse were only four miles off and fast closing in.

The Prince wasted no time in rushing downstairs and when his servant said that a roasted side of lamb and two hens were about to be placed on the table he cried out indignantly:

'Would you have me sit down to dinner when my enemy is so near me? Eat! I can neither eat nor rest while my poor people are starving.'

In the greatest haste the Prince, the Duke of Perth, Lord George Murray and Lord John Drummond mounted and rode off. Drums beat, pipes skirled and guns fired in attempts to recall the Highlanders, but only caused confusion. Officers ran about trying to rouse men who were half-naked with exhaustion and could hardly crawl.

At Inverness the townspeople were startled by the drums

beating to arms and the trumpets of Fitzjames' Horse sounding the call to boot and saddle.

The Atholl men and Camerons, the first to return from the night march, were now first on the field. The Prince was with Lochiel's regiment, with O'Sullivan, as always, close on his heels. O'Sullivan remarked admiringly that there was not the least concern on the Prince's face and that when there was the greatest danger that was when the Prince appeared most cheerful and hearty.

Now he rode along, shouting to his men:

'Here they are coming, my lads; we'll soon be with them. They don't forget Glads-muir and Falkirk and you have the same arms and swords. Let me see yours . . . I'll answer . . .' He brandished his own sword. 'This will cut off some heads and arms today. Go on, my lads; the day will be ours and we'll want for nothing after!'

Murray requested 'a little time to have another look at the ground,' but this was curtly refused by the Prince, who was impatient to see his army immediately form in order of battle. Murray, however, had seen enough of the boggy moor over which the Highlanders would be forced to travel in a charge to realise that O'Sullivan had chosen a battlefield which Cumberland would have been only too delighted to have picked out himself. Lord George then protested about the order of battle drawn up by O'Sullivan, but the Irishman, like the Prince, would be moved on nothing. He insisted there was no time for rearrangement and as for the ground it was as good a position as any.

On the other side the Duke of Cumberland was 'mightily pleased' about the choice of ground. On the way he had been wary and perplexed, thinking there must be Highlanders waiting to ambush him at every corner and behind every hillock. He could not believe that his previously wily and astute enemy would not be lurking in the dark heather waiting to pounce on him. It took several military patrols to convince him that the Highland army were actually formed on a moor. And on arrival it was at once apparent that this dejected, depleted and disorganised force were not the clans that had fought with such fierceness and vigour at Prestonpans and Falkirk.

240

O'Sullivan was galloping this way and that in a confused manner, trying to draw up the army in line of battle. Later Lord George was to remark sarcastically: 'At Culloden O'Sullivan had forty-eight hours to display his skill, and did it accordingly.' And many times he insisted, 'I am certain that neither the Scots officers nor one single man of all the Highlanders would have agreed to it had their advice been asked, for there never could be more improper ground for Highlanders.'

The Prince rode among his men, doing his best to encourage them, and they, despite their fatigue and low spirits, raised their bonnets and gave him a faint huzza. Then Charles took up his position on the second or rear line beside Fitzjames' Horse and behind the Irish picquets. There were only enough men to form two sparse lines against the three solid ones behind which Cumberland was positioned.

On some raised ground at the side of the moor, women and children from Inverness had gathered, some of them with picnic baskets eager not to miss the afternoon's excitement. Further along Annabella, Nancy, Regina, chiefs' wives and other women who were travelling with the Highland army also waited and watched.

Annabella noticed with mounting anxiety that the Highland army was vastly outnumbered. Seeing that there was a much wider distance between the front lines of the opposing armies than there had been at Falkirk, she was quick to realise that this would prove a disadvantage to the Highland method of fighting. She vividly remembered them charging with such speed that their opponents were barely allowed time for one shot before the Highland claymores hacked them down. She also saw that attached to their muskets the English had long bayonets which obviously could pin the Highlanders back out of claymore reach. Not that she was concerned as Nancy was, for the Highlanders as such. The acuteness of her concern was solely directed at the French contingents. She was just about to peer through her telescope in an effort to pick out Lavelle when suddenly the ground shuddered as all the cannon of the royal army exploded in one great roll, obscuring the Highland lines with smoke and fire. As the smoke cleared, she was shocked to see the great holes in the Highland formation. Dead bodies were everywhere. One ball decapitated the Prince's groom who was only yards away from the Prince. Another injured the Prince's grey charger and he had to mount a different horse. The messenger that the Prince had sent giving the order for his front line to charge was also decapitated and the Highland line did not move except to close up to fill the gaps as men were blown to pieces. The cannon continued to roar and severed arms and legs scattered into the air, splattering blood over the remaining men. Most of the two thousand men killed at the Battle of Culloden were in fact killed during this time before the order to charge finally reached the survivors. Then they raced through the cannon smoke like devils, shrieking, throwing away their muskets and slashing the air with their swords, only to be mowed down by volley fire and grapeshot.

The MacDonalds—in response to the Duke of Perth's cries of 'Claymore! Claymore!'—had to run for more than half a mile in the face of this unwavering fire. Their opponents, safely out of reach of frantic broadswords, slaughtered them as they came. The Clan Chattans ran into the same choking smoke and devastating fire, some of them holding their plaids before their eyes as they clambered over their dead comrades who were lying three and four deep. The regiments of McLean and MacLachlin had even further to run over boggy ground, but still they went forward, calling out as best they could, 'Another Hector!' and 'Death or Life!' And it was death for them.

Highlanders danced and threatened and roared and shrieked and ran and stopped in futile efforts to draw the enemy line, but this time the line refused to be drawn or broken. The Highlanders kept coming and falling in their hundreds, until eventually they began to turn back, first in twos and threes, then in confused and bewildered swarms.

The Prince's advisers pleaded with him not to risk his life in the heat of the action, but Charles could not believe that his invincible clans were being routed. Desperately he tried to put new life and confidence into the regiments now streaming from the field and persuade them to return. His bonnet and his wig were blown off in his feverish attempts to stop the torrent of his men's flight and he only managed to recover the wig as it fell. He kept crying out, pleading on all sides:

'Rally, in the name of God. Pray, gentlemen, return. Pray stand with me, your prince, but a moment—otherwise you ruin me, your country, yourselves. And God forgive you.'

Most of the men, who only spoke Gaelic, did not understand what he said and anyway the mouths of the cannon spoke louder.

The Prince became so distraught that Lochiel's uncle, Major Kennedy, had to grab his horse's bridle and lead him away.

A sea of tartan trickled, spurted, rolled, gushed from the field in all directions, with Cumberland's troops now wildly pursuing them, hacking at them with bayonet, sword and spontoon, or mowing them down with their muskets. Mutilated bodies were piling up not only on the battlefield but all around the countryside. The carnage engulfed the spectators.

Regina began to moan, then wail, then scream. Nancy called out distractedly: 'Calum! Calum!'

Annabella's horse reared and snorted and stamped and circled in agitation and she saw to her horror a company of dragoons ride straight through the group of Inverness women and children, trampling and slashing them as they passed. She saw a girl's head being cleft to the teeth, a baby heaved high on the end of a bayonet, a woman's face cut again and again until it was a crimson poppy stuck to the green stem of her dress. She saw a bayonet being poked in an old woman's eye.

Everywhere there was screaming. Annabella shouted:

'Jesus Christ! Where are the French? What am I to do?'

Just then, Nancy knocked Regina off the back of the horse that they were sharing and galloped into the thick of the battlefield, her long black hair streaming out behind her.

Regina, tiny among the surging mass of men, looked terror-stricken and her screams staccatoed up in a fit of hysteria. Standing helplessly screeching, she watched an English soldier, sword in hand, approaching her. And still she kept up her staccato screeching after a shot from Annabella's pistol dropped him in his tracks.

'Up behind me.' Annabella forced her snorting and squealing

horse over bodies and between Highlanders who had no shields to protect them while their opponents slashed at them with maniacal fury. 'Regina, damn you!' She shouted again: 'Mount behind, I said!'

But eventually she had to reach down and grab the girl's arm to haul her up. Once on the horse, Regina frantically clutched Annabella around the waist, hid close to her, pressed her face hard into Annabella's back.

'Oh, mistress, gallop away. Gallop away!'

Annabella ignored her plea.

'Where are the French? Can you see them?'

'To the devil with the French.' Regina wept. 'Let us away to Glasgow where we belong.'

'I belong with my Frenchman. If he goes to the devil, girl, that's where I go too!'

She spurred her horse forward. Over towards the river she thought she could see the silver-grey of the French uniform. With the help of her telescope, she discovered it was the Irish picquets who had come down from their post to save the Royal Scots from complete encirclement and whose close and steady fire was also covering the MacDonalds' retreat. Eventually after losing half their number in the attempt they too retreated, carrying with them their injured commanding officer, Brigadier Stapleton.

Over at another part the Fitzjames' Horse commanded by Robert O'Shea, who had come over from France during the winter, was fighting a similar delaying action along with Lord Elcho's men and allowing the right wing of the Jacobite army to make its escape.

Then she saw Lavelle's company, or what was left of it, struggling across the river in the distance. Immediately she kicked her horse's flanks and shouted it on.

'No, oh, no,' Regina sobbed when she saw that Annabella's intention was to cross the river. 'We'll be drowned. Look at all the others.'

The river was swollen with the recent heavy rain and from writhing slowly around fields and hills like a silver-backed snake, it had become a rapid, snapping, raging monster. Already it had swallowed Highlanders and the pursuing English.

'No, oh, mistress, for God's sake, no!'

Annabella ignored her, and the horse, whinnying with fright, floundered in.

The noise of the water was deafening. It thundered in their heads, clamped tight over their nostrils, snatched the breath from their mouths. It battered and tugged at their bodies until it tore Regina off the horse. But still she managed to cling fiercely to Annabella, who, with head down and gasping for air, fought to keep a grip of the animal with one hand and blindly clutch at the girl with the other.

With sheer force of will they held on until the horse stumbled out on the opposite bank.

Not long afterwards Nancy's lover, Calum, followed on a black horse, with Nancy close behind on a brown and they too made it safely to the other side. There they stopped for breath and looked back.

To the sound of a Fraser's pipes and with flying colours the Jacobite right wing under Lord George Murray was carrying out its retreat 'with the greatest regularity'. In square formation they faced about several times to keep Hawley's cavalry in check until the horsemen eventually galloped off in pursuit of the MacDonalds and centre regiments who had taken the road to Inverness.

The heather-covered battlefield wept blood. Never had a field been so thick with dead. Cumberland's men, with killing and dabbling their feet in the blood and splashing it about one another, looked like vast hordes of butchers.

Soon distracted camp-followers and wives were scrambling about searching for their men among the dead and wounded. There were few beggars to pillage the bodies because the beggars too had been cut down by the troopers. Others were burned to death in the Leanach barn along with wounded officers when Cumberland ordered the barn to be locked and set on fire.

Nancy said: 'What's it all been for?'

Calum sighed.

'No doubt many gentlemen who reluctantly tore themselves from their homes and families and who sacrificed their fortunes will be asking themselves that, Nancy.'

It was not long before some of the Jacobite officers were angrily asking that very question. According to Michael Sheridan, Sir Thomas's nephew, he had been ordered to carry back to the Prince all the money that had been recently given to Aeneas MacDonald to distribute among his needy followers. Lord George Murray, whose wig and bonnet had been blown from his head and his sword broken and his whole person splattered with mud, angrily exclaimed:

'It's a very hard case that the Prince carries away the money while so many gentlemen who have sacrificed their fortunes for him are starving. Damn it! If I had ten guineas in the world I'd with all my heart and soul share it with them.'

He was also infuriated because although he had pleaded that stores of meal should be sent to Badenoch in case of a reverse, he found nothing with which to feed his men. And he immediately sent a letter of angry recrimination to the Prince.

This did nothing to alleviate the Prince's fears that he had been betrayed by the Scottish chiefs and that they and Lord George in particular were treacherous. As far as the Prince was concerned, they had prevented him from reaching London and the crown of England. Now they had lost him the battle against Cumberland.

After the battle, on a road some miles from the field, the Prince was in a highly distraught and excitable state. He was with Sheridan, O'Shea and his men, and O'Sullivan. As Scots officers began to join him, he became more and more agitated. He ordered them to go to a village a mile's distance from where he was, then sent one of the Irish officers after them with the order to disperse.

Lord George Murray received his last brief royal command:

'Let every man seek his own safety the best way he can.'

No words of gratitude or goodbye; nothing but the cold order. It was not until much later after his life had been saved many times by the ordinary people of the Highlands that the Prince was able to dictate his more generous 'The Letter to Ye Chiefs in parting from Scotland, 1746'. It said:

'For The Chiefs,

When I came into this country, it was my only view to do all in my power for your good and safety. This I will always do as long as life is in me. But alas! I see with grief I can at present do little for you on this side of the water, for the only thing that can now be done is to defend yourselves until the French assist you, if not to be able to make better terms. To effectuate this, the only way is to assemble in a body as soon as possible, and then to take measures for the best, which you that know the country are only judges of. This makes me be of little use here; whereas, by my going into France instantly, however dangerous it be, I will certainly engage the French Court either to assist us effectually and powerfully, or at least to procure you such terms as you would not obtain otherways. My presence there, I flatter myself, will have more effect to bring this sooner to a determination than anybody else, for several reasons; viz. it is thought to be a policy, though a false one, of the French Court, not to restore our masters, but to keep a continual civil war in this country, which renders the English Government less powerful, and of consequence themselves more. This is absolutely destroyed by my leaving the country, which nothing else but this will persuade them that this play cannot last, and if not remedied, the Elector will soon be as despotic as the French King, which, I should think, will oblige them to strike the great stroke, which is always in their power, however averse they may have been to it for the time past. Before leaving off, I must recommend to you that all things should be decided by a council of all your chiefs, or in any of your absence, the next commander of your several corps with the assistance of the Duke of Perth and Lord George Murray, who, I am persuaded, will stick by you to the very last. My departure should be kept as long private and concealed as possible on one pretext or another which you will fall upon. May the Almighty bless and direct you.'

But despite the reference to the Lieutenant-General in this letter, the Prince never was able to rid himself of his fear and distrust of Murray and he later wrote to his father King James saying that if 'this devil' came to see him in Rome he ought to immediately imprison him. And even his father could not persuade him to feel otherwise. But before this letter, and the letter to the chiefs and immediately after Culloden, the curt order he sent telling him that every man should seek his own safety was read by Murray to the assembled officers and men. Then they said a last goodbye to each other before separating to seek what refuge they could. No one could tell if they would end on the scaffold or what would happen. The Highlanders gave vent to their grief in wild howlings and lamentations and tears flowed down their cheeks. They realised that their country was now at the mercy of the Duke of Cumberland and on the point of being plundered, and for them and their children there would be no hope.

Nancy felt harrowed and shocked at the sight of the men in such a distressed state and was glad when Calum wasted no time in galloping away. She was not accustomed to such uninhibited displays of emotion. Lowland men never behaved like this. She wondered what Calum's reactions were, but he kept ahead of her, silent and stiff in the saddle, and neither spoke nor looked back as they set off on the long journey through hills and glens in their attempts to reach what might be left of his home. She was to see much more tragic and distressing sights on the way.

Highland regiments of Cumberland's army—for there had been three Scottish regiments with Cumberland and some companies of Loudon's regiment and also the Argyll militia—as well as the English were systematically looting, burning, killing, raping, torturing and destroying everything and everyone they could find. Often their victims were not only of their own tongue but of their own name.

By the time Nancy made up on Annabella and Lavelle who had been wounded in the leg, her face had set in a hard white mask against the sickening atrocities she had seen. Annabella had witnessed them too and was so distressed that as soon as she caught sight of Nancy she leapt from her horse and ran to embrace her. Then, immediately recovering, she shouted:

'God damn you! I ought to give you a monstrously severe whipping for galloping off and deserting me. Now you'll have us all killed by dallying like this.'

Nancy shrugged. 'I'm all for getting away from here, mistress, and the quicker the better.'

Flushed with embarrassment and anger, Annabella remounted. All the time Regina had been sitting like a stone on a horse that had once belonged to a dead cavalry officer. Like the other two women, she was dirty and bedraggled, her hair was flowing free and her clothes like theirs were torn and wet and clinging to her body, showing every outline. They all rode off without saying any more and before night fell they found a house that had been looted and the occupants killed. They were thankful, however, that at least the house had not been burned and could afford them shelter until morning.

Before settling down to try and get some sleep, Annabella made a determined effort to regain her dignity by combing her hair and tidying her clothes and washing at a draw-well in the yard. She also attended to Lavelle and did what she could to clean and dress his wound. Then afterwards she lay in his arms and tenderly caressed him.

'You are mightily glad now, are you not,' she whispered close to his ear, 'that I have come with you?'

Despite his pain, he managed one of his lop-sided smiles. 'If I could find a priest I might even make a respectable woman of you.'

She laughed.

'What do I care about being respectable?'

All night she soothed him when he cried out in pain and gently caressed him and nursed him in her arms.

Nancy and Calum were sleeping at the front of the house and it was they who heard the clatter of horses' hooves in the yard outside early next morning. They rushed to warn Annabella and Lavelle before hurrying to hide in the woods at the back of the house.

But Lavelle's leg had swollen and stiffened during the night and, despite Annabella's efforts to help him, it was obvious he was not going to reach the woods in time. Regina was standing in the doorway watching.

'God damn you, don't just stand there, help him, can't you!' Annabella cried to her.

Regina said: 'There's a whole crowd of troopers. They're

coming in the front door.'

'Into this cupboard.' Annabella struggled to support Lavelle over to the kitchen cupboard and immediately she reached it she pushed him in and shut the door. Then she rushed from the kitchen to the front of the house, knocking Regina roughly aside as she flew past. Reaching the front of the house, she slowed her pace to her usual swagger and faced the troopers with head in the air and cool impudent eyes.

'Have you any food with you, gentlemen? I and my servant are prodigiously hungry. We have journeyed all the way from Glasgow to visit friends and this is what we find. A house empty of both people and sustenance. I have searched every cupboard and I'm damned if I can find a crumb.'

One of the men lumbered towards her and Annabella drew a pistol from her dress.

'Careful, sir, do not make a mistake you will regret. For one thing, I am a Whig and a Hanoverian. For another, my father is a wealthy merchant and a friend of the Provost of Glasgow and many other influential gentlemen who could easily have you hanged.'

The men sheepishly drew back and then, unexpectedly Annabella heard Regina's voice:

'It's true what she says. She is of important and wealthy Whig people. But there is a Frenchman who is for the Prince.'

'Regina!' Annabella's whole appearance changed to wild terror. She pushed the gun into Regina's hands. 'If you hate me so much, shoot me! But for pity's sake no more!'

'It's not you I hate, mistress.'

'Where is the Frenchman?' The trooper shouted and his companions crowded eagerly forward. 'We can have some sport with him.'

'Regina, no.' Annabella flung herself on her knees in front of the girl. 'Oh, please. Oh, Regina. Regina, I'm begging you.'

'You'll find him through that door in the kitchen cupboard,' Regina said.

Immediately the men lunged towards the kitchen with Annabella after them clawing at their backs like a wildcat.

Regina left quietly by the front door. The troopers' horses

were standing where they'd left them in the cobbled yard. Quickly, deftly, she rifled their saddlebags and transferred into her own saddlebag on her own horse gold and silver sovereigns and jewellery they had obviously looted. She found a gun and a sword too. Then, mounting her horse, she galloped off until Annabella's screams and Lavelle's screams and the insane laughter of the troopers faded further and further away.

The men never missed either Regina or their loot when they mounted up and rode off to find their next sport. They were much too elated.

Annabella was left kneeling on the floor distractedly nursing Lavelle to and fro like a baby. He was still alive but with an unrecognisable pulp of a face and the stench of burnt flesh thick about him.

'Oh, love,' she wept. 'What can I do? Oh, love, oh, love.' She flung back her face and with eyes closed shouted heavenwards: 'Help him, damn you, help him!'

But Lavelle died in her arms. She was still holding him tightly, still nursing him backwards and forwards, forwards and backwards, when Nancy and Calum returned. They prised him away and Calum buried him while Nancy struggled to hold Annabella back. She fought like someone crazed to reach him, to prevent the earth from covering him, to stop him becoming irrevocably lost to her. Until the grave was filled in and she flung herself on top of it.

Nancy said: 'You'll come home with Calum and me.'

'Glasgow's where I'm making for now.'

'You can't find your way back there on your own.'

'That girl. She betrayed him,' Annabella said. 'That girl. She'll head for Glasgow.'

'You're in no fit state to travel anywhere alone,' said Nancy. 'You'll do as I tell you.'

'God damn you!' Annabella lifted a ravaged face. 'I do not take orders from an impudent bitch of a servant. If I say I'm riding to Glasgow, Glasgow is where I'm going.'

Chapter 21

'Tell me, have you seen a girl with wicked green eyes and long red hair?' Annabella demanded, at the same time impatiently peering past the woman in the doorway into the hovel beyond.

The woman stared tragically, uncomprehendingly. She looked like a skeleton hiding under a plaid too heavy for her skull. Eventually she moved aside and allowed Annabella to enter. The house was dark and thick with brown shadows and an earthy smell. Moist slabs of turf were stacked together to make walls. A fire burned on the floor and smoke belched about and drifted upwards through a hole in the turf that arched overhead. Around the fire crouched five children and an ancient woman like a walnut hidden deep in a long plaid. Sunken defeated eyes rested on Annabella's yellow hair, pink flushed face and peacock dress. No one said anything. Then the first woman shuffled over on bare stiff feet to a corner and slowly returned holding out a filthy wooden bowl. Annabella stared at it in disgust. It contained a little oatmeal mixed with blood.

'No, thank you.' She waved the bowl away. She was hungry, but her hunger was nothing compared with the fury that clawed inside her head and heart. Anyway, the obnoxious offering was probably all the food the wretched family possessed and she had no wish to deprive them of it. The children's eyes clung to the bowl in anguish. Annabella grabbed a girl who looked about thirteen and dragged her in front of the woman.

'Have you seen a girl of this age? A stranger with green eyes and long red hair. Has she passed here recently? Tell me, damn you, tell me!'

Suddenly the girl said: 'My mother will only be speaking the Gaelic.'

'You tell me then, and be quick about it. I'm wasting a prodigious amount of time and I've no time to spare.'

'I have seen such a person ride through the glen. We called to her. We were anxious about our father who will be fighting for the Prince. But she hastened on and would make no reply.'

'When was this?'

'I will not be knowing exactly.'

'God damn you, you'd better know.'

'It was not very long ago. But without a clock I will not be knowing exactly.'

'In what direction was she travelling?'

'Her horse was galloping very fast towards the south.'

Without another word Annabella grabbed up her skirts and flew from the house. The girl put out a hand as if to stop her.

'Will you be telling us any news of our father?'

But it was too late. Annabella had leapt on her horse and was away. A kind of insanity possessed her. Her brain was fevering her body. Her brain was split, refusing to contain the memory of Lavelle's death, hysterical in its confusion, rejecting his mutilated face, his screams, his moans, his whimpers. Her brain stuck like a leech to another image, a cream-coloured stone set with two hard emeralds and framed with auburn fire. Her brain bloodied that face, clawed the emeralds from it, tore and trampled the fire.

She sobbed to herself as she urged her horse on through boggy heather. The animal kept sinking and stumbling and she yelled at it.

'Faster, faster, you stupid clumsy beast.' She kicked it again and again, but it only whinnied with fear and plunged deeper. Eventually she had to get off and haul it along while sinking knee-deep herself, and losing her shoes and stockings, and muddying her dress. Sheer will-power, sheer maniacal determination, made her go on pulling and sweating and struggling until she reached drier, firmer ground. Almost collapsing with exhaustion, she leaned against the horse's steaming flanks, then forced herself to mount and go on. It was a devilish job to avoid the heather. The mountains were draped with it like a lush, multicoloured plaid of copper, and deep river blue, and smoky purple, and red-brown, and golden yellow, and orange glistening from the earth like the rising sun. A vast panorama of colour kept unfolding before her eyes. Every shade of green, of gold, of silver sparkled all around. High above white mountain peaks disappeared into the heavens. But she had no eyes for beauty, or lofty grandeur, no eyes for anything but another horse on the horizon, another female figure. But there was nothing.

Dusk came creeping over the land, making shadows of trees, and spiky bushes of broom point ghostly fingers. A river barred her path, silver-grey against silver-green. She was shocked at the coldness of it as she and her horse plunged in. Emerging at the other side, her teeth were chattering and she was violently shivering as if she had the plague. Ahead now she could see a ploughed field and as she neared it she thought she could discern the figure of a man. Dismounting, she led the horse through the gathering gloom towards him. She knew that once darkness fell it was impossible to keep travelling and hoped that the ploughman would tell her where she could find shelter. But when she reached him she discovered he was crouched over a small boy of about eight or nine, as if trying to shield him. Both man and boy were dead.

Still shivering, Annabella stared around. There was bound to be some hovel nearby where the man and his family had lived. Then she spied a thread of smoke curling up from the middle of a wood in the distance. Not without some difficulty, because she was exhausted, she heaved herself back on the horse. The animal had no energy left either and despite her angry commands it dragged its feet and hung its head down.

The wood was dark and sombre with no grass, only a thick brown covering of needles. The horse drooped slowly through the silence until it came to a clearing and what had been a cottage. Fire had consumed most of the roof and walls. Charred remnants of a home could still be seen inside, a cracked jug, a cooking pot, and what looked like a woman with long black dust of hair.

Annabella closed her eyes and allowed the horse to carry her wearily past. Emotion condensed into a clear essence. The agonising memory of Lavelle's suffering, her hatred of Regina, the terrible crimes she was witnessing, mixed together to form icy tear-drops which shimmered inside her. But her eyes remained dry and she kept her face stubbornly tilted up.

It was not until she was out of the wooded area and once more in the open moonlit countryside that she slithered from the horse and on to the ground. Even the knowledge that soldiers must be in the area could not prevent her from collapsing into an exhausted sleep. Yet her sleep was neither deep nor peaceful. Macabre images pulsated continuously behind her closed lids. Screams and whimpers mixed with the squeaks and squawks of small animals of the night. The she saw Regina's closed face and heard her voice quite distinctly. Immediately she wakened and struggled to her feet. But everywhere she looked there was no one. She seemed to be alone in the world. Her horse was grazing nearby and she patted it and stroked it and rubbed her face against it before mounting. The feeling that soldiers were somewhere in the vicinity still clung to her and she wished that she did not need to ride through the open glen. She prayed as she went along for another wood to act as cover but many hot and harrowing miles seemed to pass before she came to one. Gratefully she entered its cool green, underwater atmosphere. It was as if the air itself was green, quite divorced even from the sounds of birdsong. Dappled light danced on the ends of rays of gold like candlelight through green shutters; buzzing of myriads of tiny midges disturbed from every light bright green bush as she passed. Then she heard the tinkling sound of a burn and slid from the horse to stumble over to sink to her knees and splash her face and mouth with refreshing water. It was while she was revelling in this that a hand suddenly gripped her and hauled her up. She whirled round and stared with cool impudence at the dragoon who had a coarse-grained face as red as his coat.

'Must you startle a lady like that, sir? Have you no manners?'

'I mean to do more than startle you, mistress. By God, you're a beauty, aren't you, eh?' He jerked her close to him. 'Eh?'

She wriggled provocatively and flashed him coquettish glances as her hands began caressing over his body.

'Gently, gently, sir. There is an art in this that must be enjoyed. Relax and let me show you.'

Lips parted, she raised her face to his. Suddenly he stiffened, a look of surprise straining his eyes wide as she stabbed him with the dagger she had slipped from his belt. He slithered to the ground at her feet without making a sound. Bending over him, ignoring the staring eyes, she wrenched the knife from his body, wiped the blood from it with the end of his coat and secreting it in her dress she scrambled back on her horse. It had only galloped a few paces when suddenly it was out of the woods and she was confronted with the scene of two dragoons struggling gleefully with a bedraggled Highlander.

One of the dragoons bawled: 'Forster, come back! He's here. We've got him.' He looked round towards the wood as he called and saw Annabella emerge. She had two choices. Either she turned back or she kept on. Without hesitating, she kicked and yelled the horse forward, straight at the knot of men. The dragoons were trampled down before they had a chance to race from her path. The Highlander was faster and flew towards the woods as swift and light-footed as a red deer.

Galloping hard away, Annabella stole a glance back. The dragoons were stumbling about trying to catch their panicking horses.

They would be after her soon.

Chapter 22

The flower of Highland manhood was buried under the boggy earth of Culloden Moor. It became a vast graveyard over which the wind moaned like a piper's lament and the air was for ever heavy with sadness. In that bleak place the '45 rebellion ended and with it died a nation.

The bagpipes were forbidden. To possess or carry arms was illegal. Laws were enforced to destroy the clan system and the feudal power of the chiefs. Although it was considered that all Scots were rogues, even those loyal to King George II, the chiefs who had fought on the King's side, like the Campbells, were richly compensated for their loss of 'pit and gallows' jurisdiction over their clans. The others who had sympathised with the Jacobites received nothing and were deprived of their power of life and death over their people just the same. And once they lost their power, they lost their saving grace, their parental interest in their clansmen.

But to the fast-dwindling populace of ordinary men and women of the Highlands what most immediately affected them was the legislation that banned the Highland dress. It became an offence punishable by imprisonment, deportation or death to wear the kilt, the plaid, or any clothing of tartan weave. And the mountain folk had no other clothing but the tartan plaid and kilt and nothing could be so well suited for the inclemency of the weather and the life they had to lead. Their unique clothing had been their pride too and that pride withered when colourful tartans had to be sunk in vats of black dye and mud and their kilts sewn between their legs to make breeches.

By brutality and the destruction of Highland pride the glens were emptied and the clans destroyed. After Culloden people in the Highlands continued to die and suffer agonies of mind and spirit. But in the Lowlands, and in England, others who had never seen a battle or been within miles of a battlefield wrote poems and sent praises and petitions of gratitude to the King.

> The pride of France is lily white,
> The rose in June is Jacobite,
> The prickly thistle of the Scot,
> Is northern knighthood's badge and lot;
> But since the Duke's victorious blows
> The lily, thistle and the rose,
> All droop and fade, all die away;
> Sweet William only rules the day.
> No plant with brighter lustre grows,
> Except the laurel on his brows.

At Sadler's Wells in London a ballet called Culloden was performed to delighted audiences who were thrilled by a scene which was said to depict an exact view of the battle accompanied by the exciting sound of cannon fire.

A gay new dance was invented called 'The Culloden Reel', although when English officers asked this to be performed at a theatre in Edinburgh the Castle Guard had to be called out to quell the subsequent riot. But in London a gate of Hyde Park was renamed Cumberland Gate and everywhere ladies wore the pretty clustering flower with the new name of Sweet William on their clothes.

> 'Tis he! 'Tis he! the pride of fame,
> *William* returned! the shouts proclaim,
> *William* with northern laurels crown'd,
> *William* the hills and vales resound!
> What numbers fled, what numbers fell,
> *Culloden's* glorious field may tell:
> *Culloden's* field the muse may fire,
> To sing the sun and charm the fire.

He was also fondly referred to as the 'martial boy'. The 'martial boy's' luggage had arrived some days before and contained everything including bedding, linen and furnishings that could be pillaged from the houses in which he had lived during his stay in Scotland. But even Cumberland's baggage could not rival his general's. From one Scottish hostess alone,

General Hawley had gathered literally everything she possessed but the clothes she stood up in. The distressed lady, a Mrs Gordon, wrote to her sister:

> '. . . every bit of china I had, which I am sure would not be bought for two hundred pounds; all my bedding and table linen, every book, my repeating clock which stood by the bed in which he lay every night, my worked screen, every rag of Mr Gordon's clothes, the very hat, breeches, nightgown, shoes and what shirts there was of the child's, twelve teaspoons, strainer and tongs, the japan'd board on which the chocolate and coffee cup stood. Even the larding pins, iron screws, the fish kettles and marble mortar and what the General did not desire for himself, he gave to his officers, like for example my flutes, music and cane. He also entertained lavishly and soon used five and a half pounds of my tea, seven loaves of fine sugar, half a hundred loaves of lump sugar, seven pounds of chocolate, a great stock of salt beef, pickled pork, hams, peas, butter, coals, peats, ale, verne jelly, rice and spice, some cheese, brandy, rum, sago, hartshorn, salop, sweetmeats, Narbonne honey, two dozen wash balls with many things 'tis impossible to mention, all of which he kept himself, nor would he give me any share of them, even my empty bottles he took.'

'Hangman' Hawley presented Mrs Gordon's handsome set of table china to the Duke, '. . . as an expression of affection and regard from an old hero to a young one'. His Royal Highness thanked him for the gift but had no particular liking for it, so he in turn presented it to a prostitute who had no use for it and she sold it to a dealer.

The Houses of Parliament passed a Bill to increase Cumberland's yearly income to forty thousand pounds and in addition his father gave him the lucrative sinecure of Ranger of Windsor Castle. There was extra money too for the soldiers and officers. And a campaign medal was struck in their honour. Cast in gold for the officers, it boasted a Roman bust of the Duke and the word 'Cumberland' in halo above it. On the other side of the medal was the nude figure of Apollo piercing the neck of a dragon with his arrow. There were copper and bronze copies for

259

the private soldiers.

And while hundreds of men rotted in prisons, churches and ships—'wounded and naked . . . the wounded festering in their gore and blood, some dead bodies covered quite over with pish and dirt, the living standing to the middle of it, their groans would have pierced a heart of stone . . .'—there was a special service of thanksgiving at St Paul's Cathedral. The Duke looked very splendid as he strode in wearing his dress uniform of scarlet, lapelled and cuffed in blue. The buttonholes were stitched with gold thread. His buff waistcoat was edged with gold. There was gold too on his right shoulder, a tumbling aiguillette of glittering cord. There was still more gold on the crimson baton he was carrying. He was wearing snowy-white breeches and pumps buckled in silver and his fat cheeks glowed happily in the frame of his white curled wig.

He swept off his laced beaver. The organ pealed out with 'The Conquering Hero' especially written for the occasion by George Frederick Handel. The voices of the choir rose with great emotion to the grand dome of the cathedral. And everyone was enthralled. The Archbishop of York then proceeded to preach a sermon which did nothing to detract from or to spoil the grandeur or pleasurable emotions of the occasion. There were no awkward quotations or confusing observations on the subject of brotherly love or charity or tolerance or compassion or mercy. And certainly nothing was mentioned of the Carpenter of Nazareth in his sandals and coarse cloth robe.

Nothing of this was mentioned either in the petition to King George from their General Assembly in London entitled 'A Humble address of the People called Quakers'. It said:

'. . . As none of all thy Protestant subjects exceed us in aversion to the tyranny, idolatry and superstition of the Church of Rome; so none is under more just apprehension of immediate danger from their destructive consequences or have greater cause to be thankful to the Almighty for the inter-position of His providence and our preservation . . . a preservation so remarkable makes it our indispensable duty also to acknowledge the King's paternal care for the safety of his people, of which he has given the most assured pledge in permitting one of his royal offspring to expose himself to the greatest dangers for their security.'

And the address concluded with the hope that '. . . an uninterrupted race of kings of the royal progeny would continue to be a blessing for England, Ireland, Scotland and Wales'.

The Church of Scotland address was to the Duke himself.

'Sir, That the General Assembly of the Church of Scotland has met at this time in a state of peace and security exceeding our greatest hopes is, under God, owing to His Majesty's wisdom and goodness in sending Your Royal Highness, and to your generous resolution in coming to be the deliverer of this church and nation. We might be justly charged with ingratitude to the glorious instrument of Divine Providence if we neglected to pay Your Royal Highness our most humble and heartfelt thanks for that happiness which we now enjoy.

'As for some months past the many fatigues you endured, and the alarming dangers you ran in pursuing that ungrateful and rebellious crew, filled our minds with the greatest pain: so now the complete victory now obtained over them by the bravery of your Royal Father's troops, led on by your wise conduct and animated by your heroic example, gives us the greatest joy . . .

'The Church of Scotland are under peculiar obligations to offer their most thankful acknowledgements to Almighty God, Who has raised you up to be the brave defender of your Royal Father's throne, the happy restorer of our peace, and at this time guardian of all our sacred and civil interests.

'The many late instances of your favourable regard to the ministers of the Church of Scotland and of that entire confidence that you have placed in us ever since this part of Great Britain has been blessed with your presence, must forever excite us to give the strongest proofs that we have not been unworthy of that countenance you have been pleased to give us, and of that trust with which you have honoured us.

'That the Lord of Hosts, Who has hitherto covered your head in the day of battle, may still guard your precious life . . . and crown you with the same glorious success . . . and that your illustrious name, so dear to us, may be transmitted still with greater glory to latest posterity: and that you may share at last in the eternal happiness and glory bestowed, through the Divine Mercy, by Jesus Christ, in a distinguished manner, upon those who have been eminent examples of virtue and the happy instruments of communicating public blessings to mankind, are and shall be the prayers of

    'May it please Your Royal Highness,

    'Your most obliged, most obedient, and most humble servants, The Ministers and Elders of the Church of Scotland.

      'Signed in our presence and at our appointment by

John Lumsden, Moderator.'

All this did not happen for some considerable time after the battle, of course, because news only travelled as fast as a horse and rider and it was some time before even the people of Glasgow heard of Duke William's victory at Culloden.

They learned too that an incredible award of thirty thousand pounds had been offered for the Prince, who was now hiding among the heather and caves of the Highlands. The biggest manhunt in history had been mounted, but so far no one had come forward to claim the reward. Although the government had spies among the clans who said they would betray him if they got the chance. A young lad had told of how and where he had met up with the Prince and how the Prince, seeing he was hungry, had given him a share of his meat. There was also the Protestant minister on one of the islands who had been looking forward to the opportunity of betraying the Pretender and was extremely chagrined when he had discovered too late that he had in fact given hospitality unawares to Charles Edward and his Highland boatman.

And there was the Highland chief, Coll McDonell of Barrisdale. He boasted that he would be the most likely to lead the soldiers to where the Prince was hiding because he knew the mountains better than anyone.

The news came also of another battle, this time between ships at Loch nan Uamh. Two French privateers had come to try to rescue the Prince but had only managed to pick up a band of dispirited Jacobite lords who were quite worn out with the contemplation of their utter ruin. Two ships of the Royal Navy had arrived and attacked the French ships and many men had been killed and wounded on both sides before the French ships managed to get away with the Scottish and Irish officers.

It was to take six attempts by French ships and there were to be many more men killed before the Prince was finally found and rescued by four determined Irishmen.

Celebrations for the victory of Culloden had been planned in Glasgow to take place in a couple of days' time and everyone was looking forward to them. The Grammar School was going to be closed that afternoon and in the morning instead of the usual lessons there was to be a cockfight. All the shops and counting-houses were going to have a holiday too. The two days before, everyone was busy cutting wood and gathering material for bonfires. Extra candles were being made to illuminate all windows and lanterns were being hung outside buildings on all the main streets. Flags and banners were being erected too.

Quin caught glimpses of the unusual activity and sensed the excitement as he jogged round the outskirts of the town, peeping in curiously at the perimeter like a hen pecking at grain. He determined as soon as darkness came, and he could slip safely into the wynds and closes, to find out what was going on. But his first priority was to continue his search for Gav.

Dusk was beginning to blur the edges of the city and make shadows of the trees in the countryside around him when he heard the sound of horses' hooves. Bustling round, he saw a young gentleman bobbing along wearing a white periwig, smart blue cut army coat, ruffled neck-cloth, white breeches and jackboots. He had a pistol in his belt and he also sported a sword. Quin was just about to humbly beg for money or food when the young gentleman stopped his horse and said:

'What are you doing here, Quin? You'll not find much shelter outside the city.'

Quin cocked his head. His one eye stared out. But still he could not recognise the stranger.

'Quin's been banished,' he said. 'And all Quin and the childer did was sup a drink o' water.'

'You mean Gav?'

'The verra one.'

'Has he been banished?'

'Quin's lost him. They chugged Gav away from Quin at the Tolbooth.'

'I want him.'

'Oh-ho, you too, eh? Quin's never known a poor childer to have so many folks chasing after him.'

'What do you mean? Who else is after him?'

'Merchant Ramsay a while back.'

'That's where he'll be.'

Quin jigged round and round with excitement, his hair and his hands and his coat-tails whirling out.

'Oh-ho, oh-ho. Aren't you the clever one, eh, eh? Quin never thought of that.'

The horse reared up, then cantered away, leaving Quin motionless with surprise for a minute. Then suddenly he scampered after it.

'Quin's coming,' he puffed.

'What can you do? Leave me to find him.'

'But, maister, what can a fine gentleman like yourself want with a beggar lad?'

'I'm his sister, Regina.'

Quin stopped in his tracks and the horse quickened its pace and left him behind in the empty countryside like a scarecrow with the wind flapping at his clothes.

Regina clattered past the Shawfield Mansion and along Trongate Street. Then she stopped at the Cross where the four main streets intersected. If Gav was out at all, the chances were he would be seen from here. She kept turning her horse around to peer down one street and then the other. But it was fast getting too dark to see very far and she was just about to give up and try again the next day when she caught sight of the sturdy figure in the too big jacket approaching the Cross from the High Street. She spurred the horse towards him and, startled, he turned to run.

'Gav!' she hissed, and hurriedly dismounted. 'Gav, it's me Regina.'

He stopped. Puzzlement replaced consternation.

'Regina?' he echoed.

'Never say that name again. Call me Reg or Reggie as if I were a lad.'

'Why? I don't understand. Why are you dressed in breeches? And you look so grand. How . . .'

'I stole the clothes off dead bodies.'

Gav was appalled and incredulous.

'Stole? You stole from the dead?'

'They had no longer any use for them. I was entitled to them. I deserved them because I survived. I've come a long way and it's taken me many terrible days and nights. Terrible days and nights. On my own. But I survived. I bloody well survived.'

'But, Regina . . .'

'Reggie.'

'Reggie, how . . . where . . . why . . .'

'Soldiers are killing people everywhere up north. And burning houses and barns and crops and killing cattle. The whole place is ruined, finished. There's bodies strewn about all over. Down hillsides, in glens, floating in rivers, sprawled on roads, inside the houses. Everyone's killing and stealing. I've lots of money, Gav. And jewellery. We'll be all right now. Nobody will dare kick us about or make our lives miserable. But I've got to get safely away from Glasgow before Annabella Ramsay comes back.'

Gav said:

'I'm not getting kicked about and I didn't steal or kill. Maister Ramsay has been good to me. He's sent me to the Grammar School to learn bookkeeping and one day I'm going to go as an indentured servant to Virginia.'

'To the plantations? You must be mad. Can't you see he's tricked you? He's going to sell you as a slave. Remember Mammy used to tell us how folk were sent over there as slaves for stealing.'

'I'm not a thief and Maister Ramsay wouldn't trick me. He's a good maister.'

'A good maister,' Regina sneered. 'What does he care about you? Haven't you learned yet that nobody cares about anybody? There's nothing for it in this bloody world but to take damn good care of yourself.'

He stared at her in distress, realising for the first time that it was not only her disguise that made her unrecognisable. Her whole expression and even her voice had changed. Her eyes, once large and timid, seemed to have shrunk back into her head like glittering green bullets, the muscles of her face were taut, gripping her mouth into a hard line that twisted down at the edges.

'Mammy's dead,' he said. 'They hanged her.'

She did not blink an eyelid, but the muscle of one cheek contorted, deforming her mouth as she echoed:

'Hanged her?'

Tears gushed inwards and stung other wounds. What harm had her mother ever done? All her life she had worked hard and tried to do her best for her family. Yet all she had got out of life was misery and pain. Then eventually they had hanged her. Ignorant, cruel, wicked pigs of men had hanged her.

'What are you going to do, Regina?' Gav asked.

She ignored his question.

'They'll hang you too. Or worse. The Virginia plantations!' She gave a humourless laugh. 'You're a fool!'

All the time she was speaking she could see her mother swinging on the gallows and feel the pain she must have suffered. She could hear her voice crooning . . .

> Homeward ye're travellin'
> In the soft hill-rain,
> The day long by
> That ye wearied o' the glen,
> No ring upon yer hand,
> No kiss upon yer mou',
> Quiet noo.

'You're the fool,' Gav flashed back in anger. 'And you're the one who'll end on the scaffold if you've been killing and stealing.'

'They'll have to catch me first. And recognise me. I'm not a helpless beggar girl any more. I'm a young man, don't forget!'

'What are you going to do, Regina?' he repeated.

'Reggie, for God's sake. My life may depend on it.'

'Reggie.'

'I don't know yet.' She shrugged. 'Edinburgh or London maybe. I haven't made up my mind.'

> Cold was the sky above ye,
> The road baith rough and steep.
> No further shall ye wander
> Nor greet yersel' tae sleep,
> My ain wild lass,
> My bonnie hurtit doo,
> Quiet, quiet noo.

'Until you do, why don't you attend the Grammar School with me? I'm learning bookkeeping. It's a useful thing for any lad to know who wants to get on in the world. That's what Maister Ramsay says. It costs four shillings a term. Have you got enough for that?'

'Of course,' she told him disdainfully. 'I could probably buy the whole damned school if I wanted to.'

But she couldn't buy back her mother.

'You'd get in all right. The headmaster likes people with money.'

'I can imagine!'

'Then we'd be together, even just for a wee while, Reg . . . Reggie. Oh, please, meet me there tomorrow. I've missed you and I've been so worried.'

She hesitated in wretchedness.

'If Mistress Annabella returns, you promise not to tell her about who or where I am?'

'Of course not. Do you think I'd betray my own sister?'

'Cousin. Your sister is as dead as your mother, Gav.'

'You'll be there tomorrow?'

She nodded and then as she sprang back on to her horse Gav added:

'Why are you so anxious that Mistress Annabella shouldn't know anything about you?'

But Regina galloped off without giving him an answer. He continued thoughtfully on his way to the Old Coffee House

Land where Ramsay too was deep in thought. He was worrying about Annabella.

Now that the rebel army was defeated, it seemed to Ramsay that Annabella must have been defeated and killed along with them. Probably she had never survived the journey as far as Culloden. Yet his mind kept returning hopefully to what the minister said. Annabella would not be easily quelled, not even by the mighty Duke of Cumberland. And because he felt that the minister would have more chance of God's ear, he asked him to put up a prayer every day. Encouraged by plenty of whisky, Mr Blackadder prayed most earnestly.

'O Lord, Lord. O blessed Redeemer, for pity's sake help oor Annabella. Aye, we ken fine how thrawn and wicked the lassie is and we hope you'll forgive us for asking. O Lord, Lord, in Your infinite mercy, can you no' find it in Your heart to lead her back to Glasga a' in one piece? No' so much for her ain sake but for her faither's. The poor man's fair distractit.'

Indeed it was true. From the moment he awoke in the morning until he snuffed out his candle at night, Ramsay's mind was tormented by thoughts of his daughter.

'Damn the hussy!' he told himself over and over again. 'She's never been anything but a plague and a worry to me.'

He tried to banish her completely from his thoughts, to concentrate on living his normal life and for the most part he at least looked as if there was nothing amiss. He busied himself in his counting-house. He went for his meridian and sat in the tavern with his friends drinking and talking. He visited and supped with his colleagues, Willie Halyburton, the Earl of Glendinny and the old Earl of Locheid. He paced the plainstanes with all the other tobacco lords and discussed the price of a hogshead of tobacco and how much was to be exported to the countries in Europe and how many hogsheads were lying in bond.

But all the time the figure of Annabella drifted in and out of his mind like a yellow-headed wraith. Occasionally his mind's eyes fastened wistfully on her and he would be pulled back by a colleague or friend having to loudly repeat to him something they had said. Or he would be counting up a column of figures and suddenly discover that he had got a wrong total and have to shake himself and struggle to concentrate and count everything again.

Now Griselle and Douglas had made him a grandfather, but he could not work up any enthusiasm for the baby, nor even to question the suspiciously premature birth. It was his lack of interest rather than the reverse that allowed him to be persuaded to attend the Cummers Feast and to celebrate the birth and when Gav appeared he growled.

'Away and tell Big John to hurry with the lanthorns and bring me my cloak. We've to go down the road to Maister Douglas's place, damn him!'

Douglas had a flat in Gibson's Land further down Saltmarket Street. The distance did not merit the bother of taking out and saddling up a horse, so Ramsay went on foot, striding along in his bushy wig with his head thrust forward and his hands thumping one on top of the other behind his back. Big John and Gav held up the lanterns in front and guided him safely around the ruts and potholes on the road.

Going in the other direction, Moothy McMurdo swaggered past.

'A beautiful young lassie called Mally Sime,
Is to wed Andra Gillespie in two days' time,
Mally has a fortune o' four thousand and mair,
And it's verra unusual to be rich and fair.'

Gibson's Land was a magnificent tenement standing upon eighteen stately pillars or arches and entry was through four arches into a courtyard and the stairways at the back. Trust Douglas, Ramsay thought, to set himself up in something fancy.

Inside the house, as was customary after a birth, Griselle sat in state in full dress, propped up on top of her four-poster bed on a footstool and with three white satin pillows at her back and her enormous hoops spread across the white satin bed-cover. Her wig was high and well powdered and decorated with large curling feathers and she was wearing face patches and held a long fan. There was already quite a crowd of friends milling about the bedroom paying their respects and curtseying and bowing and drinking wine. The supper was laid out and all the guests sampled the ham and fowl and ducks and hens and partridges. Then after the meat had been removed everyone suddenly scrambled to grab the sweetmeats and stuff them in their pockets. Chairs were knocked over and dishes crashed from the table and men and women pulled and pushed at one another and there was a terrible noise. After a time it quietened down again as folk concentrated once more on drinking the wine.

Ramsay came away early. He preferred whisky and he was in no mood for socialising. He could no longer feel at ease away from his own house in case, through some miracle, Annabella might have returned. When he got back he thought the miracle had happened. A candle flickered in the kitchen. But it was Nancy who emerged. Big John rushed joyfully towards her but she pushed him aside.

'Is Mistress Annabella back?'

'She's alive then?' Ramsay said.

'She was on her way home when I last saw her.'

'With Lavelle?'

'Alone.'

'Good God!'

'She'll make it. I did.'

'Why the hell didn't you accompany her and see to her? What the devil do you think I pay you good money for? I could have you whipped through the toon for this.'

'She went away on her own. I followed not long after, but there's many different paths and it's easy to get confused, especially in the dark.'

Thoughts of the many long dark nights Annabella must have travelled and was still travelling tormented him beyond words. He pushed past Nancy and into his room, crashing like an enraged bull into furniture in the dark.

'Gav! Bring the bloody lanthorn, damn you!' he roared, and when Gav ran obediently with the lantern, Ramsay snatched it from him and cuffed his ears.

'Time you were away to Virginia, m'lad. You get it too bloody soft here. I'm sick to death o' being surrounded wi'

270

useless tramps who do nothing but eat my meat, burn my candles and pocket my hard-earned sillar.'

Gav groped his way back through the dark lobby into the kitchen where one candle made a ragged patch of light that gave furtive movement to the gloom. He had no sooner reached the kitchen when Ramsay bellowed out again:

'Where the hell are you a' noo? It's time for the reading.'

Even the reading was a challenge of concentration to him and he felt keenly guilty at the frequency with which his mind wandered from God's word. But he never missed a night in front of the Bible in Annabella's bedroom even when there had only been himself and Big John.

After the reading and the prayer and ignoring the lateness of the hour, he questioned Big John, Gav and Nancy on their Catechisms before allowing them to retire. Then after sitting motionless for a long time he lifted the candelabra and went over to the corner to stare gloomily out of the dark window. Occasionally a disembodied lantern twinkled past like a firefly. Then came the slower light of the town guard swinging on its pole as he plodded through the streets. But it too was soon swallowed into the blackness. A horse's hooves beat a sudden kettledrum clatter on cobbles, then just as suddenly stopped. Silence opened like the grave. Ramsay turned away deeply dejected and went through to his own room and bed.

While outside on the stairs, crushed among a shivering flotsam of humanity, Quin waited.

Chapter 23

Gav was embarrassed and nervous when, on the way to school next morning, he saw Quin, but he bade him a polite good morning as he crushed past the crowd of bodies on the stairs. In a dither of excitement, Quin trotted after him.

'Gavie, Gavie. Quin's found Gavie.'

The dangers, the insecurities, the terrible privations of Gav's recent existence, roared like a lion at his heels along with Quin. It was as if already the good food he'd been enjoying, the warmth, the shelter, the safety, the bookkeeping lessons, everything had only been a dream. Quin was the nightmare reality. Quin was ugliness and squalor; Quin was fear and loneliness; Quin was hunger; Quin was stiff-cold nights and days with nowhere to go.

Early-morning light made cobwebs of the roof-tops and a ghostly face of the Tolbooth clock. It had been raining during the night. Quin's clothes would have been wet and they would have dried slowly as he huddled on the draughty stairs. He would have had nothing to eat or drink. Gav had not been listening to his chatter as they hurried past the Cross and up the High Street. Nor had he spoken a word, but on reaching the school he stopped and said:

'I thought you were banished.'

'Quin is! Quin is!'

'I tried to see you. I went to the Tolbooth and asked again and again.'

'Gav's a good lad, eh?'

Gav took from his pocket a piece of bread, a piece of chicken and an apple supplied to him by Nancy. He pushed them all into Quin's hands and Quin hastily crammed the bread and the chicken into his mouth until his face bulged grotesquely all over.

Gav said: 'I've got to go into school now.'

Quin couldn't talk because his mouth was so full, but his one eye strained wide and his head wobbled in bewilderment. Gav hesitated, then added:

'I'll see you tomorrow morning and explain.'

Quin nodded eagerly, but before he could gulp over the food and say anything in reply, Gav dashed into the school building.

Regina was waiting for him in the lobby and the first thing she asked was: 'Is Annabella Ramsay back yet?'

He was still shaken by the encounter with Quin and her question did not penetrate his consciousness at first.

'Are you still asleep?' Regina angrily prodded him. 'Answer me!'

'What?'

'Is she back yet?'

'Mistress Ramsay?'

'Who else, you fool!'

'Stop calling me a fool. I'm not a fool.'

'Oh, no,' she smirked sarcastically. 'You've just signed indenture papers condemning yourself to five years' slavery on the Virginia plantations because you're so damned clever.'

'You don't know what you're talking about. I'm going to work but I don't mind working. It's better than stealing or begging.'

'But you'll enjoy my money all right, no matter how I came by it.'

'No, I won't. Keep your money. I don't want any of it. I won't touch it.'

She groaned. 'You're being damned stupid again.'

'Just come into the classroom and see if I'm stupid or not. I was always cleverer than you and you know it. I was the cleverest in the whole school at the last school and I'm the cleverest in this one as well.'

'I asked you a question and you haven't answered it yet.'

'No, she's not back. Why are you so afraid of her? What have you done to anger her?'

'I had her Frenchie killed.'

'Her Frenchie?'

'They were lovers. You know,' she said irritably. 'Lovers! She loved the French pig.'

Gav's colour faded with his voice.

'Regina!'

At the sound of the name her hand shot out and stung his face.

'If you say that word again I'll kill you.'

Heartbroken tears shimmered before his eyes, blurring his vision. He wept, not because of the blow Regina had given him, but because his sister did not exist any more.

'Stop that damned blubbering,' she said. 'You'll have plenty to blubber about when you're rotting on the plantation.'

In his wretchedness he began to wonder if he had made a terrible mistake. His happy dreams of doing bookkeeping in one of Maister Ramsay's stores and eventually becoming manager began to crumble. In his heart he had always suspected that they were too good to be true. Good things like that did not happen to beggar boys. Only people who already had good things in life were given the chance of more.

Now his mind opened to stories his mother used to tell them about what she had heard about the plantations. About people starving and dying. About savages who ate people. About wild animals the like of which had never been seen in Glasgow.

His heart crashed about inside his chest as if it were determined to smash through his ribs.

He would be alone in Virginia without friend or relation. Perhaps it would be better to stay with Quin, after all. But he had signed the indenture papers and he had given Maister Ramsay his hand on it. Thinking of Maister Ramsay steadied him a little. Would a kind, clever, honest man like that trick him?

As it happened, at that very moment Ramsay was supervising the setting up of hogsheads of tobacco on the open street in front of the Exchange at the Trongate in preparation for the auction. This area, the business centre of Glasgow, fronted by the plainstanes which contained the Exchange, the Tolbooth, the Exchange Coffee House and Tavern, had been nicknamed 'The Golden Acre'. Already merchants from various countries in Europe were strolling about rubbing sample leaves between finger and thumb to test it for quality.

Ramsay's ships the *Mary Heron* and *The Glasgow Lass* were now lying at Port Glasgow. All the tobacco that was brought into Britain had as usual gone into bonded warehouses until it was time for it be re-exported. Ramsay, having taken his out to sell, would now be able to claim a 'drawback'. He had found a dishonest customs man and arranged that the certificate issued by the Customs House showed double the number of hogsheads than had actually been landed. As a result now that he had withdrawn the tobacco he got double the drawback of tax money he was entitled to. He did not consider this dishonest. Nor did the merchants who put in tobacco, took it out again, got their drawback, then re-landed the same tobacco at a different port and repeated the process again. There were so many duties on foreign goods that most respectable people laughed at the way smugglers dodged the excise man. And when the subject of the tobacco trade came up in conversation they would wink knowingly and tell of the many tricks used by tobacco merchants.

The only people not amused by merchants' ways were the Virginia planters. The merchants did not think much of the planters either. Some of them they viewed as very slippery and coarse fellows with their thumbnails grown specially long and hardened in the flame of a candle. Suspicious travellers maintained the nails were cultivated for the purpose of gouging out victims' eyes in the many rough and tumbles they became involved in. The yeomen who worked their crops claimed they needed their long nails only for the innocent reason of 'topping' the tobacco plants. At one stage, to ensure growth and strength, they maintained the top of the tobacco plant, including the bud, had to be removed.

The planters referred to men like Ramsay as 'the unconscionable and cruel merchants'. The merchants regarded the planters as spendthrifts and wastrels, quick to borrow and slow to pay. But none of this was on Ramsay's mind as he strode around with the other merchants fingering the samples of tobacco. He was still thinking of Annabella. Nancy had been so certain that Annabella was bound to arrive at any moment that she had stayed up late waiting to receive her and make her a warming dish of chocolate.

'She started off before me,' she kept repeating. 'Even if she took a longer road by mistake, she should be back by now.' He had not been able to sleep and he had heard Nancy moving about the kitchen for a long time. Then in the morning she said, 'Maister, I'll go and meet her. She's bound to be coming near Glasgow now. She's bound to be. Can I take a horse?'

He glowered at her.

'You brought a horse in, didn't you? The beast is yours. Do what you will with it.'

It was some hours ago now since she had galloped away and there was still no sign of her return. He was plagued with wicked wayward women and thinking of them he hardly heard the rhythmic chant of the auctioneer with its mellow cadences starting with the cry of 'Bid 'er up, boys!'

Then came the silent gestures of the buyers. One might wink. Another put a finger to his chest. Another raised an eyebrow. Another pulled the lobe of his ear. The auctioneer slipped his figures higher and higher:

'22-2-2-3-3-3-4-4-4.'

Until he 'knocked down' the tobacco he sang over and over again in a kind of Gregorian chant the last number of each bid:

'25-5-5-6-6-6-7-7-7-8-8-8.'

It was a colourful scene with the hogsheads piled up and the tobacco lords strolling around and the many other merchants from all over the world in their rich and vivid clothes. Hovering on the outskirts there was another motley throng. There were the tradespeople. There were the chapmen. There were the hotchpotch of men and women of all shapes and sizes with trays hanging from their necks selling Daffy's Elixir, or Tincture of Rhubarb or Tar Water or Dried Bees for the rheumatics or aromatic herbs or candy. There were the milkmaids on horseback with 'soor-dook' barrels strapped across the saddle. There were the beggars, the pickpockets, the harlots and the thieves.

But of Annabella or Nancy there was never a sign.

Nancy had just meant to ride a few miles out of town. She was certain that Annabella could not be any further away. But one mile of desolate countryside passed, then another and another. Morning gave way to afternoon, and afternoon sank slowly into evening. It would be hopeless she knew, to find anyone once darkness came. She had not even brought a lantern, but a dozen lanterns would be mere pinpricks in the vast blackness of the night.

Her horse cantered to a halt and she sat uncertainly, looking around, wondering what she should do, when suddenly she detected a movement among some trees across the other side of a river. Then out of the shadows appeared a woman on foot and hitching up her skirts she began wading across. From the distance she looked like a daffodil in the navy blue water. Nancy could not make out her features. Her defiant carriage, however, and the way she was forcing herself against the water, as if challenging it, daring it to stop her, left Nancy in no doubt.

She spurred her horse forward, then leapt down as soon as it reached the river's edge.

'Mistress Annabella!'

Annabella's hair tumbled untidily around her shoulders. Her face was pink with her exertions but black-spattered with dirt and her bare feet and legs were bruised and cut. She struggled out of the water as Nancy watched in helpless disbelief.

'Mistress, what happened?'

'Hell and damnation!' Annabella cried out. 'The bloody horse fell down a pothole and broke his leg. I've had to walk a monstrous distance. I tell you, Nancy, I have never been so exhausted in all my life.'

'It'll be morning now before we get back to Glasgow. Would you rest here for the night and start off in the morning?'

'What? Spend another odious night shivering on wet grass? Don't just stand there blethering such ridiculous nonsense. Help me to mount.'

After helping her up, Nancy sprang up to sit behind her. Then after a few minutes as the horse cantered along Annabella suddenly burst out:

'Gracious heaven, Nancy, what are you doing here? I thought you were away home with your wondrous chief.'

There was another silence before Nancy replied:

'The troopers caught up with us.'

'God!'

'They didn't get him.'

'Why not?'

277

'I shot him first.'

Annabella said nothing and after a while Nancy gave a bitter laugh.

'They thought Calum must have been kidnapping me and carrying me off and their arrival gave me my chance of freedom. I suppose if they hadn't thought that they would have raped me, then killed me. I saw plenty of women on my way back left lying dead in all sorts of indecent positions. Bloody English savages!'

'It wasn't just the English,' Annabella said. 'You saw the Scots regiments on Cumberland's side on the field and I'm damned sure you've seen them roaming around the countryside as well.'

'Bloody traitors of Campbells.'

'It wasn't just the Campbells either.'

'Are you trying to excuse what they've done?'

'Don't be a bloody fool. What happened at Culloden will always be inexcusable and what's been happening after is worse. What I'm saying is that all men are obviously capable of the most monstrous evil if they're given the chance and encouraged to it. And women too. Even children.'

'You're thinking of Regina.'

'Yes, I'm thinking of Regina.'

'Tormenting yourself with thoughts of the beggar girl won't bring anybody back or change anything. The person I blame for this whole tragic mess is his bloody Italian Highness. What right had he to come over here and stir up trouble and cause so many poor folk to be killed just because he wanted power?'

'He had courage.'

'Oh, had he! I'm not so sure. I noticed he was always at the rear in the battles. Oh, I know he marched ahead all the time on the way down to England. Oh, he was a great lad then. But when he was thwarted and had to turn back he was huffy and acted like a spoiled brat. He dragged behind and did all sorts of awkward perverse things that could have endangered the men. And as I say, in battles he was all right. He always had his lifeguards or his Irish around him for protection.'

'Hell and damnation, Nancy. I'm no Jacobite. Everybody knows that. But I hope I'm honest enough and fair enough to give credit where credit's due. When the Pretender came over here he had only a handful of men.'

'I know. But he was brought up to believe this was what he was meant to do. He believed he had a divine right to come here so that he could eventually lord it in St James's Palace. What did he care how many good Scotsmen he sacrificed in order to get himself and his father there?'

'That's still no reason to question his courage. He had courage I tell you!'

'To bloody hell with courage then. A lot of damn good it did anybody, including himself.'

Annabella sighed.

'I suppose you're right.' She was silent for a spell, then she said: 'I'll never forget it, Nancy, will you? I don't mean Jean-Paul and Calum. That goes without saying. But the whole monstrous business. I feel sick to my soul. The evil, the cruelty, the carnage, the complete lack of pity, never fades even in my sleep. I try to command such thoughts to leave me in peace, but they refuse to be banished. My mind's saturated with the blood of it all. I believe that no matter where I am after this, or what I'm thinking about, or looking at, it will always be through a stained-glass window of suffering in the Highlands.'

Detecting a crack in Annabella's voice, Nancy said:

'We're both tired. Let's stop here and rest. We'll find a dry place and you can sleep or just relax and admire the sunrise. Look how beautiful it is already. Calum told me how he used to love to watch the dawn. His home was in a glen and it was especially beautiful in winter. He said the hills and glens were more colourful then.' Nancy was looking at Annabella yet a curtain of sadness blacked out sight. 'The mountain peaks were white, but the hillsides were all different shades. Reddish brown and copper and rust and orange and yellow and navy blue and purple. In winter there was a special dewy lushness. And the trees were silver-green. He said it was so peaceful. A world on its own.'

Annabella touched her arm.

'I'm sorry. Truly I am.'

Nancy nodded, then moved away to secure the horse to a

279

bush.

'This place seems dry enough. Try to get some sleep. There's no hurry now. It doesn't matter if we don't get into Glasgow until afternoon.'

The two women curled down close to one another and lay wide-eyed listening to the small rustlings and whisperings all around them and high above the first careless song of the birds.

After the auction Ramsay paraded the plainstanes talking to his friends William Halyburton, the Provost Andrew Cochrane and the Earl of Locheid. The Earl of Glendinny had bustled home to his new bride. The men, as was customary, passed the statue on the right when going westward and in reverse order when walking eastward.

The Earl of Locheid, the owner of the tenement in which Halyburton lived, was a man in his seventies, as tall as Halyburton but as skinny and pinched-looking as his friend was fleshy and robust. Yet for all his long languorous appearance, Locheid enjoyed life. Albeit in a canny way. He laughed but cautiously, with lips tightly closed and shoulders screwed in to repress a hiccuping chest. He fornicated but did so with a certain reserve and always took a hot toddy afterwards to counteract any harmful effects of excitement. He enjoyed his food but was pernickety with it. He appreciated a dram but was careful to instruct a servant to be at hand at all times to loosen his cravat in case he choked. And rather than risk, like his colleagues when in their cups, sprawling under the table to be at the mercy of draughts and rats, he always had two servants ready with a long pole to slide through the arms of his chair and lift him away, still holding himself neatly together, until he was tucked safely in bed.

'Mm-hm.' He minced his words and chewed them over as if determined to hang on to them as long as possible. 'There's mm-hm going to be mm-hm, a celebration for the Duke's victory at Culloden I hear, mm-hm-hm-mm.'

'Aye,' Ramsay agreed, but absent-mindedly. 'Thank God it's a' over and done with.'

'Mm-hm. If ye ask me, hm-mm, Heelanders are nothing, hm-mm, but trouble. Always have been, hm-hm. Cattle thieves.

Hm-hm. Bandits. Mm-hm. Bitter, vengeful folks tae. Mm-hm. Never forgive a grudge between clans. Mm-hm. Always fighting between themselves. Mm-hm. Terrible folk!'

Halyburton loudly trumpeted his agreement.

'Ye're right, Locheid. Yer quite right. And just think what it might have been like if folks like that had got the better o' us.'

'While I agree with what you say, gentlemen,' Andrew Cochrane thoughtfully fingered his gold-topped Malacca cane, 'I think we must admit that the rebel army was civil enough while it was here.'

'Oh, aye,' said Ramsay, stung into giving his full attention. 'Oh, aye, they robbed us but they were verra civil aboot it!'

The Provost sighed.

'I suppose we'll get scant else but polite acknowledgements from the English government in reply to my letters informing them of our grievances. I fear no cash will be paid unless we go down to London and press our case for compensation to the King himself.'

Trongate Street, yellow with sunlight, was gradually emptying of people. A lumbering coach drawn by six black horses and crowded with gentlemen began creaking away. The musical bells of the Tolbooth clock and the Tron Church steeple sang in chorus like cascading water tumbling down the warm sunny air.

The four men pulled out their gold watches, checked the time, then tucked them away again before bidding each other goodbye and making for home.

The first thing Ramsay asked when Big John opened the door was:

'Is she back yet?'

'No,' said Big John. 'And Nancy's no' back either.'

Ramsay's jaw clamped forward. 'Is this no' damnable? It's whipped through the toon they need.'

'Did ye see Captain Kilfuddy and Captain Daidles?'

'No.'

'They said no' to worry, they'll be up again. They've just gone doon to the tavern.'

'Oh, I'm no' worried about them. They'll no stray far when there's celebrations to join in.'

281

Big John turned miserably away.

'We've no' much to celebrate, have we?'

'Trust in the Lord, man,' Ramsay irritably commanded. 'Trust in the Lord. If it's God's will to bring the damned women back, He'll bring them back. If it's no', He'll no'. And that's a' aboot it.'

Chapter 24

The celebration day began with an early-morning thanksgiving service.

Ramsay went to church on horseback and commanded Big John and Gav to accompany him, also on horseback.

'You may as well get used to a bit o' riding, Gav,' he said. 'There's long distances to cover in Virginia and to be a good horse rider is verra important.'

He strode from the house in front of Gav and knocked aside all the vagrants on the stairs, including Quin. Quin dodged about after them in great agitation. Gav felt irritated both at Quin and the pity he felt for him. He wished he would just go away and leave him in peace. Yet mixed with these feelings was the fear that he might still be glad of him.

'I can't see you just now,' he hissed in passing. 'I've got to go to church. You'd better be careful the bailies don't catch you. You're supposed to be banished.'

While they were saddling up the horses, he caught glimpses of Quin's grotesque face bobbing up from behind walls, jerking out from the sides of closes and screwing round corners.

Riding past on a horse that was too big for him and needed all his attention, he impatiently signalled for Quin to get out of the way. But he knew that he was still following all along the road to the church.

During the service Gav kept seeing Quin's gargoyle face in his mind's eye and could not properly concentrate on what the minister was saying. Only snatches reached him like unexpected waves of sound surging in, then receding.

'O Lord, Lord!' cried the Reverend Blackadder. 'We thank Thee for safe deliverance from manifold perils . . . Tammas McKay, what have you got yer hat on for in the kirk? If yer bare pow's cauld, just get a good grey worset wig. They're no' so dear and there's plenty o' them at Bob Gordon's for tenpence . . . Aye,

Lord, we thank Ye for demolishing oor enemies. Aye, and we'll be ready to demolish the deevil.' Blackadder suddenly assumed the position of one aiming a pistol and made a loud noise like a shot. 'We'll shoot him wi' the gun o' the gospel and doon he'll come like a dead crow. But, freends,' he leaned forward over the pulpit. 'Unless ye a' repent yer sins, ye'll a' perish.' At that moment a fly alighted on the open Bible in front of him and Blackadder's eyes gleamed. 'Aye, freends, ye'll a' perish just as surely as I'm going to ding the guts oot o' that big blue fly that's landed on my Bible.' His clenched fist crashed down with all his might, but the fly got away and he roared. 'Would ye believe it? There's a chance for ye yet!'

After the service everyone went for a leisurely stroll or a ride on Glasgow Green. Recently there had been a warning notice about gentlemen who sent their servants to exercise their horses on the Green. The notice said that gentlemen should not allow their servants to ride in such crowds and at such speed as the quantities of dust dispersed by the horses were ruining the bleachfields. Also the lives of the inhabitants from the number and fury of the rides had often been in danger.

But on this pleasant sunny day no one was in any hurry. Ladies paraded in their long waisted gowns and hooped skirts, arching round the Green like a shimmering rainbow. Some young women wore silken plaids. Many older ladies still clung to the fashion of wearing lace 'screens' or mantillas gracefully draped over their heads. Others favoured wig decorations of long curling feathers or beads or bows or brooches or a mixture of all of these things. Their male companions vied with them in peacock splendour in their different patterns and colours of silk and satin and velvet.

Ramsay cantered past his son Douglas and noticed he was dressed with even more style than usual. He sported bright pink satin damask embroidered in green and gold. He carried a muff and had long ribbons fluttering from each wrist. His wife swept along by his side with her head in the air and their maid walked behind them carrying the new baby. Both Douglas and Griselle seemed very stiff-faced and anything but happy. Ramsay wondered if they had been quarrelling. However, he did not stop to find out. In fact, after favouring them with only a curt sign of recognition, he encouraged his horse into a trot and soon left them far behind. He was impatient to get back to the house. He regretted having brought both servants with him. It was only right and proper that they should have had the spiritual benefits of the Reverend Blackadder's sermon but afterwards somebody should have stayed in the house in case Annabella came.

But when they all returned she was still not there.

The celebrations were getting under way. Fiddlers were beginning to play in the streets. The atmosphere was quickening. Bells were being rung.

'Aye, lads,' Ramsay addressed Big John and Gav, 'ye'll be wanting to go out and join in a' the excitement, I suppose.'

Gav agreed but without much enthusiasm. It was not the celebrations he was thinking about. Decisions had to be made and the future settled once and for all. He needed to talk to both Regina and Quin.

Big John gloomily shook his head. 'I'll wait here for Nancy.'

'Aye, weel, on you go, Gav. But be careful and no' be getting drunk or into any trouble. My ships will be sailing verra soon and I'm expecting you to be ready to leave on one of them.'

Regina was lodging in a tavern in Saltmarket Street, the same one in which Cameron of Lochiel had stayed in while the Highland army had been in Glasgow. Gav determined to make for there first and discuss with her what ought to be done. But again Quin accosted him on the stairs.

Gav sighed.

'I wish you'd leave me alone just now. I'm worried about what's going to happen to Regina—or Reggie, as she says we've to call her now. She's in terrible trouble.'

'Oh-ho—Reggie looked in fine fettle to Quin.'

'She's afraid of Mistress Annabella finding her. That's why she's pretending she's a lad. She says she's stolen all those clothes and things, but worse,' he hesitated and could hardly lift his gaze to meet Quin, 'she had the mistress's Frenchie killed.'

'Oh-ho, now there'll be fun, eh?'

'What would Mistress Annabella do to her, Quin?'

'March her over to the Tolbooth to be hangit. Or kill her

herself. Aye, Quin thinks that Mistress Annabella would kill Reggie herself and no' be very dainty aboot it either.'

'I'm going to talk to Regin . . . Reggie now.'

'Quin's coming.'

'It's too dangerous for you. You'll be hanged too if you're seen.'

'Quin'll dodge aboot.'

In exasperation Gav stamped away.

In the tavern Regina was sitting near the door with a stoup of ale and when she saw Quin hovering behind Gav she said: 'What's he doing here?'

'Look, Reg . . . Reggie, we'll have to decide what's to be done.'

Regina finished up her ale and swaggered out. 'With him?'

'With us all. The maister's ships are due to sail any day and I'm supposed to be on one of them.'

Quin's head cocked to one side and his face screwed up as he followed them along Saltmarket Street and round by the Cross.

'Quin's no' verra pleased.'

Ignoring him, Gav continued to address Regina: 'Could you not come with me? You don't need to go as an indentured servant. If you've plenty of money as you say, you could pay for your own passage to Virginia. Then at least we'd be together.'

'What would I do in Virginia?'

'I don't know, but surely there would be something. Maister Ramsay's got stores.'

'Quin's no' verra pleased.'

Regina turned on him. 'Go away! We don't want you any more.'

'But Quin's yer faither!'

Gav put a hand on Quin's arm and was distressed to discover it was violently trembling.

'We're just worried in case the bailies see you, Quin. Away you go outside the town until it's dark. Tonight or tomorrow morning, whenever I can, I'll come down the stairs with something for you to eat and maybe some money.'

'Quin's no' verra pleased.'

'Go on. I don't want you to get hanged.'

He trotted away rubbing his ear and his hair spiking out.

Gav said: 'You didn't need to be nasty to him.'

'Oh, who cares about that freak?'

'I do.'

She shrugged and turned her attention to the noisy crowds now thronging round the Cross and along Trongate Street. On the landing of the outside stairs some of the magistrates were raising their glasses in a toast to the victors, but so great was the noise of revelry all around that no one could hear a word they shouted. Bells pealed, fiddles scraped, pipes skirled, people screeched and danced and laughed and drank and skittered delightedly about. Then to add to the hullabaloo there came a deafening discharge of muskets from a detachment of the town's regiment.

Approaching the town from the western side, Annabella and Nancy heard the uproar and could not imagine what the cause might be. Nancy had dismounted and was walking alongside Annabella, who sat astride the horse. As they plodded along the country lane nearer and nearer the Shawfield Mansion and the beginnings of the Trongate, they could not believe their eyes and ears.

'Gracious heavens!' Annabella gasped. 'Have they all gone stark raving mad?'

Noise filled the air, deafened, stunned them. Every person in Glasgow it seemed had completely abandoned restraint and decorum. Even Letitia Halyburton was out dancing in the streets. Then Annabella's attention was caught by a figure sitting alone on the road close to the wall of the Shawfield Mansion. He was hugging his knees and hiding his face down in his lap.

'Quin?' Annabella shouted. 'Is that Quin?'

Immediately he scrambled to his feet and, seeing who called, jogged towards her.

'Aye, mistress, it's Quin.'

She stared curiously at him for a minute. His face was wet as if he had been weeping. Eventually with a flap of her hand she said:

'What is the meaning of this noise and commotion?'

Quin scratched his head. 'They tell Quin they've killed

thoosands o' Heelanders. But Quin hasn't seen them getting hangit for it.'

Annabella stared round at Nancy.

'Pox on them! They're celebrating Culloden.'

They moved into the joyful, riotous throng and were immediately jostled and pushed and manhandled. Men struggled to pull Nancy away and she clung to the side of the horse and for the first time began to weep. Stumbling along with her face buried against Annabella's leg, her wailing became louder and louder.

'Be quiet, you stupid bitch!' Annabella shouted. 'Get up here beside me.' She gave her a hand and hauled her on to the horse. Then she smashed her foot into the face of one of the men who had been pawing at Nancy before kicking the horse's flanks and yelling it on.

In the path of Annabella's horse people's laughter rapidly changed to screams of panic as they were knocked down and kicked and trampled. From one of the lantern windows Ramsay caught sight of the wild approach of his daughter with a mixture of absolute joy and utter horror. Men and women, most of them too drunk to leap out of the way, were being hurt.

He kept watching, hypnotised by the shocking sight, not only of the injured but of the skirts hitched up to reveal bare legs and thighs, the torn bodice showing flashes of shoulder and bosom, the streaming yellow hair, the beautiful untamed face. He was still standing at the window when his daughter strode into the room. It radiated to life the moment she entered it. Ramsay was so overcome with emotion he could have sobbed out loud. She was his torment, his pride, his shame, his sorrow, his overwhelming, delirious delight.

She tossed her head and looked him straight in the eye.

'Well, Papa, aren't you mightily glad to see me?'

'You've ruined that horse,' he said.

'Fiddlesticks! Big John will see to him. I'm devilish hungry. I haven't eaten for a prodigiously long time.'

'Eat then. I'm away to meet my freends at the tavern. I'll be back in time for the reading. Do you hear me, mistress?'

'Yes, Papa.'

Glowering, his head thrust forward and his hands thumping behind his back, he strode past her and out of the house.

He was too early for his other merchant colleagues but the captains of his ships were waiting in the tavern and soon they had decided that the next day the *Mary Heron* and *The Glasgow Lass* would set sail for Virginia. Shortly afterwards, when through the tavern window Ramsay noticed Gav among the crowd, he sent the tavern-keeper to tell him so that he could be prepared. Then later when Captains Daidles and Kilfuddy were leaving he noticed Gav and a well-dressed young fellow accosting the captains and addressing them very earnestly. He wondered who the well-dressed young fellow was, but the arrival of his friends put Gav and the stranger out of his head.

The Earl of Glendinny, the Reverend Blackadder, the Earl of Locheid, Andrew Cochrane and Willie Halyburton were all out to celebrate and were in a suitably happy and expansive frame of mind. Ramsay felt that now he too had something to be happy about and entered the evening's festivities with unusual gusto. Before a few drinks had passed he was thumping the table and shouting.

'Drink up, gentlemen. I give you good King Geordie!'

'God bless him!' The Reverend Blackadder's eyes rolled back with the whisky.

Willie Halyburton thumped the table and stamped his feet. 'The Duke of Cumberland!'

'Sweet William, God bless him.' The Reverend Blackadder's elbow heaved up and down again.

At the cue of 'Sweet William' they at once burst into the Whig ditty in praise of Cumberland and loudly and lustily they sang it.

'From scourging rebellion and baffling proud France,
Crowned with laurels, behold British William advance,
His triumphs to grace and distinguish the day,
The sun brighter shines and all nature looks gay.

Your glasses charge high, 'tis in brave William's praise,
To his glory your voices, to his glory your voices,
To his glory your voices and instruments raise.

289

In his train see sweet peace, fairest child of the sky,
Every bliss in her smile, every charm in her eye,
While the worst foe to man, that dire fiend Civil War,
Gnashing horrid his teeth, comes fast bound to her care.

Your glasses charge high, 'tis in brave William's praise,
To his glory your voices, to his glory your voices,
To his glory your voices and instruments raise.'

Even the Earl of Locheid joined in the singing, but in a canny
way, chewing at the words with his eyes closed and when he
laughed, and he laughed a lot as the evening's carousal proceeded,
it was carefully contained, with arms pressing against the sides
of his chest and his lips primly closed. All his life he had been a
neat and canny man and no matter how drunk, he had never
been known either to splutter or to spill one drop of whisky.

Ramsay, by this time very drunk indeed, began to roar out
another song.

'There's nowhere a land so fair,
As in Virginia,
So full of song, so free from care,
As in Virginia,
And I believe that happy land,
The Lord's prepared for mortal man,
Is built exactly on the plan,
Of old Virginia.'

They all cheered his rendering and his sentiments and joined
with him in a second rousing chorus.

Bottle after bottle of whisky appeared on the table, was
emptied and knocked aside. Wigs slipped askew, coats hung
loosely from sagging shoulders and feet flopped and fumbled up
on top of the table.

Only the Earl of Locheid remained neatly sitting upright, his
bony fingers curled round his glass like a vulture's claw.

Willie Halyburton swayed nearer to the Earl and peered close
to his face.

'Locheid's looking verra pale.'

'Och, that's no' surprising,' said the Reverend Blackadder.

290

'I noticed him passing ower to the other side to his Maker aboot an hour ago but I didn't like to interrupt the proceedings.'

'Aye, and would you look at that,' Ramsay said in admiration. 'He's never spilled a drop.'

It was now dark outside and all round the Cross in Trongate Street and High Street and Gallowgate Street and Saltmarket Street bonfires blazed and people were carousing and singing and dancing and making love. Lanterns hung from public buildings and every window in the city was illuminated with candles. All through the night the celebrations went on until daylight came and with it hissing swishing rain to douse the fires and send people scattering home.

It was early morning when Gav saw Quin and gave him some bannocks and a lump of cheese and a silver coin he had persuaded from Regina.

'Where were you last night?' he asked. 'I looked on the stairs for you. Were you out at the celebrations?'

Quin rubbed his ear.

'Auld Nick says to Quin, says he, "It's time you were visiting your mither and faither." '

'You went out to the Gallow Moor in the dark?'

'Quin knows the way.'

'Regina and I are riding to Port Glasgow. I'm on my way to meet her now. She's bought a passage to Virginia. After seeing Mistress Annabella ride into the town, she decided the further she was away from her the better.'

Quin cocked his head. 'Gavie's no' going to Virginia.'

'I don't want to be a beggar all my life, Quin, and there's work for me in Virginia.'

'Gavie's no going away.'

Gav squashed downstairs, with Quin jogging after him, rubbing his torn ear and scratching his head and agitating all over.

Big John had the horses saddled up in the back yard. Ramsay had instructed him to ride with Gav to the ship, then bring back his horse. By the time Big John and Gav had mounted, Regina came cantering in to join them.

They grouped together, the horses turning and snorting and

restlessly pawing the ground.

Regina said: 'What the hell are we waiting for?'

Gav looked down at Quin. He was sure he had never, and would never again see anyone so ugly in all his life.

'What'll you do?' he asked in a small voice.

'Who cares?' Regina said.

'You shut your mouth!' Gav cried brokenly. 'Shut your cruel wicked mouth.'

To his horror he could see tears spurting from Quin's one eye and smearing down through the dirt of his face.

Regina said: 'Good God, I didn't know you could cry.'

'Weel, you know noo,' said Quin, and jogged away as fast as he could with his coat-tails and hair flying.

Gav turned on Regina.

'I hate you.'

She shrugged.

'The harder you hate, the better it'll be for you. You'll only get hurt if you're soft. It's a cruel world. Well? Are you going to Virginia or are you not?'

Without another word they guided their horses out of the close and as they passed the Cross to go along Trongate Street, Gav looked back towards the Gallowgate and saw Quin still flying away towards the Gallow Moor crossroads and his 'mither and faither'. It reminded Gav, as his horse clip-clopped away in the opposite direction, that his mother also lay at that lonely crossroads and the pain and tightness in his chest grew unbearable. He spurred his horse on and the other two followed until soon they had left Glasgow far behind them. He wondered if he would ever see it again and now having left it perhaps for ever, it became dear to him for the very first time. The tall tenements, the arched piazzas, the plainstanes, the silver spires, even the back closes stinking with fulzie and the crowded turnpike stairs, etched a warm and urgent and never to be forgotten picture in his memory of home.

He thought of it, saw it in his mind's eye when later he stood on the deck of *The Glasgow Lass* as its sails billowed out and the old ship groaned and creaked away.

Regina stood beside him in her three-cornered hat and smart

cutaway coat, waistcoat and breeches. Her face was a stiff mask in which her green eyes smouldered. But the thumb of one hand was nonchalantly latched in her waistcoat pocket and the other hand rested easily on her sword.

Gav wore smart new clothes too. They looked like a couple of young bucks to be reckoned with. And despite his sadness Gav felt, as he was sure his sister felt too, the first stirrings of excitement as they set off for their strange adventure in a new land.

ROOTS OF BONDAGE

This book is dedicated to my dear American friends
Elizabeth and Amy Turnell

Chapter 1

The merchant ship *The Glasgow Lass* left the Firth of Clyde behind and made for the open sea. Tossing about like a tiny cockleshell in the wide expanse of water, it sometimes disappeared completely from sight as waves swelled high to engulf it. Up it would bob again though, its square sails bravely billowing.

Gav crouched against the bulwarks vomiting into the scuppers, his small freckled face white against his red hair. He longed to die. He wished he had never signed the indenture papers, never heard of tobacco ships or the Virginia plantations. All he wanted was to be back in Glasgow and on good steady land.

He glanced up at his sister, Regina, or Reggie as he was supposed to call her now because she was passing herself as a young gentleman. She was neither help nor comfort any more. Like a stranger and far older than her thirteen years, she stood stiff and controlled, hands clutching at taut perpendicular ropes.

He didn't know what to make of her. Once she had been so gentle and loving to him. They had bickered and quarrelled occasionally, it was true, but no more than was normal for brother and sister.

From the moment they heard that Prince Charles Edward Stuart and his Highland army were about to invade Glasgow, their whole lives had changed.

First their mother had disappeared. Then the beggar Quin had captured them and made them sleep in closes at night and wander the streets with him during the day.

They had tried to return home. Regina, in fact, had managed it at one point but when she came back she said the house had been taken over by the Irish and the Frenchies—Irish and French soldiers who had come with the Highland Army. The French soldiers must have done something terrible to Regina because ever since she had nursed a sick hatred for them. It had been from that time that she had changed.

He squeezed his eyes shut, then blinked to chase away his tears of regret at losing Regina as she used to be. His stomach heaved and his head ached. Never in his wildest dreams had he thought that any ship could roll and toss about so much and be so fearfully noisy. Like a giant basket made of the driest materials, squeaking and creaking and filled with iron tools falling about clanking and banging, it kept up a continuous racket. To escape from the noise and his wretched physical condition, he clung again to thoughts of Glasgow.

Regina had gone to earn money by working for Mistress Annabella, the daughter of tobacco merchant Maister Ramsay, to whom this very ship belonged. Mistress Annabella was a wild and wicked woman. She had followed the Highland army to be with her French lover and she had forced Regina to go with her. They had been at the Battle of Culloden and escaped from it. It was while they were hiding from the Duke of Cumberland's troops that Regina had betrayed Mistress Annabella's French officer.

'I had her Frenchie killed,' Regina told him bitterly and with no sign of regret.

He had not yet recovered from the shock of what Regina had done. Not only had she been responsible for the French officer dying a horrible death at the hands of Cumberland's dragoons, but she had coolly rifled the dragoons' saddlebags while they were committing the terrible deed. She had stolen many gold pieces and jewellery and other precious items.

'It was loot,' she insisted. 'It didn't belong to them.'

Then, on her way back to Glasgow, she had stolen clothes and pistols and other valuables from dead bodies that were, according to her, littered all over the Highlands.

He had not recognized her at first with her auburn hair hidden under a powdered tie-wig and a three-cornered hat. Instead of her striped skirt and green cape, she wore breeches, a long waistcoat and a cutaway coat, and a sword dangled at her hip. He had not known the pale face either with its bitter, twisted mouth. It was her eyes, hard and smouldering, yet still of the most beautiful jewel green, that convinced him, incredible though it seemed, that this smart young buck was actually his sister Regina.

He knew she must have suffered. Terrible stories had been told about the sufferings in the Highlands. But he had suffered too, living with the beggar Quin, sleeping at night in icy cold closes and wandering about the streets during the day nearly starving to death. His mother had been found, wrongfully accused of stealing and hanged, and he and Quin had had the dreadful job of burying her at the Gallows Moor.

He would still be wandering the streets if Maister Ramsay had not given him the chance to go to Virginia as an indentured servant. Regina had paid for a passage and come along too so that she could escape from Mistress Annabella. When he had asked Quin what Mistress Annabella would do to Regina if she caught her, Quin said:

'March her over to the Tolbooth to be hangit. Or kill her herself. Aye, Quin thinks that Mistress Annabella would kill Reggie herself and no' be very dainty aboot it either.'

At least Regina was safe now and when they reached Virginia, no doubt she would find some sort of work if she needed to. Of course she claimed she still had plenty of money and could do whatever she pleased, but he could not be sure if she were telling the truth or not. He wasn't sure of anything about Regina. More than once he had said to her:

'I've never stolen anything or caused anybody to be murdered. Why have you done such terrible things? I don't understand you any more.'

'You're a fool,' was all Regina deigned to reply. 'You've sold yourself to slavery on the Virginia plantations.'

She paid no heed to his protests or his explanations of how Maister Ramsay had stores in Virginia and how he had to help with the bookkeeping and perhaps one day become a Stores' Manager. It was a great opportunity for him. Maister Ramsay had given him the chance after discovering that he had been to school and could read and write and count and speak Latin. Not many children were as clever as him. He had been the cleverest in the whole school. He had even been smarter than Regina and she was older by two years and could read and write too.

But now, crouched against the bulwarks, miserably seasick and wet to the skin with the sea swathing across the deck and sucking back through the scuppers, he didn't feel smart at all. The cloying smell of tar and mildewed canvas wasn't helping his stomach. The sight of other passengers vomiting did nothing to allay his symptoms either.

The other passengers were all women who had been charged with stealing or vagrancy and whose punishment was to be deported to Virginia to work on the plantations. Some had babies in their arms and small children clinging to their skirts.

Some of the women were leaning against the starboard bulwarks weeping helplessly as they watched the shores of Scotland shrink away into the far distance until they disappeared over the horizon. Behind them, inside and underneath the longboat, the farm animals brought aboard for fresh meat and milk cackled and squawked and screeched in a flurry of protest at being pitched about.

Large waves collected, heaved the ship skywards, rushed beneath, then disappeared as rapidly as they'd come while every timber creaked and every sailor hollered. It was some time before Gav recognized one particular voice aimed at the passengers, including himself. It was Mr Gudgeon, the first mate, bawling orders to get below.

Gav staggered to his feet.

'I'm down in the hold,' he told Regina. 'I wish I could stay with you.'

'Stop whining,' Regina said. She had a cabin at the stern of the ship. It was small but at least she had not to crowd in with a lot of strangers.

He flushed angrily.

'I'm not whining. I only thought we should try and stay together because we've only got each other now.'

He tried to walk away with some dignity but was soon toppled from his feet by the tilting deck and had to crawl as best he could towards the steerage hatch. Getting down the ladder was no easy feat either, but with desperate concentration he managed it.

The steerage was a pit of gloom. After the hatches were

battened down, the only light came from one lantern. The dark wooden beams absorbed the fitful yellow light and, screwing up his eyes, he could barely discern the huddled figures of the women and children. Coils of rope, spare sails, old junk and sea charts lay heaped around. He could hear the thick slimy water slopping to and fro in the bilges and every now and again rats' eyes redly flickered. He lowered himself down on to a coil of rigging.

Up on deck, Regina made her way along, with the help of anything steady she could lay her hands on, towards her cabin. It had been the first mate's living space and she had paid him a deal of money for the use of it. He was a greedy man and a bully too, by all accounts, with his coarse, pocked face, red bull neck and a voice like the hull of a boat being scraped over sand.

She felt nauseated, but by sheer will-power controlled the heaving of her stomach. Raindrops furiously pattered the deck, then mixed with hail and blasted in on gusts of wind, snatching her breath away.

But despite the wind and the pitching and tossing of the ship, sailors were springing aloft to shouts from the mate and bosun to furl the royals and top gallant sail and haul up the mainsail. In no time, the little vessel was running before the wind, tearing through the water as if she'd never be able to stop.

Regina did not relax until she had groped her way inside the cabin but, even lying on her berth, she had still to cling on grimly to prevent herself from being flung to the floor. She heard the order passed from the captain to the mate to batten down the hatches, and she wondered how Gav was faring. She knew that what he said was true. They should stick together and she resolved at the first opportunity to ask for Gav to be allowed up to share her accommodation. No doubt more money would accomplish the change. Money could do anything. Money had secured her escape from Glasgow and so saved her life and money would give her a fresh start in the new world.

She felt confident and safe despite the discomforts of the ship and the uneasiness her first glimpse of the vessel's figurehead had inspired. The gaudily painted sculpture, with its bright blue eyes and flowing yellow hair, bore an uncanny resemblance to

Annabella Ramsay. No doubt she, being the owner's daughter, was the 'Glasgow Lass' of the ship's name and also had been the model for its figurehead.

Regina had no wish to be reminded of Mistress Ramsay. Not that she bore the woman any grudge. Mistress Annabella had always been decent enough to her. Indeed, at Culloden she had saved her from an Englishman's sword. No, it had been Mistress Annabella's Frenchie she had hated and feared. She would see him killed again were it possible, her only regret being that she had to leave Glasgow to prevent Mistress Annabella finding her and taking revenge.

Outside, the wind seemed to be abating but she could hear the seamen lustily singing:

> 'Ooh! Haul away from the windy weather, boys,
> Haul away, boys, haul away!
> Ooh, haul away and pull together, boys,
> Haul away, boys, haul away!
> Ooh! Haul away for the merchant's money, boys,
> Haul away, boys, haul away . . .'

Lying clinging with all her might to the sides of her berth, for the ship was still rolling from side to side, she wondered how long the voyage would take. She had been told that a good fast run could make Chesapeake Bay in Virginia in four or five weeks but that the ship was very much at the mercy of the weather—especially the prevailing winds. Ships could be blown a hundred miles or more off course and the journey could take months. Many ships never reached their destination and were wrecked off some unknown rocky shore.

Her heart palpitated at the thought. Her mouth went dry. For the first time the enormity of what she was doing pierced home. The insecurity of the ship, the uncertainty of her future in a strange land, obsessed her. Tales she had heard about women and children sold into slavery and about cannibals filtered back through a mind stiff with fear. She doubted if even money could save her from such horrors but it was the only protection she had. She longed to scramble from the berth and open her sea chest so that she could count yet again the coins that she possessed. She was always counting them, gazing at them, feeling them, listening to the sweet music of them clinking over her fingers like a golden waterfall that never quite succeeded in slaking her thirst.

As soon as the motion of the ship became steadier, she did get up and creaked open the chest, but she was too nervous in case one of the officers or seamen should open the cabin door and discover her secret hoard. After only a few seconds she shut it again. As she looked out of the window, the sea and the horizon swooped high and plunged low and made her nausea return but she determined to overcome it and left the cabin for a breath of fresh air.

Stepping out on deck, she was hailed by the captain who was standing on the poop with an eyeglass tucked under his arm. He was a large man with a plump belly straining over his breeches and out of his blue coat. He was throttled by a huge black stock and his white hair, topped with a three-cornered hat, was tied back in a black bow.

'Found your sea-legs yet, Master Chisholm?' he called.

She went up to join him.

'I feel better now that the storm has abated, sir.'

He laughed.

'Storm? Storm? Only a merry breeze, boy. Wait a wee. Wait a wee. Ready for your dinner, eh? Andra's putting it on the cuddy table right now, I'll wager.'

'Andra?'

'Andra Doone, oor cook.'

Suddenly there was a cry of 'Sail-ho!'

Captain Kilfuddy raised his eyeglass.

'Aye. Looks like a fine brig.'

Swinging round Regina saw a ship come bowing and curvetting and plunging and rearing towards them.

'Have the trumpet brought up, Mr Gudgeon!' the captain called and the chief mate relayed the order in a louder, harsher tone. Soon the long speaking trumpet was brought up and the signal flags got ready in case they only managed to get near enough for a 'bunting talk'. But Captain Kilfuddy said he hoped to board her. To his obvious disappointment, however, he was unable to do this. Although the other ship was skilfully steered within twenty yards of *The Glasgow Lass*, both vessels were making a fair wind and scudding along at eight knots an hour. All the two captains could do was shout to each other.

'Whence come?'

'Where bound for?'

She was the ship *Annie Cruthers* of Glasgow bound for the West Indies.

A wave of the hand and they were gone. Regina watched the vessel as it shrank away and finally faded from sight. Her uneasiness had returned with the talk of boarding. A terrible thought struck her. What if Mistress Annabella had been on that ship?

But she strangled the thought at birth. Mistress Annabella had no idea where she was. Only the beggar, Quin, and Gav knew that she had left on board ship and dressed as a boy. Anyway, Maister Ramsay would never allow his precious daughter to stravaig away again. Not after her last adventure in the Highlands. Gav had told her that the man had been nearly demented with worry. Anyway, Mistress Annabella had gone to the Highlands under the protection of her precious Frenchie. She would never dare leave Glasgow on her own and on a long and perilous journey to Virginia, even if she wanted to.

Regina was convinced of this. Yet, as four bells were rung, heralding six o'clock and the evening meal, she went down to the cuddy absent-mindedly.

She was remembering Culloden. She was standing on the verge of the moor helplessly watching as the defeated Highland army streamed away in all directions pursued by Cumberland's troops. She had been hysterical with fear as one of the soldiers, his sword already dripping with blood, lunged towards her. Mistress Annabella's pistol had dropped him in his tracks.

'Up behind me!' she'd shouted, forcing her snorting and squealing horse over bodies and between Highlanders and Englishmen, slashing at one another. 'Regina, damn you. Mount behind me, I said.'

Mistress Annabella had eventually reached down and grabbed her by the arm and hauled her up. She'd clung frantically round

Annabella's waist, pressed her face into her back, and cried out:

'Oh, mistress, gallop away. Gallop away.'

But her pleas had been ignored.

'Where are the French? Can you see them?'

'To the devil with the French, mistress,' she had wept. 'Let us away to Glasgow where we belong.'

'I belong with my Frenchman. If he goes to the devil, girl, that's where I go too!'

Then she suddenly spurred the horse forward. She had seen, struggling across the river in the distance, what was left of her Frenchman's company.

Kicking the horse's flanks, she shouted it on.

The river was swollen with the recent heavy rain. It was like a raging torrent and it had already swallowed Highlanders and the pursuing English.

Regina went icy cold remembering the terror of it and the way Mistress Annabella forced the horse, whinnying with fright, to flounder in. It had been a nightmare struggle and only by sheer force of will had they held on until the horse stumbled out on the opposite bank.

Mistress Annabella was a wild and determined woman. But her merchant papa was a stubborn and powerful man. He was going to marry her off to the minister, she'd heard.

Regina smiled grimly to herself. Pity the poor preacher!

Chapter 2

'Papa, how can you use me so cruelly?' Annabella's eyes strained wide in an effort to challenge the existence of tears. Yet they kept misting sight and spilling over. Ashamed, she tossed her head and flicked at them with her fingers. 'You know I cannot thole the obnoxious man.'

'The match is for your own good,' Ramsay growled. 'You need a settling influence. As God's my witness, I've tried, Annabella. But you're a wicked, wayward lassie. I've obviously failed you.'

'No, no, Papa.' Even though she was despondent her voice remained as light as thistledown.

'Aye, so. It's the truth and I don't mind admitting it. But the minister's a dedicated man of God. He'll soon squash you down.'

'Merciful heavens! Is that what you want for me, Papa? To be miserable and cast down?'

'I want you to walk in the way of the Lord and you've never learned how to do that. For all the teaching you've had here. For all the readings I've given and all the times I've questioned you on your catechisms. Well, we'll see what the minister can do now.'

'That long visaged melancholy idiot will do nothing but drive me mad.'

Her father suddenly crashed a fist down on the oval table in the centre of the room at which they were both sitting.

'Watch your tongue, mistress. It was a flogging offence in my day to speak ill of the minister and you could still be punished.'

'Fiddlesticks!' She bounced from her chair, ringlets and skirts flying. Restlessly she began pacing the room. She was wearing a dress the colour of autumn leaves, with a low-cut front that revealed the bulge of her breasts. Creamy lace frothed from the front and from the elbows. Her hair, smoothed back from her face and hanging in curls, sparkled like sunshine above the coppery-coloured dress. 'Anyway, sir,' she said, 'there is no punishment more vile than being married to the Reverend Mr Blackadder.'

Ramsay had the open Bible before him and looked as stern as any minister. But his enormous curly black wig, the three-cornered hat which he always wore in the house and the richness of his satin waistcoat stamped him for what he was—a wealthy tobacco merchant.

He had just dined on broth and salt beef and a sup of ale followed by a reading from the good book for Annabella's benefit. Normally he only gave a reading first thing in the morning and last thing at night but since Annabella's recent sinful behaviour, he felt it necessary to attend even more conscientiously to her spiritual welfare. Now he said,

'You're wrong there, mistress. The Lord would guide me in many ways of chastisement and paths down which to guide you so you could rid yourself of your wicked pride and thrawnness. No more gold pieces for you, mistress. No more fine clothes and falderals like sedan chairs when you go out. No more of these creams and potions you plaster on your face.'

Annabella stamped her foot but her voice betrayed concern as well as temper.

'Do not vex me too much, sir. You know perfectly well that I am sorely tried at times for want of clothes and falderals, as you call them, that befit a lady of my position. As for creams and potions, if I painted my face as I have heard it said English ladies do, then you might have cause for complaint. But I do not. A little skin lubrication occasionally to protect myself from the ravages of a Scottish climate, that is all I have ever used. And the cream is made very cheaply by Nancy and myself.'

'Aye, well you can do without her for a start.'

'You cannot deprive me of a maid, sir.'

'Oh?' Ramsay raised a bushy brow. 'Can I no'?'

'It is unthinkable. We have not enough servants as it is. There is only Big John and Nancy and she complains enough about our lack of a washerwoman. You must employ more servants, not less.'

307

He lowered his brows again and his voice acquired an acid tone.

'I can do whatsoever I choose, mistress, and I choose to have less.'

'But Papa. Who will do my hair and wash the floors and empty the chamberpots?'

'You will. And everything else that needs done. Maybe you've been such easy prey to the devil because you've had too much time on your hands. And you've been too much exposed to temptation. That has got to be changed and if you're going to remain in my care it behoves me to see to it. You'll never put a step out of this house without a chaperon in future. Either myself or Letitia Halyburton will accompany you. And when you're not attending to household duties, you will read this Bible and write out your catechisms. Evenings we'll spend in readings and in prayer.'

Annabella came back to the table and sat down. The table was in her bedroom where they ate and sat and entertained. It was a long, low-ceilinged room with white plastered walls, a bare wooden floor, and a hole-in-the-wall bed draped with curtains the colour of claret and a pink satin valance. When the bed drapes were closed they were flush with the walls, a warm splash of colour against the white that completely hid the set-in bed. Opposite the bed was the large open fire with an easy chair positioned on either side. Annabella's own chair was covered in red silk velvet. The one her father sat in was bigger and more solid, like himself. It was patterned with large flowers in maroon and blue on a fawn background and had wings and rolled arms.

The curtains at the window were the same purplish red as the bed-drapes but they gleamed lighter and warmer like a sunset in the reflection of the fire. The fire crackled, sending tongues of orange darting across the floor and ceiling, jerking them closer together. On the oval table in the centre of the room a candle had been lit to allow Ramsay to read the spidery print of the Bible. It made a gentler glow, its amber flame bowing and curtsying in the draught.

Most Glasgow families dined and entertained in their main bedroom, even those who had a dining-room. A dining-room was never aired or used unless on very special occasions when guests came from afar, or if there wasn't enough room in the main bedroom.

'Oh Papa,' Annabella sighed. She knew him well enough to realise that he would carry out his threats to the letter. He was a dour, determined man and many a long, weary, punishing hour she had spent with him in prayer in this shadowy room with its heavy-hanging ceiling beams. It was the thought of endless Bible readings, catechisms and prayers that settled the issue, not the indignity of menial work. If forced to she would have hitched up her skirts and washed the floors and to hell with him. But she needed to be allowed some freedom to enjoy life elsewhere to make up for the hardships of home. She couldn't thole being a prisoner of prayer as well.

She could manage the minister. It was monstrous and damnable to be married to such a man but at least she would not be a prisoner in his house. More than likely he would be drunk half the time and not know where she was or what she was doing.

She made one more attempt to persuade her father, however.

'Don't you think I've been punished enough? I dearly loved Monsieur Lavelle and I saw him horribly killed before my eyes.' Her chin tipped up but she looked away.

'He died in my arms, Papa. I was mightily distressed.'

It was no pretence. She still had nightmares about that terrible day during the time of the uprising when they had been hiding in a deserted house and Nancy had come running to warn of a party of dragoons approaching. Jean-Paul had been wounded in the leg but she had managed to help him through to the kitchen and secrete him in a cupboard. Then she'd hurried back to meet the dragoons at the door of the house. With her head in the air, she had raked them with a cool impudent stare.

'Have you any food with you, gentlemen?' she'd inquired. 'I and my servant are prodigiously hungry. We have journeyed all the way from Glasgow to visit friends and this is what we find. A house empty of both people and sustenance. I have searched every cupboard and I'm damned if I can find a crumb.'

One of the men had lumbered forward and she had drawn a pistol from her dress and warned him.

'Careful, sir, do not make a mistake you will regret. For one thing, I am a Whig and a Hanoverian. For another my father is a wealthy merchant and a friend of the Provost of Glasgow and many other mightily influential gentlemen who could easily have you hanged.'

The man sheepishly drew back and she had thought everything would be well when suddenly she heard the voice of her other servant, Regina Chisholm. Never to her dying day would she forget the sound of it or the words uttered with such callous deliberation.

'It's true what she says. She is of important and wealthy Whig people. But there is a Frenchman who is for the Prince.'

She still crumpled inside with terror at the memory of the words. She had immediately pushed the gun into Regina's hands and cried out.

'If you hate me so much—shoot me! But for pity's sake say no more!'

'It's not you that I hate, mistress,' Regina said.

'Where is the Frenchman?' the trooper shouted and his companions crowded eagerly forward. 'We can have some sport with him.'

'Regina, no.' She had flung herself on her knees in front of the girl. 'Oh, please. Oh, Regina. Regina, I'm begging you.'

But all her entreaties were to no avail.

'You'll find him through that door in the kitchen cupboard,' Regina said.

Ramsay's voice growled through Annabella's grief.

'The Lord's ways are verra strange and awesome at times. But we maun accept them with good grace.'

'Not the Lord's way, Papa.' She picked at the burnished folds of her dress, eyes lowered so that he could not see the expression in them. 'It was that wicked girl who caused Jean-Paul's death. But she'll need the Lord's help when I find her.'

'You may as weel put the lassie out of your mind. God alone knows where she is now.'

'She was making for Glasgow. Highland people I questioned saw her riding south.'

'Aye, weel, you've looked and she's no' here.'

'I'll find her. The beggar Quin might know.'

'He's been banished from the town long since.'

'I'll find her.'

Ramsay half rose, pushing his face closer to hers. She did not raise her eyes but could see the curls of his wig, and his neck-linen like snow above the dark glimmer of his satin waistcoat.

'You'll do as you're bid and put the lassie out of your mind. Finding her would only mean another bloody murder—for you're capable of such wickedness, Annabella. That's what worries me and obliges me to trust the saving of you to the minister.' He reached for his coat and, after donning it, swirled on his scarlet cloak. 'I'm away back to the counting house. I'll be seeing Blackadder in the tavern tonight and we'll fix a date.'

Annabella sat listening to the heavy thump of his feet leave the bedroom, cross the lobby and echo away down the tenement stairs. It took all her courage and will-power to prevent herself from crumpling over the table and indulging in a wild paroxysm of weeping. Fighting with her trembling lips, she called out.

'Nancy! Nancy, damn you, where are you hiding yourself now?'

The maid sauntered into the room and stood, black hair straggling over one shoulder, hands on hips. Her white shirt hung loose revealing the creamy skin of her shoulders and most of her breasts.

'I wasn't hiding.' Her voice had a husky provocative quality that matched her smouldering violet eyes.

'Don't contradict me, you impudent baggage. I've enough to put up with without you. Indeed, misfortunes appear to be overwhelming me.'

'What now?'

'Papa is setting the date for my marriage to the minister. I'm too agitated for words.'

Nancy shrugged.

'He's got a nice house round in the Briggait.'

'I like the house well enough. It's the ugly black crow that lives in it I'm complaining about.'

Laughter made a gurgling noise in Nancy's throat, and immediately Annabella grabbed a fan lying nearby and sent it

311

flying through the air.

'Devil choke you! This is no laughing matter. It's a dastardly outrage. I would have none of it had Papa not threatened to have me cruelly confined.'

Nancy picked up the fan and, all the time admiring and fingering its jewel colours, she went over, hips swaying, to where Annabella sat.

'You could do worse.'

'Worse?' Annabella squealed. 'Gracious heavens, have you gone mad? How worse could anyone get?'

Reluctantly returning the fan, Nancy shrugged again.

'I don't think he'll beat you or misuse you.'

Annabella rolled her eyes.

'Lord's sakes. Better if he did. Anything would be better than having to listen to his long and heavy preaching for the rest of my life. It's bad enough on Sunday. When he's not moaning and weeping and wringing his hands, he's caterwauling like an old tom cat.'

'You know fine you won't listen to him.'

'Or he's so prodigiously intoxicated he can't stand.'

'There's nothing wrong with a man who can take a good dram.'

'Damn it, Nancy, whose side are you on?'

'There's no use crying over spilt milk. You might as well make the best of it. Do you want to take the air? It's quite a nice day outside and a wee turn about the streets might cheer you.'

Annabella grabbed up her fan and agitated it in front of her face, creating a rainbow of colour.

'No, I'm too vexed to go abroad today. My head pains me. I think I'll lie on top of the bed and see if I can sleep.'

'Will I make you a cup of chocolate?'

'Oh, very well.'

She flounced over and through the curtains of the hole-in-the-wall bed. There she lay wide awake and in a tremble on top of the salmon-coloured bedspread.

'Pox on the bloody minister,' she kept thinking. 'Pox on him! Pox on him!'

312

Chapter 3

Jemmy Ducks looked after the animals that were brought on board to provide milk and fresh meat. He was a lean, leathery man with ears like wings and eyes that protruded as if constantly startled. His left leg had been smashed years ago by a fall from the main mast and it dragged uselessly as he walked. But he could hop about at no mean speed when he had to, for instance, when he was chasing the hens and ducks and goats and pigs about the deck in order to catch them and make them snug for the night.

The hull of the longboat was nearly hidden by temporary wooden erections that housed the animals and inside it were the hen coops. But as Jemmy sat talking to Gav the pigs and goats were rooting busily on the deck between the poop and the foc'stle and the ducks and geese were enjoying themselves paddling in the wash about the lee scuppers.

'I've got to keep a weather eye on them hogs, Gav. A very weather eye.' Jemmy pointed to one of his bulbous eyes as he spoke. 'After a few weeks afloat them hogs are apt to develop a taste for a live leg of mutton.'

'They attack the sheep?'

'Not that I blames them.' Jemmy hastened to the defence of the pigs. 'I defies anyone to point the finger at them hogs. Them hogs gets hungry same as anyone else.' He scratched indignantly under the arm of his red shirt and then attacked his head making his pigtail dance up his back. 'No, no, Gav, I defies them. Tell me, I asks, what do you do when you're hungry? Why, I'll tell you, I says, and I told them. You bash their brains in with one of them belaying pins. Then you gobbles them up, legs and trotters, brains and all.' He sighed. 'And them's such cheerful creatures, Gav. Hogs are happy at sea.'

Gav looked doubtful. The pigs were stuttering about the small deck like drunk men in a hurry. As the ship rolled to one side, they scampered to the other, their trotters scraping and slithering. They kept getting in the way of the seamen too and one man, getting harassed beyond endurance, removed the offending animal with a mighty kick. Immediately Jemmy scrambled up angrily shaking his fist.

'Damn your eyes! That's old George you're mauling aft.' To Gav he added: 'George is my favourite. I likes them all but George is the clever one, Gav. I teaches him tricks. I dreads the day when they'll come and shatter George's headrails. They says I gets too partial towards them animals, Gav. And they're right. Many's the time after dinner I've felt as though I've eaten an old messmate.'

'The goats seem cleverer at balancing,' Gav said.

'You're right there, Gav, and I can't deny it. Them goats have marvellous sea-legs. And never was a beast easier pleased with his vittles. Them goats smacks their lips over anything from shavings from Chips the carpenter's berth to old newspapers or logbooks.'

Gav looked impressed and Jemmy continued enthusiastically.

'Great old sea-dogs them goats are. Many's a hard gale they've weathered.'

'I hope we don't have any gales before we get to Virginia.'

'We're bounds to get them, Gav. Lots of them. There's no denying it.'

'Oh, well,' Gav made a show of nonchalance; 'I think I'll take a turn about the deck and stretch my legs while I can.' He struggled to his feet. 'Have you seen my . . . my cousin, Reggie, anywhere?'

'I've come athwart him, but not spoke him. He's not a friendly young salt like yourself, Gav, and I don't minds saying it.'

Jemmy's bulbous eyes followed Gav as he tried to adapt his steps to the easy roll of the ship as she met the slow, steady swell. The deck was an untidy crush of women and children, pigs, goats, sheep, geese and ducks. The only part of the ship with a little free space was the high poop deck where Captain Kilfuddy was taking the air by pacing back and forth. For a minute or two Gav clung to the bulwarks and gazed admiringly up at the old man.

He was strutting to and fro with his hands clenched behind his back, his barrel belly jutting forward and his three-cornered hat squashed well down on his brow. Suddenly he stopped, peered upwards, then said to the mate:

'Hands aloft to trim the topsails, Mr Gudgeon.'

The mate bawled down to the bosun who, in turn, shouted at the men, who leapt immediately to the rigging.

Gav watched, fascinated and overawed by their courage as they clambered up shrouds and along the yardarms until they were like flies against a swinging sky. It was amazing how different seamen were to men on land. It wasn't only their courage and capacity for hard work. They even looked different. Some were small, some tall, some lean, some hefty but they all had a drooping posture, their corded neck muscles disguising the breadth of their tapering shoulders. Their heads sunk low and seemed to jut from their chests, bowed by years of crouching in the foc'stle. They had square hands lumpy with callouses, surmounted by small, torn, dirty nails stained with tobacco and tar. Across the steel-like bands of muscle in their forearms were rope burns from sheets ripped from their grasp by the power of storms. Their gait was a swinging lope accompanied by the heavy fleshy slap of naked feet on their natural environment, the wooden deck of a sailing ship. They were almost like throwbacks to earlier men, people adapted for this special way of life.

The captain addressed the mate again and the mate relayed the order through the bosun to the men who started pulling on ropes and singing cheerily.

'Oh, they call me hanging Johnny,
Away, boys, away,
They says I hangs for money,
Oh, hang, boys, hang.
And first I hanged me daddy,
Away, boys, away,
And first I hanged me daddy,
Oh, hang, boys, hang.
And then I hanged me mother,
Away, boys, away,

315

Me sister and me brother,
Oh, hang, boys, hang . . .'

A sudden lump in Gav's throat pained him so much it made his eyes water. The hanging shanty reminded him of his mother and, turning away from the poop deck, he groped along towards the bows of the ship, trying not to listen.

On the foc'stle some off duty sailors were lighting their pipes from the wick kept there closely guarded by a sentry because fire was an ever present danger on board. 'Chips' the carpenter was sitting enjoying a smoke. So was Andra Doone, the cook.

'Have you seen my cousin Reggie?' he asked Andra, a small fat man with a patch over one eye and a twisted back that kept one of his shoulders permanently hunched high against his ear.

Gav had learned that cooks on board ship and carpenters and the man who looked after the animals were always called 'idlers' by the seamen and, with the exception of the carpenter, were usually men with some sort of injury or deformity.

Andra sucked deeply at his pipe. He was even more superstitious than the rest of the men and saw ominous signs in the most innocent events.

'That's a strange thing. He's been seeking you. And you've been seeking him. And neither of you meeting. It could be a sign the ship's going to blow off course.'

'Where is he now?' Gav asked, impatient to take his leave because the cook always made him feel apprehensive.

'Well,' Andra took another slow thoughtful suck. 'If you don't find him in the cuddy, I reckon he's lost.'

As fast as he could Gav made his way back to the stern and into the low-ceilinged room where the officers and cabin passengers had their meals. In the centre of the room stood a table with a bench at either side, all secured to the floor. A window looked out of the stern of the ship and there were two berths on each of the walls at right angles to the window. These berths were usually occupied by wealthy passengers but, apart from Regina, the only passengers on this voyage were steerage ones like himself.

Regina sat like a carved statue on one of the benches. She was

316

a slight figure in a green coat with gold buttons and fawn lace cascading at her throat and cuffs.

'Where the hell have you been hiding yourself?' she demanded. 'We should stick together, you said. We've only got each other now, you said.'

'I wasn't hiding. I was just talking to Jemmy Ducks.'

A nerve pulled at Regina's cheek, tightening her mouth.

'What a mess you're in. Where are your fine new clothes?'

'In my sea-chest.' He gazed defensively at the too big jacket his mother had once bought from a rag woman. The sleeves were so long they hid his hands and the shoulders drooped low. His hat had come from the same source and was also several sizes too large but his thick mop of curls prevented it from flopping down over his face. 'There's nothing wrong with these for on board ship. I want to keep my new breeches and jacket for when we arrive at Virginia.'

Before he could say any more he was startled by the chief mate, Mr Gudgeon, bursting into the cabin, grabbing him by the ear and jerking him outside.

'You listen to me, m'lad. It's the steerage for landlubber tramps like you. If you come near the poop, the quarterdeck or the cuddy again, I'll throw you over the side.' He gave Gav's ear a twist, making him yelp with pain. 'Are you listening, lad? Do you know what'll happen to you if I throw you over the side? The sharks'll have you. They'll have you, m'lad.'

With a punch he sent Gav hurtling down to land on his face on the main deck. Trying to suppress tears of pain and humiliation, Gav picked himself up. Blood trickled from his nose and seeped into his mouth as Jemmy Ducks came limping alongside him.

'Cheerily, shipmate. Cheerily. He's mauled you a little fore and aft but at least he hasn't sent you to the bilboes. If you splashes your face in the scuppers, I dare say you'll survive.'

Gav glanced back and saw Regina standing at the door of the cuddy, her face expressionless. He felt broken-hearted and allowed himself to be led away by Jemmy without protest.

He remembered the time when Regina and he would have braved anything to protect each other from harm. He remembered how, hand in hand, they used to grope their way to and from school on dark winter mornings and nights. He remembered how she clutched him close to her as they passed the bridge over the river Clyde. She knew he was afraid of the lepers who floated across from the Gorbals hospital like ghosts in their hooded cloaks, their clappers eerily echoing. He remembered how she shielded him from the prancing horses in Trongate Street and Blind Jinky's snarling dog in Tannery Wynd where they had once lived.

Not that he had been a coward. There wasn't a boy in the school he hadn't fought and beaten. Or if a crowd of boys set upon him, as they often did because of his red hair like his Highland grandfather, he went down fighting and he never cried.

'Whig pigs!' he used to call them. But it didn't seem to matter any more about Whigs or Jacobites. Prince Charles and his Highland army had gone. Now he and Regina had left Glasgow too and everything, including Regina, was different. He felt at a loss. He didn't know how to cope on his own in this new situation.

Jemmy Ducks drew him down beside the longboat.

'We all knows Mr Gudgeon, Gav. And the quicker you knows him, the better.' He pushed his big-eyed face closer to the child's smaller bloodied one. 'There's no denying that Mr Gudgeon stows away more grog than he can steadily carry. So you heeds what I says and steer clear of him, eh?'

'I was just trying to see my . . . I was just trying to see Reggie.'

'Not that I blames you, Gav. No, no. But the poop's the poop and the foc'stle the foc'stle. And if you goes up there again, he'll have you, Gav. What I says is, if you don't steer clear of him he'll have you. Mr Gudgeon always has to have somebody.'

Remembering what the chief mate had said about throwing him to the sharks, Gav's chest tightened with anxiety.

'I'll try,' he managed shakily. 'But I wish I could get speaking to Reggie.'

Then, as if to prove Jemmy's point, there was a sudden fracas on the deck and Mr Gudgeon was seen striking Mr Jubb, the second mate, over and over again on the face. The latter, a slender, blond-haired man, was not retaliating but trying to retain some sort of dignity while attempting to escape. Mr Gudgeon was lurching after him from side to side of the deck with poultry and feathers flying around them.

'If I say you were late on watch, Mr Jubb,' he was roaring, 'you were late on watch. I'll have none of your bloody jaw, sir.'

Animals squawked and women screamed but Mr Jubb never uttered a sound.

'Why doesn't he say something or do something to defend himself?' Gav asked Jemmy.

'I'll tells you why, Gav. I'll tells you. If Mr Jubb returns them blows, he's put in irons. Yes, it's down in the bilboes for him.'

The Captain called over all the rabble.

'Mr Gudgeon! Mr Gudgeon, sir! Will ye come aft? You too, Mr Jubb.'

'The captain's the man to sort them out. That's when old Captain Kilfuddy's himself. But I'll tells you something else you oughts to know. Sometimes the captain's not himself.'

'What do you mean?'

'I means what I says, Gav. Sometimes the captain's himself.' Jemmy tapped his head significantly each time he said the word. 'And in charge. And sometimes he's not himself. And when he's not himself, he's not in charge. Now do you gets my meaning?'

Gav nodded uncertainly. Darkness was beginning to creep around and he was far from happy. Apart from missing Regina, he felt worried about how to keep out of Mr Gudgeon's way. It had been bad enough trying to hide from enemies in Glasgow with its many closes and wynds, but the ship was tiny in comparison, a cramped dangerous place from which there was no escape. He realized the safest place for him was probably the steerage but it was a terrible thought to go down to that stinking hold to lie in the gloom with rats scuffling over him.

The night before he had wakened to the sound of a gentle rustling. Then, by the feeble light of the lantern, he'd seen a monster rat jump from one of the sea-chests and walk towards where he was huddled against the bulkhead. Too terrified to move in case it would bite, willing himself not to cry out and waken the women and younger children, he lay in agony watching it climb over his bare feet. He could feel its scratching nails on his skin. It made its way up one side of him and then, crossing where his head was pillowed, its progress was hindered by an entanglement in his hair.

Tears and sweat streamed from his face and it took all his courage to refrain from crying out. It seemed an age before the rat freed itself from his curls and walked down the other side of him and away.

Afterwards he'd sobbed himself to sleep, repeating Regina's name over and over again as if believing that somehow the broken-hearted repetition of the word must reach her.

'Where do you sleep?' he asked Jemmy Ducks.

'I sleeps with the rest of the crew in the foc'stle, Gav. What makes you ask?'

'Can I stay with you? I don't like it down in that steerage place. Can I sleep in the foc'stle with you, Jemmy? I won't take up much room or be any trouble. Please?'

Jemmy scratched his head, making his pigtail jig about.

'If you asks me, Gav, the foc'stle's no better a place than the steerage. Not that I blames you for not liking it. I defies anyone to like it. No, no, I defies them. But the foc'stle's no better, that's what I says.'

'But I'd be with you. You're my friend, aren't you? And friends should stick together?'

Jemmy looked taken aback. All eyes and ears, he stared at Gav. Eventually he said:

'You're right, Gav. And I can't deny it. Them's true words you spoke.'

Gav brightened.

'I can come with you?'

'I've work to do first. Them animals have to be rounded up and made snug. You'd best keep out of sight until I'm ready. Or stow yourself away in the foc'stle when Mr Gudgeon's not looking and I'll meets you there later.'

Gav nodded. Then, after Jemmy hopped away, it occurred to him that just in case Regina tried to get in touch, he ought to tell her that he was changing to the foc'stle. Struggling to his feet, he peered cautiously around. The moon was half-hidden by small white clouds and the sails stood out like silhouettes. The ship seemed to be in the exact centre of an empty circle of shimmering ocean. It was quiet on board except for the usual straining and groaning of wooden spars rubbing together. He hesitated, wondering if he dared go right aft where Regina's cabin was situated. Probably it would be Mr Jubb who was on watch now and it would be all right. Still, he couldn't be sure and he eventually decided to make straight for the foc'stle.

It turned out to be a small dark cave right up in the bows with no warmth and no light except that of the moon glistening through the square scuttle. Triangular in shape, it was full of vague huddles of men, ropes and sails. It stank frowstily of bilge water, sweat, tar and mildew, and by the feel of the slushy planks of the floor, it had never been dry for years and would never dry again. Everywhere there was water.

Gav shivered. It was very dark and cold and he wished that Jemmy would come. Dim outlines of sleeping sailors gave him scant comfort and no desire to move away from the path of grey light afforded by the scuttle. But he was tired and the ship was beginning to roll and heave about, making it difficult for him to stand. Groping to one side, he found a coil of rope and lay down on it and before long he had to cling to it as best as he was able because of the increasing movement of the ship.

Then suddenly the dark shadow of a head appeared at the scuttle and the bosun's voice shouted.

'All hands ahoy! Tumble up here and take in sail!'

Men fell about and struggled into clothes and rushed for the ladder and in a matter of minutes, Gav was alone. He felt frightened by the pitching of the vessel, the increasing anger of the wind and the lightning that had begun to sizzle and flash. At one point, he cried out loud as the ship lurched so far to one side he thought it would never rise again.

The men were making a terrible noise on deck too. He could hear the loud and repeated orders of the mate, the heavy tramping of feet and the creaking of blocks.

Unable to stand being on his own any longer, he scrambled up and tried to reach the ladder to the scuttle. But it took several

321

terrifying minutes of being tossed from one side of the foc'stle to the other before he finally grabbed the ladder, clung on, then slowly edged his way upwards.

Chapter 4

'Hear ye, hear ye goodfolk o' the toon,
There's going to be a horse fair held right soon,
Along the Trongate they'll be put through their paces,
Come along tomorrow and see the races.
Ride the beast first to put him to test,
Before ye buy make sure it's the best.'

Moothy McMurdo clanged his bell as he strolled along, his tattered green frockcoat flapping in the breeze and showing a wide expanse of orange breeches. His cocked hat was jammed forward on a head flung back to give full range to his great bell-like voice.

'To dance to there will be penny reels,
Tents where they'll sell cheap whisky,
A fiddler will help ye kick up yer heels,
No' just horses will be frisky.'

Annabella watched McMurdo from the window of her bedroom. The Ramsay tenement, known as The Old Coffee House Land, was situated at the corner of Saltmarket Street and Trongate Street and it commanded an excellent view of the business centre and the market place where four main streets intersected. Trongate Street ran from the west, Gallowgate Street from the east, High Street from the north and Saltmarket from the south and the River Clyde.

On the corner of the building there was a lantern-shaped projection above one of the arches that opened into shops and warerooms below. This lantern-shaped projection meant an extra dimension to Annabella's room and gave it three windows, each with a different view. It was through the one facing into Trongate Street that she was watching Moothy McMurdo go shouting and swinging his bell.

She sighed and turned to Nancy who was washing the floor in a leisurely fashion, hands on hips, bare feet shuffling a wet

323

cloth around, red and white striped petticoats swinging.

'At least the horse market will be a diversion. I have persuaded Papa, not without some difficulty I confess, to promise that a horse can be part of my dowry and that I will be allowed to choose it myself.'

'The date's fixed then?'

'Yes, more's the pity. The hateful calamity will be in two weeks' time.'

Nancy stopped for a moment to give her a piercing look.

'Does it really bother you that much?'

'Gracious heavens, Nancy. Wouldn't it bother you? I try to keep my courage up. I try to be of good cheer. I've never believed in wasting time with fruitless lamentations but oh, the minister, Nancy. Of all the men in Glasgow, why did it have to be him?'

'The maister's told you why often enough.'

'Oh yes, he wants my spirit broken. He wants to see me a quiet wee, obedient wee, douce wee minister's wife. Well, wife I will be, but quiet, obedient and douce I certainly will not!'

With a small smile Nancy continued her lazy shuffle.

Annabella bristled.

'What are you smirking for? You surely don't think I'd let such a man as the minister get the better of me?'

'No, mistress. I was only thinking that the Reverend Mr Blackadder doesn't know what's afore him. It's almost possible to feel sorry for the poor man in his innocence.'

A trill of laughter took Annabella aback. Hastily she stifled it with her fan.

'Losh sakes, don't make me laugh. It's no laughing matter.'

Tears had in fact been fast building up inside her and threatened at any time to flood out and drown the whole preposterous idea of marriage to Blackadder. Yet at the same time she longed to laugh. Laughter, like her energy for enjoying life, strained for release. A deeper sadness remained in secret places. There were still times alone in bed at night, when she wept for Jean-Paul Lavelle. But his death was too terrible to be kept at the forefront of her mind. She locked it away along with the emotions it aroused and she as seldom as possible allowed herself to look at it. At the best of times she was an impatient young woman with little, if any, concentration. Neither was it in her nature to be morose, and despite the ravages of emotions like grief and vengeance, a mischievous butterfly kept rising up and fluttering about inside her.

'But as you say,' she added, with a frisk of her fan, 'I might as well try and make the best of it. I'll set to as soon as possible and brighten up that gloomy house of his. It's commodious enough but sadly in need of new curtains and cushions and the like.'

'Don't forget the minister's not a wealthy man like your father.'

'If he can't afford me, he should never have entertained the idea of making me his wife. I'll fly into a pretty passion, I can tell you, if he denies me a few yards of silks and velvets.'

'I suppose the maister won't see you stuck.'

'He's bringing Blackadder home with him today so you'd better tell Big John to get the whisky bottles lined up.'

Nancy giggled.

'I wonder if he'll be as drunk as usual on his wedding night.'

'If he does, he'll never catch me. I'm a lot more nimble than him even when he's sober.'

Another noisy character was now making his way along the Trongate. He was a tall angular man, hung about from top to toe with clanking, jangling kitchen utensils and he was calling out:

'Roasting-jacks and toasting-forks!'

He rolled the initial 'R' so long and loudly that it echoed down the streets like a clap of thunder. It had been raining earlier and the rutted earth of the Trongate looked as if it were dotted with sparkling pier glasses. The roasting-jack man was heedlessly trudging them and getting his bare feet and breeches soaked.

Rain had also polished the Tolbooth across the road. Annabella stared idly at it, wondering if there were any prisoners inside. Sometimes passers-by could hear them groaning. At other times, hands could be seen straining out through the bars appealing for food, or for money with which to bribe the guards.

It was a huge building of five storeys with barred windows on each floor. Its principal front was on the Trongate but a portion of it looked onto the High Street. There was also a crown-topped steeple that jutted out a few feet and had a special entrance guarded by a half-door with spikes on top, and a sharp-eyed turnkey.

The main entrance was up the outside stair, called the hanging stair, to the door on the outside landing or balcony. It was here that the gallows were set up when there was a hanging. The stocks and the pillory were in front of the Tolbooth too and the Ramsay tenement was much envied because it afforded such a good view of everything of interest that went on.

Annabella had always enjoyed the thrill of a hanging like the rest of the town. But she never had any patience with the punishments meted out to the breakers of the Sabbath. In fact, she had often risked being put in the stocks or pillory herself in order to help them. Many a poor wretch in the stocks, who had done nothing worse than comb her hair or laugh on a Sunday, had been grateful for Annabella's protection. She thought nothing of standing in front of the victim, shouting abuse at his or her attackers and daring them to throw another missile. Or she had given defiant sups of whisky to similar victims who were nailed by the ear to the pillory.

'But Papa, Papa,' she kept trying to explain to an outraged Ramsay. 'All they have done is act in a perfectly natural manner. I cannot see why it should be such a sin and a crime to take a stroll on the green or hum a merry tune or look in a pier glass on a Sunday.'

'No, that's your trouble, mistress!' her father always roared. 'And you never learn, for all I've told you and for all the readings I've given you from the Good Book. You're a wicked and sinful lassie.'

She could see him now emerging from the tavern accompanied by the minister. They were both tall men but Ramsay had the heavier build and was more prosperous looking in his long curly wig and scarlet cloak and shoes buckled in silver. The Rev Mr Blackadder picked his way gingerly beside him with a watchful eye on the muddy road that could ruin his best stockings.

He was a man of many moods, watchful and cautious like now, or at other times, when he was in the pulpit, throwing all restraint to the winds and working himself into a veritable frenzy of rhetoric. He had a long lantern-jawed face with keen dark eyes, high shoulders and long limbs. A black tie-wig covered his head and he wore a dark blue coat, a grey waistcoat of almost the same length and blue breeches with knee buckles.

'Here they come,' Annabella said. 'Hell and damnation!' She swished across the room, flopped down on a chair and impatiently tapped her fan on the table.

Soon she heard her father's heavy tread on the stairs and the quicker pace that betrayed the eagerness of the other man.

He bowed at the same time as rubbing his hands when he entered.

'Uh-huh. It's yourself, Mistress Annabella.'

Annabella flounced into a curtsy.

'Minister.'

Ramsay said: 'You'll take a glass?'

'Och, aye. I never say no to a wee dram.'

'Indeed it's true, sir,' Annabella said.

Ramsay pulled at his nose and glowered a warning at Annabella from beneath bushy brows. But Mr Blackadder seemed happily unaware of Annabella's jibe. With one eye he admired his glass filling with amber fluid and at the same time inquired:

'And how are you today, Annabella?'

'As well as can be expected in the circumstances, sir.'

'Uh-huh. Oh, well,' said the minister mistaking the circumstances referred to for her recent adventures with the Highland army. 'The least said about that the better. God bless this whisky,' he added before emptying his glass and smacking his lips. 'I've had a wee word with the Reverend Mr Gillespie and he's agreed to say the prayers over us.'

Ramsay signalled to his servant, Big John, to give the minister a refill and Big John, dwarfing the low-ceilinged room, lumbered over to do as he was bid. Then Ramsay said:

'And Letitia Halyburton is willing to have the marriage feast at her place. It's bigger and she's got more servants and there's her girls to help her. I'll pay her well for all the food and falderals, of course. Still, it's verra obliging of her.'

Annabella flicked her fan open and flapped it rapidly in front of her face. Her brother Douglas was married to Griselle, one of the Halyburton sisters. And Griselle's father, William Halyburton, was a tobacco merchant like her father. She could just imagine how primly pleased his wife Letitia Halyburton would be at the coming wedding.

Long ago she'd insisted,

'Mistress Annabella, you are too perjink and disrespectful. You need someone to discipline you. The minister should do very well.'

Griselle and her sister Phemy would have a prodigiously enjoyable time too, snickering and giggling. The only person who would not savour the wedding would be herself. She swallowed down the lump of chagrin in her throat.

'Very obliging indeed, sir,' she sarcastically agreed with her father.

One thing was certain, she would see all the Halyburtons and her father and the minister choke in hell before she would allow them to witness her distress. As if in preparation for this she shut her father and the minister out of her mind. Instead she concentrated her attention in the fading light of the window on the ornaments on the mantelpiece—dainty porcelain figures and snuffboxes painted in bright colours and gilt—on the silver candelabra, and on the big Bible on the table, its black grain a coarse contrast to its gossamer leaves with their golden, gleaming edges.

Her father and the minister continued to converse and drink together. At one point they burst into a drunken duet and a psalm rollicked up to the ceiling.

> 'To render thanks unto the Lord, it is a comely thing,
> And to Thy name, O Thou most high, due praise aloud
>   to sing.
> Thy loving kindness to show forth,
> When shines the morning light;
> And to declare Thy faithfulness
> With pleasure every night . . .'

The summer's evening gradually emptied of sunshine. The

moon slid over to fill its place. Curtains were drawn, candles lit, their flickering deepening the shadowy folds of the bed-drapes.

Annabella remained at the table straight-backed and dignified in her lavender silk dress with silver trimmings, her white powdered hair and her black face patches.

At long last the Reverend Blackadder was hoisted to his feet by Big John and escorted home. Her father swayed away to his own room, head dropping forward, wig askew, mouth struggling to form the words of the psalm and sing them into his chest. Only when he had safely disappeared and she could hear him groping about and muttering in his own bedroom through the wall did she dare to relax. She flung herself into the darkness of the hole-in-the-wall bed in a puff of hair powder and a rustling of skirts.

But as Nancy loosened her hoops and tugged off her gown and petticoats, all she allowed herself was one muffled—

'Hell and damnation!'

The horse fair had been proclaimed by the magistrates at the Cross in front of the Tolbooth and before an eager, jostling crowd. A moist sun sparkled over scarlet capes, snowy shirts, cravats and frilly mob caps. It picked out coats the colour of sky and grass and earth. It flashed against shoe buckles. It made shimmering rainbows of gowns, petticoats and plaids.

'It's going to be a lively day,' Nancy remarked as she and Annabella emerged from the close. She was hugging her tartan plaid around her. Annabella, flushed like a rose with excitement, was wrapped in a royal blue cloak.

Excitement sizzled in the early morning air. People milled about from Saltmarket Street up to the Cross, along Trongate Street past the Tolbooth and the Exchange, past the Guard House and down Stockwell Street to the Briggait.

Between the houses on the south side of the Briggait and the river was the slaughterhouse, the stench of which spread far and wide. Beside the slaughterhouse stretched a spare piece of ground. It was here that the pavilions or 'shows' were set up.

The freakish, beak-nosed Punch and Judy squawked and screeched and fought to be heard above the bedlam of the crowd. Proprietors of booths added to the shoutings and clangour in their efforts to attract customers to come and see their displays. Jugglers, giants, dwarfs, fat men and women frolicked about, and creatures in the last stages of consumption were exhibited as living skeletons.

Big drums boom-boomed, small drums beat a fast tattoo. Fiddles scraped and trumpets brayed. Shameless pimple-skinned hizzies displayed themselves half-nude and capered about on raised stages, kicking up their legs and running on their toes and spinning round and round on one leg.

A brutish man skinned live rats with his teeth, quick as a flash, one after the other.

Annabella gave a squeal of distress and hurried past, pushing and gesticulating at people to remove themselves from her path.

'Let's go back to Trongate Street and watch the races,' she told Nancy.

The horses were on show from the old bridge right up Stockwell Street, but it was along Trongate Street that they were tested for pace and wind. Although the rain had stopped and sunshine added colour to the spectacle, the ground was spongy and the horses' restless hooves were turning it into quagmire.

Nancy was having difficulty in stumbling along in her bare feet. Annabella, in her wooden pattens supported on iron rings, could scarcely keep her balance.

'Losh sakes, Nancy, hold my arm to steady me. Already my stockings and skirts are spotted with this monstrous mud.'

'Here's the minister. He'll support you.'

'Uh-huh.' Mr Blackadder came hurrying to greet her. 'Can I give you an arm, Mistress Annabella?'

Stifling a sigh at the sight of his scarecrow figure she managed to reply pertly.

'That I will allow, sir.'

She linked arms with him and somehow the touch of his flesh reminded her of Lavelle. The memory brought a stab of need as well as pain. Desperately struggling to ignore her feelings she said,

'Nancy was just remarking on how early the proceedings have started. Already the recruiting parties are marching round the streets banging on their drums.' She favoured him with a sparkling sideways glance. 'Are you not tempted, sir?'

'No,' the Rev Blackadder replied dryly. 'No' by recruiting parties.'

'Why, sir,' Annabella laughed. 'Do I detect that you have a sense of humour? Even perhaps a tiny spark of gallantry?'

'I'm just as God made me, Annabella.'

Crowds were pressing in on either side of Trongate Street as the first horses appeared from Stockwell Street and reared and snorted and pawed the ground. Their riders, mostly the local aristocracy and merchants or sons of the same, fought for control of the animals, before suddenly cracking their whips and sending them racing along the street with mud spurting up from either side.

Women squealed and giggled hysterically and flurried about as their skirts and capes were splashed. Men drew them further back for protection, glad of the excuse for putting an arm round a lady's waist or shoulders and holding her close, which only made her squeal and giggle all the more.

Blackadder elbowed a path for Annabella through the crowd. Rubbing shoulders with elegantly dressed ladies and gentlemen were ragged beggars and orphan children, soldiers in red coats, country women in homespun plaids, country men in blue tam-o'-shanters and girls in striped petticoats.

'Oot o' the way. Behave yoursels. Let a lady pass when you're telt.' Then to Annabella with a shake of his head: 'I shudder to think o' the mortal sins that'll be committed before nightfall. As sure as God's my witness, Annabella, the devil will be rampaging about Glasgow this day.'

Reaching Stockwell Street, they turned the corner and tried to get a good view of all the horses.

'Down there!' Annabella pointed as best she could between bobbing heads and bonnets. 'The one being held by the red-faced farmer in the grey waistcoat. See what a proud beauty that one is.'

Blackadder's long face strained with worry as they struggled towards it.

'Haud on, Annabella. Haud on. It seems gey frisky to me.

That beast would kick you to kingdom come as quick as look at you the way its loupin' about.'

'I like anything with spirit. You haggle about price while I test the animal.'

She snatched the reins from the farmer-owner, ignoring Blackadder's cries of protest.

'Annabella, you're surely no' going to race the beast. Mistress Annabella, come down off that at once. Let one of the farm-lads or . . .' he added in wretched agitation, '. . . me if you must.'

She laughed.

'That's mightily obliging of you, minister, but I must not. Now, unless you want trampled into the mud, I suggest you step out of my way.'

The horse went nudging, prancing, snorting, bucking through the crush of other animals and people until it reached the top of the Stockwell and joined the tumultuous assembly of horses on Trongate Street.

The riders, all men, greeted Annabella's arrival with bantering shouts and guffaws of laughter, but she shouted back at them.

'Pox on you all. Let the race begin. I swear I'll beat the lot of you.'

Then suddenly a pistol was fired and with great gusty yells and cracking of whips, they were off.

The wind tore at Annabella's hooded cloak, wrenched it high behind her, slashed her chest and face, snatched her breath away. She felt delirious with joy for the few minutes of the flight. When she reached the Cross at the other end and dismounted in a swirl of skirts, she was flushed and bright-eyed and trembling with excitement. At first she thought she had won, but then noticed that another rider had made it before her by a few seconds. He was a big man in a black coat and knee length boots. He had a coarse face with a broken nose and a wide yet cruel mouth.

Annabella's flush deepened as she became aware of him staring at her. She tipped up her chin.

'The thrill is in the game, sir,' she said, 'not the winning of it.'

He gave a small bow at the same time as patting and stroking his horse. Then he remounted and galloped back to the Stockwell.

Chapter 5

At first Gav could see nothing for hail and sleet racing through the air. Blindly he struggled from the foc'stle scuttle, then grabbed on to some rigging to prevent himself from being washed overboard. The tiny ship was plunging madly into a giant sea that kept burying the forward part of the vessel. Within seconds he was soaked to the skin and gasping for breath.

Lightning sizzled and flared and flashed on the water all around making the ship appear to be in the centre of an inferno, and thunder rolled over the decks like a broadside of cannon. Gav remained pinned to the rigging, too terrified to move one way or the other. Despite the noise of the storm he could hear Mr Gudgeon's voice roaring orders and the bosun bawling out so quickly after him that their voices fought together with the raging wind.

Then suddenly there was only Mr Gudgeon's voice and his hand grabbing Gav's jacket and jerking him along. Gav screamed and struggled but failed to free himself and hardly knew what was happening until he landed with a painful thud in the steerage and the hatch was battened down. The pain of his fall took his breath away but he was relieved that he hadn't been tossed overboard. All around him women were screaming and children were sobbing and everyone was fighting to hang on to something, anything to prevent themselves from being flung from one side of the ship to the other. Gav kept a grip of the hatch ladder and clung on grimly until the storm quietened. The ship still heaved and sent his stomach leaping and plunging but at least it seemed to have escaped the wildest patch of weather.

He tried to settle down to sleep for what remained of the night but there was such a weeping and wailing going on that sleep proved impossible. One woman in particular was creating a frightful racket. Every few minutes she let out a piercing scream that tailed off into an animal-like groan, only to work up to a crescendo of ear-splitting noise again.

Unable to stand it any more, Gav struggled across to where she was lying.

'The storm's over now, mistress.' He tried to give comfort. 'You're in no danger. Don't be afraid. Everything's going to be all right.'

The woman's large dark eyes gazed at him through the gloom. Perspiration was running down her face and her long hair was plastered wetly against it. She managed to gasp something and, although he did not understand what she said, he immediately recognized the language as the Gaelic. His mother had originated from the Highlands and had often sung to Regina and himself in that language. He turned to a woman nearby who, like most of the others, was being wretchedly seasick in whatever space or corner she could find.

'What is she saying? Do you understand the Gaelic?'

Supporting herself against the bulkhead, the other woman shook her head.

'We're all from Glasgow. She's the only Skye woman. She's in labour with child and God help her and the bairn when it comes.'

The Skye woman gave another scream of agony. Gav felt unnerved by her suffering. He had to do something. Wondering if there was a chirurgeon on board, he groped his way back to the hatch ladder and waited for what seemed a hell of endless time until the hatch was opened. Indeed, the shaft of daylight spilling down and trickling faintly to every side revealed what looked like hell. Bodies were helplessly strewn about and sobbing children clung to mothers who were too ill to bother with them or even protect them against the army of rats splashing and noisily quarrelling about the floor.

Thankfully he scrambled up the ladder and once on the deck went straight to the longboat and Jemmy Ducks.

'There you are, shipmate.' Jemmy greeted him. 'When you weren't in the foc'stle, I says to Andra Mr Gudgeon's had him. He's had him, I says.'

'He caught me on deck during the storm last night and flung me down into steerage.'

Jemmy scratched his pigtail.

'Not that I blames him for that. The deck's no place for a lad in a storm. There's no denying it, Gav. You were a danger to yourself and to Mr Gudgeon's men. Verra busy them men are in a storm and they don't like folks getting in their way.' He sighed. 'I don't minds admitting it, Gav, I have a terrible struggle with them animals at times like that. They panics, y'see, and flutters and squacks and squeals and batters about something cruel.'

Suddenly Gav remembered about the Skye woman.

'There's a woman in steerage needing help. She's having a baby. Is there a doctor or a chirurgeon on board?'

'I always says there should be. I had a cow once and she pined away and died long before we reached Virginia. I never did find out what ailed that cow.'

'Surely somebody could help.'

'Chips tried his best. Yes, yes, I admits that. Chips tried his best for Henrietta but it was no use.'

'I mean for the Skye woman.'

'It's Chips for her too, Gav. It's Chips for everybody. He pulled them teeth.' He stretched his lips into a grotesque grin and indicated several black spaces. Then suddenly he pointed his fingers upwards. 'No, no, I tells a lie. The Captain sees to some things, Gav. He's got his responsibilities but they're not to steerage folks and that's a fact. No, no, it's Chips for them.'

'I'd better go and tell him,' Gav said and then added wistfully, 'I wish I could get something to eat. My biscuits have got all wet down there and the rats have been at them.'

Jemmy's eyes, protruding from a brown, leathery face, strained cautiously around.

'I knows some friends who can maybe help.' He jerked a thumb in the direction of the hen coops. 'Them hens has helped me out many's the time. I'm hungry, I tells them, and out they comes with an egg. Them hens are great friends to me, Gav, and I don't minds admitting it.'

After a great deal of stealth and precautions to ensure that he would not be found out, Jemmy slipped Gav an egg and stood in front of him to hide him from view while Gav sucked hungrily at it.

Feeling considerably cheered, he went to tell Chips the carpenter about the Skye woman and then, when returning, his attention was caught and riveted with delight by a school of porpoises leaping and tumbling and bobbing all round the ship. But he was exhausted with lack of sleep and after a while he decided to go down to the foc'stle for a doze.

He found some of the crew sitting making and patching clothes by the light of the scuttle. They greeted him in a friendly enough manner and did not object when he made a bed for himself on top of some sails. He fell immediately into a deep sleep and dreamt that he was in the hole-in-the-wall bed in his old home in Tannery Wynd. He was cuddled between Regina and his mammy and his mammy's tartan plaid covered the three of them. The bed-doors were tight shut and everything was safe and cosy. Even when mammy got up and opened the bed-doors and went over to poke up the fire and put on the porridge pot, he still felt a warm, happy glow inside.

Soon they would have their porridge and milk, maybe bannocks and ale as well. As usual, at night after they came home from school, mammy sang to them. It was then he wakened and realized that the singing was not mammy's. Mammy was dead. He sat up rubbing at his eyes.

Echoing down from the deck came sailors' lusty voices:

'Oh, it's pipe up, Dan, when yer feelin' kind o' blue,
With a half-drowned ship, an' a half-dead crew,
When yer heart's in yer sea-boots 'n the cold is in yer
    bones,
An' ye don't give a damn how soon she goes to Davy Jones,
When it's dark as the devil an' it's blowin' all it can,
Oh, he's worth ten men on a rope is Dan!'

He didn't know what to do. The dream, or rather the wakening to the realization that it was only a dream, weighed him down with sadness. It took all his courage to keep tears at bay as he struggled into his big jacket and jammed his hat over his mass of curls. When he returned on deck, the first thing he saw was Jemmy Ducks excitedly chasing a gay coloured rooster round the decks. He couldn't help giggling at the sight and then,

336

after glancing towards the poop to make sure that it was Mr Jubb's watch and not Mr Gudgeon's, he joined his friend in the chase. Suddenly, just when the rooster was within the eager grasp of both Jemmy and himself, it leapt up flapping and squacking in indignation and escaped overboard.

'Damn his eyes!' Jemmy wailed as they watched the animal fluttering helplessly down among the rolling waves. Its glowing plumage looked strangely out of harmony with the dull slate colour of the water as it sat drifting away astern. 'Damn his eyes,' Jemmy repeated brokenly as he turned and limped away.

Respecting his need to be alone with his distress, Gav didn't follow him and it was while he was still standing gazing overboard that Regina approached.

'You'd better watch that pig of a mate doesn't catch you again. You know what he said about keeping to steerage.'

'It's Mr Jubb on duty just now.'

'I know that,' Regina said impatiently. 'But Gudgeon's still on the ship, isn't he?'

'He keeps picking on me.'

'I know that as well. The men call him bully Gudgeon. He's just a pig.' Her mouth twisted. 'He looks like one as well.'

'I'm down in the foc'stle now.'

'Does he know?'

Gav shook his head.

'Not that it's much better.'

'There isn't much room in my cabin and there's only one berth but we'd be able to squeeze in together . . .'

'Oh, Regina!'

Immediately her hand stung across his face.

'Reggie,' she hissed at him.

Swallowing as best he could, he nodded his head before dutifully repeating, 'Reggie.'

'It means asking him.'

'He doesn't like me.'

'He likes money, I'll wager.'

'Jemmy says he's always got to have somebody to pick on.'

'He can find somebody else. He can pick on your precious Jemmy.'

Gav was silent. Eventually he managed:

'When are you going to ask him?'

Regina shrugged.

'First chance I get. It isn't easy to talk sense with him when he's always so drunk. Did you see him falling off the poop?'

Gav shook his head and Regina smiled grimly.

'He staggered and fell down the stairs. There was such a thump I thought he'd gone through the quarter deck. I was the only one who dared laugh. Serves you right, I said, for bullying Gav Chisholm.'

Gav didn't look at all happy. He was thinking that the incident and Regina's behaviour would do nothing to help his position. If anything, the mate would hate him and try to bully him all the more.

He gazed anxiously around.

'Maybe I'd better get back to the foc'stle now.'

'Being afraid of him won't help you.'

'It's all very well for you to talk.' Anger reddened Gav's cheeks. 'You're all right. You're safe enough. And you're older and bigger than me,' he flung at her before stamping away.

He hadn't gone very far when he stopped in surprise. The captain was shuffling along the deck towards him. He was wearing soft floppy shoes and no coat and he had a woolly stocking hat pulled over his tangled hair.

'Aye, and who might you be?' he asked Gav.

'Gav Chisholm, sir.'

'Are you any relation to the red-headed family that has the next farm to us?'

'I . . . I don't think so.'

'Where's my wee sister?'

'Your sister, sir?'

'My Minnie said I was to keep an eye on her. An awful wee lassie she is. She'll be in the daisy field again.'

The hair crept up the back of Gav's neck. The old man was obviously mad. Yet at the same time, he couldn't help feeling sorry for him. He looked so pathetic with his shirt hanging over his breeches and his long tangled hair and woolly hat.

'Don't worry, she's all right,' he said kindly. 'Your mammy's

338

found her.'

The wrinkled, weather-beaten face brightened.

'I'm obliged to you, Gav Chisholm. I was verra worried aboot oor Hester.'

Just then Mr Jubb approached and, ignoring Gav, murmured something to the captain and led him away towards his cabin in the stern.

Jemmy came limping over shaking his head.

'They're greasing the board.'

'What do you mean?'

'Chips and his mate. They're getting ready for a burial. Somebody in steerage has died. Captain'll have to say a few words before he sends her down to Davy Jones' locker.'

'He's gone mad.'

'No, no, Gav. He's just not himself at times. He'll come all right again, you'll see. Mr Jubb helps him. Mr Jubb's good with the captain when he's not himself.'

Gav felt upset.

'I wonder if it's the Skye woman who's dead. My mammy came from the Highlands. She spoke just like the Skye woman.'

'Happens all the time, Gav. Folks dies all the time on ships. Last voyage we had five folk died. Time afore that we had seven. As often as not, we has shipmates dies as well.'

'With seasickness?'

'No, no. It's not the seasickness that shatters your hull and rigging, Gav. It's the scurvy or the ship-fever or the flux. Them's the terrible things.'

A little knot of women were huddling on deck with plaids draped over bent heads and children clutching at them. Seamen too were gathering and standing quietly around. The board was set up and Chips brought the body sewed in sailcloth and weighted to make sure it went to the bottom.

Eventually Mr Jubb came back with a happily smiling Captain Kilfuddy, cocked hat slightly askew, black stock muffling too high up over his chin, coat and skirt flapping loose in the breeze. They stopped beside the board which was balanced ready on top of the bulwarks.

'Aye,' said Captain Kilfuddy patting one of the children on

339

the head, a pale-faced little boy of about three. 'And what game do you like best, eh? Crinky? Or cross tig? My wee sister's aye at the peevers but it's bools and peeries and fleein' dragons for me.'

Mr Jubb put a hand on his arm and bent closer to murmur in his ear. The captain turned on him in surprise.

'Say a few words? I've just said a few words. Who are you?'

Mr Jubb had a vague, hunted look as if he was trying to shrink into himself and disappear. Yet he always managed to retain a certain air of dignity. He murmured again.

The captain said:

'Prayers? No, I canny mind any prayers. But there's a verse my Minnie says.' He beamed around the silent crowd, then cleared his throat.

> 'When Faither Time goes hirplin' doon life's hillside,
> And locks once raven, noo as white as snaw,
> We'll keep oor hearts from grow'n sad and weary,
> With thinkin' o' the days so long awa',
> The bairnies with their laughin' and their daffin',
> Will help us to forget lang days o' pain;
> The songs they sing when softly falls the gloamin',
> Will make us live oor youthful days again.'

A woman began sobbing and Chips who was holding the board shook his head at Mr Jubb. 'It's no use, sir.'

'Here's another one my Minnie likes.'

Captain Kilfuddy held up a hand.

> 'They're slowly slippin' from our ken
> The freends we loved so weel,
> As mists in autumn gloamin's fa',
> Along the valleys steal;
> And though the day's last rosy beam,
> May light some lofty Ben,
> The shadows seem to deeper grow
> Within the wooded glen.'

Mr Jubb made one last attempt and the old man repeated his words in surprise.

'Commit this body to the deep?' Before he could say any more, Chips and his mate tipped up the board and the body disappeared with barely a splash. Gav turned away from the scene and without a word walked towards the foc'stle. Then, once alone in that dark cave, he wept.

Chapter 6

Annabella had not liked the look of the man. There did not seem much refinement about him and when, after the race, she had rejoined Nancy and Blackadder, she was irritated to find him close by and staring at her again. In fact, everywhere they went—crushing through the crowded streets, admiring the shows down by the river or strolling on the Green—he was to be seen towering behind them, his hefty thighs gripping his horse's flanks. Eventually even Blackadder noticed.

'Jist a minute, Annabella. I must have a wee word with this gentleman.'

Annabella raised a sarcastic eyebrow.

'Gentleman, sir? He looks more like a monstrous pugilist dressed in gentleman's clothes.'

'Aye, weel, be that as it may. What I'd like to know is, why he keeps traipsing after us. He's been somewhere about us the whole day.'

Annabella couldn't help admiring Mr Blackadder's unexpected show of courage.

'Careful, minister,' she warned as he marched across and peered up at the stranger.

'Huh-huh, and who might I ask are you, sir?'

'Harding.'

'I dinna ken the name.'

Harding glanced in Annabella's direction.

'Is she Merchant Ramsay's daughter?'

Annabella bristled.

'If you must refer to me, sir, pray have the courtesy to dismount and speak directly to me.'

He did not dismount but stared with eyes shadowed beneath heavy brows.

'I do business with your father.'

Then he reined his horse to one side and cantered coolly

away.

'Well!' Annabella said. 'What a monstrous ill-mannered oaf. What's it to me even if he is doing business with Papa?'

She dismissed the stranger from her mind. It was time to return home. She was beginning to feel hungry and there was the Assembly to prepare for in the evening.

The Assembly was being held in Merchants' House, or Briggait Hall as it was sometimes called, because it was situated in the Briggait.

It meant 'high dress' of course and she bid Nancy smooth and pin her hair over a front pad and then arrange it in ringlet curls at the back. Then they went into the closet and the maid gave it a good powdering. Out of the closet again, Nancy fastened on the corset which made Annabella's tiny waist look even tinier. Then on went her panniers and her low-cut silver petticoat, decorated from bosom to hem with row after row of satin bows. Annabella loved the slippery feel of the satin and the sound of it rustling and swishing about her. A ribbon with matching bow was fastened round her neck. Next came the open gown of the same sparkling blue as her eyes, white silk stockings and high-heeled blue satin slippers. She stuck a couple of patches on her face and selected a fan on which were painted cherubs gracefully entangled with coloured ribbons and posies of flowers. Then she viewed herself with satisfaction in the pier glass over by the window. She swooshed round and round and held her arms stretched out and provocatively raised and wiggled her shoulders making her bosom nearly spring right out of her corset. As it was, everything but the nipples was showing.

Big John had already summoned a sedan chair but it took some time to squeeze herself into it and arrange her voluminous skirts before the chair men could set off at their usual round plunging trot. The carrying shafts were quite flexible and pliant and the chair men in their haste to fit in several engagements caused the chair to bounce up and down and swing to and fro at an alarming rate. In retaliation for this extreme discomfort, Annabella gave the men a piece of her tongue before flouncing away through the pillared entrance of Briggait Hall.

Annabella swept along the lobby, ascended the staircase and

entered the hall with fan fluttering. It was one of the largest halls in the town, being about eighty feet long and thirty feet wide. Round the walls hung portraits of Benefactors to the Poor of the Merchants' House and from the centre of the roof dangled a large and beautiful model of a fully rigged ship. It was well-lit with many candles and there was a fireplace at each end.

A fiddler was merrily scraping and beside him, anxiously surveying the dancing throng and as stringy as a fiddle bow, stood the dancing master, Dougie Clegg. Many's the time at his weekly dancing lessons he had put Annabella and the rest through their paces. At the lessons there was no fiddler and Dougie hummed the tune, kept the time and gave instruction in deft and rapid rotation.

> 'Up lads, noo!
> Ta teedleum ta toodleum.
> Up lassies too!
> Ta teedleum ta toodleum.
> Toes in a line noo!
> Ta teedleum ta toodleum.
> Let everyone boo!
> Ta teedleum ta toodleum.
> Toots, Jean Gibb, ye're a' wrong, you!
> Ta teedleum ta toodleum.
> Turn round about noo!
> Ta teedleum ta toodleum.
> Doon the middle noo!
> Ta teedleum ta toodleum.
> Stand back Jock Tamson, you!
> Ta teedleum ta toodleum.
> Join hands noo!
> Ta teedleum ta toodleum.
> Toots, ye're a' wrong thegether!
> Ta teedleum ta toodleum.
> Tam Wilkie, ye're a gowk!
> Ta teedleum ta toodleum.'

But now he just stood tapping his cane to the fiddler's tune and peering at the feet of the dancers.

The Widow Aberdour came sailing towards Annabella, more billowing and resplendent than the ship that hung from the ceiling. She was the one who was in charge of the proceedings

344

and who arranged the partners. Her hair glistened with diamond and ruby brooches, and a ruby necklace on a heavy gold chain sparkled round her neck. Her purple gown was generously fringed with black lace at bosom and elbow and she brandished a jewelled snuffbox and a purple fan with a gold tassel.

'Ah, Mistress Ramsay!'

'Mistress Aberdour.' Annabella sank into a graceful curtsy. 'You are well, I trust?'

'Indeed. Indeed. I shall dance a merry tune until I am a hundred.' The widow carolled with laughter. Then she made high beckoning motions with her fan and trilled, 'Mr Harding, sir. Mr Harding!'

Annabella flushed when she saw the big man pushing towards them. He was not wearing elegant flowered or patterned silk or satin like the other gentlemen but a black coat, buff coloured waistcoat, breeches and black boots.

'Mistress Aberdour,' Annabella protested indignantly and in the man's hearing. 'This . . . this person is wearing boots and a sword!' Then turning to Harding she said, 'It is not fitting, sir.'

He shrugged.

'I can't do anything about the boots. I did not bring any shoes with me. But I'll remove the sword if it eases you.'

Unsheathing the weapon, he tossed it onto a nearby chair.

Widow Aberdour raised her fan high.

'Splendid! Splendid! Mr Harding! Mistress Ramsay!' And with hands heavenwards, she swooped triumphantly away.

Annabella fanned herself as if about to faint. She was too furious for words. She had been looking forward so much to the ball, knowing that the Rev. Blackadder would not be there, frowning as he did on such 'wicked frivolities' as he called them.

'I am from Virginia,' Harding said.

Annabella paid him not the slightest attention.

'I have a plantation inland from the James River. I deal with your father's stores.'

Annabella allowed her gaze to stray among the dancers. Many of the men were prodigiously handsome and belonged to local aristocratic families. It was really too cruel of the Widow Aberdour to partner her with this ugly brutish creature. But no

345

doubt he had influenced her in his favour with money, if not with flattery. Mistress Aberdour was very prone to both.

'Your father's a robber.'

She switched her full attention to him.

'What did you say, sir?'

He bared his teeth in a humourless grin.

'I thought that would waken you up.'

'How dare you insult my Papa. How dare you, sir!'

'I can dare very easily for it is the truth.'

'Papa ships goods to Virginia and sells them in his stores. He is perfectly entitled to profit by his endeavours.'

'Granted. What he's not entitled to do is charge outrageous prices to people who, because of their isolated position, have no choice but to buy from him. Nor ought he to enmesh us in such debt that our tobacco crop is pledged to him sometimes for years ahead.'

'Huh!' Annabella gave a trill of sarcastic laughter. 'I see now what your position is. You are monstrously inefficient and mightily in debt, sir. You envy my Papa who is plagued by neither of these things.'

'You do not know what you are talking about, mistress. It is I and men like me who pay for the fine clothes on your back and the good food in your belly.'

' 'Tis monstrous and damnable that you should speak to me like this.'

'Anger suits you,' he remarked without smiling. 'You're a damnably beautiful woman.'

'I do not care for compliments from you, sir.'

'It was not intended as a compliment. I stated a fact, that was all. Now let us dance. That was what you came for, was it not?'

'I certainly did not come to the Assembly with either the desire or the intention of dancing with you. That is a fact!'

He cupped a hand over her elbow.

'Well, you are going to dance with me.'

'Remove your hand, sir. I do what I like. You have been a prodigious irritation to me the whole day long. I refuse to countenance any more of it. I demand an explanation of your behaviour.'

346

'I had heard much talk of you. I was curious to see what kind of woman it is who not only followed the rebel army and braved its battles, but survived the rigours of the long journey back alone and unaided.'

'Well, now you have had a good look.'

'Yes.'

An irrepressible surge of mischief mingled with her anger. Her eyes sparkled with both.

'And what, pray, are your conclusions?'

'I believe you would be admirably suited for life in Virginia,' he replied with a grimness that she could not fathom.

'Virginia?' She gasped incredulously. 'Are you actually imagining me working on a Virginia plantation?'

'I am imagining you as my wife.'

'Losh and lovenendie!' She couldn't help laughing. 'So you came to the market for a wife as well as a horse, did you? Well, as far as I'm concerned, sir, I'm not one of those females who are herded up like cattle and shipped across to Virginia because planters need wives. Your imagination is inflamed. Here is another fact for you. I am promised to the minister. The Reverend Mr Blackadder and I are to be married in less than two weeks' time.'

A look of disgust contorted his face.

'What a bloody waste!'

'Guard your tongue,' she said, trying to be serious. 'Now let us dance.'

He moved clumsily and every time she pirouetted round his ugliness caught her by surprise. He had a big-boned face. His brows reminded her of an overhanging cliff. His eyes were caves of darkness. His nose had a broken bridge and was twisted to one side. His mouth was wide but with an upper lip that could tighten back like a snarling animal.

She resigned herself to spending the evening with him and making the best she could of it. Eventually, laughing and breathless, she told him:

'Dancing with you, sir, is like dancing with a bear. I am prodigiously exhausted.'

'I shall take you home.'

'Indeed you shall not. You may call a caddy to summon a sedan chair and that will do very well.'

She swished past him towards the door, rapidly flicking her fan in an effort to cool herself. He strode after her down the stairs and out into the summer's night. Clouds were scudding across the moon, blackening the town then suddenly lightening it again.

She turned on Harding impatiently.

'Well, sir? I am waiting for a sedan chair.'

'First let us stroll on the Green and enjoy the evening air. It is too fine a night to waste.'

She laughed in astonishment.

'You are mad! It is late. We have no lanterns and I am not wearing pattens. My slippers would be ruined.'

'We have the moon for a lantern. As for your slippers—the earth is dry now but if it will make you happy, I will carry you.'

Before she could object, he had swept her off her feet and was carrying her along Bridge Street towards the Low Green and the river.

Kicking furiously and with a fine display of silk stockings, she punched his chest and cried out:

'It does not make me happy, sir. Put me down, this instant. I wish a sedan chair.'

'Why have two men carry you when one man can do the job?'

'Because the one man is an impertinent scoundrel and he is carrying me in the wrong direction. My Papa shall be told of this, I am warning you.'

'I am not afraid of your father.'

Reaching the Green he passed a clump of trees and put her down. Moonlight snuffed out for a few minutes and they stood close together in the pitch blackness. She thought she heard in the distance the lapping of the river. A veil of light wafted back and, as if waking from a dream Annabella said

'This is preposterous. Why have you brought me here?'

'Because I wanted you.'

'Wanted me?' Her voice betrayed an edge of concern. 'You surely do not mean . . .'

'I mean what I say.'

'Mr Harding, you spoke earlier about imagining me as your wife. This is no way to persuade me, sir.'

He moved towards her and she pushed out her hands to ward him off.

'Here? Now?' She tried to laugh. 'Anywhere with you would be monstrous and inconceivable, Mr Harding. But . . . but . . .' Words failed her. She could not believe what was happening.

His arms encircled her waist and jerked her towards him, making her punch his chest and kick his shins.

'Mr Harding, I do not want you. If you are a gentleman, you cannot force me.'

'I am not a gentleman, Annabella.'

She felt breathless and in pain as his mouth fastened over hers. She wept and kicked and struggled but could do nothing to prevent him pulling her down onto the grass. She screamed and sobbed in humiliation as his hands tugged at her clothes. Then, pinned helplessly under the bulk and weight of him, she moaned as he forced himself again and again into her body.

Afterwards he rolled onto his back and allowed her to struggle up, but when she took flight and disappeared away through the trees, he scrambled to his feet calling after her.

'Come back you little fool.'

Annabella paid no heed. In a panic of distress, she bumped into trees and tore her dress on bushes and lost her slippers in her frantic efforts to escape and reach home.

She could still hear the echo of his deep harsh voice as, clutching her mud-stained skirts about her, she raced up Saltmarket Street. Stones and lumpy earth cut into her feet and horse dung splattered her stockings. Sobbing with relief, she reached her close and stumbled through to the back yard. The narrow stone stairway in the tower projection at the back of the building was packed with sleeping beggars and orphans. She fought to get past, trampling over them in the darkness until she reached the first landing and the door to her father's house. Not caring if she awakened her father, she loudly tirled the door-pin. But it was Nancy who opened the door, holding up a guttering candle. Seeing her mistress's gown, once a smooth satiny blue, now crushed and stained with grass and mud, she gasped.

'Laud's sake, what's happened?'

She lit the way into Annabella's bedroom. For a minute or two Annabella fought for dignity. Her chin tipped up and she began in a voice straining to be light and bright:

'A most astounding incident occurred . . .'

Then suddenly the strain was too much and she buried her face in her hands.

Chapter 7

'The less you have to do with the likes of him the better,' Nancy insisted.

'He cannot be allowed to get away with his outrageous behaviour towards me last night. I refuse to countenance such a preposterous idea. I'll make him pay.' Annabella's voice was bitter. 'Oh, I'll make him pay, Nancy. I'll lead him a merry dance, I can tell you. First, I'll disarm him by doing him the honour of allowing him to marry me. Then I'll set about making sure that he'll regret the match. Oh, how he'll regret it. Already he imagines me as his wife. Already he imagines me admirably suited for life with him in Virginia. But he could never imagine the subtle miseries that I am capable of inflicting. There's a lot more in life than brute strength, Nancy. A lady has many other weapons.'

'I don't doubt that, and I can understand you lusting for revenge, but surely to marry the man is going too far. You'll be punishing yourself as well as him.'

'Can you think of any other or better way to get at him? No doubt he will be returning to his plantation in Virginia soon. As for punishing myself—I am between the devil and the deep blue sea, am I not? It is either marry the minister and stay in Glasgow, or marry the planter and go to the New World. At least there will be the excitement of the voyage over and finding out about life in Virginia. Life there will be a challenge, Nancy. It will be a challenge too to get the better of that obnoxious oaf of a man.'

Nancy smoothed at her long black hair as if she was lazily stretching.

'I suppose you've never really seen yourself in the minister's house in Briggait.'

'No indeed.' Sitting at the small tea-table, she lit up that corner of the room with her frilly mob cap perched on top of her golden hair, and her yellow and green sprigged cotton gown. She

351

sipped the hot chocolate Nancy had made for her and tried to draw comfort from it.

Her experience of the previous night had harrowed her more than she cared to admit. It wasn't just the unexpected and brutal attack on her person. It was the dreadful humiliation of the whole occurrence. Had the outrage been perpetrated in her bedroom, or even in his bedroom, it would have been bad enough. But to abduct her to the Green and defile her on the filthy earth as if she were no more than a common serving wench was too terrible to contemplate. The wounds to her dignity and pride were by far the most painful and deep-seated.

The only way she felt she could burn away the scars of these wounds was by seeking revenge of them. Yet she trembled inside with confusion and uncertainty. She refused to acknowledge her secret confusions as fear or any other kind of weakness. She had always been a woman of prodigious spirit and daring. Now was her chance to put these qualities to the test. Deciding not to waste another moment, she pushed aside her cup and flicked off her mob cap. It lay on the floor like a patch of snow on rich earth.

She went over to the closet at the other side of the door and Nancy lit candles because it was a black box of a place and too far from the room windows to get any light. Annabella settled herself on the chair in front of the looking-glass and peered close at it as she stuck on a couple of face patches. Then Nancy helped to cover her up with a powdering gown before putting on her wig and starting to powder it. This made a terrible mess as the powder was sprayed upwards so that in falling it could settle evenly on the hair. Both women coughed and spluttered and sneezed and eventually Nancy protested.

'I don't know why you have to have your hair dressed or go to any bother at all for him.'

Annabella spluttered into a hanky, then waved it about in front of her face so that she could breathe more easily.

'I must look my most dignified and ladylike. I'm going to teach that brutish creature a lesson, I tell you.' Slipping out of the powdering gown she thankfully escaped from the cupboard back into the bedroom accompanied by a puff of powder dust.

352

'Hurry up and shut that door,' she called to Nancy who emerged behind her irritably shaking her own hair and clothes. 'Do you think I should change my dress?' she added to the maid, unable to prevent anxiety tightening her voice.

Nancy rolled her eyes.

'What's wrong with the dress you've on?'

'Damn it, printed cotton isn't very impressive, is it? Bring my white and mauve striped silk and my white quilted petticoat and my straw hat with the mauve ribbons.'

Nancy shrugged. She couldn't make up her mind if Annabella was angry and in love or humiliated and afraid. Perhaps a mixture of all four? But because she was not sure of her mistress's mood she did not know how to react. The idea of Annabella being afraid was unnerving. Any man who could upset Annabella like this was someone worth fearing.

'Let Big John and me come with you,' Nancy said after Annabella had donned the gown with its low *décolleté* and long narrow waist. 'This man sounds evil. He's a danger to you.'

'I refuse to have any show of fear. You may accompany me if you wish but there will be no need for anyone else. The brute would not dare harm me under Mistress Aberdour's roof.'

Nancy had already discovered that Harding had lodgings with the Widow Aberdour who lived along the Gallowgate.

'Oh, all right,' Nancy reluctantly agreed and after fetching Annabella's cloak and her own coarser plaid, both girls left the house.

From the close at the top of the Saltmarket it was only a short distance round by the Cross into the Gallowgate. Crow-stepped gable tenements with arches, or piazzas as they were called, under which tradesmen had shops or booths, lined either side of the street. One such shop had been a great favourite of Annabella's when she was a child. There she had been able to purchase delights such as sugarallie, liquory-stick and deil's dung.

The Widow Aberdour's tenement was next to the white-washed thatched-roofed Avondale Arms Inn and she often accommodated the overflow from that place. Above the Inn there hung a board on which was written:

'All ye that pass through Gallow Moor,
Stop in Helen Whitehead's door,
She's what will cheer man in due course,
And entertainment for his horse.
But you that stand before the fire,
Maun just sit down by good desire,
That other folk, as well as you,
May see the glow and feel it too.
Your pipes lay by when stables you request,
Or flame from you to me may prove severe.'

Nancy and Annabella entered Mistress Aberdour's close and climbed the stairs to the first flat where she lived. The widow opened the door and flung her hands high at seeing them. A frilled cap of flowered lawn covered her head and her ample figure sported a sacque, a pleated gown falling in graceful folds from the shoulders and a full, flounced skirt.

'Why, Mistress Ramsay! Come away in, do.'

Annabella bobbed into a curtsy.

'Madam. I have business with Mr Harding.'

'Mr Harding? Mr Harding?' the widow cried heavenwards. 'That gentleman is far, far from here.'

'What do you mean, Madam?'

'Why, he galloped away for Port Glasgow at the crack of dawn. His ship sailed for Virginia this morning.' She swooped up her hands again. 'Mr Harding will be far, far away now. But do come in, do.'

'No, I cannot.' Somehow she managed another curtsy. 'But I thank you for your kind offer of hospitality. Good day to you.'

'And a good day to you, Mistress Ramsay.' The Widow Aberdour's voice sang merrily after Annabella and Nancy as they escaped back down the stairs.

Outside on Gallowgate Street, Annabella stopped and gripped the corner of the building for support. Never, in the lifetime that Nancy had known her, had she seen Annabella look so distraught. Her face had turned as white as her hair powder and a patch on her cheek stood out vivid black. Mauve and white silk ballooning unheeded in the breeze revealed high heeled slippers and indecent amounts of white silk stockings. Nancy made a clumsy effort to hold down Annabella's skirts and mumble words of comfort.

'It's all right. Don't fash yourself.'

Annabella struggled for composure. On top of everything else, to be so humiliated in front of her maid was unendurable. Inwardly she cursed herself for babbling out her foolish plans of revenge and of marriage to Harding. At last she managed to brush Nancy away and take charge of her own skirts.

'Of course it is all right. Pox on the monstrous man. I am well rid of him.'

A beggar in a long blue coat crushed close to her as she stepped briskly along the street.

'Will ye help a poor cripple, mistress?'

She knocked him aside shouting,

'Out of my way, you filthy dog!'

And the old woman who approached crying. 'Gingerbread, gingerbread, buy my hot gingerbread,' received equally rough treatment.

'There are far too many beggars and peddlers and such prodigious nuisances cluttering the streets,' she railed at Nancy. 'It is time Papa did something about it. He is on the Town Council, is he not? It is monstrous and damnable that a lady cannot walk the streets without being pestered and agitated like this.'

The tune of the Tolbooth clock added to the street noises and everywhere people were calling, 'Caddie! Caddie!' Horses were whinnying and clip-clopping, carriage wheels were squeaking and groaning and rattling over bumpy earth, and children were singing.

Annabella hastened her pace until she was almost running. The sun was dappling buildings and making people's clothes look fresh and new and jewel-coloured, but she felt like winter inside. It was a relief to reach her house, march into her room and shut the door. She leaned her back against it for a minute or two, head high, nostrils flaring. She would not weep. She would not. She kept commanding herself. But as she tore off her cloak and flung it to the floor, a giant wave of tears overcame her and she sobbed out loud to the empty room.

'I have been cruelly used. I hate him. I hate him. May he be damned and rot in hell!'

Later, although more composed in her person, she could not eat any dinner. Her father peered at her.

'Aye, you're looking verra wishy-washy. I told you that prancing about at Assemblies would do you no good. The minister warned you against such wicked frivolities as well. You should have paid more heed to him, if not to me, mistress.'

'Yes, Papa.'

'What ails you, Annabella?'

'Only some trifling head pains, Papa.'

'It's a verra strange thing for you to be ailing. Never have I known the day.'

'Well, sir, you know it now.'

'Aye. Maybe punishment for your sins is catching up with you. The Lord works in strange and mysterious ways.'

'Indeed he does, Papa.'

She wished he would retire so that she could go to bed. Yet she had no desire to be alone with her thoughts. Tomorrow, she resolved, she would gallop her new horse the whole day. She would travel for miles and enjoy the scenery and the good weather but when tomorrow came she had not the heart for it and lay listlessly abed. Nor could she be bothered getting up the day after.

Nancy said:

'The maister's worried. He says to fetch the doctor.'

'Fiddlesticks,' Annabella said. 'Can a lady not have a rest in bed without such a prodigious fuss being made? I refuse to see Doctor Scobie. He's a fool of a man and he will only bleed me.'

Talking of bleeding reminded her that she should have had her monthly bleeding by now. Surely this could not mean that she was pregnant.

'Hell and damnation!' she suddenly yelled.

'What's wrong now?' Nancy gasped.

'Nothing's wrong, nothing, I tell you! Get out of my sight, you stupid fool of a girl. I refuse to allow anything to be wrong.'

Nancy rolled her eyes and turned towards the door.

'The maister says to fetch the doctor.'

'No! No! No!'

The muffled cry came from deep in Annabella's pillow. But Nancy had already left the room, banging the door shut behind her.

Within the hour, the doctor and her father were calling for permission to enter and she was shouting back at them telling them to go away. Her father made to open the door and finding it locked, battered on it in a fury.

'Annabella, open this door at once, damn you!'

'Go away.'

'How dare you disobey me. You'll pay for this, mistress. I'm warning you.'

The doctor took his turn of thumping and bawling.

'Ye're a wicked lassie, Annabella Ramsay. Do as ye're faither bids ye. D'ye hear?'

'Go away, I said.'

At last they gave up and left her alone and in silence until morning when she got up and dressed and opened the door and seemed as bright and pert as usual.

Her father said,

'Are you not ashamed?'

'Ashamed, Papa?'

'Aye, ashamed.' He sat down at the oval table in the centre of her bedroom, a grim figure with scowling face under an enormous curled wig.

'Papa, Papa, I am sorry if I displeased you. Truly I am. But I cannot abide Doctor Scobie or his little black worms. And see, I am fully recovered without them.'

He glared at her, his stare raking over the neatly brushed-back hair and the small face with the fragile bluish tinge to the skin under the eyes.

'You still look gey peely-wally to me.'

'I swear I am recovered, Papa. I will prove it to you with how much breakfast I will eat.'

'There's cloth arrived from London and silk and lace from France. I'll have some sent up for you to choose from. It's high time you had everything ready for your wedding.'

'The mantua maker is nearly finished a dress.' She hesitated then added casually, 'There was a man at the Assembly who said he did business with you. A Mr Harding, I think his name was. A coarse ugly fellow.'

Her father glowered with anger.

'Aye. An impertinent scoundrel as well. He had the gall to come over here to argue his right, his right mark you, to ship his produce directly to Europe. I soon put a stop to that. You need ships then, I said. Well, ye'll get none here. And I had a wee word with all my freends and made sure that not one ship anywhere would convenience him. Aye, that soon put him in a rage. It was well seen the Glasgow merchants were all related by blood or marriage, he accused. I readily agreed. I told him it was good business that it should be so and it would fit him better to be attending to his own business of planting tobacco in Virginia instead of meddling with our affairs in Glasgow. It's a damned conspiracy, he shouted, and I thought he was going to draw his pistol or his sword. He's a dangerous and violent man. If I had known he was going to be at the Assembly, I would have forbidden you to attend, Annabella.'

If only he had, she thought. Her life seemed in ruins and she hardly knew how to start picking up the pieces. For the first time she listened not only attentively but desperately when, after breakfast, her father gave his usual reading from the Bible. And she prayed fervently to herself that the bleeding would start soon and she would be spared not only the inconvenience of being pregnant but the monstrous punishment of carrying such a man's child.

But no reading and no prayers brought any comfort. She found herself living two lives, one outward and one inward. Outwardly she appeared her usual pert and vivacious self, if at times somewhat absent-minded. Inwardly she felt distracted. Her mind struggled this way and that like a penned animal fighting for escape and only succeeding in injuring itself. She paid no attention to time passing and when it was the evening before her wedding and friends came for the ceremony of feet-washing, she laughed and frolicked with the rest as if nothing was amiss.

First of all she had Nancy bring a pail of soapy water. Then a wedding ring was borrowed from one of the married women and Annabella flung it into the pail.

Then, amidst much squealing and laughing and splashing all the unmarried girls fell upon the pail and tried to find the ring. For whoever found the ring first would be the next among them to be married.

After that she removed her slippers and stockings, hitched up her skirts and placed her feet in the water. It was the task of unmarried girls to wash the bride's feet and afterwards stain them and her hands with henna. It was the custom too for the bride's attendants to paint her eyebrows with shiny silver antimony.

Even after they had all gone and she was left alone, Annabella could not really believe her fate. The candles had been snuffed out and she lay in the hole-in-the-wall bed watching the firelight crouch and leap like witches and devils dancing. Shadows swelled and shrunk around the room making the porcelain figures on the mantelpiece join in the macabre dance. Even when she closed her eyes she could still see red red blurs glimmering and the figures dancing.

Occasionally in the strange, hazy world between waking and sleeping a thought pierced her like an arrow: tomorrow night she would be married to the minister.

But when eventually she drifted into sleep, it was to dream of a tall man with his hair tied back from a craggy broken-nosed face. A man with massive shoulders and muscles like balls of iron. A man with a deep snarling voice.

'Come back, you little fool. Come back!'

She awoke with a start and sat up violently trembling. But there was no-one there.

Sunshine made a yellow haze of the room. Then Nancy entered, hair untidy, violet eyes still heavy with sleep. Yawning, she said,

'Come on, mistress. It's your wedding day. You'd better not keep Mr Blackadder waiting.'

Chapter 8

It was a calm night with only a gentle breeze blowing and the ship slid over the water leaving a wake of white froth. On such a night the ship seemed to swell up and grow bigger. It was in full bloom now and looked a beautiful and mysterious sight with its sails puffed out yet perfectly still. But Gav knew by now how quickly weather could change on such a long sea voyage and that a calm often came before a storm.

He and Regina had arranged to meet on deck, watch the sunset together and perhaps talk of plans for their future in Virginia. Regina told him she did not sleep well and often came on deck to watch the sunset or sunrise.

The last shades of day were lingering on distant waves when Gav noticed the strangeness of the sky. On a dark blue lowering expanse floated light yellow clouds tinged with various colours of the evening. A strong tint began reflecting on the ship's shrouds and rigging until it was a golden ship gliding over golden water.

'I don't like that,' Gav said, glancing anxiously around. Now even the calm sea looked ominous. A sea-bird shrieked as it passed.

Regina shrugged.

'It means we're going to have another storm, I suppose. We'll be lucky if we ever reach Virginia.'

'Don't say things like that.'

She pointed down at the water.

'The swell's starting already.'

'Have you spoken to Mr Gudgeon yet?' Gav tried to change the subject.

'Oh, yes. I spoke to him all right and he took his revenge for me laughing so heartily at him when he fell. I could tell by his ugly face when he refused my request.'

Gav could not hide his disappointment. He had been depending on spending the rest of the voyage with Regina in the comparative comfort of her cabin. He missed her terribly and also, as Jemmy had warned, the foc'stle was little better than the steerage as far as comfort was concerned.

'He said, "The steerage is the place for tramps like him," ' Regina went on. 'I nearly laughed again and told him that he was a fool and had been fooled all along because you were with the crew in the foc'stle. You'd spent no more than a night or two in steerage.'

'You didn't tell him, did you?' Gav's freckled face screwed up with concern.

'No, don't worry. Your secret's still safe.' Then, her voice losing some of its sarcasm, she added: 'Pity about sharing the cabin though.'

As they stood talking in the half darkness with the golden shadows tinting the ship, it began to pitch and roll and waves grew like mountains and reared high on either side.

'I'm fed up with this.' Gav tried to sound gruff.

'Well, it was your idea to come to Virginia, not mine.'

'I couldn't turn down the job when Maister Ramsay offered it to me. It was either that or spend my life begging with Quin. And you had to get as far away as possible from Mistress Ramsay.'

'Stop complaining then. We can't do anything about the weather.'

He swallowed with difficulty, then nodded.

'It'll be all right when we get to Virginia. Maister Ramsay said the weather was fine and warm there.'

Regina rolled her eyes.

'Must you believe everything he tells you?'

'Och, you're just suspicious of everybody. Why should Maister Ramsay lie to me?'

'To persuade you to go as a slave to the plantations of course.'

'I'm not going anywhere as a slave. An indentured servant's different.'

'How is it different?'

Gav wished Regina wouldn't keep worrying him. He was troubled enough without her sharpening the edge of his anxiety.

'I've to get my clothes and my food.'

'They'll have to feed their slaves, I suppose.'

'I know!' he said suddenly brightening. 'My indenture papers are only for five years. That means I'll be free when I'm sixteen. And all indentured servants get fifty acres of land when they're free.'

Regina's mouth twisted.

'If you live that long.'

Gav stuffed his hands into the pockets of his jacket and tried to look as if he didn't care. Eventually he said:

'I'm going back to the foc'stle.'

Regina shrugged and looked away as if it wasn't any interest to her where he went. Hurt and near to tears, he walked as best he could along the rolling deck. Loneliness slid around him like a snake, cold and frightening. It separated him from his surroundings so that he was unaware of where he was going or who was there. He groped through the shadows for the foc'stle scuttle.

'One of the crew now, are you?'

Mr Gudgeon's voice alerted him and he gazed up at the man's red face with its snout-like nose and tiny eyes.

'I don't think they mind me being with them.'

'If you're crew, you're not supposed to think. You're just supposed to work.'

Gav stared down at his feet, not knowing what else to say or do.

'Well, get working then,' said Mr Gudgeon.

Nervously Gav looked up again.

'I don't understand, sir.'

'You don't know what to do, eh?'

'No, sir.'

'Well, I'll tell you. Get up the shrouds and out on the yardarm.'

Gav's eyes widened with fear. He had often watched with bated breath as seaman clambered up the cobwebs of ropes stretching from each side of the ship high into the masts. He had marvelled at their courage and dexterity when they performed the apparently impossible feat, especially in stormy weather, when they climbed out onto the yardarms. The idea of himself attempting such dizzying heights brought paralysing terror. He could neither move nor utter a sound.

Mr Gudgeon rasped louder.

'Up the shrouds with you, I said.'

Still Gav could not move. Mr Gudgeon's face darkened from red to purple and he grabbed the little boy by the ear and propelled him across the deck.

'Up!' he roared.

He leapt onto the shrouds himself and dragged Gav with him. Then he balanced on the top of the bulwark with one hand clutching the ropes and one hand jerking and pushing the child.

'Up, I said. Up with you. Higher, damn you. Higher!'

As Gav clung desperately to the ropes, the ship heaved from side to side and there was nothing but sea beneath him and the sea and the yellow horizon kept swinging about and swooping up and making him feel sick.

Then, unexpectedly, Mr Gudgeon gave a different kind of cry, making Gav twist his eyes round. To his horror, he saw a shadowy Regina batter at Mr Gudgeon's legs with a belaying pin making him lose his balance on the slippery bulwark. Swinging out with the pitching of the ship, he still managed to cling to the rigging with one hand until a wave like a black mouth rushed up and swallowed him.

'Man overboard!' Gav shouted. 'Man overboard!'

'Come down and be quiet, you fool,' Regina commanded.

He climbed down, refusing her proffered hand.

'We can't just let him drown.'

Pushing her aside he ran, stumbling from side to side and clutching at whatever he could, until he reached aft where the bosun was talking to the helmsman.

'Man overboard!' he shouted again and the cry was immediately taken up by the bosun until it echoed like a chorus all over the ship.

A boat was quickly got out and four men began rowing in the direction that Gav indicated. The sea was so high that nothing could be seen of the mate. The boat kept disappearing too but eventually Captain Kilfuddy, looking through his spying glass, shouted:

'I see him. He's still struggling to swim. They're pulling towards him. He's going down . . . No, wait, I think they've got him. Aye, they're hauling him up.'

It took another half-hour in the gathering dark and swelling sea before the boat struggled alongside and hoisted Mr Gudgeon aboard.

Regina came and stood beside Gav and the rest of the crew. She waited silently and with apparent unconcern.

Gav said,

'He looks dead.'

The captain had produced a knife and said:

'Tie up the arm.'

'What's going to happen?' Gav asked Jemmy Ducks.

'He's got to be bleeded, Gav. And if that don't work, they tries rubbing and other things.'

Captain Kilfuddy hesitated, knife poised.

'You got to be gey careful,' he explained, 'no' to hack into an artery instead o' a vein.'

At last he made an incision. No blood came however. As a result friction was applied. After some considerable time, when that failed, the application of salt was tried and strong volatiles.

Gav watched with confused emotion. He wanted the man to recover so that Regina would not be guilty of causing his death. Yet, at the same time, he feared his return to consciousness and hoped he would die so that Regina would be safe.

Two hours passed without the smallest symptom of returning animation, then suddenly blood spouted from the arm for a few seconds and as suddenly stopped. Ten minutes after that the limbs became stiff and the colour of the skin changed.

Regina turned away saying:

'If he wasn't dead before, he's dead now.'

Gav followed her in silence. Regina glanced at his face, sickly white beneath its dusting of freckles.

'Why are you looking so miserable? You didn't like him any more that I did.'

'You killed him,' Gav whispered incredulously.

'It was either you or him. You would have fallen off the rigging and drowned if you'd gone any further.'

'I might not have.'

'You were terrified.'

Gav bristled.

'But I kept on climbing. You would have felt frightened too if you'd been up there.'

'Anyway, you don't need to worry about Bully Gudgeon any more. Now you can move into my cabin.'

He could not deny he was glad of that.

'I suppose,' he conceded uncertainly, 'if you thought you were saving my life, it wasn't really murder.'

'It's only a word,' she said, looking away.

The poop lanterns sent light lurching up one side of the darkness then the other as Regina groped for his hand and led him into the cabin. She had left a lantern lit inside but its candle had burned low and was barely a pinprick in the gloom.

'The berth's broad enough for both of us,' she said. 'The floor's wet with water coming in the window. But they've put the dead-lights up now.'

'What's the dead-lights?' Gav asked faintly.

'Wooden shutters they nail over the windows to keep the sea out when there's going to be a bad storm.'

'I don't mind the storm so much now that I'm with you,' Gav said, climbing into the berth beside her. Huddled close to his sister with her arm protectively across him, he felt almost happy. It was like how it used to be when mammy was alive.

They didn't speak any more but lay for long sleepless hours in the blackness of the berth listening to the wind moaning and howling in a hysteria of anger that creaked the ship over on one side then hurled it over to the other.

Eventually Gav said:

'This is the worst one yet, and the longest. It must be near morning now.' The words were no sooner out of his mouth, when there was a terrific crash outside on the deck. 'What was that?'

He could feel Regina's heart pounding against his back but her voice sounded calm.

'One of the masts gone perhaps.'

'Should we get up?'

365

'Why?'

'To look. Or . . . or to be ready in case they're going to abandon ship.'

Regina gave a mirthless laugh.

'If this ship breaks up, I can't see what chance the longboat would have. But probably it's time we were up anyway, so we'll take a look if you like. Hold on tightly though.'

Carefully they climbed from the berth and after a long time and many painful attempts, they reached the cabin door and Regina managed to open it. Immediately a gust of wind sprayed them with salt water and through it they saw the ship rearing up until it seemed she might reach the perpendicular. Sails that had bellied and cracked were now ripped to shreds and the topmasts were bent like willows.

Regina struggled to shut the cabin door again but wasn't strong enough. At last, between them, they managed it.

Then they waited, hand in hand, in the darkness of the cabin.

Chapter 9

Captain Kilfuddy creaked open the door, peeling away a slice of darkness.

'Ah, there you are, Master Chisholm. I thought we'd lost you. You look gey pale, the pair of you.'

Gav and Regina blinked in the bright light of day and Gav asked:

'Are we going to be shipwrecked?'

'Och, not a bit of it. It was just a merry wind and it's all but finished now.'

Gav stepped cautiously out of the cabin. Some of the crew were busy cleaning up the deck. Others were bending new sails although there was still quite a strong wind and the sea was rolling and frothing about.

He and Regina were glad to be on deck for a breath of fresh air.

'Look!' Gav pointed excitedly at a whale heaving its massive body out of the water. 'It's bigger than the ship. What a giant.'

In a minute the whale disappeared again but by the time Gav and Regina reached the bulwarks, porpoises were joyfully playing and chasing each other about, rolling, diving and leaping from the water.

Jemmy Ducks came hopping and limping over beside Gav and Regina.

'It'll be land-ho soon, shipmates. I sees the signs, smells them too.'

'What signs?' asked Gav.

Jemmy sniffed loudly and deeply, making his face pinch in and his ears stick out.

'Pine trees. Sometimes I smells them from as much as sixty leagues off shore.'

Gav sniffed again and again.

'I can't smell anything but salty air.'

'You've just not learned how, Gav. This is your first voyage but many's a hard gale I've weathered. Many's the time I've been glad of the signs. Damn my eyes, there's some more.'

'Where?'

'Them bits of flotsam. Them logs and branches. Them plants. And look, Gav, the sea's not deep blue any more. That sea's offshore green.'

Gav began bouncing about with excitement. There were land birds skimming the crests of the waves now.

'Land-ho! Land-ho!' he shouted in great joy.

'No, no.' Jemmy shook his head, making his pigtail jerk to and fro. 'Don't be heaving-to yet, shipmate. I tells you, we've maybe two or three days sailing before us. It depends on wind and weather. Them winds are devils. Many's the time we've been in sight of the Chesapeake and them winds have blown us verra near back to Glasgow.'

'Once I'm on land, I'll never, never go to sea again.'

'Them's the verra words I've said myself. Never again, I says. But I did haul up my anchor, Gav. And you will too.'

Gav couldn't imagine it. He longed to set foot on solid earth once more and hoped he would never feel the pitching and tossing of a ship again as long as he lived, although at the moment it was entrancing to watch the porpoises playing and the giant whales spouting.

Soon he saw the mariner's lead being swung out into the water and Jemmy explained that it had been greased with tallow so that whatever lay at the bottom would stick to it. At the parallel where the Chesapeake joined the Atlantic the bottom consisted of mud mixed with sand and small oyster shells. If the lead brought up this mixture then, said Jemmy,

'Our latitude's thirty-seven degrees north, Gav, and the Capes of Virginia lies dead ahead.'

Regina appeared not to be listening to Gav and Jemmy's conversation. Elbows leaning on the bulwarks, she was gazing absently into space. She was not sure whether she would be glad to reach Virginia or not. She had no idea what she was going to do when she got there. Would it be best to continue acting the part of a boy, she wondered. Not that she had any fears of

Mistress Annabella finding her in this far-off land. But it might be easier for a boy than a girl to find work or buy a piece of land, or do anything. Perhaps she could be employed in Ramsay's store along with Gav until she had a chance to look around and see what other opportunities there were.

'Look! Look!' Gav shouted again. Flying fish with white bodies and black wings were rising out of the water and skittering above the waves with dolphins pursuing them. Sometimes they soared into the air for ten to twenty feet before dropping back with a gentle little splashing noise into the continual swishing of the water.

Regina wished time would stand still and she would always remain like this, shut inside herself, never reaching anywhere, never needing to make any decisions, just standing staring out at the vast ocean. But sadness came to blur the edges of her rigidity and hang heavy on her like a black cloak. It cut her off even further from the frolicking life in the water, from Gav and Jemmy chatting, from the sailors energetically working the pumps and singing.

'. . . Oh, pump away in merry, merry strife,
Oh, heave away for to save dear life,
Oh, pump her out from down below,
Oh, pump her out and away we'll go.
The starboard pump is like the crew,
It's all worn out an' will not do,
Leave her, Johnny, we can pump no more,
It's time we wuz upon dry shore.'

Without saying anything, Regina turned away. Gav did not notice her go. He was too thrilled by everything that was going on and interested in what Jemmy was telling him. She went to the cuddy and sat at the table with white knuckled hands in front of her. Lack of sleep screwed her on a rack between wakefulness and repose. Nightmares born of the darkness refused to die. Flitting about like shadows they haunted the daylight hours, straining her with anxiety. She longed for some haven where she could relax and rest and have no need to worry about anything or anybody. But life was a snake pit where nothing could be expected except evil abuse. Anything different had to be fought for or paid for and she was girding herself to do both.

She'd heard that the Colonies were always desperate for servants of any sort so that there should be no difficulty getting a job beside Gav in Ramsay's store. But it would only be a temporary measure. One day she would have a store of her own. Or something even bigger and better. One day she would have servants serving her. The certainty of this gave her some satisfaction and lightened her spirits so that later during what was known as a 'smooth spell', she was able to enjoy the first cooked meal she and Gav (or anyone else for that matter) had had for several days.

It was impossible not only to cook in the galley when it was stormy but for anyone to walk from the galley to the table with the food. Many a man had lost his reviving hot drink of tea before reaching the foc'stle. Many a dish of salt beef had ended in the scuppers.

That night the weather remained calm and she took a lantern on deck and stood gazing at the sea's looking-glass surface speckled with star dust. A gentle breeze was blowing the ship over the dark water leaving a wake of silver fire. The fairy image remained with her long after she returned to her cabin and lay awake, as still as a corpse, listening to the creaking and groaning of the ship.

She was still awake when morning came and Gav scrambled happily from the bunk. It seemed as if she had lain the whole night long with eyes and ears alert. Yet black spaces in her memory indicated that there must have been occasions when sleep crept up on her.

'Regina! I mean Reggie,' Gav hastily corrected himself. 'Come on, we don't want to miss the first sight of land. Jemmy says we might reach the Chesapeake today.'

But it was not that day but the next before they heard the cry of 'Land ho! Land ho! Land ahead on the larboard bow.'

Everyone was jubilant. Even Mr Jubb could not contain his excitement. His face flushed and his eyes shone. Captain Kilfuddy frisked about the deck and rubbed his hands with glee. He was quite cranky with delight.

'Och, what a wonderful science is navigation!' he cried out. 'Is it no' astonishing, Maister Chisholm, that we've safely crossed thousands of miles of trackless ocean and found land again? The verra land we planned to reach.'

'Indeed it is, sir,' Gav agreed.

'Let us a' thank God,' said the captain, taking off his hat and gazing heavenwards, 'for our preservation from the perils of the deep. We thank ye, Lord. Aye, we thank ye.'

Then he thumped his hat back on and grinned delightedly round at everyone again.

By that afternoon they had reached the Chesapeake—'The Noblest Bay in the Universe'—and they were sailing deep into the James River.

Gav feverishly chattered all the time. The New World had obviously cast a spell over him and Regina couldn't blame him for being so impressed. She had never expected to see such thickly wooded shores or trees of such enormous proportions. The forests looked ancient, primeval. They had a reverent gloom that was awesome and frightening. Everything was giant size. Foot long bullfrogs made the deep bellowing sounds of oxen, enormous turtles sunned themselves on the river banks and swam with their heads out of water. Shoals of fish packed the river, and there were whales and porpoises in abundance. The water was black with ducks and when they took flight there was a great rustling and vibration like a storm coming through the trees. Wild geese were everywhere too and they rose in such enormous numbers that the noise made by their wings sounded like a whirlwind.

Flocks of four or five hundred turkeys could be seen hustling along. Some must have weighed fifty pounds and more.

At last, through the tangle of undergrowth and the forests of giant pine and oak and chestnut, clearings began to appear and projecting into the muddy waters of the river were the rough wood landings of the plantations.

The Glasgow Lass billowed along on a fine breeze until she reached the wharf which was backed by the log warehouses and sheds where hogsheads of tobacco had been collected ready for shipping. Nearer the backcloth of trees could be seen the timber building that served as the store. There was a jailhouse too with a scaffold and pillory. In front of the jailhouse stretched a large clearing. Over on one side stood a cluster of log cabins of various sizes, some with large brick chimneys built out on one wall from ground to roof. Some had curtains at sparkling glass windows and all the doors lay open. From all directions people were hastening to the wharf to welcome the ship as it glided in. Negro slaves ran to catch the lines and warp the vessel into the side.

A gang plank was made ready and down strutted Captain Kilfuddy into the dusty bilge-stinking heat wearing his hair tied back in a bow and a large black stock muffling his neck and chin. He was greeted by the store manager, Mr Speckles, who, despite his shifty eyes, looked and was genuinely glad to see him. Mr Speckles was a lonely skeleton of a man with a pale scurfy face and nails bitten down until there was a red rim protruding at the end of each finger.

The Virginians did not like store managers to whom they owed a great deal of money and Mr Speckles, like the other managers of the stores in the chain that stretched deep into the interior, had been advised by the Glasgow tobacco lords not to become too friendly with the neighbouring planters. They were also forbidden to marry. Shiploads of women had been sent over to Virginia from Scotland for the purpose of supplying wives for planters and other men but storekeepers were supposed to concentrate all their time and attention on nothing but business.

'And what have you got for me this time, Cap'n?' he queried, his eyes jerking furtively this way and that.

'All that ye asked for and more, Mr Speckles,' the captain announced proudly. 'There's everything from linens, damask, gloves, china teacups, silver plates, cutlery, fine furniture, pots and pans and tools, to convicts and indentured servants.'

'Thank the Lord for the servants. How many lassies did Maister Ramsay send me?'

'No lassies, Mr Speckles. Just one lad. Gav Chisholm's the name. Aye, but there's another who's willing. A cousin of wee Gav's. As smart a young lad as any, I'll wager.'

'Ah, well, a servant's a servant. One's better than none and two's even better. There's plenty planters here, as you can see,

Cap'n. They're waiting for the goods being ready for sale in the store. But they're even more anxious for servants. Some of them aren't too keen on having Negroes in the house. Even in the fields they're more of a hindrance than a help at first. They're slow and clumsy and that's not much use when seedlings have to be transplanted.'

'The convicts are women. Most of them quite hale and hearty.'

'Good, good.'

'Here's the lads I was telling you about.' The captain raised his voice. 'Maisters Chisholm. Over here with ye. Aye, there ye are.' He beamed at them when they arrived at his side. 'Aren't they a smart looking pair, Mr Speckles?'

'Indeed, indeed. If you come into the store I'll take you upstairs and show you your room. My living quarters and my counting house are above the shop. It's best, I think, that you should be where I can keep an eye on you. We'll talk business later. Will you come up as well, Cap'n, and I'll give you a dram.'

Mr Speckles was wearing a brown tie-wig, a dusty looking green frockcoat and breeches, a long brown waistcoat and brown buckled shoes. He walked in a jerky fashion with his hands tucked underneath the tails of his coat and puffs of dust spurting up from behind his heels.

'You've given your orders to unload, I've no doubt.'

'Aye, aye,' said the captain. 'Everything's under way, don't you worry, Mr Speckles.'

But just to make certain, Mr Speckles stopped at the door of the store and blinked back at the wharf. There, sure enough, were Mr Jubb and the bosun shouting orders to the men who were busy unloading the cargo and singing so heartily they all but drowned out Mr Jubb's and the bosun's cries. Later these same men would come ashore gaily rigged-up in varied costume. Most wore white stockings, loose white duck trousers, blue jackets and checked or striped shirts. Some swaggered ashore wearing gay sashes full of pistols and cutlasses. They would make for the path through the trees that led to another clearing and the Widow Shoozie's tavern.

Mr Speckles heaved a quick little sigh. Even the thought of a

373

woman tormented him. The need for one continually clawed at his innards, distracting him from his work making him absent-minded and a prey to secret acts with his slaves and himself that he was bitterly ashamed of. With an effort he banished such thoughts from his mind.

There was an outside wooden stair at the side of the store that led to the living quarters and the counting house and as he climbed it, he gripped his hands tightly under his coat tails, making them bulge and flip.

Reaching a narrow inside passage at the top of the stairs he indicated where Gav and Regina had to go and then led Captain Kilfuddy into the counting house. At an open window there was a table and chairs where they settled to savour their dram. From the window could be seen *The Glasgow Lass*, her masts like fragile threads compared with the trees crowding in on either side of the clearing.

Mr Speckles said:

'I've had a hard time on my own these past few weeks, Cap'n. My clerk and two servants died of the fever and a woman slave was drowned. All since I've last seen you. I'm dogged with bad luck, sir. Dogged by it.' He fingered his glass round and round, never raising his eyes from it.

'Aye,' the captain agreed. 'That's verra true. You get more than your share of stormy weather, Mr Speckles. But be of good cheer, you're not shipwrecked yet.' The old man raised his glass. 'Yer good health, sir.'

Mr Speckles nodded, lifting his own glass but his eyes not quite reaching the same height.

'Safe journey back to Glasgow, Cap'n.'

While the two men were downing their whisky, Regina and Gav surveyed their new home. The walls of the room were made of huge logs and the chinks were filled with clay. There were two bunk beds, a table dark with stains, and two chairs. From the glassless window they could see a vegetable patch and a tiny cornfield. The corn had been planted between tree stumps as that part of the forest had been cleared. Then there was the forest itself like a gigantic wall.

Heat shimmered like yellow steam outside but inside it was

dark brown and comparatively cool.

'Isn't this marvellous?' Gav said.

Regina shrugged.

'I suppose it's better than sleeping in filthy cold closes in Glasgow.'

'Maybe later we'll get time to go exploring. Do you think I should change into my old clothes now?'

'No, better wait until he's spoken to us and told us what our duties are.'

'Are you going to be a girl again?' Gav asked.

Regina looked away. She felt afraid of anyone knowing she was female. Yet for how much longer could she hide her swelling breasts and rounding hips.

'Mind your own business,' she said.

Chapter 10

Annabella decided to wear scarlet on her wedding day. Letitia Halyburton and her daughters Griselle and Phemy had tried pleading, cajoling and bullying her into the white satin dress trimmed with silver. Or even the flowered silk. But Annabella was adamant. She was wearing the scarlet taffeta and to hell with the lot of them.

Griselle said,

'It's not even fashionable any more. Everyone's wearing delicate pastel shades in London.'

Griselle was very proud of the fact that she had been to that far-off city and never missed an opportunity of bringing up the fact in conversation.

'I don't care a damn what they're wearing in London.'

'But, Annabella . . .'

'I do what I please and I wear what I please.'

Griselle's lips primped. She had a draw string mouth like her mother and was stiff-backed like Letitia too.

'You may wear what you please, Annabella, but I don't think it pleases you much to be marrying the minister.'

Annabella flicked out her fan and tipped her head high.

'I dare say, Mistress Griselle, I'll be as happy, if not happier, married to Mr Blackadder as you are to my brother Douglas.'

Griselle flushed. Douglas was a fop and not renowned for any strength of character. It had often been said that the devil had been at work in the Ramsay house and twisted everything about so that Annabella had all the spunk and her brother was the delicate, giggling female.

There was no need to persuade him to dress up. At that very moment he was at home fussing and fluttering into his frilly shirt and his suit of flowered silk. He would also have painted his face as the gentlemen of fashion did in England but he hadn't the courage to withstand the wrath that the sight of cosmetics would explode in his father.

He was to be the bridesman and was expected to appear at the Ramsay house within the hour and escort Annabella to the church. His father's displeasure at the perfumed powder he'd used on his wig would be hard enough to bear. By the time he reached the house, however, his father had left for the church and the bridesmaids were waiting eagerly for his arrival. Everyone was on tiptoe with anticipation it seemed, except the bride.

Annabella was sitting in her bedroom like a queen, head held high, fan flicking. Her eyes were wide open yet she did not seem to be looking at anyone or anything.

Twice Phemy had to say,

'Annabella, dear, your brother has arrived and we are ready to form the procession.'

Then suddenly Annabella bounced to her feet and swooped towards the door like a flame setting the room ablaze.

Everyone hustled excitedly after her, hitching up skirts and petticoats to protect them from the dirt of the turnpike stairs leading down to the back yard.

Outside the close in Saltmarket Street a piper was waiting and when he saw Annabella approaching like a whirlwind, he hastily set his pipes skirling to the tune of 'Fye, let's a' to the Bridal.' Behind him the bridal procession formed in readiness to follow the piper up Saltmarket Street, round by the Cross and along Trongate Street to the church. The bride was supported on one side by Douglas, the bridesman, and on the other by a young bridesmaid called Netty. Douglas and Netty linked arms with Annabella and from Netty's left hand and Douglas's right was held a white scarf which festooned across the figure of the bride. Behind them were two young girls bearing a scarf in the same way and behind them again fluttered Griselle and Phemy and another girl called Sukie. The sun sparkled the bridesmaids' wide-skirted yellow and blue and silver satin gowns and made riotous gardens of the flowered silks which Douglas, Griselle, Phemy and Sukie wore.

The procession drew the attention of crowds of townspeople who either leaned from windows to watch or jostled about on either side of the street or merrily joined in. Children skipped after it too and blue-coated beggars and one-eared thieves and tousy-haired harlots. People clapped their hands and danced up and down and there was a great babble and buzz of laughter and of excitement that almost drowned the music of the pipes.

The church was packed inside and the heat of the day had increased the stench of living bodies as well as those long dead. The earthen floor was continuously being dug up and human bones kicked aside to make room for fresh bodies. People complained about the bones and the smell of them to no avail. But no-one was in the mood for complaining today as they crushed aside to make way for the bridal procession.

The sun's long fingers rainbowed through the stained glass windows patchily illuminating the gloomy interior of the church.

Mr Blackadder was waiting in front of the pulpit. He looked taller and thinner than usual in his new blue coat and breeches, white silk stockings and buckled shoes. He wore a tie-wig well powdered and carried his three cornered hat primly under one arm. Staring solemnly round at Annabella, he seemed to her more like an undertaker viewing a corpse than a bridegroom gazing on his bride. Not that she appeared a picture of happiness herself. To her this was more of a funeral than a wedding. Her life was ending. It was about to be buried with her freedom. Yet, liveliness refused to fizzle out. She had an almost irrepressible desire to poke her tongue out at Mr Blackadder, to do something, anything, to shock him and the tightly packed jostling congregation behind them. Long-faced idiot, she thought, giving her intended husband a stare prickling with impertinence before they separated to opposite corners to untie all the ribbons and knots about their persons. After being modestly surrounded and helped by her bridesmaids with this task, Annabella sauntered back.

In front of Mr Blackadder and Annabella waited the Reverend Mr Gillespie, hands clasped on top of fat belly, eyes patiently resting heavenwards. He performed the marriage ceremony like that, said the prayer, gave the exhortation and the benediction. Then the bride and groom again retired to separate corners this time to tie all their knots before leaving the church at the head of the procession led by the piper playing *She's wooed and married and a'*.

They crossed the street and crushed through the archway alongside the Halyburton warerooms and into the close at the back. Then up the stairs everyone squashed and hustled until the Halyburtons' door was reached. There they stopped to watch the bridesmaid and bridesman break an oaten cake over the bride's head before distributing the pieces among the company. Pieces of bride-cake were next thrown over the bride and bridegroom's heads to signify prosperity. Finally a glass of whisky was handed around before they all entered the house. Once inside a bottle of whisky was passed round sun-wise and healths drunk again.

Letitia Halyburton was proud of the fine feast she had prepared and stood at the head of the table, rigid-backed, with hands clasped beneath her long bosom as if holding it up.

For the guests to enjoy there was roast mutton, a roast pike, legs of mutton boiled with capers and served with walnuts and melted butter, a side of beef, a dish of rabbits all smothered with onions, reindeers' tongues, brandered chickens, cows' udders and eyeballs, and in the middle of the table balanced a pyramid of syllabubs and jellies.

'Come away in,' Letitia ordered briskly. 'Lift a plate off the sideboard.' She flicked her closed fan in the appropriate direction. 'Bride and bridegroom first. Now over to the table. This way, Mistress Blackadder. Tuts, Annabella,' her voice sharpened. 'You're Mistress Blackadder. Wake up, girl.'

Everyone laughed uproariously at Annabella forgetting her new name.

'Annie, Nell, Tam,' Letitia rapped out to servants. 'Help the folk. Willie,' she addressed her husband, 'cut the meat.'

Soon everyone was milling and squashing and chatting round the table and fast demolishing all the food it held.

Letitia found a plate for herself and cleared a path to what was left of the meal by striking everyone before her a sharp blow with her fan.

'Aye, Mistress Blackadder,' she said, finding herself next to Annabella. 'That's taken the wind out your sails.'

Annabella stared at the older woman who was busying

herself heaping a plate with food.

'What has, Mistress Halyburton?'

'Getting married, of course.'

Annabella laughed.

'Losh and lovenendie, you are very mistaken if you think marriage has made any difference to me. I feel the same today as I did yesterday. I do assure you of that.'

'We'll see how perjink you are tomorrow, mistress.'

'You mean after I'm bedded?' Annabella gave another trill of merriment. 'I am intrigued by your line of thought, Mistress Halyburton. Can it be that you do not know I have been bedded a prodigious number of times before? To know a man is no new thing for me.'

'Tuts, Annabella! Have you no shame? Hold your tongue! Someone might hear you.'

Annabella prettily pouted her lips over a spoon so that she could suck in creamy syllabub. Then she said,

'There's scarce a young woman in this town by the time she has been taught to spin but has also learned some houghma-gandie. Why not be honest about it?'

'You make the mistake, Mistress Blackadder, of judging everyone like yourself.'

'Fiddlesticks, Mistress Halyburton. I'm perfectly aware that no other woman could compete with me. Ask any man!'

Letitia's sallow face flushed a dark maroon.

'You are a shameless strumpet, mistress, and if it wasn't for your father's sake and the fact that our families are related by business and marriage, you would never be allowed to crack an egg in this house.'

Annabella shrugged and sauntered away, apparently enjoying her syllabub. In actual fact she felt sick but she would rather be damned than let anyone know it. Her bleeding was now over two weeks late and such a thing had never happened before. She must surely be pregnant. Conscience as well as her general malaise now bothered her. She did not care an oatcake for Mr Blackadder, yet his innocence of her condition made her feel guilty.

Not that her condition was her fault. Thinking of the man

responsible fevered her with such fury and bitterness she could barely conceal her agitation.

It was a relief and a cover of sorts when the dancing time came and everyone spilled out of the house, down the stairs and out onto Trongate Street. At least there was no need for conversation then and her flushes of distress could pass for the heat of the dance.

To the sound of the pipes, she and Mr Blackadder led off the first reel and everyone joined in with much laughing and screeching and rumbustious good spirits. Annabella flung herself into the merrymaking with a wildness that eventually became a worry to her sister-in-law Phemy. The little pock-face creased as if in pain.

'Annabella, you have me quite fluttered. Are you well?'

'Dear Phemy, you are always seeking someone to concern yourself with. But have no fears for me. I am having a prodigiously magnificent time.'

The Reverend Mr Blackadder was having a grand time too. Normally he frowned on the frivolity of dancing but as it was his wedding day he had rashly decided to throw all caution to the winds and was prancing and leaping about like a long-limbed horse.

He had obviously practised unusual restraint in his drinking, however. Normally before an evening's carousal had finished, he was incapable of standing up. He either slipped quietly underneath his host's table and into a deep slumber or he was carried home by servants.

This wedding night had reduced him to a state of hiccoughing inebriation but he was not helpless. Bottles of whisky kept being pressed upon him, only to be eased aside by a cautious and surprisingly steady hand.

He was still on his feet when the night ended. Dancing and kicking up his heels he led the multitude of guests and townspeople to his house in the Briggait. At the entrance he stopped, and to the encouraging cheers and shouts of the onlookers, he managed to lift Annabella into his arms and stagger over the threshold. The door shut leaving them in total darkness.

'Put me down, sir,' Annabella said. 'Get a lantern from

somebody before they all go away.'

'Uh-huh. Aye.' He fumbled with the door and managed to swing it open and call out, 'Willie Tampson, where do you think you're going with that lanthorn? Hand it ower, man. It's as black as sin in here.'

The lantern's yellow light wibble-wobbled over the inside stair and, through the open doorway of the kitchen on the right, Annabella caught glimpses of a dresser. On it pewter plates winked. Two chairs and a table flickered beside an inglenook fire. From a ceiling beam dangled a string of onions and a large ham. Mr Blackadder said,

'There's plenty of space in the kitchen and this bit lobby for the servants. Oor room's upstairs.'

He led the way unsteadily but with great concentration. Annabella had to gather up her skirts, carry them over one arm and manoeuvre her hoops sideways, the stairs were so narrow. There were two bedrooms, one on the first landing and another attic room up another rickety flight of stairs. They entered the first room which had oak wainscoting and a ceiling painted with coloured shapes like fruit. It was of decent proportions as far as Annabella could discern by the feeble light of the lantern. It contained a hole-in-the-wall bed draped with dusty brown material, a table in the centre of the floor, a bookcase with leaded glass doors, a mahogany lowboy, a grandfather clock in the corner, and some chairs.

Without a word, Annabella undressed and climbed into bed. Mr Blackadder's fumbling fingers took longer. After much pitching and rolling like a ship on a stormy sea, he won a battle with his nightshirt, then sank onto his knees at the side of the bed.

'Gracious heavens, what are you doing now?' Annabella groaned.

'Just saying my prayers.'

'Which one, sir? For what I am about to receive, the Lord make me truly thankful?'

'Aye,' said Mr Blackadder, climbing into bed. 'Maybe so, maybe so.'

Annabella stiffened her body and closed her eyes. She refused to give in to tears and later, amazed at her husband's energy, she had no strength to do anything but sleep.

Chapter 11

'You may call me Erchie, noo,' the Reverend Blackadder informed Annabella but she greeted the news with neither interest nor enthusiasm.

'I am entertaining cummers today, sir. Must you sit in this room?'

'I've my sermon to prepare. God's word can't be neglected, Annabella.'

'His word would be none the worse off being attended to upstairs in the attic. Or in the tavern, for that matter. Other men do their business there.'

She tweaked at the new bed drapes then smoothed a hand down their velvety richness.

'You've an unfortunate way of putting things, lassie. A verra unfortunate . . .'

'In the church, then,' Annabella interrupted impatiently. 'Do not ruffle me, Mr Blackadder. Griselle and Phemy are coming and we've servant and household problems to discuss. You will be a prodigious nuisance.'

Mr Blackadder reared up as if to take offence but, remembering Annabella's splendid condition, he eased himself back down again. The thought of having a son or daughter with Annabella's comely appearance and his own excellent character secretly delighted him. In this connection he was forever sending prayers of gratitude winging upwards.

'You're premature in your thanks, Mr Blackadder,' Annabella told him. 'The child could have my character and your looks.'

But the minister remained undaunted.

'Uh-huh, there's nothing wrong with the attic, I dare say. I'll just go up there for a wee while.'

'You'll be nearer the source of your inspiration,' Annabella flung at him as he passed clutching his big Bible, his quill pen and some papers.

He turned at the door to eye her sternly.

'Uh-huh, many a true word is spoken in jest, mistress.'

She rolled her eyes at his retreating back before plumping up the embroidered cushions on each chair. Then she tenderly unpacked her china teacups and saucers from the kist under the bed. As delicate as eggshells, they were painted with a few little strokes from which hung pink cherry blossom. She had other even finer china which had rice grains and flower patterns inset round the cups and if you held one up the light could easily be seen to shine through. But on this occasion she decided to use the painted cherry blossom set. Hesitating between the table in the middle of the floor and the smaller side table over in the corner, she eventually spread a snowy linen cloth on the large table. Each corner of the cloth had an embroidered cluster of pink roses and a festoon of ribbon a similar blue to the velvet curtains. She had stitched the embroidery herself and felt a glow of pride when she gazed at it. Even Letitia had grudgingly admitted that she was good with a needle. Carefully she arranged the cups and saucers and plates on the table. Then from the lowboy she fetched a cake and placed it in the centre of the table. It glistened black as coal with fruit and filled the nostrils with its spicy aroma. Next came a plate of sugar biscuits with the crunchy crystals quivering and winking in the light of the fire. The firelight also danced in the silver of the teapot and sugar and cream dishes her father had given her as a wedding present.

Annabella sighed with satisfaction as she surveyed the scene. The burning logs gave a cosy red glow to the room, accentuating the blue sheen of the curtains, the sparkling white of the table cloth and the lustre of the dishes.

Overcome with delight, she clapped her hands in admiration of the scene. Then she sang out,

'Nancy! Nancy!'

'I'm not deaf,' Nancy grumbled when she arrived upstairs from the kitchen. 'There's no need to raise the roof.'

'There's no need for you to be in such a monstrous black mood. Haven't I told you I'm arranging for more help in the house. Griselle and Phemy have word of someone. They are coming this afternoon. So you'd better hurry and get the tea made. They'll be here any minute. Nancy!' She summoned the maid back again and swirled round and round making her white muslin dress flutter out like butterfly wings. 'Do I still look prodigiously beautiful? My hateful condition is not in any way apparent, is it?'

'With these hoops how could your swollen belly be seen? Anyway, why do you worry? Everyone knows your condition and the minister for one is as pleased as punch.'

'Pox on the minister. I do not care what he thinks.'

She was wearing a satin petticoat of sky-blue under her gown and a blue ribbon to match was fastened round her throat with a neat bow in front. Her hair was drawn back in curls and there was a glow to her face that made her look even more beautiful than usual.

'So many women,' she said, 'let themselves go to wreck and ruin until they look like monstrous frumps when they are *enceinte*. I refuse to allow any man to reduce me to such a pitiable state.'

'You look all right. I'm away to make the tea.'

After Nancy disappeared Annabella glanced around the room again. The colour of the curtains was picked out in the paintings of fruit and other designs on the ceiling beams. The walls were panelled with oak wood, a shade darker than the lowboy, and the gold lettered books in the bookcase added a special richness to the place. She was tolerably well satisfied with the house, except that it needed more servants in it to cook and clean. Nancy insisted that she was supposed to be her personal maid and should not be wasting time with so much cooking and house cleaning. This was true enough, but efficient servants were not so easily come by. Nor were they over anxious to be employed in a minister's household. Their lives were joyless enough on a Sunday without living under the eagle eye of the minister every day of the week. This Annabella could understand. Sunday had always been bad enough in her father's house but since she had been married it was purgatory.

She had done everything to try and escape from it without success. Only last week she had tried to escape in sleep during her husband's long, long sermon, but although the minister had not noticed her, he had spied another sleepy member of the congregation and wakened the offender by calling to him,

'Andy McKay, you are sleepin'. I insist on your waking when God's word is preached to ye!'

Andy McKay had called back,

'Look at your ain seat, minister, and you'll see a sleeper forby me.'

And he'd pointed to the minister's pew where she was dozing wrapped snugly in her cape with its hood pulled well forward over her face.

'Mistress Blackadder,' the minister had called out loudly, making her jerk. 'Stand up!'

She felt furious. It was quite a common occurrence, she knew, for members of the congregation to be commanded to stand up in public and receive censure for some offence or other, but how dare he humiliate her. For a long minute she struggled between remaining seated and indulging in a public battle of wits or standing and being done with the situation as quickly as possible. One was as bad as the other. Eventually she stood up, trying to convey to him by furious meaningful looks that she would wreak her revenge on him later.

He leaned forward on the high pulpit, arms across the Bible, face stern.

'Mistress Blackadder, everybody kens you're nae angel. But even angels would have mair sense than to shut their eyes and lugs to God's word. We'll have a hymn noo and we'll a' sing with a' oor might and see if that'll help ye to wake up and pay attention.' He strained over the edge of the pulpit to where the precentor sat at a desk underneath. 'Dauvit, stop your snuffin' and sneezing. Put away that snuffbox and attend to your business.'

The snuffbox snapped shut. There was the dirl of the 'pitchfork' on the book-board and old Dauvit began bellowing out lines for the congregation to repeat after him.

Normally this was the only diversion of the long dreary imprisonment in the church because Dauvit made many mistakes, both in words and tune, and many a surreptitious giggle he had provided for her. On this occasion, however, she was still scarlet-faced and fuming at the minister and hardly noticed Dauvit and the congregation's unfortunate rendering of the line 'And for His sheep He doth us take' as:

> 'And for His sheep He'd
> And for His sheep He'd
> And for His sheep He'd
> -oth us take.'

But later, despite anger still fizzling inside her, she could not control a twitching of the lips when the precentor, faithfully followed by the multitude, exclaimed:

> 'Oh! Send down Sal
> Oh! Send down Sal
> Oh! Send down Sal
> va-tion to us.
> And we shall bow-wow-wow
> Bow-wow-wow
> Before the throne.'

It was not quite as hilarious as the occasion when the female voices in a choir had to repeat by themselves:

> 'Oh! For a man
> Oh! For a man
> Oh! For a man-sion in the skies.'

But it was enough to relieve some of the gloom and boredom and take away the keenness of her humiliation. As long as she could keep her sense of humour she would keep her sanity, she kept telling herself. But it was no easy task at times.

The tirling of the door-pin rasped through her thoughts and she whisked from the room and pattered downstairs, deftly manoeuvring her skirts as she went to welcome her two sisters-in-law.

There had been a time when she had considered them a monumental bore, but now with the restricting influence of the minister and her pregnant condition, they were a very welcome diversion.

Phemy's scraggy face peeked out from beneath a dark green

tartan plaid. Griselle's prettier features and highly coloured cheeks were accentuated by the scarlet of her hooded cape.

'Mistress Griselle, Mistress Phemy.' Annabella greeted them with a graceful curtsy and they curtsied prettily in reply. Then they all crushed upstairs. 'How is my brother Douglas today, Griselle?' Annabella inquired after they had divested themselves of their wraps and seated themselves in her bedroom. Douglas had been suffering from a feverish chill and was confined to bed.

'He'll survive,' Griselle remarked dryly. 'Although you would not think so with the fuss he's making.'

Annabella laughed.

'Gracious heavens! Are men all the same! My husband had the toothache the other day and, upon my word, the howling and yowling of him might have been heard in Edinburgh.'

Phemy giggled a little behind her hand but she said:

'Poor Mr Blackadder. What did you do to ease him, Annabella?'

'I passed him the whisky bottle and he eased himself.'

'The Earl of Glendinny,' said Phemy, referring to her own husband, an elderly widower who lived upstairs from her father, 'has been coughing more of late.'

Her father had chosen the Earl to be her husband and she had sensibly agreed when her father had pointed out that she was lucky to get anybody, far less a tobacco merchant with three stout sailing ships. She knew that with her small stature, pocked beaky face and straggling hair, she was no beauty. But she had a sweet singing voice and a kindly nature and she and the old Earl rubbed along easily enough.

'He is quite amenable to my ministrations, however. He supped the honey and herb mixture I gave him with very little coaxing.'

'Pray let me offer you some tea,' said Annabella, as Nancy entered the room and placed the silver engraved teapot on the table.

Griselle said:

'I am surprised at the minister allowing you to indulge in tea, Annabella. There is a great deal of agitation against it among the clergy.'

'I know, but I made such a prodigious fuss he was glad to agree. You knew my father gave me this handsome silver service?'

Phemy sighed.

'It is lovely, Annabella. Oh, and I do enjoy a cup of tea, don't you?'

'Indeed I do, Phemy. Let us be monstrously indulgent and wicked and have several cups.'

Both Griselle and Phemy giggled as they accepted their tea, Phemy with hunched up shoulders like a bird, Griselle straight-backed and prim-lipped.

After a few sips, Griselle said:

'We visited Mistress Netty yesterday and as usual she entertained us on the spinet.'

Annabella rolled her eyes.

'That girl makes a perfect toil of music. I swear one day she'll bore me to sleep.'

'Well, well,' said Griselle. 'At least she won't be able to make you stand up and be chastised for it.'

Annabella flushed and Phemy hastened to say,

'It was there I heard about this serving woman, Annabella. Her name's Betsy and she has a very decent character.'

'Damn her decency,' Annabella said. 'Can she make good collops?'

'Her cooking,' Griselle said, 'leaves a lot to be expected but she's young enough to train.'

'What age is she, pray?'

'Thirteen.'

'Hardly more than a child really,' Phemy said.

'About the same age as that monstrous Regina Chisholm was when she was supposed to be serving me. What an odious child she turned out to be.'

Griselle looked smug.

'Well, you can't say I didn't warn you, Annabella. I did warn you but in your usual headstrong fashion you paid no heed.'

'Betsy seems a nice girl,' Phemy said. 'I'm sure you'll be all right with her, Annabella.'

They were just enjoying their second cup of tea and sugar

biscuit when Mr Blackadder's long face appeared round the door. Then the rest of his lanky body eased itself into the room.

'Uh-huh. Aye.' Once in he leaned over in a low bow. 'There you are, ladies. Aye, it's yourselves. And verra welcome, as usual. Where did you put the whisky, Annabella?'

'There is a bottle on top of the lowboy. There in front of your eyes, sir.'

'Och, aye. So it is.'

'Why don't you join us and give us your chat, Mr Blackadder?' Phemy said kindly.

Annabella said,

'Mr Blackadder is busy preparing his sermon.'

'Aye. There's a lot of sin going aboot and it needs a lot of talking to.'

'What good does talking do, I wonder,' Annabella said.

'Uh-huh, och, well, I think I can hold my own with the stocks, the pillory and the hangman's noose.'

'I don't know what the world's coming to.' Griselle tutted and shook her head. 'Wickedness gets treated in much too soft a fashion, that's the trouble. There should be more offences punished by hanging. It's the only way. If we allow a child to steal a crust of bread today, nothing in our larders will be safe tomorrow.'

Phemy looked worried.

'I think hanging children is going a bit too far though, Grizzie.'

'Tuts!' Grizzie said impatiently. 'Stealing is stealing. They hang children all the time in London. With my own eyes I've seen whole cartloads of children, some no more than six or seven years of age, being taken through the streets to the gallows. I remember the bright coloured dresses of the girls.'

'Poor wee things,' murmured Phemy.

'If it were left to people like Phemy,' Griselle addressed Annabella and the minister, 'nothing or nobody would be safe.'

'Uh-huh. Aye. There's a lot of wickedness in the world. There's no fewer than six adulterers, twelve fornicators and fifteen breakers of the sabbath coming up before the Kirk Session this week.'

Griselle tutted again.

'The devil's busy, Mr Blackadder.'

'Aye,' the minister agreed. 'Verra busy.'

Annabella's thoughts were still on Regina. At last she said:

'I'd like to see that monstrous red-haired devil hanged all right. And maybe I'll see it yet.'

Chapter 12

Regina's job was to serve in the store. Gav was set to work on the ledgers in the counting house. Mr Speckles halved his time between upstairs and downstairs. The store was a long windowless room with double doors that lay open all day in the summer months. It had three counters, one at each end and one facing the doors in the middle. The light from the doors served most of the room but a lantern hung at each end to illuminate the shadowy corners. The floor, the walls, the counters were all cluttered with a great variety of articles. Even the ceiling was used as storage space and hens nested in the beams.

A box of nails was heaped on top with spades and hoes. Gloves, hooks and eyes, and buttons crammed other boxes. Ribbons like rainbows streamed from yet another. Prayer books and Bibles soared high on shelves like black mountains. Bales of serge, canvas, silk and taffeta made a wall on the counter behind which Regina could disappear from view. Stays and hoops for ladies dangled on the wall, the hoops bouncing and rolling about like giant balls when anyone brushed against them. On the floor sacks of coffee and wig powder squashed against barrels of whisky and chests of tea. Above them, strings of pumpkins festooned the wall. The air hung heavy and still, pungent with smells of coffee and tobacco and the carrion pelts that were spread over one of the counters.

The comparative darkness inside the shop made it look cool, but it was not. Regina wore only breeches, shirt and waistcoat. Long ago she had discarded her shoes, stockings and wig and she had her auburn hair tied back in a bow as most of the men did. But many gentlemen and ladies wore wigs, especially when visiting the store from one of the neighbouring plantations or when joining a ship to take them further down river to one of the bigger plantations which had their own wharfs.

But whatever reason they came to the settlement, once there

the gentlemen sauntered about discussing the state of their tobacco crop, grumbling about the store prices, the laziness of their servants, or the problems of catching runaway slaves. There were no proper paths or roads, only earth scuffed bald of grass except for fringes of green around cabins and tree stumps, and as the planters strolled in the blazing heat dust whitened their top boots and breeches. The brassy sun made the back of their throats taste metallic, and sweat dribbled down their eyebrows to hang glimmering like a spider's web with droplets of dew.

The windows of the houses flashed like diamonds and all the doors lay wide in the hope of sucking in a breeze from the river. But down by the sheds and warehouses it was no cooler. Steam rose from the water and shimmered wooden hulls and delicate giant masts. Only in the forest where the sun could not penetrate, along the tobacco road, in the slave quarters, or further along in Widow Shoozie's tavern was it tolerably cool.

But despite the heat men enjoyed walking around or gathering in the clearing in the centre of the settlement in front of the jailhouse to bet on cock fights.

Ladies put their heads together, happy at the chance of a gossip in one or other of the houses and sipped home-made peach brandy. They chattered about the latest fashions or their last trip to Williamsburg, or the news the ships had brought from Scotland or England. Or they exchanged recipes for puddings and potions or dramatic tales of confinements.

Regina was kept busy in the store, although there were quiet times too. Then she was able to escape and be on her own. Sometimes she went down by the creek and fished with rod and line. But it was a favourite place for the young lads of the settlement and if any of them appeared she slipped quietly away. There was a tree with a hollowed-out trunk on the way to the creek and often she would crouch in there and stay hidden for hours. Since she had been forced by the heat to discard her coat, the lack of the cover it had afforded worried her. But her waistcoat was long and not too tight and so did not reveal the true contours of her body. Even so, she found herself receiving unwelcome attention, not because of her shape but because of her hair and smooth complexion. And most of all, people remarked on the vivid green of her eyes.

One woman had laughed and said to Mr Speckles,

'Never did I dream, sir, that I would be envious of a lad's appearance. But I swear he is the most handsome I have ever seen. Such skin, Mr Speckles. Such skin and those eyes, sir. Never has an emerald been so green. If it were not for a certain hardness of expression both of the eyes and the mouth, he could pass for a young girl.'

People watched her and she hated the intrusion of their attentions. She especially hated Mr Speckles who stank of stale sweat and whisky and who sniffed a lot and had shifty eyes that often followed her. They quickly slithered away when she turned on him or suddenly stared up. But they kept ferreting back again to annoy her. She didn't like the man. She didn't like his flaky face and moth-eaten wig and filthy handkerchief forever trailing and fluttering from his back pocket. She didn't like his sunken eyes and consumptive appearance. She hoped he might die of the consumption or the fever or the flux so that she and Gav would be left on their own. They could run the place, she was sure. In no time they had picked up how things were done.

They dealt mostly with small planters and offered credit and paid for the planters' tobacco crop mostly in goods. There was an acute shortage of coin in the colony and everyone, even the ministers, got paid in tobacco. This shortage of coin meant that the planters could not do their shopping anywhere else but the Company's store. There they were allowed to buy goods up to the limit of the tobacco they produced. In the store all the goods on display were marked with two prices, a 'cash' price and a much higher 'goods' price. Those who paid in money or tobacco were allowed the lower cash price. Those who wanted credit, however, had to pay the higher goods price. Already it was obvious to Regina that once a man got into debt, it was difficult for him to pay it off. His debts just kept increasing and most of the planters' next year's crops were already mortgaged to the store.

Now she understood why Glasgow merchants like Ramsay

were wealthy. Even if they sold tobacco at a loss, the tobacco lords would still be rich on the profit from their retail stores. It was obvious too that the planters did not like the tobacco lords or their store managers, although sometimes Mr Speckles entertained one or two of them in the counting house to a bottle of whisky or wine and a game of cards. In letters from Ramsay he was told to do this to encourage good feeling and good business, and cases of wine and whisky were shipped over from Glasgow for this very purpose. Mr Speckles was also advised to allow the planters to win at cards. But even though he did this conscientiously, he was not a popular man with them. More often than not he gambled and drank with the tradesmen on the settlement, or the ships' captains when there were ships at the wharf. Often he went to the tavern, and when he wasn't furtively watching Widow Shoozie he caroused and gambled with back-woodsmen or trappers or whoever might be there.

Gav said he was sorry for him and took upon himself the task of getting Mr Speckles safely to bed every night. Sometimes he had to go out looking for him and half drag the drunken man back to the store before divesting him of his filthy garments and helping him into bed.

'Let him rot,' she told Gav. 'Or get one of the slaves to see to him. Why should you worry?'

'Why shouldn't I?' Gav replied. 'He's kind to me and I like him.'

Gav was easily pleased and there had always been a softness about him despite his efforts to appear tough. He had even liked the beggar, Quin, and had wept when they had parted in Glasgow. Quin had been ugly and deformed and had made them beg for him.

After she had got money of her own and she and Gav were ready to leave Glasgow, she had soon told the ugly Quin that he was no longer wanted. But Gav had actually seemed worried.

'What'll you do?' he'd asked the beggar.

'Who cares?' she'd said.

And Gav had cried out,

'I care! So you shut your cruel, wicked mouth.'

Gav would never get anywhere in the world. But she would.

Her golden pieces were still safely locked in her sea-chest. Meantime, she was learning fast about everything and everybody and gaining much invaluable experience.

She still was not sure of course what she could do. There might be the possibility of buying some land from one of the planters. Land was one commodity there was plenty of. Perhaps she could grow tobacco and become wealthy on that, but she would have to be careful that she did not get into debt like most of the others.

All this meant remaining as a young man. She did not know of any laws in Virginia preventing a female owning land or property. (Most taverns were apparently owned by women and the Widow Shoozie had a good sized plot at the back of her place.) But it might be easier as a man. She kept telling herself that her disguise was only for business reasons but in her heart she knew she was far too afraid of being a woman.

She still had nightmares about that terrible day when she went to the house in Tannery Wynd to look for Gav but found instead that it was crowded with French and Irish soldiers. They had been part of the army of the Stuart Pretender who had invaded Glasgow. One of the Frenchmen had grabbed her, whimpering with terror, into the hole-in-the-wall bed. Soon her whimpers had panicked into screams and she had gone on screaming as one man after the other had climbed into the bed on top of her. Eventually she was left dumb with shock, with blood pouring from between her legs.

She shrank from going to sleep at night in case the nightmare would return to terrify her. Over and over again she tried to convince herself that all men were not like those drunken animals of soldiers. Here in Virginia, for instance, men seemed to regard females very highly. A girl had barely reached her teens before she was snapped up in marriage. Only the other day the thirteen year old daughter of the carpenter had made a very good marriage. Regina knew she would have no problem finding a husband—perhaps even a rich husband—but the thought of a man, any man, defiling her again sickened her beyond measure. She could not bear to contemplate such horror. No, much better and safer to conceal the fact that she was a woman and increase her wealth and position by other means.

She was so deep in thought about her ambitions that she had not heard a customer come into the store. Suddenly he came into focus. He was peering closely at her across the counter.

'Ah! So you are not dead,' he said. 'You looked like a corpse standing there.'

'Oh, no,' she assured him. 'I'm very much alive, sir.'

It was Mr Harding from one of the biggest of the plantations in the interior. A huge, ugly man, he wore his hair tied back in a black ribbon notched into swallow tails. His dark moody eyes had a disconcerting habit of sharpening and riveting someone with unexpected attention, as he was doing now with Regina. She willed herself not to flush or flinch under his scrutiny. His wife trilled out.

'I do declare, I do declare, Master Reggie, you gave me quite a start. My poor little heart went pitter-patter, pitter-patter until I thought poor little me was going to faint.'

She was a fragile wisp of a woman with a face like a pearl button under her wig, and a wide hooped gown in which she seemed lost. Coquettishly she swooped up a fan from which a tassel bobbed and swung.

'As if this terrible heat wasn't enough.'

'May I offer you a chair, Mistress Harding?' Regina asked.

'That's mighty civil of you, mighty civil of you, sir.' She collapsed into the chair with a puffing of skirts and a rolling of eyes. 'I cannot think of a less salubrious place. One day it's unbearably hot and the next day, or that very evening, it has turned so cold I could just die, just die, Master Reggie.'

'I believe it is caused by the variable winds.'

'And there's nothing we can do about it,' Harding growled, 'so stop your damned complaining.'

His wife flushed but widened her eyes and flapped her lashes and fan.

'I do declare, I do declare, you are such a tease, Mister Harding.'

'Is her last order in yet?' Harding said, ignoring her.

It occurred to Regina that here was one man who did not

regard women very highly, especially his wife.

'I'm very sorry, sir. The ship has obviously been delayed. She should have been in a week ago. But we're expecting her any day. If you could return next week—'

'No, I could not. I've more important things to do than ride all the way out here every week.'

His wife rose in distress, thinking of the potions that she was depending on from a highly recommended chirurgeon in Glasgow. There were times she felt so weak and sickly she felt sure she was going to die.

'Oh, Robert, Robert. There are things I need. I need badly. You could easily send the carriage and some of the slaves.'

'Sit down. You don't know what you're talking about. This is the busiest season of the year on the plantation.' He turned to Reggie. 'Deliver them.'

'Deliver them?' Regina echoed.

'That's what I said.'

'But it is at least a day's ride and I've neither horse nor carriage. There were quite a few items in the order, sir. Including cases of wine for yourself. It would need a carriage.'

'Then you shall have a carriage. There is one at the black-smith's just now.'

'But, Robert, dear,' Mistress Harding's voice trembled and she prayed that she would not succumb to one of her breathless attacks. The pain in her chest and the choking sensation were very frightening and she never knew what to do about them except pray and keep calm. 'How shall I return to Forest Hall today?' she asked.

'You shall ride side-saddle behind me, madam, or take one of the slave's horses.'

She could have slipped down onto the floor with utter fatigue at the mere idea.

'But I cannot, I cannot.'

'Then you do not get your precious items from Scotland.'

She blinked and tried not to look miserable. But her face had gone an ugly putty colour and she could no longer contort it into a smile. She knew it must be terrible for a robust man like her husband to have to suffer such a weakling as herself and she was forever trying to appear bright, cheerful and normal in her manner and also to be gay and attractive in her dress, but nothing seemed to work as successfully as she hoped. She kept trying because she thought Robert was a wonderful person and was honoured to be his wife.

Regina thought Harding was a brute of a man. He was as big and muscley as his wife was tiny and frail. His dark hair was tied back from a broken-nosed face and he wore an open necked shirt and carried a whip. It was said of him that he abused his slaves but she could imagine him being equally cruel to his wife.

He was a brute, but then all men were brutes. She managed to give him one of her small polite smiles.

'How do I return to the store, sir? That is, if I manage to handle a carriage and a pair of horses and find my way to your plantation.'

'Ah, no easy task for a young lad, I agree. But you have a determined look about you, Master Chisholm. I have an idea that once you make up your mind to achieve something, you achieve it.'

'Once I make up my mind, sir.'

Harding laughed.

'You will be well rewarded, never fear. You shall have a horse of your own from my stables.'

Another dry smile.

'Your order will be delivered.'

Mr Speckles became quite agitated when later she told him. He stuffed his nose with too much snuff and went into such a paroxysm of sneezing that he spilled the rest of his snuffbox all over his coat and looked dirtier and more repulsive than ever with eyes inflamed, wig askew and nose and mouth dribbling. But Mr Harding was an important customer and he had no choice but to agree in the end between snuffles and rubbings with his oversized hanky. He gave her what directions he could of the route to Harding's plantation. She must try to keep to the tobacco road, he said. Only it wasn't really a road, just a track through the trees made by the hogsheads of tobacco being dragged along from the plantations to the wharf every year for shipping to Glasgow. At the same time he kept moaning and muttering, half to himself,

'I'm dogged with bad luck. Dogged by it. I've lost two clerks already. The devil has me by the coat-tail in this God-forsaken place.'

Regina said,

'I have no intention of getting lost, sir. The journey will be of no concern to me once I master the horses. If Mr Harding can successfully travel through the forest, so can I.'

Yet secretly she was afraid. All the settlers, including grown men, feared the forest and were continuously working to clear it. They dreaded the darkness of the trees and the wild beasts and savages they concealed. The high branches whispered a constant reminder of a wilderness unconquered. Men seldom ventured into it alone and even Harding, when he came to the store, always had several slaves with him. Yet, a horse was no small prize. It was one of the symbols of wealth and comfort and security and she had pledged her life to acquiring these things.

Gav said,

'You can't mean it, Reggie. Nobody goes deep into the forest on their own.'

'Don't worry,' she said. 'I'm not asking you to come with me.'

'I don't think Mr Speckles would let me but . . . I . . . I could ask him if you're really set on going.'

He looked so wide-eyed with fear that she gave a burst of laughter.

'I said don't worry. I don't want you to come.' Then seeing his miserable expression, she added in a kinder tone, 'I'll be fine with a carriage and two fast horses, Gav, and I shall be there in no time. When I return with the horse he has promised me you shall have a turn of it whenever you like.'

His face brightened.

'Will you let me help to look after it too?'

'Of course.'

When she was not serving in the store she practised taking Harding's carriage and horses round the settlement until she felt confident at handling the reins. But she did not go near the forest, not even as far as the tavern.

Then one day a ship was sighted coming up the river in full

401

sail. It was *The Glasgow Lass*, the same ship that had brought them over from Scotland.

Gav was delighted to see Jemmy Ducks again and introduce him to his new friend Mr Speckles. Gav had a talent for attaching himself to the most horrible and useless of people.

She was glad, yet sad, that his attention had been diverted from her adventure as he listened to Jemmy Ducks tell of *The Glasgow Lass's* brush with pirates and how she had outsailed the pirates' ship and escaped being boarded. For a long time now she had been aware of this aloneness, this distance between herself and other people, even Gav. She shrivelled from any closeness, as if it were a snake poised ready to crush the life from her.

Knots of people had gathered at the wharf, planters in fancy waistcoats and tricorne hats, backwoodsmen in fur hats and stiff patched deerskin and their women in tattered homespun. Other men who lived in the settlement wore Scotch bonnets and their women's aprons and bonnet strings fluttered in the breeze.

Negro slaves unloaded the ship and trudged backwards and forwards from the wharf to the store, their backs stooped under heavy boxes and barrels.

Later other larger barrels or hogsheads filled with tobacco leaves would be rolled onto the vessel ready to be shipped back to Glasgow. From there it would be sold and distributed all over Europe.

But for the moment, Regina was not interested in the tobacco. She now had Harding's order and wasted no time in packing it into the open carriage. No sooner had she started to do this than the whisper flew round the crowd at the wharf and they turned around and hustled to the store and stood there nudging one another and whispering. Actually they weren't sure of what attitude to take to the event or to Regina. They regarded her as a handsome but cold young man and somehow different from them. She had always been polite when they went into the store on business but outside she was in the habit of keeping herself to herself and speaking to no-one.

She spoke to no-one now, sitting ready, tight lipped and hard-eyed, the reins held easily between her fingers. Mr Speckles' snuff-stained fingers pushed a tinder-box onto her lap, muttering something about needing it to light a fire and Gav came running up with Jemmy Ducks limping and hopping beside him and begged her to change her mind. Ignoring him, she flicked the reins, made a clicking noise through clenched teeth and sent the horses cantering away. A cloud of dust bowled after her, hiding her from view until eventually she disappeared into the black mouth of the forest.

Chapter 13

As Regina moved through the hush of deep woods, it was hard to take comfort from the fact that these trees furnished so many implements of survival for the settlers. Gun stocks were fashioned from black walnut. Boat ribs came from the tall oak trees. Axe-handles, singletrees, and wagon hubs came from hickory and black gum. The finest tree was an evergreen, the great white pine. It soared over the wilderness often two hundred feet high and more, and provided the light but strong wood for houses and boat planking and ship's masts.

Now, for Regina, all they did was shut out the sun.

Her progress was considerably slowed by bronze-tinted turkeys that every now and again swarmed across her path. More than once the horses had been frightened by them and reared up whinnying in panic. It was only with difficulty that she was able to pacify them and urge them on.

She was afraid, yet at the same time she began to experience an exhilaration that was akin to enjoyment and the deeper she penetrated into the forest, the less afraid and the more at home she felt. Jogging along further and further away from the settlement and people, her body swaying to the rhythm of the horses, it would have been easy to believe that she belonged in this lovely place, as if she were an animal herself and the forest was her refuge and shelter.

She stopped eventually to eat some of the food she had brought. Nearby the river sent stars winking through the undergrowth. She chewed her cornbread, savouring more intensely than the food the strange happiness penetrating into the deepest, most secret cores of herself. Perched in the small open carriage, the reins draped loosely on her lap and crumbs of cornbread spotting her breeches, she wondered why it was she felt so content. It had taken her by surprise. She had been prepared for nothing but terror. Certainly she was retaining an alertness to danger and her eyes missed none of the movements in the bushes and trees all around her, but the danger was worrying her less and less. The animals of the forest, she decided, were as wary of her as she was of them.

It was in man that the real danger lay. She thought of Robert Harding with anger. He had forced her into taking this journey, not caring if she became lost in the wilderness. She pitied his wife who seemed like a feeble moth fluttering hopefully around him, despite being constantly swatted away.

Resentment against Harding rose like a stone to her throat. It tightened the muscles of her jaw and neck until she was unable to finish her cornbread. She wrapped it and put it aside before picking up the reins and jerking the horses into action. The carriage jarred and leapt on the rough earth and she was forced to strain the horses back until they resumed their previous slow pace.

She tried to banish thoughts of Harding from her mind. He possessed concentrated maleness which she found far more frightening than any thoughts of wild beasts in the forest. Everything about him was disturbingly intense. Most of the men who came to the store had dusty brown or faded grey hair. Harding's hair glinted blue-black. Most of the men's skins were dirt-lined and pocked. His skin was taut and nut brown. Most men were either fat or thin. He was huge, with a flat belly and rock hard muscles in arms and thighs. His eyes set deep under craggy brows could be penetrating or brooding. His broken nose twisted to one side over a wide mouth that took on a strange tightness when he laughed. It gave him a cruel appearance and hardened the aggressive masculinity about him.

With a determined effort, she concentrated on her immediate surroundings. Somewhere high above her, the squawking of birds had a hollow echo as if they were contained in a drum.

Would Gav be given forest land like this when he finished his indenture, she wondered. Most settlers had to begin by gnawing into the woods, burning or hacking down trees to make a clearing so that they could build a log cabin and plant some Indian corn between the stumps. It would be hard work but it would be well worth while. Happiness filled her veins like wine.

She and Gav would build a good life. They wouldn't need to care about anybody. She would buy extra land with her gold coins and they would grow tobacco and one day they would have a decent sized plantation. The forest would be their friend, isolating them from other people, a wall surrounding them and keeping them safe.

Cantering along through the trees, she felt alone in the world and queen of all she surveyed. It was a good feeling. It grew inside her like a myriad of bubbles floating up to her head. She could have gone on and on into eternity like that savouring the aloneness, being exhilarated and soothed at one and the same time. Being interested too. Peering at trees and bushes and plants of all shapes and shades and sizes. Soaking up the endless variety and wonder of it all.

Until eventually she stiffened with surprise at the unexpected sight of people. A man on foot wearing buckskins carried an axe and a gun, and a sweating woman with frowsy hair trudged behind him clutching the rim of a spinning wheel and a bulging sack. Several little boys and girls, each laden with a bundle, straggled after her. A horse loaded high with baggage was topped with a kind of wicker cage in which a baby had rocked to sleep. At the end of the procession a cow lumbered along with a bed and a bag of meal tied on its back.

The man stopped to greet her and on an impulse she passed down her cornbread to be shared among the children. The man and woman told her they were moving westward, seeking a new place to settle, and she wished them a brief 'good luck' before snapping the reins and gee-upping the horses into action.

Soon she was alone again and glad of it. Glad of the long hushed hours. Glad of the rhythmic clopping of the horses and the rattling of the carriage lulling her once more into dreams. But the realization that it had become colder gradually began to pierce her consciousness. She became aware too of night sounds coming from the undergrowth, sudden rustlings that just as suddenly stopped. She became aware of the chirping of crickets and the shouting of tree frogs, and fireflies gleaming in the bushes.

She decided she would have to stop and light a fire before it got any darker. Mr Speckles had said there would be a clearing and house where she could seek shelter for the night but so far she had not seen one. Unhitching the horses, she tied them to a tree, then gathered fuel before fighting with the tinder-box. At last she managed to get a fire going. She lit a lantern too and, before hanging it on the carriage, she held it up and swung it round, sending its puny beam scraping at the edges of the black wall of trees surrounding her. The horses pricked their ears and shifted restlessly but she sat very still gazing into the fire, her back relaxed against the carriage wheel. In the blackness quite near to her the wings of a large bird flapped.

She was thinking of Gav again and their plans for the future. They would build a log cabin to start with. Everyone did that. Usually it had only one room. Two at the most. But eventually, when they began to sell tobacco and make a profit, the log cabin would just be used for their slaves. She and Gav would have a bigger, better house by then. They would paint it white and it would have white pillars and glass windows like the plantation mansions she'd seen from the ship as it sailed up the James River. They would have a garden too with flowers as well as vegetables and herbs. Inside there would be every comfort. They would have furniture made by English cabinet-makers, graceful chairs and sofas upholstered in velvet and rich brocade and a rosewood spinet and a japanned tea table. They would have carpets too and feather beds and snowy white bed-linen and table-linen. And silver and china and glass. They would have decanters and goblets and teapots and bowls and platters and pitchers and candlesticks and spoons and knives and forks. She saw it all, a warm luxurious, inviting picture in the crimson frame of the fire.

She heard the dismal yelling cry of wolves, but did not resent them. They were a natural part of the forest. She accepted them, just as she accepted the fact that the forest had an affinity with the wildness in her.

She dozed a little, her head drooping down onto her chest, then jerking up again as if she were suddenly not sure where she was. Several times she roused herself to toss more wood on the fire, until watery fingers of light, sparkling like glass, cut through the darkness of the trees. The forest was still dark. It was always dark in the forest. But during the day sunlight dribbled down like delicate coloured icing on a chocolate cake.

She hitched up the horses, climbed stiffly onto the front of the carriage and set off again. It wasn't long before she came to the house that Mr Speckles must have meant.

'Hallo-o-o-o, the house' she called as Mr Speckles had instructed. Then she waited at the edge of the clearing. Hens squealed and fluttered in panic round the doorway at the unexpected sound of her voice. And hogs bumped and snorted their protests in all directions. A long loose string of a man appeared with a rifle drooping under one arm. She recognized him as Jud Norton. He and his wife Ada, paid occasional visits to the store.

'I'm Master Chisholm from the store. I'm bound for Forest Hall, the Harding plantation. Could you oblige me with directions from here?'

Jud leaned against the doorway, not saying anything, as if holding up the rifle in the crook of his arm didn't leave him enough strength. His greasy hair straggled loose, and a long beard accentuated his sunken jaws. From behind him, in bare feet and bulging homespun gown, Ada appeared, cleaning floury hands on hips.

'Yep.' She pointed to one side of the house. 'Just keep goin' nor' nor' east. 'Taint more'n ten miles from here. But you'll be wantin' something fer your stummick first.'

Regina guided the carriage between the tree stumps, jumped down and secured the horses to a tree.

'Thank you. I'd appreciate something to drink.'

'Some fresh milk mebbe? And cornbread?'

'That would be fine.'

She squashed past Jud, who was still draped against the door lintel, and accepted a stool beside the table. It was roughly made with knots and holes in the wood and one leg shorter than the others.

Answering his own unspoken question, Jud said,

' 'Taint likely you came across any Injuns. They're like foxes, them fellers.'

'I didn't see any.'

408

Jud spat on the earthen floor of the cabin.

'Nobody sees them fellers till they're ready to show.'

Regina sipped at the wooden bowl of milk Ada gave her.

'Are there many around here, do you think?'

Before Jud could answer, Ada cut in.

'Don't you go speakin' agin.'

'What fer?'

' 'Taint no use agitatin' Master Chisholm. You jest drink your milk, Master Chisholm. It'll perk up your spirits some.'

Jud gave a slow easy shrug. It was obvious by the look of him that he didn't do much work around the place, Regina thought. She had heard, of course, that many backwoodsmen were lazy at everything except begetting children. It was the wife who was the industrious one. With her spinning wheel, loom and dye pots, she produced clothing, blankets and quilts. She made soap and candles, from the woods she picked herbs and roots for purges, emetics, syrups, cordials and poultices. As often as not she could use a gun, not only to kill animals for food but to protect her home from wild beasts and Indians.

The milk and the cornbread refreshed Regina and she wasted no time in setting off on her journey again. Ada came out to stand between the tree stumps to wave her goodbye but Jud remained propping up the lintel.

As the mantle of the forest closed around her again, she couldn't help remembering what he had said about Indians, although the one or two Indians who came to the store always seemed peaceful enough. They padded in with a heap of skins, laid them on the counter and stood silently waiting for a few beads and baubles and perhaps a jug of whisky in exchange. They had dark hair and eyes and high broad cheekbones like Harding, and, like all men, they could not be trusted.

The thought of them made her uneasy. But she was soon soothed again by the splendid isolation of the forest, the rhythmic clop-clopping of the horses' hooves and the branches flicking cobwebs of light overhead. She was sorry when the trees began to thin out and then alternate with blackened stumps until there, in the midst of them, ghostly white against the shadows of the trees, stood Forest Hall.

Chapter 14

Forest Hall was a double storeyed mansion made of wood with a frontage of pillars and an outside staircase. To Regina it looked magnificent, a fairy palace shining through the gloom. Yet it had a lonely threatened air, as if it knew that it was only a matter of time before the tight fist of the forest closed in and suffocated it.

'Hallo-o-o-o-o, the house!' she called, weaving the horses between the trees, dust rising and shivering the air.

As she came nearer to the house, she noticed that its glass windows were draped with dirt. Paint blistered and flaked from walls and pillars, baring patches of brown, and the wooden stairs were concave and splintered at the edges.

At the sound of her carriage, slaves came shambling round from one side, some of the men wearing only tattered shirts and no breeches. A girl and a boy both showing marked signs of puberty were completely naked.

Suddenly the front door opened and Harding stood on the wooden platform between the stairs, his thumbs hooked in the top of his breeches. A wide-sleeved shirt with a frill down the front hung open to reveal black hair curling against brown skin. His mouth drew back in a grin that showed teeth as startlingly white as his shirt.

'So you've actually done it.'

With difficulty, Regina climbed down and relinquished the reins to one of the slaves. She was stiff and sore, and from her tangled hair to her bare feet she was covered with sweat and dust.

'Well, sir,' she said. 'Where is my horse?'

He suddenly let out a roar of laughter.

'By God, sir, you deserve it. I never for a moment thought I would see you standing there on your own.'

'I am not afraid of the forest, Mr Harding.'

'Then there can be very little you are afraid of.'

'I have enough will to conquer any fears that may assail me.'

'You are a young man after my own heart, Master Chisholm. Come in and be refreshed with some food and wine. But first, let Old Abe find you a new coat and breeches.' Without looking at him, he beckoned to a black man with stooping shoulders and a shaved grey head. 'Go with him and he will show you where to wash and dress.'

Her feet made a hollow echo on the stairs and balcony then smacked into the hall. It was dark and cool. A flow of air, sweet-scented with herbs and flowers, drifted in from an open door at the far end. With it a shaft of light heavily laden with dust spread across the floor. Flies bustled about and left their droppings like smudgings of grey paint on banisters and wainscoting. A chandelier made a high-pitched protest in the breeze.

Regina followed Old Abe up a staircase and along a corridor to one of the bedrooms. It had a four-poster bed without curtains but a mosquito net hung over it from a hook on the ceiling. The windows darkened the room with dirt and the floor was bare. The only other articles of furniture, apart from the bed, were a kist and a wash stand on which stood a blue and white jug and bowl, criss-crossed with brown hair-cracks.

Old Abe began rummaging in the kist, spilling clothes onto the floor in his search for something suitable. At last she said,

'You're wasting your time. Nothing of Mr Harding's could possibly fit me. I'm so much smaller than he is.'

'Yes, suh. But these ain't what Mr Harding wears. These'n extra clothes.'

They found a handsome green plush coat eventually and brown breeches. Ordering Old Abe to wait outside until she called him, she washed her face in the bowl of water, combed and tied back her hair and donned the new clothes. They were heavier than her own and had a luxurious feel about them. They gave her a sense of importance and when she allowed Old Abe to lead her back downstairs, she followed him with a swagger. He stopped at a door at one side of the hall. It opened into a drawing-room where her host waited with a whisky bottle in his hand ready to pour out drinks. Behind him was a large fireplace

411

from which dead wood-ash overflowed. Above the mantelpiece hung an ornate gold-framed mirror and on the mantelpiece itself were green and gold vases, a miniature by Tassie, two snuffboxes and a long churchwarden pipe. On one side of the fireplace stood a table crowded with bottles and glasses. One wall of the room was lined with leather-bound books and a tall clock with a face of brass stood in the corner. An Axminster carpet added to the luxury of the settees and chairs covered in rich brocade. Yet the room, like the rest of the house, had a drab, neglected look. The windows were dull with grime. The carpet was so dusty that the colour was practically indistinguishable and cobwebs straggled from the ceiling candelabra.

'Where is Mistress Harding?' Regina asked. 'She is well, I hope?'

Harding passed over a glass and she noticed how broad and brown his hand looked.

'No, she is not,' he said, 'but then she seldom is. She has been moaning and groaning in bed ever since journeying back from the store. The slaves will all be naked before she gets down to making any clothes for them and the house in ruins for lack of proper housewifery.'

'It's a long, hard journey for a lady. I'm not surprised she's feeling poorly.'

He gave a bitter laugh.

'Oh, I'm not surprised, sir. I've been bedevilled for years with the weak-livered creature's uselessness.'

'She can't help being weak and female. It does you no credit to speak of your wife like that.'

His eyes flashed at her like those of a wild animal and she noticed for the first time that they were tawny streaked.

'You dare criticize me in my own house?'

She was taken aback by his anger.

'Forgive me, Mr Harding. I didn't mean to give offence. The fatigue of the journey has made me forget my manners.'

'Drink up your whisky.'

She gulped some down, then looked around.

'It's a very grand house.'

'It's nothing of the kind.'

412

'I've never been in such a large house in all my life. It's very grand to me, sir.'

'You must have seen some of the bigger mansions from the ship on your way up the river when you first came to this country. The really wealthy men own those plantations on the river banks.'

'But this is one of the biggest plantations in the interior, I've heard.'

'That's true,' Harding agreed. 'Oh, make no mistake. I am proud of what I have. That's why I'm bitterly dissatisfied that I have no son to carry on the place.' His mouth took on an ugly twist. 'I will never forgive the useless, affected creature who lies upstairs for failing me in this. Later I'll show you around but now we must eat.'

He strode from the room and she followed him into a dining-room panelled in yellow pine. A table was set with fruits and vegetables of every kind along with several different types of meat and fish, oysters, crabs and terrapins. Slaves surrounded the room, drooping back against the walls, but as soon as Harding entered, they shuffled forward, bumping into one another in general chaos in their efforts to lay out plates and serve the food. One of them splashed too much wine into Harding's glass, spilling it over onto his hand.

'Sorry, suh. I'll jes' mop you up, suh.' The slave hastily attempted to dry the wine with a napkin but with a wide swing of his arm, Harding knocked the man staggering back.

'Get away, you fool.'

Regina kept her attention lowered on her plate.

Still clutching the bottle the slave hurried over to her.

'Yo want a smitch o' wine, suh?'

'Yes, thank you,' she murmured.

'Well,' said Harding. 'Don't just sit there gawping. Eat!'

She felt a glow of malicious satisfaction in the knowledge that Harding did not enjoy a happy relationship with his wife and that he was so obviously cast down because he had no son and heir. Serves him right, she thought. If he was so keen on having a strong, spirited woman for a wife, why didn't he have the sense to marry one. She realized, of course, that most marriages were

413

arranged like business contracts and that few men actually chose their wives for any other reasons but financial ones. No doubt Mistress Kitty was offered to Harding with such a tempting dowry of land or money or both that he was not able to refuse. She couldn't really blame him for that. There was very little she wouldn't do for money herself or the pleasures that money offered like the meal she was now relishing.

Since she had come to Virginia she had managed to get enough to eat, but only of plain food like cornbread or mush. In Glasgow for most of the time she had been near to starvation. First at her home in Tannery Wynd she had known little other than porridge. Then later, at the mercy of Quin, she had survived on filthy scraps either stolen or begged for. Never, either in Glasgow or the settlement, had she dreamed of consuming such a meal. She ate steadily, packing herself with as much as she could hold, savouring every mouthful so that she would always remember it.

'You like good food, I see,' Harding remarked.

'I appreciate all the good things of life, sir.'

'What can you know of the good things of life, Master Chisholm?'

'I have enough intelligence to recognize them and appreciate them when they are offered to me.'

He laughed.

'I believe you. Well, have you finished appreciating the food?'

'Yes.'

'Come then. I will show you around.'

Across the hall from the drawing-room and dining-room was a long ballroom lined with high-backed grey chairs like rows of dead people long forgotten.

'Most planters have a yearly or twice yearly ball,' he explained. 'That way everyone's able to meet and exchange news. Otherwise we seldom see each other. There's such distances between plantations. This ballroom is seldom used, however. My wife is usually not fit enough to entertain.'

'I'm sorry. It must be very lonely for you both. These vast distances are what impressed me most when I came to this country,' Regina said.

414

Harding shrugged.

'I'm not averse to my own company.' He pointed towards the ceiling. 'Do you appreciate that crystal chandelier brought over from England with much difficulty and expense?'

'It's beautiful.'

'My wife's pride and joy,' he said, his top lip drawing back into a humourless smile. 'That and some china dishes and silver knick-knacks. Foolish fancies for things often overcome her. At the moment she has taken a fancy for you. You'd better come up and see her.'

'Yes, of course.'

She followed him out of the ballroom and up the stairs. As they passed a slave in the hall, Harding shouted,

'Light some bloody candles. It's as dark as the tomb in here.'

'Yes, suh.'

They turned left at the top of the stairs and at the end of the corridor Harding stopped and swung open a door.

'Master Chisholm,' he announced abruptly.

Kitty Harding was propped up in a four-poster bed. The mosquito net and the curtains were crushed untidily back. The curtains and the bedmat were so dirty it was impossible to tell what colour they were. But Kitty herself was a riot of vivid hues. A scarlet robe was fastened with an emerald brooch at her bosom and at her throat was a necklace of sapphires. Strings of pearls and plumes decorated her powdered wig and her face was spotted with patches of various shapes.

'Robert . . . Robert . . . my dear. And Master Chisholm, Master Chisholm.'

She stretched out a hand and Regina bowed politely over it.

'Mistress Harding. I trust your health is improving.'

The windows were closed and there was a hot stench of unemptied chamber pots. Something that looked like a flea sprang from Mistress Kitty's wig. She coquettishly fluttered her fan.

'Oh indeed, indeed. And all the better for your kind inquiry. I do declare, I do declare you look mighty handsome, young sir.'

On the wall above the fireplace hung a child's sampler worked in blue and red cross-stitch: 'Kitty May Colington

415

1728.' Open fans were propped up along the top of the mantelpiece, along with a crush of fashion-babies or dolls dressed in fine clothes. There was also a china cup and saucer, an ornate clock and several snuffboxes. A green velvet armchair and a needlepoint footstool sat in one corner and a table with a candelabra and a litter of books filled another. A kist lay open with gowns, petticoats and stays spilling from it and flaunting their gaudy tints.

'Do sit down, Master Chisholm. Oh, I do declare, I'm so pleased to see you.'

'I'm showing him around,' Harding said from the doorway. 'We'd better go outside before it's too dark.'

Blinking with disappointment, Kitty managed a tremulous smile. It had taken a terrible effort of will to gather enough energy to prepare herself for the visit. As soon as she had heard Regina arriving, she had dragged herself about the room to find her robe and jewellery in a determined effort to look her best.

'Of course, Robert, dear,' she said lightly. 'Of course. Of course.'

Harding gripped Regina's arm, levered her from the room and crashed the door shut. But before going outside, he stopped downstairs in the hall and smoothed his hand against one of the panels. To Regina's surprise, it swung open. He lifted a candle and held it forward to reveal a narrow stairway.

'There's a couple of secret rooms down there,' he explained, 'in case of Indian attack.' He closed the panels again and replaced the candle before turning away. 'So far we've never needed to use them. The tribes around here are peaceful enough. But occasionally more warlike tribes come down from the north and attack the plantations. Mostly the smaller ones through. The danger faced by the biggest plantations—the ones further down the river with their own wharfs—is from pirates.'

She followed him across the hall to the front door.

'Pirates surely don't come ashore.'

'Indeed they do. They've kidnapped slaves and owners alike before now.'

It was still light outside and a scented breeze swayed the long grass. Some of the grass around the building had been cut short but there was nothing like a formal lawn. Too many stumps and trees crowded too near the house, their tall branches twisting into unexpected postures, their roots humping up.

Standing to one side of the house and slightly behind it was a cluster of whitewashed wooden buildings. One was a large kitchen in which crowds of half-naked slaves blended into dark corners. Harding allowed her no more than a glance inside. Another building was a storehouse. There was also one in which Harding did business and kept his plantation accounts. It had a counter on top of which sat a crock of quills, an ink-pot, a slim white pipe and a box of snuff. Behind the counter was a handsome leather chair. Nearby shelves were filled with ledgers.

The overseer's house came next. Then a low stone-lined 'spring-house' in which icy water curled round crocks filled with dairy produce and perishable goods. Across the path at right angles to the storehouse and overseer's house and facing the back of the mansion were the stables and the barns in which the tobacco leaves were stored and cured. Even further away from the mansion and hidden by a clump of trees stood the rows of rough shacks which housed the slaves. There was also a blacksmith's forge.

More woods opened out onto tobacco fields and miles of black fencing made of upturned stumps, their roots writhing as if in some macabre dance.

It was dark by the time they strolled back along the path towards the house and fireflies were rapidly winking all around. The moon made mist of the trees and through the mist tree-frogs croaked.

Regina said,

'My kinsman, Gav, tells me that after he serves his indenture he could receive fifty acres of land.'

'That is so. And some clothing, an ox, a gun and a few farming tools.'

'I wonder,' Regina murmured, 'if I can wait until he is ready.'

'You will be entitled to land at the same time as Gav. You came across together, didn't you?'

'Yes, but I'm not indentured. I paid my own passage and I'm free to choose what I do with my life and when.'

'Indeed? Well, I told you I admired your spirit, young sir. There will always be employment for you here if you want it.'

Walking along beside him, their silence broken only by the chirping of crickets somewhere in the darkness, she wondered if working for Harding might be her opportunity to learn how to run a plantation until she was old enough to buy one for herself.

Eventually she murmured in a cautious tone.

'I am in no hurry, Mr Harding. But I will give the matter serious and careful thought.'

He chuckled.

'You do that, Master Chisholm. You do that.'

Chapter 15

'Did you ever see such a sturdy laddie?' Mr Blackadder asked proudly as he poked a long bony finger into the baby's cradle. 'How does the name Mungo sound to you, Ramsay?' he asked Annabella's father. 'That was St Kentigern's other name. He was a bishop of Glasgow away back in the sixth century.'

Ramsay stood gazing down at the cradle. He was an imposing figure in his large curly wig and rich clothing, and a handsome man too in his own dour-faced way. As he admired his new grandson, however, his eyes softened.

'Aye, Mungo will do verra well, minister. The Lord has blessed you with a grand lad.'

'Uh-huh, aye, he has indeed. Uh-huh.' He could hardly take his eyes off the child and Annabella laughed when she came into the room.

'Are you two still there? Gracious heavens, the pair of you will be taking root beside that cradle.'

'You're still as perjink as ever I see, mistress,' her father remarked drily. 'It would take more than a birth to take the wind oot o' your sails.'

She planted a quick kiss on his cheek as she passed.

'Don't pretend you aren't pleased with me, Papa. I'm prodigiously clever to have produced a lusty child like Mungo with such ease.'

'Careful noo, Annabella.' Mr Blackadder's face tried to compose itself into a stern expression. 'Pride's a terrible sin.'

'Fiddlesticks!' Annabella said.

She hadn't thought she'd even like the child, imagining during her pregnancy that it would be a constant source of shame to her, and a painful reminder of the humiliation she had suffered. But she couldn't find any hatred in her heart when she looked at it. Indeed, she enjoyed sweet pangs of pleasure every time she saw the little pink face and plump legs and arms. It was a

419

beautiful child with her perfect skin and bright blue eyes. There was nothing of Harding about it. She still hated the man but the child she loved with unashamed delight.

'If you're staying, Papa, for pity's sake take off your cloak and sit yourself down. I'll pour out some whisky.'

'No.' He held up a hand. 'I must away. I've business to attend to. I just happened to be passing and thought I'd call in and see how you were.'

'Losh and lovenendie, Papa, what a liar you've become.'

'God forgive you, Annabella!' Mr Blackadder cried out in alarm. 'Will ye haud yer wicked tongue. Have some respect for yer faither.'

Annabella laughed.

'You did come to see your wondrously beautiful grandson, didn't you, Papa? Be honest now.'

'I came to visit both Mungo and yourself, mistress, and now I must away.'

'Uh-huh, ye'll be back again soon, Maister Ramsay. You know ye're aye welcome,' said Mr Blackadder, seeing him out of the room and downstairs to the front door. On his return to the bedroom he stared uncertainly at the cradle. 'Do you no' think it'll disturb Mungo if I have the catechism examinations and questioning in here, Annabella? I could verra easily talk to the folk in the attic.'

Annabella rolled her eyes.

'Sit down and stop fussing and spoiling the child. He'll have to get used to noise and people going about. Later when he's older, the attic can be his room. But must they come so often? You're always visiting them. You question them here, you question them there. Why can't you just mind your own business?'

'It is my business, mistress. God has instructed me to chide the careless, reprove the thoughtless, rebuke the erring, denounce the hardened and obdurate and question everybody about all things.'

'Fiddlesticks!' she said impatiently.

'One of these days,' Mr Blackadder warned solemnly, 'you'll be struck down dead for your impudence. Oh, and another thing,' he added, 'there's the visiting preacher, a young man new to the call. I said he could come and break an egg with us later.'

He drew in a chair at the table, set some paper in front of him and a candle near his elbow, then picked up a quill.

Annabella groaned to herself. One minister in the house was bad enough, two was very hard to bear.

'Gracious, heavens, Nancy,' she shouted, grabbing her fan and flapping it in annoyance. 'We haven't got all night. Send the first one up and let us get on with the doleful business.'

'Will ye haud yer tongue,' the minister chided sharply. 'You're the one that's needing examined more than anybody. You're a disgrace.'

Annabella rolled her eyes but said no more. She wondered if she should light an extra candle. Already the room looked half asleep. The grandfather clock in the corner gave a wheezy sigh then donged with melancholia. Mr Blackadder's quill scraped across a yellow pool of light. She gazed at his lowered head and high-hunched shoulders and felt no rancour against him. She just wished he was married to someone else, that was all. Occasionally the full impact of her position would hit her but it was panic she felt, not hatred or malice against Mr Blackadder. More often than not she just did not believe that she was truly condemned to spend the rest of her days and nights tied to the minister in this oppressive house with the quill forever sleepily scraping and the clock's brass heart mercilessly beating her life away.

It was almost a relief when the first person to be questioned appeared, a little girl who shuffled in wiping her nose on the back of her sleeve. The minister interrogated her long and sternly, his face straining forward into the candlelight, shadows scooping deep hollows in his cheeks and eyes. The droning of his voice and the heat from the fire and the steady ticking of the clock had a soporific effect, and Annabella had to keep straining her eyes wide and giving sudden flutters of her fan to keep herself awake.

The little girl, however, was concentrating as much on Mr Blackadder as he was concentrating on her. At last he came to the final query.

421

'Uh-huh, aye, Mary, and why did the Israelites make a golden calf?'

Mary thought for a minute and then, determined not to be beaten at the last gasp, answered,

'They hadn't enough silver to make a cow.'

Annabella giggled behind her fan and the minister eyed her reprovingly before correcting then dismissing the child. Afterwards he scratched conscientiously at the paper in front of him again. There was little entertainment to be had from the others who came trudging up the stairs, however, and she became so bored with it all she was glad when the young minister arrived and put a stop to the proceedings.

He was introduced as Mr Adair and he reminded her of her brother Douglas. He was not so foppish in dress, of course, but there was a fussy, almost feminine, affectation about him. As the evening progressed she could see that his affected and priggish manner was even beginning to irritate Mr Blackadder.

'You'll have a glass o' whisky, Mr Adair?' he invited, but Mr Adair flung up his hands and cried out in his high pitched voice.

'I really do not drink, sir. Nor do I approve of drinking.'

'Uh-huh, well, well, that's a gey queer way to be. But you'll have a pipe with me then.'

'No, no, Mr Blackadder. I really do not smoke.'

'Uh-huh, do you eat grass, Mr Adair?'

'Eat grass, sir?' Mr Adair raised his brows in surprise. 'Eat grass? No, I do not eat grass. What makes you ask that?'

'Weel, weel,' said Mr Blackadder dryly, 'ye can go yer own way, for if ye neither smoke, nor drink, nor eat grass, you're neither fit company for man nor beast.'

Annabella laughed.

'Pay no heed to Mr Blackadder, Mr Adair. He is in one of his moods. Tell me, what is the subject of your sermon on Sunday?'

Mr Adair fluttered his hands again.

'Oh, Mistress Blackadder, Mistress Blackadder, that is what I keep asking myself, for it is really a most terrible problem. What will I preach about? What will I preach about? I really do not know what to preach about.'

'Just preach aboot a quarter of an hour,' Mr Blackadder said.

Afterwards in disgust he told Annabella:

'That man's no' going to be any use as a preacher. I'll have dug the guts oot o' five Bibles before he ever gets started.'

Annabella could not deny this. Mr Blackadder was never stuck for something to say when he mounted the high pulpit.

The following Sunday, for her benefit she was sure, he spoke for nearly six hours on the proud, unjust and vindictive man and he added, eyeing her meaningfully,

'*Woman!* Uh-huh! Aye, even although many's the time the proud, the unjust and the vindictive escape from the hand of man, as they too often do, aye, but in the dread day of vengeance they'll no' escape from the Lord. The lofty looks of man.' Another beady stare. '*And woman* shall be humbled. The haughtiness of men *and women* shall be bowed down. Aye, the Lord shall bring them low. They shall drink of the wine of the wrath of God. They shall be cast into the lake of fire. They shall die the second death.'

Not that she allowed any of his gloomy and terrifying forecasts to frighten her. Though after so many long weary hours every Sunday and often when he preached during the week as well, it was easy to become depressed. But her depression never lasted long and by the next day her jaunty spirits would have bounced back again. Along Trongate she would parade or along by the Green, ablaze with colour in her wide hooped skirts and swirling cape, with fan aflicking and head held high.

But often stepping back into the tiny dark lobby of the house in the Briggait and climbing the narrow stairs to face another long evening with Mr Blackadder hunched over his Bible, it was a sore struggle to keep her spirits up.

For hours she would sit trying to concentrate on a piece of embroidery, listening to the scraping of Mr Blackadder's quill or his muttering to himself as he composed his sermon, or his lengthy readings, or melancholy prayers and she would long to scream.

If it had not been for Mungo she would have run away, either on her own or with any gallant gentleman willing to take her. But she could not leave the child. Mungo was the only true pleasure of her life and she loved to dandle him and play with

423

him and bring a smile to his rosy-cheeked face or hear him chuckle.

She tried to keep alive her passionate hatred for Harding but it faded with time, as did her vengeful feelings against Regina. She did not forgive them for what they had done to her. For longer and longer periods of time she just forgot them. Hatred and vengeance could find no permanent darkness in her from which to draw nourishment and grow.

But as she said herself:

'Gracious heavens, I feel sorely tried and cruelly confined. It is making me prodigiously restless. If something, anything, doesn't happen soon I shall be obliged to fly the country!'

Griselle and Phemy tutted at her and Phemy said:

'I beg of you, Annabella, do not talk in such a wild and wayward manner. You have us all in a flutter.'

Griselle tightened the drawstrings of her mouth.

'We remember the last time you flew off, even if you don't, mistress. It nearly killed your poor father with worry.'

'Fiddlesticks. Papa is made of sterner stuff than that. Anyway, just think of the adventure, the fantastic experience I had.'

'Traipsing about the Highlands with an army of barbarians is not an experience we have any taste for, Annabella,' Griselle said. 'I would have thought it ought to have been a lesson to you.'

'Oh, indeed it was, Grizzie. It taught me how to survive, amidst monstrous suffering and hardship. I'm not so easily fluttered.'

'Now that winter's upon us again,' Phemy said, 'there's nothing for it but to try and content your mind and settle yourself, dear. When the nights are so long and dark and the roads so bad, there's very little even you can do. Just try and think yourself fortunate to have such a bonny son and a good husband and a nice little house.'

'If somewhat cramped,' added Griselle who had a much larger, roomier place.

Once, in exasperation, Annabella said to Mr Blackadder:

'Do you never feel restless? Do you never have any curiosity, any desire to see what lies beyond the boundaries of Glasgow?'

424

'No, indeed I have not,' he answered firmly. 'This is where God put me and this is where I stay. I trust in the Lord, Annabella. The Lord knows best.'

'It may be best for you, sir, but it's no damned good for me.'

'Annabella! Haud your wicked tongue. You'll be cursing and swearing in front of the bairn next.'

'This endless boredom is enough to make a saint swear.'

'You're nae saint, mistress.'

'It's the same routine in Glasgow, day in, day out. At six o'clock in the morning the rider arrives with the post and newspapers. Then the gun's fired at the Cross to summon the businessmen. Then you all gather in the taverns to collect and assimilate the news. Then at eight o'clock, back to breakfast you all come. After that it's off to the counting house for father and the other merchants. You write your sermon or make your rounds until dinner. Then it's work again until about eight. Supper at nine, family prayers and early bed. All I ever do is attend to Mungo. That is when I get the chance, for Nancy fair dotes on the child. Or I entertain a few cummers of an afternoon. That is all.'

'Uh-huh. What else should there be?'

'I've never even been to an Assembly for an age.'

'Aye, weel, I've never held with such fripperies and you're still feeding Mungo.'

'He's nearly a year old. I shall not be feeding him for much longer.'

'No matter. I'm no' having you going any place where ye might be led into sin and temptation.'

'Oh, fiddlesticks! I shall go mad in this boring place if I don't do something or go somewhere.'

She realized of course that it was not really Glasgow she was complaining of. She had always managed to find some sport and gaiety in the town before her marriage. It was Mr Blackadder that was really the thorn in her side and the depressing influence. Although, to be fair, there were worse ministers than him going about the town and she sometimes breathed a sigh of relief that her father had not chosen one of the others. At least Mr Blackadder was capable of caustic wit now and again and he had a certain amount of kindliness in his nature.

There were others like the Reverend Gowrie who were more like disciples of the devil than men of God. At least they seemed so to her. To themselves they were holy men doing God's work with great and zealous concentration. At the Reverend Gowrie's church there were always several people being pilloried underneath his pulpit. There was always someone standing at the church door barelegged and clad only in a gown of sackcloth. A large notice hung round their necks to shame them and tell the congregation if they were adulterers or fornicators. The Reverend Gowrie never tired of seeking out sexual offenders and questioning and punishing them.

Of course, as well-known faces appeared in the place of ignominy, smiles and smirks and whispers passed from one to another in the congregation and even young lairds and members of the aristocracy came to enjoy the entertainment. They were quite safe from punishments because, apparently, God only wished to punish the poor. Such diversions, she had to admit, rendered the services less dreary. But his conscientious persecution of pregnant girls came a bit too near home to be felt amusing. Indeed, since she had had a baby herself, she felt nothing but pity and indignation for the poor creatures and the merciless way they were treated. Frequently, rather than face the trial of being pilloried and admonished by the minister, often for as much as twenty-six Sundays in succession, they fled the country. Some committed suicide, others in their terror destroyed their offspring in the hope of concealing their fault. Scores of women, condemned to death for child-murder, had confessed that the dread of the pillory was the cause of their crime.

Mr Blackadder, of course, had done his share of rebuking girls on the pillory. But he had grown wary of these forms of church discipline since it had become known that Scottish women were the greatest child-murderers in the world and many people were thinking that appearances in church for scandal actually caused these murders.

'It's a terrible worry and problem,' he confessed to Annabella, 'to know what to do for the best.'

Child murder continued with terrible frequency, however,

and long ago the Scots Parliament had passed laws of great rigour to suppress so prevalent a form of murder. The General Assembly ordered Mr Blackadder and all the ministers to read from their pulpits the Act against concealment of pregnancy in solemn warning. Yet, so many women continued to be executed for the crime that sometimes they had to be hanged in batches at one time.

'It's a sad world,' said Mr Blackadder.

Often he said that. Just suddenly, in the middle of what he was doing or saying or writing.

'Uh-huh, aye, it's a sad, sad world.'

And more and more often she was agreeing with him.

Chapter 16

Annabella dreamed of donning her most beautiful dress and powdering her hair and being carried in a sedan to some elegant ball. Often she remembered the ball given by Prince Charles Edward Stuart during his stay in Glasgow and how she had danced the minuet with Jean-Paul Lavelle and with the handsome Prince. She remembered the many-candled chandeliers and the brilliant colours of tartans worn by the Highland Chiefs.

Oh, such gaiety, such elegance, such light, witty bantering conversation—how she longed for it now. How she sighed too for a lover's courteous and flattering attentions. Often, out taking the air in her fur-trimmed cloak and hood and matching muff, or shopping at the booths wearing a mask to protect her face and pattens to protect her satin slippers, she pertly eyed the men who passed either on foot or clopping along on horseback. She played guessing games with herself as to the potential as gallant paramours of this young buck royal with blue cloak and gold trimmed cocked hat, or that soldier in the scarlet coat. But the young bucks were too young and the soldiers very coarse fellows.

The long dark nights of winter dragged on like a prison sentence until she knew every splinter, every rough patch, every pattern of dark stain on floor or wood-panelled walls. She knew off by heart every title (and often large parts of the text) of every book behind the leaded glass doors of the bookcase. Titles like *Revelation and Sermons by That Eminent Servant of the Lord, Mr Andrew Gray*, and *Rules of Good Deportment* and *Sanctifiction of the Lord's Day* and *Glimpse of Glory* and *Case of Conscience*.

She knew how many purple pears were painted on the ceiling-beams, and russet apples and bunches of black grapes. She knew the way the curtains rippled in the draught and the delicate dance of the candle flame. She knew the regular rhythm of Mr

Blackadder's quill pen and the way his hair straggled forward as he crouched, high shouldered, over the table.

Not that she just sat idly gazing around all the time. She kept herself as busy as she could with her embroidery and the mending of table linen and bed linen and the sewing of shirts, because Mr Blackadder could not afford a sewing maid. The training and supervising of Betsy and her cooking efforts in the kitchen took up a considerable portion of every day. Betsy was now fairly proficient in making dishes like barley broth, or cockie-leekie soup, haggis or oatmeal farles, minced collops or boiled goose. But when it came to preparing a sheep's head for sheep's head broth, or partan-pie made with dressed crab, or Naple's biscuits, or ratafia cream or tanzie custard, she was reduced to blubbering into her petticoats. Over and over again Annabella had to patter downstairs and into the kitchen to attend to some culinary crisis when Betsy had given it up as hopeless and burst into loudening wails of panic.

Nancy refused to have anything to do with her.

'She's the cook. Let her get on with it,' Nancy always said and Annabella felt like wringing her neck.

'Losh and lovenendie, a lot of help you are. The pair of you are driving me to distraction.'

'I do my own work,' Nancy insisted. 'I don't ask her to help me.'

'Pox on you, you lazy strumpet. You do as little as possible. You've always been the same.'

Then she would have to show Betsy yet again how to make Mr Blackadder's favourite sheep's head broth. She would scrape and brush the head herself and take out the glassy part of the eyes. Then she would split the head with the cleaver and lay aside the brains and clean the nostrils and gristly parts before putting the head into the pot to boil with mutton, barley, peas, carrots, turnips, onions and parsley.

Betsy would dry away her tears and curtsy her thanks and promise, with wide-eyed earnestness, that she understood everything perfectly now and that she would certainly be able to do it all herself the next time. But the next time she would be howling into her petticoats again.

In a way, Annabella was glad of these sorties into the kitchen. At least they made a daily diversion and the kitchen was a pleasant enough place with its inglenook fireplace with stools at either side close into the fire and further out a rocking chair and across the other side a dresser with gleaming pewter plates. It was always cosy in the kitchen with mouth-watering smells of roasting meat, lemons, oatmeal, herbs and spices of all kinds. The flurry of kitchen activity required enough concentration to banish Annabella's other more distressing and depressing thoughts.

She was also much relieved by the brief celebrations for Hallowe'en and Yule and New Year when there was feasting and the men indulged in shooting matches, football and other diversions.

On Shrove Tuesday there was a bit of excitement in the town when all the schoolboys took a fighting-cock to school and on payment of twelve pennies to the master, the cocks were pitted against each other in the schoolroom in the presence of the gentry of the neighbourhood. It was amusing how afterwards the schoolmaster eagerly gathered up the dead cocks. They were apparently regarded as a sumptuous feast by his family who ate nothing but oatmeal for the rest of the year.

But cockfighting was a man's sport and of no great interest to her.

On the first of May the Beltane Festival was fun for everyone when bonfires were lit and everyone danced round the flames. It was about this time that she saw the chance of a really exciting reprieve.

The General Assembly of the Church of Scotland was held in Edinburgh every year. It had never been of any interest to her before her marriage and in the first year Mungo had been too young to travel any great distance. Anyway it had never appealed to her. In fact, she had been glad to get rid of Mr Blackadder for a few weeks. But now it assumed obsessive importance, not for the Assembly itself but for the chance to visit the capital city. She had never been to Edinburgh and could imagine there must be all sorts of pleasures and excitement there, things to see, places to visit, people to meet. She became quite feverish with anxiety

430

when Mr Blackadder showed little if any enthusiasm to take her.

'But you must allow me to accompany you, sir. I insist. It is inconceivable that I should be left here to languish on my own. I refuse to do such a thing.'

'Aye, weel, ye can't go, mistress, and that's all there is aboot it.'

'Why can't I go?' She stamped her foot. 'Why, I say? Why, sir?'

'You know verra weel. Ye can't leave wee Mungo. Nor can you take the bairn along.'

'Of course I can take him.'

'Annabella, lassie, you obviously don't know the long and dangerous journey it is to Edinburgh. The roads are that bad it's aye a miracle when anybody gets there. But it's no' just the roads. There's Egyptian sorners and all sorts of dangers to contend with.'

'Oh, pooh to the sorners. I'll soon send them packing with a flea in their ear. As for the roads, I'll get Papa to borrow a lumbering coach and six fine horses from one of the gentry who are his customers. If necessary, he would pay for the use of it when it is to secure the comfort and safety of his daughter and grandson. And we can take Nancy and Betsy along to see to our needs.'

'Uh-huh, aye. Even if you persuaded your father into such an extravagant and foolish action it would neither guarantee your safety nor your comfort. That road's enough to bump the guts oot o' anybody and we'd be verra fortunate if we got there in a day and a half.'

'I don't care about the time. Time I have prodigiously plenty of, Mr Blackadder. Time lies uncommon heavy on me here. I shall pine away and die if you do not take me.'

'Wheest, Annabella, ye've no' to talk like that.'

'I'll talk in whatever way I wish, sir, and if I say I'll die, I'll die. I swear this past winter has been the most monstrously tedious in my whole life. I feel a spiritual indisposition and a decay of the soul. I am deeply dejected, sir.'

'Uh-huh, weel, you aye seem cheery enough to me.'

'I do not go about with a long, melancholy face, that is true.

431

I try to keep your home a happy place, Mr Blackadder. I try to be a good wife. Surely I deserve to be indulged in this. How can you even think to go without me. I am mightily distressed, sir.'

'Och, dearie me, you're an awful lassie, Annabella. Och, I suppose if you must come, you must come.'

Immediately she brightened. Her eyes shone. Clapping her hands with excitement, she kissed him on the cheek.

'I'm obliged to you, Mr Blackadder. I shall speak to Papa right away.'

Her father did not readily agree but she persuaded him in the end and he arranged for the use of not only my Lord Knox's lumbering coach and six fine horses but three footmen as well. Two of the footmen were to stand behind armed with long poles to prise the coach out of the ruts and one was to run in front to give warning of any obstruction.

Mr Blackadder made his will and they set all their affairs in order before they began the journey. The young maid Betsy wept copiously with fear and distress at going so far from her family who all turned out, howling and lamenting, to see her off. Others came too to share the excitement of the departure and to gaze in admiration at the coach. Gudewives and maids strained from tenement windows all around. Children skipped about or stood gazing in open-mouthed wonder. Gentlemen cantered up on horseback to wish the travellers well. Ruffians leered and nudged about. Ladies crowded close, skirts swaying in a riot of colour, handkerchiefs waving, to call,

'Safe journey. God be with you.'

And in the same breath they gossiped to each other about how it was a disgrace to be travelling with a child on such a dangerous journey and how Annabella's gown was far too fashionable to be proper for a minister's wife.

Such was the clamour and crush and excitement around the carriage, it was only with the utmost difficulty and roaring and cursing that Big John managed to get the horses and the crowd moving.

Mr Blackadder screwed his head out of the carriage window and yelled up protests to Big John at his shocking language, but his voice was drowned by the noise of the crowd until eventually with a mighty crack of Big John's whip they were away.

Annabella's cheeks burned scarlet with joy as the coach thundered along Gallowgate Street and out the deserted country road to Edinburgh.

'Oh, what an adventure,' she cried out. 'Nancy, Betsy, it is a wondrous adventure, is it not?'

Betsy wailed and Nancy glowered,

'If anything happens to this bairn, mistress . . .' She could have murdered Annabella. There she was, not giving the slightest thought for anyone but herself, completely oblivious of the danger and discomfort they were all in. There she was, radiant in her froth of a gown the colour of apple-blossom and a milkmaid straw hat perched on her curls and tied under her chin with bright blue ribbons to match her eyes.

'Oh fiddlesticks, Nancy, nothing is going to happen to Mungo. Look how he bounces up and down and laughs and enjoys himself already. He is his mother's son.'

She hugged and kissed the little boy who was being held, not without some difficulty, on Nancy's knee. Then she peered with interest from the window. At first she caught glimpses of moorland and then gently rolling countryside and trees and broom. But there was nothing gentle about the rough and pitted road on which they travelled. Soon it was impossible to concentrate on scenery as they pitched about from boulder to boulder.

'What is that devilish footman about?' Annabella shouted. 'Is he not supposed to run in front and warn us about such things so that we may go round them?'

Grimly Mr Blackadder hung onto his hat.

'Aye, I warned ye, mistress. It's no' so pleasant noo, is it?'

'You have not answered my question, sir. Why are we bumping and swaying down into pits and crashing and leaping over boulders like this? Why do we not avoid these hazards?'

'There's no way of avoiding them, that's why. Unless you want us to get stuck in a ditch.'

'Command him to remove the boulders.'

'Haud yer wheest! He's removing as many as he's able.'

By the time they reached Linlithgow and the Change House

433

where they were to stay the night, they were so jarred and tossed about they were barely fit to stagger from the coach. And had it not been for their weary and painful condition, they would not for a moment have remained there.

The inn was a mean thatched hovel, with dirty rooms, dirty food and dirty attendants. The table at which the footmen, Big John, Nancy, Betsy, Mungo, Mr Blackadder and Annabella ate was greasy and without a cover. The butter was thick with cowhairs. The coarse meal was served without a knife and fork and they were forced to use their fingers. When one tin can was placed on the table to be handed round from mouth to mouth, Annabella objected in no uncertain manner.

'How many mouths has this repulsive object been to before it has reached us? Remove it from my sight at once, do you hear, and bring me a clean glass. Clean, I said! Shame on you, sir, for keeping such a monstrous filthy house. It is a dastardly outrage, that a lady and gentleman have to suffer such shocking indignities.'

But what they suffered at the meal was nothing to what they had to put up with later. The beds were stinking and crawling with bugs and fleas. Annabella refused to go near hers. She sat the whole night on a chair, her apple blossom skirts bunched up around her, her feet still in their blue satin slippers resting on a stool. She ordered the others to do the same or to lie on the floor if they preferred. As a result, in the morning when they set off again they were not much refreshed.

The road did not improve and several times when the footmen, no matter how hard they struggled with the poles, could not budge the carriage from a deep hollow, they had all to clamber out to lighten it. On one occasion Mr Blackadder had to help the other men in their struggle to budge the wheels. When his good black coat and breeches and white stockings became splashed with mud he shook his fist at Annabella and howled,

'This is all your fault, mistress. You and your damn lumbering coaches. If I had been riding along by myself on my ain horse there would have been none of this bother.'

'Don't you dare raise your voice and fist at me, sir,' Annabella fumed, and when Mungo began to cry with fright, 'Now look what you've done.' To make matters worse Betsy began to screech and Annabella whirled on her and soundly slapped her face. 'You useless girl. Stop that monstrous caterwauling this instant.'

She began to think they were fated never to reach Edinburgh until at long last she caught her first glimpse of the place. Away in the distance, high on a hill of rock, towered Edinburgh Castle. The sight cheered her immediately. It seemed to put new energy into the footmen and Big John too and they urged the horses forward as hard as they could.

Soon they were approaching the West Port. Edinburgh was a walled city with various Ports or Gates. Once inside the West Port, Annabella was immediately struck by the height of the tenement buildings towering ten to twelve storeys in the air on either side of them. The long High Street was particularly impressive with wooden-faced gables turned to the streets, the projecting upper storey making piazzas below. Underneath these pillared piazzas were the open booths where merchants displayed their wares. Some had spread them on the pavement in front of their shops. In the middle of the street near the lofty St Giles Cathedral were stalls crammed with woollen stuffs, linen, pots and all sorts of articles. In the second or third flats of the Luckenbooths—a row of tall narrow houses standing in front of St Giles and blocking the High Street—the best tradesmen had their shops. Other shopkeepers carried on their businesses in cellars to which the customers descended by worn stone steps so narrow that it was hardly possible to turn and too dark to see.

In front of the houses were painted signs indicating the article in which each tradesman chiefly dealt. Over one window a periwig advertised the presence of a barber. A likeness of stays or a petticoat showed ladies where they could buy these articles.

The street was seething with a vast panorama of humanity. There were few coaches in the narrow steep streets but innumerable sedan-chairs swayed about in all directions carried by Highland porters yelling in Gaelic at anyone who got in their way.

Young ladies in gigantic hoops swept along on either side of the street, their heads and shoulders draped with gay silken plaids, scarlet and green. Faces adorned by patches were mostly concealed by black velvet masks held close by strings, the buttoned ends of which were held by the ladies' teeth. In their hands they wielded huge green paper fans to cool themselves and by their sides hung little snuff bags. On their feet were red high-heeled shoes in which they tripped lightly along. Stately old ladies walked with precision and dignity with pattens on their feet and canes in their hands.

There were judges wearing large wigs and carrying their hats under their arms; advocates billowing along in their gowns on the way to the courts in Parliament House; and there were ministers by the dozen in their blue or grey coats, bands, wigs and three-cornered hats.

Ragged and dirty but swift and alert caddies were running with parcels and messages to different parts of the town.

Merchants assembled at the Cross, near St Giles, to transact business and to exchange news and snuffboxes. Other men about town met and gossiped.

Annabella was entranced by the busy, noisy scene yet at the same time she was shocked at the dirt and odour of the place. The causeways were broken and stinking with filth. Big gurgling gutters, in which ran the refuse of a teeming population, provided garbage for crowds of pigs who came poking their snouts and grunting with satisfaction.

When Annabella alighted from the coach she had to gather up her skirts and take every care to prevent her gown and stockings from being spotted or specked.

The footmen took the coach away to stable it and the horses, and Mr Blackadder, Annabella, Mungo and the other servants made their way down the narrow Wynd to the close where they would be staying. A cousin of her father was giving them hospitality and they lived up the steepest and narrowest staircase Annabella had ever climbed. It, like the other inside staircases of Edinburgh was really an upright street and just as busy.

The dark stairs with their stone steps worn and sloping with traffic were as filthy as the streets, and at each door they passed they were assailed by the repulsive smell and sight of the 'dirty luggies' which contained all the filth and fulzie that would be tossed from the windows when the bells of St Giles rang out ten o'clock.

In Glasgow the fulzie was decently deposited out of windows into the back yards of the houses so that the streets remained comparatively clean and pleasant places for ladies to walk on. In Edinburgh, Annabella discovered, everything was slung out of front windows with a cry of 'Gardy loo.'

The cry was usually heard too late and many a drenched periwig and foul-stained three-cornered hat was borne dripping and stinking home. At the dreaded hour of ten o'clock, when all the abominations of the town were flung out and the terrible smells—sarcastically known as 'the flowers of Edinburgh'—filled the air, citizens burned sheets of brown paper in their houses in attempts to dispel the odours that wafted in from the streets.

It was no easy task for Annabella to crush her hoops up the stairs which were jostling unceremoniously with all sorts of people besides the residents. There were porters carrying coal, fishwives with their creels, men carrying the daily supplies of water for each flat, barbers' boys with retrimmed wigs all squeezing past one another as they struggled to get up or down.

At last, somewhat puffed and dishevelled, Annabella managed to reach Cousin Rob's door. Cousin Rob and his wife, Kirsty, greeted them with enthusiasm and a shower of kisses. Cousin Rob was a mouse of a man, all twitching and blinking, but merry with it. His wife rustled like an autumn leaf in a brown dress.

'You'll drink a cup of tea right away,' she said. 'I've got a pot ready made. In fact, I was just having a cup and a gossip with a neighbour when you came to the door. I'll get my cup back and tell her you've arrived.'

'She went rustling over to the open window of the drawing-room and raised her voice out the window.

'That's oor kinsfolk arrived, Mistress Fleming. I'll take my cup back if you're finished with it and see you later.'

The lady she addressed was at a window in one of the houses opposite. But the path between the houses was so narrow and the houses so overhanging, it was quite easy for Kirsty to stretch out and retrieve her cup.

She shut the window and began busying herself, admiring Mungo, questioning Annabella and Mr Blackadder and pouring out tea.

'My, my, what a fine big lad. Do you like your tea strong, Annabella? Isn't he the spitten image of his grandfather? Tho' I can see a wee bit of you as well, Mr Blackadder. Are you going to the Kirk Assembly tonight, sir? Help yourself to my fruit cake. Or there's awful nice wee cookies. Would you like to go to the Dancing Assembly, Annabella? Or do you not feel fit after your journey? Isn't that a lovely wee man?'

The room was low-ceilinged and ill-lit but Annabella could see that it had a finely carved marble fireplace of grey threaded with reddish brown, and the walls were oak-panelled. Two hole-in-the-wall beds were concealed with brocade curtains of a rich dark colour similar to Kirsty's dress. The room boasted a highly polished table with hand-turned legs, a rosewood spinet and a writing table, and everything was crowded with silverware and ornaments of every hue and shape. Annabella sorely envied some of the pretty *objets d'art*.

The tea quickly revived her and her spirits began to soar.

'Indeed, Cousin Kirsty, I feel prodigiously fit,' she assured the older woman. 'And I can hardly wait to step the minuet at one of your Edinburgh Dancing Assemblies.'

Chapter 17

'I can swim as good as anyone,' Gav shouted. His freckled face was flushed and his hair wet and tousled. He fastened up his breeches and finished drying himself with his shirt.

The young man he angrily addressed was a large blubber of fat topped by a sneering, pocked face. George Clow was the only son of a planter who had his own wharf further down the river but who occasionally came up to the store or to the wooden church which had now been built on the settlement, or to visit Widow Shoozie's tavern. Eighteen-year-old George was much adored by his father and everything George had ever done from tormenting slaves to associating with whores had been looked upon with a loving and indulgent eye.

Gav had tangled with him before and disliked the youth intensely. But some of the other planters' sons weren't so bad and when they gathered like this at the creek for a swim they often enjoyed riotous good fun together and their laughter and shouts would echo through the trees. George was the only one who kept reminding Gav that he was little better than a slave and treating him as such.

On this occasion, Clow was in a tormenting mood and had ducked him several times under the water and held him until Gav thought he was going to drown. Then all the boys and himself had had a race and he, being the youngest and smallest, had struggled in last, much to the laughter of the others and the loud taunting of Clow.

Gav was about to say more in retaliation when he caught sight of Regina. She came strolling along to settle on a tree stump some distance away. Then, drawing a knife from her belt and picking up a bit of wood, she began to whittle. He didn't think she was near enough to hear what was going on but she would be able to see himself and George and the three other lads who were snickering and fooling about.

'I thought red-haired people were supposed to have a wild temper,' George was saying, bouncing around him now with fists raised. 'So come on, Rusty. Let's see you go wild.'

Gav felt apprehensive in case Regina would become involved. Since the incident on the ship with Mr Gudgeon, Regina had become even more of an unknown element. He was fast developing the belief that anything Regina might do would always be worse than anything that could happen to him alone. He didn't mind taking a beating. He had survived many beatings at school in Glasgow. Regina had never interfered then and he couldn't understand why she had changed so much. In those days she had cringed timidly away from violence of any kind but she had been of great comfort to him afterwards. He could always depend on her for comfort and sympathy as, hand in hand, after school they had made their way home. Now he could depend on nothing as far as Regina was concerned. There was never any telling what she might do.

It was because of this that he swallowed his pride and backed away from Clow.

'I'm not afraid of you, George Clow,' he said truthfully. 'I could soon ram my red-head into your fat belly and take the wind out of you if I wanted to. Only I haven't time just now. I've got to run back to the store.'

'Rusty doesn't want to run away, y'see,' Clow addressed the other boys. 'Rusty just wants to get back to work, y'see. Rusty loves working in that miserable oven of a store, y'see. Rusty just adores it, y'see. Can't get back quick enough, y'see. But I don't think we should let him go back to that rotten ol' place, do you?'

Giggling, the boys jostled closer. Gav knew that his tormentors would never let him live it down if he ran. But at least it would be the end of the incident as far as Regina was concerned. So, after dodging this way and that to avoid hands trying to grab at him, he managed to hare away as fast as he could. After a few minutes, however, he realized that the feet were no longer pounding after him and, screwing his head round, he saw why.

Clow had discovered a new quarry. He and his friends were now swaggering towards Regina. Gav didn't hesitate. Back he flew.

'Reggie's my cousin,' he said breathlessly. 'And he just minds his own business. He doesn't want anything to do with you.'

Regina was still sitting, eyes lowered, silently whittling.

'Reggie doesn't want anything to do with us, y'see,' George told his friends. 'Reggie's just a trashy servant like his cousin Gav here, y'see. But he thinks he's better than us, y'see.'

Gav stood in front of her.

'All right,' he said, putting up his fists. 'I'll fight you now.'

They all howled with laughter until eventually Clow said,

'Did you ever see such a sight? Reggie here is a good head bigger than Gav but he hasn't even the nerve to look up, far less stand up. He prefers to hide behind his wee cousin, y'see. He obviously can't fight, y'see. I wonder if he can swim, eh? Let's strip him off and fling him in the river. If he sinks we'll know he can't swim, y'see.'

Suddenly Gav lowered his head and lunged at Clow like a young bull. It winded the older boy, all right, but he soon recovered and flung Gav roughly aside. Then just as he was about to grab Regina and the others were moving in with whoops and yells of excitement, Regina's knife suddenly flashed up and down, up and down.

Everyone stopped. They stared in horror at Clow's arm. It had burst open to reveal lumpy flesh from which blood swelled up and overflowed. Clow gave one long, high-pitched scream.

In a shaky voice Gav said:

'Quick, you'd better get him back to the settlement and somebody to help him before he bleeds to death.'

Without a word the boys stumbled rapidly away, half holding, half carrying, a grey-faced Clow.

Gav stared at Regina in distress. She was still gripping the knife but she was wide-eyed and shivering like a terrified animal.

'Oh, Regina,' he said.

She dropped the knife but still didn't say anything. She seemed incapable of speech. Her face had the waxy look of death but a nerve twitched and quivered at one side of it.

Gav picked up the weapon and wiped it clean on some grass. She put her hand out for it and he gave it back to her and helped her to her feet.

'We'll have to go back, Reggie. But don't worry, I'll tell everyone they were tormenting us.'

Regina gave him a grotesque jerky smile.

'You know perfectly well that servants are always being tormented. If you don't, you're a fool. It's normal sport to the likes of them. Do you think that pig's father's going to think his precious son's done anything wrong by having a bit of sport with me? And his father's a burgess, remember.'

'Maister Ramsay's other ship's in just now. Maybe we could stowaway aboard and get back to Glasgow.'

'Don't be stupid. You like it here. You and your shifty-eyed friend.'

'I'll stick with you. We'll be all right.'

'You are a fool. This has nothing to do with you. You didn't stab him. You're all right.'

'I'll stick with you,' he repeated stubbornly.

'We'd never make it to the ship. We'd be in full view of the settlement.'

'We could hide in the forest until it's dark,' he suggested unhappily, his eyes already anxious with visions of wild animals and savages.

'No, they'd set the dogs on us like they do to the niggers. They'd get you as well. You were right the first time. I'll have to go back.'

'Maybe nothing will happen,' Gav said without conviction as they slowly set off.

Regina did not say anything until they came near the settlement. Then she stopped and turned a stiff face to him in which green eyes shone with fear.

'I'll have to go in on my own.'

'I'm here. I'm staying with you.'

'Please walk slowly back along by the creek. Then wait there for as long as you can. Promise me you will.'

'But that'll take ages,' he protested. 'I'm not afraid of anything happening to me. I want to be with you.'

'I know. But it would only make me feel worse. Please, Gav. Oh, please. Stay away as long as you can.'

He swallowed unhappily.

'All right.'

Without another word between them Regina walked away. As he watched her go she seemed to shrink into herself and become smaller. He had believed she possessed great courage when she had gone into the forest and he had admired her. But now she did not look at all brave. The sight of the cringing, barefooted figure, hair like ruby wine in the sun above the long loose waistcoat, made his heart pain him and tears sting his eyes. He dropped onto the ground to sit cross-legged, arms hugging round knees, head hidden in lap, miserably nursing himself. When he looked up again Regina had disappeared. He could hardly bear to think what was already happening to her. No doubt she would be immediately flung into gaol, a windowless cabin with a raised platform in front to hold the scaffold, the whipping post and the pillory. Probably she would be fastened into the pillory and everyone would throw things at her.

As he began his journey along by the creek, he sobbed with distress and at the same time tried to wipe away his tears. He wouldn't let them. He would stand in front of Regina and protect her. He would throw things back at them. He would chase them away. It was an agony for him to be walking in the opposite direction from his sister and several times he was tempted to turn and race back, but he had given his promise and he knew Regina meant what she said about feeling worse if he was there. She was such a queer person at times, he just didn't know what to make of her or what to do for the best.

After he'd seemed to wander for miles he crouched on the ground, sobbing and wiping at his tears, trying to keep his promise to her to wait for as long as possible. Eventually he began walking back until the settlement came into view and he couldn't keep from breaking into a run.

A crowd was overflowing from the store and he guessed that they were deciding what was going to be done with Regina. He wondered as he flew towards them if she was in the store too, perhaps being defended by Mr Speckles. Or had she been already locked in the gaol? Then he remembered that there were already a couple of slaves in the gaol waiting to be strung up this afternoon. Noble and his wife, Honey, were two runaways who

443

had been found stowed away in Ramsay's ship the *Mary Heron*. Apparently their master had been going to sell them separately and, to avoid being parted, they had run away. That might only have meant a whipping but they had taken with them one of their master's coats and a good wool cape belonging to their mistress. And stealing was a hanging offence.

There were more people than usual in the settlement because of the ships being in. Sailors in loose petticoat-breeches and striped shirts with pistols and sabres stuck in sashes, and large cocked hats atop tied handkerchiefs, brushed shoulders with planters in many buttoned, brightly coloured coats and waistcoats, shirts and cravats, white silk stockings, and silver buckled shoes. Ladies decked in frilly caps and tight bodices stiffened with whalebone and lace-trimmed petticoats flaring from panniered overskirts, crowded expectantly among maids in mob-caps and short striped dresses, bib aprons and bare feet. Farm workers in brown breeches and English smocks, coloured neckerchiefs and straw hats elbowed and crushed about beside other workmen in green coats, waistcoats and muslin cravats, with their hair in pigtails. Rawboned, big, bearded back-woodsmen chawed tobacco and spat indiscriminately while children hopped about and dogs barked at the edges of the crowd.

'What's happening?' Gav shouted when he reached the milling throng. At the same time he tried to struggle into the store but one of the backwoodsmen plucked him back as if he were no heavier than a tobacco leaf.

' 'Taint no use tryin' to git in ther'. The gabbin's over fer now. If you hightails over to the gaol, you'll git a good view.'

The crowd was surging in that direction now and Gav ran along with it, ignoring the stones slashing at his feet and the clouds of dust making him splutter and cough.

First the runaways, Noble and Honey, were dragged out. They were both young and they were sobbing and clinging to one another. In a flurry of hysterical clutching at Noble, Honey fell up the stairs to the scaffold and laughter immediately howled out from the crowd, drowning the broken-hearted sobbing. But Gav was near enough to hear the girl cry out to her

444

husband,

'Why can't I be with you? Why can't I?' Then loudly, urgently, ' 'Taint you I'm angry at. 'Taint you, Noble.'

They strung the young man up first, and perhaps because he was young, he took a long time to die, twitching and kicking spasmodically, as the rope swung slowly from side to side. After they hauled him down, the woman tried to crawl across to him but she was grabbed, silent now, as if in a daze, and hanged quickly. Then Regina was dragged out. No longer wearing her waistcoat, she was clad only in a loose shirt and breeches. She was frantically struggling. Somebody shouted,

'String 'im up as well.'

Another voice said,

'We agreed on a whipping.'

'String 'im up.'

Then suddenly Gav noticed Mistress Kitty at the front of the crowd. She had become separated from her husband in the rush and crush and looked dishevelled. Her wig hung askew and her silk fichu had come undone leaving one shoulder bare.

'Master Reggie serves us well in the store, in the store,' she cried out. Never before in her life had she suffered such extreme agitation. Master Reggie had been kind to her, had treated her with respect and her gratitude to him knew no bounds. In desperation she fluttered up her hands and shrilled out, 'Mr Harding and I ask that he be spared, be spared.'

'If it's to be a whipping, get on with it then,' somebody else shouted.

Harding pushed towards his wife and said,

'You hold your tongue, woman. Don't you put words into my mouth.'

'But, Robert, Robert. Poor Master Reggie has always been so civil to me, so civil to me, sir.'

'He has committed a crime and deserves to be punished.'

Gav squeezed between them.

'Let me pass. I've got to stop them.'

Harding grabbed him by the scruff of the neck.

'No, you have not.'

As he struggled to free himself, Gav could see rope being

445

twisted round Regina's waist as she was fastened to the whipping post. A man wielding a long handled whip suddenly tore her shirt down to her waist. There was a gasp from the crowd and the man with the whip shouted:

'Dammit, sir! It's a female!'

Harding loosened his grip in surprise and Gav struggled forward and clambered up the steps until he reached Regina. Clumsily he tried to cover up her nakedness until George Clow's father dragged him off and flung him aside.

'It makes no bloody difference,' he roared. 'This no-good slave tried to kill my son.'

'She isn't a slave.' Gav sobbed. 'She's my sister, Regina.'

Kitty Harding swayed around clutching a lacy handkerchief to her brow.

'I do declare, I do declare, I feel quite faint and breathless, quite faint and breathless.'

The first lash of the whip sent a red thread snaking rapidly across Regina's back. Kicked every time he tried to get up or move towards Regina, Gav sat on the ground moaning and moving his head from side to side, trying to shut out the awful picture of his sister becoming covered with blood, and what was even more shocking, the silence of her. Not once did she scream. In Glasgow many men and women had been whipped and their screams had racketed round the town. Regina's silence was truly terrible and when they eventually cut her down, she slithered to the ground like a rag doll, without even a moan. The crowd dispersed to enjoy a chat about what had happened or to forget about it and go about their normal daily business. Gav scrambled forward.

'Regina, oh, Regina.'

Her eyes were closed and she was hardly breathing. He struggled to put his arms around her and raise her up but she proved heavier than he expected. Then suddenly Mr Speckles was towering over them like a giant skeleton with skeleton fingers and dusty clothes hanging loosely on him and two bright blotches burning high on his cheekbones.

'I'll help you, Gav. We'll get her back to the store between us.'

'Thank you, sir.'

Gav renewed his attempts to raise Regina but Mr Speckles said,

'You take her feet, Gav. I'll lift her there.' Crouching down he slid his hands under Regina's armpits and round until his fingers pressed into the sides of her breasts. 'Lift, Gav, lift.'

They shuffled their way down the stairs and then walked jerkily, trying to avoid bumping or being bumped by groups of people standing gossiping or strolling about. A drunken backwoodsman in dyed buckskin with yellow fringes swayed forward, peering close at Regina.

'Good-lookin' little varmint, ain't she, eh?'

Ignoring him they hurried past, Mr Speckles edging sometimes backwards, sometimes sideways. Awkwardly they climbed the stairs at the side of the store and manoeuvred Regina into the room that she and Gav shared.

It was cool and brown with only a narrow slice of sunlight warming the air and floor and changing them to gold dust.

'Don't lie her on her back,' Gav warned as they made to put her on one of the bunks. 'I'll have to try and bathe it.'

'That's right. You go and fetch water, Gav.'

Something about the man's voice and the way he was staring at Regina made Gav feel reluctant to leave.

'There's water here in this bowl. It's all right, Mr Speckles, I'll attend to Regina.'

'I've ointment downstairs in the store.'

'She's beginning to come round.'

Regina's mouth was twisting and her fingers were clutching at the patchwork quilt. Mr Speckles moved back a pace or two muttering.

'I'll go and fetch it.'

Then with his rapid jerky walk he left the room.

'Regina, you're all right now. You're in your own bed and I'm going to bathe your back and put healing ointment on.'

Her eyes opened wide.

'It's all right,' he repeated. 'There's no need to be frightened. I'll look after you.'

'Don't let anyone near me,' she said.

'I won't, Regina.'

447

'No one.'

'Not even Mr Speckles, I promise. He'll probably have started serving in the shop and be too busy to come back up anyway. I'll run down and get the ointment. I won't be a minute.'

It was as he suspected. The shop was busy. A planter's wife was strolling around, her skirts swishing against a pile of dead turkeys, feathers gleaming like fish scales in the gloom. A serving-maid was examining the brooms propped upside down in an old whisky barrel. A man in a sky-blue coat and a lace cravat was critically examining his bill by the light of the doorway. Gav wriggled past him and ran over to Mr Speckles who was standing behind the counter hugging his skinny body as if he was cold.

'The ointment's over by the basket of vegetables,' he said without looking at Gav and the boy wasted no time in scrambling across to grab it.

Before he could get out the door again, however, Mistress Harding in her wide tulle skirts had frothed in front of him, her face too small under her curled wig.

'How is your poor sister, your poor sister, Master Chisholm?'

'She's very upset and her back's in a terrible state. I'm going to bathe it and dab on this ointment. I hope that'll help her.'

'Poor little thing. Poor little thing.' Mistress Harding held out a miniature brandy flask. 'Give her this also. It will strengthen her. It will strengthen her, Master Chisholm.'

'You're very kind, Mistress Harding.'

Mistress Harding seemed short of breath and to be having difficulty in moving her chest when she spoke.

'Your sister has often done little kindnesses to me, young sir. I do not forget such things. I do not forget.'

Just then Harding came striding up to them. He was wearing a white nankeen coat that accentuated the width of his shoulders and deepened the colour of his skin and hair.

'What are you chattering on about now, mistress? I have finished my business here.'

She managed a light tinkling laugh.

'You're such a tease, Robert dear. Such a tease.'

Gav slipped away and in a few minutes he was up the stairs

448

and beside Regina again. Then came the ordeal of trying to bathe the blood from her back and put on the ointment. He got the job done and secured a bandage of sorts with a towel around her. Then he helped her into a fresh shirt and gave her some more of the brandy. She managed to thank him and tell him she felt easier.

She lay on her stomach with her tear-stained cheek twisted against the pillow and when he took her hand and held it she tried to smile.

After a time her eyes closed and he sat listening to the sounds echoing in the heat haze outside the room. Men and women talking and laughing, horses whinnying and clip-clopping, carpenters sawing, sailors singing. It seemed as if nothing had happened, nothing had gone wrong. Yet he was harrowed beyond words and a strange apprehension had begun to creep over him. Unconsciously he tightened his grip on Regina's hand.

Chapter 18

Mr Speckles did not dare keep the news from Ramsay and so he sent a letter back with the *Mary Heron* telling of how it had been discovered that the boy 'Reggie Chisholm' was really a girl called Regina.

'. . . I am dogged by bad luck, sir. I have lost assistants before. But it is not my humble self I am thinking of when I crave your kind permission to keep this girl at work in the store. Your business is my prime concern, sir, and she is of valuable help to it. I do earnestly assure you of this. She applies herself diligently to all tasks and is quiet and modest in her manner. Indeed, sir, she rarely speaks at all, unless to be polite and helpful to your customers. . . .'

When the ship sailed Gav reminded Regina that it would take many weeks, if not months, to reach Glasgow and a similar time would pass before one or other of Ramsay's ships managed to return to the settlement and bring a reply. So she had plenty of time before needing to worry about other employment.

'Maister Ramsay might decide to keep you on, Regina. I don't see why not. And it won't be so very long now until my indenture's finished and I get my own land. Think of that, Regina. We'll build our own house and live in it and grow our own food and tobacco.'

'You've still about three years to go.'

'It'll soon pass, you'll see. And I told you, we'll not even need to worry about Maister Ramsay until next year.'

Regina wasn't so sure. All sorts of vague and shadowy spectres haunted her. Would Ramsay tell his daughter about her? She didn't think he was the type of man who would discuss business matters with the female members of his family. But what if, on this occasion, he did?

Gav said:

'He wouldn't tell her, Regina. I know he wouldn't.'

'How do you know?' she scoffed.

'Because of how she ran away to the Highlands after the Frenchman. Maister Ramsay was so cast down with worry about her, he wouldn't want to risk unsettling her again.'

'Maybe he'll want revenge on me because of the Frenchman.'

'Of course he won't, Regina. Why should he? He hated the man. And if it wasn't for you causing the Frenchman to be killed, Maister Ramsay would never have got Mistress Annabella back. I'm sure Maister Ramsay won't cause any harm to you, Regina. He's really a kind man.'

Regina's mouth twisted in derision but at the same time she had to admit to herself that what Gav said made sense. No one knew better than Ramsay what a reckless person his daughter was. Surely he would guard his tongue very carefully when Mistress Annabella was around. Yet with men she could be sure of nothing except harm and so apprehension continued to claw at the edges of her existence.

The only happiness she could draw from her daily routine was when she was alone in her bedroom. There she unlocked her sea-chest and gazed upon and touched her golden coins and dreamed dreams of the security and the help they would one day give to both Gav and herself. She didn't know exactly how much land would cost but she had heard it was cheap, and of course in this vast country it was certainly plentiful. When it came nearer the time for Gav to get his, she would find out about prices and buy some acres next to Gav's, so that they would have a decent sized plantation between them. Maybe she could manage to get some land fronting the river like most of the wealthy planters. And she would employ carpenters to build a decent house, not just a tiny windowless cabin like those of most of the indentured servants who had become free men. Perhaps she would have enough to send to Scotland for elegant furniture and china dishes and chandeliers as well.

And Gav and she would live in comfort and safety. No one would dare threaten them then or misuse them or put a foot near them. They would be safe.

She couldn't feel safe here in the settlement. Not any more. Men stared at her since she had begun dressing in girls' clothes.

She had bought material from the store, and with the help of a paper pattern and much good advice from Mistress Harding, she had managed to make herself an over-gown of green cotton with yellow petticoats and a yellow frill at her elbows. She grew her hair long and pinned it back from her head but left one long curled lock to dangle over the front of her shoulder.

Mistress Harding said:

'I do declare, I do declare, Regina, you're quite the most beautiful, the most beautiful little thing I ever did see. But there's suffering on your face, child, suffering on your face. That's what's wrong with your poor little mouth.'

Harding had been there at the time and he had said impatiently:

'I don't see anything the matter with her.'

'Just a little hardness, Robert dear. Sometimes there's a hard little twist. But it's not poor little Regina's fault. Any more than it's your poor little Kitty's fault for always being ill.'

Regina felt some sort of bond grow between herself and Mistress Harding but she viewed the relationship with caution amounting to suspicion. Why should such a woman be so interested in her? Surely they had nothing in common. Mistress Harding was foolishly affected in speech and a restless butterfly in manner. In contrast, Regina seldom spoke unless she had to, and she had no use for conventional niceties of manner like curtsying or fluttering eyelashes or using a fan. But Mistress Harding was very keen that she should learn. Mistress Harding, it seemed, had come to look forward to her visits to the store for this very reason. She had acquired not only a liking for Regina but a passionate interest in making something of her.

Once, in her husband's presence, Mistress Harding had sighed and said:

'You are a strange and mysterious creature, Regina. Strange and mysterious and that is how a woman should be. I do declare, you are no ordinary little servant miss. You have means, have you not? And you have an education, an education.'

'I have a little money of my own,' Regina admitted cautiously. 'And I can read and write and count. I know some Latin too, but not as much as my brother.'

'Your talents are wasted here, Regina. Wasted here, my dear.

You should be in a household of quality, a household of quality. Living with a fashionable family, Regina. As a tutor or the like.'

'If you're hinting that the girl comes and works at Forest Hall, mistress,' Harding sneered, 'she'll have a long wait before you produce a family to tutor.'

Kitty Harding flushed and flickered her fan and fluttered her eyelids and cried out:

'Oh, oh, I do declare, what a clever idea! What a clever idea. Regina, you must come and live with us at Forest Hall. You can be my maid-companion. My maid-companion.'

As politely as possible, Regina refused. To be a maid, or even a maid-companion, was not one of her ambitions.

She had other offers too, mostly from men. These also she refused. She didn't like the way the men looked at her or spoke to her, especially those who paid her compliments. Sometimes they addressed Mr Speckles.

'A fine looking young filly you've got there, sir. Too damn good for this place. A ripe cherry like that should be picked and enjoyed, sir. Time she was married. With whom do I make the arrangements?'

Mr Speckles had muttered that he would make inquiries in his next letter to Glasgow, while his eyes darted across to steal furtive looks at her.

When they spoke of marriage direct to her, she answered them in a voice that was like a tight cold fist. Talk of marriage added to her uneasiness and the attention she received hedged her about like a restricting fence. She was particularly unnerved by Mr Speckles' hungry glances and a couple of times she had been startled on opening the bedroom door to find him standing outside. Once she had wakened during the night with a terrifying feeling that he was in the room. In panic, she had called on Gav and with difficulty he had groped for the tinder-box and lit a lantern. The smoky yellow light revealed no one. But she remained convinced that only a few minutes previously someone had been hovering near her.

She thought she would never survive the long winter nights. It was terrible to feel unsafe while she slept. As a result, before spring came again, she had decided to accept Mistress Harding's invitation.

'We've got to separate now,' she told her little brother. 'But you've only two years to go and I'll come and visit you at the store as often as I can. Just keep thinking of the time when you'll be free and we'll have our own house and our own plantation.'

Gav tried to look brave but his voice trembled.

'But, Regina, why do you need to go? You're all right here with Mr Speckles and me until we get our own place. I don't want you to leave me.'

'I'm not all right. You don't understand.' She turned abruptly away from him. 'I'm going and that's all there is to it. And don't dare start blubbering. You're not a child any more.'

She waited for the Hardings' next visit to the store with mixed feelings. In all her sixteen years of life she had only been separated from Gav once before and that was when Mistress Annabella had taken her as her maid to the Highlands. That had been a dreadful experience. She remembered the loneliness as well as all the other terrors. She had missed Gav all the time, although she had never admitted it. She could not be honest and open with her feelings like him. To be like that was to her a crumbling of defences, a leaving open for unexpected attack, a vulnerability that could lead to the destruction of the soul. She guarded her feelings with great care.

Mrs Harding could not contain her delight when she learned of Regina's decision. Her mittened arms and gauzy dress fluttered and flapped and made her look like a grotesque yet delicate winged butterfly about to blow away.

'I do declare! I do declare!' she carolled to everyone in the store. 'I am the happiest and luckiest of human beings.' And tears shimmered in her eyes as she alighted on Regina and kissed her.

Regina was embarrassed and looked away. The woman was only hiring a maid after all. Even a maid who was to act as a companion surely didn't warrant such a fuss and commotion.

Harding's face was a cold mask. Eventually he said:

'If you're coming, you might as well come now. I'll get one of the slaves to collect your belongings.'

He was a strange man. When he had thought she was a boy

he had shown every interest in her. Indeed, remembering the sumptuous meal and hospitality she had received from him, it occurred to her that he had been very civil. Now, as a girl, she seemed no longer to exist as far as he was concerned.

After seeing to her luggage and collecting her cape, she said an abrupt goodbye to Gav. But he ran after her as she walked away to join Mistress Harding in the carriage.

'Regina.'

'What is it?' she snapped irritably. 'How many goodbyes do you want me to say?'

Looking pale and hurt, he hesitated. Then suddenly grabbing her, he hid his face in her neck.

She pushed him away.

'For goodness sake, you're always such a baby.'

He flushed the colour of his thick mop of curls.

'I am not.'

'Yes, you are.'

'I am not.'

She climbed into the open carriage and without looking at him again said,

'Well, goodbye then.'

'Goodbye,' said Gav.

The carriage creaked over the rough earth of the clearing in front of the jailhouse. Then it weaved a path between the stumps and towards the track that led alongside the quarters and past Widow Shoozie's tavern into the forest. No sooner had it done so than a feeling began to grow in Regina that she had made a terrible mistake in deciding to leave Gav and her job at the store. The feeling terrified her, yet she remained frozen in her seat of the carriage unable even to turn round.

Mistress Harding chattered happily all the way and she wondered how she would be able to stand her for any length of time. Surely her silly talk was enough to drive anyone mad. Her green eyes stole a glance at the older woman. Even on the hottest days Mistress Harding wore a wig decorated by bows or beads or little ornaments or a mantilla of lace. It wasn't until later that Regina discovered it was because Kitty Harding possessed a thin dusting of hair through which the white skin of her scalp was plainly visible. Feathery lines at her brow and eyes gave her an anxious look when she wasn't smiling, but she smiled a great deal. She was smiling now and her chatter echoed through the trees of the forest like a strange tireless species of bird.

After a while Regina stopped listening. Occasionally she glanced over at Harding who was riding sometimes further ahead, sometimes at one side of the carriage. She wondered what was going on behind those jutting brows and eyes deep-set like slivers of coal.

When darkness fell, a bed was made for Mistress Harding across the two seats of the carriage and Regina tucked a cover over her before settling herself down underneath, between the carriage wheels.

Harding sat staring moodily into the fire the slaves had lit. He seemed unaware of the howling of the wolves all around. But the slaves were jittery and restless and, although Mistress Harding hid her head beneath the cover, her jerky high-pitched cries of distress could be heard competing with the racket of the wolves for most of the night.

Regina tried not to think of Gav lying alone in the room above the store but all sorts of worries about him came to plague her. Now that he had not her to look after him, would he be all right with Mr Speckles? Would the planters' sons torment him and bully him? What if he took ill?

Despite the harassment of her thoughts, she sank into a deep sleep and dreamt that Mr Speckles had crept into Gav's room and Gav had awoken screaming with fear. She jerked awake herself unable to believe for a minute or two that the silver rays of early morning were shimmering through the tops of the trees and that there was no Gav calling her name.

Mistress Harding was dozing and lay with the cover fallen half off and wig askew. From her mouth with its little threads that betrayed the beginnings of wrinkles, a trickle of saliva glistened.

'Mistress Harding,' Regina said. 'Can I help you up? We're ready to move away.'

She awoke with a splutter and a jerk and with Regina's help struggled into a sitting position.

'Oh, oh! Thank you, my dear, thank you. Oh, oh, what a dreadful dreadful night. I shall be so glad, so glad to get home. I shall be glad too of a reviving cup of chocolate. You shall have one too, Regina. You shall dine with us. Because you are employed as my companion, you shall have the same status as a tutor and live like one of the family. Like one of the family, my dear.'

The carriage jerked and creaked away. Horses' hooves thudded. All around and above them the forest was rustling and cracking and flapping into life.

Mistress Harding struggled to straighten her wig and they both attempted to tidy their appearance as the carriage swayed and bumped along. Regina felt resentment at Harding for ordering the driver to start off so suddenly, not allowing Mistress Harding or herself enough time to get organized or settled. He was a selfish, insensitive man with never a thought for anyone but himself.

She was stiff and tired and irritable and felt nothing but regret that she had decided to join this ill-matched pair. But then when Forest Hall eventually came into view, she experienced a thrill at the thought that she would be living in this grand place. It was a far cry from the streets and closes of Glasgow where she and Gav had spent many a cold and miserable night with the beggar Quin. Never again would she have to suffer such deprivations. This resolve took shape inside her like a diamond, hard and pure and beautiful. She savoured it as she alighted from the carriage and entered the house side by side with Mistress Harding.

'Now that we're home, Regina, now that we're home, you must call me Mistress Kitty. Westminster, Westminster,' she called to one of the slaves. 'Bring our chocolate into the drawing-room. Bring it into the drawing-room before poor little me faints clean away. Oh, oh, Regina, it was a dreadful journey, was it not?'

In the drawing-room Harding went straight to the whisky bottle and poured himself a glass while Regina helped Mistress Kitty off with her cape and passed it to a slave. The older woman flopped into a chair.

'I do declare, I do declare, that journey will be the death of me yet. The death of me yet.'

'Oh, be quiet, woman,' Harding said without looking round. 'I'm sick of your lily-livered whining. If only you would die!'

Regina's eye glittered.

'That's a terrible thing to say.'

'It's all right, my dear.' Mistress Kitty's voice was high and quavery. 'Robert doesn't really mean it. Not really. He's such a tease of a man. Such a tease of a man.'

Harding flung a sarcastic glance in Regina's direction.

'Don't you come all self-righteous with me, mistress. You nearly killed the son of a friend of mine. And what did you do in Glasgow, I wonder, to warrant your escape from that place disguised as a boy?'

Regina glowered hatred at him before looking away.

'Here is the chocolate. Here is the chocolate,' Kitty cried out. 'This will help us all into a better humour.' Gratefully she sipped at hers. 'Do sit down, Regina. Sit down, my dear. Is that the only gown you have? The only one?'

Regina nodded over her cup of chocolate.

'Green suits you, of course, and the gown is very becoming, very becoming. But we must find you something to change with. I have so many gowns. Dear Robert is most generous, most generous. You must try them on for size, Regina. We will choose some pretty gowns and petticoats for you. Oh, oh, we will have such fun, such fun. Are you not glad you came?'

Thinking of the gowns and the petticoats, Regina was able to say:

'Yes.'

Chapter 19

'I don't care if the Provost of Edinburgh himself attends these Dancing Assemblies. I tell you dancing is a temptation to sin,' Mr Blackadder insisted. 'Promiscuous dancing is a seductive temptation to sin, lust and worldliness.'

Annabella groaned and rolled her eyes. Her husband crashed his fist down on the table as if it were the pulpit.

'Annabella, it's an incentive to sensuality and the places where they're held are nurseries of vice.'

'Oh fiddlesticks!'

'I'm telling you, mistress.'

'I know what you're telling me, sir, and I wholeheartedly disagree with you. I repeat, all the best of society meet at balls and I will be chaperoned by Cousin Kirsty. What harm could possibly befall me? My heart is set on going, Mr Blackadder. I did not suffer that monstrous journey from Glasgow to Edinburgh for nothing.'

He was late enough as it was for his Kirk Assembly, otherwise he might have prolonged the harangue, but in exasperation and for the sake of peace, especially in someone else's house, he eventually agreed that she could go.

The narrow lane leading to where the dancing was held was a-riot with coloured sedan chairs and their gaily attired occupants. From tall overhanging tenements people leaned out windows to get a good look, and underneath a noisy mob jostled on the cobbles to witness the fine sight of ladies in richly embroidered gowns and gentlemen in bright silken coats making their way into the close. From there they climbed the winding turnpike stair to the ballroom, the ladies holding their hoops and concentrating on manoeuvring them through the narrow passages.

At the end of the ballroom, under a wall bracket in which a candle flared wildly in the draught, sat the imposing figure of the

Lady Directress. It was she who organized and contrived everything and everybody. The ladies gathered at one side of the room and the gentlemen at the other. Eventually the Lady Directress picked out a lady and gentleman to minuet, then another and another, swooping this way and that, making brusque indications with her fan that the ladies and gentlemen leapt to obey. After several minuets were walked with much formality and dignity, all stood ready for a country dance.

Annabella enjoyed the dancing, but she had to admit to herself that the evening was not as good fun as many she had experienced in Glasgow. Here, dignity was rigidity and, although there was much ogling by the ladies and sighing by the men, no conversing or closeness was allowed by the tyrannical Directress.

The ballroom was not even comfortable, with cold air whistling up from the draughty staircase and smoke billowing in from the pipes of the footmen who waited at the entry.

Then, as St Giles' bells rang out eleven o'clock, the Lady Directress with firm dignity waved her fan, the music abruptly ceased and the ladies and gentlemen dispersed.

Annabella discovered that the gentlemen saw their partners home to their flats and then they adjourned to a tavern for the custom of 'saving the ladies.' This meant each man proposing a toast to the lady of his choice. He drank to her beauty and to her glory and to anything else he could think of. He drank vowing to die in her defence and the one who drank most and fell unconscious last was the victor.

In their respective homes the ladies had a cup of chocolate and a gossip before peeling off their hoops and stays and retiring to bed.

It was all rather disappointing and did nothing to cure Annabella's restlessness and dissatisfaction with life. But she made the best of a few days' visit to Edinburgh all the same. What she enjoyed much more than the ball was the afternoon she spent at a 'consort.' There artistic noblemen and lairds performed Italian sonatas on flute, hautbois, violoncello and harpsichord. Never to her knowledge had there been such an occasion in Glasgow and she looked forward to boasting of the experience to Grizzie and Phemy when she returned home. She

460

had fluttered coquettish glances over her fan at Lord Colington, one of the performers, and later he had given her a very charming bow and presented her with his snuffbox. She had been chatting and laughing with him and having such a delightful interval when it was spoiled by a pert madam with long swinging earrings who claimed him as her 'dear husband.'

The journey home to Glasgow was not only uncomfortable but depressing. She felt very low in spirits at the thought of going back to the dreary routine of life with Mr Blackadder in his cramped dismal house with its bookcase full of Bibles and religious publications. Unable to make conversation with Mr Blackadder or the servants or even to talk to Mungo, she closed her eyes and pretended to be sleeping for most of the way. Although in fact it was impossible for anyone to sleep with the coach heaving and jerking and jarring so much.

As soon as she arrived at the Briggait she went straight to her bed, so heavy was her depression. Lying in the gloom, she listened to the monotonous tick-tock, tick-tock of the clock that stood in the shadowy corner.

Then Nancy's feet thudded down from the attic room.

'I've put Mungo to bed,' she said. 'Can I bring you a cup of chocolate or something to make you feel better?'

'No, there is nothing here to help my condition,' she sighed.

'It isn't like you to be so downcast. What's wrong? Are you with child again?'

'Gracious heavens!' Annabella cried out. 'No, I am not.'

'What ails you then?'

'I don't know.'

'Will I tell Mistress Griselle and Phemy to call tomorrow?'

'Yes, they will want to know all about Edinburgh.'

Thoughts of telling her friends about the journey and stay in Edinburgh brightened her a little and when Griselle and Phemy came she appeared her normal, lively self, although Griselle noticed that she looked paler than usual. Her father noticed too when he called later that evening.

'You're gey pale and dreamy looking, Annabella. Are you sickening for something?'

She laughed and gave him a kiss.

461

'Papa, Papa, I am indeed.'

'For what may I ask?'

'You would not understand. I hardly understand myself. But all the spice seems to have gone out of my life and it is very dull fare indeed.'

'You should think yourself lucky, mistress. You have a husband who does not misuse you and a bonny bairn.'

'Yes, Papa.'

'And you've just had a visit to the capital city.'

'Yes, Papa.'

'I knew it would do you no good to go there. A turn in the country would have done far more for you. A ride to Port Glasgow would have brought the colour back to your cheeks.'

'What is there in Port Glasgow, Papa?'

'It's a verra nice wee place. All the ships come and go from there.' He hesitated, then said: 'I'm riding there tomorrow on business. You may ride along with me if you've a mind to.'

She had no particular fancy to see Port Glasgow, but anything was better than nothing to break the monotony.

'That's most civil of you, Papa. I will look forward to it.'

Indeed she did begin to look forward to it and early next morning she rode up Saltmarket Street and waved cheerily to her father who was waiting astride his horse with his scarlet cloak billowing out behind him. They cantered off together and soon left Glasgow far behind and were alone in the open countryside. The road deteriorated as they came nearer the port until there was no road at all. Then, after clopping through thick woods, they had to slither the horses down a rough track on a steep hill. From the hill the view was breathtakingly beautiful and shimmering bays and peninsulas and surrounding mountains of purple could be seen.

Port Glasgow nestled down in a bay that was a forest of ships' masts. Whitewashed houses ran in a semicircle with many closes at the front and gardens at the back. The houses were two storeys in height with high pitched roofs and crow-stepped gables. Behind the houses stretched a building of immense length and Ramsay explained that this was the rope works.

They went to a tavern for a glass of ale with which to refresh

462

themselves and found the tavern busy with sailors and masters of ships as well as local farmers and tradespeople. Supping her ale, Annabella became intrigued with some of the conversations going on around her. Sailors were telling of fearsome adventures aboard ship, of being boarded by swashbuckling pirates, of storms and shipwrecks on tropical islands. Others enthused on the marvels of Virginia.

'It's a new world all right,' someone said. 'A different world, a fantastic world. Everything is giant size and the numbers of birds and beasts are truly incredible. I tell no lie when I say I have seen flights of birds miles long that blacked out the sun. When such a flight rises in the air it is like roaring thunder.'

Someone else said:

'There are many great mansion houses along the banks of the James River. Huge places, each with a ballroom, outbuildings and slave quarters. Plantations have their own carpenters, coopers, blacksmiths, tanners, curriers, shoemakers, spinners, weavers, knitters and even distillers. A plantation's like a complete city.'

Someone else again:

'There are towns too and the streets are gay with scarlet, gold-laced uniforms and brightly coloured coats, and women's dresses. And there's gilded four-wheeled chariots and coaches drawn by four or six horses wearing shiny silver-mounted harness. And they're driven by bewigged black servants wearing colourful livery. And there's glass enclosed sedan chairs carried by Negro slaves in splendid uniforms.'

Annabella could see it all. How exciting it sounded. Her eyes sparkled, her cheeks glowed.

'Aye,' her father said with some satisfaction. 'You're more like yourself already.'

She favoured him with a happy smile.

'Indeed, Papa, I feel prodigiously cheered. I thank you for bringing me.'

'I have business to speak with the customs officer. He will be arriving soon. Away you go and have a look around. You can meet me later.'

'Very well, Papa.'

The first thing she noticed was that the streets were infested with hogs and she was reminded of Edinburgh in this respect. But of course the Port of Glasgow was little more than a village compared with Edinburgh. The original village had been called Newark after the ancient Newark Castle. Then it grew to the New Port of Glasgow and eventually became known as Port Glasgow. The castle was a large turreted mansion with crow-stepped gables and cable mouldings and it sat right on the water's edge.

An exhilarating breeze was gusting her curls about as she cantered along and she could see white horses foaming the water and merrily seesawing the ships. She had never felt so happy and alive for years.

She could hear sailors singing.

'Now if you want a merchant ship to sail the seas at large,
You'll not have any trouble if you have a good discharge,
Signed by the Board o' Trade an' everything exact,
For there's nothin' done on a Limejuice Ship contrary to
    the Act.
So haul, boys, your weather mainbrace and ease away your
    lee,
Hoist jibs and topsails, lads, an' let the ship go free.
Hurrah, boys, hurrah; we'll sing this Jubilee;
You can keep the Navy, boys, a Merchant Ship for me.

Gazing at the bobbing vessels in the bay she thought that here was the gateway to real adventure and a great longing came over her to dash aboard one of the ships and set sail for faraway, fantastic lands and a new and wondrously exciting life.

Once such a thought came into her mind there could be no denying it. She wanted to journey across the sea. She wanted to go to Virginia. She itched to put the thought immediately into action, but it was such a revolutionary idea that even she realized it would never come to pass unless she acquired patience and used all the womanly wiles at her disposal.

Her mind busied itself with plans. Instinctively she knew that this was one whim in which her father would not indulge her. But what if her husband decided to go to Virginia? Her father would not go against the minister. The more she thought about this, the more she was certain that her only chance lay through Mr Blackadder. But how to persuade Mr Blackadder to take such a giant step, that was the problem. Mr Blackadder did not even like going to Edinburgh and only stirred himself to face the journey because he felt it was his Christian duty to attend the Kirk Assembly.

Suddenly Annabella had the clue. If she could persuade the minister that it was his Christian duty to go to the New World . . .

Her heart raced with joy. Surely it was not beyond her intelligence to accomplish such a feat? She could hardly wait to get back to Glasgow and her husband. On the return journey, in fact, she whipped her horse into a lather until her father, barely able to keep up with her, lost his temper and bawled,

'Damn it, Annabella, if you're no' at one extreme, you're at the other. Compose yourself, woman, or I'll take the whip to you.'

Never before had Mr Blackadder come home to such a good dinner or such a beautiful and charming wife.

The narrow lobby and the stairs had been washed and the bedroom floor was shining as well. A crisp white cloth graced the table and on top of it sparkled the best rice grain china and silver tea-service. The royal blue bedcurtains were looped back to reveal the bed resplendent with white satin bedcover.

A log fire blazed merrily and enclosed the room in a rosy hue. Annabella, magnificent in powdered wig and patches, tightly laced bodice and voluminous golden skirts, billowed into the room carrying a steaming dish of sheep's head broth.

Mr Blackadder hardly noticed. He had been out late doing his rounds of visiting, catechising and questioning and he was fatigued and out of humour with his flock.

'They're an impudent, ungrateful bunch,' he said.

'Indeed they are, sir,' Annabella agreed, depositing the dish on the table and making dash at Mr Blackadder to stuff another cushion behind his back. 'They do not appreciate your prodigious talents.'

He slid her a look of surprise tinged with suspicion.

'Uh-huh, aye, that's true enough. Auld Mistress Logie was showing me the new horse on the farm and I heard her calling the beast Blackadder. When I questioned her about this, she had the temerity to say it was because it bore a distinct resemblance to me.'

With an almost superhuman effort, Annabella suppressed her hilarity and instead creased her face into what she hoped had an appearance of sympathy.

'The woman's in her dotage. Her farmer son should keep her locked in the house. She is a madwoman, sir, to talk in such a ridiculous way.'

'Uh-huh, aye, weel. Mind you, it was a fine-looking beast.'

'I do not know how you can thole them. You have the patience of a saint, Mr Blackadder.'

'Uh-huh. Aye.'

'They do not deserve you.'

'Have you by any chance been having a wee tipple, Annabella?'

'Why no, sir. I have been the whole day with my Papa.'

'Oh aye. At Port Glasgow. And how did ye get on there?'

Annabella wiggled to the edge of her seat with enthusiasm, her golden dress shimmering in the firelight.

'I was much intrigued with it, sir.'

'Indeed. Uh-huh.'

She suddenly swooped up and across to the table.

'Look what I have for you. Come do, sit in and enjoy it, Mr Blackadder. You will feel better after supping such a delicious broth.' Then, no sooner had he taken the first sup, she burst once more into eager speech. 'It is a wondrously beautiful place nestling at the foot of a green hill with sparkling water in front and purple and blue hills across the water and all around.'

'You'd see the ships.'

'Oh, I did, I did and it was a truly wondrous sight, Mr Blackadder. There was a prodigious number of seamen there too and they told of many fantastic adventures.'

'Uh-huh. Aye, they can spin a yarn all right.'

'They spoke much of Virginia and told of what a prodigiously beautiful place it was. Only I was disconcerted to hear that there are savages there.'

'Aye, I've heard about them.'

'Does that mean they do not know about The Word?' she enquired, using his own phrase.

'Aye, it does indeed.'

'But that is terrible.'

'Uh-huh.' He supped his broth and smacked his lips over it in obvious enjoyment.

'They say the settlers are little better. They perambulate on the Sabbath and comb their hair and cook their food and sing bawdy songs . . .'

'Annabella!' He banged down his spoon. 'Control yourself! Don't even think such wickedness.'

'But they said . . .'

'Wickedness! Wickedness!' His voice rose, pulling him up from his seat.

She leapt to comfort him and push him back down.

'I agree, sir. I agree, Oh, it is indeed too terrible to contemplate. They have not enough good men like yourself. That is the trouble with Virginia. God's work is being monstrously neglected.'

Mr Blackadder was boiling with indignation on God's behalf.

'The wicked rascals. The sword of God's wrath will smite them down. Come the terrible day of judgement they will be cast into the eternal fire.'

'Ah, many's the time I've heard you preach long and heavy on that very subject, Mr Blackadder. If only these terrible Virginians could have heard you. It might have been the saving of them. Let me help you to another bowl of broth.'

She did not press the subject of Virginia and the terrible sins committed there any further that evening but it kept cropping up on other occasions when they were in company or when they were on their own, until one day Mr Blackadder unthinkingly remarked,

'I've a good mind to go over there and tell the sinners what I think of them.'

And Annabella immediately flung her arms round his neck and cried out,

'Oh, Mr Blackadder, you've had the call. Rest assured, sir,

that I will not shirk my duty. When you go to save the souls of the sinners in Virginia, I will be there by your side.'

'Haud on a minute, Annabella,' he cautioned, somewhat taken aback. 'These things can't be rushed into.'

'I trust you to know your duty, sir, and have the courage to carry it out. You've never lacked a sense of duty or courage before.'

'Uh-huh. Aye. But there's other things to consider, Annabella. And other folk.'

'I am not afraid to journey to the New World.'

'But there's wee Mungo.'

'It will be a splendid new life for him. And when he gets older he can supervise Papa's stores or whatever business Papa needs him to attend to in Virginia. What is there for him here?'

'Och!' Mr Blackadder had never looked more worried and uncertain. 'But hang on a minute . . . hang on . . .'

'And I know you have always had a prodigious concern for Mungo,' Annabella said and gave him as passionate a kiss as she could muster.

Eventually he had been not so much persuaded as harassed into agreeing, and Annabella rushed around telling everyone the news that they were emigrating to Virginia. He had no sooner nodded his head when he was caught up in all the arrangements for leaving. There was so much to do he hardly had time to realize what he was doing.

Annabella flung herself into the business of packing and preparing for the journey with great zeal and energy. Sometimes, when Mr Blackadder was not there, she swirled around the room singing,

'I'm going to Virginia! I'm going to Virginia!'

Nancy, who felt secretly disturbed by wild tales of cannibals and giant beasts, muttered dourly,

'Maybe you'll find more over there than you bargained for!'

Chapter 20

Mr Blackadder made them all kneel down, Annabella, Nancy, Betsy, and little Mungo. The deck creaked and groaned beneath them and above sails bellied and cracked.

'God the Father Almighty.' He clasped his hands and rolled his eyes heavenwards. 'For the love of Jesus Christ, His Son, by the comfort of the Holy Ghost, the one God Who miraculously brought the children of Israel through the Red Sea, and brought Jonah to land out of the belly of the whale, and the apostle St Paul and his ship to safety, from the troubled raging sea and from the violence of a tempestuous storm, deliver, sanctify, bless and conduct us peaceably, calmly and comfortably, through the sea to our harbour, according to His divine will, which we beg; saying, Our Father . . .'

'Our Father . . .' the others trailed after him with small mutters compared with Mr Blackadder's ringing funereal tones.

Immediately afterwards the women scrambled up to catch a last glance of Port Glasgow. As they sailed along, the white houses of Port Glasgow and then of its neighbour Greenock glittered on the edge of the river. Behind them groves of trees rose over each other against a background of hills.

Towards the mouth of the Clyde, other vessels were billowing along, their sails sparkling white against the blue of the water and the purple and green of the hills. It was a beautiful sight and the little cluster of women at the bulwarks now joined by Mr Blackadder gazed at it in silence. Then Betsy began to wail.

'For any sake! If you don't stop that infernal yowling,' Annabella snapped, 'I'll throw you overboard. And don't you dare start either,' she rounded on Nancy who glared back in an effort to hide her real feelings behind a front of anger.

In truth, Nancy had never felt so harrowed since that awful day in the Highlands after the Battle of Culloden when the dragoons had caught up with her and Calum, her Highland lover. She had shot him rather than allow the redcoats to have him. She had seen what had happened to Annabella's lover, Jean-Paul Lavelle. Regina Chisholm had betrayed where Lavelle was hiding and the redcoats had dragged the wounded man out and put him through the most dreadful tortures. She would never forget the sight of the dying Lavelle in Annabella's arms afterwards, his face and head burned unrecognizable, a mass of black flesh.

She had shot Calum rather than have him suffer as Lavelle had suffered, but it was a terrible thing to have to do.

And this was a terrible thing to have to do, to leave the shores of one's own country, to tear out one's own heart.

It was like saying goodbye to Calum all over again.

'I never made a damned sound,' she said to Annabella.

'No, but your face is as long as a fiddle. You'd think we were going to our death instead of to a new life.'

'For all I know we are going to our death.'

'Fiddlesticks! How many times have I to explain to you? We are not going to live in the middle of a forest or anywhere isolated or uncivilized. We are going to a wondrously gay metropolis. We are going to the capital city of Williamsburg.'

'I'll believe that when I see it.'

'Ignorant strumpet! There's no telling you anything.'

'Now, now, Annabella,' Mr Blackadder intervened. 'Haud yer wheesht. We're all a wee bit upset at leaving our native land. I dare say you are yourself.'

It was true. Despite her eagerness to be away on the great adventure, strange pangs contracted her chest and throat. The beautiful coastline of Scotland now pulling away seemed to be tearing something from her as it went. She kept blinking with pain but she said,

'It never does any good to mope and wail, sir. And I'll not allow anyone to agitate the child.'

'Uh-huh, aye. You're no' to upset wee Mungo, Betsy. So do what your mistress bids ye.'

'I'm going to promenade the deck, Mr Blackadder,' Annabella announced. 'Would you care to join me?'

'Uh-huh. Aye.'

'Then give me your arm, sir.'

Not that there was far to go. The ship was small and cramped. Everywhere there was rope strewn about. Pigs grunted around and geese and ducks waddled past. Somewhere a cow mooed.

Then an exciting scene caught her attention. A warship lay at the tail of the Bank and men from it were boarding a merchant vessel that had been making its way up river. The merchantmen were fighting to prevent their ship being invaded by the Navy and there was much shouting and clashing of swords.

'Gracious heavens!' Annabella said. 'What is happening, Mr Blackadder?'

'It's the press gang,' her husband explained. 'Your father's lost many a good able-bodied man that way. The navy ships lie in wait for the merchantmen returning from long voyages and set upon them and capture most of the crew for service in His Majesty's ships.'

'Isn't there anything Papa or anyone can do?'

'Och aye, most times they land the younger members of the crew at Fairlie and let them make their own way home over the hills to Greenock and Port Glasgow. But och, the press gangs still get them. Armed landing parties search all the inns and taverns.'

'It's a wonder to me how Papa manages with all these worries and difficulties. Yet he continues to prosper. He must be prodigiously good at his business.'

'Uh-huh, aye. He's been very good to us. Sending letters of introduction to all those important people in Williamsburg will make sure we get a bit of help to find our way around it and get settled. Although we're going to a town instead of to the settlement on the river where his nearest store is. The settlement would have been handiest for us with his ships always calling with news and stores, and the settlers and savages there would have been more in need of a minister.'

'Papa thought it would be more congenial for me in the town. Papa is very considerate. And we could hardly argue with him when he was giving us such a large sum of money. We should be able to purchase a commodious dwelling place with that. I hope you made sure, sir, that our furniture and possessions are safely

471

stored in the ship. I do not want my fine china teacups or anything else broken or damaged.'

'I have Captain Kilfuddy's word on that.'

'It can be monstrous stormy, I am told.'

'I hope not, mistress. My stomach feels gey queasy already.'

But the weather remained calm until they were well out in the Atlantic Ocean. Then a squall blew up and gradually increased until it blew a full gale. Mr Blackadder rocked and groaned as if in torment and was very sick into a bucket in between desperate roaring prayers. Fortunately Mungo slept through stormy nights and seemed to enjoy the pitching and tossing of the ship. At least he showed not the slightest sign of panic or fear. On one occasion he had actually laughed. Annabella and the others had been sitting at dinner in the cuddy when a heavy sea broke over the poop. It smashed the skylight and a lamp that was hanging in the cuddy was thrown through the air and broken to pieces. The ship lay almost over on its beam ends and everyone's dinner landed in their laps.

After the first shock, Annabella had joined Mungo in his fit of giggles but the others had reacted with a mixture of acute distress, exasperation and anger. Mr Blackadder had been furious and shouted abuse at her. But he made the mistake of struggling from his seat to do so and was hurled across the cabin by another lurch of the ship. He landed in such an undignified position on his bottom on the floor that Annabella only laughed all the louder.

'You cruel wicked hussy!' he yelled at her. 'The ship could be going to the bottom of the sea and everyone in it for all you care. You do not seem to realize the uncertainty of life, mistress.'

'It is better to laugh in such circumstances than to moan, sir.'

Staggering to his feet he had gripped the table and clung on, pushing his face close to her.

'There is nothing to laugh at in drowning in cold water, mistress. Especially when below that cold water there awaits for you an eternity of fire and brimstone.'

She tossed her curls.

'I refuse to drown, sir. I have set my mind on seeing Virginia.'

But even she became sorely tried as the storm continued

unabated for several nights and days. The dreadful creaking of every part of the vessel, the screaming of the wind, the roaring of the sea and the hollering of the sailors made sleep impossible. At one point their cabin door flew open with the force of the waves that were pounding over the ship's decks. A green swell of water burst in to swish back and forward on the floor. But calm returned eventually and the ship sailed sweetly, lazily shouldering through light seas. Then Annabella was able to wear her white muslin dress with the side panniers that kept it wide and showed her lilac-coloured petticoats.

The only other stir of the voyage was when Captain Kilfuddy thought he had sighted a privateer. Being a merchant ship they did not carry many guns, but the few six-pounders they had were hastily made ready. Sailors bent to the tackles and raised the gun-ports. Powder and shot were rammed home and each sailor had his slow match alight even before the guns were run out through the open ports. But they drifted into a mist that soon thickened into fog and they were able to lose the privateer without a shot being fired.

There certainly was a miraculous thunder and lightning storm as they entered Chesapeake Bay, but it soon passed and they glided up the James River on a mirror-like surface.

Her father had arranged that they should stay overnight at the mansion of one of the riverside plantations and from there travel overland to Williamsburg which was situated between the James and York Rivers.

'You could go further up to the settlement but there isn't enough accommodation at the store and the nearest tavern is Widow Shoozie's. That's no fit place for a lady and I forbid you to go there. It's frequented by seamen and peltry traders. The seamen are bad enough but the peltry traders lead loose and vicious lives and corrupt all who come in contact with them.'

She had assured him that she had no desire or intention of going anywhere near an establishment of such low repute.

'I expect it will be filthy and bug ridden as well,' she said, remembering the horrible place in which they had to spend the night on the way to Edinburgh. 'You have no need to worry, Papa. I would much prefer the comforts of a planter's mansion house.'

He had explained that it was the custom for planters on these isolated situations to offer hospitality to anyone who happened to be in the vicinity. It could be a lonely life cut off by long distances from neighbours and news and they were only too delighted to see and talk to anyone.

This particular planter was not a customer of her father's, but they had met some years previously.

'I've sent him a letter so you'll be expected,' her father said.

But she had not expected the grandness of the house that sat up on the hill from the wharf at which they landed. Even the driveway up to it was impressive with its level and gleaming white surface made of crushed oyster shells. Sheep grazed on the velvety lawn in front of the house which was made of red brick and had carved white wooden pillars and white shutters and doors. The sheer size and spaciousness of everything compared with the flats and houses in Glasgow took Annabella's breath away, but she quickly recovered and swept into the hallway with head held high and fan briskly flicking.

Never in her life had she seen such chandeliers and furnishings and ornaments and richly liveried servants. Not even in Mr Glassford's house had there been such splendour.

Later, in the privacy of the bedroom allocated to them, she enthused about everything to Mr Blackadder.

'I'm struck all of a heap, sir. Are you not impressed? Have you ever seen such magnificence? Everything is such an uncommon size.'

'Uh-huh. Weel, it's a big country. They've got room to spread themselves, I suppose.'

She danced round the high-ceilinged room with arms spread out.

'It feels good to have room to spread oneself. Oh, it feels prodigiously good.'

'That's enough of your wicked frivolity.' He mopped his face. 'It must be the devil gives you your energy, mistress. It's hot enough to melt a candle. It's not natural to be so frisky in such heat.'

'It surely must agree with me, Mr Blackadder, for I feel

474

wondrously well.'

'Uh-huh, aye. You'll feel quite at home in hell no doubt.'

She laughed and flopped into a chair, energetically fanning herself.

'I cannot wait to set off for Williamsburg. It's uncommonly kind of our host to put his carriage and servants at our disposal.'

'Aye, Mr Burleigh seems a civil enough man. We could never have found our way to Williamsburg without his help. He tells me he plans to visit the town in the autumn so no doubt we'll have the chance to return his hospitality then.'

'I shall cook a splendid meal for him and Mistress Burleigh. Betsy is not nearly proficient enough for such an important occasion.'

'Uh-huh. Aye. He says he may be able to help me with a church. One of the ministers in the town is old and ailing and not expected to last much longer. I could assist the poor man, he says, with a view to eventually taking over his flock.'

'Then we have nothing to worry about. Did I not tell you everything would go prodigiously well, Mr Blackadder?'

Mr Blackadder did not look at all convinced.

'Uh-huh. Aye. We'll see. We're no' there yet.'

But she was already there in her imagination. Conversing, dancing, flirting with all sorts of wondrously charming, elegant and interesting people. Still fanning herself and smiling dreamily, she closed her eyes and saw it all.

Chapter 21

'Slowly, slowly, my dear. Yes, that's better. That's better.' Kitty Harding fluttered around Regina who was curtsying with gown spread wide and head lowered. 'Now keep your arms stretched out like that. Such pretty arms. Such pretty arms. Don't move for a second, or two, then, taking plenty of time, gracefully rise again. Oh, oh, the way you slowly raised you head, that was much better, much better. Any gentleman meeting your eyes flashing up like that, like glittering emeralds, my dear, would be devastated. I do declare he would be quite, quite devastated.'

Seeing Regina in the ball gown reminded Kitty of when she was young and had attended balls. She had never been as beautiful as Regina, of course. But there had been a big-eyed fragility about her that some beaus had found quite appealing. She didn't think Robert had ever admired her, though, not in the way the other young men had. It was not his fault. She had just not been the type of woman he wanted or needed. But her father and his father had arranged the match. Her father had been most generous in the matter of her dowry and he had also helped Robert's father with a substantial loan and saved him having to face some sort of distressing business crisis, she couldn't remember exactly what.

She hadn't wanted to marry Robert any more than he had wanted to marry her, but after the knot had been tied, love had blossomed and multiplied and grown inside her until she could not contain it and it burst forth and showered over him in a thousand affectionate words and acts. He tried to respond at first. She remembered the times he tried to respond. It was because of those precious moments in the early years of their marriage, and because she still loved him, that she forgave his every unkind word or deed now.

Perhaps if she had been more robust, perhaps if she had been able to give him a son, their relationship and their lives together might have been different. But she had developed terrible fatigues and breathless attacks and so many aches and pains and distresses of one kind and another. She had been a terrible trial to poor Robert.

'I don't want to meet men,' Regina said. 'I just want to stay here alone with you.'

Tears shimmered Kitty's gaze.

'Oh, oh, how sweet, how sweet. Dear, dear Regina. But life must be lived and we must have balls and attend balls and you must meet presentable gentlemen. Gentlemen of quality and substance, one of whom you must marry. You must marry. I cannot be so selfish as to keep you to myself for ever and ruin your own sweet life.'

'But I don't want to marry. Nor do I need to. I have a little money of my own.'

Mistress Kitty sent tinkles of laughter this way and that.

'A little money. A little money. My dear, what good is a little money? You need a man of wealth and property who can give you a beautiful home and beautiful things. Every woman needs to get married. It isn't good for a woman to remain single. Not good at all.'

Regina was not so sure. She had been making full use of the library at Forest Hall and she had learned a thing or two in the process. For instance, a single woman might own her own property, contract debts, sue and be sued in court, and run her own business. But a married woman, so far as the law was concerned, existed only in her husband. He had the use of all her real property and absolute possession of all her personal property, even the clothes on her back, and he could bequeath them to somebody else in his will. He was entitled to beat her for any faults. He had complete power over any children of the marriage and could also give directions in his will as to who was to care for them after his death. A wife's duty was submission to whatever a husband commanded.

It was far better and safer to be single, as far as Regina could see. So long as you had money, of course.

'What's the use of being married if it only means being ill-used and miserable?' she said.

'My dear, why should you be ill-used or miserable?' she said. 'You are.'

Colour mounted quickly in Mistress Harding's face making her look feverish. She felt hurt and distressed, not for her own sake but for Robert's. Robert tried so hard. Regina did not understand and she did not like Robert. She did not seem to like men in general, but Robert she detested in particular. She was a strange, unhappy child and in fact she and Robert had much in common in their natures.

'No, no, my dear Regina. Mr Harding teases me a little in company but he really is a most chivalrous gentleman when we are alone. It is only his gruff manner in public that you see. But that is not the whole man, not the whole man. Robert is a very complex character. You do not understand, my dear. You do not understand.'

Regina believed she understood very well. Robert Harding despised his wife. If she had produced a son he might have forgiven her silly ways, but she had not and he had dismissed her as useless. They no longer even shared the same room. Often he upbraided her in Regina's hearing, if not exactly in her presence. Only the other day she had been sitting outside in the garden. The window of the sitting-room had been open and she had heard him raging at Mistress Kitty for not managing the house slaves in an efficient manner and not seeing that the meals were properly cooked and served on time. Mistress Kitty had been reduced to tears when he had threatened to have the slaves whipped. She could never abide violence of any kind.

Regina had gone into the room and asked if she could be given the authority to organize the house slaves in future and take a more active part in the running of the house so that she could be of more help to Mistress Kitty. She refrained from saying that doing nothing all day but listen to Mistress Kitty's chatter was nearly driving her mad. And if her lessons in proper social behaviour were only aimed at ensnaring a husband, this did nothing to make her feel any easier.

Harding had agreed to her suggestion but in his usual abrupt manner.

'Yes, it's time you did something useful for your keep. From now on I hold you responsible for the running of this house.'

She had suspected that because she was young and for most of the time of silent disposition, the slaves might take this as weakness. In order to dispel any such ideas right from the start, she ordered them to line up in the hall and told them in no uncertain manner that if they did their work well they would be treated well. If they did not, they would be whipped immediately and without mercy. However, her icy manner and her glittering eye convinced them more than any words could that she was someone to be feared.

But what made them really hate her was the way she cut down on the house slaves and sent most of the them to work in the fields under the whips of Negro foremen and the white overseer and, of course, Harding. House slaves were considered much superior to field slaves and the work in the house much lighter and safer. To be degraded to the fields was both humiliating and frightening.

'It's ridiculous having so many slaves in the house,' Regina told Harding. 'Just look at them in the dining-room. All they do is get in each other's way. Two or three properly trained men or women serving table would be far more efficient.

He shrugged.

'The house is your province. I have given you the authority. Do whatever you wish.'

So from about thirty house slaves, Regina chose only ten. For the kitchen, she chose Callie Mae, Flementina, Minda and Infant. Jenny was to attend to the bedrooms. For a personal servant for Harding, Old Abe. For serving at table, Joseph, Westminster and Melie Anne. For cleaning the floors and windows and emptying the chamberpots, Big Kate.

After dismissing the others, she lined the ten up and told them what she expected of them.

'Instead of thirty of you, there are now ten. That means you will have to work at least three times as hard as you did before. And work at least three times more efficiently. If you do not, you will be punished and sent to work in the fields. Someone else will be brought in to replace you.' She detailed to each of them their special jobs, but told them that they had also to do whatever

479

extra duties were required. 'There's a spinning wheel and a loom in the kitchen. Let them never be idle. All of you women must see to that. Melie Anne, you see that the downstairs rooms are kept dusted and polished. Each man is a general factotum. A man of all work,' she explained when they looked puzzled.

Next she found a bale of calico and a quantity of coarse linen and persuaded Mistress Kitty to get down to the job of making dresses for the women slaves and shirts for the men.

'We must teach them to cut and sew the clothes themselves eventually. Meantime, we have no choice but to see that they are decently covered.'

'But, Regina dear, dear Regina,' Kitty fluttered, 'the niggers don't feel the cold, even in winter, even in winter.'

'I wasn't thinking of their feelings,' Regina said. 'We will cut and sew the clothes together and drink mint juleps and talk while we work. It will be a pleasant diversion.'

So they had basket chairs set out on one of the patches of grass in front of the house that had been cut short and a table put between them to hold their drinks and one of the slaves worked a shoo-fly while they sat sewing. Mistress Kitty sat slumped almost double, making her look like a tiny, deformed old woman. Regina looked straight-backed and graceful with a wide brimmed straw hat shading her creamy skin. She kept a small, polite smile on her face as if she was listening and appreciating Mistress Kitty's incessant talk, but all the time her mind was far away on her own imaginary plantation where there would only be peace and silence.

Sometimes during the day they sat in the drawing-room where trees near the window filtered in the sun, making stripes of light and shade, amber and earth brown. The room now gleamed with polish. The mahogany of the desk vied with the wall panelling in tawny lustre. The brass firedogs and the brass face of the tall clock glittered like gold. The silver candelabra dangling from the ceiling and the other decorating the desk shone like looking-glass. On top of the desk too was a sweet-smelling bouquet of roses.

At all times Regina discouraged gossip or laughing with the slaves. The slave women used to tell Mistress Kitty all sorts of nonsense as well as their troubles. And more than once, since Regina's arrival, Mistress Kitty had gone to the quarters to administer medicine to a sick Negro child.

But idle chatter didn't get rooms cleaned, food cooked properly or meals served on time. Since Regina began seeing to things, she firmly discouraged this useless gossiping. If she came into a room where Mistress Kitty was chattering and laughing with a servant, she said a polite 'excuse me' to Mistress Kitty, then dismissed the servant. Or, if the latter was supposed to be doing some job in the room, she gave her a sharp command to get on with it before guiding Mistress Kitty firmly away.

She could feel the slaves' dislike of her harden but she did not care. To her they were alien creatures with their black skin and tight frizzy hair and as much savages as the Indians or forest people. Only the Negroes were more dangerous than the Indians because they were not only all around but inside the house. She kept a pistol and a knife under her pillow at night and always had a dagger secreted about her person during the day.

But, so far, the coldness of a look or the sharpness of a word had been enough. She had not needed to call in the help of the overseer with his whip. She still had plenty of time to spend with Mistress Kitty, of course. She helped her dress, kept her wig in good shape and made sure she was comfortably settled in bed for her afternoon nap. Every morning after she had given the slaves their orders and organized what was to be cooked for meals, she strolled with Mistress Kitty around the outside of the house or down the path past the clearing in front of the barns and stables or past the quarters and through the wooded area to the tobacco fields. But usually that was too far and too exhausting for the older woman. Mistress Kitty never tired of showering her with clothes and other gifts and continued with great enthusiasm to coach her in the social graces. Then one day she announced, as if presenting her with the most exciting gift of all:

'Regina, Regina, now I can tell you. Everything is arranged. Everything is arranged and you are coming with us.'

'To the store?' Regina's eyes brightened. It would be good to see Gav again. Not a day had passed but she had not thought of him with some anxiety.

481

'No, no, heaven forbid, heaven forbid,' Kitty cried out. 'I would not be so happy at the thought of that journey. No, no, my dear. It is the Public Time, the Public Time.'

Regina looked puzzled and her voice acquired its stiff, guarded tone.

'I don't know what you're talking about.'

'Twice a year there are the Public Times when all the planters and everybody, absolutely everybody, goes to Williamsburg. The gentlemen attend the Assembly in the Capital Building. I believe they vote and discuss the country's affairs. But, more important, my dear, more important are all the balls and entertainments. Such balls and entertainments you never did see. I do declare, there is even a theatre, a theatre!'

Regina felt disappointed. She would rather have visited the store and been reunited with Gav.

'I was hoping,' she said, 'to have seen my brother.'

'You shall, you shall, Regina. But after our Williamsburg visit, my dear. You can arrange to accompany Mr Harding. He will be going to the store on business. But first you must have a gay time at all the balls in Williamsburg. Oh, oh, I will be so proud of you, my dear.'

All her married life she had suffered such an acute sense of failure. Sometimes the pain of her own inadequacy was almost unendurable. Nothing she ever attempted turned out right. Over the years, humiliation had heaped upon humiliation. And it was all her own fault. She did all sorts of foolish little things like forgetting to put the sugar in Robert's favourite pudding in her anxiety to please him and cook it herself and get it exactly right. Or she took ill and collapsed while she and Robert were entertaining guests and caused distress and embarrassment to everyone.

The last straw, of course, had been when she ruined their lovemaking by taking one of her breathless turns while he was on top of her. Her chest had felt as if it was caving in and the pain had been frightful. Nevertheless, she would have endured the pain in silence, would have died of it, rather than have let Robert know and cause him any embarrassment. But a choking, breathless attack had taken complete possession of her. Robert withdrew immediately. Then he dutifully did what he could to help. He had always conscientiously done his best for her but they had never shared a bed again.

She felt sorry for him. Sorry that his life was such a desert. Sorry that he had no passionate woman to share his bed. Sorry that he had no beautiful wife to show off to his friends. Sorry that he had no son to carry on his name. She wept for him in the night under the covers of the giant four-poster bed in which her tiny, curled up body was hardly visible, even during the day.

Now she pitied him all the more because she had the comfort of Regina and his life was still barren. Sometimes, timidly, like a mouse darting into her conscious mind, she thought of Regina giving pleasure and comfort to Robert to make up for her own inability. She suspected that that was why she had wanted Regina to come to Forest Hall in the first place. But the thought made her feel guilty and every time it crept into her mind, she clasped her hands tightly together and closed her eyes and prayed that God would forgive her for such wicked thoughts. As if she had not been enough trouble to Robert without putting temptation in his way and encouraging him to commit adultery, a sin for which he could be made to suffer terrible punishments and indignities at the hands of the minister of the church. And what of poor Regina? The child trusted her and was fond of her too. How kind she had been and how conscientiously she had worked since coming to Forest Hall. Now she must do her best for Regina in return. She would be the belle of the ball and both she and Robert would be so proud of her.

They began packing right away and Regina had never seen Mistress Kitty so excited. Her small, sickly face was blotchy with colour, her eyes shone and she chattered so much that Regina had to stop her.

'If you don't calm down I won't go.'

'But you must, you must, Regina. You are like a daughter to me, a daughter.'

Sometimes Regina suspected the woman was half-mad.

'If you don't calm down, you will be taking one of your seizures. Then neither of us will be able to go.'

'Of course, of course, you are quite right, my dear. Quite right.'

After that she had at least tried to take the business of packing and preparing for their visit to Williamsburg at a slower, quieter pace.

Regina embarked on the preparations and the journey with mixed feelings. Her natural inclination was to shrink into herself and have nothing to do with people and new experiences. At the same time she was curious to see the town and discover what kind of grand houses there were there and what treasures the shops held. Maybe she would not need to send to Glasgow for furnishings for the house that she and Gav would one day own. Perhaps in Williamsburg she would find everything they would need.

She had to admit also to some secret satisfaction at the thought of entering a ballroom, dressed in as grand a fashion, if not more grand, than any lady who might be there. It was a lot better than shivering outside in the street, shoeless and stockingless, watching ladies being carried in their sedan chairs to the balls as she'd often done in Glasgow.

Glasgow seemed very far away now, in time as well as distance. Only occasionally she thought of the huddle of streets with the Cross and the Tolbooth at its centre. The town meant nothing to her but suffering and deprivation. Yet thinking of it helped to harden her resolve to see that she and Gav had a good life here in Virginia.

Bitterness came to twist her mouth. She would have a good life all right. She would go from strength to strength, and she would get wealthier and wealthier and more and more powerful. Nothing and nobody was going to stop her.

Chapter 22

Annabella was both charmed and dismayed by her first sight of Williamsburg. The coach emerged from the forest of tall straight pines and turned the corner past what she later learned was the Capital Building, and there was the long Duke of Gloucester Street, the main thoroughfare of Williamsburg. It certainly was attractive with its trees on either side and pretty white or red brick houses. In front of each house stretched a green lawn and a multicoloured display of roses and neat box hedges and paling fences. The air was heady with perfume, despite the thick dust rising from the sandy road and the hogs and cattle straying about.

What dismayed her was the quietness of the place. There were attractive looking shops and taverns, but no people as far as she could see except one or two liveried black servants ambling along.

Her anxieties were soon settled, however, when her host and hostess, Lord and Lady Butler, assured her that the town would be a seething mass of humanity at what they called the Public Time.

'You will wish that it could be decently quiet like this again,' Lady Butler said. 'One does, you know. There is such a rabble at the Public Time. Of course, one finds the balls an elegant meeting place for one's friends and acquaintances. And one sees the latest fashions in gowns. There people know how to behave. But outside and elsewhere . . .' She twitched with distaste. 'One has to contend with such noise, such crush, such rabble.'

Annabella had not met Lady Butler before but her father had introduced her to Lord Butler during one of his visits to Glasgow and they had given him hospitality during his stay. He was a fat, jolly looking man with scarlet cheeks, a white powdered wig tied at the back, and much frilly lace on his shirt. His wife was richly dressed in a gown of purple and gold brocade and Annabella got a glimpse of black silk stockings with a silver thread at the side. Much bejewelled with ruby rings and long ruby and gold earrings, she never smiled except out of politeness and to people she thought were important enough. She was too snobbish for Annabella's taste but she was glad of the introductions Lord and Lady Butler gave and also of their help in the finding of a suitable house. It was small and modest compared with the Butler residence, but it was still far roomier than Annabella had ever been accustomed to, either in her father's house or in Mr Blackadder's house in the Briggait.

To begin with the ceilings were much higher, and instead of dark panelled woodwork the walls were painted white. There was a longer lobby than they had had at home in Glasgow, and on one side a light oak stairway led up to two bedrooms. Downstairs was a decent sized living-room to the front and a smaller dining-room to the back. A back door led outside to a kitchen building which surprised Annabella greatly. She soon learned, however, that kitchens were always separate from houses.

In the bedroom she shared with Mr Blackadder they put the furniture they had brought from Glasgow which made Mr Blackadder feel more at home. But, of course, they had to buy a bed and they had purchased a sturdy oak four-poster which, to please Mr Blackadder, she had draped with the same royal blue velvet curtains that had graced their bed in the Briggait.

The extra rooms downstairs, however, meant spending a considerable sum on new furnishings and she was delighted with the comfort and cheerful appearance of the rooms. Although the living-room's chintz-covered chairs and settee with matching curtains were admittedly not luxurious, they were pretty and gay. The two windows looking onto Francis Street let in lots of sunshine and in between them hung a rather grand looking-glass with a gilt frame and an eagle with wide spread wings on top. Beneath the looking-glass sat a small mahogany table on which a vase of flowers added a glow of colour. Another little table, also bright with flowers, graced the centre of the room and on the wall opposite the door stood a beautiful Japanned highboy.

The floor was of light oak and the rug, picking out the darker shades of the chintz, covered the floor in front of the redbrick fire. The fire basket had brass knobs topping the front legs, and a long brass poker, and brass and leather bellows lay on either side of it. A chest decorated with brass and containing logs stood nearby. Of course Nancy and Betsy complained of all the polishing the brass needed to keep it sparkling but it added such a lovely glow to the room, especially when the log fire burned bright and reflected in it.

In the dining-room she had put the dresser from the kitchen in the Briggait and added an oval drop-leaf table, half a dozen windsor chairs and a windsor settee, all in a dark glossy wood. Annabella wanted to paint the wood white or some other pretty colour, but Mr Blackadder put his foot down and simply would not allow such a frivolity, in the same way as he absolutely forbade her to have a spinet.

Lady Butler said there would be a ball at the Governor's Palace and no doubt they would all be invited. Annabella was looking forward to the Public Time with great excitement. Her enthusiasm, however, was not shared by Mr Blackadder. He was tolerably content with his church and found Williamsburg a pleasant enough place to look at, but the climate made him irritable and had a generally debilitating effect on his constitution.

It had been hot and thundery at first and the clay of the tobacco fields was baked hard and dry. There had been much lightning during the night. It kept flashing across the heavens, making the sky switch from black to bright blue. It was certainly most disconcerting. It kept Mr Blackadder off his sleep and made him weary next day. Nights were never quiet enough for him. Indeed, it had taken Annabella some time to get used to the clamour and feverish activity of nights in Virginia. Fireflies winged and winked like thousands of red eyes and the squeaking and chirping of crickets continuously attacked the senses. During his daily round of visiting, Mr Blackadder had plodded along the sandy streets trying to keep to the patches of shade. But he could not escape the dust stirred up by every horseman and carriage that passed and he soon developed a cough.

He complained of the flies too and the mosquitoes and Annabella shared his horror of the ticks which attacked anyone who ventured into the long grass or sat on a tree stump. Nor did she like the cockroaches that plagued the house. The tortoise she had been advised to keep to live off the cockroaches was not particularly attractive either.

Rain had come for a few days to change the town from a parched place of choking dust to an equally unpleasant one of dripping and steaming damp. The sweet smell of damp clung to everything. It sickened curtains and clothes in closets. It cast a cloud over the varnish of paintings. It brought green mould overnight to bloom wetly on the covers of books.

But throughout all these unpleasantnesses and discomforts Annabella kept her spirits up by thoughts and plans and preparations for the Public Times. She was looking forward to giving hospitality to Mr and Mistress Burleigh and perhaps to entertain and be entertained by new friends she would meet.

She said to Nancy:

'Thank the Lord for the Public Times. Gracious Heavens, I could not abide this place without such a prospect. It does not contain more than a thousand souls and that includes the Negroes. In Glasgow there were nearly twenty thousand inhabitants. And think of the prodigious number of gentry among them. Why, here there are no more than ten or twelve gentlemen's families constantly residing in the town besides some merchants and tradesmen.'

'They've all bigger houses here though.'

'Yes, indeed. That was something I was most gratified to note. Wouldn't Mistress Halyburton and Griselle and Phemy be wondrously impressed I must write and tell them.'

Mr Blackadder sighed.

'I wish I was travelling back with the letter.'

His eyes were continuously red-rimmed, an irritation caused by the dust, and his cough was most troublesome, especially at night.

'Uh-huh, aye, not that I would relish the journey, but to see Glasgow again would do my heart good.'

'Do not be downhearted, sir,' Annabella encouraged, hastening

488

to pour him out a strengthening glass of whisky. 'You will be uncommonly diverted during the Public Time and that is very soon now.'

'Fairs and frivolities are the work of the devil and are no' going to divert me from the path of righteousness.'

'Of course not, Mr Blackadder, of course not. What I meant was that you would have so many more souls to save then.'

'Uh-huh. Aye. We'll see.'

'And your church will be full to overflowing.'

But even this prospect did not do much to lighten Mr Blackadder's load of depression.

'Damn the heat,' Annabella thought.

'I can sympathize with your indisposition, Mr Blackadder,' she said. 'This heat is a hateful calamity and one we were not led to expect.'

'Uh-huh. It doesn't seem to have indisposed you that much.'

'I was somewhat discommoded at first but I have acclimatized myself wondrously well I must admit. But it is nearly autumn already. Soon it will be winter. The heat cannot last much longer. And you must admit, the Virginian skies are always the most beautiful blue.'

Mr Blackadder sighed and she felt a pang of concern for his drooping, bleary-eyed figure. He had never been a cheerful man but he had always had a measure of caustic wit and wiry physical strength. She kept shooing him off to bed early and she and Nancy concocted various potions for him, for he absolutely refused to take the ones they obtained from the apothecary's shop.

Fortunately Mungo was of sturdy constitution and played about the house and garden with happy unconcern. As a baby he had possessed her blonde hair, but already at three years it had darkened considerably and his skin, once a delicate pink, was now quite brown with the sun. Sometimes she thought she saw a look of his real father about his eyes, especially when the child was angry or in a tantrum. But she scarcely remembered what Harding looked like now and seldom gave him a thought.

It had crossed her mind, of course, that he was somewhere in Virginia. But knowing what a vast country it was, and how far away some of the plantations were, she believed the chances of bumping into him were very remote indeed.

Even if his plantation did happen to be within travelling distance of Williamsburg, she doubted if he would be the type of person to appreciate the gay social life. He was the kind of coarse brute who would shun the elegant Public Time, she was sure.

Any thoughts of such an unpleasant nature were soon completely banished from her mind, however, when the Public Time began and coaches started to arrive by the dozen and clatter down Duke of Gloucester Street and all the other streets. Not to mention innumerable horsemen and people on foot. There was little room for the sedan chairs and they were fearfully squeezed and jostled. Dust rose in great clouds from the busy, noisy scene and it became more and more crowded.

Annabella could scarcely believe her eyes and ears and Mr Blackadder was nearly demented.

'I've had to fight my way through a mob of planters,' he gasped on his arrival home, dusty and dishevelled and in obvious distress. 'Fight my way through, mistress. They're crowded in front of that Raleigh Tavern bidding for slaves and acting like common rowdies for all their lace cuffs and brocade waistcoats and silver buttons. The devil choke ye all, I told them. May ye all rot in the pit of hell where ye belong.'

'Gracious heavens, Mr Blackadder, do not shout at such a pitch. You will frighten Mungo. Let me straighten your wig. It is not like you to get into such a monstrous state. Nancy, run quickly and bring Mr Blackadder a dram. Sit down, sir, and quieten yourself, I implore you.'

But no one seemed able to be quiet any more.

Outside in the jammed streets, drivers of carriages roared curses at their horses and each other. Street peddlers shouted their wares and covered the market square with stalls. Youths had noisy sport chasing greased pigs, or cudgelling, or yelling themselves hoarse at cock fights where steel spurs slashed through feathers and flesh. Men roared with excitement and bet large sums of money on dog fights and bull baiting.

Annabella had been subject to some harassment herself when

490

she had been out. Wishing to make a purchase at one of the shops and venturing on foot being impossible for the rough crowds, she had taken a sedan chair. Even then, however, she had been badly shaken and tumbled about and had not only to shout at the chairmen but lean from the chair and sharply strike some ruffians with her fan to make a decent path for herself.

However, she was looking forward to her first ball that evening. Mr Blackadder had refused to attend, but Lord and Lady Butler were calling for her in their carriage and taking her. Lady Butler and herself had already discussed over dainty teacups and cookies what gowns and petticoats and jewellery they would wear. Also they had chosen the fans and snuffboxes they were to carry.

The coach was fancifully carved and gilded and drawn by six horses wearing shining, silver mounted harness. It was driven by bewigged black servants wearing scarlet livery. Although it was roomy inside, the dresses worn by Annabella and Lady Butler filled the carriage to overflowing.

The night was alive with lanterns and when they arrived at their destination servants made a path for them, holding up lanterns fastened to poles. Annabella had not felt so gay and happy and excited for years. She swished into the ballroom with every bit as much dignity as Lady Butler and with much more panache.

A footman called out as they entered:

'My Lord and Lady Butler and Mistress Blackadder!'

The room was a blaze of colour and a flutter of fans. Annabella tipped up her head and, blue eyes sparkling, stared around. She could see that already she had caught the admiring attention of several handsome gentlemen.

Lord Butler, obviously proud of her, said:

'Allow me to introduce you to some of my planter friends, my dear. I fear they will never forgive me if I do not.'

He raised his hand and she accepted it.

'I will be delighted to meet them, sir.'

He led her to a nearby group who immediately 'made a leg'. She curtsied very prettily and before she had time to draw breath one of the gallants captured her and led her away to step a dignified minuet.

He was a very richly dressed gentleman, someone of wondrous importance, she felt sure, judging by the envious glances of the other women. She felt proud and happy. She was walking on air.

Chapter 23

Mistress Kitty said,

'I do wish we could afford a house in town, a house in town, Regina. So many of the planters do have houses here. It must be so much pleasanter, so much pleasanter than having to reside at a tavern. I do declare the taverns are so crowded, they'll burst at the seams one of these days. They'll surely burst at the seams.'

The Raleigh Tavern would have been a pleasant enough place had there not been such a crush. It was a long white-gabled building with many windows now streaming with candlelight. A lead bust of Sir Walter Raleigh stood above the door and on benches under the taproom windows gossiping people crowded. In front too were hitching-bars where saddle horses with drooping heads waited for their owners.

Normally the rooms were elegant and comfortable especially the Apollo room with its long, highly polished table and its half-panelled walls. Over the fireplace the wood panels covered the walls up to the ceiling and beside the fireplace deep cushioned chairs invited the visitor to relax. Or, if they preferred, they could sit at the spinet where music was always propped ready on the stand and vases of flowers and a candlestick graced the top of the instrument. But now the parlour, the public bar, the dining-room and even the ballroom were far too packed with visitors to afford any proper relaxation and the smell of liquor and food and sweat was almost too much to bear.

Regina was glad when Mistress Kitty and herself were able to retire and leave Mr Harding to carouse with his friends. Mistress Kitty and she had to share a tiny room and Regina thought the older woman would never stop chattering and go to sleep. All Mistress Kitty could think of and talk of was the grand impression they were going to make at the ball.

'My dear Regina, I do declare I can hardly wait till they see you, hardly wait till they see you. They will be impressed with our beautiful little *protégée*. They will be so impressed. Yes, all the ladies and all the gentlemen. And Robert will be so pleased and proud. Oh, Regina, I do so long to do something to please him and make him happy. Dear Robert, he really has been very patient and good with me, and he has been forced to suffer so much. So much. Poor Robert's life had been ruined because of me.'

At last her chatter stopped and she sunk into an exhausted sleep. Regina listened for a time to her snoring before going over to the window and gazing out at the broad Duke of Gloucester Street. Lights flickered warmly from every house. Carriages jingled past with lanterns aglow and fireflies flitted tirelessly under the shadows of the trees.

She was impressed with the thoroughfare and its houses and shops as she was with the whole of Williamsburg. The town was laid out in parallel streets which were intersected by others at right angles. She liked its handsome square in the centre and the public buildings at either end of the main street, the college and the capitol.

The public buildings and the Governor's Palace were made of red brick. Most of the other houses were of wood covered with shingles, but all had a handsome appearance and some of the gardens were very beautiful indeed.

She imprinted everything firmly on her memory so that she could tell Gav in accurate detail when next she saw him. One day they would have a town house here. She would tell him that too. Thinking of him made her contract inside with pain. The ball, the grand houses, the town, meant nothing compared with her longing to see him again and make sure that he was all right. Sometimes she had fearful premonitions that something was going to happen to him and she would never see him again. She suffered one now but immediately crushed it and turned away from the window, her face hard, her mouth twisted down.

Damn the stupid woman and her infernal snoring. Even in sleep she couldn't keep quiet. It was all she could do to prevent herself from snatching at a pillow and thumping it over Mistress Harding's face. She lay resenting the woman for most of the night and next day listened to her happy, excited chatter in a dour silence that barely concealed her distaste. What did she care about entertainments and balls, or the stupid fops and the proud and haughty dames that attended them. They could all sink and drown in the James River for all she cared.

She dressed without enthusiasm in the open gown Mistress Kitty had chosen for her. It had very wide rustling skirts and frills of lace at the elbows.

'I do declare, I do declare, Regina, that taffeta is as vivid and glossy a green as your eyes.' Mistress Kitty was in raptures. 'And the golden yellow of the petticoat is such a beautiful contrast and the lace trimming is very fine, very fine. Now your fan, my dear. Oh, oh, I do declare, I have never seen anyone look so beautiful, so beautiful.'

Harding made no comment when he saw her. It was as if she were a blind spot in his eye or a blank in the horizon. As they sat in the carriage together they seemed miles apart both in attention and appearance. Yet people could have been forgiven for mistaking her for his daughter. There was something of the same hard-eyed look about them both.

'We usually arrive much earlier than this, much earlier than this,' Mistress Kitty prattled on, 'but this time I am glad we are late. I do declare it is much better that we are late, much better that we are late. Robert dear, will you please lead us in one on each hand? I on one hand and dear, dear Regina on the other.'

Both Harding and Regina ignored her. Regina was annoyed that they were late. She had no desire to make an exhibition of herself and have all eyes turned on her. Mistress Harding would be embarrassment enough in her too large plumed wig, and gown patterned with giant blue flowers and crowds of green leaves.

The ballroom was full of people when they entered but it was the glittering chandeliers and rich furnishings that impressed Regina and caught her attention. She was hardly aware of the coloured flunkey strutting forward in readiness to chant our their names.

In the middle of the ballroom Annabella was dancing a minuet with Mr Carter Cunningham. By this time she had learned that he was one of the wealthiest planters in Virginia. He was also stunningly handsome and his courteous attentions and obvious admiration were floating to her head like champagne. Never since she had known her dear Jean-Paul Lavelle had she felt so light in spirits, although at the same time, her secret sadness stretched fingers of pain through her frivolous spirits to tug at her heart. As usual, she hastily ignored these disturbing twinges. She closed her mind to them. It was such a beautiful dance, such a splendid occasion.

Over in the far corner a sheaf of black-coated, white neckerchiefed fiddlers accompanied by a gentleman on the harpsichord were giving a stately rendering of a minuet. The rest of the room was a dream of rustling, swishing colour. Ornaments and plumes and loops of beads swayed and sparkled against high powdered wigs. Jewels flashed at ears, throats, wrists and fingers. Enormous skirted, low-fronted gowns of gold and silver and purple and blue and pink and amber and flame floated along in graceful time to the music.

Then, suddenly, the dream changed to a nightmare. From quite near a footman chanted out:

'Mr Robert Harding, Mistress Kitty Harding, and Mistress Regina Chisholm.'

Annabella felt faint and sick. Colour drained from her face. Her feet faltered. She couldn't see the grand ballroom any more. The candles snuffed out. She was left in frightening darkness and from the darkness came Jean-Paul's tortured face. She heard his screams mingle with her own. She smelled the burning flesh of him. She cradled him in her arms not knowing what to do to stop the horror of his suffering.

And all the time she knew that the girl Regina Chisholm had been the cause of his torment, had told the dragoons where she had hidden him. She could see her now, a barefooted, pale-faced filthy urchin with long tangled hair and tattered clothes.

With a moan of distress, Annabella stumbled towards her, then hit out with all the strength of pent-up years of horror and grief too terrible to be endured. Again and again, her nails tore and clutched and jerked.

Then, suddenly, Robert Harding pulled the girl away and Annabella became aware once more of the candlelit ballroom and the rainbow of ladies' gowns and gentlemen's coats. Only now the ladies and gentlemen were no longer stepping a stately minuet. Everything was confusion with ladies screaming or hiding shocked faces behind fans and gentlemen waving lace-edge handkerchiefs in efforts to revive them and calling out words of comfort and concern in loud and harassed tones.

Robert Harding's voice thundered over all the rest making them fall silent and listen intently.

'Madam, I realize that Mistress Chisholm must have done you much harm to have forced a lady of your quality to such an extremity. I will see that Mistress Chisholm is soundly whipped.'

In a low voice Annabella said,

'You are a fine one to talk about someone harming me. Remove your hand from my arm and step out of my way.' Then in a louder tone for everyone to hear, 'There is no need for you to whip the wretch. I have done my own whipping. Anyway, nothing will ever bring back the gentleman whose death she caused. Pox on her. She no longer concerns me.'

Regina clutched her torn dress over her breasts. It was spotted with blood from scratch marks on her face and neck. Her hair powder had been mostly shaken off and her hair looked fiery-red against the remaining streaks of white. She pushed her way through the crowd to the entrance hall. There an excited flunkey told her that Mistress Harding had been taken ill and he had helped her into a side room. Regina ordered him to fetch their carriage and then to return and assist her to get Mistress Harding into it.

Regina took it for granted that Mistress Kitty had either fainted or taken one of her breathless turns. As soon as she; saw her, however, she realized that this time she had suffered a different kind of seizure. She was lying on a sofa with her eyes closed and one side of her face was contorted as if it was made of wax and someone had squashed it up. One side of her body too was twisted out of shape, shoulder hunched, arm bent, hand raised, fingers splayed.

'Mistress Kitty?' Regina said without going over.

There was no reply. Turning, Regina went back into the hall. The coloured footman met her.

'The carriage is at the door, Miss Chisholm.'

'Hurry into the ballroom and tell Mr Harding his wife has taken ill.'

'Yes, Miss Chisholm.'

He scuttled off and in no time breathlessly returned again.

'Master Harding he say she always taking ill and for you to attend to her, Miss Chisholm.'

'Damn the pig!' Regina thought. 'May he burn in hell!'

'You carry her out then.'

'Yes, mistress.'

At the Raleigh Tavern, the slave driving the carriage carried the still unconscious woman inside and upstairs to the bedroom.

'Go and fetch a doctor,' Regina told him.

She lit candles, then stood looking down at Mistress Harding. She wondered if she were dead, and if it would be worthwhile undressing her and making her comfortable in bed. As it was, she lay on top of the coverlets and no doubt was tightly laced in her stays. She was still standing debating the question in her head when the doctor arrived.

The first thing he did was to bleed Mistress Kitty. Then he burned shavings of hartshorn under her nose. And when she eventually showed signs of life, he forced a stimulant between her twisted lips. Some of it overflowed from her mouth and trickled down her chin and neck. Her eyes, open now, stared tragically up at Regina.

The doctor said:

'See that she's undressed and comfortably settled. I will make another potion and call again in the morning to administer it.'

Regina nodded, then after he'd left she began the awkward task of getting her out of her hooped gown, petticoats and stays. And all the time the eyes stared and not a word was said.

Regina pulled the bed clothes up round Mistress Harding's chin. Then she went over to gaze out the window. It was only then, in the stillness of the room, that she began to realize she felt far from well herself. The scratches on her face and neck stung, she ached from head to toe with bruises and her temples throbbed.

The memory of suddenly being confronted with Mistress

Annabella made her feel sick. The shock of the unexpected sight kept crashing across her like cold waves. She shivered violently. Clutching tightly at herself she tried to control the shaking of her body and the chattering of her teeth. But it was no use. Stumbling over to the bed, she jerked off the top coverlet and wrapped it around herself. Hunched inside it and still agitating like a devil possessed, she returned to the window and collapsed into a chair.

She remembered the way Harding had grabbed her and flung her aside and she hated him until she thought her head would burst. She remembered his voice when he addressed Mistress Annabella. She remembered the way his hands had sought to comfort Annabella. She remembered what he had said. His words echoed and re-echoed in the dark chambers of her mind.

'I shall see that Mistress Chisholm is soundly whipped.'

Whip her, would he? She would remember that. And she would remember the expression in his eyes when he looked upon Mistress Annabella. Mr Harding had a weakness. Yes, she would remember that.

Chapter 24

Williamsburg was aflame with gossip and excitement. Everyone, from the highest Lord and Lady and wealthiest of planters down to the lowliest of slaves, was chattering breathlessly about what had happened at the ball.

The minister's wife . . . yes, the minister's wife, of all people, had actually, would you believe it? . . . had actually pounced upon another guest, had attacked her, had struggled, had hustled about, had fought like a mad thing. It was unheard of. It was wicked. It was shocking.

The speculation about the reason or reasons for the attack snowballed around the town gathering impetus as it scurried from mouth to mouth. Everyone was eager to see if Annabella would have the nerve to turn up at the church in full view of everyone. Also, they were impatient to discover how the minister was taking his wife's dreadful behaviour and what his reaction would be. As a result, on the Sunday immediately following the ball, the church was packed to overflowing. People were crushed so tightly together that once they had pushed and jostled their way inside the building, they found it impossible to raise an arm or shuffle a cramped foot.

Annabella was well aware of the stir she had caused and had lost no time in telling Mr Blackadder of what happened. Better that the news should come from her than from anyone else, she decided.

'You knew of what happened to my Frenchman who was fighting with the Highland army,' she said.

'Uh-huh. Aye. I heard something of it,' Mr Blackadder replied cautiously.

'I followed him to the Highlands.'

'Aye. It was a very foolish and dangerous thing for any lassie to do. You might verra easily have been killed at one of his battles.'

500

'I followed him because I loved him and I cared nothing for the danger. And after he was wounded at Culloden and the Duke of Cumberland's men were after him, I hid him in a deserted farmhouse. A party of dragoons arrived on the doorstep but I was successfully getting rid of them and my Jean-Paul would have been safe. Then that girl, that red-haired wretch with the eyes like a cat, suddenly spoke up and betrayed him. I went on my knees to her. I begged her to have mercy and spare him but she did not. For no reason at all she told the dragoons who he was and where he was.' Annabella took a deep breath. 'As a result Jean-Paul Lavelle died a most horrible death.'

'Uh-huh, aye, weel. I can't see the point in going over all that now.'

'The point is, Mr Blackadder, I saw that wicked fiend of a girl at the ball. Suddenly her name was announced and she was standing there as calm and cold as she had been that last time I'd seen her. It brought it all back to me, sir, and I set upon her. I do not mind admitting it. Nor do I have any regrets. I have vented my feelings. That is my way. Now I care no more about the wretch.'

'You attacked her, you mean?' Mr Blackadder paled. 'With your bare hands? In front of everyone?'

'I did.' She tossed her curls. 'I pulled her hair and scratched her face and tore her dress and with prodigious energy I kicked and punched her all over.'

Mr Blackadder groaned and rolled his eyes.

'You'll be the talk o' the toon!'

'Oh, yes, indeed. I am well aware of that, sir. I dare swear Williamsburg has never made such a wondrous buzz.'

'I don't know how you have the nerve to face them again.'

'Oh, I have plenty of nerve, sir.'

'Uh-huh, aye, that's verra true. You'll be going to church as usual then.'

'I am donning a wondrous new gown especially for the occasion. I will be carrying my best ivory handled fan and wearing my sapphire earrings and bracelet.'

Mr Blackadder sighed.

'God forgive you, Annabella. You're an awful lassie.'

When the time came Annabella swished into the church with fan flicking and gown and jewels sparkling like a blue sun. Right to the front to the minister's pew she went and bounced down onto the seat in a shimmering cloud of hooped silk. The people who had been outside the church waiting to see her arrive, all began crushing and pushing to squeeze inside the building until it was so jam-packed they could not close the doors. The beadle and the precentor tried their best, struggling and puffing and cursing and getting crimson-faced. Eventually they gave up and left them open.

There was a hush as the Reverend Blackadder climbed the high pulpit. A tremor of feverish expectation rippled from wall to wall as he gripped the edge of the pulpit and leaned forward to fix the congregation with a beady eye.

Suddenly he roared out:

'Gossip! Aye, gossip! That's what the sermon's aboot today. That insidious tool of the devil, the loose tongue. Aye, and do you know what it says in the Good Book? Do you know what the Lord God says aboot it?'

Mr Blackadder paused meaningfully, accusingly and the congregation visibly shrank in their seats.

'Behold, how great a matter a little fire kindleth! And the tongue is a fire, a world of iniquity. So is the tongue among our members, that it defileth the whole body, and setteth on fire the course of nature; and it is set on fire of hell.

'For every kind of beast, and bird, and serpent, and thing of the sea, is tamed, and hath been tamed of mankind.

'But the tongue can no man tame. It is an unruly evil, full of deadly poison.' Straining further forward he lowered his tone dramatically.

'Do you hear that? Do you hear? It's unruly. It's evil. It's deadly. It's poison. And I'll tell you another thing, it's damn hypocritical as well. Aye, just you think on it.

'It says: "Therewith bless we God, even the Father; and therewith curse we men, which are made after the similitude of God." Out of the same mouth proceedeth blessing and cursing. My brethren, these things ought not to be . . .'

Annabella could not help feeling impressed and even a little

502

proud of her husband. She had never thought much of his ranting and ravings before and she usually managed to think of other things to while away the time his sermons. On this occasion, however, she, like the rest of the congregation, was all attention as he expounded on the evils and dangers of gossip and went on, in a voice that echoed in every corner of the church, to ring out another quotation:

'Speak no evil one of another, brethren. He that speaketh evil of his brother, *or his sister*,' he added knowingly, 'and judgeth his brother, *or his sister*, speaketh evil of the law, and judgeth the law. But if thou judge the law, thou art not a doer of the law, but a judge.

'There is one lawgiver, who is also to save and to destroy: who art thou that judgest another?

'Go to now, ye that say, today or tomorrow we will go into such a city, and continue there a year and buy and sell, and yet again. Whereas ye knew not what shall be on the morrow. For what is your life?' He ended with tears in his eyes and much emotion. 'It is even a vapour, that appeareth for a little time, then vanishes away.'

There was a silence only broken by miserable sniffling from the congregation. Then Mr Blackadder noisily blew his nose and said quite cheerily.

'Uh-huh, aye. Weel, I suppose we'd better have a wee prayer noo.'

Afterwards when everyone spilled back outside, Harding was the first one to approach Annabella, bow, and enquire after her health. Lord Butler came next, followed by his wife, albeit in none too warm a fashion. Then Mr and Mistress Burleigh paid their respects.

Public gestures from these people, Annabella knew, were all she needed to assure her of being once more accepted into Williamsburg society. She returned home along the tree-lined street on her husband's arm, with a gay and thankful heart.

Her feelings of ease, however, were short-lived. Mr Blackadder had no sooner gone visiting his parishioners when Harding called at the house. Nancy came first to tell her that he was waiting in the hall. She was unusually agitated.

503

'Take my advice, mistress,' she urged. 'Let me send him packing without further ado. Don't risk having any words with him, I implore you.'

'Don't worry, Nancy,' Annabella said, 'I have no interest in conversing with such a man. Tell him I do not wish to see him.'

Nancy went to do as she was bid but in a matter of seconds Harding's giant, rock-like body had come bursting into the room, dwarfing it, making the bright chintz of chairs and curtains shrink and fade.

Annabella said,

'I see you have not changed, sir. You are still as brutish and ill-mannered as ever.'

'Will I go and try to find Mr Blackadder, mistress?' Nancy asked.

'No, that will not be necessary. I believe that Mr Harding will soon realize he is not welcome here and leave. I will call you if I need you, Nancy.'

Reluctantly Nancy left the room and immediately they were alone Harding said,

'I have never sopped thinking about you.'

Annabella raised an eyebrow.

'Indeed?'

'I am sorry if I distressed you at our last meeting but . . .'

Annabella let out a sarcastic tinkle of merriment.

'Distressed me? Distressed me, sir? Surely you should say raped me. You are usually a man of blunt speech, are you not?'

'No, I am not sorry that I possessed you. That I can never be. Knowing your beautiful and exciting body has been the delight of my life.'

She laughed again.

'Come, come, sir. It is a pretty speech. But how can you be such a prodigious liar. To say that our brief association meant anything to you is not borne out by facts. You rode away to Port Glasgow that very same night and sailed for Virginia without even a word to me. Nor did you make any attempt to contact me since.'

'It was no use. Everything was hopeless. I am married.'

'It is a pity you did not think of that sooner.'

504

'I had been drinking solidly all day.'

'Oh, shame, shame. You are claiming drink as an excuse?'

'No. I was desperately unhappy. I heard about you and saw you and realized that you were the only woman for me. One way or the other I had to have you.'

'Am I supposed to be flattered, sir? For I am not.'

'It was selfish and brutish of me to take you by force. I repeat I am truly sorry that I caused you distress.'

'I accept your apology. Now goodbye.'

'Have you no pity?'

'Pity? You want my pity, Mr Harding?'

'If you cannot give me your love.'

She laughed.

'I certainly cannot give you love, sir.'

'Give me your friendship then.'

She arched a brow.

'Why should I?'

Suddenly he shouted:

'Because I ask you to, damn you!'

She laughed again, this time with genuine amusement. She did not know what to make of him. Protestations of love seemed strange coming from such a rugged, broad-shouldered bull of a man. His eyes smouldered with what looked more like fury than affection.

'If you laugh at me again,' he said, 'you cruel, impertinent, wild and beautiful hussy, I shall take you over my knee and thrash you.'

'You have a prodigiously violent nature, Mr Harding. I am the minister's wife, don't forget.'

'I cannot bear the thought of you tied to such a man.'

'My husband, sir, is a wondrously good man. I refuse to countenance a word said against him.'

'Your loyalty does you credit. But I still say your life is wasted with him just as my life is wasted with the person I am married to.'

'Ah, yes, you think we would have been better married to each other.'

'I do.'

'What makes you think that, Mr Harding? I care nothing for you.'

'I would make you care.'

'By thrashing me, no doubt.'

'We could have a full and exciting life.'

'Fiddlesticks!'

'Come here!'

Before she could answer, he had grabbed her into his arms and his mouth was on hers. She struggled and eventually freed herself but not before she had experienced a disturbing emotion. It was like an electric storm, thrilling yet frightening and not in the least pleasant. She felt convinced that, like the electric storm, it was better to be without such an experience.

'I think it's time you left, Mr Harding,' she managed, escaping to the door and calling on Nancy before he could touch her again.

He hesitated, his eyes glistening like knife-points and making her flinch and look away. Then without another word he strode from the room.

'Damn the monstrous creature,' she thought afterwards. 'Damn him! Damn him!'

Chapter 25

'Is Regina seeing to your every need?' Harding asked his wife. As he stood at the end of her bed, the whip he was holding kept tapping impatiently against one of his riding boots.

Back home and propped in her own four-poster bed at Forest Hall, a patchwork quilt tucked high round her twisted face, Kitty Harding was still unable to speak. But she managed to nod her head.

'I have ordered Doctor Mason to attend you regularly until you are cured.'

She nodded again, her eyes wide with gratitude. He turned abruptly away and, as if unable to remain a moment longer, strode from the room. Regina waited for a few minutes, glancing round to see that everything was in order and going over to straighten the coverlet on the bed. But when Mistress Kitty's hand reached out seeking hers she drew away.

'I'll send Jenny up to keep you company. I'm going out for a walk but I'll come back and read to you.'

She left the silent, stuffy room, clean now but still cluttered and claustrophobic, and descended the stairs. Collecting her cloak on the way she left the house and went round to the kitchen building. The kitchen was also much cleaner than it had been in the past. Wooden tables and shelves had been scrubbed, pans and kettles gleamed, joints of meat hung in neat rows from the ceiling beams.

'Jenny,' Regina called sharply. 'Go upstairs and sit with Mistress Harding until I return.'

The wind was blowing hard and she had to put up her hood and hug her cloak around herself. But she was glad to escape from the house so that she could think in peace. In the bedroom that she shared with Mistress Kitty she was constantly aware of the older woman's eyes upon her. It was an even worse distraction than her prattling voice had been. She had not been able to gather enough nerve to take over another bedroom for herself but she had ordered a large closet in Mistress Kitty's room to be cleared and a bed put in there. So at least she was not forced to sleep with the woman any more.

As she walked along, head bent against the wind and cloak tugging and flapping, she mulled over her recent visit to Williamsburg. The attack in the ballroom crept about at the back of her mind like a spider but, shrinking away from it, she tried to concentrate on Williamsburg's spacious houses and gardens sweet-smelling with flowers and rustling with trees. The shops, too, had been places of attraction with their stocks of coloured silk petticoats, aprons and hoods, dress caps, stomachers and knots, French flowers for trimming, silk gloves and mitts, leather and brown thread, fine Irish muslins for ladies' gowns and many other articles.

One day she and Gav would visit Williamsburg from their own plantation and they would wander around these shops making purchases. Already she had begun compiling lists of things they would need for their house as well as for their persons. The personal articles would be mostly for Gav because she had many gowns and other possessions that Mistress Kitty had given her.

She had made inquiries about the price of land, too, but it was not so much that expense that worried her. Slaves would have to be bought to work their plantation. Tobacco growing needed a great many workers if it were going to be a paying proposition of the kind she envisaged. She wondered if it might be better to make do with Gav's fifty acres at first and have enough slaves to work it. Then, after Gav and she had sold a couple of crops, and could afford it, they could buy more land. Such thoughts and dreams obsessed most of her waking hours. She was more truly in the house and on the plantation that one day she and Gav would own than she was in the house and plantation owned by Robert Harding.

'What are you doing out here?' Harding's voice slashed unexpectedly through her thoughts. He reined his horse to a halt near her. She could smell it and feel the steam from it and feel the little earth tremors as it pawed the ground.

'Walking and taking the air. I left Jenny with Mistress Kitty.'

'It's pouring with rain,' he said.

She hadn't noticed the rain, so deep and safe had she been in her dreams. Now, looking up at Harding, she became aware of icy water whipping her cheeks and blurring her vision. She said:

'I suppose I'd better turn back.'

'You can ride with me.' Suddenly, leaning down, he hoisted her up to sit side saddle in front of him.

His arms enclosed her on either side as they held the reins and she felt the jerk of his body hard against hers as he kicked the horse's flank to urge it on. She sat as still as the movement of the horse permitted, her stillness coming from deep inside. It was as if she were spiritually paralysed or waiting like a cornered hypnotized animal. Eventually Harding said:

'You're a strange female. What age are you?'

'Sixteen, nearly seventeen.'

'My wife had hopes of marrying you off.'

'I've no wish to be married.'

'Why not?'

'I don't like men.'

He gave a short burst of laughter.

'That could soon be cured by the right man.'

'No.'

'You'll have to marry sometime.'

'No.'

'It may not always be possible for you to live here.'

'I'll live somewhere else.'

'Now that you're such a beauty, no wife would trust you in her house.'

'Your wife did.'

'My wife is a fool.'

Regina would have liked to say, 'She was a fool to have married you,' but she hadn't the nerve. Instead she lowered her head and muttered,

'I have my plans.'

'Yes, I don't doubt that. I've often wondered what schemes you were hatching during your long silences.'

Keeping her head lowered and her gaze averted she made no

509

reply. His nearness and the way they swayed together in tune with the animal beneath them tortured and confused her. His arms, like two iron bars imprisoning her against the heat of his body, made her feel safe, yet at the same time in terrifying danger. Never before had she been so glad to see Forest Hall.

He lifted her down and no sooner had her feet touched the ground that she hurried away into the house. Running up the stairs she did not look back to see if Harding had followed her indoors, but she heard another of his abrupt humourless laughs before she burst into the bedroom. After ordering the servant to leave, she shut the door. Leaning against it taking deep breaths, she felt too distressed to care about Mistress Kitty's large eyes riveted upon her.

She couldn't understand what was happening to her. She seemed to be breaking up into two people. One part of herself hated all men, was sickened and revolted by them; another part was causing her fear and confusion by unexpectedly different reactions to Harding. There were times when one part of herself actually admired him, admired his hardness, his abrupt dogmatic manner, even his craggy face and hefty muscular body.

Now more acute and frightening feelings were taking possession of her. Trembling against the door, she struggled to quell them. The tingling excitement of Harding's body rubbing against hers as they swayed together on the horse. The easy strength of his arms as he lifted her down. The closeness of him. The heat.

Stumbling away from the door she tore off her cloak and flung it aside. Then she dabbed at her face with the cool water in the jug on the washstand. Feeling calmer she sat down in front of the dressing-table and with slow determined strokes brushed her hair and arranged the long thick curl that hung over the front of one shoulder.

All the time, Mistress Kitty's eyes watched her through the looking-glass. As last she rose and went out of the room to call down to Jenny that she would have her meal with Mistress Kitty instead of in the dining-room. Then, picking up a book, she went over to sit by the bed, but not too close so that Mistress Kitty could not reach her to touch her. She read without interest or feeling in her voice. The spiders were multiplying in her mind but she was ignoring them. She was thinking of the bedroom she would have in her own house. She was thinking of how she would go downstairs and have her meals with Gav and of how they would be happy and safe together.

Her voice was still droning on when the door opened and Harding towered in the doorway.

'You'll come downstairs and have your meals in the dining-room as usual, mistress.'

'I want to stay with Mistress Kitty.'

'You'll do as you're told.' With that he swung the door shut.

She sat with head bowed staring at the book yet unable to continue reading it. Eventually she said,

'I hate that brute. I wish I had never come here.' It was as if they were two magnets and their hatred was drawing them together. The thought terrified her. 'I hate him. I wish I was back at the store with Gav. But it won't be long now until his indenture is finished. Then we'll have our own place and I won't need to care about anyone.'

Gav often thought of the time he would be free but he did not think of it in the same way as Regina. He was happy working in the store. Since Regina had gone he worked mostly downstairs and he enjoyed meeting and talking with the folk who came in to do business. He had plenty of help too in the shape of Tom, another, younger indentured servant and also Booster and Coolidge, Negro slaves purchased by Mr Speckles on behalf of Master Ramsay. There was Mamma Sophy too, who cooked for Mr Speckles and himself. Mr Speckles enjoyed a good dram but unfortunately did not have the constitution to contain it. Often the morning after having had a few too many, he was unable to lift himself from his bed. There he would moan and groan and feebly writhe about, hair straggling across a sickly green face, skeleton fingers plucking at the blankets.

Mamma Sophy would cluck her tongue and shake her black head and say,

'Liquor goin' be the death o' that pore man.'

And she would puff up and down the stairs with tempting

511

delicacies to try and put some strength back into the invalid. But many's the time she complained about how inconvenient the layout of the store building was.

'What they make this stair outside fo'? And why's the eatin' room not downstairs? And what's this kitchen hut stuck on the back o' the store fo'?'

But as she scolded herself most of the time, nobody paid much heed to her.

More and more Mr Speckles depended on Gav to run the place. Gav didn't mind in the least. He thrived on the extra responsibility. The longer he worked in the store, the more he realized that that was what he wanted to do. One day he would be a store manager, just as Master Ramsay had predicted he would. Regina was wrong about Ramsay. Back in Glasgow she had spoken of him with hate and prophesied that he meant to ruin Gav's life by sending him to Virginia and that he meant to sell him to the plantations as a slave.

Regina was wrong about a lot of things. She thought they were both looking forward to living on some lonely piece of land deep in the forest when his indenture was finished. But he viewed the prospect with nothing but horror. It wasn't the task of clearing the land and building a log cabin that worried him. He wasn't afraid of hard work. He'd grown into a strong, hefty lad and could fell a tree and saw wood with the best of them. No, it was the loneliness he had no stomach for. Regina was different from him. She liked to be on her own. She seemed to shrink away from people all the time. Whereas he was always reaching out to them. Often he thought of giving up the idea of having land and just continuing to work at the store after his indenture was finished. But it worried him to disappoint Regina.

'You can't think of her all the time,' Abigail Hershy, the blacksmith's daughter, told him. Abigail was the same age as him. She had fair hair tied in a knot on top of her head with a few wispy tendrils escaping around her face.

'Yes, I can,' he protested. 'She's my sister. We've only got each other.'

Abigail fixed him with one of her earnest unblinking stares. 'People get married, you know.'

Gav had never thought of that. He thought of it now. Then he shook his head.

'Not Regina. She hates men.'

'Lots of girls say that. They don't really mean it. She's bound to get married. All girls do.'

Gav didn't look convinced but he didn't say anything and eventually Abigail said,

'You'll get married too.'

He had never thought of that either. He stared at Abigail and was surprised to see her face become crimson. It was quite an interesting face really. Serious brown eyes contrasted with a cute little turned-up nose and dimpled chin. He liked Abigail and they had become firm friends. He liked her father too and sometimes helped him in the forge.

'I suppose I will,' he said at last, 'but any land I take and any house I build will be here in the settlement.'

'A man needs a wife,' said Abigail, who had an honest and practical nature, despite her weakness for blushing.

'That's true,' Gav agreed. 'Especially in a country like this.'

'And plenty of sons to help with the work. My poor father was unlucky. He only had me.'

'Now you're being silly,' Gav said. 'How could anyone be unlucky who had you?'

Her blush deepened but she looked pleased. He was pleased too. No, more than pleased. Happiness warmed up inside him and soothed through his veins. He felt ten feet tall.

He smiled at her and, after a minute of gazing earnestly, searchingly into his eyes, she smiled too.

Chapter 26

Annabella thought a lot about Harding's visit. She found him a bore and a coarse one at that. She liked pretty manners and speeches and elegant dress. She admired lightness and brightness and a quickness of mind as well as of tongue and Harding possessed none of these things. All he had to commend him was a certain animal attraction, a sexual magnetism, something very basic and physical.

Did she want a sexual relationship with Harding just for its own sake? She decided not. She had an active enough sex life with Mr Blackadder. No, it was not sex alone she craved from life. Sex was only acceptable to her as an integral part of a relationship that contained many other more important things. It was part of a delightful game. It was the reward, generously and warmly given, for elegant and chivalrous behaviour, for witty repartee and tender phrases, for sweeping bows and gentle kissing of hands, for beautifully worded declarations of devotion.

Try as she might, she could not fit Harding into this picture of an *affaire de coeur*. If he contacted her again, she would have to be ready with a good excuse to avoid him. As it happened, an excuse came in the form of Mr Blackadder who took a fever and needed nursing attention. So the next time Harding was in Williamsburg and called on her, she made sure that Mr Blackadder was in the drawing-room along with them. He hadn't fully recovered and was lantern-jawed and too weak to walk more than a few steps unaided. Nancy and she had half-carried him downstairs and propped him onto one of the chairs. Then, while Harding was in, she fussed around Mr Blackadder with wifely concern, tucking a rug over his legs and another around his shoulders.

'She's an awful lassie, this, Mr Harding.' Mr Blackadder tutted and shook his head. 'She just canny seem to keep her hands off me. Aye fussing around.'

514

'I envy you, sir.'

'Aye, weel,' Mr Blackadder reluctantly conceded. 'I suppose we should count oor blessings.' A light flared up in his gaunt, colourless face. 'We've a son, you know. A real sturdy wee lad.'

Harding looked surprised.

'No, I did not know.'

'Aye, he's called Mungo. Annabella, tell Nancy to bring him through so that Mr Harding can see for himself.'

'Some other time, Mr Blackadder. I've already instructed Nancy to take him out for a walk.'

She had no intention of ever allowing Harding and his son to come together. Her only worry was that someone might see the resemblance the child had to the man. Already Mungo was developing Harding's sturdy build, rather than Mr Blackadder's lean one. Already there was a look of Harding about the child's face, especially when Mungo was glowering in displeasure or when he was in a temper. But Harding normally only came to Williamsburg twice a year at the Public Times and seemed to have few friends. She was sure he would soon tire of pursuing her, especially when she made matters as difficult as possible by sticking like a leech to Mr Blackadder's side.

'Shall I fetch you a dish of gruel?' she asked her husband now, plucking his rug closer round him and whisking back a few stray locks of hair from his forehead.

'You ken fine I'm sick and tired of the stuff.'

'But it's wondrously strengthening with some whisky in it.'

'The whisky'll be strengthening enough without the gruel.'

Immediately she hastened across the room to pour a glass and then back to hold it eagerly to Mr Blackadder's lips. But in her eagerness she tipped it too fast and he spluttered and nearly choked.

'Damn it, Annabella,' he protested, managing to fight off her comforting hands and rise from his chair. 'Can you no' leave me in peace?' Turning, hunched up like an old man, rigid with irritation at the intensity of her devotion, he addressed Mr Harding,

'You'll have to excuse me, sir. I'm no' myself these days. I'm away upstairs for a wee nap.'

515

'I'll help you,' Annabella said.

'No, you will not.'

'But you'll never manage the stairs.'

'Then I'll go through to the settee in the dining-room.'

'But, Mr Blackadder . . .'

'You just haud your tongue and attend to our guest,' he snapped and shuffled determinedly from the room, banging the door shut behind him.

Annabella had no choice but to stay with Harding. She went over to gaze out of the window. Eventually he said,

'You don't belong here. You belong in my house, with me.'

'Losh and lovenendie. I cannot think why you say such things. I do assure you, you are monstrously mistaken. I belong here, with Mr Blackadder.'

'You cannot mean that.'

Impatiently she began flicking her fan. He was such an arrogant boor. Why should she not mean what she said?

'Mr Harding, can I offer you a glass of whisky? My husband would be most upset if I did not obey his instructions, and I am sure you do not wish me to cause him any distress.'

'I don't care a damn for your husband. He can sink into hell for all I care.'

Annabella flushed with annoyance.

'I can see that you do not care, sir. But I do.'

'My God, how beautiful you look,' Harding groaned. 'I could kill you for looking so beautiful and tormenting me like this.'

She rolled her eyes.

'Gracious heavens, I cannot compliment you on a pretty turn of speech, Mr Harding. It is obviously something you have no talent for.'

'I'm no bloody sugary-mouthed fop.'

'Never let it be said!'

'Now you are laughing at me, damn you.'

'Laughing? Laughing, sir? My lips have never betrayed a quiver.'

'I can see the laughter in your eyes.'

'Ah, I cannot help what you see in my eyes.'

'Nor can I help the love you see in mine.'

516

'Not love, sir, lust.'

Suddenly he roared at her.

'That is not true!'

She turned away, her fan agitating. There was such a terrible emotion in his voice she regretted her words and realized for the first time that in his own way Mr Harding did love her. The thought was more than a little frightening. Surely she had done nothing to encourage such an emotion.

'You should not have come here, Mr Harding,' she managed eventually, 'and I am sorry if I have caused you distress.'

'I wanted to come.'

'That may be so, but the fact remains you should not have come. No purpose can be served by such visits.'

'Annabella!'

His voice acquired a husky, animal-like urgency and she felt revolted by its coarseness. Then the memory of the time he had raped her ruffled her with panic. She fought to discipline her unruly fears.

Damn the man! She would not allow him to make her so afraid of him.

'Well, sir,' she said, with an impertinent arch of her brow. 'If you do not wish to accept a glass of whisky, you might as well go. That is all the hospitality I can offer you.'

He glowered at her and she stared back at him with all the impudence she could muster.

'Goodbye, Mr Harding. Now, if you'll excuse me, I have my husband to attend to.'

And with that she swept from the room. Safely through in the dining-room beside Mr Blackadder, she listened anxiously for sounds of the other man leaving before helping her husband upstairs to bed.

Mr Blackadder did not feel as well as he'd thought. But when the time came for the reading that evening, he told Annabella to summon Nancy and Betsy.

'What you need is a rest, not a reading,' Annabella said crossly.

But he perched in bed with the book on his lap, leafing

517

through its gossamer pages. Annabella flounced to the door shouting:

'Nancy, Betsy. It's time for the reading.'

They stood round the bed and Mr Blackadder began,

'Wives, submit yourselves unto your own husbands, as unto the Lord. For the husband is the head of the wife, even as Christ is the head of the church: and he is the saviour of the body . . .'

Annabella rolled her eyes but fortunately Mr Blackadder did not notice, so intent was he in tracing the words with a long bony finger. It was all Annabella could do to prevent her toe from tapping with impatience. She thought he was never going to stop droning on. Mr Blackadder could be such a bore at times. It was really quite painful. The room was stuffy because the windows had to be kept shut to prevent the dust from outside making him cough and the air stank of the linseed oil with which she had rubbed his chest. She yawned with the heat and was greatly relieved when at last she could escape from the room.

Yet there was nothing very diverting downstairs. With a sigh she left the house to wander round the garden in order to pass a little time. Other households she knew of had bookshelves with novels to make pleasant reading, but Mr Blackadder would allow none of those in his establishment. Nor did he allow a gaming room. In every other house she knew there was a billiard table and tables for playing cards. She kept telling him that billiards and cards were perfectly proper games for ladies and gentlemen but Mr Blackadder's caustic reply was:

'They're no' mentioned in the Bible.'

Round and round the garden she went, her high-heeled shoes and the edges of her gown becoming more and more dusty.

During Williamsburg's quiet or sleeping times, as they were called, the town was like a cemetery with only the occasional afternoon visiting or small dinner party to enliven the empty hours. Carter Cunningham had been at the last dinner party she had attended at the house of Lord and Lady Butler. He had just returned from a visit to far-off London and she had been enchanted when he had presented her with a 'fashion-baby' that he had bought there. It was a doll dressed in the latest style in every detail and she could hardly wait to have copies made of its

518

clothes. It was so clever of Mr Cunningham to have thought of such a gift.

A tall man with laughing eyes, he was popular with the gentlemen as well as the ladies. He was not only elegant and charming but an enthusiastic gambler and he enjoyed gaming with the men. Even she had been shocked when she had heard of the amount of money he could lose. But apparently he was so wealthy, the money didn't matter. His plantation was self-sufficient, a complete town in miniature. He had an army of servants and slaves working every sort of trade and supplying his every need, and he had been heard to say:

'I do not require money. I have not a bill to pay. A coin can rest undisturbed in my pocket for many moons. I am completely independent.'

He had been to Glasgow too and brought letters and news from her father and friends.

'There is now a stagecoach running from Glasgow to Edinburgh twice a week,' he told her.

She was thrilled and incredulous.

'A stagecoach from Glasgow to Edinburgh, Mr Cunningham? Why, sir, you'll be telling me there's transport from Glasgow to London next!'

Phemy had produced a daughter, and a son had been born to Griselle. Annabella felt a pang of homesickness at the thought of Phemy and Griselle. She missed their company. Yet she had met plenty of amusing people in Williamsburg and she had no real regrets about coming to Virginia. It was a new and exciting country. It suddenly occurred to her that it didn't really matter where she was—in Glasgow or Virginia. She would still feel depressed at times. Living with Mr Blackadder this could not be altogether avoided. She would just have to make the best of it and be of good cheer where and when she could.

She was just gathering up her skirts to step indoors again when a familiar voice cried:

'Mistress Blackadder!'

She swung round to see Mr Cunningham standing at the garden gate.

'I was strolling along Francis Street on my way to meet a

519

friend,' he said. 'And I was admiring the flowers in the gardens when I caught sight of the most beautiful flower of all.'

She flicked out her fan and went over to him twinkling with delight.

'Mr Cunningham, can I tempt you to step inside for a glass of whisky?'

'You are always a temptation, mistress.' He picked up her hand and tenderly kissed it. 'But, alas, for the moment I must resist. I am expected elsewhere, and I am unforgivably late already.'

She pouted prettily.

'And tomorrow you return to your plantation.'

'I shall be back for the Public Time. I look forward to seeing much of you then.' His eyes narrowed roguishly, then suddenly he made a deep, sweeping bow. 'Mistress Blackadder.'

Arms stretched wide, she sunk into a low curtsy.

'Mr Cunningham.'

With joy in her heart and wings on her feet, she sped into the house. In the living-room Nancy was putting some linen away in one of the drawers of the highboy. She turned when Annabella burst into the room.

'I've put Mungo to bed but he refused to sleep until you go and say goodnight to him.' Then suddenly noticing Annabella's flushed face and dancing eyes she asked: 'What's happened? Where have you been?'

Annabella laughed.

'It's none of your damned business where I've been. But as a matter of fact I've been taking a stroll round the garden.'

Nancy arched a brow.

'It seems to have done you a power of good.'

'Indeed yes, I feel in uncommonly good spirits.' She pirouetted around. 'Now I'll run and kiss Mungo goodnight before going to chat with Mr Blackadder. Bring me a cup of chocolate to the bedroom.'

In Mungo's back bedroom with its carved and painted furniture in red and white oak and sycamore, the child added to her pleasure by hanging round her neck, gazing at her with obvious love and pride and saying:

'You're such a pretty mummy.'

She blew a shower of kisses from the doorway before leaving him and pattering along to the main bedroom. The room was shadowy and had an immediate depressing effect on her. The stuffiness and the smell of linseed oil was so dense, it could almost be touched. Mr Blackadder, a slight figure in the big four poster bed, had dozed off to sleep with the Bible still open on his lap. His head hung down and slightly to one side. His mouth sagged and he was gently snoring. She removed the Bible and put it over on the table. Then she tucked the clothes around him and smoothed back a lock of hair that had slid over his face. It was grey at the temples, she noticed. Mr Blackadder looked quite elderly. Of course he was old enough to be her father.

She sighed and went over to sit at the window. Behind her the shadows gathered and the grandfather clock monotonously tick-tocked. With her fair ringlet curls, her rose petal skin and neat little figure in low-necked, wide-skirted gown, she looked like the fashion baby Mr Cunningham had given her. Balancing her elbows on the window ledge and her chin on the back of her clasped hands, she fluttered her mind over the latest fashions and the gowns she would like to make or have made and the gay parties she would like to have and to attend.

Her mouth curved into a smile as she imagined herself stepping the minuet, jigging merrily around in country dances, and having sparkling jewel-bright conversations. At the same time she was surprised by tears springing to her eyes. Immediately she flicked them away and jumped to her feet, protesting out loud.

'Pox on that lazy strumpet, Nancy. Is she never bringing my chocolate?'

A lump tightened in her throat as she went downstairs and out to the small kitchen building at the back of the house. Low voices could be heard coming from inside and when she entered, Nancy and a man jerked apart.

'Oh, Lord,' Nancy groaned. 'Your chocolate. I forgot.'

'I am not surprised,' Annabella said, eyeing the man who by his plain dress was not a gentleman but uncommonly handsome all the same. The man gave a small bow.

'It was my fault, mistress.'

'Of that I have no doubt,' said Annabella. 'Who are you?'

'My name is Morgan West.'

Nancy said, 'He's a farmer. I'll bring your chocolate through now.'

'Make sure you do,' Annabella said. 'I wish to talk to you.'

She felt uncommonly disturbed. Nancy and she had grown up together and, although their personalities often clashed, there had always been some sort of bond between them stronger than the usual mistress-servant relationship. Often they giggled and gossiped together like old friends. She was hurt that Nancy had never mentioned this Morgan West. Yet she knew that Nancy could be very deep and secretive. It was time the candles were lit but she felt too fluttered to search for the tinder-box. Pacing about in agitation her hoops bounced against the chairs and made the curtains fly to one side as she swept past.

'You sly wretch!' she burst out as soon as the servant entered.

Calmly Nancy laid down the cup of chocolate and lit the candles on the mantelpiece. They quivered feebly through the gloom.

'I was going to tell you when things were settled.'

'Were you indeed?'

'Things aren't settled yet.'

'Pox on you. I am mightily distressed.'

'I wouldn't leave until you got somebody else.'

'Huh! I wouldn't allow you to.' She swished across and picked up the chocolate.

Nancy left, closing the door quietly behind her. Annabella remained, blinking at the candle-flame.

Chapter 27

'Please,' Regina said in a low voice. It seemed as if Harding was taking a fiendish delight in tormenting her. More than once during these past months he had gone to the store and refused her permission to go too. He no longer even allowed her to accompany him on his visits to Williamsburg. Day in and day out she was imprisoned with Mistress Kitty. Time was passing and she had to speak to Gav and discuss their plans. 'I must see my brother.'

'Your duty is to stay here and look after my wife.'

'The Negroes dote on your wife. The only danger to Mistress Kitty while I'm away would be from them fussing over her too much.'

She was tempted just to leave for good but restrained herself from any such rash action. In the first place she had nowhere to go. For all she knew there could be another servant sharing Gav's room by now and anyway, she had no guarantee that Mr Speckles or anyone else would give her shelter. Not that she wanted to be in the position of having to ask Mr Speckles or anyone for help. She did not trust anyone.

'And it's only for such a short time.'

'Oh, very well,' he agreed at last.

Her relief was intense and she could hardly wait to set off on the journey. They took the carriage to collect the supplies but Old Abe drove it and she and Harding rode their own horses.

The settlement was the same as she remembered it. Its log cabins and church and tobacco sheds squatted between stumps. The large clearing in front of the gaol was just as lumpy and dusty, and from the gaol came sounds of moaning and wailing. The windowless store hadn't changed either, or the wharf jostling with tall delicate masted ships. One of the ships was a man o' war. The other was *The Glasgow Lass*.

Inside the store a Negro slave was polishing the counter.

Another was sweeping the floor. A lanky white lad with hair tied tightly back was serving a customer.

'Is Gav upstairs?' she asked him.

'Don't know, mistress.'

Although the place looked much the same, there was a strange, unwelcoming atmosphere about it. She didn't feel at home. She was an outsider. But then she had never felt at home anywhere since her mother disappeared and she no longer belonged at Tannery Wynd in Glasgow.

She went upstairs to the counting house where she found Mr Speckles bent over a ledger, his hair like tangled straggles of greasy wool. But there was still no sign of Gav.

'Where's my brother?' she asked.

Mr Speckles' eyes seemed more furtive and evasive than ever.

'Eh, I think he'll be eating his food along by the creek.'

She hurried downstairs again without another word. Gav and she often used to go and sit by the creek and somehow it pained her to think of him being there without her. Panic twitched behind a stiff face. Had her brother been unhappy and lonely? How could she have stayed away for so long? She would never forgive Harding for not allowing her to come sooner.

At last she saw him come strolling through the trees. How tall he looked. Quite a young man. He still had his stock of red hair and freckles but his plumpness had hardened into muscle.

'Regina!' he yelled when he caught sight of her. And before she could say anything, he had rushed at her and was hugging her off her feet and making her laugh and choke for breath.

'Gav, you fool, let go of me.' Then suddenly she saw the girl. 'Who's that?'

Grinning happily, he turned round.

'Abigail, this is my sister, Regina. Regina, this is Abigail. It's so good to see you, Regina. Don't you look grand? Are you married yet, eh? Has some wealthy planter snapped you up? You certainly look prosperous. Doesn't she look splendid, Abigail?'

'I like your gown,' Abigail said. 'I don't suppose Gav will ever be able to afford to buy me gowns like that. But I won't mind. As long as I have him.'

524

Gav was gazing at Abigail with great pride and joy. Regina's mind fuddled. Who was this girl with the plain face and the strong will behind the candid brown eyes?

'Gav, I must speak to you. I'm not here for long.'

'Of course. Go ahead. I've lots to tell you too. Oh, it's so good to see you again, Regina.'

He linked arms as they walked towards the store. Abigail on one side of him and Regina on the other.

'Alone,' Regina said.

'Oh, it's all right to talk in front of Abigail. We've no secrets from each other.'

Abigail released his arm.

'That's right. Gav and I are very close. But I've work to do. So I'll leave him alone with you for a little while.' She smiled. 'But only for a little while.'

Gav laughed and pretended to aim a punch at Abigail's chin.

'I can't get rid of her at all. She sticks to me like a leech. It's terrible.'

'Tell your sister about our plans, Gav.'

'Which ones? We've got so many.'

'Tell her, Gav.' Then to Regina: 'Goodbye, Regina.'

After she'd gone, they went up the stairs to Gav's room.

'I share this with Tom now. Did you see him down in the store?'

Regina's eyes tried to convey the anguish she felt.

'He's a nice lad,' Gav went on. 'We get on well together. Many a good laugh we have over a game of cards. He tries to cheat but I'm too clever for him. Of course Tom just does it for fun. He's really very honest . . .'

'To hell with bloody Tom,' she suddenly burst out.

Gav looked taken aback.

'Why did you say that? He's never done you any harm.'

'What about our plans? Your indenture will soon be finished.'

Gav hesitated.

'You still feel the same then?'

'Of course I still feel the same. Why should I feel any different?'

'Oh, hell, Regina, you're a beautiful woman. You're bound

to get married sometime. It's a miracle you're not married already. Women are so scarce here, even if you were as ugly as sin the chances are you'd be married. Surely you haven't been passing up chances because of our silly childish talk.'

'Silly childish talk?'

'If you buried yourself away in some isolated little patch of land, you'd never get married. You're far better where you are, meeting people at balls and things.'

'I don't want to get married.'

'Regina, you've got to be practical. Who's going to support you for the rest of your life? Who's going to feed you and clothe you—not just this year or next year but when you're old?'

She stared at him speechlessly.

'I know you have a few gold coins and pieces of jewellery hidden away, but it's not enough. It's not enough, Regina. It won't look after you for the rest of your life. It won't even give you the kind of security you imagine you need.'

'I thought . . . I always thought . . .'

Gav sighed and put an arm around her shoulders.

'I know what you thought. And of course I'd never see you homeless or starving. All I'm saying is there's no need for that. It's natural and proper that you should get married and have a husband to provide for you. Just as it's natural and proper that I should get married and provide for my wife.'

'Abigail?'

'Yes, I'm going to continue working in the store. I'll clear a bit of the forest over there and build a cabin and plant enough corn and vegetables and herbs to feed us. We'll have a good life and be happy. I know we will. Abigail's father is going to help by making us tools and cooking utensils. He's a wonderful man, Regina. What a size he is and as strong as an ox. I often help him at his forge. It's a lot harder work than in the store, I can tell you.'

Face lowered, Regina began fumbling in her purse. Eventually she brought out a gold coin.

'Take this, I hope it will be of use to you.'

'Regina!' He hugged her with gratitude, but she pushed him away.

'I must go now.'

'So soon? Surely not. You can have my bed and I'll sleep on the floor.'

'No, I'm going to the tavern. It's time you were back at work.'

'Then, I'll see you tomorrow before you return.'

'No.'

'But Regina . . .'

She walked away leaving him helplessly shaking his head. Outside she mounted her horse and rode it towards the path through the trees that led past the slave quarters to the tavern. She seemed to be dangling over a precipice, not knowing how to hang on, not even knowing what to hang on to.

The tavern was a two-storeyed wooden building set in a clearing at the crossing of two tobacco roads just beyond the cluster of huts where the Negro slaves lived. It looked a dull and desolate place with black tree stumps strewn about it and tall trees crowding menacingly close. But smoke was curling up from one of the chimneys and when she drew nearer, she heard laughter and shouting.

Inside sailors were having a carousal. Some were crouched over tables. Others were sitting or lying on the floor. One had a parrot perched on his arm. A skinny dog rooted about.

Shouts and thumping of fists on wood started up when they saw her, and as she crossed the crowded room to talk to the Widow Shoozie, one seaman lurched across her path. She pushed him aside and he fell against a chair, upturning it with a clatter as he landed on the floor.

'I am with Mr Harding,' she told the widow, 'and I wish a room at once.'

The old woman hesitated but only for a moment. Nervously she curtsied,

'Yes, mistress. Follow me, mistress.'

Once alone in the room, Regina shut and locked the door. She would make Harding pay for her accommodation. The other gold coin in her purse would not be so carelessly given away. She regretted giving one to Gav. Why should she give him anything? He was no better than any other man. He had betrayed her. He had ruined her life. Hatred sucked the blood from her veins, leaving her dizzy. She stumbled across to the bed and collapsed on top of it. She clenched her fists. She buried her face in the pillow. She couldn't understand what had happened. How could Gav desert her for this girl he'd only known a comparatively short time? This stranger.

She and Gav had been like one person all their lives. How could he not want her any more?

Memories of their childhood together came hurtling towards her like daggers in her back. Dusk sank into darkness but she did not stir to light a candle. Drunken noise swelled and receded downstairs, slurred voices and sleepy song. Occasionally the parrot squawked.

Then silence blanketed down only broken by the clicking of crickets and the distant howling of wolves. Slowly darkness faded into light. The forest began chirping and twittering. Still she lay, rigid as in death, until eventually there was a pounding on her door and Harding called:

'Are you in there?'

With difficulty she moved.

'Yes.'

'We're ready to go.'

When she opened the door he stared at her curiously.

'Are you ill?'

'No.'

'What's wrong then?'

'Nothing's wrong.'

He hesitated, then shrugged. She followed him downstairs and they mounted their horses and rode away and never once spoke again during the long journey back to Forest Hall.

'Regina.'

It was the first word Mistress Kitty uttered. It rolled around like a too large ball writhing and swelling her mouth. Again she fought to push it out,

'Regina.'

'Good,' said Regina. 'You're improving.'

Another desperate struggle produced,

'Thank you.'

'There's no need to thank me. I've only done what I've been

paid to do.'

Kitty Harding shook her head.

They were sitting outside, Kitty like a wooden timber doll, Regina leisurely wafting a fan from side to side.

'I think you should exercise your bad arm and leg more,' Regina said. 'It would surely be more strengthening than the bleeding the doctor does. At the rate he's going, you'll soon have no blood left.'

Kitty tried to smile. She was touched by Regina's concern for her. No invalid could have a more capable and conscientious nurse. Indeed, the care Regina took of her went far beyond the call of any sense of duty. If the girl had been her own daughter, she could not have been more kind and attentive. She loved Regina almost as much as she loved Robert and, strangely enough, she had come to feel as sorry for the girl as she did for the man.

Deprived of speech, her other senses seemed to have sharpened and she knew that Regina was being more and more troubled by an attraction for Robert. There had been times when she had witnessed Regina's distress at its most acute. She had seen the burning cheeks, the anguished eyes, the pulse beating fast in the creamy throat. There had been other occasions in Robert's presence when she had noticed Regina's cold mask slip. Robert had not been aware of the passion in the green eyes on those occasions when they had burned hungrily over him. He had been smoking a pipe, or reading a book, or writing a letter, or perhaps walking from the room. The look only lasted a few seconds and always came furtively when Robert's attention was safely turned away.

Kitty sighed to herself as she looked across at Regina who was absently fanning herself and gazing unseeingly towards the forest. Regina kept insisting she hated Robert but, poor, bewildered child, it was obvious that she not only admired but passionately desired the man. Kitty felt a pang of guilt. She had been the cause of Regina coming to Forest Hall and therefore being put at risk. Robert was much older than the girl and she had not detected the slightest sign of any emotional attachment on his side. Of course, men never fell victims of their emotions in the same way as women. They had physical needs which included the need of a woman's body. But they could fulfil that hunger in the same way as they devoured a meal. Afterwards they were able to forget the woman as easily as they forgot the meal, until the next time they felt hungry. That's how Harding was.

Guiltily she gazed at Regina again. Knowing that she was not fit enough to supply Robert's physical needs, had her real reason for bringing Regina to Forest Hall been simply to supply that need? But she had never wanted the poor child to be hurt. No, not even deep in her subconscious mind had she wanted that. Yet she ought to have known that Regina would grow to love Robert. Wasn't he the kindest, handsomest, most wonderful of men?

Regina was thinking of the state of Mistress Kitty's health. It was now a constant source of worry to her. Not because she particularly cared for the woman, but the fact had to be faced that if Mistress Kitty died, Harding could, and no doubt would, dispense with her services. Then what would she do? Where would she go?

Her eyes slid round to the white pillared house. If only she could have a place like this for her very own. It was in surroundings like these that she now felt she belonged. Yet what Gav had said was true. For some time she had suspected that her cache of gold coins alone would not be enough to fulfil her dreams. Her money plus Gav's land and Gav's help in building a house and planting and selling a tobacco crop could have created a potentially prosperous situation. But without Gav it was useless. She could buy a few acres but who would help her to work it? Or she could buy a house in Williamsburg but how could she clothe herself? How would she eat? As Gav had reminded her, it wasn't just the present time she had to think about. It was the rest of her life.

A cool breeze rustled her gown and switched her attention back to Mistress Kitty.

'Are you cold?'

Mistress Kitty nodded at the same time as trying and failing to say:

'A little.'

Regina jumped up, calling to one of the slaves.

'Joseph! Help Mistress Kitty back to her bedroom.'

At first she tried to encourage the older woman to walk a few steps on her own. But Mistress Kitty was far too feeble. Her legs, like wisps of cotton thread, did not have enough strength to support her unaided.

Once Mistress Kitty was settled back in bed again, Regina collected her cloak and left the house. It was her habit to get away on her own as often as possible. She cut round the side of the house, passed the outbuildings and the quarters, and walked along the path through the woods to the fields. Some of the fencing skirting the fields looked like rows of witches in tortured positions. It had been made with black tree stumps dragged from the ground by oxen and turned upside down so that their broken-off fang-like roots seemed to be twisting round each other in a grotesque dance.

There was other, newer fencing too, and the fences snaked round and bridled the wilderness for hundreds of acres.

She wanted a place like this. She wanted it. Why should that selfish, arrogant brute have all this while she had nothing. There was something basic about owning land that gave the kind of security she needed. Such was the desperation of her need that, as she hurried along, hugging tightly at her cloak, she began to imagine that it could be hers, almost that it was hers already.

Somewhere, somehow, there was a way.

Then it occurred to her that perhaps in showing her antagonism to Harding so plainly and so often she had been endangering her position more than Mistress Kitty's death even could. After all, even if Mistress Kitty did not die, he could still replace her with someone else if he had a mind to. It surely followed too that it Mistress Kitty died, he could still employ her to run his house if he had a mind to.

For the first time she realized that it was on herself and how she could influence Harding, not his wife, that her future depended.

When she returned to the house, she read to Mistress Kitty for a while before going down to tell Jenny to take up her tray. Then she went in to have her meal in the dining-room with Harding.

There were two silver candelabra on the table and the warm light on the yellow pine walls gave the room a golden glow. Harding's black hair, tanned skin and white shirt made a startling contrast. She always experienced something of a shock when she saw him.

She was stiff-backed in her blue brocade gown and quilted satin petticoat. Her hair glimmered like ruby wine, the long curl dangling over the front of her shoulder accentuating the creaminess of her skin.

The slaves served the meal, the silence only broken by the tinkle of cutlery against china. Gradually, a sense of well-being and satisfaction soothed over her as she ate. Every now and again, her gaze wandered over the curves of the mahogany sideboard and its silver serving dishes, the lustrous mahogany of the chairs and table; the rich reds and blues of the carpet. No one more keenly appreciated the good things of life than she did. She tried never to think of the past, but sometimes memories of her life in Glasgow sucked her into a tunnel of fear. It seemed incredible that she had once begged in the streets in her bare feet, had slept with criminals in filthy stairways, had eaten revolting scraps of food from the stinking pockets of Quin.

She shuddered and returned to her thoughts of the afternoon. She must not endanger her position by showing antagonism. Eventually she managed to fix a cool green stare on the man opposite. His attention was concentrated on his food and he seemed completely unaware of her existence. Gradually, however, he sensed her eyes upon him and looked up.

Her mouth twisted into a smile. He stared at her.

'Mistress, I believe that is the first time I have ever seen you smile. It's a poor effort. But the effort was made. I wonder why?'

Her fork toyed with the food before her.

'I am sorry if I've appeared over-solemn, Mr Harding.'

'Are you indeed?'

'I will try to be more pleasing in future.'

'Pleasing?' He laughed incredulously. 'You?'

She didn't dare raise her eyes.

'What do you mean?' he added.

'Like yourself, sir, I always mean what I say.'

'You are actually likening yourself to me?'

She shrugged.

'Maybe we are not so different as you think.'

'Mistress Chisholm,' he said. 'I have never been so deeply suspicious of you as I am today.'

She smiled again.

'Will you excuse me, Mr Harding?'

With a rustle of skirts she rose and left the room. In the hallway she hesitated. The thought of going upstairs to be closeted with Mistress Kitty for the rest of the evening held little attraction. Most evenings she sat reading in a corner of the drawing-room. Sometimes when Harding was at home, he sat by the fire reading. Sometimes he wrote, his quill scraping and scoring at the silence between them. Perhaps tonight he would retire early and leave her to enjoy her own company. She decided to take the risk and went into the drawing-room.

A log fire crackled in the fireplace, shooting out arrows of light. The pendant flame of the candelabra shivered in the draught and as she lifted it and took it over to the bookshelves, its amber flame trailed unwillingly behind her. She selected a book and sat down. No sooner had she done so than Harding entered. She did not glance up until he came over to her. Without a word he lifted the candelabra, took it over and with it lit the other candles on the small table beside his chair before returning it. Then he poured himself a whisky and leaning back in his chair, sampled his drink.

'You want to go to Williamsburg, is that it?' he said eventually.

'No.'

'You want something, mistress.'

'At the moment, Mr Harding, all I want is peace to read.'

His eyes narrowed.

'Yes, something's crystallizing in that icicle of a brain. Take care, Mistress Chisholm. Take great care.'

533

Chapter 28

'I told you you were doing too much.' Annabella helped Mr Blackadder off with his coat. 'You've more than enough to cope with when you visit the merchants and tradespeople in town without riding for miles across country to outlying farmers and planters.'

'Uh-huh. Aye. They've got to be catechized as well.'

'Fiddlesticks,' she said, deftly undoing his waistcoat. 'Your health comes first. I will not allow you to continue over-straining yourself like this, sir.'

She attacked his breeches, ignoring his indignant struggles to hold on to them.

'You're an awful lassie, Annabella.'

'You have a fever again. Your face is monstrously inflamed.'

'Damn you, I just feel a wee bit shivery and tired.'

Nancy said:

'I don't think he rightly recovered from the last time.'

'Nor do I,' Annabella agreed. 'I told him he returned to his duties too soon. Quickly, quickly, to bed with you. Nancy has put a warming pan in.'

'Will you stop harassing me, woman,' Mr Blackadder protested but he was shivering so violently, he was glad of his wife and Nancy's help to hoist him between the sheets.

Annabella smoothed and tucked the coverlets high around him, then she dabbed at his face with her handkerchief.

'We have some of the potion left from the last time, have we not, Nancy?'

'Yes.'

'Bring it then.'

Mr Blackadder had begun to mutter and moan and by the time Nancy had returned with the potion, his face was scarlet and shiny with rivulets of sweat. They propped him up and with much difficulty Annabella forced some of the liquid between his

534

lips. But his condition continued to grow worse instead of better until his eyes became glazed and he tossed restlessly about. Occasionally he called Annabella's name.

'I am here. I am here,' she kept assuring him. Then to Nancy: 'Gracious heavens, what can we do?'

'Will I fetch the doctor?'

'He will only bleed him but perhaps on this occasion it might help. I do not know. I am prodigiously fluttered. Yes, go on, fetch him, Nancy.'

After the maid left, Annabella dipped her handkerchief in a bowl of water and gently bathed Mr Blackadder's face. Nancy was a long time in returning. The room had darkened and Annabella was stiff with sitting crouched over the bed. Mr Blackadder was still murmuring and moaning and shouting her name. Nancy lit a candle and held it over the minister while the doctor examined him. Then, to Annabella's disgust, he fastened a cluster of leeches to either side of Mr Blackadder's face. She loathed the writhing black worms. Eventually she cried out:

'These monstrous slugs are distressing him. I will not have him tormented like this. Remove them at once.'

'I was just about to, Mistress Blackadder.' From under his long wig the doctor eyed her severely. 'He has been bled enough. Now I will give him a febrifuge pill.'

'And what is that, pray?'

He took a pinch of snuff before answering.

'It is made with powdered Peruvian bark, oil of cinnamon and powdered red coral and it is for reducing his fever. I will leave you seven more. Give him one each night and morning in a little barley water.'

'Very well.'

Nancy took the candle to light the doctor's path to the door where his carriage waited, lanterns swinging in the cool night breeze.

When she returned upstairs to the bedroom she said to Annabella:

'You're tired. Do you want me to sit with him while you have a sleep through in Mungo's room?'

'No, light another candle and leave it by the bed. I'll stay and watch him. He might be agitated if he called my name and I did not answer.'

'Maybe the pills will help.'

'Gracious heavens, I hope so. He is on fire with fever and suffering monstrous pain by the sounds of him.'

Nancy moved in a pool of yellow towards the door.

'Call me if you need me.'

The door closed leaving blackness except for the finger of light near Mr Blackadder's pillow. His breathing had become fast. It sawed through the silence like a tireless carpenter. And every now and again he gave a roar.

'Annabella!'

And her voice came close.

'I am here. I am here.'

Until, unexpectedly, his breathing stopped.

Rising from her crouched position, she lifted the candle and held it over his face.

'Och, Erchie!' she said brokenly, reproachfully. Then she closed her eyes and tipped up her head, nostrils quivering. She stood like that for a long time before going to tell Nancy.

In the days that followed she kept herself busy and went about the preparations for, and then the funeral itself, with brisk efficiency. It was not until it was all over and the many guests and mourners had gone that she retired to her room and shed helpless tears.

Nancy pushed open the door saying,

'You've been overtiring yourself.'

'Losh sakes, don't just stand there gawping at me then. Fetch me a reviving cup of tea. Do something!'

Nancy went away muttering and rolling her eyes and Annabella shouted after her,

'And I'll have none of your impudence, you sly, black-haired bitch. You and your bloody farmer. Never a word did you say to me of where you met him or when.'

She snatched up her fan and rapidly jerked it to and fro. She would have to write to her father and tell of her predicament. How could she continue to keep a house and a growing son with no money coming in? She felt vastly alarmed. Yet as time passed, her usual courage and bouncy spirits came to her rescue. If necessary, she would live on credit until money came from her father. She would manage somehow. Every day she busied herself with household duties or with attending to Mungo. Sometimes, while arranging flowers in a vase near the window, she would peer out, expecting to see Mr Blackadder's long, lean figure come plodding along Francis Street. Then she would remember that she would never be seeing him again and a tightness would come to her throat.

But she determinedly swallowed it down. Sometimes she sang a little song to cheer herself as she whisked busily about the house. She tugged the chintz covers from the settee and chairs and rubbed and scrubbed at them herself in a tub in the kitchen. The curtains were washed too and all the woodwork and brasses energetically polished. She also made frequent batches of biscuits and cakes, much to Mungo's delight. No one was allowed to be either idle or gloomy. Several times she chastised Betsy for weeping and howling, 'Poor Mr Blackadder! Poor Mr Blackadder!'

'Losh and lovenendie, will you stop your fruitless lamentations. He's gone and that's an end to it.'

Then one day, not long after the Public Time had started, Robert Harding called.

'Annabella!' He strode across the room towards her and attempted to take her into his arm but she indignantly pushed him away.

'How dare you, sir. You would try to take advantage of my unfortunate position.'

'I have just heard. Why didn't you answer my letters? Why didn't you write and tell me?'

'Mr Harding, it is quite simple. I had no desire to answer your letters. As for telling you of my husband's death—I did not see any reason for doing so.'

'I can look after you now.'

'No, sir, you cannot.'

'You have no longer any excuse.'

'Excuse? You are mad, sir. You think my husband was no more than an excuse to keep your advances temporarily at bay?

537

I see I will have to speak plainly to you, sir. To say the least, you are obviously a monstrously stubborn and arrogant man.'

'Don't think too harshly of me. I have suffered greatly. My marriage was a tragic mistake and the only relief from misery I have enjoyed for many years started when I first saw your face. I could not tear my eyes from you. You were testing a horse on Trongate Street, remember? But I first saw you approaching through the crowds on Stockwell. As soon as I caught sight of you and the proud, wild way you carried yourself, I knew you must be the daring beauty I had heard so much about.'

'Mr Harding, there is no point in talking like this.'

'Since then you have haunted my every hour. I dream of holding you, possessing you again as I did that night.'

'That is enough, Mr Harding.'

'We are meant to be together.'

She stamped her foot in exasperation.

'No, we are not. We are not, sir. I think of you only as a monstrously crude and infuriating creature and you are the last person on earth with whom I would choose to share my life.'

'In time you will think differently.'

She rolled her eyes.

'Mr Harding, how blunt do I need to get? I had a higher regard for my husband than I could ever have for you.'

'I do not believe you.'

She began flicking her fan.

'There is another man, Mr Harding, a charming gentleman of my acquaintance that I hope to see during the Public Time. He is a trifle catched by me and I by him . . .'

He moved forward and she thought that he was going to fell her with one blow. Then he hesitated, turned abruptly and left the room. She ran across to the window and watched him stride from the house, mount his horse and gallop away.

She sighed.

'Poor Mr Harding.'

Still, it had to be done. Such a man could make a lady's life a misery, she felt sure, and she had no intention of allowing herself to be disturbed by someone so lacking in sensibility. No doubt he would soon forget her by drowning his sorrows in a carousal with the noisy mob of planters now filling the 'Raleigh Tavern'. Probably he would indulge in a harlot or two. That would be more in keeping with his coarse and unruly passions. Yet she had to admit that when Mungo came into the room, she felt a pang of conscience, even perhaps of regret and she experienced the same wrench of the heart that she remembered feeling on the ship coming to Virginia when she gazed on the shores of her native land for the last time.

'Can we go for a walk, Mummy?' Mungo asked.

Kneeling down in front of him, she took his hands.

'No, it is not possible during the Public Time. We can walk no further than the garden for the streets are so crowded and filled with such monstrous abominations. They have put several privy houses in the street and they empty their filth onto the apparel of anyone who happens to be passing. And even the hogs and the cattle protest noisily at the crush. But perhaps I can persuade Lord and Lady Butler or some other friend to give us the use of their carriage so that we can take a short outing. Would you like that?'

'Yes.'

'Perhaps we could catch a glimpse of some of the wonders of the fair.'

The child's eyes lit up.

'Oh, yes, please. Please, Mummy.'

She rustled to her feet.

'I shall see what I can do.'

Mr Cunningham possessed a very grand carriage and he was a most obliging gentleman. No doubt if she made her need known to him, he would put his carriage at her disposal. She expected a call from Mr Cunningham at any time. As soon as he heard the news he would come. And just as she expected, it was not long before Nancy showed him in.

'Mistress Blackadder.' He made a deep, slow bow.

'Mr Cunningham.' She spread her skirts and bowed her head in a curtsy.

'I was shocked to hear of your distressful bereavement.' He took her hand and for only a brief moment pressed his lips to it. 'May I offer you my sincere condolences. The Reverend Mr

Blackadder was a fine Christian gentleman.'

'Thank you, Mr Cunningham. He was indeed.'

'If there is anything I can do, dear lady, please do not hesitate . . .'

After inviting him to sit down and ordering Nancy to serve some tea, she told him of her conversation with Mungo.

'My carriage is at your disposal,' he said at once.

He was such a wondrously delightful man.

They sipped tea together and conversed pleasantly for some time before he rose to take his leave.

'Can I look forward to the pleasure of seeing you at the next Public Time, Mistress Blackadder? Or am I being too insensitive in view of your recent loss?'

'Locking myself away and indulging in fruitless lamentations will not bring back my husband, sir. Yes, of course, I will be attending the social occasions of the next Public Time.'

His eyes glimmered when he smiled.

'Mistress Blackadder, you are unique—a sensible woman as well as an enchanting one.'

Chapter 29

The pink fragrance of roses mingled with the dark leather smell of books and the waxy aroma of polished wood. Silver and amber slats of light heavy with dust sloped in, painting lustrous patches on furniture and floor. Outside, trees made secret whispers and crickets and birds joined in a chorus of chirpings.

Mistress Kitty, Regina and Harding sat round the unlit fire in silence as if in three separate worlds of their own. A table between them held china teacups and a silver tea-service.

Regina, dressed in a gold velvet gown and satin petticoat, poured the tea. Then she proceeded to help Mistress Kitty to drink from one of the delicate cups. In one hand she held the cup to the older woman's lips. With the other hand she held a napkin ready to dab away any rivulets of tea that overflowed.

Harding lit a pipe and sprawled back, glassily watching the smoke drift into the air. Mistress Kitty felt so worried about him she could not drag her eyes from his face. Several times she allowed tea to spill from her mouth and Regina had to catch it in the napkin and take great pains to dry her face.

Kitty had never seen Robert look so unhappy. Her heart was sore for him. She longed to break from the prison of her failures and weaknesses and be of comfort and help to him. But she knew she could not.

As soon as the tea ritual was finished, Regina said,

'Time to go upstairs now.'

She acquiesced thankfully. It was good to sink back into the feather nest of her bed and have Regina prop her pillows at exactly the right height and leave one of her favourite books conveniently beside the hand she was able to use. She was able to move both sides of her body more and more each day but her breathless turns still tended to plague and exhaust her.

'Is there anything else you want?' Regina asked.

Kitty hesitated. Then with difficulty managed,

'I'm worried about Robert.'

Avoiding her eyes. Regina smoothed and tidied the bedcovers.

'There's no need. I must go now. I have things to attend to.'

'Worried about Robert,' Regina's mind echoed sarcastically as she returned downstairs. If only Mistress Kitty knew. All Robert was out of countenance for was having his attentions rejected once and for all by Mistress Annabella. The last time she had been in Williamsburg she had met Nancy and Nancy had told her how Harding had called on Mistress Annabella after Mr Blackadder's death and how Mistress Annabella had sent Harding storming away in a terrible temper and he had never written or returned since.

Later, she'd bumped into Annabella and, after a few minutes' polite small talk, Annabella had suddenly asked in a sad voice:

'Why did you did it?'

'A crowd of French pigs raped me.'

'I see.'

'No, you don't.'

'It's better to forgive and forget.'

'Better for who?'

'For you.'

'I'll never forget.'

Annabella shrugged before moving on.

'I pity you,' she said.

Harding was still in the drawing-room, his teeth clenched over the stem of his long white pipe. Then, unexpectedly, the overseer was ushered into the room. Harding laid aside the pipe.

'Is there something wrong?'

'Don't know.' The overseer's grubby skin and crushed clothes looked out of place in the immaculate room. At least Harding was always clean in his person and linen. 'Big buck called Coolidge brought this letter for Mistress Chisholm.'

Regina struggled to stifle an upsurge of anxiety.

'That must be from my brother.'

The overseer handed the letter to her and after being dismissed by Harding, left the room.

She broke the seal and read under the date,

542

'My dear Regina,

Abigail and I are to be married in three days' time. I hope Mr and Mrs Harding will allow you to attend the ceremony. It is being performed in Abigail's old home (for we have a new home built ready for us to move into). The ceremony will take place at noon and will be followed by a feast and dancing in Mr Matleck's barn. (Mr Matleck is a friend of Abigail's father.)

We had not expected to be able to marry so soon but everyone in the settlement helped with the building and furnishing of our house and I am so happy and eager to be wed.

I hope you are well and happy too, Regina, and I look forward to seeing you.

Your loving brother,

Gav.'

Regina passed the letter to Harding. His eyes skimmed over the paper then he returned it saying,

'I planned to go tomorrow to collect some stores. You may travel with me.'

She shrugged.

'I don't want to go.'

'To your brother's wedding?'

'He'll be happy enough without me there. And his Abigail will be even happier.'

She could not prevent the note of bitterness entering her voice.

Harding said,

'Jealousy is an ugly emotion, mistress. It does not become you to be jealous of your brother's happiness, or his young bride.'

Never before in her life had Regina felt so furious. Rage flared up and flashed out before she could control it.

'How dare you lecture me on what emotions I should or should not have. You, of all people!'

He rose immediately from his chair, his hand shooting out and catching her by the wrist as she made to turn away. She cried out in pain at the hardness of his grip and the way it jerked her back round towards him.

'Don't you forget, Mistress Chisholm,' he said, 'that you are

543

a servant in my house. You keep a respectful tongue in your head and you do as I say. And I say you travel with me to the settlement tomorrow. Now go and tell my wife and make the necessary arrangements for her welfare until we return.'

As soon as she managed to wrench herself free, she swept from the room, up the stairs and along the corridor to Mistress Kitty's bedroom. Once inside though, a fit of trembling like a fever took possession of her and she covered her face with her hands.

'Regina, my dear, my poor, dear girl,' Kitty said.

'I hate him. I hate him. He's an animal.'

'No, no.'

Regina took a deep breath and lowered her hands. Her wrist was discoloured with bruised blood and it throbbed painfully.

'We're going to the settlement tomorrow but don't worry, I'll leave instructions for the slaves. You'll be all right.'

Tears trickled down Mistress Kitty's face and noticing them, Regina hastened to dab at them with a towel from the wash-table.

'There's no need to distress yourself. We won't be away for long. I didn't want to go at all. It's that brute who's insisting.'

For a minute Mistress Kitty's mouth struggled to form words, then she gave up and closed her eyes. Regina smoothed and tidied the bedclothes before leaving the room to go and talk to the slaves.

The kitchen was stifling. Heat blanketed out from the open fireplace. An iron swee was positioned over the blazing logs like a black arm. Hanging from it a kettle steamed and a large cooking pot kept erupting like an angry volcano. The door of the brick oven lay open and a sweating Callie Mae was retrieving a tray of scones. From a ceiling beam above the fireplace green herbs hung to dry. Beside them dangled yellow and rust coloured yarns that some of the other slaves had spun, dyed and woven.

Regina wasted no time in issuing her instructions. The steam was marking her velvet gown and the heat was making it drag and cling, causing intense discomfort. As soon as possible she swept away from the kitchen building and back to the cool of the house.

She was still furious with Harding. He hardly ever left her thoughts now. While sitting talking or reading to Mistress Kitty her mind's eye followed his bull-shouldered figure as he strode along the path to his office or rode leisurely around the plantation. While she was busy on a piece of embroidery, the colours blurred until she could only see his face. While in the same room she stole furtive glances at him. She hated him. She had always hated him. But now the emotion was acquiring frightening proportions. His selfish, arrogant, cold, domineering, overpowering, animal presence was beginning to obsess her every waking moment. Even at night, lying in the narrow bed in the closet off Mistress Kitty's room, listening to Mistress Kitty's snores and the rustling and creaking of trees and the strange wild sounds echoing from the forest, the awareness of him was as strong as her own heartbeat, as close as her own breath.

Gav felt proud and happy. Life was good. People were good. The people of the settlement made quite a frolic of house-raising and his had been no exception. The men and boys had helped him clear a good acre of forest. Then they lent a hand in the building of a sturdy two roomed log cabin. The women had made beef and vegetable stew and spoonbread to sustain the workers. Then, after the house had been completed, there had been much hilarity and singing and dancing in which everyone joined. They'd had tournament tilting as well. Several wooden hoops had been hung from a crossbar in the clearing in front of the gaol. Then some of the young bucks, himself included, had mounted their horses, levelled a lance and at full gallop tried to run it through a hoop and tear it free. He had freed the most hoops and so gained the right to name Abigail 'The Queen of Love and Beauty.'

Now he was going to marry Abigail. He could hardly believe his good fortune. And when he saw Regina emerge through the trees his happiness was complete. She came slowly, a slim yet awesome figure in a velvet riding coat the colour of chocolate and a cold, expressionless face

Beside her rode Mr Harding.

Mr Harding wished him well and in a rush of courage, born

545

of his great happiness, he invited the planter to join in the festivities if he'd a mind to. To his surprise and delight Mr Harding accepted and soon everyone was crowding around Abigail's father's house and the ceremony was being performed. Only a few people could be accommodated inside. Those included Mr Harding and Regina. They sat staring in front of them with an odd kind of intensity that seemed to have little to do with Abigail and him.

Afterwards in the barn, however, they feasted and drank copiously with the rest and soon lost much of their seriousness. Then later, when the dancing was in full swing, he saw Regina whirl round and round with Mr Harding in wild abandonment. Regina had always been a person of frightening extremes. He thanked God that Abigail was such a sensible, well-balanced, natural kind of girl. You always knew where you stood with Abigail.

The dancing went on until morning but by that time a party of young ladies had taken Abigail up a ladder to the loft and put her to bed there. A delegation of young men then took him up. Then there was the ceremony of throwing the stocking. The bridesmaids stood in turn at the foot of the bed with their backs towards it. In that position and with much giggling, they threw a rolled stocking at the bride. The groomsmen in their turn, aimed at the groom and the first one to succeed in hitting the mark was supposed to be the next one married.

He had not seen Regina and Mr Harding leave but he'd been told afterwards that they had collected their stores and ridden away followed by their wagon and slaves.

He hoped Regina would come and visit him once he and Abigail got settled in their own home. It wouldn't be as grand a place as no doubt she had become accustomed to, but as well as working in the store, he would plant and care for flax and corn and vegetables and eventually fruit trees on his land, claiming more space from the forest as he needed it. Abigail would cook and bake and make soft soap and dip candles and spin and weave. They would create a comfortable and happy home. He had never been more sure of anything in his life. And he often thought how lucky it was that fate had led him to this big, exciting country where so much was possible.

The drinking and the dancing had flung Regina's mind into turmoil. Even the silent journey through the forest had done nothing to quieten and soothe her emotions. It had been raining and the sparkling moisture gave a fresh and alive feeling in the dense, virgin woods. The leaves were a vivid, translucent green from which water dripped slowly, suddenly in heavy splashes. Bird song trilled high in the trees. Wet, earthy smells titillated the nostrils. Excitement vibrated in the air. As they went deeper, as it became darker, she was aware of animals lurking soundlessly in the shadows. Shadows closed in all around. And all the time as her body undulated to the rhythm of the horse, warm and strong against her flesh, she was aware of Harding riding beside her, not saying anything, not even looking at her. His presence, especially in that dark wild place, became a torment to her.

She hated him. His ability to cut himself off, to be completely independent and self-sufficient frightened her. He had had a weakness for Annabella but he had soon hardened that weakness away. She felt unsafe and insecure. Her whole existence had come to depend on this man, was painfully entangled with his, like the roots of the trees that surrounded and shut off Forest Hall from the rest of the world.

The house was waiting for them on the edge of the wilderness like a white skull, its windows black sockets. It was as if long ago it had been abandoned. Yet she felt more than ever that it was a part of her, that she belonged to the place, and it belonged to her.

Inside, Harding's wife slept. Regina stood at the end of the four poster bed and stared at the woman through the ghostly grey of the mosquito net. What a useless creature Kitty Harding was. A mere wrinkle of skin and bone beneath the coverlet, her balding head with its few dry wisps of hair hardly denting the pillow. This was the mistress of Forest Hall? It was so unfair. This creature did nothing for Forest Hall. And she was certainly no use to her husband. She did not even understand him. Her loyalty to him, or to the imaginary picture she treasured of him, was pathetic. Robert Harding was an arrogant and ruthless man. He wanted only two things of a woman; a son to carry on his name and gratification of his animal passions. That was his weakness. It hadn't been love for Annabella. He wasn't capable of love. He had felt only lust for Annabella's body. Granted, Annabella was very beautiful and could incite the passions of most men but the thought edged cautiously into her head—couldn't her own beauty match Annabella's? Hadn't she been much admired while working in the store? The implications of this fact in relation to Harding were now inescapable. There could be no doubt of what she must do. By pandering to his lust she must make herself indispensable to him. She must set out to attract him, not repel him. Then one day, because Mistress Kitty could not possibly drag out her pathetic life for much longer, she could be mistress of this house.

As she undressed and put on a flimsy robe, triumph made her shiver, yet at the same time she felt sick with fear. The candles in the hall lent a feeble light and as she stopped and listened at the drawing-room for the clink of Harding's whisky glass, the gold of her robe had a metallic glimmer. She opened the door and went in. The room was empty. The curtains had been drawn and a fire glowed in the hearth sending exploratory red fingers over the sandy grain of the books, the silky sheen of the upholstery, and the burnished copper of her hair. The brass face of the tall clock in the corner matched her robe. She lit a candle.

Harding would be down for his glass of whisky, she was sure. He always came into the drawing-room for a drink before retiring. Panic nearly overcame her and caused her to fly back upstairs. Childhood terrors returned. She was trapped in the hole-in-the-wall bed struggling hysterically against the French soldiers.

She had a sudden ridiculous longing to rush to Mistress Kitty's room and cling to her for comfort and protection as, long ago, before even the animal soldiers, she had found comfort and protection from her mother. After the soldiers there had been no one. No mother, no comfort, no hope. She had been alone, all the time fighting for survival, fighting to protect herself. And she was alone now.

She was standing beside the bookshelves holding a book and

trying to stop her fingers trembling as she turned the pages, when Harding entered. She did not look round until the whisky bottle clinked and splashed against his glass. When she did will herself to turn, he was standing with his back to the fire, legs apart, a glass in one hand and his other hand hooked in the top of his breeches. He had discarded his coat, waistcoat and neckcloth and wore only tight buff-coloured breeches and a white shirt hanging open to his waist showing brown skin and black hair.

She forced herself to meet his eyes, deep-set and tawny-streaked, containing only darkness and danger like those of a wild animal. She thought she would die with terror. She remembered the strength of him as he had whirled her round and round in the wedding dance. She wanted to run from the room. But somehow she could not even look away. At last he said,

'Come here.'

Conscious of her thin robe and how it revealed the contours of her body, she managed to carry her terror across the room and stand helplessly in front of him.

He took a mouthful of whisky, savoured it in his mouth without taking his eyes from her and then flicked the loosely tied belt at her waist. Her robe slithered open. He raised an eyebrow.

'No protests?' He finished the whisky and laid aside the glass. She didn't move, just stared up at him. He smiled his cold smile at her. 'No modest fumblings?' One hand slid round the back of her neck. 'No struggles?' His fingers entwined in her hair, painfully twisting it, straining her head to one side. 'No fighting to defend your honour?' He pulled her against him until their bodies touched.

She moaned at the feel of him and passion that was even stronger than hatred engulfed her. She was no longer in control of her actions. Nor did she have any understanding of them. Her fingers clawed him closer to her as if every inch of her body was thirsting for the touch of him. She cried out in surprise and terror and ecstasy as his lips met hers and his tongue forced its way deep into her mouth. Then he swung her into his arms and carried her out of the room and upstairs.

Mistress Kitty heard the heavy footsteps on the stairs, heard the door of Robert's bedroom kicked open, heard the noisy creaking of his bed, heard Regina's cries and moans. Then silence. Mistress Kitty wept. At the same time she tried to feel glad that Robert and Regina had found fulfilment. But she felt lonely and lost. Tomorrow she would be all right though. She would be all right. Regina and Robert would come to see her. They would take care of her. They had always been so good and kind. Lying like a ghost under the mosquito net in the four poster bed in the cluttered room in the stillness of the house, Mistress Kitty sobbed, 'Dear Regina. Dear Robert. They deserve each other.'

Along the corridor in another room a light still burned. Regina lay beside the sprawled sleeping figure of Harding as if hypnotized by the candle. Its flame added fuel to the fire of her conflicting emotions. She thought of the soldiers and the hatred and loathing of all men that had poisoned her life since she was a child. But now, other feelings were suspending her on a cloud of sensuous pleasure. She could not come down to earth and go to sleep. Long after the candle had gone out, her eyes remained staring at the darkness. She kept telling herself that all she wanted was the gossamer threads that bound her to Mistress Kitty to be finally broken. Then she would be mistress of Forest Hall. Then she would be safe. She would not need to care about Harding.

She hated him. She had always hated him. But, as she drifted in and out of sleep during the long, dark night, her fingers, cautious as feathers, would float out and touch him to make sure that he was still there.

Chapter 30

It was the Sleeping Time in Williamsburg, the lazy lull between the Public Times when the long Duke of Gloucester Street stretched empty and quiet. Dust sighed and settled down, only to stir with the occasional unhurried plod of a liveried servant going on an errand for his master or mistress. Sometimes an elegant sedan was carried along with a lady relaxing inside, leisurely fanning herself. Cattle wandered slowly over the market square chewing the cud and every now and again swishing at flies with their tails.

Francis Street had the same drowsy quality. Sleep dragged heavily at the hot air like snores. Life was suspended. Only the crimsons and purples and yellows of the flowers in the gardens bloomed with vibrant energy.

Inside her house in Francis Street, Annabella was dressing to receive some of her late husband's congregation who had sent a note to say they would be calling. Nancy was helping her, or at least trying, in her own way, to be of help.

'You can't wear your cherry hoop,' she repeated dourly, stubbornly.

Annabella snatched it from her.

'Impudent wretch! Don't you dare tell me what I can or cannot wear. If I say I shall wear my cherry hoop, I shall wear my cherry hoop.'

'But what'll they think? You're supposed to be in mourning. You're supposed to wear black.'

'I do not suit black. It makes me feel prodigiously dejected and cast down. And I refuse to be cast down. I tell you I am wearing my cherry hoop, and my white embroidered petticoat.'

'Well, for God's sake, at least don't let them see what you've done to this bedroom.' Nancy helped Annabella into the garments in none too gentle a fashion.

'What's wrong with the bedroom? It looks wondrously

cheerful and bright since I put up the new bed-drapes and curtains.'

'That's what's wrong with it. Everything in Mistress Sharp's bedroom was black after Mr Sharp died, black bed linen, black nightwear, black . . .'

'Gracious heaven!' Annabella interrupted with a shudder. 'What an odious practice. I shall have none of it.'

Nancy rolled her eyes.

'Just look at you! Well!' she shrugged. 'Don't say I didn't warn you.'

Admiring herself in the pier glass Annabella sent her wide hooped skirt swaying this way and that. Then she caressed the little bulges of breasts above the tightly laced stomacher with its pink satin bows.

'I think I look very beautiful and elegant.'

'It's what they'll think that's worrying me.'

'Pox on them. I don't care a fig what they think.'

'Can you not even have a bit of consideration for poor Mr Blackadder?'

'I gave Mr Blackadder my consideration while he was alive and while it mattered. Nothing can affect that pile of bones in the churchyard except worms. There's the door! Go and answer it at once. I'll be down as soon as I choose a fan.'

'At least carry a mourning fan.'

'Will you go away and do as you're told? I'll do as I like.'

She decided against a mourning fan, as, for one thing, it would look incongruous against her bright gown, her merry blue eyes, and golden hair. For another, she did not believe in all the fuss and bother about black. What did it matter about the colour of one's clothes except that they should enhance the person wearing them? What did it even matter about so-called mourning? Going about with a long face didn't bring back the dead. She had done her best for Mr Blackadder. She had been a good wife. Now she was a wife no longer. And that was that. Certainly there were times when she missed him. There were times when in the privacy of her bedroom she wept. But she wasn't the kind of person who could live in the past, and more and more it was Carter Cunningham who occupied her thoughts.

552

She had not seen him since the last Public Time. Nor had she expected to. The planters had their plantation business to attend to and seldom had either the time or the inclination to make the long journey to Williamsburg during its sleeping time. But she had hoped for some indication that he had not forgotten her. A little gift, or a note delivered by one of his slaves would have been much appreciated.

But no note had come. She toyed with the idea of sending Nancy with a polite inquiry. But so far, pride had prevented her. In the first place, she had no coach and Nancy would have to make the journey on horseback. Then, in courtship, and surely if one was honest that was what their relationship must now be, in courtship the man should take the initiative. It wasn't a case of conforming to custom in doing this. She enjoyed being paid pretty compliments, and flirted with, and pursued by an elegant gentleman like Mr Cunningham. But the customs of courting in Virginia were too ritualistic to suit her taste. In her view, they were hypocritical. Not only had a proposal to be made in an atmosphere of strict religious formality, but the lady had to be approached with fear and trembling as if she were some kind of saint. The gentleman had to prostrate himself before her, either literally or figuratively. She had to pretend to be surprised and distressed at the mere idea of marriage and only after much protestation could she agree to consider the gentleman's proposition.

Annabella, it was true, had a coquettish turn of nature, but she had a flair for freedom too and could not abide anything that smacked of restriction, especially if it were religiously inspired.

Still wondering if she ought to send Nancy with some sort of communication to Mr Cunningham, she pattered downstairs and into the drawing-room.

Mistress Sharp and Mistress Blair waited with solemn faces and straight backs, their hoops smothering the chintz sofa. Mistress Sharp's black bombazine gave her pinched face a waxy, corpse-like appearance. Mistress Blair's deep purple silk accentuated the broken capillaries on her cheeks and nose. They rustled to their feet to greet Annabella with dignified expressions of sympathy that immediately collapsed with shock at the sight of her.

'Mistress Sharp!' Annabella dropped a curtsy. 'Mistress Blair!' She curtsied again. 'How kind of you to come.'

'We cannot stay,' Mistress Sharp managed. 'We have other calls to make.'

Mistress Blair's purple cheeks quivered.

'We only came out of respect for Mr Blackadder. A fine Christian gentleman.'

'Indeed he was,' Annabella cheerily agreed. 'But surely you will stay for a dish of tea? My maid is preparing it. I was looking forward to a pleasant *tête-à-tête*.'

Mistress Sharp glared in mounting disapproval.

'I would have thought that this was hardly an occasion for pleasure.'

'Oh?' Annabella's brows lifted and she flicked open her fan. 'And why not?'

'Really!' The ladies gasped at one another. Then Mistress Blair rounded on Annabella.

'Your heart should be heavy with grief, mistress, not light with wicked frivolity.'

'Gracious heavens! A dish of tea and a pleasant *tête-à-tête* is surely neither wicked nor frivolous? And with respect, Mistress Blair, you do not know what is in my heart.'

'We know what is on your back, though,' Mistress Sharp cut in. 'And it's not a mourning gown. It's a disgrace!' And with that the two ladies swept from the room and the house.

Nancy came in and put the tea things down on the table.

'I warned you.'

Annabella selected a sweetmeat and nibbled daintily at it.

'Silly cows. What do I care about them?'

To be honest, though, she felt somewhat surprised and hurt. Later, when she invited other acquaintances to tea and they sent a servant with a note saying they could not come but offering no explanation, she felt even more so. Not that she showed her distress, even to Nancy.

Eventually she told the maid:

'I have decided to send you with a note to Mr Cunningham. I am prodigiously bored and cannot wait until the Public Time to see him.'

Nancy was shocked.

'You can't make advances to him like that.'

'Advances! Advances!' Annabella flapped her hands. 'All I'm doing is sending him a polite little note asking him how he is and telling him how I am.'

'He'll know perfectly well what you're doing.'

Suddenly Annabella giggled.

'It's what I want to do that should intrigue him.'

'You're hopeless.'

'Not at all. I am full of hope. I have always been an optimist. I refuse to be anything else.'

With much groaning and grumbling Nancy was eventually persuaded to set out on the journey to the Cunningham plantation. Unknown to Annabella, however, she stopped off for a night at Morgan West's farm on the way. It was only with much reluctance, and irritation at Annabella, that she left the farm and spurred her horse on once again. But her resentment at having been forced to make such a tiresome expedition was fanned into fury at the rude way she was treated when she arrived at the Cunningham mansion.

She went boldly to the main door instead of the kitchen, having been instructed to hand the letter to the master and not some forgetful slave. The door was opened by a liveried Negro, but before she could say a word to him a lady with a pocked face and no rings on her fingers came harassing to the door complaining shrilly:

'What is it now, Samuel?'

The slave stepped aside to reveal Nancy with the letter in her hand.

'How dare you come to the front door of the house?' The woman's voice screeched high with anger. 'The kitchen is the place for servants.'

'I was told by Mistress Annabella to deliver this letter into Mr Cunningham's hands and I didn't expect to find him in the kitchen.'

'Impudent hussy! Give that to me!' Before Nancy could do anything the women had snatched the letter from her hand. 'I'm the mistress of this house.'

'But Mistress Annabella . . .' Nancy protested.

'Mistress Annabella! Oh, yes, I know all about her. Just you go right back this instant and tell her to leave Mr Cunningham alone.'

With that she banged the door shut in the maid's face and hurried back upstairs to her cousin's bedroom. Clusters of leeches were still sucking at his neck. His head rolled feebly about and his fingers wandered and twitched in futile efforts to free himself. All night, indeed for several nights now, she had struggled to nurse the delirious man. Not that she minded. She would nurse him for the rest of his life, attend to his every need, run his house, do anything he wanted if only he would ask for her hand in marriage. Despite the fact he had had amorous adventures with many women, she and Carter had remained friends and she often came from her papa's plantation to visit him. She lived in the hope that one day he would realize what an excellent wife she would make for him and agree to her papa's proposal that it would make a sensible match. She lived for and dreamed of the day when she and Carter would stop being friends and he would begin courting her. After all, he could at least be certain that she wasn't after his money, like most of the penniless creatures he had become mixed up with in the past. Her papa was almost as wealthy as he was.

When she came on this visit, she had seen immediately that something was amiss. Her cousin was not his gay amusing self at all. It soon became obvious that he was ill and she persuaded him, not without some difficulty, to retire to bed. She was thrilled at the idea of being needed by him, and set to work with a will to look after everything. She dreamed happy dreams of him realizing at last that he could not live without her, of him reaching out to her and calling her name.

But it was Annabella's name he kept calling.

Angrily, tears of frustration spurting from her eyes, she tore up Annabella's letter and tossed it into the bedroom fire.

Nancy felt like weeping as well. Tired after the journey, she had expected some decent hospitality; a refreshing meal in the Carter kitchen, perhaps a glass of ale or home-made wine with which to wash it down before turning her horse towards home, first of all to Morgan West's farm and then to Annabella's house in Williamsburg. She felt so annoyed and insulted by her experience at the Carter place that she made up her mind there and then that it was the last time anyone would be able to call her a maid. When she reached Morgan West's farm she told him that she would accept his proposal of marriage. A date was settled and everything arranged. The only snag was the prick of guilt she felt at having to break this news to Annabella almost in the same breath as telling her that Carter Cunningham had another woman.

'Pshaw!' Annabella tossed her curls. 'She could be anybody. A servant. A relation perhaps. There is a perfectly innocent explanation, I'm sure. Mr Cunningham is a gentleman.'

'I told you what she said. And if you ask me he's nothing but a gambler and a womanizer. That man has had more women chasing after him than any other in the whole of Virginia.'

'How do you know? You are only a common serving maid.'

'It's common knowledge.'

'Gossip, you mean. I tell you, Mr Cunningham is a gentleman. He will explain everything when he calls to see me at the Public Time, as he promised.'

Nancy rolled her eyes. Annabella seemed hell-bent on getting hurt and there was nothing she could do about it. Not that she felt over-worried. Annabella was a lot tougher than she looked.

Nancy married Morgan West quietly and without any fuss, as they had arranged. She did feel a pang of regret when it came to actually saying goodbye to Annabella. They'd been together a long time. But neither of them shed any tears at parting. Indeed, Annabella seemed almost indecently cheerful, pattering around, showering her with gifts, laughing, waving, wishing her every happiness. The last she saw of Annabella was the dainty figure, like one of the flowers in the garden, recklessly throwing kisses, her vivid skirts swaying, her hair shimmering like gold in the sun.

What she did not see was Annabella flying back into the house and tossing herself on to the sofa to weep with wild and heartbroken abandon. She quickly recovered, of course, and was soon looking forward eagerly to Carter Cunningham's visit, and to all the other excitements of the Public Time.

But when the Public Time came the female society of Williamsburg rejected and froze her out with every means as its disposal. She received no invitations to any of the balls. Tea parties gathered and gossiped in houses all around her but she was never included. Dinner guests in all their rustling finery spilled from carriages and rainbowed into dining-rooms, but she was never among them.

Not that she sat at home and moped. In the first place, she was kept very busy with the running of the house since Nancy had left. She still had the young maid, Betsy, but it had been distressing to lose Nancy. She had been a lazy impertinent strumpet at times, and they had fought like wildcats, but they had been friends too, as close as mistress and maid could be.

But it was not seeing Carter Cunningham again that cut the deepest. She was not only hurt but humiliated by the fact that the Public Time came and went and he never called to see her. She had been so confident that once he found out she was not being invited to the social functions he would immediately appear and whisk her away in his carriage to the very next ball. If he had led her in, no one would have dared to spurn her or turn her away. But he had not come and she had heard nothing from him.

'Pox on him!' she cried, and stamped her foot and agitated her fan. 'Pox on the monstrous man. I care not a fig for the abominable scoundrel.'

But she did care. During each day she managed to retain her bright exterior and chatter gaily to Mungo or Betsy. Alone at night though, acutely sensitive to the creaking and clanking of carriages in Francis Street and the flare of passing lanterns in the room, she often lost the battle with tears. They trickled down and wet her embroidery or the book she was pretending to read. Until suddenly, she made her decision.

'We are returning to Glasgow,' she announced to Betsy. 'I refuse to sit here and mope a moment longer. Glasgow is a prodigiously exciting and friendly city. I will have a wondrously good life there. I know I will!'

So she whisked into immediate preparations, and swept on to the very next ship setting sail for Scotland.

When a slave galloped into Williamsburg with a letter for her, he found a deserted house and, returning to the Cunningham plantation, he told his master that Mistress Annabella had gone.

Chapter 31

Regina laid down her fork, looked across the dining-room table at Harding and said:

'I want to accompany you to the horse fair.'

He lit a pipe.

'It's time you improved your manners, mistress.'

'I don't understand.'

'You talk like a spoiled child. It's always "I want".'

'I say what I mean.'

He blew smoke into the air.

'You mean you want a horse.'

She shrugged.

'Mr Harding, may I,' she said, 'accompany you to the horse fair?'

He gave one of his harsh, abrupt laughs, then silence fell between them once more. Eventually he said,

'I have other business to see to. People to see. Slaves to buy.'

'I see no reason why I should not accompany you.'

'So be it.'

He looked away, dismissing her, losing interest in her. She felt irritated and had a compulsion to force his attention back to her again but managed to control it. After all, she had got what she wanted. Or at least she soon would when they attended the horse fair. Every time she thought of the visit it gave her a secret shiver of pleasure.

Williamsburg was teeming with people, and so noisy that they heard the place long before they passed the Capital Building and cantered into Duke of Gloucester Street.

Impeding the movement of carriages and horses and sedan chairs were bearded trappers dressed in buckskins and fur hats, servant women in white mob caps and scarlet cloaks, gentlemen in smart coats and waistcoats and buckled shoes and masked ladies in a rainbow of panniered gowns and capes. Tinkers astride ponies carried moulds and soldering irons in their saddlebags and travelling shoemakers bore the tools of their trade on their backs.

Harding said:

'It's hardly worthwhile washing and changing our linen. In this dust we'll be filthy again in a matter of minutes.'

Nevertheless, Regina ordered water to be brought to her room and she felt much refreshed after washing away the sweat and grime of the journey and changing into a cream coloured silk gown with a blue quilted petticoat. Then they both enjoyed a hash of lamb and a bottle of claret in the Apollo Room sitting at its long, highly polished table. Eventually they sauntered out and along the leafy tree-lined street in the direction of the Market Square. The horses for sale were being led around a roped-off section at the far end of the Square. Harding pushed his way towards it and she followed, glad of his big body protecting her from the crush of people. All around, peddlers were eagerly offering kerchiefs, laces, finger and earrings, blue, crimson and yellow beads, buckles, buttons and bodkins. Farmers' wives had spread vegetables and eggs and home-made cider and peach brandy on stalls.

Reaching the roped-off area, Harding said

'How about one of those stallions?'

She eyed the stallions being paraded, and said,

'No, thank you.'

A white man who was obviously the owner of the horses kept signalling the Negroes who were leading them round to stop so that he could go over each animal with his hands and explain its fine points.

Harding bid for one of the stallions and eventually succeeded in buying a powerful beast with a black satiny coat. It secretly frightened Regina. It seemed to have too much uncontrolled and uncontrollable energy. The Negro had a terrible struggle to hold its head and, as he hung grimly on to the bridle, the horse's mane flew about and its tail lifted like a banner and it swung round on its hindquarters, whinnying loudly.

Regina chose a chestnut gelding. It was a beautiful yet gentle animal and seemed to take to her right away, nuzzling its head against her, its muscles rippling with pleasure under her hand.

She was more happy and relaxed than she had ever been before in her life. The happiness warmed inside her, melting the hardness and creating an area of dangerous vulnerability in the armour of her cool.

She left Harding to complete the rest of his business on his own and began pushing her way through the crowd towards Duke of Gloucester Street. Dust scraped underfoot and puffed up with waves of heat to parch her throat and nostrils. Suddenly she felt nauseated and her struggles to free herself from the crowd increased. For several days now she had been plagued with bouts of sickness and dizziness and this discomposure frightened her. Not being in control of herself meant being at someone else's mercy. She fought to banish this terror from her mind. All she needed was rest. After she had relaxed in bed for an hour, she would be perfectly all right. However, she had only taken a few steps inside the entrance of the Raleigh Tavern when she crumpled into a heap on the floor.

When she regained consciousness she was sprawled on top of the bed with a Negro servant in a white bib apron fussing around and a man in a long curly wig staring severely down at her. He introduced himself as Doctor Simmonds and, after questioning her in detail, he announced that she was pregnant, adding:

'I see you're not wearing a wedding ring, mistress. I must report this sinfulness to the church.'

'You'll do no such thing, sir,' she managed coldly. 'I have every intention of getting married. What is your fee?'

He told her the amount in tobacco but she said,

'I prefer to pay in coin.' Then, reaching for her purse, she opened it, handed him a generous sum and making the words sound like a curt dismissal, said:

'Thank you for your services.'

She dismissed the servant too and lay for a long time alone in the room without moving.

'If only Mistress Kitty would die,' she kept thinking. The woman would be better dead. What sort of life had she with an ugly, twisted body that was no use to herself or her husband. If only Mistress Kitty would die, Harding would marry her to give his unborn child a name. He wanted a proper legal heir, not a bastard. If only Mistress Kitty would die, everything would be all right. She would be safe as the mistress of Forest Hall with her fruitfulness as an extra hold over Harding. If she could have one child, she could have others.

Lying watching the white curtains puffing playfully at the open window, her hair like burnished copper against the snowy pillows of the bed, she wondered if she ought to tell Harding about the baby. She decided against it. Instinct cautioned her to wait.

The rest in bed refreshed her and she was able to get up and, after brushing her hair and tidying the creamy silk folds of her gown over her blue petticoat, she went downstairs to join Harding in the dining-room. They shared a meal of green pea soup, a leg of mutton and a codling tart with cream. Then she returned upstairs to read a novel while Harding went for an evening's carousal with friends.

The next day they returned home. When they arrived, Regina, followed by Harding, climbed the outside stairs and entered through the pillared doorway. The glass chandelier in the hall tinkled lightly in the breeze until Old Abe shut the door.

Regina addressed Harding:

'I'll go upstairs straight away and see that Mistress Kitty is all right.'

Mistress Kitty was propped up in bed in her scarlet robe and powdered wig, and she had an open book on her lap.

Jenny was sitting on a chair close to the bed and she rose when Regina entered.

'Light the candles,' Regina told her. 'It is too shadowy in here for Mistress Kitty to read in comfort. See that they are lit in my room too and hot water ready in my jug.'

The slave left the room and Regina stood at the foot of the bed.

'You have been well, I hope?'

For a minute or two the older woman couldn't speak. It was as if her last dregs of energy had trickled away and she had not even the strength to bring a light of welcome to her eyes.

'Oh, Regina, Regina. I have missed you. I have felt so ill and weak.' She paused, labouring desperately for enough breath. 'I'm so glad, so glad you're back.'

Then, slowly, she managed a monstrous smile. Regina shrank inside at the ugliness of it, but she betrayed no hint of her revulsion. The smile clung on, screwing up one side of the death-coloured face and bulging one eye.

Kitty put out a hand to Regina, but she ignored it and walked over to the window. She gazed down at the thinned out area of trees in front of the house. Black stumps and patches of grass alternated with the trees and a ribbon of brown earth snaked around them and away into the black wall of the forest. How cut off this house was. It could be the only house in the world. Mistress Kitty and Harding and herself could be the only people in the world.

Her hands strayed to the front of her waist and suddenly the reality of her situation gripped her like a pain. She could not bring herself to turn from the window and face Mistress Kitty. It was as if she was immobilized forever in the middle of the wilderness with the deformed woman. Horror entangled them like the forest undergrowth.

'I must go and wash and change my clothes.' Her voice was tight and cautious and she walked towards the door without allowing her eyes to stray anywhere near the other woman. 'I'll return at teatime.'

Mistress Kitty loved to have afternoon tea in the drawing-room. Three o'clock had become the focus of her life. She watched the clock, counting the minutes until it came.

It was a ritual. Regina arrived in the bedroom at exactly three o'clock each day and called for Westminster or Joseph to carry her downstairs. Wrapped snugly in a blanket, she would be whisked along the corridor with its panelled walls and silver wall brackets holding individual candles. Then down the wide curve of the stairs, across the bare wooden-floored hall and into the drawing-room. There, Regina made sure that she was comfortably settled in her chair and she, Robert and Regina sat together sipping tea from delicate china cups.

On the afternoon after they returned from Williamsburg,

Regina poured tea from a silver pot. She placed Harding's conveniently near to him, then she held a cup close to Mistress Kitty and helped her to sip from it. Every now and again she dabbed at the older woman's face with a napkin to mop up the rivulets of liquid that overflowed from the loose, contorted mouth.

'Would you like a sugar biscuit?' Regina asked.

Kitty darted her husband a furtive, apprehensive look. She longed for a biscuit but knew she wasn't yet clever enough at eating. If crumbs of half-chewed pieces of food tumbled from her mouth, would Robert be upset, she wondered.

Regina saw the look and was irritated by it.

'Here, take one.' She could not conceal her impatience. 'Hold it in your good hand. You can do it perfectly well.'

Kitty concentrated fearfully on bringing her trembling leaf of a hand to her mouth. Then, managing it, she gave a moan of distress when the biscuit broke against her lips and crumbled down her neck and down onto the floor.

Harding's anger immediately erupted towards Regina.

'For God's sake. Look after her properly. This daily farce will have to stop. My wife would be far better served in the privacy of her bedroom.'

Regina's mouth twisted with bitterness.

'Better for you, you mean.'

'Watch your tone of voice, mistress. Don't you ever imagine that you are safe from a whipping, because you are not. When I say that my wife would be better served in the privacy of her bedroom, that is what I mean.'

'It does her good to come downstairs.'

'Does her good?' Harding's lip drew back in a sneer. 'Look at her!'

Kitty's crumb-speckled mouth contorted in its efforts to form speech, but failed.

'She can hardly breathe.'

Regina was prevented from retorting by the high-pitched moan of panic that Mistress Kitty managed to squeeze out.

'Keep calm.' She addressed the older woman sharply. Then hastening over to the door, she called for Westminster who immediately came running. 'Carry Mistress Kitty upstairs to bed,' she ordered him.

The Negro servant snatched up the woman as effortlessly as if she'd been a scrap of gauze and hurried upstairs with long strides, taking them two and three at a time.

Regina followed him at a slower, more dignified pace, daintily holding up her skirts to prevent them from brushing against the stairs.

Once in the bedroom, she dismissed Westminster, propped Kitty up in the bed with plenty of pillows and tucked the bed covers around her. This done, she proceeded to administer Peruvian bark and camphor. Then, as usual, she stood back and waited for the cure to take effect.

She was as sick of the daily farce as Harding was. She didn't enjoy watching the revolting spectacle of Kitty drinking tea and making a disgusting mess with food any more than he did. But Harding was to blame for upsetting her. He would be the death of his wife one of these days with his brutish and insensitive manner.

It was then it occurred to her that this might be the best thing that could happen. Why was she fighting all the time like this to protect and help Mistress Kitty? Why was she so meticulous in her efforts to look after this useless wreck of a woman? She was keeping her alive, yet knew she had to die. She must die.

Regina stared at the tiny face, the wisp of body. This was all that was preventing her from being safely married to Harding and mistress of this house. Conscious of the child ever growing inside her, a panic of desperation nearly overcame her. All she needed was to crush a pillow over that face to close those tragic staring eyes for ever. Then they would all be free. She had actually taken a step towards the bed when Mistress Kitty quavered out,

'I'm sorry. I'm sorry, Regina.'

'I'll go and make you a strengthening gruel,' she managed in her icy, distant voice.

Outside on the landing, she had to lean on the banisters for a few minutes before she felt able to return downstairs and face Harding again. She felt waves of nausea engulf her. The blood sucked from her veins leaving her weak and her skin prickling. Willing herself not to faint, her knuckles whitened over the banister and she took big, slow breaths.

When she eventually reached the drawing-room, she was relieved to find Harding gone. The dishes had slops of tea left in them. Saucers and plates and table and carpet were all spotted with crumbs. Cushions were dented. The logs in the fire had collapsed and spewed out ash. The air was stale with pipe smoke. Suddenly, unexpectedly, she felt tears shimmering across her eyes. Dabbing at them, she fought to breathe deeply and calmly again. Being with child, she decided, had a most disturbing effect on the whole constitution. She hated Harding for being the cause of her vulnerable and therefore dangerous condition. She had a curious fenced-in feeling that made her restless. Yet, at the same time, she experienced an urgent need for absolute security. Her life was now continuously torn by conflicting emotions. Her hatred of Harding was no less real because of the physical passion she felt for him. She tried to stifle the passion, to freeze it away, even to reason with it. She would stare at him coldly and tell herself, 'He is ugly. It is not logical to feel attracted by him.' Often she convinced herself and an icy distance stretched between them across which he made no attempt to reach her.

Now, standing alone in the drawing-room, she covered her face with her hands. She couldn't go on like this. Each day she was becoming more uncertain and afraid of what tomorrow might bring. She was not sure what Harding's reaction would be when he found out about her pregnancy, and she felt ill with indecision and distress. She kept asking herself what he would do; what could he do? He couldn't marry her as long as Mistress Kitty was alive. If only Mistress Kitty would die. She was half-dead as it was. What perverse fate was keeping her clinging on to her futile mockery of a life? If Mistress Kitty stayed alive for much longer and the pregnancy became obvious, Harding, or for that matter his wife, could throw her out to starve, the terrible fate of so many other servants from other houses in the colony. She would be up before the church session. She would have to suffer all sorts of punishments, deprivations and humiliations. Her only hope was if Harding was free and then learned of the pregnancy. That way he had the chance of acquiring a legal heir by marrying her. He might not take that chance but she felt almost certain that he would. She knew how much he had always wanted a son and how bitterly disappointed he was that Mistress Kitty had never provided him with one.

Regina poured herself a glass of whisky in the hope that it would give her strength. She was drinking it when she heard the familiar sound of Mistress Kitty's bell. Automatically she hastened from the room and upstairs in answer to it.

Mistress Kitty looked like a piece of melted wax stuck to the pillow. The bell lay on its side on the coverlet where it had fallen from her hand. At first it seemed as if she was too feeble to talk, but then she managed to whisper:

'Did you forget, my dear?'

'Forget?'

'The gruel. I feel so weak.'

'Of course. I don't know why it went out of my mind. I'll see to it immediately.'

Regina called Jenny and told her to fetch a bowl of gruel. She had never seen Mistress Kitty look so weak. Even after being fed the gruel she did not rally as much as she usually did, although the hot sweet liquid helped. But by the time she was settled down to sleep for the night she seemed tolerably comfortable and content.

Regina had moved to a bedroom of her own, and in its welcome privacy she undressed slowly, then before slipping into bed, examined her body in the pier glass. Already her abdomen looked swollen. She felt like sobbing with fear and apprehension, but no tears came. She lay stiffly, dry-eyed under the coverlets with the candle flickering on the table beside the bed. To relax into sleep was impossible and she was still awake when Mistress Kitty's bell began its hollow chime.

Regina could imagine the feeble hand struggling to jerk the bell first one way, then the other. She tossed aside the bed covers, grabbed the candle holder and without stopping to don a robe, she hastened along the corridor and entered Mistress Kitty's room, the door of which always lay open at night. The bell had fallen on to the floor, and Kitty was gasping for breath. Regina lit the candle by the bed so that she could prepare her potion and give her relief. It was while she was doing this that she noticed Mistress Kitty's eyes, bulging with distress, fix on her abdomen. Then their eyes met. The older woman was still fighting desperately to breathe and her eyes pulled away and sought the potion on the bedside table. But Regina continued to stare at her as if frozen; as if incapable of ever moving again. Then suddenly she lifted the candle and left the room, shutting the door behind her.

Jenny, who slept in the cupboard under the stairs, had just reached the landing when Regina said,

'I have seen to Mistress Kitty. Go back to bed.'

Then she waited at the top of the stairs holding the candle high until the servant disappeared.

Back in her own room she climbed into bed and covered her head with the blankets; She waited in an agony of apprehension and suspense to see what the morning would bring. As she half-hoped, half-dreaded, it brought screams of grief from Jenny and shouts of,

'Pore Miz Kitty! Oh, pore Miz Kitty!'

She put on a robe and went along to the older woman's room. On the way, she met Harding.

In silence they gazed at the dead woman. She had been half out of bed and Jenny was lifting her and putting her back against the pillows again.

'Close her eyes,' Regina said, beginning to weep. 'Close her eyes,' she repeated, before turning away to go and get dressed.

She did not know if she wept because of sadness or exhaustion or relief. Nor did she care.

She stood at her bedroom window and stared out at the wilderness. She had never felt so much a part of it. Like one of the forest animals stirring to greet another day, a fountain of triumph rose within her and all she could think, again and again, was:

'I have survived.'

Then she thought:

'Now let tomorrow come.'

SCORPION IN THE FIRE

To Roger Davis

Chapter 1

Six sweat-lathered, black horses raced ahead of the billowing cloud of dust. In the middle of it bounced and jerked the coach from Port Glasgow with Will Bramstone, better known as Old Brimstone, clutching the reins and cracking his whip as he goaded the horses on to greater effort. Clinging to the back with one hand and blasting with all his lungs at the horn was his partner Hamish.

Inside the coach, Annabella tried to steady herself in order to peer out the window and catch the first glimpse of Glasgow. Through the trees on the right she had caught flashes of the River Clyde and the occasional tiny boat with its sail flapping and sparkling. Straight ahead against the blue of the sky, she sighted the silver spires of Hutcheson's Hospital, the Tron Church and the Tolbooth. Further over to the left reared the College in the High Street. Down to the right near the river glinted the Merchant's Hall. Crowded underneath and around these lofty edifices were the crow-stepped gables of the Glasgow tenements, and lower still huddled the thatched cottages and hovels.

Her father had told Annabella that many changes had taken place in the seven years that she'd been away. She made an attempt to lean out to get a closer look but a breeze grabbed the wide brim of her straw hat and nearly tore it from her head.

'Hell and damnation!'

She bounced back on her seat, curls escaping untidily and cheeks afire.

Her father, Adam Ramsay, drew down his bushy brows at her.

'Compose yourself, woman. That's no way to talk in front of the child.'

Mungo was as excited and curious as she was. He had only been a year old when he left Glasgow and had no memories of the place. He tried to stand to see out but the mad dance of the

573

carriage whipped him off his feet. Annabella laughed as she hoisted him up.

'That'll teach you, sir.'

'Teach me what, ma'am?' he said, trying to quell her hilarity with one of his smouldering, grown-up stares.

He was dressed like a gentleman in miniature with a green, knee-length coat, long waistcoat in a lighter shade and a three-cornered hat the same chocolate colour as the inside of the carriage. His hat had been knocked askew and his breeches darkened with the dust of the carriage floor. He looked like a little ruffian despite his silver-buckled shoes and green silk brocade.

'To remain in your seat and behave yourself,' Annabella said.

'I want to see Glasgow.'

Ramsay growled.

'Hold your impatient tongue, sir. You'll see it soon enough.' Then to Annabella, 'It's well seen he's taken after you, mistress, and not his father, God rest his soul. And I'll warrant you've been sadly neglecting his spiritual teaching. How well does he know his catechisms?'

'Mr Blackadder was very diligent in his instruction, Papa. Never a day passed but he didn't give us all a reading and question us on our catechism.'

'Your husband, God rest his soul, has been dead nigh on two years. How diligent have you been, mistress? That's what I want to know.'

'I have been sorely tried these past two years, Papa, but I have done my best in the circumstances.'

It had indeed been a difficult and vexing time since Mr Blackadder's death. It had taken months for the news of her plight to reach her father in Glasgow and months again for the money that she requested from him to arrive back in Virginia. In the interval she had been forced to borrow from friends. At least, she had naively imagined people like Lord and Lady Butler were her friends. They had made her a substantial loan but at the same time emphasized that it was only a matter of business because of Lord Butler's association with her father. Socially, they had ostracized her, as if with the loss of her husband she had lost the last shreds of respectability.

Of course, the Williamsburg society had only grudgingly accepted her after the first ball she'd attended at which she had attacked Regina Chisholm. Regina had betrayed Annabella's lover to the English dragoons after the battle of Culloden. Jean-Paul Lavelle had died a horrible death as a result and she had no regrets about what she had done to Regina Chisholm that night when she had unexpectedly come face to face with her at the ball. Williamsburg society would have ostracized her right there and then had it not been for Mr Blackadder preaching hell-fire and damnation at all of them the following Sunday.

In the old days in Glasgow Regina had been her maid. Now she worked for tobacco planter Robert Harding in Virginia. As usual, thoughts of Harding disturbed Annabella. Not so much because he had once raped her. She was a generous-hearted, exuberant woman, incapable of nursing the black emotions of hatred or revenge for very long and she had forgiven Harding for his assault upon her. What continued to irritate and disturb her was his more recent protestation of love and his stubborn determination to make her his mistress. He was a coarse brute of a man with very little refinement of manners. She did not remember seeing him wearing anything more elegant than a black coat, beige-coloured breeches and jackboots. Never, to her knowledge, had he sported a snuffbox, nor ever kissed her hand or paid her a pretty compliment. She would rather die than allow such a boor of a man to know that he was the father of her son.

Even Mr Blackadder, with his dry pawky wit, could turn a clever phrase to his advantage. She was glad that she had never disillusioned Mr Blackadder in his belief that Mungo was his child. He had been so fond of the boy.

Harding had been insensitive enough to force his way into the house not long after Mr Blackadder's death and once again insist that she should succumb to his animal passions. It had been the devil's own job to get rid of him that day and she had only succeeded by saying,

'There is another man, Mr Harding. A charming gentleman of my acquaintance that I hope to see during the Public Time. He is a trifle catched by me and I by him . . .'

The charming gentleman of her acquaintance was Carter Cunningham. They had met several times at the social occasions of the Public Time when all the planters and others from outlying farms and plantations came to Williamsburg to vote and to enjoy themselves with their families and friends. She had not foreseen then that the female society of Williamsburg would reject and freeze her out with every means at its disposal.

She no longer received invitations to any of the balls. Tea parties gathered and gossiped in houses all around her but she was never included. Dinner guests in all their rustling finery spilled from carriages and rainbowed into dining-rooms but she was never among them.

Not that she had sat at home and moped. In the first place, she had been kept very busy with the running of the house since her maid Nancy had left to marry. She'd still had the young maid Betsy, but it had been distressing to lose Nancy. After all, they had grown up together in Glasgow. She couldn't remember a time when she hadn't known the girl. She had been a lazy, impertinent strumpet at times and they had fought like wild cats, but they had been friends too, as close friends as a mistress and maid could be.

But it was not seeing Carter Cunningham again that cut the deepest. She was not only hurt but humiliated by the fact that the next Public Time had come and gone and he had never called to see her. She had been so confident that once he had found out she was not being invited to the social functions he would come and whisk her away in his carriage to the very next ball. If he had led her in, no one would have dared to spurn her or turn her away. Mr Cunningham was one of the richest tobacco planters in Virginia. But he had not come and she had heard nothing from him.

'Pox on him!' she remembered crying out to the empty room and stamping her foot and agitating her fan. 'Pox on the monstrous man. I care not a fig for the abominable scoundrel.'

But she had cared. During each day she had managed to retain her bright exterior and chatter gaily to Mungo or to Betsy. Alone at night, though, acutely sensitive to the creaking and clanking of carriages in Francis Street and the flare of passing lanterns in the road, she had often lost the battle with tears. They had trickled down and wet her embroidery or the book she had been pretending to read.

But all that was behind her now. Here she was ready and eager to begin life again in Glasgow despite the fact that she was nearly thirty. No one could tell her age by her appearance. She was still a beautiful woman with hair like sunshine and eyes as blue as a summer's sky. And the low-fronted velvet gown, the same shade of blue as her eyes and the ribbons of her hat, showed that she had a shapely little figure.

The coach was rollicking along now between high parallel hedges and past thatched cottages. Hamish toot-tooted his horn and the vibration and noise brought a flush of excitement to her cheeks.

'Look, look, Papa,' she cried. 'Over there before the Shawfield Mansion there's another wondrous place.'

Her father remained sitting, hands bunched over the gold-topped Malacca cane propped between his knees. Without glancing round he said,

'That'll be George Buchanan's latest ploy. You'll remember Buchanan who built that other house? He called it Mount Vernon after his Virginian friend, George Washington's place. Well, now he's built this place and called it the Virginia Mansion. He's opened up a street there too. He's called it Virginia Street. Wicked vanity and pride is swelling the heads of too many tobacco merchants these days.'

'You mean everyone is building mansions like that?'

She was astonished and thrilled. The Virginia Mansion was most impressive with its pavilion-shaped roof with chimney stalks in the centre and its handsome balustrade running along the eaves. A triangular entablature rose above the centre projecting part of the building and on the pinnacles elegant stone vases and ornaments were placed.

'A wicked waste of money,' her father said. 'What's good enough for our fathers is good enough for us.'

'Fiddlesticks. There's got to be progress.'

'It's vanity, I tell you. Nothing but vanity and puffed-up

pride. The Lord will smite them down.'

'Oh, Papa!'

'Hasn't He already shaken the threatening rod of His wrath at Glasgow in these past few years?'

'You mean the rebellion?' She laughed. 'Prince Charles Edward Stuart was the threat, not God, Papa.'

'To have had our own town invaded and our merchants all but bankrupted is no laughing matter, mistress.'

'If they are building mansion houses they are well on the way to recovery, sir.'

She held onto her hat as the carriage jolted and jarred every bone in her body. She was aching and exhausted but the fact that at last they had arrived in Glasgow infused her with new energy. The high bushes and banks of yellow broom and the thatched cottages had shrunk away behind the coach and she was able to get a close look at the Virginia Mansion as they passed it. Then the Shawfield Mansion. Then came the tenements and the lively, crowded Trongate Street.

It reminded her of Williamsburg at the Public Time, but the Public Time only happened twice a year. At other times the town of Williamsburg was quiet and deserted. Here in Glasgow it was crowded and noisy and busy and exciting every day of the year except Sundays. The Williamsburg streets were wider and the houses much larger with gardens all around, but it was good to see the Glasgow tenements again. They were tall, stately structures of stone with gables to the front, resting on a row of piazzas. Into these piazzas or covered archways, people were crowding to see the goods displayed or to squeeze into the dark shops or booths behind. Out in the open air of Trongate Street there were stalls higgledy-piggledy all over the road but especially around the Cross attended by market women in blue duffle cloaks with hoods drawn forward over their heads.

Hamish blew violently at his horn but it was only with much difficulty that they cleared a path and swung right down Saltmarket Street and into their close. Yet even at the back of the building people were doing business. Beside the middens and dung heaps, byre-women milked cows and butchers bloodied the earth with meat for sale.

578

Annabella had to sit for a few minutes after the coach came to a halt outside the round tower stairway. Even then it took all her will-power and the helping hand of her father to ease her to the ground.

'Losh and lovenendie. A more dreadful road cannot be imagined. It was a miracle that the coach did not overturn.' Spreading out her skirts she dusted them down as best she could. Her stays dug into her waist and breasts and she felt bruised and stiff. 'Are you all right, Mungo?'

The child had struggled from the vehicle unaided and was standing wide-eyed watching the butchers hacking at carcasses with long knives. The men were covered in blood. Blood had dried darkly on their clothes and glistened scarlet on their hands and arms as if they had no skin.

Then suddenly into the close came a bustle of ladies shepherding a young lad of about Mungo's age in a blue silk coat.

'Annabella! Annabella!' the ladies called.

Annabella clapped her hands in genuine delight.

'Mistress Halyburton! Griselle! Phemy! Oh, it is wondrously good to see you again.'

Mistress Halyburton was a rigid-backed woman in a mahogany-coloured dress and powdered hair.

'Aye, Mistress Blackadder.' She managed to subdue her pleasure before favouring Annabella with a prim kiss on the brow. 'Still as perjink as ever, no doubt?'

Her daughters were more enthusiastic in their embrace. Griselle's ruddy cheeks vied with the flame-coloured dress she was wearing. Even Phemy's pocked unhealthy face was coloured with excitement and the colour, if not the face, made a pretty contrast against her turquoise gown. Both young women hugged Annabella until she had to push them away.

'Losh sake, if I don't get a cup of tea or a dram or something to revive me after that monstrous journey, I shall drop in my tracks and you shall have to carry me upstairs.'

With squeals of sympathy they grabbed Annabella's arms and swooped her towards the protruding round tower at the back of the building. The stairway was dark and they had to lift their skirts to protect them from the dung and urine of tramps and vagabonds who had slept on the stairs during the night.

Annabella screwed up her nose.

'Lord's sakes,' she said, 'what a noisome place!'

'It's no different from when you last saw it, mistress,' Letitia Halyburton snapped.

'More's the pity,' Annabella said.

She had forgotten how cramped and filthy the tenements were. She was accustomed to much better things now.

'What a fine big lad Mungo has turned out to be,' Phemy said when they arrived in the flat. 'I have a little daughter, as you know, but I couldn't bring her out today. She has a feverish cold.'

'I'm looking forward to seeing her, Phemy.'

Letitia gripped her hands beneath her long bosom and raked Annabella with an accusing stare.

'Your Mungo doesn't bear the slightest resemblance to Mr Blackadder.'

Annabella loosened the ribbons of her hat, willing her hands not to tremble.

'Indeed he does not, Mrs Halyburton. I have always said that Mungo has more a look of his grandfather than his Papa. The Ramsay strain must be strong,' she laughed, 'because I see my brother Douglas in your son George, Griselle.'

Griselle stiffened with displeasure. She had no great love for her husband, Douglas Ramsay, and regarded him as a weak-willed, affected fop.

'He may look like his father but he takes after me, nevertheless.'

'I'm glad to hear it,' Annabella tossed aside her hat, then with a big sigh gazed around. 'It's good to be back.'

And she meant it, despite the low-beamed ceilings and tiny windows filtering in thin slices of light. Despite the noise bombarding the room from outside. Despite the chattering of women and the guffawing of men. Despite the rhythmic tattoo of horses' feet. Despite the racket of street cries.

'Bellows to mend!' a man with lungs like bellows was roaring.

'Knives to grind!' chanted another.

A woman was singing:

'Herrings, fresh herrings. Come buy my fresh herrings!'

A man selling rabbits slung on a pole which he carried on his shoulders joined in the bedlam:

'Rabbits, rabbits, ho!'

Another was loudly competing with,

'Buy my goose, my fat goose!'

'Lavender!' A young woman joined in the chorus. 'Lavender, sweet lavender!'

Annabella felt like singing too. There was a bouncy rumbustiousness about Glasgow that suited her and already her senses were tingling with excitement for the interesting, lively, challenging times to come.

'I've ordered chairs for the four of us,' Letitia said, swinging her skirts over one arm in preparation to leave. 'Your father can bring the boys.' She had prepared a meal at her own house along Trongate Street to celebrate Annabella's return. Annabella's brother and Griselle's husband, Douglas Ramsay, was going to be there, also Phemy's husband, the Earl of Glendinny, and Andrew Halyburton, brother of Griselle and Phemy. 'Where's Nancy and Betsy?' she added, suddenly remembering about Annabella's maids.

'Didn't you know about Nancy? She married a Virginia farmer,' Annabella laughed. 'Losh sakes, there's so much to tell you, I'll be talking for days. Betsy's here, though. At least, she will be. Her folks were meeting her at Port Glasgow. She'll be starting work again tomorrow. Not that she's much use. I dare swear I'd be better without her. Although I'll need somebody by the look of this place. It has been monstrously neglected.'

Letitia's drawstring mouth pulled tighter.

'Your father's a stubborn man. I've been telling him for years to take a wife. There's many a decent widow woman would have been glad to have him. But no. Not even a housekeeper would he look at.'

Annabella glanced around. Earlier in the day sunshine had pointed with amber fingers at greasy stains on plaster walls and wooden floors that in the past Nancy had so often washed. Now shadows pulled the ceiling lower and weighed down the dark oak, making the room in which they were all crowded look cramped. It was Annabella's bedroom and the main room of the house in which all entertaining was done. She fluttered around it like a butterfly, brightening the place with gaiety and colour, yet accentuating its darkness and gloom.

'Papa, Papa,' she cried out. 'I am ashamed of you, letting the house go to rack and ruin. Now I'll need at least one other servant as well as Betsy to get everything put to rights.'

Ramsay glowered.

'Big John managed fine.'

Annabella rolled her eyes at the mere idea of her father's clumsy giant of a manservant managing anything. Still, she couldn't help feeling cheered and refreshed since she had washed her face and changed into an open gown of violet satin with a quilted yellow petticoat. The sleeves were tight to the elbow and then opened into treble flounces of lace-edged gauze. The stomacher-front bodice was wide and low, making her father roar out:

'In the name of decency, Annabella, cover yourself. You're practically naked.'

'Oh, fiddlesticks, Papa. A wide *décolletage* is the fashion.'

'I like your hat, Annabella,' Phemy piped up. 'We're still wearing the plaid here.' She twirled the hat round on the tip of her fingers making its ribbons flap out. 'Are you putting it on again?'

'No, not tonight.'

'How does it stay on with such a shallow crown? And such a big brim surely catches the wind. Is that why the brim is cocked up front and back?' Phemy was a sparrow of a woman with frizzy hair secured back in a straggle of ringlets. Her mother towered above her, rigid-backed, with hands clasped at the front of her waist as if supporting her long bosom.

'There's nothing wrong with the plaid, mistress.'

'No, mother.'

Annabella said, 'It's most fashionable to have the ribbons dangling down at one side but if it's a very breezy day, I often tie them at the back under my hair or at the front under my chin.'

Griselle raised her brows and Annabella was reminded of

how like her mother she looked; the same straight back, the same long thick hair. Even her cheeks, once a pretty pink, were darkening into purple like Letitia's.

'I would have thought, Annabella, that away in the back of beyond among savages and wild animals, fashion would have been the least of your concerns.'

'Gracious heavens, I wasn't living in the forest, Grizzie. I was in Williamsburg which is prodigiously civilized, I can assure you.'

'Tuts, you always were a terrible one for exaggerating,' Letitia said. 'Cover your nakedness with a cloak and we'll be away.'

Annabella couldn't help giggling. Obviously to them anything outside of Glasgow was not worth considering. Though Griselle was very proud of the fact that once, long ago, she had visited London. But even London had apparently palled in comparison with the great things Glasgow had to offer.

'We've so much to tell you too, Annabella,' Phemy chattered breathlessly as they picked their way down the stairs. 'The town's so much bigger now, didn't you notice? But no, you would be too shaken up and tired.'

'She'll have plenty of time to view the town,' Letitia said. 'First things first.'

Annabella supposed the older woman meant seeing the rest of the family. Or perhaps enjoying the meal she had prepared. Certainly it was a relief not to have to tackle cooking so soon after she had arrived and especially in her father's cramped kitchen.

The four sedan chairs and the eight chairmen were waiting in a line in the back court. Annabella manoeuvred her hoops in, then plumped herself down, her silver powdered hair like the heart of a flower with violet petals puffing up all around her.

The chairmen heaved the chair up and loped through the close and out into Saltmarket Street. In a matter of minutes they were at the Cross. Cramped though their tenement was inside, it occurred to Annabella that from the outside the place where they lived was quite a respectable-looking grey stone building. The Ramsay house occupied the second storey at the corner, having windows on Trongate Street but also three little windows, one facing each way, in a lantern-shaped projection overhanging the corner. On part of the ground floor, behind the pillars of the arched piazza, was the Old Coffee House Tavern. Already candles flickered in the Tavern windows and shadows of men in cloaks and cocked hats wibble-wabbled inside and sounds of merriment kept punching the mild autumn air.

Four streets met at the Cross. Saltmarket Street from the south and the River Clyde, Gallowgate Street from the east, High Street from the north and Trongate Street from the west.

The chairmen turned left into Trongate Street and trotted resolutely, heads down, through knots of gossiping populace. Stalls were being dismantled and a profusion of goods, such as wooden churns, tubs, pails, bowls, plates, as well as meat and fowl and vegetables and shoes, wheeled away on hand-carts or packed in sacks and then slung over the backs of stall-holders or pack-horses.

Across the rough dirt road stood the Tolbooth, a magnificent edifice, five storeys high. It had a tower on the corner of Trongate and High Street with a clock and a crown-shaped steeple. In front of the Tolbooth building in Trongate Street was a large outside stairway made up of two sets of stairs, one on the west side and one on the east, joined by a platform or gallery which was used as the place of execution. It also served to exhibit all those condemned to stand in the pillory.

Annabella wondered if there were still as many Sabbath breakers being pilloried. The Glasgow Sabbath had always seemed to her an odious imposition. It began in the Ramsay household by a reading of exercises from the Bible. Then at ten o'clock the family set forth to church, returning at half past twelve to lengthy prayers, followed by a little cold meat or an egg. No cooking was allowed. Back to church at two o'clock where they were preached at until four or five. Then home again to be questioned on their catechism and to meditate and say private prayers until supper time. After supper her father gave another reading, then more prayers or singing of hymns until bedtime.

Nothing else was allowed and searchers or inquisitors could

enter houses and arrest anyone who danced, hummed a tune, combed their hair, washed, carried water or swept their house. People were arrested and pilloried for 'profanely walking' outside. Children were punished for playing.

How Mungo would react to such restrictions Annabella dreaded to think. In Williamsburg she had insisted that he behaved with some decorum on the Sabbath but there had been very little preaching and catechizing since Mr Blackadder died.

She peered out of the sedan chair window to make sure that Mungo was following with his grandfather and his cousin, George. At first she could see no sign of them. There was only a gaggle of gossips in red and white striped petticoats and white cotton caps tied with red ribbons, and men wearing flat, blue, Kilmarnock bonnets like giant scones on their heads. Two dogs fought noisily in a cloud of dust. Then she saw her father striding along, his cane thumping the ground, his scarlet cloak billowing like a ship in full sail, his thick shoulder-length wig topped by a three-cornered hat. On either side of him hurried his grandsons, Mungo determined to keep pace with as big, rapid strides as he could manage, George trotting lightly, breathlessly, all the time out of step.

George kept reminding Annabella of her brother, Douglas, the boy's father. He had the same lean features and long neck and the vivid blue eyes common to all the Ramsays. Though Adam Ramsay's had hardened into grey.

She waved her fan out the window chuckling to herself. Already Mungo had something of the same dour look of his grandfather, although the child was only eight. The worst of it was, he looked even more like Robert Harding. Relaxing back as best she could in the bouncing, swinging chair, she allowed herself a few thoughts about Harding. The night he'd raped her seemed like a dream now. She had been partnered with him at a dancing assembly and afterwards, instead of calling for a sedan chair to take her safely home, he had swept her off her feet and, despite her protests and struggles, had carried her to the Green. No finesse, no courting, no pretty turn of speech, no delicate persuasion could be expected from a man like him. If Harding wanted something, he took it. Years afterwards when they had met again in Virginia, he had tried to excuse his monstrous behaviour by blaming a mixture of drink, his passion for her and the wretched state of his marriage to Kitty Harding. She had forgiven him eventually, especially after meeting his wife. Kitty was a feeble affectation of a woman and no use as a wife to a man like Harding, especially since her illness.

She supposed that by now Kitty would be dead and Harding more suitably married to his fiery-headed housekeeper, Regina. More suitable as far as being alike in their characters, that is. They were both strong-willed and determined but of the two, Annabella thought that Regina was the worst. How could anyone be more cruel and vengeful than Regina who, long before either of them had met Harding, had betrayed poor Jean-Paul after the battle of Culloden.

Annabella sighed. It had to be admitted, of course, that her struggle on the Green with Harding was nothing compared with what had caused Regina to hate men so much. Regina had been a mere child when she had been sexually attacked by not just one man but a crowd of French soldiers.

The jar of the chair stopping and being laid down jolted Annabella back to the present.

'Hell and damnation!' she cried, struggling out with hoops swaying to reveal flashes of white silk stockings. 'Watch what you're about, you ruffians, or I'll have you thrown in the Tolbooth.'

She smoothed her hair and plucked her gown into shape while Letitia emerged from one of the other chairs and promptly cracked both her chairmen on the head with her fan. Phemy and Griselle giggled discreetly behind mittened palms.

'Come away, come away.' Letitia shepherded them all into Locheid's Land, as the tenement building in which she lived was called. The building was on the same side of Trongate Street as the Tolbooth and the Exchange but further west. Like most of the other buildings it was fronted with arches and pillars on the ground floor and on the first floor above this archway was the Halyburton flat. It was bigger than the Ramsay's, having four rooms and kitchen, compared with the Ramsay's two rooms and kitchen. Entry to the building was through one of the

586

archways to the back and into Locheid's Close. From there the ladies crowded up the dark turnpike stair to the first landing. Letitia tirled the door-pin, filling the darkness with a noise like a harsh-throated crow. Muffled voices and shufflings issued from inside, then the door creaked open. Letitia pushed it wide.

'Where's the candle, Kate?' she demanded of the old hunchback in the lobby. 'The nights are drawing in. It's high time it was lit.'

'Yer aye getting on to me for being wasteful. Can ye no' make up yer mind? Oh, there ye are, Annabella. Look at her!' she suddenly shrieked. 'What a disgrace! Everything's bare but her bum.'

Letitia brushed the servant aside.

'Away and tell Nell to come and help at table and less of your snash.'

'Snash is it?' The old woman shuffled away, muttering to herself. 'A wicked disgrace. She should be nailed by her lug to the pillory. And what's wrong with me helping at the table, eh?'

All the doors off the lobby were open and there was just enough light from the main bedrooms to guide them through the gloom.

The first person to greet them in the bedroom was Annabella's brother, Douglas. As foppish as ever in a high-fronted wig with roll curls at either side and lots of lace frills in his shirt and ribbons streaming from his wrists, he came mincing towards her, arms outstretched.

'Dear saucy brat,' he said and kissed her hand. 'I do declare I feel quite pleased to see you.'

'And so you should after all this time,' Annabella said pertly but she gave him an affectionate kiss on the cheek before smiling around. 'I'm prodigiously pleased to see all of you. Andrew!' She offered him her hand. 'Tell me, why haven't you persuaded Suky to marry you yet?'

Andrew's scurfy face had inflamed beetroot-coloured patches and at Annabella's words they rapidly spread across his cheeks. He was a small, round man with small, round eyeglasses which he snatched off and busily rubbed.

'Not my good fortune.' He replaced his glasses to scratch

587

himself vigorously behind one ear. 'Lord Dinwoodie. Suky favoured him.'

'Gracious heavens, you mean she married someone else?'

Annabella wasn't as surprised as she affected to be. Suky was the sonsy daughter of the Earl of Locheid who owned Locheid's Land and lived upstairs and, although Andrew had courted her desperately for years, it had never seemed very likely that he would capture Suky's heart. Or anybody's heart for that matter. Andrew was anything but a romantic figure with his bloodshot eyes and wheezy breath.

His mother sniffed. 'Aye, she'll be ruing it by now.'

'What makes you say that?' Annabella asked.

'He's a right wastrel.'

'Lord Dinwoodie?'

'The very one.' She hitched her shoulders back and tightened her mouth. 'Never away from gaming tables and cockfights and the like. She hardly ever sees him. And it's no more than she deserves. She could have had our Andra.'

Head lowered, Andrew fumbled with his snuffbox.

'Not my good fortune.'

'And him that well placed,' Letitia went on, 'since his father crossed to the other side. You knew the gudeman had gone to meet his Maker?'

Annabella accepted a pinch of snuff from Andrew's box.

'Yes, Papa sent me the news in one of his letters. I was mightily distressed to hear of his passing.'

'Nothing to be distressed about,' Letitia said.

The Earl of Glendinny, Phemy's husband, had been hovering in the background. Now he shuffled forward, head bent as if his wig was too heavy. Then, after waiting until Annabella had enjoyed a good sneeze and dabbed at her nose and mouth with a lace handkerchief, he greeted her with a quaver of pleasure. He was more than thirty years older than Phemy and his looks rivalled those of his wife in lack of beauty. In his prime he had been a big, muscly man with a nose like a pear and ears like turnips. But at nearly seventy, he had shrunk, leaving his ears and nose the same size but his skin loosely hanging from eyes and chin.

'Weel, weel, Annabella. My, you haven't changed a bit.'
Letitia clasped her hands primly in front of her waist.

'Aye, still as perjink as ever. Come away now, the supper's ready and waiting.'

A table was laid at the other end of the room from the russet-draped four-poster bed and near enough the fire to benefit from its light and comfort. On the table sparkled a white cover, silver candelabra and Letitia's best china dishes with their gold edges glittering. Annabella clapped her hands in appreciation.

'Mistress Halyburton, you have surpassed yourself. That table is magnificent. Look, Mungo!' she called to the little boy who had just arrived with his cousin and grandfather. 'Did you ever see such delightful food?'

There was a boiled leg of mutton, a roast loin of pork with peas, pudding and parsnips; a roast goose, salmon, lobsters and crab, and a cushie doo pie. A mountainous confection of syllabub graced the far end of the table along with a silver dish of slate biscuits and golden brandy snaps.

'Aye,' said Letitia looking and sounding as if the whole thing was more of a disgrace than a delight. 'Eat it then. That's what it was made for. Nellie?' she rapped out in a louder voice. 'Where are you, woman? You're supposed to be slicing the meat.'

Annabella fluttered her fan.

'Losh and lovenendie, after that journey I feel quite faint with hunger.'

Virginia seemed far away in another world now, almost as if it had never existed. And Nancy and Regina and Robert Harding and Carter Cunningham were like ghosts with no substance in reality.

Yet, memories of Cunningham and the way he had deserted her when she needed him still had the power to hurt.

'Pox on the scoundrel,' she thought as she whisked towards the table. Carter Cunningham wasn't the only man in the world.

Chapter 2

Regina Chisholm and Robert Harding sat at opposite ends of the long dining-table. Two candelabra quivered tongues of light around the room, picked out yellow pine walls, reflected in the glassy mahogany table and high-back chairs, gave a golden heart to the silver plates and cutlery. Three Negro slaves waited in the background, one at either end of the table and one at the sideboard. Only the tinkle of cutlery broke the silence.

Regina took satisfaction from remembering how she had managed to organize the house. Everything had been so different when she had first come to Forest Hall and when Harding's wife was alive. Kitty Harding had never been any use. Even before her illness she had allowed the slaves to do what they liked. She had been incapable of meting out the slightest discipline. On the contrary, laxity and domestic chaos had been encouraged by her chattering and laughing with the servants and visiting them in their quarters to minister to their ills. The house had been neglected. Meals had been ill-cooked, never on time, and served in a ridiculously slapdash manner.

For the most part, Harding had given up trying to make his wife more sensible and efficient. Occasionally he had erupted in a violent temper that only reduced Kitty to tears and put her into such a flutter that she had to retire to bed. More often than not he had contemptuously ignored her. It had been on one of the occasions when he had been upbraiding his wife that Regina had seized her chance. She had asked if she could be given the authority to organize the house slaves in future and take a more active part in the running of the house so that she could be of more help to Mistress Kitty. What she did not mention was that doing nothing all day but listen to Mistress Kitty's silly talk had been nearly driving her mad.

Harding had agreed to her suggestion but in his usual abrupt manner.

'Yes, it's time you did something useful for your keep. From now on I hold you responsible for the running of this house.'

After that she had firmly discouraged idle gossiping. If she had entered a room and found Mistress Kitty chattering and laughing with a servant, she had said a polite 'excuse me' to Mistress Kitty, then dismissed the servant. Or if the servant was supposed to be doing some job in the room, she had given her a sharp command to get on with it before guiding Mistress Kitty firmly away.

She had made it clear to the slaves that if they disobeyed her commands, they would be severely punished. But, in fact, there had been less violence than before when Harding used to vent his rage at his wife's futility by ordering the overseer to whip the slaves. Or he had whipped them himself. The fact that they now suffered less punishment, and that although she was strict she was fair, did nothing to make them like or appreciate Regina. They hated her far more intensely than they hated Harding, if they bothered to feel anything for him at all.

From what they had heard from other slaves, or from what they had previously experienced themselves, he was no worse than many other masters and better than many more. Whipping, even to death, was one of the less barbaric of the punishments commonly meted out.

Regina knew the slaves hated her because she had banished so many of them to the fields. Through a haze of auburn eyelashes she stole a glance across the table at Harding. What a coarse, ugly-looking brute he was. Her mouth acquired its hard twist as she stared at him. His hair was tied back from his big-boned face, its blackness accentuating the tan of his skin and his dark eyes. His nose was broken and twisted over a wide mouth, the upper lip of which could tighten back like that of a snarling animal.

Lowering her eyes to her plate again, she picked neatly at her food with a silver fork. She hated this man so much that even to look at him made her heart lurch wildly and her pulse career out of control. She could hardly believe that her life was now so ensnared with his. At one time she had dreamed of leaving and starting a small plantation with her brother, Gav. Gav had been due fifty acres of land when he had finished his indenture in one of Master Ramsay's stores. Helped by looted gold coins she had stolen from the saddlebags of dragoons after the battle of Culloden, they could have bought some slaves and built up a good place of their own. For years she had dreamed and planned and lived for that day. But, like all men, Gav had proved worthless. He had suddenly announced that he was marrying a blacksmith's daughter called Abigail, a plain-faced girl with a serious stare and hair pinned tightly up on top of her head.

She remembered returning from the settlement after Gav had broken the news to her. She had been at the store with Harding to collect supplies. Later, riding back, when the forest had begun to thin out and in the shadow of the trees that were left in ragged disarray, she had seen Forest Hall again and it had occurred to her that this was the kind of place she had been aiming for. A two-roomed cabin of the kind small planters usually began with would not have given her space to breathe or to have the kind of privacy she treasured. But she did not want simply to serve in a mansion like Forest Hall as companion-housekeeper. She wanted to be mistress of a place like this. There was a stillness, a bleakness about the building that matched some secret place within her. Yet there was dignity, too, with the double outside stairs and pillared doorway.

But she knew that far from being mistress of the house, she was in a dangerously insecure position. Now her future as well as her present was utterly dependent on Harding.

She resented being dependent on him. He obsessed her thoughts. Continuously aware of him, she saw his face in everything she did. When she was in the same room, her eyes kept stealing furtive glances in his direction. Though there had been times, at Gav's wedding for instance, when she and Harding had whirled round and round together in a dance that went on most of the night and seemed to let loose a kind of madness in them both.

The night after the wedding when they had returned to Forest Hall she had undressed, put on a flimsy robe and stood watching the snoring Kitty Harding for a few minutes before going downstairs. What a useless creature Harding's wife was, she remembered thinking. A mere wrinkle of skin and bone beneath the coverlet, her balding head with its few wisps of hair hardly denting the pillows. This was the mistress of Forest Hall, she remembered thinking. It was so unfair. This creature was no use to Forest Hall and she was certainly no use to her husband. Nor did she even understand him. Her loyalty to him, or to the imaginary picture she treasured of him, was pathetic. Robert Harding was an arrogant and ruthless man and he wanted only two things of a woman—a son to carry on his name and gratification of his animal passions.

His lust for a woman's body; that was Harding's weakness and she had decided to use it to advantage.

That night, in the drawing-room, she had shut the curtains and lit the candles. Then, trembling with fear, she had waited for Harding to come down for his usual nightcap of whisky. At first she had not been able to look round when he came into the room. All she'd wanted was to fly upstairs to Mistress Kitty's room to seek comfort and protection from her just as long ago she'd sought comfort and protection from her mother. The whisky bottle clinked and splashed against his glass before she was able to force herself to turn and face him across the room.

He had been standing with his back to the fire, legs apart, a glass in one hand and the other hooked in the top of his breeches. He had discarded his coat, waistcoat and neckcloth, and wore only buff-coloured breeches and white shirt hanging open to the waist showing brown skin and black hair. Conflicting emotions fought for supremacy inside her. Memories of the time when the soldiers had raped her made her feel sick with terror. She never wanted another man to touch her as long as she lived. Yet, as she met Harding's eyes, dark and tawny-streaked like those of a wild animal, she experienced a terrifying need for physical contact with him.

At last he said, 'Come here.'

Conscious of her thin robe and the way it revealed the contours of her body, she had managed to carry her terror across the room and stand helplessly in front of him.

He had taken a mouthful of whisky, savoured it in his mouth without taking his eyes from her and then flicked the loosely tied belt at her waist, making her robe slither open.

He had raised an eyebrow.

'No protests, Mistress Chisholm?' She had not been able to move and had just stood staring up at him. He had finished his whisky and laid aside his glass. 'No modest fumblings?' One hand had slid round the back of her neck. 'No struggles?' His fingers had entwined in her hair, painfully twisting it, straining her head to one side. 'No fighting to defend your honour?'

He had pulled her against him and at the touch of his body against hers, she had moaned at the feel of him and the passion even stronger than hatred that engulfed her. Then suddenly he had swung her into his arms and carried her out of the room and upstairs.

Since that night she had moved from where she normally slept in Mistress Kitty's room to a bedroom of her own. At first it had been plainly furnished with bare floorboards and only one rug beside the undraped four-poster bed. Gradually she had persuaded Harding to supply her with a luxurious Turkey carpet, two Turkey worked chairs, a Russian leather chair, a pier glass, a walnut chest with drawers, an elegant candle-holder, and rich brocade curtains and valance for the bed.

But she had not deigned to fawn or flatter or plead for what she wanted as his wife used to do. She informed him coolly and bluntly. At first he had told her with equal bluntness to go to hell. But afterwards when he had come to her bedroom he had found the door locked against him. She had lain stiffly in bed listening to his snarling commands.

'Open this door, damn you. Open it, or I'll kick the bloody thing down.'

She ignored him. She had seen herself in the pier glass in the corner, propped up on pillows in the large four-poster bed like a ruby-haired, milky-skinned doll, and had wondered at how cool and still she looked. There had been no sign of the panic beating its wings inside her like a caged bird. He had begun to kick the door and hurl his weight against it until the lock burst and the wood flew back and exploded against the wall.

She had stared at him with green icicles of eyes which did nothing to betray the shock she always experienced when she saw him. The black of his hair and brown of his skin made a startling contrast to the white of his shirt. His overhanging brows made pits of his eyes. His twisted nose and tight upper lip gave him a demonic look.

'This is my house, mistress,' he said, 'and if you ever lock a door of it against me again, I will have you whipped.'

'You wouldn't dare.'

'Oh, wouldn't I?' he had said, coming slowly towards the bed. 'But the whip is not the only way to beat you down, mistress.'

She had not struggled with him but she had not been able to control her little animal-like moans at his brutality. She had not realized that he could be so cruel. Plunged back to the time when she was a child and the soldiers had raped her, each one more shocking and monstrous than the last, she was overwhelmed with terror at Harding's unexpected behaviour towards her.

But a few days later the luxurious Turkey carpet had been laid in her room. It had been a victory that had done nothing to reduce her fear and one that she viewed with wariness, not understanding the thought process behind it.

Since that night she had not dared to lock her door. Nor had he shown her the same brutality. When she struggled against him, beat her fists against his chest and tossed her head from side to side on the pillow moaning uncontrollably, it was not because he was causing her pain. Sometimes, in fact, when he fondled her breasts and his mouth opened over her nipples he was almost gentle.

She despised him for his weakness, if weakness it was. She could never be quite sure. She hated him for humiliating her, for making her a victim of his strong animal magnetism, for firing her blood over and over again until she felt drunk and didn't know what she was doing or saying.

Yet there could be no doubt of the fact that she needed him now that she was carrying his child. She wondered if this was a good moment to tell him and almost blurted out her secret before remembering the slaves hovering in the background waiting to serve them at the dining-table. She dropped her eyes to her plate again. Tomorrow, immediately after breakfast, she and Harding were setting out for Williamsburg where Harding had business to attend to and more slaves to buy at the market. It would be better to wait until they returned and he hadn't so many other things to occupy his attention. He hadn't wanted to take her at first, but she had insisted. It was too soon after Mistress Kitty's death for her to feel completely at ease in the house alone. She had longed for Mistress Kitty to die. Yet the strange thing was, now that she was dead, she missed her. She missed her morning visits to the older woman's bedroom to make sure that she'd spent a comfortable night. She missed talking to her and organizing all her comforts like a table by her bedside with her little bell that she could ring when she needed a fresh supply of reading materials, or fruit juice, or enough threads for her embroidery frame, or for attention if she didn't feel well.

Regina often heard the bell in nightmares now, saw the feeble hand struggling to jerk it first one way, then the other, heard its hollow chime. She would wake suddenly and jerk trembling into a sitting position. Her palms would fly to cover her mouth to muffle moans of distress while perspiration coursed down her face and mingled with her tears. She tried to tell herself that the poor woman was better dead. Mistress Kitty had suffered so long with her breathless attacks. Then after her stroke she had been unable to walk, and even to talk or eat had been a tortuous business.

She had done everything humanly possible to help Harding's wife. After every nightmare she would keep repeating this to herself. She had nursed Mistress Kitty and seen to her every need with obsessive conscientiousness; no one knew that better or appreciated it more than Mistress Kitty herself. But Mistress Kitty had begun to suspect something was wrong, and from then on she had been in an impossible situation. She remembered the first frightening occasion when Mistress Kitty asked in her breathless, butterfly voice:

'My dear child, something is causing you concern. Please tell me what it is, please do. You know that I love you like a daughter, like a daughter. I would do anything to help you.

Anything.'

She had immediately retreated behind a stiff mask and replied coolly:

'Nothing is amiss. Do you wish to come to the drawing-room for tea? Mr Harding still insists that you should not be coming downstairs because the effort makes you so breathless.'

'Dear Robert, I appreciate his solicitude. But I get bored, so bored with my bedroom. It is so nice to have tea in the drawing-room with you both, with you both.'

She had called to Westminster to come and carry Mistress Kitty downstairs, then drawn back the bedcovers, swivelled out the two skin-covered bones that were Mistress Kitty's legs and arranged her tidily into her robe as if she was a child. Then she hoisted her to her feet to await the slave's arrival in the room. One side of Mistress Kitty's face and body was still twisted and she felt as fragile as an autumn leaf.

Downstairs, propped opposite her husband at the drawing-room fire, she allowed Regina to hold a cup of tea to her lips and help her to drink it. In between sips she had breathlessly chattered.

'Listen to the singing birds, the singing birds. Aren't they lovely? There's more of them now than when I was a girl, I am sure, yes, I am sure. Did I hear you go out last night, Robert? I hope there was nothing wrong, dear, nothing wrong.'

'I went out hunting.'

'But, dear Robert, it was so late, so very late.'

'When it's for raccoon and possum it's best done on foot and by the light of the moon and stars.'

'I do declare! I do declare! I'm quite fluttered at the thought of you alone in the forest, alone on foot.'

'I had the dogs with me.'

'I remember at my daddy's place, at my daddy's place. There was always hog killing after the first frost. All the neighbours gathered to render down the fat in great black kettles. And all the children chewed on the crackling, on the crackling.'

'We have hog killing here,' Harding said.

Mistress Kitty sighed again.

'Ah, but it's not the same as when I was a child. It's not the same. I remember the smells of the smokehouse and all those hams and shoulders and sides of bacon.'

Mistress Kitty's voice echoed on and on in Regina's mind, with the woman's twisted grey face and bulging eye. In spite of the fact that looking after her had become more and more of a torment and her death a release, she still clung to the routines and the memory of how hard she had worked.

At one time she had even dressed and undressed Mistress Kitty but eventually she had excused herself from this task by explaining that she was burdened by so many other duties in the house and had not enough time. There had been some truth in this, of course. It was not just a case of supervising the slaves and seeing that they cleaned the house and served the meals properly. One day she would have the kitchen slaves trained to cook properly but as it was she had to do much of the cooking herself as Callie Mae, Flemintina, Minda and Infant were useless at anything more than the most basic of dishes and could not read the recipe books that she conscientiously studied. Then there were physics to make up, not only for Mistress Kitty but for the slaves as well. There were always slaves going down with some illness or other and Harding had told her that it was the duty of the mistress of any plantation to attend to sick slaves.

'But because my wife cannot fulfil this duty, it must fall on you,' he'd said.

The quarters were quite a distance beyond the other outbuildings and were separated and hidden from them and the big house by a thickly wooded area. But the stream that passed all the other buildings and kept the butter and cream in the spring-house cool and fresh also sparkled past the quarters. They consisted of rows of huts facing each other across a space of soil. At first she never ventured more than a step or two inside the doorway of any, her mouth twisting at the obnoxious smells, the untidiness, the droppings of fowl and ducks. Her hand twitched back her skirts from fleas and lice as she rapped orders at whoever in the family was well enough to look after the sick person.

Mistress Kitty, before her illness, had actually hurried along the path through the trees to the quarters as if she enjoyed the chore and the slaves crowded around her with equal eagerness to report the latest gossip about the progress or otherwise of her 'poor patients' as she called them.

When Regina went, silence cleared a path before her. The old man sitting in front of a hut scraping at a violin stopped playing. The barefooted children in short ragged shifts stopped dancing to the tune. Mothers in doorways dandling infants melted away into shadowy interiors.

She hated any contact with poverty. It was too painful a reminder of what she had suffered in Glasgow. But slaves cost a lot of money and, although it was Harding's money and not hers, she was still reluctant to waste it. She made the medicinal potions to the best of her ability and began issuing orders for the quarters to be kept clean and tidy and any sick people to be properly cared for.

No doubt Harding would be wasting quite a bit of money at the market in Williamsburg. At markets and fairs there was always plenty of cockfighting and bull-baiting and nigger-fighting to bet money on. Not to mention the games of cards and box and dice in the taverns.

Chapter 3

When the time came to go, it was decided that it would be more comfortable travelling on horseback. To travel in any sort of carriage was an ordeal. On some of the rough paths through the forest, even in open country, a carriage could be literally jolted to pieces or sucked deep into a swamp or crashed onto its side in a pothole. But Westminster was instructed to follow them with the wagon.

Setting out, Regina clopped at a leisurely pace behind Harding. She was dressed in a bottle-green riding-jacket shaped like a man's coat with large gold buttons and gold facings. The long buttoned waistcoat was green and the full petticoat yellow. She also wore leather gloves and a large, feather-fringed tricorne hat. Harding's muscular jackbooted legs gripped the sides of his horse from under a voluminous triple-caped riding-cloak. She twisted round towards the house before entering the forest, almost expecting to see Mistress Kitty as usual propped in a chair at her bedroom window like a lost soul in a haunted place. But there was no one there.

It was a golden autumn day and Regina took what pleasure she could in breathing in the leafy air. Falling leaves swooped and twirled and sparkled in the sun, and rustled and crackled under the horses' hooves. An earthy, mouldy smell clung thickly in her nostrils. Yet at the same time, a keen frosty tang sharpened other perfumes and enlivened the senses. Sounds vied with each other too, like an orchestra rich in unexpected changes of rhythm. Birds trilled, squawked, chirruped. Larger animals creaked cautiously through the undergrowth. Hogs rooted and grunted. Flights of wild pigeons clapped like thunder overhead, darkening the sky and snapping the limbs of trees when they landed. Dusk was beginning to settle and crickets chirped tirelessly. Fireflies began their rapid winking.

She was glad when Harding said, 'There's a clearing ahead.

There will be a house where we can seek shelter for the night.'

When they reached the edge of the clearing, Harding hailed in a loud voice:

'Hallo-o-o-o-o! The house!'

Then, as they slowly followed the wagon track winding among the stumps and half-burned log-piles, he repeated the call several times.

The cabin squatted in the shadow of mighty elm, hickory, ash and chestnut trees. Its walls consisted of hewn logs notched into one another at the corners. The cracks between them were stuffed with moss, sticks, straw and clay. It had a clapboard roof and a log chimney. Some hogs snorted together at one side of the door and at the other on a plank shelf were a basswood basin, a gourd of soft soap and another basin for drinking water from the wooden pail that sat below. A bare patch among the weeds showed where the soapy water had been thrown. A man stood at the front of the cabin and a woman was shading her eyes in the doorway trying to make out if she knew the visitors.

Harding dismounted and said,

'Harding's the name.' Then with a jerk of his head in Regina's direction, 'Mistress Chisholm. We seek shelter for the night. My slave can sleep beneath the wagon.'

The man scratched his beard, yellow-stained with tobacco.

'Dan'l Howell. And tha's m'old woman, Martha.'

The 'old woman' was no more than thirty but already she had lost her freshness, and hair that had once been glossy and golden now straggled in greasy strands around her face. Her skin had a parched look, and lines like wagon tracks criss-crossed it. A cluster of bare-bottom children dressed only in torn linen shirts appeared, clinging in timid confusion to her tattered homespun skirts. Brushing them off like flies, she stepped aside to allow Harding and Regina to enter the cabin. It was dark inside and the air was thick with the smell of wood-smoke from the fire and carrion from the fresh pelts drying on the wall. A spinning wheel, a table made of split slab supported by legs set in holes, and a few three-legged stools made in the same way, were the only articles of furniture. Two forks attached to a joist held a rifle and shot pouch. There was an iron kettle, a frying pan, a few pewter spoons and steel knives, some wooden trenchers and mugs, and that was all.

The poverty and discomfort of the place and the cold earthen floor reminded Regina of the home she had once shared with her mother and Gav in Tannery Wynd in Glasgow. Although at least there they had had what in Glasgow was known as a hole-in-the-wall bed. It had wooden shutters to keep out draughts and, huddled in it with her mother and Gav, with her mother's plaid tucked over them, they had been tolerably warm and comfortable.

Here there was no sign of a bed of any sort.

'You'll be awantin' supper. Cain' offer you much,' Martha said, already attacking the fire with a poke and thumping the frying pan on top of the embers.

'I will pay you well,' Harding said.

Daniel Howell spat on the earthen floor.

'We ain't askin' yo' to be payin'.'

Martha put pork to sizzle in the pan.

'But we ain't refusin' either,' she said.

As well as pork they had Indian corn that Martha had beaten in a hand mortar and then baked in the hearth as a hoecake. The food was washed down with home-made cider and, although nothing in comparison with what Regina had become used to at Forest Hall, the meal at least satisfied her hunger. But despite the food inside her, and the log fire crackling, she felt depressed and bitterly cold.

The cabin's one window had no glass or shutters and blasts of icy air sent shivers down her back. Cold breezes also beat in through loopholes cut to enable the settlers to shoot at attacking Indians. For a time a candle had been lit but it soon blew out and Martha did not light it again, explaining that there was no point in wasting the candles that she had taken so much time and trouble to make. The sensible thing to do was to sleep when it got dark and get up in God's own light.

This they did, all lying down like a flock of sheep on the floor in front of the fire.

Regina was disgusted. She lay listening to the squeaking of the rats in the rafters fighting to be heard against the howling

602

and creaking of the wind in the trees outside. Again she was reminded of her life in Glasgow and there was nothing she hated more than to be reminded of the horrors of that. The sound of the rats, the hardness of the floor, the bitter cold dragged her unwilling mind back to the time when Gav and she had slept on stairways with the beggar, Quin. In those days she had wakened in the morning almost too frozen to move and was forced to drag her stiff limbs about the streets begging filthy scraps to eat.

Never again would she allow herself to suffer such deprivation. She felt herself shaking as much with fear as with cold. Edging closer to Harding's mountainous back, she touched it to make sure that he was still there, that her life in Forest Hall wasn't just a dream.

Oh, the luxury of her four-poster bed there, the thick carpets, the glass windows, the elegant furniture, the crystal chandeliers and silver candelabra. Lying awake and shivering in the backwoods cabin, she experienced a sudden need to empty her bladder but willed herself to ignore it. She could not face rising in the fire-tinged dark and going outside to squat in the howling blackness of the forest. At Forest Hall there were chamber pots that fitted out of sight in commodes and the slaves emptied the pots every day. Still thinking about Forest Hall, she drifted in and out of restless sleep until daylight came to sweep away the dark.

Martha was up first and splashing water outside the open door. Soon she had ham and eggs sizzling in the frying pan and the smell of it cut through the less pleasant odours of animal pelts and human bodies. Regina felt stiff and aching and Harding had to help her up. She brushed down her clothes as best she could before going out to splash her face with water from the bucket and dab herself dry with her handkerchief. Her face was always pale and made a startling contrast to her ruby-coloured hair and emerald eyes, but today she was even paler than usual. Strain pulled at her eyes and mouth, giving her a hard, tense look. She could eat no breakfast, accepting only a few sips of milk, but she said a polite 'Thank you. Goodbye,' before taking leave of Martha and Daniel Howell.

On their way again, they passed a string of pack-horses and

peltry traders laden with brass kettles, rum, red lead for Indian face-paint, axes, gunpowder, lace hats for chiefs and small mirrors for young bucks to hang around their necks on rawhide lanyards.

Regina noticed that some of the traders had only one eye. Others had mutilated ears and noses and she was reminded that Daniel Howell had part of an ear missing.

She remarked on this to Harding and he said,

'There is a lot of rowdyism and fighting between backwoods people.'

'But how can they become so mutilated?'

'It's the custom to mutilate the loser in a fight by biting off his ear or nose or gouging out his eye. Sometimes they go as far as castration.'

'Barbarous,' Regina said. 'But then, most men are.'

Harding gave one of his abrupt humourless laughs then they clopped along in silence for a while with the wagon trundling along some distance behind. Westminster was singing quietly to himself:

> 'I've got a mother in de heaven
> Outshines de sun,
> I've got a father in de heaven
> Outshines de sun,
> I've got a sister in de heaven
> Outshines de sun,
> When we get to heaven, we will
> Outshine de sun,
> Way beyond the moon.'

Eventually Regina asked:

'What causes so much fighting? Do they become inflamed with drink?'

Harding shrugged.

'I've known fights to start over quite trivial matters. One has called the other a thick-skull, or a buckskin, or a Scotchman. Or one has mislaid the other's hat, or knocked an apple out of his hand, or offered him a dram without wiping the mouth of the bottle.'

'Fools,' Regina said.

The only other person they saw on their journey was a woman wearing nothing but a short gown, crouched on the log step of a cabin, smoking a pipe and viewing the nearby creek through a cloud of mosquitoes.

As they rode through the tall pine woods that led into Williamsburg, the sun spangled the branches and sent arrows of golden light shooting across their line of vision. Somewhere in the distance, Regina could hear the tinkle of a bell and despite the sunshine her body turned to ice.

'Is there something wrong?' Harding asked, noticing her pale stiff face.

She managed to shake her head. It would be a church bell or the handbell of a schoolmaster summoning the children to their lessons. The thought of children made her keenly aware of her pregnancy again. That was what was upsetting her. Being with child made one oversensitive and disturbed both physically and mentally.

Closing her eyes she allowed the horse to lead her along and tried not to listen to the faint, haunting chimes of the bell.

The coffle snaked slowly across the green, a black shadow on the landscape of white faces and multicoloured clothes. The line of men and women all spancelled together hobbled towards the auction platform. Some clutched a small assortment of belongings wrapped in a handkerchief or ragged piece of cloth. Others carried limp bundles on their heads. A few of the men had a bundle tied to a stick and slung over one shoulder. Others had no belongings at all, or just a small treasure like a broken comb, a cracked teacup or a scrap of coloured cloth small enough to hold in one hand. Several of the women nursed babies in their arms. Children, some hardly old enough to walk, trailed along, big-eyed with fear, or blank-faced with fatigue and confusion.

The coffle was herded to one side of the wooden platform, where the slaves stood in a tangled knot as if being as close together as possible afforded some comfort and protection. But a crowd of white people, mostly men, began separating them out and ordering them to strip off. Harding moved forward too and Regina, following him, said,

605

'What are you going to do?'

She felt agitated. The slaves she was in the habit of seeing were those belonging to Forest Hall and, even then, it was mostly just the few who worked in the house. They were well-fed and healthy-looking. Even the field slaves at Forest Hall did not have the frightened, vulnerable look of these pathetic creatures. Or, if they had, she'd never noticed it. But what shocked her more than anything was the way they were forced to strip off and allow the white men to handle and finger them.

'It's no use buying a pig in a poke,' Harding said. 'We've got to see what we're bidding for.'

In horror she watched a loose-mouthed, red-necked farmer fondle the small breasts of a girl of about twelve. Then the man's horny fingers began probing between the girl's legs. All the time a little boy was clinging to her arm.

The girl and boy were obviously brother and sister, and they reminded Regina of herself and Gav at that age. There was something about the girl's stiff silence and the boy's mop of curls.

Memories too of the time she had been molested and raped rampaged back. Pushed and jostled in the eager, busy crowd, she felt sick and panic-stricken. All around her, white hands were sliding over black skin, were cupping testicles, or breasts, were spreading buttocks. Voices crowded in on her too.

'Shuck down your britches . . . Shuck off that dress . . . This looks a prime buck . . . well muscled . . . heavy-hung . . . Here's a prime wench . . . well titted out . . . Run catch that stick, boy . . .'

Suddenly the auctioneer was banging his gavel on the table up on the platform and the sale was ready to begin.

'Bring on the youngest saplings first,' he shouted.

Another white man grabbed one of the children and hauled her onto the platform. She was a little girl of about three, dressed only in a ragged shirt that barely reached her buttocks. The man jerked it off, leaving her naked. The auctioneer shouted.

'Rosabell, out of Sally by Tom. Fair percentage of human blood from dam who is octoroon. What am I bid, gentlemen?'

Harding made no bid for the child who was sold eventually to a giant of a man with one eye and a beard like a prickly bush.

When the brother and sister climbed onto the platform, Regina said,

'I want them.'

Harding stared round in surprise.

'Why?'

'I need servants young enough to train for house duties.'

The auctioneer was saying,

'Lunesta and Little Sam. Can be sold together or separately. Both out of Violet, sired by Joseph. Royal Hausa, and some human blood from sire.'

'There's plenty running about the quarters,' Harding said.

'I want those two.'

'All right, buy them yourself.'

His voice was like a blow on the face. She winced but replied coolly, 'I don't know how to bid.'

He shrugged.

'Then you're not going to get them.'

The bidding had started and she glanced around, face stiff, heart palpitating with distress. Eventually she signalled by raising her hand but a man a few yards away brandished a newspaper at the auctioneer and the price immediately jumped. She raised her hand again. This time a man twirled his cane and the price took another brisk leap upwards. She continued to signal, terrified by the price but determined not to be beaten.

Eventually the auctioneer's hammer came down.

'Sold to the lady with the red hair.'

Then the sale went on.

'Angelina, prime dam, with six month old sucker called Lizzie . . .'

She waited until Harding had purchased his slaves then she strolled with him back to the Raleigh Tavern where they were staying the night. She passed the printer's house, the storehouse, the milliner's shop and the silversmith's, without noticing any of them. She was not even aware of the scent of roses from the gardens of the houses or the singing sound of the trees. She was not only feeling emotionally distressed, she was suffering physically as well. Waves of sickness and nausea kept rising inside her and it took all her energy and will-power to fight them down. She wished there was someone who cared about her and to whom she could turn for advice and help but there was no one.

Mistress Kitty had been kind and generous and the memory of her affection and generosity came back like a pain. She hated Harding but she had never hated Mistress Kitty. As far as she was aware she had never uttered one unkind word to the older woman. She realized that Mistress Kitty had always had an affection for her and this she had secretly treasured. The only other people in her life who had ever shown any feeling for her were her mother and Gav. Her mother had long ago disappeared and Gav had gone out of her life too. His love had been stolen by somebody else. Mistress Kitty's love had been like a solitary flame in the wilderness of her life. She had not wanted it extinguished.

She could eat no supper in the Raleigh Tavern that night and Harding eyed her curiously but said nothing.

The next day they set off for home. Harding had purchased several slaves, both men and women, and of course there were the two children that Regina had bought. All of them were packed into the wagon, and Harding and Regina rode ahead of it.

It was good to see Forest Hall again because it now indeed meant 'home' to her. She didn't care that it had no formal garden or lawn like some plantation mansions. She liked its strange wild look and the unexpected luminosity of it that glimmered from among the trees.

Westminster drove the wagon along the path that wound round the right hand side of the house, then round the back to the left and down past the storehouses to the barns and stables. The storehouses and office and overseer's house ran down the left edge of the path and faced onto it. But the barns and stables were some way over on the right and backed onto the woods. They faced the rear of the big house, or what could be seen of it from that distance through the trees and stumps and long grass.

Westminster stopped the wagon at the stables, unloaded the slaves and left Matthew, the stable boy, to attend to the horses

608

and wagon while he led the new slaves further along the path through the woods at the back of the stables until they came to the quarters.

By this time Harding and Regina had entered the house and Joseph had taken charge of the horses they had been riding.

Halfway up the stairs on the way to her bedroom Regina stopped and called back to Old Abe:

'Westminster's at the quarters. Send someone to tell him to bring the new slaves, Lunesta and Little Sam, up to the house.'

'Yes, Miss Chisholm, ma'am.'

The stairway curved gracefully into an open landing on either side. She turned left until she came to the room at the end. Then she stopped. Automatically she had made straight for Mistress Kitty's room and for a moment, standing there gripping the door-handle, she really believed that if she opened the door she would see Mistress Kitty propped up in bed, eager to welcome her with the monstrous smile that screwed up one side of her face and bulged one eye.

'Oh, Regina, Regina, my dear,' she'd say, clasping her hands underneath her chin in delight. 'Poor little me's so pleased to see you, so pleased to see you. Tell me all about Williamsburg, do.'

And she'd reply:

'We had a very successful time. We bought fine horses and several slaves. And amber beads for you and a pretty fan and some silks and velvets . . . But wait, I'll send Jenny for a hot drink for both of us and after I go to my room and take off my coat and wash my face and hands I'll come back and we will have a long talk . . .'

It seemed incredible that Mistress Kitty's room, when she slowly creaked open the door, lay neat and clean and empty.

Regina took a deep breath and turned away. She tried to tell herself that she was being ridiculous. She had never felt that she needed anyone before. And anyway there were still Gav and Abigail and now their twin children Bette and Jethro. But she only saw them very occasionally. The journey to the settlement was a long and arduous one and could not be taken during the winter, for the tobacco road could be a dangerous quagmire. In the spring also, when the freshets came rushing down from the hills, overflowing the rivers and flooding the lands, it was sometimes impossible to travel. She remembered in Glasgow the River Clyde sometimes overflowed its banks and flooded the lower parts of the city around the Briggait, the foot of Stockwell Street, Saltmarket Street and the Green. On these occasions she and Gav could not go to school. But that was nothing to the devastating Virginian freshets.

The autumn was usually the best time for the journey to the settlement and she had gone with Harding when he went to the store on business. She had stayed at the tavern overnight, however. She had no desire to pig it with Gav and his family in their tiny two-roomed cabin. But she had drunk tea with them and Abigail had treated her civilly, although she suspected that Gav's wife had no great liking for her. The children were much too young as yet to appreciate the presents she brought. Not only did she take fancy sweetmeats which she had cooked herself, but expensive toys she made a point of purchasing for them when she visited Williamsburg.

This time she had bought Jethro a drum and a soldier's hat and Bette a beautiful little silk gown. The gown had been a mistake, she realized now. By the time she saw the child again, she might have outgrown it.

In her own room she went over to the pier glass and stared at the ashen face in its fiery frame. It was all Gav's fault. They should have been together on their own plantation. He should have kept his promise. If they had been together in their own home, on their own plantation, she would not be here in Forest Hall now. She would not have Harding's child inside her. She would not be having nightmares about Mistress Kitty.

Chapter 4

It had rained so constantly in the past few days that living in Glasgow had become like living at the bottom of a pond. Not a heavy downpour battering and shaking windows and roofs, but a steady drizzle like a cloud of fog enshrouded the Tolbooth and the surrounding tenements, blurring outlines, blackening windows, making the roads a bog of mud and giving a dismal appearance to the city.

Hardly a soul ventured out. Not even a caddie could be seen to run an errand or fetch a sedan chair. Annabella had to send Betsy to the well for drinking water and the girl returned miserably shivering with her towsy hair like cobwebs sticking across her face. Her large eyes overflowed with rain that dribbled down her face and neck.

'Don't stand there looking so sorry for yourself,' Annabella scolded. 'Go and get dry at the kitchen fire.'

Later she'd gone through to the kitchen to find Betsy crouched beside the fire in a cloud of steam.

'You stupid girl.' Annabella snatched a wooden spoon from the table and flung it, scoring a direct hit on Betsy's back. The girl howled out in pain.

'I couldn't help it, Mistress Annabella. I didn't mean it.'

Annabella rolled her eyes.

'What are you bleating on about now?'

'Whatever it is I've done wrong, Mistress Annabella. Oh, I didn't mean it. I didn't mean to do wrong! May the Good Lord Jesus be my judge.'

'Never mind bringing the Good Lord Jesus into it. Haven't you enough sense of your own to take your gown off to dry it and give yourself a rub down with a towel? No wonder you're forever sniffling and streaming with colds. And don't clasp your hands like that as if you're down on your knees praying.'

Betsy crumpled forward in a spate of sobs, burying her face

in her lap, rolling backwards and forwards like a ball with a wet tangle of hair sticking out in front. It was as much as Annabella could do to prevent herself from giving the ball a good kick. What controlled the impulse more than anything was the idea that Betsy, in her own infuriating way, would be pleased to get a kicking. Betsy liked any excuse for a broken-hearted howl and weep.

Annabella stamped her foot instead.

'Stop that infernal blubbering. You'll drown in your own self-pity one of these days. Big John's down at the stables. Go and tell him to saddle up my horse.'

'Oh, Mistress Annabella!' Betsy unrolled and clasped her hands again. 'You're surely not going out in all this wet? The roads are thick with mud. I'm all black and sticky with it right up past my ankles.'

'I am not in the least surprised to hear it, Betsy. Your filthy footprints are all over the floor. And I am mightily glad that Mistress Griselle has invited Mungo and me for tea today. What with the wretched rain and your long-visaged melancholy appearance, I feel quite cast down. Hurry now. Go and do as you're told. Mungo can share my saddle.'

'What about me?'

'Oh, you can stay moping by the fire, if you wish. But don't fall asleep and let it go out, do you hear?'

'Oh, God save us, you'll catch your death, and poor wee Mungo. Oh, the poor wee soul.'

She started rocking and weeping again.

'Gracious heavens,' Annabella cried out. 'Must I kick you down the stairs before you will go and do as you're bid? I am away to put on my cloak.'

Mungo was waiting in his double-caped coat and three-cornered hat. He looked quite grown-up for his eight years. His cousin, George, was a year older but looked much more delicate and immature. The boys got on well together, however, and Mungo was glad of his company. He missed his friends in Williamsburg and as he had not yet started school in Glasgow the opportunity had not arisen to make new friends.

'I have made some sweetmeats,' Annabella told him. 'You

can take them as a present to your cousin.'

'Thank you, Mother.' He lifted the box from the table, tucked it under his arm and stood watching Annabella fasten her cape and pull the hood well forward over her hair.

On an impulse, she dropped a kiss on his brow. Sometimes she felt so proud of the sturdy little figure with the brown eyes and dark straight hair, she could not resist indulging in a quick kiss or hug. She struggled not to pet the child too much and spoil him, though. Griselle had coddled and ruined poor George. Apparently she even insisted on a sedan chair to carry George to and from the grammar school. There would be none of that nonsense for Mungo. Mungo would have to fend for himself outside and inside of school, and school could be tough. She remembered only too well her own struggles to survive the torments of a bullying dominie whose tawse seemed an appendage of himself. She did not recall ever seeing the man without this instrument of torture in his hand.

Childhood was the proving ground for adult life and only the sturdiest in body and spirit survived.

'Come away, then,' she said. 'I'm ready and willing to brace the infernal weather if you are, sir.'

He preceded her down the tower stair, clearing a path for her through the beggars and orphans who huddled together for shelter on every step. He took pleasure in shouting and kicking at them as he had seen his grandfather doing.

'Out of the way, you filthy dogs. Make a path for Mistress Blackadder.'

'Wait!' she commanded when they reached the foot of the stairs. 'There's no point in wading through all that monstrous mud if we can avoid it. Betsy!' Shading her eyes with a gloved hand she shouted to the blur beginning to take shape through the Scotch mist. 'Tell Big John to bring the horse across here.'

They waited until the animal, led by Big John, came whinnying and sidling about in protest at being dragged from the warm stable into the cold. Steam rose from its silver and grey flanks and spouted from its nostrils and the smell of the stables still clung.

Annabella patted it.

613

'Steady, boy.'

After she had mounted with a swirl and puff of cloak and skirts, she ordered Big John to lift Mungo up beside her. They set off at a trot with mud spattering high all around. Vagrants sheltering in other back stairs off the courtyard peered out to see what was happening but shrank hastily back from the fountain of mud as the horse splashed past.

Annabella was glad of the warmth and protection of Mungo's body against hers but she did not lower her head to hide her face from the wet. Rain, she had heard, was good for the complexion and it certainly gave the skin a tingling sensation that was most exhilarating. Once through the close and out onto Saltmarket Street, she jerked and kicked the horse to the right and they went galloping down towards the river.

'Whee!' she squealed and Mungo laughed along with her. George would have not only been frightened at the reckless speed but horrified by the filth spraying up and spoiling their clothes. George was a nervous and fastidious boy.

Annabella reined in the horse when they came to Gibson's Land, the tenement in which her brother Douglas and Griselle lived. It was a stately building standing on pillars and entry was through arches into a courtyard and stairways at the back. At Douglas's stair she tied the horse to the hitching post, then bunching up her skirts, she called,

'Race you upstairs.'

Griselle's flat was on the first floor, but even so Annabella was breathless when she reached it and it took her a moment or two before she could regain her composure.

Griselle looked affronted.

'What a way for a lady to behave. And in front of the child too. Will you never learn, Annabella? Look at you, soaking wet and covered in mud. And look at the child. He'll catch his death.'

'We both will,' Annabella managed to gasp, 'if you keep us standing out here in the draughty landing.'

'Tuts. You've got me so fluttered. Come away in.'

A fire was merrily dancing in the bedroom. It tossed yellow light about the ceiling and walls making the candlesticks, the four-poster bed, the long pier glass, the table and chairs all appear to jig about too.

Annabella made straight for the fire, swinging off her cloak and throwing it to Griselle's servant.

'I always think this is a prodigiously lovely room, Griselle. The ceiling is as low as ours but it is so much bigger and better proportioned in every other way. And I do admire your paintings. It is damnable of Papa not to allow me to have paintings in our house. He insists they are frivolous and works of the devil. The devil choke him!'

'Annabella!' Griselle's purple cheeks paled. 'You'll be punished for speaking in so wicked a manner.'

Douglas rose from his seat at the table and came to greet his sister, one hand daintily outstretched and the other patting his high-fronted wig. At the same time, he said to his wife,

'No need to get into such a tither, Grizzie. My dear saucebox of a sister will be perfectly all right. I dare swear she's in league with the devil.'

Annabella raised her hand for his kiss.

'What keeps you indoors today, brother? Should you not be with Papa in the counting house?'

He sighed and plucked a lace-edged handkerchief from his frilly cuff. Dabbing it to his nose, he said,

'Alas, I had the makings of a cold this morning and did not think it wise to venture out.'

'Fiddlesticks and poppycock! You just did not want the rain to wash off your monstrous face paint.'

Flicking his handkerchief at her, he turned away.

'Pshaw! You imagine yourself a woman of fashion. Yet you do not know that it is all the rage in England for men to wear powder and paint. Ladies too. So what do you think of that?'

'I don't care a fig what they do in England. I do what I like, and I do not like face paint. I think it looks clownish.'

'All right, all right, my cockie. But I'm not the only one in Scotland to paint my face, you know.'

'Oh, yes,' said Annabella. 'You mean some of your gamester friends. I don't admire their painted faces either, but I have always thought it cruelly unfair of Papa never to allow me to attend the gaming tables. I have missed much excitement in life

615

by being so confined.'

Griselle said,

'The diversion of cards and dice, however engaging, Annabella, are more often provocations to avarice and loss of temper than mere recreation and innocent amusement. If it were not for the fact that we meet so many of the landed gentry at the tables, we wouldn't attend. Did I tell you that we've been invited to stay for a few days at my Lord Knox's estate?'

'No!' Annabella was suitably impressed. 'I wonder if I dare risk the tables now that I am a widow. Papa has no right to stop me. I'm neither a child nor an innocent young girl any more.'

Douglas sighed.

'Dear Annabella, I would not advise it in your case. I would be on Papa's side in this. You are a person of such extremes, I fear the cards would be your ruination.'

'Fiddlesticks! What possible harm could a game of cards do to me?'

'Sister dear, there is nothing that wears out a fine face like too many indulgences at the card tables and the cutting passions which attend them.'

Annabella laughed. 'Passions, indeed!'

'It is true. People become worn out with the passions of the tables. So many female gamesters have hollow eyes, haggard looks and pale complexions and I have known women to be carried out half-dead. I have seen a woman of quality gliding by in her sedan-chair at two o'clock in the morning like a spectre in a flare of flambeaux.'

'Gracious heavens!'

'Overindulgence in anything is a sin,' Griselle said. 'You'll take a drink of tea, Annabella?'

'Indeed yes, I would enjoy a cup, Grizzie.'

As she poured tea into the delicate china cups, Griselle said to Mungo,

'Strip off your wet shoes and stockings and breeches, Mungo. George, give him your dressing-gown before he gets his death of cold.'

'I am perfectly fit, Mistress Ramsay,' Mungo said, 'and not in the least cold.'

Griselle bristled.

'You watch your impertinent tongue, young sir. Go at once and do as you're told.' Then to Annabella, 'Mr Blackadder would never have allowed him to speak like that.'

'He was only telling the truth. Oh, Grizzie, you have made your delicious almond biscuits.'

Griselle's mouth quivered with pleasure.

'Yes, I do make a good biscuit.' She arranged herself neatly on a chair and began pouring milk into cups and handing them around. 'Douglas, stop fiddling with your cuffs and pass your sister the biscuit plate. And you'll not taste a better gingerbread than that one anywhere in Glasgow, Annabella.'

Annabella munched at a crisp nutty confection, then after a sip or two of tea, helped herself to another one.

'Phemy and her daughter did not come, then?'

'Of course not.'

'I seem fated not to meet that child.'

Douglas dabbed at the corner of his mouth with his froth of lace handkerchief.

'She's a fine girlie.'

'I didn't expect her to arrive when I saw what the weather was like,' Griselle said. 'Little Jemima's a delicate child. Only the likes of you would behave in so rash a manner, Annabella. Not one with any sense would put a foot outside their doors on such a day. Oh, there you are, boys. That's better, Mungo. It's a little tight across the shoulders and somewhat short for you, but it'll do. Wrap it over and tie it properly, then come over by the fire and have some tea.' Then turning to Annabella, she added in an accusing tone, 'That boy's built like an ox.'

Annabella laughed.

'Rather a small one, Grizzie.'

'Mr Blackadder was such a thin, delicate-made man.'

'Oh, good gracious alive, Mr Blackadder might have been thin but he was prodigiously tough all the same.'

'Not tough enough to survive Virginia,' Griselle observed acidly. 'That poor man should never have been dragged out to that heathen place.'

'That's why he wanted to go. Because he believed there were

617

so many souls to be saved. And he wasn't dragged.'

'Did Papa really venture out to the counting house?' Douglas asked.

'Of course! He is made of sterner stuff than you, brother. I've said it before and I say it again. Mungo takes after him.'

'Tuts, on such a day it wasn't wise, Annabella. The rain shows no sign of letting up and it'll be dark by the time he returns and dreadful underfoot.'

Annabella shrugged and helped herself to a piece of gingerbread.

'I dare say he's been out on rainy days before.'

'Eat up, boys.' Griselle gazed fondly at George then patted his head. 'Have another biscuit, Geordie.'

'Yes, Mama.' George waited until the grown-ups weren't looking before popping a whole biscuit into his mouth. Mungo chuckled in appreciation at the bulging-eyed antics of his long-necked cousin. Then he followed suit by stuffing a whole biscuit into his mouth. Unfortunately, everyone's attention was on him when he did it. Annabella gave him a smart clip across his face that left one ear scarlet and stinging and made bits of biscuit all but choke him by jerking down his throat. George could hardly contain his giggles.

'I must ask you to remember your manners, sir,' Annabella said. 'You put me quite out of countenance with your behaviour.'

'When is he starting the school?' Griselle inquired.

'I'll take him on Monday. I was giving him the chance to see Glasgow first so that he could find his way around and not get lost.'

'Aye, bairns are disappearing too often these days and it's not with getting lost. They're kidnapped by beggars and gypsies.'

Mungo glowered.

'Beggars or gypsies better not dare touch me. I'll soon send them packing with a flea in their ear.'

Douglas nibbled at a biscuit, his scarlet lips puckering greasily.

'Dear sister. He sounds just like you.'

'He'll be none the worse for that, sir.'

Griselle went to the door and called to her maid to come and light a candle.

'See how dark it's getting already,' she remarked returning to her seat by the fire. 'You're always welcome, as you know, Annabella, but you were very foolish to come today. You haven't even brought a lantern.'

Douglas fluttered his handkerchief under his nose.

'I will, of course, give you the use of a lantern, Annabella, but I regret I cannot accompany you safely home. Not in, my condition. I feel like the ghost of a dead dog.'

'Oh, good gracious alive!' Annabella laughed. 'We live in the same street. I just need to point the horse in the right direction. There's no danger of passing our close either because there's always candles and lanterns in the windows and the Old Coffee House lighting up the entrance.'

Mungo and George went over to the other side of the room to play and their recurrent laughter made a pleasant background.

'That's a particularly handsome likeness of you.' Annabella gazed up at the portrait of Griselle that hung above the mantelpiece. It was very serious, of course, but then Griselle seldom smiled.

Griselle tutted in annoyance.

'I wish I'd worn my cherry velvet instead of that lavender silk.'

'You suit the lavender gown very well. Tell me, what kind of dancing assemblies have you been having? Is the Widow Aberdour still hale and hearty?'

'Haven't you heard?' Griselle jerked her chair closer in preparation for an enjoyable gossip.

The fire's scarlet glow reflected on the three figures grouped round it. It sent port wine shadows smoothing out behind them as they talked undisturbed by the candles slowly nodding their yellow heads in the draught at the other side of the room.

At last Annabella said,

'Papa will be home soon and expecting his supper. I had better go. Is it still raining, do you think?'

Griselle jerked her head towards the window.

'Listen to it. It's coming down harder than ever.'

'Ah, well!' Annabella bounced lightly to her feet snapping shut her fan. 'There's no use moping about it. Mungo, get your

619

breeches on and look sharp about it.'

'Och, Mother . . .'

'Mungo!'

'If the child wants to stay, let him,' Griselle said. 'He'll be company for George and it's a pity for him to get soaked again.'

Annabella hesitated.

'Please, please, Aunt Annabella,' George pleaded, bulging-eyed and thin-necked like a fragile young giraffe.

'Oh, all right.'

The boys hopped about hugging one another in delight while Griselle called to the maid to bring Annabella's cloak and a lantern.

'I'll bring it back tomorrow,' Annabella said, 'and I can collect Mungo at the same time.'

'Very well. Tell your father I was asking kindly for him.'

Douglas dropped a kiss on Annabella's brow.

'And you will explain to him about my regrettable indisposition, won't you, dear saucebox?'

'I will do my best.'

They carried candles with them to see her to the front door and then, before she said goodbye and stepped out onto the pitch black landing, Douglas lit the lantern for her with one of the candles.

'Goodbye, Mungo,' she called just before the door closed behind her.

The lantern-light seesawing back and forth revealed huddles of ragged people crouched in corners neither sleeping nor talking. She picked her way down the stairs to where she could hear her horse nervously whinnying. Then suddenly, just as she reached the last few steps, she was astonished to feel water lapping at her ankles. It seemed incredible that it could have rained so much while she had been with Douglas and Griselle. She had an urge to hasten back up and tell them but she controlled the impulse. After all, there was nothing Douglas or Griselle could do. And it would only make them worry about her all the more.

Her shoes and stockings would be ruined, not to mention her petticoats before she even reached the horse but once mounted she would manage home all right. Hitching up her skirts at the same time as trying to keep a grip of the lantern, she gingerly descended the remaining steps.

Outside of Glasgow, Donald McPhee, the shepherd, peered from his cottage window. The cottage was perched on top of a steep bank on one side of the river. Across the other side were the fields in which his sheep grazed and rising from them the hills that encircled the whole valley. The river snaked this way and that, sometimes looping around clusters of trees that dipped low across the water as if they were drinking from it. Sometimes it disappeared among the overlapping bulk of the hills. But tonight Donald saw by the light of the moon and by the occasional flash of lightning that the river had no shape any more. All the land glittered darkly with water.

'I'd better try and get the sheep across,' he told his wife.

She wrapped her plaid over her head and round her shoulders and lifted the lantern without saying anything.

Immediately they stepped outside the wind attacked them, tugging and tearing at their clothes like a mad dog and pelting them with rain, spasmodically, viciously.

'Hold the lantern up,' Donald roared in competition with the high-pitched raving of the wind and the echoing cracks of thunder.

The lantern's puny flicker did little to help guide them to the path that led down to the bridge. But clouds scudding across the moon sent flashes of silver to light up the narrow wooden structure and the swollen river foaming across it. Over at the other side sheep were standing knee deep in water bleating miserably. The bridge shivered under Donald's feet and, keeping a cautious hold of the hand rail, he forced a path across it.

On the other side he waded over to where the sheep were bunched. But as soon as he reached them and made to grab one they all scattered out in panic. Cursing, he splashed forward and made another lunge. This time he managed to get a grip of one and haul it back. Floundering about he at last succeeded in lifting the struggling animal and stumbled with it towards the bridge.

The return journey was even worse. He couldn't get a grip of the rail because of the weight of the struggling animal he was carrying but he managed to stagger back and fling the sheep down. His wife then chased it up the bank onto the high road behind the cottage. Stopping to regain his breath, he returned for the next one.

To and fro he went until his clothes hung heavy on him with water and the river like a monster raged louder and louder over the bridge and round his legs. Each time he went back to the meadow the water there seemed deeper, making his task more difficult.

It was on one of his return journeys that he thought he saw his wife waving and signalling to him. He thought he heard her shouting too. But he could not be certain. It could have been the wind playing tricks with her plaid, and giving one of its high-pitched screeches. Then, before he could think any more, a towering wall of water, grotesquely spiked with tree-trunks, thundered on top of him. He was engulfed in a crescendo of noise. The bridge flew from beneath his feet. He was plunged into the torrent to be whirled and tossed about and rushed along with the flotsam and the flood towards the town.

Adam Ramsay had retreated to the stairs of his counting house where he stood moodily waiting for his clerk to bring one of the small boats tied down by the riverside. He wondered if the water had reached Saltmarket Street and seeped into cellars and warehouses and ruined the tobacco and other precious commodities stored there. Something would have to be done about the river. It would have to be deepened, dykes would have to be built, some way would have to be found to prevent flooding of the southern streets of the city.

Usually it never reached as far as his home and warehouse at the Trongate corner of Saltmarket Street. But his counting house, the other buildings in the Briggait and those at the foot of Stockwell and Saltmarket Street had been awash more than once before. And many a cow and sheep had been drowned on the Green. One or two humans as well.

He thumped his hands behind his back and thrust his

bewigged head aggressively forward. Where was that fool of a clerk? It was getting dark and not a candle lit to guide his path down the stairs. Water kept lapping gently, monotonously.

'Sanny Crompton!' he suddenly shouted. 'Where the hell are you? I didn't send you to build the bloody boat!'

'Coming, maister, coming,' a distraught voice answered. 'But it's no' easy. It's worse than you think out here. There's a wind birling me about like a peerie.'

'You've oars, haven't you?' Ramsay bawled. 'Row, damn you, and be quick about it.'

Suddenly the boat skimmed into view and rammed noisily against the stairs on which Ramsay was standing. It splashed filthy water up over his shoes and breeches and made him roar out again.

'What the hell . . . ? I'll have a few words to say to you tomorrow, sir. By God I will.'

The clerk hobbled about trying to help Ramsay into the boat.

'Och, it's a terrible night, just terrible.'

'We've had floodings before. Stop your whining, man.'

However, he couldn't help being worried by the fact that it was still raining and he was somewhat disconcerted to see that the water had reached the Trongate end of Saltmarket Street although it wasn't quite deep enough to float the boat into the back close. At least not with the weight of Sanny and him in it.

He climbed out cursing furiously at the discomfort of icy water lapping up his legs.

'Well, don't just sit there gawping,' he told the other man. 'Get out and shove it to the foot of the stairs and secure it to the hitching post, or better still, heave it into the tower to keep it dry. If the rain goes on like this, it could fill the boat by morning. After you see to the boat, get away home.'

Sanny lived up the High Street and well away from any danger or discomfort from the river.

The wind was singing a sad song inside the tower stair as he squelched his way up in the dark. Vagrants were huddled back against the walls. He couldn't see them but he could hear them chittering with the cold. Somewhere among them a child wept.

He tirled the door-pin, then waited impatiently in the pitch black landing. Straining his ears for Betsy or Big John's feet in the lobby, all he could hear was the whispering in the stairs behind him and somewhere nearer the busy squeaking of rats. Then, as if from far off, Annabella's voice called:

'Betsy, where the hell are you? Open the door at once.'

He couldn't think why Annabella kept Betsy as a servant. The girl was always howling and crying or getting into panics. Either that or she was curling up in front of the fire and falling asleep. Sometimes he wondered if Annabella was as perjink and unconcerned as she made herself out to be. She often raged at Betsy but in actual fact she was far too soft with the girl. Betsy was supposed to cook all the food but as far as he could see, Annabella did most of the cooking herself. She should have been flung out on the streets long ago. Any servant living under his roof, using his candles, eating his food, had to work for their keep. He'd had to work hard all his life. Nobody had given him anything for nothing. He suddenly battered at the door with his fist.

'Betsy, damn ye!'

Her high-pitched wail came trailing from the direction of the kitchen and grew louder as it reached the door. As soon as it creaked open a crack, he punched it wide, nearly knocking both Betsy and her candle to the floor. An amber glow from his daughter's bedroom guided him towards it. The claret-coloured curtains and bed-drapes were drawn and a fire flung out orange flames of light over the japanned pier glass, picking out its raised figures of peacocks and flowers. It reddened the mahogany of the highboy too and made the gold drawer handles gleam. One candle would have been all that was required to add to the fire's brightness. Yet Annabella was sitting calmly stitching at her embroidery with a candelabra holding three candles on the table in the centre of the room. Another candelabra stood on the tea-table beside the bed.

'You'd think this was an assembly hall,' he protested indignantly. 'Candles cost money, mistress. And don't you forget it.'

'You're very late, Papa.'

'Do you wonder, in weather like this?'

'Is it still raining, then?'

'I had to come home in a bloody boat.'

She looked up.

'Lord's sake, it's not as bad as that, surely?'

'Are you calling me a liar?'

Putting aside her embroidery she rustled to her feet and went over to peer out the window. When she opened the curtains she immediately felt an icy dampness from the glass. Moonlight and the occasional lantern of a passer-by revealed Trongate Street to be clouded with rain and a quagmire underfoot.

Her father said,

'Not there. Saltmarket Street and further down by the river. The counting house must be near waist deep by now.'

'It's a good thing that Douglas's place is one up.'

'Aye. If the water splashed into his place he'd be as much use at saving his furniture or his family as that blubbering fool of a lassie through there.'

'Gracious heavens, I hope it doesn't get any worse.'

'Aye. I'm away through to take these wet shoes and breeches off and get into my dressing-gown. See that my food's on the table by the time I get back.'

After he left the room she plucked aside the curtains of the other window and tried to get a good look at Saltmarket Street. But there were no lanterns there and the moon kept playing hide and seek. She caught brief glimpses of the grey outline of buildings opposite silhouetted against a smoky sky. Then darkness. Sometimes the moon reflected in water sending icicle fingers pointing down the street. How much water there was she found it difficult to judge. There might only be a few inches. Or it could be a couple of feet deep. Picking up a candelabra, she went through to the kitchen trying to squash the uneasiness she was beginning to feel.

'What are you sitting there for? You lazy slut. Get the food through to the table. And where's Big John?'

Betsy's eyes filled and a tremor attacked her lips.

'He went to see to the horses. Said they'd be feart and restless. I'm feart as well, mistress.'

Annabella rolled her eyes.

'You're always the same. What are you afraid of now?'

'The river's lapping about the streets.'

'Well, just think yourself lucky you're not out there. Now get the dinner on the table. Don't have me telling you again.'

No sooner had she returned to the bedroom than her father entered. He had removed his long curly wig and was wearing a dark blue nightcap over his shaved head. A royal blue dressing-gown braided with gold was wrapped around his tall frame and cloth slippers had replaced his buckled shoes.

'Where's Mungo?' he said.

'He wanted to stay with his cousin. I'll collect him and bring him home tomorrow.'

'If I'd known you'd been so foolish I would have collected the lad and brought him back with me in the boat.'

Annabella hesitated.

'Do you think I ought to go and fetch him?'

'The bairn will be in bed by now. Dragging him out at this time of night would do more harm than good. You should never have left him there. Now he's missed the reading. I doubt if Douglas even sees to his family's prayers.'

'It's not missing the reading and prayers I'm worried about, Papa.'

'Oh, aye, I can believe that. You've never been much concerned with the word o' the Lord. But He'll catch up with you yet. In His righteous wrath, He'll strike you down. For all the wicked things you've said and done in your life, the Lord God will . . .'

'Papa, the Saltmarket's a slope, isn't it?' she interrupted impatiently.

'It's got a wee bit of a slope, aye.'

'So the water will be deeper at Douglas's end.'

'The water would have to rise ten feet or more to flood their place, woman.'

Betsy came snivelling in with a steaming tureen of soup and laid it on the table. Then she stood wiping at her nose and eyes with her sleeve.

'Go and bring the mutton and the chicken pie, then,' Annabella said. 'You've only got the soup, the salmon and the oatcakes here.'

626

She settled herself opposite her father at the table.

'Yes, of course, Papa; It couldn't possibly do that.'

She ate her soup daintily. No more was said. The fire crackled occasionally through the silence. Then there was the hoarse craw-craw of the door-pin.

'That'll be Big John,' she said.

A few minutes passed, then both Betsy and Big John came through, each carrying platters of food which they placed on the table.

'I've taken the horses up to Alick's stables,' Big John said. 'They didn't like the water lickin' round their legs.'

'Aye, the Lord has opened up His heavens tonight,' Ramsay said, smacking his lips over his soup.

Annabella cried out.

'Pox on you, Big John! You're dripping water all over the floor. Away through to the kitchen and get your dinner.'

'Yes, mistress.'

'He's brought a cold wind in with him too,' she added, shivering.

'Eat up your soup,' her father said. He poured himself a generous glass of claret and drank deeply at it before attacking the pie.

Afterwards he had a leisurely pipe by the fire. Finally came the reading and the prayer.

'God is our refuge and our strength, a very present help in trouble. Therefore, will we not fear, though the earth be removed and though the mountains be carried into the midst of the sea; though the waters thereof roar and be troubled, though the mountains shake with the swelling thereof. Selah . . . be still and know that I am God . . . The Lord of hosts is with us . . . the God of Jacob is our refuge. Selah . . .'

Annabella listened uneasily to the wind beginning to bluster outside and later, lying in the hole-in-the-wall bed watching the fire's red glow in the darkness, she could not sleep for the rattling of the windows. She must have drifted off eventually because she woke with a start. The fire had gone out and the darkness would have been complete had she not opened the curtains before retiring. Faint glimmers of moonlight freckling the rain made

627

fast moving patterns on floors and walls. The windows were still rattling but it was not the wind that had wakened her. Listening intently she scrambled out of bed. Yes, there it was again. People were shouting for help. She sped across to the window.

'Gracious heavens!' she cried out loud. 'Papa, Papa! Betsy! Big John!'

Saltmarket Street had disappeared beneath a torrent of water. The piazzas, the warerooms, the bottom flats of the tenements were awash and people were struggling waist deep in water to reach the High Street. Tables and chairs were being swept along. The body of a sheep floated past.

In vast alarm she turned away. Her father, like a ghost in his long white nightshirt, was standing in the bedroom doorway holding a candle high.

'Papa, tell Big John to get the boat ready,' she said. 'I must go for Mungo.'

Chapter 5

Douglas hadn't been able to sleep. He lay trying not to listen to the rain beating against the windows and the wind howling like a pack of wolves outside. His mind wandered unhappily from one thing to another. He felt guilty at allowing Annabella to go home unescorted on such a wild night. Of course, he knew it was ridiculous to harbour such worries. Annabella was better able to take care of herself than he was. She never worried about anything. Nor had he ever known her to suffer from even the mildest indisposition. Had he gone out with her this evening in such a storm of rain and wind, he would have been laid low with a fever afterwards. He had a most delicate constitution. This had always been a matter of embarrassment and regret to him. It had also been the cause of much suffering when he was at school. There had been some dreadfully coarse fellows at school and despite, or perhaps because of, his timid overtures at friendship, they had tormented him and pummelled him unmercifully.

He had been glad of a fever in those days because it kept him away from that frightful place. He remembered one boy in particular, Jedediah Burt, an ugly bovine creature with a huge face and tiny eyes. He had been a farmer's son and the only thing his warped brain, if he had a brain at all, could understand was cruelty. The torments that ignorant lout had made him suffer did not bear thinking about; the twisted arms, the hair torn out by the roots, the kicks in the groin. He remembered one time being bound hand and foot and left hanging by the waist from a tree. He remembered the height of it and the creaking of the branch as he swung backwards and forwards. He remembered the way his heart panicked and the overpowering sickness he felt.

One of the worst times though was when Jed and his bucolic followers heaved him into the river and held him down until his lungs were at bursting point and he was certain he was going to drown. Ever since, he had been terrified of the water and could not bring himself to put a toe near it even for the sake of teaching George to swim.

He adored the child and could deny him nothing as a rule. In this, however, and in the matter of the sedan to take George to school, he was in perfect agreement with Griselle. Annabella could say what she liked, he wasn't going to allow dear, sensitive George to be subjected to the frightful tortures he had suffered as a child. Poor George would have enough to bear at the hands of the dominie while he was inside the classroom. Often the dominie was worse than the cruellest of his pupils.

He had never been so glad to say goodbye to anyone as he had to the dominie who had taught him. That last day at school was also his twelfth birthday and oh, what a blessed day it was. Immediately afterwards he had gone to university and, although life there was difficult and exhausting, it had been sheer heaven compared with the school.

Then, of course, had come the apprenticeship with Papa which included the journey to Virginia and a spell travelling around his stores. That had been another ghastly time. Annabella had made her journey and stay in Virginia sound so exciting and pleasurable. He had been violently seasick and nearly died on the way. Then during his stay in Virginia he had been attacked by the flux and the fever and would certainly have died had it not been for the conscientious nursing of a widow lady at the settlement who also dosed him with herbs and potions. After that he'd visited Venice and France.

Lying in the four-poster bed with the bedcurtains drawn all round and Griselle far away in sleep, Douglas felt a weight of depression descend on him. If only he could have remained in one of those delightful places. Ah, the cultured, elegant, sensitive ladies and gentlemen he had met in Venice and Paris. What style they had. What conversation. Glasgow was so parochial in comparison, so narrow in outlook. The ordinary people even looked askance at the clothes the tobacco merchants wore. They didn't realize that the scarlet capes and jewelled buckles and satins were the common garb of the Venetians and other merchants of the world. The trouble was, most Glasgow folk had never been beyond Trongate Street.

Tobacco merchants, including his Papa in his younger days, were men of daring and vision. They possessed a business acumen that was truly astonishing. After all, Glasgow had once been nothing more than a tiny salmon-fishing village. Before the union of Scotland and England Glasgow hadn't been allowed to trade with the colonies. The trade then had been completely cornered by the London, Bristol, Whitehaven and other southern merchants. As soon as Glasgow men were allowed to trade with Virginia, they shot ahead. In no time they had wrenched the vast majority of trade in tobacco from the English merchants who had held it for over a century. This little out-of-the-way place had become the greatest tobacco trading centre not only in Britain but in the whole of Europe.

They'd built up other trades as well. Instead of taking over empty ships to Virginia to collect the tobacco, they started the manufacture of other goods in Glasgow. Then they filled the holds of their ships with everything the Virginians could need. These things were made by Glasgow citizens and kept them busily employed and included linens, saddlery, delf, ironmongery, ropes and a host of other goods.

But the cleverest move that men like his father had made was to start up a chain of stores on the James River and further inland. They had stocked all the stores with goods and put a store manager in charge of each. There were many stores, especially deep in the wilderness. There they catered for the needs of the planters, although he realized that there were times when some of the planters called the tobacco lords 'the unconscionable and cruel merchants'.

On the other hand, the merchants often viewed the planters as spendthrifts and wastrels who were quick to borrow and slow to pay. As far as he could see, when he was travelling in Virginia, most of the planters had a very comfortable life and didn't appear to be suffering any deprivation. On the contrary, the obvious wealth of some of these men was staggering. He had seen enormous mansions owned by men who had hundreds and often thousands of black slaves to pander to their every whim.

But it was such an enormous, such a rough, tough country

631

and the mansion houses were far too isolated from each other for his taste. No, he much preferred life in Venice or Paris, although life in Scotland was beginning to be more tolerable since he had begun to be accepted into the society of landed gentry. He and Griselle had already spent a few nights at the estate of no less a person than the Duke of Dunleden. There they had met a very civilized company where face paint and fashionable clothes and gaming were not in the least frowned upon, far less laughed at.

Annabella would have enjoyed it there, and no doubt if she made up her mind to it, she would be accepted too. All her life Annabella had got what she wanted. She had always been Papa's favourite. Papa tried to hide it but really he doted on the girl.

He felt another stab of guilt. Was he jealous of his sister? Was that why he had tried to discourage her from any thoughts of indulging in gaming? Was it not true that he did not relish the thought of Annabella completely outshining him if she broke into the exclusive circle in which he was only now beginning to win a grudging acceptance?

He decided that, although it was true he did suffer from pangs of anxiety in this direction, he had been sincere in his concern for Annabella's fate if she became a gamester. She was, as he'd said, a person of extremes and he had seen ladies ruined in health, wealth and happiness from overindulgence at the tables. He was genuinely fond of his sister and would not wish any harm to befall her.

He sighed again. It would have given more ease to his mind if he had escorted her safely home. At least he would have been able to sleep afterwards, although even then it might not have been so easy with such a storm raging. He thought about getting up and looking out of the window. He plucked aside the bedcurtains until he could see, by the glow of what remained of the fire, the shadowy outlines of the crimson upholstered chairs. They too looked as if they were smouldering fires. The hanging clock on the wall whirred and struck with leisurely unconcern. Gracious heavens, he thought, he had been lying awake for hours. It would soon be morning. He decided to get up and pour himself a stiff dram and see if that would induce slumber.

632

Tutting to himself, he eased himself out of bed as carefully as possible so as not to disturb Griselle. If he didn't manage to get some sleep he would not be fit to go to the counting house again and Papa would be angry. He was always failing Papa in one way or another. Poor Papa, he was such a generous man, such an excellent father. He wished he could do something to make Papa proud of him. But he couldn't help it if his delicate constitution kept letting him down. Long ago he'd given up fighting it. He'd reconciled himself to being a failure in Papa's eyes. Although Papa's view of him still hurt.

His nightshirt flapped against his legs as he tiptoed across the floor. Suddenly Griselle's voice startled him.

'A lot of good it is you tiptoeing about like that. With the storm making such a racket you could stamp across the floor and nobody would hear you.'

'Isn't it frightful?' Douglas said. 'I couldn't sleep a wink. I thought a glass of whisky might help. Would you like one, my dear?'

'Yes, all right. Light a candle and put some more wood on the fire, will you?' She sat up and jerked the bedcurtains properly open. 'It soon gets cold in here.'

Douglas knelt down in front of the fire, his nightshirt billowing out and causing a draught that made him shiver. He lit a candle and took it over to the bedside table. From it he lit another to put on the sideboard so that he could see properly to pour out the drinks. But first he crouched down by the fire again and threw on some logs. Straightening up, he caught a glimpse of himself in the long pier glass in the corner over near the window. How thin his face looked under the purple night cap. It had high cheek bones, a long pinched nose with flaring nostrils and arched aristocratic brows. A handsome face, he had been told, but to him it only looked embarrassingly delicate, like his maypole body and spindle legs. He had heard that in London men were padding their calves and special pads could be bought for this purpose. He wondered if he dared . . .

'Hurry up then,' urged Griselle. 'You'll catch your death of cold. Why didn't you put on your dressing-gown? And look at you with your bare feet. Is it any wonder that you're plagued

633

with fevers?'

'I'm sorry, Grizzie,' Douglas fluttered over to the sideboard. 'You are quite right, of course. I do not know what I would do without you, dear girlie.'

The wind screeched outside and rattled wildly at the windows. The curtains agitated about. Suddenly he realized he was chilled to the bone and his feet had stiffened and stuck like blocks of ice to the floor. As a rule he always wrapped himself in something warm before venturing from the bed but he had been dazed with fatigue and lack of sleep on this occasion and his mind had been wandering on to too many other things. Chittering and trembling, he poured out the drinks and hurried back to put them on the bedside table, then clamber in beside Griselle.

The whisky made him feel better and he relaxed back against the pillow, grateful for its warm, melting glow.

Griselle said,

'Listen to that rain. It's just never stopped. What was that?' She jerked out a hand and gripped his arm, alerting him.

He listened but there was only the angry sound of the wind and run.

'Do you think it was one of the boys calling?' he asked. 'I don't suppose they're able to sleep in this monstrous racket either.'

'I thought it came from outside.'

He was silent for a second or two.

'I still don't hear anything but if it will make your mind easier, dear girlie, I shall get up and look out the window.'

He said the words with good grace and patted her hand. But it was an ordeal to leave the warm cocoon of blankets and brave the cold again.

'Put on your dressing-gown and slippers,' Griselle said.

'I doubt if even the bellman would venture out on a night like this, my dear.'

'There it is again. Someone called out.'

This time he thought he did hear feeble cries intermingle with the powerful roaring of the elements. Easing the curtains aside, he peered out the window. At first the scene that met his eyes didn't register. Rain was streaking and smudging the glass and

634

through it the moon wobbled like a stub of wax, making dancing shadows of roof-tops. Then he saw the water.

'Dear Jesus,' he moaned.

'What is it? What's wrong?' Griselle tossed aside the blankets and fumbled into her dressing-gown and slippers.

'Dear Jesus,' Douglas's voice tightened up a note towards hysteria.

'Out of my way!' Griselle pushed him aside then immediately cried out in alarm, 'Oh, Douglas, oh, my God!'

Douglas turned away from the window willing himself not to succumb to the panic that was threatening to burst in his head and leave him witless.

'We'd better get dressed.' He went groping and trembling over to the chair where he'd left his shirt and breeches.

Griselle flew after him and began tearing off her night things and wriggling into a petticoat and gown.

'What are we going to do? You're supposed to be the man of the house. For God's sake, do something!'

The buttons of his shirt kept escaping from his fingers.

'Don't just stand there,' Griselle shouted.

'I'll bring the boys through.'

He stumbled towards the door and then had to come back for a candle. Outside in the lobby he leaned against the wall and prayed for strength.

'Dear Jesus, help me! For the sake of Griselle and the boys, please help me.'

They were asleep. It seemed incredible that in the midst of such an uproar they should be lying so still and with such innocent, peaceful faces.

'Geordie, Mungo,' he quavered, 'wake up like good fellows.' Leaning over the bed, the candle flame all but blowing out in the draught, he gave each child a shake. They wakened grudgingly, groaning with protest. 'Quickly now, bring your clothes through to the fire and get dressed there.'

'It isn't morning yet, Papa.' George's voice sounded babyish and bewildered in his half-sleep. 'It's still dark.'

'Yes, my cockie, but there's a bit of a storm. Nothing of great moment, you understand, but Mama and I would feel better if

635

you were beside us.'

Mungo was already up and pulling on his breeches, and before Douglas had helped George into his dressing-gown, Mungo had donned his shirt, waistcoat, stockings and shoes.

'Don't go near the window,' Douglas anxiously warned.

'Why not?' Mungo wanted to know.

'Oh, do come through like good fellows.'

There was an edge to Douglas's voice that surprised Mungo and made him stare at his uncle intently. Douglas was always so merry and light-hearted. George said his Papa had never once scolded him. On the contrary, he was splendid fun and often played with him. George said they had great hilarity when they were alone together and he much preferred his Papa to his Mama.

Through in the main bedroom the fire was blazing and all the candles were lit. Griselle was pacing the floor, kneading her hands together. Immediately Douglas and the children entered the room, she pounced on George and hugged and kissed him as if she had not seen him for years.

'Mama!' George was outraged at being subjected to such an indignity in front of his cousin. He stamped his foot and beat at her with his fist. 'Leave me alone. Papa, tell Mama to leave me alone.'

Douglas fluttered up his hands.

'Grizzie, will you let the lad get dressed? And keep away from the windows, all of you.'

'Trust you to say a thing like that.' Griselle straightened up, coldness stiffening over her. 'We should do quite the opposite. The only way we'll get safely out of here is by a boat going past that window. We'll have to make ourselves both seen and heard there.'

'Dear girlie, I could have done that. The children needn't have been worried just now.'

'How can a boat go past the window, Papa?' George asked, giggling a little behind his hand and making Mungo erupt into chuckles too.

Griselle crushed them with a look.

'That's enough of that. The town's flooded and it's no

laughing matter.'

'Well, well, it never does any good to mope, as my dear saucebox of a sister would say.' Douglas made a brave attempt at jocularity. 'I'll box your ears for you if you don't put on a cheerful face, she would say.'

'Oh, be quiet,' Griselle snapped. Then she jerked the curtains aside. 'Hurry up, boys, come over here and stand by the window. We'd better open it so that we can call out. Get your coats on so that you won't be too cold. And bring my cloak. Trust you to allow both the servants to go home tonight, Douglas.'

'Well, my dear girlie, they are brother and sister and their mother is dying. We couldn't let one go to see her without the other, especially on such a wild night. And as far as we could tell, we didn't need them again until morning.'

'They'll see her on the other side eventually. They didn't need to go stravaiging away to Bell's Wynd tonight.'

'Last night it is now,' Douglas said. 'Just look at the time. Gracious heavens, aren't you young fellows up early this fine morning?'

The boys giggled again

'The rain's stopped,' Griselle said, peering out.

'There! What did I tell you?' said Douglas in a bright, shaky voice. 'It is a trifling adventure. We shall be perfectly all right.'

'Tuts, don't be ridiculous, Douglas. The river's obviously burst its banks. It's going along here like a raging torrent. We're in mortal danger and there's no use hiding from the fact. Surely somebody will have managed to get a boat,' she said, peering out again.

He fetched her cloak and helped her to wrap it round herself, all the time keeping his face averted from the window.

'Open it, then,' Griselle said.

He stood staring at her helplessly, as if waiting for her to speak again.

'Open it. sir!'

Turning, he saw the water again so terrifyingly near the room it didn't seem possible. He thought he was going to faint. Closing his eyes, he leaned against the window before somehow

637

managing to wrench it open. Then he slid away from the aperture, feeling his way along the wall.

Mungo pushed passed him.

'Gracious heavens! Look, George, it just needs to rise another few feet and it'll be inside the room.'

George crowded between Griselle and Mungo at the open window.

'Lord's sake!' he gasped.

The wind scampered round the room and snuffed out all the candles. But they could see by the moon's silver light, except when clouds scudded across it and left them in darkness for a few seconds. Then like a curtain it was pulled aside and moonlight opened everything up again. They could see the low-ceilinged room, the crimson upholstered chairs, the rumpled bed, its white linen brightening the shadows, the heavy gilt-framed portrait above the fireplace of Griselle wearing the lavender dress. It now looked a ghostly grey and the china vases underneath it had acquired a cold gleam.

Safely clear of the window once more, Douglas said,

'I'd better go and fetch my coat. It's devilish cold. I think I'll bring my muff as well.'

The whisky bottle drew him towards it first, however, and he gulped over another glassful in the hope it would inject some heat and strength into him. His nerves had turned to feathers and were floating, fluttering free in his body, making him light-headed. The whisky gave him some warmth which was comforting, yet it did nothing to dispel the icy nightmare that surrounded him.

'It won't help us any if you get yourself drunk,' Griselle called over to him, making him suffer immediate pangs of shame and remorse.

'I'll go and fetch my coat and muff,' he repeated. 'Don't worry, my dear girlie, we are going to be perfectly all right.'

In the lobby, he held the candle up and peered around. The doors to the kitchen, the other bedrooms and the closet were all tight shut and the closed-in feeling of the lobby gave him a transient impression of safety. He clung to it with gratitude, closing his eyes for a long minute to help steady himself. When he widened his eyes again, he caught a glimpse of water trickling in under the outside door. His mouth parched with terror. The water could not possibly have risen at the back of the building to such a height. It must only be a little rain that had been blown under the door by a gust of wind. Tearing his eyes away and trying not to look in the direction of the outside door again, he opened the closet and pulled out his coat. Then, clutching it against his chest, he was about to stumble back into the main bedroom when the tirling of the door-pin stopped him.

He crumpled with relief. If someone was at the door, the water couldn't have risen that far. Putting the candle down on the lobby table, he struggled into his coat, hurrying to see who was there. When he opened the door he was taken aback to see not one person but a crush of ragged humanity pressing close.

'You've got to let us in, maister,' the nearest beggar pleaded with Douglas. 'We'll drown out here on the stairs.'

Douglas fluttered his handkerchief in front of his face to try and dispel the stench of the man and at the same time peer beyond him at the mob of ragged men and women on the stairs. Some of them were waist deep in water and were balancing children up on their shoulders.

'Oh, good gracious alive, what am I to make of it?'

'If we could get to the front and shout for help from your window there would be a chance of folks hearing us and seeing us.'

'All right, all right, my cockies. But look here, you must . . .' He was taken aback by the speed with which the crowd took up his invitation. Indeed, he was swept aside and almost knocked to the ground in their desperation to enter. People splashed up the stairs to the dry landing and stumbled gratefully into the house shedding pools of slimy water all over Griselle's best rugs. Hastily recovering himself, Douglas called after them.

'Look here, you fellows, you must keep back until you're told. My family are at the window and they must come first.'

In the bedroom, Griselle swung round and halted the rush with an outraged face.

'What is the meaning of this? How dare you enter my house!' She glared furiously at Douglas. 'Have you completely lost your wits, sir? Why have you allowed these thieves and vagabonds to enter my house?'

'They hadn't anywhere else to go, Grizzie.'

'That is no concern of yours, sir. Your responsibility is to me and these two boys.' She jerked her head towards George and Mungo who were propped on the sill of the open window.

He fluttered over to pose protectively in front of the children. Then he shook his hanky in the direction of the bedraggled group crowding together at the other end of the room.

'You'll wait there like good fellows, won't you?'

The beggars looked menacingly out of place in the richly furnished room. Their deformed and emaciated bodies, their skeleton faces and protruding eyes had an aura of desperation that worried Douglas.

'You'll be all right,' he said. 'We'll all be perfectly all right if we simply wait and . . .'

Suddenly George called out excitedly.

'There's a boat! There's a boat!'

And like an avalanche, the crowd plunged forward, sweeping Griselle and Douglas aside, knocking George and Mungo off-balance and sending the two boys tumbling down into the water.

From the boat, Annabella and Big John saw a couple of figures like silver dolls fall from the dark cave of the window. A violently struggling mob of people was gesticulating from the window and shouting and pleading for help. Then they discerned Griselle fighting her way to the front to lean out and scream:

'Geordie! Geordie!'

Big John quickened his pull on the oars but the water was turning past them with the rapidity of a mill lead and even he found it difficult to force the boat to breast the current. At the same time, Annabella saw Mungo surface and strike out towards them. In a matter of seconds they had reached each other and she was dragging him into the boat beside her. Once Mungo was safe, she called across to Griselle,

'It's all right, Grizzie. We'll get George too.'

As if hearing her voice, George surfaced some way from the boat, struggling, choking, sinking, gasping up and sinking

640

again. Big John flung down the oars.

'I hang on, mistress.'

The boat rocked wildly, nearly sending Mungo and her after him as he dived into the water. Reaching the spot where George had gone under, Big John kicked up his feet and disappeared. Annabella held her breath in an agony of suspense as she watched Big John surface several times and look helplessly around.

Eventually Mungo said in a shaky voice,

'It's too late, Mother. George has gone. He has drowned.'

'Fiddlesticks. If I say Big John will find him, he will.'

And sure enough the servant eventually bobbed up with George. When he reached the boat, Annabella was ready and waiting to lift the child inside and try and minister to him.

Griselle was still screaming broken-heartedly. Annabella said to Big John.

'Do you think we could get Griselle and Douglas out of there without all that mob jumping on top of us?'

Still in the water and clinging to the side of the boat, Big John thought for a minute before managing a reply.

'I'll swim over, then climb in the window and hold the crowd of vagabonds back. Then you bring the boat over and the mistress and maister can drop down.'

'Very well.' Annabella was breathlessly working on George in an attempt to bring him back to consciousness. But still without effect.

'I told you he was drowned,' Mungo said.

'If you don't be quiet I'll throw you back in.'

Big John was soon clambering up to the window and, using his head and fists as battering rams, cleared a space and hoisted himself into the room. Then he heaved the beggars back and for the first time Douglas came into view. He staggered against the sill as if he was going to faint but quickly reached out to comfort the distraught Griselle. She pushed him aside and Annabella barely had time to manoeuvre the boat underneath the window before Griselle had lowered herself into it.

'Geordie.' She snatched the little boy into her arms and rocked backwards and forwards with him tightly clutched

641

against her.

Douglas was in the boat now and Big John shouted,

'Take it away. I'll dive in and swim after you.'

Annabella said, 'We'll hurry straight back with him, Grizzie. Papa will know what to do.'

But by the time they reached her father's close and stair, she knew in her heart that George was too far gone to recover. Nevertheless she snatched him from Griselle and raced upstairs shouting as she went.

'Papa, Papa, quickly, open the door.'

Her father was waiting on the landing holding a candelabra towards the stairs.

'Are you all right?'

'Never mind about me. It's George.'

'Bring him through.'

He led the way to his room with big thumping strides, the candle flames fluttering back in the rush of air. They bled the child and massaged him and worked on him until the cold light of day was shrinking the candles, and the fire in the grate had sunk into ashes. At last Douglas wailed,

'It's no use. It's no use. Can't you see?'

Griselle whirled on him.

'You're no use! What do you know? You useless, spineless wretch. Just hold your tongue.'

With a big sigh Ramsay straightened up.

'No, he's right. The lad's gone. It's God's will. Nothing we can do can change it.'

'No.' Griselle shook her head.

'It's God's will,' Ramsay repeated.

Annabella put an arm round Griselle's shoulder.

'Come on through to my room and sit down. I'll get Betsy to bring a cup of tea with a wee drop of whisky in it.' Then to Big John who had been hovering in the doorway anxiously watching, 'Tell Betsy to stop her howling this instant and bring us all a cup of tea with whisky. And get into some dry clothes and take a good dram yourself.'

'Yes, mistress.'

'And Big John,' she shouted when she reached her own

bedroom. 'There's still a glimmer in this fire. Build it up before it goes out. It's prodigiously cold.'

She had not realized how chilled she was until now. Her breasts hung heavy against her like balls of ice. She seemed to be moving in a nightmare. Her room looked strange in the bleak half-light and unfamiliar with so many people at such an early hour.

Betsy came rattling in with the tea-tray, her face scarlet and swollen.

'Oh, dear Jesus,' she sobbed. 'Poor wee George is drowned.'

'Be quiet, or I'll beat what little wits you have out of you,' Annabella snapped. 'Put the tray down before you break my good china. And I hope you saw that Mungo took his wet clothes off and bedded himself down by the kitchen fire like I told you.'

'Yes, mistress.'

'Well, don't just stand there. Go pour Big John a good dram. And keep that fire burning bright through there.'

Big John lumbered into the room with a bundle of wood under one arm and a bucket of coal in the other and before Annabella had poured out and handed round the tea, the fire was crackling and blazing.

'You're shivering,' Annabella said to Griselle. 'Let me put some more whisky in your tea, then drink it down. It will ease you. Douglas, you have some too.'

'Thank you, dear girlie.' His voice trembled and he looked paler than the white paint on his face. A waxiness pinched the corners of his mouth and his long sliver of nose.

Griselle said,

'I'll never forgive you. You killed my son.'

'Compose yourself, woman,' Ramsay growled. 'He was Douglas's son too. And he was my grandwain.'

Griselle gave a bitter laugh.

'You never cared about Geordie. And neither did Douglas.'

'Grizzie, how can you talk in so wicked a manner?' Douglas's empty cup rattled so much on his saucer he had to put it down. 'I loved the dear boy. I'm sure Papa did too.'

'Lies. Lies.'

643

'Griselle,' Annabella protested. 'I know how you must feel but it won't bring George back and it won't make you feel any better to fly into a passion against Douglas.'

'I'll never forgive him.'

'Forgive him for what? It was the beggars who made the boys fall into the water, wasn't it?'

'They would never have been there if the stupid, useless wretch hadn't let them in.'

Ramsay swung round, his face incredulous.

'You allowed a crowd of thieves and vagabonds to enter your house?'

'They were waist deep in water on the back stairs and some of them had already drowned. I'd seen their bodies floating away.'

'Oh, aye, so you decided you'd send your son's body to join them?'

'Papa,' Annabella interrupted. 'This is monstrous and damnable. You know perfectly well he did no such thing. Drink your whisky, sir, and let us have no more of this outrageous behaviour.'

'Devil choke you, Annabella. You've an impertinent tongue.'

'You're as much to blame as anyone,' she said. 'You're on the Town Council. Why can't something be done about the river to prevent it overflowing like that? I'll tell you one thing. I'm not going to stay here and endanger my own and my son's life again.

'And where will you go, pray?' Her father raised a sarcastic eyebrow. 'You haven't two bawbees to rub together.'

'No, but you have, Papa. You could quite easily have a mansion like Mr Glassford's built on the outskirts of town.'

For a moment, Ramsay was so astounded he couldn't make a sound.

'A mansion?' he managed eventually. 'A mansion? By God, I'll grant you one thing, mistress, you've nerve.'

'You have money, Papa. You are one of the wealthiest men in Glasgow.'

'Aye, but I wouldn't be for long if you had your way. I can see that.'

'Would you rather stay here and risk losing another grandson?'

He glowered at her from under bushy brows.

'We were in no danger here and fine you know it, mistress.'

'No, I do not know it. Nobody knows how stormy it's going to be and how far the water is going to rise. And we might not have had a boat here last night. Think of that.'

'Oh, he'll think of it all right,' Griselle said bitterly. 'He'll think of his precious Mungo. But nobody thought of my wee Geordie.'

Douglas fluttered towards her.

'Grizzie, Grizzie, you know I . . .'

'Get away from me,' Griselle said.

Ramsay sighed again.

'You'd better send Big John for Letitia and Phemy.'

Annabella rose. 'Yes, Papa. I'll go and tell him.'

The heat in the kitchen was as thick as a blanket and the place reeked of whisky. A fire glowed poppy red under the black iron pot hanging from the swee on a chain. Big John snored at the table, his head collapsed onto his arms. Betsy was hiccoughing backwards and forwards on the rocking-chair on one side of the fire. On the other side slept Mungo wrapped snugly in a plaid.

Annabella shook Big John's shoulder, making him snort and jerk awake.

'You'll have to go and fetch Mistress Letitia and Mistress Phemy,' she said. 'Tell them they're needed but don't divulge why.'

He nodded, his rugged, good-natured face sad.

'I got wee Geordie out as quick as I could.'

'Indeed you did,' Annabella assured him. 'No one's blaming you. It's just a misfortune and we're all mightily distressed. But there's no use wasting time in fruitless lamentations. Away you go and do as you're told.'

She returned to her bedroom to find Griselle had disappeared.

'She wants to lay the bairn out herself,' Ramsay said. 'She's through with him now.'

Annabella went over to gaze out the window. The rain had long since stopped and the water had calmed and appeared to be shrinking towards the river. In a few days it would have completely subsided. The streets would be filthy quagmires littered with the flotsam from houses and warerooms. Carcasses of cows and sheep would hump up like black hillocks. Thousands of drowned rats would clutter the markets.

The Tolbooth bells cheerily chimed in a new day.

Chapter 6

Kneeling beside Mistress Kitty's grave, Regina absently changed the flowers. She felt sick with apprehension. Now that his wife was dead, what was to stop Harding deciding there was no place for her any more and putting her out of the house. She had nowhere to go. She kept telling herself that it was a ridiculous idea. Why should he do such a thing? He liked sleeping with her, didn't he? This knowledge brought scant reassurance. He could get other women to share his bed. Even the fact that she was carrying his child might not make any difference if he wanted to get rid of her. How many masters before him had got servants pregnant and then disowned them?

Anyway, she daren't continue putting off telling him about the child.

It had been warm earlier but now the cool evening air ruffled the long grass and made her shiver. Rising, she carefully arranged her gown and petticoat. She wanted to go indoors for a cloak and wait until later when Harding would come into the house before speaking to him. But she couldn't stand her secret torment a moment longer.

She walked stiffly round the back of the house and along past the storehouse to the office. He was sitting at a desk surrounded by ledgers and was dipping his quill into an inkpot when she entered. His eyes flashed up in surprise. Then he waited, without saying anything.

'I'm with child,' Regina announced abruptly.

Suddenly he flung back his head in a burst of laughter.

'You pig,' she said. 'I might have known you would act like this. You coarse, unfeeling, brutish pig. I loathe and detest you.'

And before he could say anything, she had swept away again, her skirts swishing, spurting up dust from the path.

Later, in the dining-room as they sat at opposite ends of the long table, she could feel his eyes glimmering across at her with amusement. Ignoring him, she kept forcing herself to eat. Eventually he said,

'It was your manner of telling me that made me laugh. It was so like you.'

He said no more and they finished the meal in silence. Afterwards, in the drawing-room, he poured a glass of whisky for them both. She sat sipping hers on the embroidered chair. He stood with his back to the fire, glass in hand. Every now and again he savoured a mouthful of whisky. She could have killed him. She raised her eyes to meet his and saw his mouth twist into a smile that had no softness about it.

'You are still amused?' she inquired.

'No, I am pleased.'

She kept her face stiff and expressionless.

He raised his glass. 'Here's to my son.'

'*My* son.'

After a pause he said, 'What is going on in that icebox of a brain now, I wonder?'

'You have no claim on me.'

'Ah!'

'I am not even indentured to you.'

He put down his empty glass. 'You are tied to me by stronger bonds than that.'

'I don't know what you're talking about,' she said coldly. The smile pulled at his mouth again.

'What a goddam liar you are. You even lie to yourself.'

'I could walk out of here tomorrow,' she said.

'Could you?'

'And you could get another woman to accommodate you.'

'True.'

'And another bastard child.'

'My son must have my name. We must be married.'

'What makes you so sure I will marry you?'

He turned away to pour himself another drink.

'Send one of the slaves with a note telling the preacher to come,' he said, ignoring her question.

It took her a minute or two to swallow down her anger and inquire in a smooth, polite tone:

'Do you wish any guests to be invited for the ceremony?'

'Invite all your friends.'

His eyes glimmered across at her again, making her flush, but she managed to keep her voice cool.

'You know I have no friends.'

'There's Nancy, Morgan West's wife.'

'I only see her occasionally in Williamsburg. I was referring to the people you do business with and carouse with in Williamsburg and elsewhere.'

'I have no need or wish for them. At least not on my wedding day. Invite your brother and sister-in-law. They can stay for a few days.'

'Very well.'

And so Joseph was sent with a note to the preacher and a letter to Gav.

Gav was worried about Mr Speckles, the store manager. The old man wasn't keeping at all well. He never served in the store now because standing behind the counter was too tiring. Also the smells of the pelts, the tobacco and the spices never failed to trigger off his cough. It was terrible to see Mr Speckles in one of his coughing spasms. The poor man could hardly hold his bundle of bones together. The coughing was such a strain, in fact, he often retched up blood. The doctor was seldom in the settlement. He spent most of his time travelling around, visiting and living for long periods with one or other of the wealthy planters. But when he did come, he gave Mr Speckles a dreadful concoction that only made him retch all the more. The doctor also advised that the already exhausted man should take vigorous exercise, particularly horseback riding because horse smell was good for weak lungs. It didn't seem to do Mr Speckles any good.

The Indian medicine man's potions hadn't been of much use either. Even old Mrs Adamson's herbs had not effected a cure. It was she who treated most of the settlement's ills. She could boast of considerable success with 'the chills' or 'the shakes' as some folks called the disease that plagued so many of the settlers. Children seemed especially vulnerable to it. Some child or other was always taking chills at school. Gav had seen boys swimming down by the creek and one of them taking a chill and the others sitting round him on the bank until he'd had his chill out. Then they all went off together as if it had never happened.

Mrs Adamson had made a big difference with her sassafras tea and her quinine. But no matter what she tried with Mr Speckles, it never made one bit of difference.

Now he was barely able to hunch over his desk in the counting house and push a quill across a ledger.

Gav had to supervise the store, the two young indentured lads and the two Negro slaves who worked in it. His duties were many and varied. It wasn't just a matter of serving in the store or seeing that the place was well stocked with goods. More and more he was having to keep the ledgers as well. There was the long tobacco book in particular in which he had to record the movement of individual hogsheads, as the casks of tobacco were called. Every hogshead was identified by a particular mark and number. The mark was a special design chosen by the planter. It could be a combination of letters interwoven, or a crow's foot, or whatever the planter's whimsy suggested.

Another important account book that now fell to him to keep was a small ledger called the 'pocket book'. In it he carefully recorded sums due to the store. Storekeepers were supposed to carry this book on their persons at all times but especially at any public occasions where planters were likely to be gathered. There the storekeeper would have the opportunity to inform his customers tactfully as to their standing.

But Mr Speckles was no longer fit to attend public occasions. Accounts had not been made up for the Public Time in Williamsburg, for instance. And even planters who had made the journey specially to the store for the purpose could not be furnished with a proper statement of what they owed. Poor Mr Speckles was getting extremely confused and tried to escape to the tavern as often as possible. When he was not able to shuffle that far, he imbibed freely from a bottle he kept in the back pocket of his coat. Often as he crouched over his desk, his shaky hand would drop the quill, fumble for the bottle, then take quick furtive swigs from it. Sometimes it made him cough and he all but choked.

650

The planters had started to complain about the state of Mr Speckles, and the state of the account books. They threatened to write to Glasgow and complain to Mr Ramsay. Eventually, in desperation, Gav had taken the initiative and organized everything himself. Night and day he had been working on the books until he had them up to date. Then he had gone to the Public Time in Williamsburg and seen many of the planters there. He had been sorry, however, on one occasion, to miss Mr Harding who was a very good customer. He had met Nancy who used to be maid to Mistress Annabella Ramsay. Nancy was now married to a farmer called Morgan West who was also a customer at the store. She and Morgan quite often visited the settlement and he enjoyed chatting to her about old times in Glasgow, but on the occasion when they'd met in Williamsburg she had told him that he had just missed not only Mr Harding but Regina as well.

Nancy had bumped into Regina in a Williamsburg shop where Regina had been buying household goods. Gav was glad that his sister had found such a comfortable home, and he was secretly relieved to be free of any worry or responsibility for her. Mr Speckles was enough to cope with. Regina would have been too much. Much as he loved her, he realized that his sister could be a very strange creature at times. He had never really understood her. Sometimes she seemed so cold and unfeeling, it was bloodcurdling. There were times he didn't dare think about. Times like the one on the voyage over to Virginia when he was being forced to climb up the shrouds by the bullying first mate. Mr Gudgeon had been standing balanced on the slippery bulwarks and suddenly Regina had attacked his legs with a belaying-pin, making him lose his balance and fall overboard.

Mr Gudgeon had drowned. Gav had been sick with fear in case the captain would find out that Regina was to blame and have her hanged for murder. She betrayed not the slightest emotion. She only said,

'You would have fallen from the shrouds. He would have caused you to drown. It was him or you.' Then with a shrug, 'Murder's only a word.'

He remembered too how, after the battle of Culloden, she

had betrayed Mistress Annabella's French lover. Then she had taken looted gold from the saddlebags of English dragoons. Not content even with that, on her journey back to Glasgow she had also stolen clothes and valuables from the dead. He had been especially horrified at this but she had only shrugged again and said,

'They had no use for it.'

Yet she could be affectionate too. And extremely kind. She had always been good to him and now she was most generous to his children. He wished she would bring Abigail a little gift sometimes, though. She was very cool with Abigail; polite but cool. It was as if she had never forgiven Abigail for marrying him. More than once he had tried to tell her how ridiculous it was still to hanker after their old childish dreams of working a plantation between them. Long before he'd ever thought of Abigail, he'd realised that for him it would be more of a nightmare than anything else. To live alone with Regina in the wilderness had never held any attraction for him. It would never have worked and it had nothing to do with Abigail. He told Regina this in no uncertain terms but it was like talking to a brick wall. When that closed look came over Regina's face, there was just no getting through to her. Still, he was sorry he'd missed her in Williamsburg. He couldn't help worrying about her and he was glad when eventually a note came from Regina inviting him and Abigail and the children to come and spend a few days at Forest Hall.

Abigail wasn't so happy about the visit.

'You've no need to worry about her, Gav. That woman is more than able to take very good care of herself.'

Gav sighed. Abigail obviously didn't like Regina any more than Regina liked her. Although, to be fair to Regina, she had never once said a word against his wife. He wouldn't allow her to, of course.

'Abby, you don't know Regina as I do. Anyway I've business with Mr Harding.'

'Pooh, that could wait. He'll be here in a few months.'

'He might. Then again he might not. My business with him can't wait that long. I must get all the books balanced. Everything's got into a terrible muddle since Mr Speckle's health has broken down.'

'There's something about that woman . . . I'm sorry, Gav, I know you're fond of her but I can't help the way I feel. The less we have to do with Mistress Regina, the happier I'll be.'

But she didn't say any more and he made the necessary arrangements to travel to Forest Hall. Booster, one of the slaves, helped him load the wagon with their trunk, and after Abigail and the children had clambered on, Booster climbed alongside Gav and, long guns on their laps, they set off along the tobacco road. Soon Booster was singing lustily, more to cover up his fear of the forest than from good cheer, Gav suspected.

'No more auction block for me,
No more, no more,
Many thousand gone.

No more driver's lash for me,
No more, no more,
Many thousand gone.

No hundred lash for me,
No more, no more . . .'

The wagon rocked and creaked and jarred over bumps on the rutted earth and Gav didn't enjoy the journey any more than Booster or Abigail did. He puffed at his pipe and gave every appearance of calm, but the deeper they travelled into the wilderness and the more the wall of trees closed in on him, the more nervous he felt. But the prickles of unease were nothing to the spiritual depression the forest imposed on him. It was so gloomy and oppressive, like a giant echoing tunnel with no end. He had never made the journey to Forest Hall before, and now it amazed him that not only Regina but even Mistress Kitty had managed it in the past. Regina, like Abigail, had a toughness about her, but Harding's wife should surely never have been subjected to such a long and arduous expedition.

It seemed eventually as if he had been journeying for a lifetime, and the settlement and his cosy cabin had disappeared into another world. He was beginning to feel he would never see it again or ever reach Forest Hall, when suddenly he caught a glimpse of it between the trees. It could have been a ghost. The hair prickled up the back of his neck. He saw it again, grey-white and evanescent against the rugged brown tree trunks. It had a spectral look that did not change as they came nearer and saw its pillared facade and the double stairs fronting its tall doors.

Neither he nor Booster nor Abigail spoke. Then eventually he cleared his throat and managed to cry out:

'Hallo-o-o, the house!'

Why had Regina invited him and his family? he suddenly thought. She had never shown any need for company before, although of course her letter had been cool and brief enough.

'Isn't that so like her?' Abigail had said. 'That's not a warm family invitation. It's not an invitation at all, it's a command.'

He felt uneasy, but he called again as the wagon rattled a path between the trees and stumps:

'Hallo-o-o, the house!'

Regina sent for the young slaves, Lunesta and Little Sam. 'I want you to look after Bette and Jethro while they are staying at Forest Hall,' she told them. 'See that they are well cared for and amused.'

Lunesta was a skinny child with her frizzy hair parted down the back of her head and tied tightly with two scarlet ribbons given to her by Regina. Delighted at being allocated such a responsible job, she immediately pounced on plump little Bette and managed, after a breathless struggle, to lift the child in her arms.

'I'm goin' to show you the squirrels, Miss Bette.' She puffed towards the door. 'One of them's so tame he eats out of my hand. Little Sam, you bring Jethro.'

As they went out, Callie Mae entered carrying the tea-tray.

'Go after them and give them a biscuit each,' Regina told her, then began pouring tea and handing cups around. She noticed Abigail looking a little worriedly after the children, and added,

'Don't worry. I've told Callie Mae to keep a firm eye on them.'

Gav smiled ruefully over at Abigail.

'Our whole house could fit into this one room.'

'There's nothing wrong with our house,' Abigail said firmly. 'It's a nice, cheerful, cosy place.'

Gav laughed.

'Well, as long as you're happy with it.'

'We can always build on another room if we want one.'

'Yes, I know.' He turned to his sister. 'But fancy you going to be mistress of such a grand house, Regina. You could never have imagined such a thing happening when you were in Glasgow, could you?'

'I don't like to think about Glasgow,' she murmured, averting her face as if the mention of the place pained her.

'Oh, I do. Not that I pine for it, you understand. Virginia is home for me now. But I often think of dear old Quin and hope he's all right. And you know, Glasgow wasn't such a bad place.'

'Huh!' Regina rolled her eyes. 'Dear old Quin! How you can talk of him with affection I just cannot understand.'

Abigail said, 'I can.'

Regina fixed her with a disdainful look.

'You never met him. He was a beggar, a thief and a liar. He was also as ugly as sin.'

'He was ugly, that's true,' Gav admitted, 'but all the same . . .'

'It's also true that he was a beggar, a thief and a liar.'

'He was kind to us,' her brother insisted stubbornly. 'Without him we would have starved or worse.'

Regina's mouth twisted.

'He was no use to me. He didn't save me from anything.'

'Oh, I don't know . . .'

'No, you don't.' Her voice flew unexpectedly out of control but she quickly recovered it. She even managed a small smile. 'Would you like a biscuit or a piece of cake?'

Every now and again, outside the window, the children's chatter made a chorus with the chirping of the birds.

Harding remarked,

'Lunesta and Little Sam seem to like looking after the children, and the children seem to be enjoying themselves too.'

'They can keep them.' Sitting on the embroidered chair, Regina looked like a painting with her wide-skirted shimmering yellow dress and chestnut hair. Behind her the mahogany desk had a dark red glow that was enriched by a bowl of sweet-scented roses.

'Keep them?' Abigail echoed. 'What do you mean?'

'Bette and Jethro can keep the slaves.'

Gav smiled. 'It's a kind thought, Regina, but shouldn't you ask Mr Harding's permission?'

Harding laughed.

'Do you think I would sit silently allowing anyone to give away my property sir? I certainly would not. Those two slaves belong to your sister and she can do whatever she wishes with them.'

'I wish Bette and Jethro to have them,' Regina repeated. 'But only on condition that you never allow Lunesta and Little Sam to be sold separately, Gav. Can I have your word on that?'

'Of course. But, Regina, are you sure you know what you're doing? Slaves cost a lot of money.'

Regina shrugged.

'There are plenty of other slaves at Forest Hall.'

'You're very generous. I appreciate how kind you are to the children. And so does Abigail. Don't you Abby?' He appealed to his wife who gave Regina one of her disconcertingly direct stares.

'I hope, Regina, that when you have a child yourself, you will give us an opportunity of doing something for it.'

Regina avoided the unwavering brown eyes. 'She knows of my condition,' she thought. The smug, self-righteous, little bitch. She's all right. She's never been trapped. She's never had to suffer. She's never been forced to do anything she didn't want to do. First a doting father and now a doting husband. What does she really know about anything?

'When is the preacher coming?' Gav asked.

'Later this evening,' Harding said. 'But come, finish up your tea and I'll show you around the plantation, Gav.'

'Great!' Gav enthused and gulped over what remained of his tea before rising and following Harding from the room.

He thought the master of Forest Hall was a decent sort, despite his abrupt manner. Probably a strong character like Harding was just the type Regina needed to cope with her strange moods.

Outside, Harding waved an arm in the direction of the trees.

'There's too many, too near. I mean to clear more of them. But it's such a devil of a job.'

'I heartily agree!' Gav shook his head. 'Burning's the only way to make decent progress.'

'I know, but it would be too dangerous so near the house.'

'Yes, I see your problem. They darken the place, though. A pity. It's a handsome house.'

'I like it. I think your sister does too.'

'Yes, I must confess it's much too isolated for my taste. But I'm sure it suits Regina very well.'

They strolled along the path that wound round the side of the house then round the back and along past the outbuildings.

'That's the kitchen.' Harding nodded his head towards the first building but didn't bother to show Gav inside.

But he did allow him to inspect the storehouses, then the office building and the overseer's house. From there they crossed the large dirt clearing that fronted the barns and stables and Harding ordered Matthew, the stable boy, to saddle up a couple of horses. Behind the stable was a peach and apple orchard and Harding told Gav that they made a fair amount of fruit brandy. They continued on horseback through a rather wooded area. Harding pointed over to the left through the trees.

'There's a stream runs behind the outbuildings and all the way along there past the quarters. Further back, where it passes the outbuildings, I had a spring-house built over it. It keeps all the dairy produce fresh and cool.'

Soon they were passing the rows of huts that made up the quarters.

'You must own a goodly number of slaves, Mr Harding.'

'I haven't bought as many as some of the plantations I know. But I choose good healthy bucks that breed well. Here are the tobacco house and smoke house,' he said as they proceeded on their way. Then he waved an arm at the tobacco fields now meandering in all directions and divided by zigzag wood fences. 'And here is the cause of all our labours.'

Gav was impressed at the size of the plantation. He realized that there were bigger places along the banks of the James River. Nevertheless, Harding owned a lot of good land. Regina was very lucky to be marrying such a man. As they returned to the house, he couldn't help remembering Harding's first wife. He wondered what had happened in the end and when exactly she had died. Since he and Abby had arrived at Forest Hall, Mistress Kitty's death had only been briefly mentioned.

'I was sorry to hear that Mistress Kitty had died,' Gav said eventually. 'When did it happen?'

'She'd been slowly dying for a long time,' Harding said. 'I knew she'd never get over that seizure she took in Williamsburg. Regina never lost hope but that was just because your sister is a devilishly stubborn woman.'

Gav couldn't help grinning.

'That I must admit, sir. But you will manage her very well, I'm sure.'

'Oh, I intend to.'

After a pause Gav said: 'That was a most unfortunate incident in Williamsburg. With Regina and Mistress Annabella, I mean.'

Harding made no comment and after another pause, Gav remarked,

'Of course, Mistress Annabella had always a wild streak in her character.'

'She had good reason for acting as she did.'

Something in his tone of voice made Gav flash Harding a curious look, but already the planter had dismounted and his boots were thumping up the wooden outside stairs of the house. One of the slaves met him in the hall.

'Miss Chisholm say to tell you the preacher arrived, sir, and she and Miss Abigail are upstairs gettin' dressed.'

'We'd better get ready too,' Gav said.

Harding shrugged.

'It's only a simple ceremony. There's going to be no one here but ourselves.'

'Yes, I know, but women like any excuse for dressing up. It does no harm to humour them.'

Upstairs in the bedroom that he and Abigail had been given,

he confessed to his wife,

'I always thought Regina was a bit of a queer character but there's something odd about Harding as well.'

Abigail was putting on her stays and her soft pink breasts bulged up as she tried to tighten them.

'Yes, your sister and that man are well matched. Here, help me with this, Gav. Pull the laces as tight as you can.'

He shook his head.

'Why you want to bother with stays I don't know. You've a perfectly nice little waist without torturing yourself into this.

'I've no intention of looking like a backwoods frump while your sister floats around like an elegant fashion baby.'

'Oh, all right.' He stuck his knee into her back and pulled the laces while she grunted and gasped and wriggled herself up.

'He seems a decent enough sort all the same,' Gav said. 'It's just that he's got such an abrupt manner.'

'You always look for something good in folk, Gav. I suppose that's one of the things I love about you. But I can't be as generous-hearted as you. I don't like your sister. I don't like Mr Harding and I especially don't like this gloomy house. It gives me the creeps. I'll be glad to get back home.'

'I don't know why you've taken such a dislike to Regina. Or to Mr Harding for that matter. Neither of them has done you any harm. Quite the reverse. Just look what Regina did today. Have you any idea what two slaves like that would cost? And think what help they'll be to you back home.'

Abigail sighed.

'I suppose I am being a bit unfair.'

He dropped a kiss on her neck.

'Or jealous?'

'Not of their possessions, Gav. Definitely not of that.' She hesitated, then with some reluctance managed to add, 'But I suppose you're right in a way. Perhaps I'm afraid she'll come between us somehow.'

'What nonsense!' Gav turned her round and took her in his arms. 'How could Regina or anyone come between us? You know, for such a sensible woman you do get some idiotic ideas into your head.' He kissed her long and lovingly. 'Now finish dressing and let's go down and see my sister happily married.'

'She doesn't look very happy.'

'She will be. In her own way.'

He began whistling a cheery tune as he changed into clean linen and breeches, and finally donned a blue coat with large cuffs and fancy buttons, and a pair of shiny, buckled shoes. He was a pleasant-looking man with hair a lighter, brighter red than his sister's. His hair was also thick and frizzy whereas hers was smooth and glossy. They both had fair creamy skins but Gav's face was blotched with many freckles. His eyes were pale grey-green. His sister's eyes were as vivid a green as any emerald.

'I'm glad you're not like her,' Abigail said.

'Abby!' Gav shouted with exasperation.

'All right! All right!' Abigail flung up her hands. 'I'm sorry. Your sister has been very kind and I shouldn't criticize her.'

'Well, damn it all, will you stop doing it?'

'All right! All right!' She suddenly laughed. 'I couldn't be jealous of the kind of life they lead here anyway. Can you imagine there being any diversion at Forest Hall like everyone enjoys at the settlement? Spinning matches, candle-dippings, quilting parties.'

'Log-rollings, house-raisings, corn-shuckings,' Gav added with a grin. 'A spell at Forest Hall is maybe what you need to stop you being so sassy.'

She knew he was only joking but she had to struggle with herself to prevent an angry reply from escaping. Normally the most even-tempered of women, she found the effect on her of anything to do with Regina disturbing to say the least. She fastened on her petticoats and gown and then stared at herself in the pier glass. Her hair never gleamed darkly like Regina's. It was wispy and faded in comparison. She had such a plain face too and Regina was so beautiful.

She sighed.

'What's wrong now?' Gav asked.

'Nothing.' She smiled at him and took his arm. 'This is Regina's day and I hope it will be a very happy one for her.'

Chapter 7

'This is the Reverend Mr Kerr,' Harding nodded towards the preacher. 'Reverend Kerr, Gav and Abigail Chisholm.'

Abigail gave a little curtsy, making her coffee-and-cream-coloured gown billow out.

'I'm happy to meet you, sir.'

'Well,' said Harding, 'now that we're all here, we'd better get on with it.'

Abigail and Gav stole a glance at one another.

The preacher rubbed his hands.

'Eh, yes, yes, indeed, Mr Harding. Well, eh, you and eh, the bride stand over here, if you will.'

Regina wore a green silk gown over wide panniers and a gold quilted petticoat. The green was the same emerald colour as her eyes and a vivid contrast to the long auburn curl that hung over one shoulder. Gold earrings dangled from her ears and she held a fan painted in colours of rich ruby red and purple and gold and green with a carved ivory handle.

Harding towered beside her, broad-shouldered, and rock-solid in comparison with her creamy shoulders and arms, and the pale perfection of her face with its silky sweep of lashes and small even features. Yet her mouth was tinged with hardness, and an aura of strength about her seemed to defy and compete with his.

The house was quiet and still as the preacher's voice droned on. Bette and Jethro had been put to bed for an afternoon sleep. Outside the window insects buzzed continuously.

The preacher stood with his back to the fireplace and above it the gold-framed mirror reflected the scene. Beside the fireplace, on top of the desk, pink and yellow and white roses sparkled with diamonds of water that had sprinkled over their petals when Melie Anne filled the bowl. A few petals had dropped off and curled wetly on the polished mahogany.

661

The room was a bower of shadows, the trees only allowing amber light to speckle in. The tall clock in the corner caught a gleam on its brass face but tick-tocked cautiously on.

Through in the kitchen some slaves had gathered and were talking in low voices.

Jenny was whispering.

' 'Tain't right so soon after poor Miss Kitty's dyin'. That poor woman ain't right settled in her grave. An' somethin' happened that night. Somethin' bad,' she added darkly.

'Wish you wouldn't keep sayin' that,' Westminster complained. 'You're goin' get us all in a heap o' trouble with that tongue o' yours.'

Old Abe said:

'Miss Kitty was fond o' Miss Regina an' Miss Regina was fond of Miss Kitty. 'Tain't no use denyin' it.'

'You're a fool,' Jenny hissed. 'You're gettin' so old an' blind you cain't see what's stuck up in front of your nose. That red-haired little devil hated poor Miss Kitty, hated that poor woman somethin' wicked. That devil, she was the death of Miss Kitty, I just know she was. She wouldn't let me near Miss Kitty's room that night. And she'd shut the door and Miss Kitty's door was never kept shut at night.'

'You're the wicked one,' old Abe said. 'Sayin' such things. I ain't blind an' I saw Miss Regina awhimperin' and aringin' her hands. That poor gal was agrievin' for Miss Kitty.'

Callie Mae gave Jenny a nudge.

'It's time you watched your tongue in front o' them saplin's.' She nodded towards Lunesta and Little Sam who were sitting together in the corner eating a meal of corn-pone. They gazed big-eyed back at the knot of servants.

They were thin, gangly children who had never been away from their mother until now. They had lived with her on the Dakwood Plantation until the master there died and his daughter had sold the plantation and most of the slaves.

Mistress Dakwood had kept their mother to go with her as a body servant to the new place. But she didn't want them. Their mother had wept and pleaded and they had wept and pleaded but it had made not the slightest difference. They had been separated from their mother and sent to the auction block just the same.

Now they had been bought by Mistress Regina and sometimes Little Sam ran errands and carried things for her. Lunesta was learning to sew and look after Mistress Regina's clothes and she also helped her to do her hair. Both children felt shy and nervous in their new surroundings and they were more than a little afraid of their new mistress, although they were thankful that so far she had been good to them. Not good in the same way that their mother had been, not warm and loving and hugging. Not even the soft-talking kind of good. But that couldn't be expected of white folks. At least not to niggers.

But Mistress Regina allowed them to sleep in the kitchen, allowed them food to eat, and didn't kick them about or beat them. Most important of all, she had allowed them to stay together. They were grateful to her for that and felt they owed her a sense of loyalty. Later, going back to the big house after eating their corn-pone, they discussed what they'd heard in the kitchen.

Lunesta said.

'Ain't that Jenny wicked, though?'

'She sure is.'

'It's just terrible how some folks talk. They just open their mouths an' let any old thing fall out. Lies, lies, lies. Some folks just cain't help tellin' them.'

'Like Big Zeph at the Dakwood Plantation? Weren't he the one? But he didn't say no wicked things. More like stories. Folks liked listenin' to Big Zeph.' He chuckled. 'Some o' his lies were awful mirthmakin'.'

Coming to the end of the short walkway that joined the kitchen to the back, they entered the house. Immediately they arrived in the hall they stopped and stood shyly holding hands. Harding and Regina were saying goodbye to the preacher at the front door. Then Harding returned to the drawing-room. Regina was about to follow him when she noticed them standing in the shadows. She stared at them for a minute and they stared back, overawed by how beautiful she looked. Suddenly she beckoned them to follow her into the dining-room.

On the sideboard was a dish of vanilla fudge and to their astonishment, she held it out to them. They just stood transfixed, gawping at the sweets.

'Well, go on,' Regina said. 'Take a piece each. Take two pieces each.'

Eyes enormous and whites showing, they stared up at her trying to decide whether or not she was meaning to trick them into doing something wrong just so that she could punish them for it.

'Go on!' she urged again.

Apprehensively they both stretched out, plucked at a piece of fudge and, never taking their eyes off Regina, they eased it into their mouths. The taste was sheer delight. Never in their lives had they experienced such bliss. They gave themselves up to the complete concentration of chewing and swallowing.

'Did you enjoy that?' Regina asked.

'Yes, Miss Regina, ma'am,' they nodded enthusiastically.

'All right, I can't stand here all day. Take your other piece.'

They pounced eagerly this time and Little Sam, quite carried away, burst out with his mouth full:

'I just knew you wasn't wicked like she said.'

'Who said?' Regina snapped, her manner changing as if a sheet of ice had suddenly hardened between them.

Both children's palms flew to their mouths.

'Answer me!' Regina's hand shot out and struck Little Sam such a blow across the face it made tears spurt from his eyes.

He started to sob and to tremble violently and Lunesta grabbed him in her arms and babbled out as quickly as she could:

'Jenny. She say you're wicked, Miss Regina, ma'am. It was Jenny. She was telling everyone you did somethin' bad to Miss Kitty that was the death of her. But no one's believin' her. Everyone's sayin' how good you was to Miss Kitty. Old Abe, he says Jenny's the wicked one and Callie Mae told Jenny 'tain't right to say such wicked things.'

The blood left Regina's face. She stared at the children without seeing them.

Mistress Kitty's bell was ringing. She could hear it echoing along the corridor from Mistress Kitty's room. Immediately she tossed aside the bedcovers, grabbed the candle-holder and without stopping to don a robe, hastened along the corridor to administer what help she could to the older woman.

The bell had fallen on to the floor and Mistress Kitty was gasping for breath. Regina lit the candle by the bed so that she would have plenty of light with which to see to prepare Mistress Kitty's potion and give the suffering woman relief. It was while she was doing this that she noticed Mistress Kitty's eyes, bulging with distress, fix on her abdomen. Then their eyes met before the older woman, still fighting desperately for breath, pulled her eyes away to seek the potion on the bedside table.

Regina continued to stare at her as if frozen. Then suddenly she lifted the candle and left the room, shutting the door behind her.

Jenny, Mistress Kitty's body slave, who slept in the cupboard under the stairs, had just reached the landing when Regina said:

'I have seen to Mistress Kitty. Go back to bed.'

She waited at the top of the stairs holding the candle high until the servant disappeared. Then she glided silently to her own room.

In the morning, Jenny had found Mistress Kitty dead. But Mistress Kitty had been suffering and dying for many months. Her eventual death had been a blessed release for everyone, including Mistress Kitty herself.

'Everyone's sayin' how good you was to Miss Kitty,' Lunesta repeated, near to tears. 'We all knows it, Miss Regina.'

'Come with me, both of you,' Regina said, suddenly sweeping from the room, across the hall and into the drawing-room.

Harding and Gav were relaxing back in their chairs beside the fire enjoying their pipes. Abigail was leafing through a book.

'What's wrong?' Harding asked when he saw Regina's stiff face, and the two sobbing children at her back. Regina jerked them forward.

'Repeat to the master what you've just said. Go on!' She punched Lunesta's back, making the words tumble out again.

Harding's eyes flashed with anger.

'Tell Callie Mae to come here,' he snapped at the terrified

child.

Both Lunesta and Little Sam ran from the room and Harding said to Gav:

'I've never had any time for disloyal troublemaking niggers.'

Gav didn't say anything and in a few minutes a wide-eyed Callie Mae appeared.

Harding said:

'I'm going to ask you some questions, Callie Mae, and you'd better answer them truthfully. If you don't, you'll be punished. Do you understand?'

'Yes, Master Harding.'

'What was Jenny saying in the kitchen just now?'

Callie Mae lowered her eyes.

'Come on, speak up. Was she saying things about your mistress?'

'Yes, Master Harding.' She spoke regretfully, sadly. She didn't want to get Jenny into trouble but knew it was inevitable.

'What did she say?'

Callie Mae hesitated, then with a trembling voice, murmured:

'She said 'tain't right you and Miss Regina gettin' married so soon.' She looked up anxiously. 'Jenny was so fond o' Miss Kitty and she was so upset at Miss Kitty dyin'. I don't think she's got over it, Master Harding. That's why she's sayin' these things.'

'Just answer my question.'

'She . . . she said somethin' happened that night.'

'What did she mean?'

'I don' know and she don' know either. She don' know what she's sayin', Master Harding. She's just upset. Somethin' bad happened, she said. She thinks Miss Regina made poor Miss Kitty die. But we all knows poor Miss Kitty was dyin' with her breathless turns. Only Jenny never would believe it. Just 'cause she didn't want it to happen, I suppose.'

'All right. Now tell Old Abe to come through.'

Tears suddenly welled up in Callie Mae's eyes.

'Yes, Master Harding.'

When Old Abe arrived he was questioned too, and then Joseph and Westminster and Melie Anne, who had also been in the kitchen at the time. Eventually Harding sent for Jenny so that he could speak to her. Joseph came back, however, and said that Jenny must have run off as she was nowhere to be found.

'Oh, has she?' Harding said grimly. 'Well, get the dogs out and saddle up my horse.' Rising, he turned to Gav. 'Do you want to come along for a bit of sport, Gav?'

Gav, who was still puffing at his pipe, shook his head.

Harding shrugged.

'Suit yourself.'

Regina said:

'What are you going to do with her when you find her? String her up?'

'No, but she'll wish I had before I'm finished with her. I'll have her tongue pulled out.'

Then before leaving the room he said to Gav: 'We'll have a game of billiards when I get back. I shouldn't be long.'

A silence held the room after he left. Regina went over to the window and stood looking out. Eventually she said:

'I wonder what way she went? Unless the dogs can smell her out, it won't be easy to find her in the forest.'

Abigail put aside the book she had been holding.

'Regina, I hope you mean to speak to your husband and persuade him from the harsh punishment he spoke of.'

'Why should I?' Regina said without turning round.

'Well, if you don't know, there's no use me telling you.'

Regina felt needled by Abigail's quiet, self-righteous voice. Easy for her, she thought bitterly. Sitting there safe and sure of her doting husband. Everything went right for Abigail. Nothing terrible or frightening happened to spoil Abigail's wedding day.

'Regina!' Gav said in a sharper tone. 'It's you I'm thinking about. What sort of person are you allowing yourself to become?'

'Allowing myself to become?' Regina echoed derisively, coming over to sit opposite Gav and stare at him. '*Allowing* myself? My God!'

'You weren't like this when you were younger and we were together.'

Yet, even as he said it, a frightening doubt was taking shape at the back of his mind. Had there not always been something terrible about Regina? She had caused Mistress Annabella's

667

French lover to be horribly killed. She had caused the first mate of the ship *The Glasgow Lass* to fall overboard and drown. What was she not capable of? He felt nauseated with horror. Could it be that the slave, Jenny, was telling the truth and Regina had caused Mistress Kitty's death?

He fixed his sister with an agonized gaze. She looked so beautiful, a defiant blaze of colour with her fiery hair, emerald eyes, golden jewellery and shimmering gown.

'Remember how it used to be at home?'

'Oh, I remember all right, Gav. In fact, I remember Glasgow a lot better than you. You say remember how it used to be at home, as if everything was happy and good then. Well, it wasn't. It wasn't good when we lived with our mother in that hovel in Tannery Row . . .'

'Regina, you don't mean that . . .'

She gave an incredulous laugh.

'Don't mean it? Why shouldn't I mean it?'

'Mother was good to us.'

'She fed us slops and kept us in a filthy hovel with harlots debauching upstairs and a blind fiend and his vicious dog next door who continually terrified us.'

'It wasn't Mother's fault that we were poor any more than it was her fault that she got caught up with the Highland army, or wrongfully hanged for stealing.'

'And I suppose it wasn't the beggar Quin's fault for kidnapping us and making us beg for him each day and sleep in filthy cold closes every night.'

'It wasn't really, Regina . . .'

Her mouth twisted.

'No? Well, it's not my fault that Jenny is going to be punished by having her tongue pulled out.'

'If you'd just try and have some compassion and understanding for other people.'

'Why should I? No one's ever had any compassion or understanding for me.'

'That's not true and you know it.'

'What the hell do you mean by that?'

Abigail rose.

668

'Gav, you and your sister can fight for as long as you like but I have a headache and I'm going upstairs to lie down.'

'I'm sorry, Abby.' Gav rose too. 'Perhaps a walk in the air would do you good. I'll come too.'

'No, I'd rather go upstairs. Anyway, if we're leaving tomorrow I'd be the better for resting today.'

'You don't need to leave tomorrow,' Regina said. 'You can stay the week if you wish.'

'Thank you, but we really do need to go. We've chores that need attending to at home.'

'Yes, the work soon piles up at the store too,' Gav added. 'I can't afford to stay away.'

'Very well.' Regina picked up her embroidery and began calmly stitching.

Gav's and Abigail's eyes met before she left the room.

'Regina.' Gav tried again once they were alone but his sister cut him short with an unexpectedly savage voice.

'Why don't you just mind your own business?'

With a sigh he picked up his pipe. Outside he could hear the barking and baying of the dogs. Sometimes the sounds were loud and clamorous, sometimes they were muffled and faint as if from a far distance. Then for a long time there was silence except for the cheeping and twittering of the birds and the rustling of the trees. Eventually Abigail came back downstairs and Regina ordered the evening meal to be served, although Harding had still not returned. When he did arrive he announced triumphantly:

'It took me longer than I expected, but I got her all right. I've locked her up until tomorrow. I'll have all the slaves gathered to watch the punishment. It'll be a warning to them.'

'Abby and I will be setting off for home first thing in the morning,' Gav said. 'We've a lot of work waiting to be done.'

Harding poured himself a glass of whisky.

'You must come again.'

'Well, I don't know about Abby and the children. It's a long tiring journey for them, but no doubt I'll be back on store business.'

'I'll get one of the slaves to pack some food supplies in your wagon. Come on, let's have that game of billiards.'

Gav followed him from the room but his mind was still troubled. It was as if nightmares like creeping mice were hiding in his head. By the time morning came and he and his family were taking their leave of Forest Hall he was ashamed at the relief he felt to be free of the place and its occupants. Just before the wagon rumbled away his eyes met those of his sister and he imagined he caught a glimpse of the timid, vulnerable Regina he had once known.

But before he had gone far into the forest he could hear the plantation bell ringing to summon all the slaves to the clearance and he knew that that was where Harding and Regina had gone too.

The plantation bell hung from a wooden erection in the clearance in front of the barns and stables on one side and the office and overseer's house on the other. The remaining sides of the square were wooded areas. The trees that faced the barns and backed onto the big house had been cut down and thinned out until most of them were like giant stools squatting in the shade of those trees that were left. On the other side of the clearance, opposite the office and overseer's house, rose the forest like a huge wall.

The bell had been donging out for some time before Harding and Regina walked round to the back of the house and along the path until they came to the office. There they mounted the steps and turned to face the gathered throng of Negroes.

'Move back all of you. Leave a space in from here,' Harding shouted. 'Where's the smith?'

'Here, Master Harding.' A big Negro, stripped to the waist and showing bulging muscles, stepped forward.

'Have you your pliers and knife ready?'

'Yes, Master Harding.'

Harding puffed leisurely at his pipe as he looked at the silent crowd. By his side Regina stood like a tropical flower in her green dress and vivid hair. Eventually Harding spoke to the waiting crowd:

'If there's one thing I won't have it's a disloyal, troublemaking

670

liar of a nigger. I've never wasted any time with no-good niggers and I'm not going to waste any time now. Especially a no-good, troublemaking nigger who tells lies about her mistress. Let what's going to happen to her be a lesson to you all.'

The overseer and the driver and the smith had taken up positions at the foot of the stairs and Harding now addressed the overseer and the driver.

'Mr Blakely and Minos, fetch Jenny the house servant.'

Soon part of the crowd erupted in terrified screams as the overseer and driver dragged a hysterical Jenny to the front of the stairs.

'I'm sorry, Miss Regina, ma'am. I'm sorry. I'm sorry, Master Harding. I didn't mean what I said, I swear I didn't mean it. Please don't hurt me. Oh, please.' Sobbing wildly she flung herself on her knees at the foot of the steps, only to be dragged up again by the two men.

'Hold her good,' Harding said, 'so as the smith can pull her tongue and make a nice clean job of it.'

Jenny's screams changed to mindless, high-pitched, staccato bursts of terror. But she managed one other cry of:

'Miss Regina!'

It was the last thing she ever said.

Chapter 8

The four streets leading from the Cross in Glasgow had a most elegant appearance with their arched and pillared piazzas and covered arcades. The Trongate especially boasted splendid edifices like the Tolbooth with its tall crown-shaped steeple and musical chiming clock. Next to the Tolbooth, the Exchange had long attracted much attention because of the faces carved in stone above the arches of its piazzas. There were spacious coffee houses and comfortable taverns. There was the Tron Church with its two large bells that rang out at six, eight and ten of the clock at night, and at six in the morning all the year round.

But the streets that met at the Cross in such silvery-grey stone splendour all dwindled away into humble thatched cottages and mean hovels of overhanging wood and outside wooden stairs. Trongate Street had the Shawfield Mansion at its western extremity, but after that, it too was a straggle of bushes and trees and cottages. To most of them was attached a malt barn and other outhouses. These houses were occupied by maltmen who prepared ale one day and delivered it on the next to the citizens. Other cottages had orchard gardens.

It was in this area that the Western Port or Gate of the city had once stood and the narrow road still bore the name Westergate as a reminder. In the Westergate aristocratic mansions had begun to be erected side by side with the cottages, making a curious contrast which strangers and travellers never tired of remarking on.

The Ramsay mansion rose up from the ground on which two cottages and their rambling orchard gardens and outbuildings had stood. When it was completed there would be very little garden left; only a small patch at the back and none at all at the front. At either side maltmen's cottages hugged close to the mansion walls, leaving no space in between. But no space in between was needed. Tradespeople had plenty of open countryside at the back of the property through which to bring their goods and a door had been provided as a rear access to the house. This was as much a novelty and a delight as anything to Annabella. To think that tradespeople would not need to drag filthy coal and water and other necessities all through the place! It meant an enormous improvement to the quality of life. For a start, the house could be kept so much cleaner.

The Ramsay mansion was one of the last dwellings before the row of elm trees and the wild countryside of heather and broom. But opposite the house was the dwelling and yard of a keeper of sedan chairs, and his cottage was often flanked by elaborate, painted chairs, some with curtained windows. Annabella thought it was a stroke of great good fortune to have such a place so near. She realized that it would not be easy to walk the distance from there to the Trongate or elsewhere to visit friends or go to the market or attend an assembly.

Trongate Street in winter, indeed in summer too, was potholed and difficult enough to manage on foot. But by the time it dwindled into the narrow Westergate, it had the extra hazard of slithering dung from the farm animals as well.

Mungo House, for that is what they had decided to call it, was going to be a very grand place and Annabella felt proud and happy as she showed Phemy around it. At the front, a short double outside stair with an iron railing led up to a tall oak door with iron studs. It opened in halves into a square hall.

Phemy clapped her hands in appreciation.

'Oh, Annabella, how lucky you are. Everything is absolutely splendid. When will you be moving in?'

'There's still the furnishings to organize and of course the workmen aren't quite finished yet despite my prodigious urgings.'

'Shame on you, you've been driving them like slaves right from the start. I wonder that the poor men have managed any sleep.'

'You like the hall, then, Phemy?'

'It is so bright and airy. Oh, I do think it's a great advantage having such a high ceiling and I love the cupola with the little windows round it.'

'Isn't the staircase marvellously elegant? Isn't it a difference from our monstrously filthy tower stairs in the Saltmarket?'

Phemy's sharp-nosed, birdlike face tweaked this way and that.

'It's a pretty colour scheme. Oh, I do like it, Annabella.'

Walls and ceilings were a delicate apple green separated by a frieze of white and gold and all the doors were gleaming white. Annabella skipped over to the first door on the right and Phemy hurried after her. It led into a fair-sized square room with a single window looking out onto the Westergate.

'This has to be the living-room, Phemy. Where Papa and I and Mungo can sit. There's a drawing-room upstairs for entertaining guests. And there's a dining-room across the other side of the hall and a kitchen at the back and even two little rooms for the servants.'

'Rooms for servants!' Phemy squealed incredulously. 'Lord's sake, what next?'

They sped back to the hall, their hooped skirts swishing and seesawing. The dining-room was the colour of peaches and also had a window facing the Westergate. Its walls were ornamented with festoons of fruit and flowers in realistic shades and looked very pleasing and inviting.

'But you haven't a dining-table at home, Annabella. In fact, you can't have nearly enough furniture.'

Annabella giggled.

'Papa has gone this far, he might as well go the whole hog and purchase a dining-table and a few other bits and pieces.'

They swept out of the room and up the stairs.

'There are three bedrooms just for sleeping in, Phemy. Imagine . . . three bedrooms! And just for sleeping in! And, hold your breath . . . this is my wondrous, dazzling drawing-room.'

'Annabella!' Phemy clasped her hands under her chin in rapturous admiration. 'Annabella, a crystal chandelier!'

'Think how many candles it will hold and how bright it will make the room. Oh, Phemy, I have always felt so cast down and cruelly confused by dark, dismal and incommodious places.'

'You will be happy here, Annabella. Surely you will.'

Here there were festoons of flowers and also raised ovals on the panelling on which were beautifully painted landscapes.

'None of the rooms are over-large. Yet they are not small.'

'They're larger than the rooms in the Saltmarket or the Trongate, Annabella. I do envy you.'

'Well, why don't you get your gudeman to build a mansion for you? He could afford it.'

Phemy gave a quick little shrug.

'The Earl could never stand all the commotion of moving, I'm afraid. Poor Glendinny's very frail.'

Annabella shrugged.

'Then you would be a widow like me—only luckier because you would be wondrously wealthy. Poor Blackadder was very lacking in bawbees.'

'Annabella, you flutter me, talking like that.' Phemy tried to give Annabella a reproving look but was shocked to find herself giggling instead. She hastily squashed her hilarity behind a mittened palm.

Annabella skimmed away towards the bedrooms.

'See, there are closets for hanging our clothes in. It is so much better than folding them into kists, don't you think? But of course I will still use the kists for storing the household linen.'

'Such a lovely view at the back.' Phemy pressed her pocked face against the bedroom window. 'What a difference from looking out at a back close crowded with beggars and suchlike. And, oh, the smell of grass and flowers and trees instead of dunghills and fulzie, Annabella.'

'There's got to be dunghills and fulzie wherever you are but out here the farmers are quick to remove it to use on their fields.'

'Will you be taking Mungo away from the grammar school? It's such a long rough walk for the poor wee lad, especially when it's dark.'

'It does seem more sensible to change to the school in the Westergate when it's so much nearer. Yes, I expect I will.'

They returned to the front door and, whisking their petticoats over one arm, they carefully stepped across the rough track of road to the sedan keeper's yard.

'I'm sorry Griselle couldn't manage,' Annabella said. 'How is she, by the way?'

Phemy sighed.

'No different from what she was when you last saw her.'

'The best thing she could have done was have another child.'

'Yes, but you know what she's like.'

'I do indeed. She would not allow Douglas to touch her with a barge-pole now, far less with his . . .'

'Annabella!'

'It is true. It is Douglas I am sorry for now. I know she is your sister, Phemy, and naturally you are fond of her. Lord's sake, so am I, but she is treating her gudeman with monstrous cruelty. Her tongue is like a dagger continuously whittling away at him.'

'I know, I know.' Tears welled up in Phemy's eyes. 'Oh, poor Douglas. He suffers it all as best he can but he must feel sorely tried and very unhappy. He has always been so fond of Griselle and so kind to her.'

'If he were more of a man and less of a milk-sop, he could stop Grizzie's infernal flyting.'

'I really don't see what he can do, Annabella.'

'He could knock a few of her teeth out for a start.'

'Annabella! You're fluttering me. Please don't talk in so wild a manner.'

'Or he could complain to the magistrates and have her put on the ducking stool. After a few duckings in the river she would have little breath left for flyting at Douglas.'

'Oh, please stop, Annabella. I can't bear even to think of such a thing. And after all, poor Grizzie lost her child.'

'Women are losing children all the time with the fever and the pox and God knows all what. But they don't keep blaming their gudemen and making their lives a misery.' She raised her voice in the direction of the chairman's cottage. 'You are keeping ladies waiting, sir. Make haste at once.'

A man like a leek in a long green coat and white breeches emerged from the front door of the house, bending his head so that it would not knock against the lintel.

'Och, it is yourselves, Mistress Blackadder and Mistress Glendinny,' he said in a lilting Highland accent. 'I am chust after telling the men at the back. They are coming round this minute. Aye, it is a grand day, is it not?'

'Indeed it is, Mr MacLintock,' Annabella replied, flouncing

open her fan and proceeding to flap it energetically in front of her face. 'If somewhat warm. I fear the sun does nothing for a lady's delicate complexion. We should have worn masks, Phemy.'

'Och, the chairs will be giving you shade and here they are now. When is it you and your family are moving to the Westergate now, Mistress Blackadder?'

'Soon. Soon, Mr MacLintock. I am greatly looking forward to it.'

'Aye, chust so. Good-day to you, ladies.'

Phemy wriggled into one chair and Annabella arranged her skirts into another, the chairmen hoisted up the poles and they were off.

Annabella peered out at the cottages and mansions on either side of the country road. Most had the rutted grass-tufted road right up to their front doors. Some had ragged bushes growing close to their walls. Some had trees spreading in front of windows, cutting out light. Others had the sparkling waters of St Enoch's burn running between them. Others again had orchard gardens like coloured shawls draped round their backs.

They passed the Buck's Head Inn, then the Black Bull Inn with its sign creaking in the breeze. Then one or two more cottages before they came to the tenements of Trongate Street.

The chairmen loped along at a steady pace, making the chairs swing and bounce. Suddenly Phemy rapped on the roof and made her chairmen stop. Seeing this, Annabella signalled for her sedan to be put down too. They opened their doors and leaned out. Phemy called over,

'Have you time to come with me to pay Griselle a little visit just now? Talking of her has made me worry about how she is. I haven't seen her for a few days.'

'You worry too much about everybody, Phemy. But all right. I'll come if it will ease you.'

They wriggled back into the sedans and the chairmen shut the doors before setting off again. Along past the Tron Church, then the shipping booths like dark caves behind the walkways underneath the arches. The booths had half-doors and sometimes the owners could be seen leaning over these doors gazing out at life passing by under the piazzas and out on the road. The statue of King William, the hero of the Boyne sitting astride his horse, reared up in front of the Exchange building. The Tolbooth towered over the Cross, its musical bells singing out as the chairmen turned right and trotted down Saltmarket Street.

Annabella glanced out at her close as she passed just to check that Betsy was not lounging about gossiping with other servants instead of preparing the dinner. Once a crowd of serving-maids gathered at a well or a close-mouth, they completely forgot about the work they were supposed to be doing or what errand they had been sent out for. There they would cluster, water stoups or baskets or milk pails discarded in the dirty road at their feet while they stood, arms cheekily akimbo or comfortably folded over bosoms, laughing and chattering.

A rush of ragged children suddenly filled the street with screaming. A dog barked and weaved about behind them as if it was herding sheep. It disappeared round by the Cross, sweeping the children and the noise away with it. There was only an old woman left. Weighed down by a sack on her back, she moved slowly and intoned into herself with every step.

'Carrots and turnips, ho! Carrots and turnips, ho!'

The sedans manoeuvred in between the pillars of Gibson's Land and through the archway to the back of the building. At the foot of the stairs leading to Griselle's flat, the chairs were lowered and Annabella and Phemy struggled out.

'I dare swear I'll make as much use of my horse as a sedan when I'm living at the Westergate,' Annabella said. 'It is monstrously hot and uncomfortable in these chairs, no matter what Mr MacLintock says.'

'I suppose we shouldn't really complain about the heat, Annabella. It'll be winter soon enough.'

Phemy tirled Griselle's door-pin and as they waited for Griselle to come Annabella clasped her hands to her bosom, gave a rapturous sigh and gazed heavenwards.

'Imagine, just imagine! I'll be living in my magnificent house by then and entertaining like a queen.'

'Come away in.' Griselle held herself primly as she led the way through to her bedroom. Her wooden mask of a face revealed only slits for eyes and mouth. Her skin was sallow and her cheeks purple-veined. 'You'll drink a cup of hot chocolate with us.'

'Hallo, Douglas,' Annabella greeted her brother and held out her cheek for a kiss. 'I didn't expect you to be home at this hour.'

He kissed her, then fluttered up his hands and eyes.

'Alas, I am plagued with these frightful headaches. Today I could not see to count the columns of figures and Papa had to send me home.'

'He's alive though,' Griselle said.

Douglas gave a fleeting ghost of a smile.

'And how are you, dear girlies? Sit down, do. I shall tell the servant to prepared you some of this delicious chocolate.'

'I'll go and tell the servant,' Griselle said. 'You can't do anything right.'

Her skirts swished like a broom scraping the floor as she left the room. Douglas lifted his cup of chocolate with shaking hands and lowered his head to take a sip.

Annabella studied him. His dress was still that of a fop and a dandy. Yet, at the same time, he had a neglected look. His wig was unevenly powdered as if he had done the job absent-mindedly. And tufts of it that should have been curls spiked out grotesquely. Powder dusted over the shoulders of his coat and his neckcloth looked limp and grubby as did the ribbons trailing from his cuffs. He still used white and scarlet face paint but it was patchy and smudged, giving him the appearance of a pathetic failure of a clown.

'We are well, Douglas,' Phemy said. 'Don't worry about us. Oh, I'm so sorry your health is not robust. I wish there was something I could do to help. Perhaps if I brought you some of my strengthening broth.'

Douglas looked up with anxious eyes.

'No, no, dear girlie. I fear Griselle would not be pleased.'

'Hell and damnation, brother!' Annabella cried out. 'Have you no spunk at all? What does it matter if Mistress Griselle is pleased or not?'

Douglas gave one of his tremulous smiles.

'It may not matter to you, sister, but it is of vital importance to me.'

Flicking out her fan, Annabella set it in angry motion.

'Fiddlesticks and poppycock! To the ducking-stool with her, I say. I have a good mind to suggest such a course of action to Papa.'

'Oh, no!' Both Douglas and Phemy cried out in distress. 'Oh, Annabella!'

Douglas put his cup down, spilling some of its contents onto the table.

'Oh, oh, you have me so fluttered, Annabella. Now look what I have done.' He began trying to mop up the spilled chocolate with his handkerchief.

'Gracious heavens!' Annabella protested. 'You have servants who can do that. You pay them to perform menial tasks. And you pay Griselle to see that the housework is done. What is the use of keeping a dog if you bark yourself?'

'Dear saucy brat,' he tried to laugh. 'You were always the same, even as a child. Nothing or no-one worried you over-much, or for very long.'

She shrugged.

'What good does it do? Your precious Griselle would think a lot more of you if you acted more like a man.'

'You do not understand.' He sighed. 'Poor Griselle . . .'

'To bloody hell with Griselle . . .'

'Annabella!' they cried in unison again.

'Pox on her, I say!'

'Pox on who?' Griselle queried, entering the room followed by a maid servant carrying a tray of steaming chocolate.

Douglas fluttered his hanky in agitation.

'Pox on the workmen who are taking such a fiendishly long time to finish Papa's mansion.'

'You fool,' Griselle said. 'Everybody knows that mansion has gone up faster than any mansion has ever gone up before. Your tongue's as useless as every other ridiculous-looking part of you.'

'Grizzie . . .' Phemy wailed but she was interrupted by Griselle's sudden shriek of fury.

'Look at my good table. It's in a pigsty you should be. You

680

filthy worm. Can't you even drink a cup of chocolate without doing something wrong?'

'Grizzie,' Annabella said in quite a pleasant tone of voice. 'I am not in the least surprised that no one visits this house any more or that I am the only friend you have left in the world. It is a misery and embarrassment to sit in the same room with you and listen to your vile tongue constantly lashing your gudeman.'

There was silence for a minute or two while they all sipped their chocolate. Then Griselle said:

'You're all right, mistress. You've always been all right.'

'Now, Grizzie, that is not true. I have had my misfortunes, and my sad losses.'

'You lost a lover.'

'And a husband.'

'If that was all I'd lost, I'd be a happy woman today.'

Phemy's face twitched into a spasm of distress.

'Griselle, you must pray to God to forgive you and to soften your heart. It is wicked to talk the way you do. I'm afraid you will be punished. I'm so worried about you.'

'It is all my fault, dear girlie.' Douglas rose with a flapping of arms. 'Truly it is. It is I who should pray to be forgiven for causing such wretchedness. Now I will relieve you of my company so that you can have a *tête-à-tête* without further disturbance.'

'Are you returning to the counting-house?' Annabella asked.

'Not him,' Griselle replied. 'He lies abed most days. It's all he's fit for.'

'Sometimes I am quite overcome by deep dejection.' Douglas posed at the door, trying to smile and fluff out his cuffs. 'And I am fit for nothing else, it is perfectly true.'

Suddenly Annabella pattered over to him and kissed his cheek. Phemy quickly followed and did the same.

'We will see you again soon, brother.'

'Yes, indeed. Indeed we will,' Phemy agreed.

His painted chalk-white face and strawberry lips blurred into the shadows of the lobby as he withdrew. Annabella shut the door and swung round.

'You shrew! You bloody fishwife!'

'Oh, Annabella,' Phemy wailed.

'Isn't he lucky,' said Griselle, 'to have a woman to fight for him? Of course, he hasn't enough guts to fight for himself.'

'You could have done a lot worse than marry my brother.'

'Tuts, you really must control that ridiculous imagination of yours, Annabella. You're letting it completely run away with you.'

'You are allowing your monstrous tongue to run away with you, mistress. Take care. I might take a fancy for tearing it out.'

'Douglas is very kind and considerate, Griselle,' Phemy said. 'He killed my son.'

'Poppycock!' Annabella snapped. 'If anyone is to blame for George drowning, Griselle, it is yourself. You should have allowed him to learn to swim. If he had been able to swim he would not have drowned.'

Phemy's palms flew to her mouth. In acute concern she stared at her sister to see what effect Annabella's words were having. Griselle's face appeared more wooden than ever. Without moving a muscle, she said,

'Get out of my house.'

'You always coddled him and babied him. It was a wonder poor George was able to walk.'

'Get out.'

'I am going. But just you remember, mistress, that if Douglas was as spiteful and unforgiving as you, he could be making your life a misery by reminding you of your responsibility in killing his son.'

'Oh, Annabella,' Phemy sobbed. 'How could you be so cruel?'

But Annabella had whisked away, banging the door shut behind her. She felt furious; furious at Griselle, furious at Douglas, furious at herself for allowing either of them to spoil the happy mood she had been in about moving to her new house.

'Pox on them,' she thought, flouncing down the stairs and out through the back close. In Saltmarket Street she was nearly knocked over by a crowd of people running up towards the Cross.

'How dare you, sir!' she railed at the nearest man. 'Have you no manners?'

The man doffed his hat and 'made a leg' but it was done in unseemly haste.

'Beg pardon, ma'am.'

'One moment, sir.' She detained him from scampering off. 'What is all this prodigious rush?'

'The stage is due to arrive from Edinburgh, ma'am.'

A flush of excitement brought immediate colour to her cheeks and sparkle to her eyes.

'Where?'

'The Saracen's Head in the Gallowgate.'

She let him go and began waving her arms about and shouting,

'Caddie! Caddie! A chair, a chair!'

She would have hitched up her skirts and run all the way up the Saltmarket and along the Gallowgate but it would have taken some considerable time and she did not want to risk missing the great event.

A caddie in a brown coat and flat tam-o'-shanter took up her cry. Down Saltmarket Street he gusted like the wind, waving his arms and roaring.

'A chair! A chair!'

He disappeared round the Briggait and soon returned with two chairmen trotting at a brisk pace with a sedan bouncing on its poles between them.

In a matter of minutes she was snug inside it and swinging along towards the Gallowgate.

Before she had gone to America the place where the Saracen's Head Inn now stood had been an ancient and neglected graveyard, called St Mungo's after Glasgow's patron saint. It had been overgrown by grass and nettles, nearly hidden amongst which had been a few narrow grey stones much encrusted with fog and deeply set in the earth, marking the graves of the long departed.

Now, miraculously, an inn stood there. Not an ordinary tavern or ale-house with the usual sign above the door saying 'Good Entertainment for Man and Beast' but a hotel with thirty-six bedrooms and a large ballroom at the back with a fiddler's loft. It had a yard at the back too with stables numbering sixty stalls. It was also a great Posting House and here were to be got the only post-chaises and gigs in the city.

The inn had a large signboard outside the main entrance. It displayed a Saracen fierce and bold with staring eyes and half-drawn scimitar, painted in strong brilliant colours.

Annabella rapped on the sedan to signal the chairmen to stop when they reached the inn but it was only with some difficulty that they squeezed a place for it near the main entrance. The stage had just arrived with its bugle still loudly blaring and its six horses steaming and rearing up and pawing the air and snorting and whinnying with excitement at all the cheering crowds jumping and struggling and pressing all around. The chairmen elbowed a space for Annabella when she stepped out of the sedan and she was able to view with delight the fashionably dressed strangers who alighted from the coach. Who were they, she wondered, and what news and titbits of gossip and scandal had they brought from the capital city?

There was an aristocratic woman in a cherry velvet hoop with broad double bands of gold trimming. She wore a large-brimmed hat decorated with enormous feathers and she held a mask on a stick in front of her face. She stood preening and posing and swirling her skirts as she waited for all the others to alight. Suddenly a rough fellow from the crowd pounced on her, knocking aside her mask and shouting:

'Welcome to Glasgow!'

Then he gave her a noisy kiss. The woman's male travelling companion was a long narrow-shouldered man with a stiff, sticking-out hem to his silver-spangled coat. He flung up his arms in dismay but that did not stop more ruffians shouting and grabbing and kissing the other women passengers until the whole party, men and women, were forced to fly into the Saracen's Head Inn screeching with harassment, hats and wigs askew.

Annabella could not help giggling as she bunched up her skirts and squeezed her way back into the sedan chair. It had been an amusing diversion and she could hardly wait to get home to tell Betsy all about it.

But when she arrived back at the house in Saltmarket Street breathless from running up and round and round the tower stairs, she did not get the chance to tell Betsy anything.

The servant's eyes were enormous and her voice conspiratorial.

'There's a gentleman visitor waiting to see you. And you'll never guess who it is.' Betsy pressed her hands against her bosom in a dramatic pose. 'When I saw him I had such a turn, mistress. I thought, dear Jesus, my eyes must be deceiving me . . .'

Annabella stamped her foot with impatience.

'Gracious heavens, tell me who it is.'

And then, who should she see standing in the doorway of her bedroom but Carter Cunningham from Virginia.

Chapter 9

Usually Annabella was quick to recover her poise no matter what surprising or vexatious situation fell upon her. On this occasion, however, she found it difficult. She had been deeply hurt by Cunningham's desertion of her in Virginia. Although, of course, she had refused to allow the matter to cast her down and she certainly did not betray her feelings to anyone.

Now she was glad of the half-dark lobby to hide the distress and confusion in her face. She fumbled for her fan, then began flicking it with apparent unconcern, as she swept towards the bedroom.

'This is indeed a surprise, sir,' she flung at him in passing. 'It has been such a long time, I barely recognize you. But welcome to Glasgow. Can I offer you a glass of whisky?'

He made a graceful bow.

'Mistress Blackadder.'

Willing her hands not to tremble, she poured out a whisky and handed it to him.

'I think I will join you,' she said, pouring another.

He smiled.

'To our renewed acquaintance.'

She clinked glasses with him, unable to say anything. But the whisky soon warmed her and steadied her, although her heart pattered at the sight of him. What easy elegance he had in his claret-coloured coat with its large buttons and cuffs and lace frothing at his neck and wrists. What a penetrating grey-green his eyes were. Like marble chips. Yet there was a glimmer of mischief about them that gentled their hardness.

After a moment or two of silence while he stared at her in the most disconcerting fashion, he said:

'What must you think of me?'

'Think of you, sir? I do not know what you mean.'

'Since we last met . . .'

'Since we last met I confess I have scarcely thought of you at all.'

'Ah, how could anyone so beautiful be so cruel.' He sighed. 'Yet, it would appear that I deserve it. I did promise to call on you in Williamsburg and I did not keep that promise. Or so it seems.'

With a graceful twist of her wrist, Annabella opened her fan.

'You talk in riddles, Mr Cunningham.'

'When I called you were gone.'

'Indeed. And are you usually a year late in paying your calls, sir? If this is your habit you cannot blame your friends for thinking little of you.'

'Ah, but surely it goes without saying that I did not stay away from anyone so beautiful and charming as yourself from choice.'

She raised an eyebrow.

'You were being kept prisoner, Mr Cunningham?'

'In a way that is true.'

'In what way is it not true?'

'I had such a fiendish and recurring fever that for many months I did not know where I was or what was happening to me.'

Annabella was nonplussed.

'I'm much surprised to hear it, sir. And sorry too. I hope you have made a good recovery.'

'Indeed yes, Mistress Annabella. Although I am somewhat fatigued after the voyage. I came straight here, of course.'

'Your ship arrived at Port Glasgow?'

'Yes, this morning.'

'And you have braved that prodigiously rough ride in this heat and so soon after such a long voyage?'

He bowed.

'To see your lovely face again and to hear your voice has made the journey well worth the taking.'

'Why, Mr Cunningham, how gallant.' She tossed him coquettish glances and fluttered her fan. 'I can almost find it in my heart to forgive you.'

'Dear lady . . .'

Moving closer, he lifted her hand to his lips.

Without removing it, she said,

'But it was a devilishly long time to expect me to wait, sir.'

His lips warmed round from the back of her hand and moved deep into her palm, sending a tickle of delight through her. His kiss smoothed up over her wrist and the bare part of her arm. She had almost forgotten what it felt like to be made love to in this delicate and charming fashion. How dull and how chaste her life had been since her marriage and widowhood. Not one lover had she had in years.

Mr Cunningham glanced up and she allowed her eyes to twinkle provocatively, invitingly at him over her fan. He slid his arms around her waist and kissed the hollow of her neck. Averting her face, she wriggled away.

'Mr Cunningham!'

'Annabella, my dear . . .'

'You flutter me, sir.'

'I adore you.'

He made to embrace her again but she held him at arm's length.

'My father will be arriving home at any minute for his evening meal. You will join us, I trust?'

'Thank you.' He bowed. 'You are most hospitable.'

She rustled over to the table and poured him another whisky.

'Do sit by the fire and make yourself at home. I must go and tell my servant to set an extra place at the table.'

She favoured him with a warm smile before skimming from the room. Betsy was flying across the lobby when Annabella opened the door.

'You lazy good-for-nothing trollop,' Annabella railed at her as soon as she reached the kitchen. 'You were spying on me.'

'No, mistress, oh, no, no,' Betsy wailed. 'Oh, for the sake of dear sweet Jesus, don't beat me, mistress.'

Annabella stamped her foot and shook both fists in exasperation.

'I'd like to beat you black and blue.'

'Oh . . . oh . . .' Betsy's wail loudened and tears spurted from her eyes. 'Oh, dear Lord, save me.'

'If I find you with your ear to my door again, nothing will

save you. And I will tell you another thing. If you do not smarten up your appearance as well as your ways, I will not take you with me to Papa's grand new house in Westergate. I cannot have someone like you in such a place. Look at you! Your hair is a disgrace. I do not believe you ever comb it, far less wash it. It must be moving with lice. And you are getting monstrously fat and filthy all over. Papa's new house is sweet and clean and smells of flowers and that is the way I wish it to stay.'

Betsy clasped her hands as if in prayer.

'Oh, please, mistress, don't make me wash, please don't. As sure as God the father of us all is my witness, I'll get my death of cold.'

'Pox on you! Get washed, I say. And if you do not wash yourself I will come through here and do the job for you. I am warning you, Betsy. But first set an extra place at the table.' She rolled her eyes. 'Hell and damnation, it would have to be a simple meal of boiled fowls today. But thank goodness I made a syllabub. Be careful when you bring it through. That with the sheep's head broth and fruit and cheese and some of my plum cake and almond biscuits should make the meal at least a tolerable one.'

If only she had known beforehand that he was coming she could have prepared such a splendid meal. How much more impressive it would have looked too in the dining-room of Mungo House. She imagined the sunny peach-coloured room furnished with a long dining-table and high-backed chairs. On the table was a grand pyramid of shellfish. A dish of roast venison and a boiled ham richly ornamented also graced the table. There were fillets of beef marinate too, and dishes of partridges and ducks' tongues. She sighed as she returned to the bedroom and saw its dirty windows and low ceiling and dingy plastered walls. Everything seemed so cramped and dismal now, she wondered how she had managed to survive in such a place. Already in spirit she was away and living free and light as air in the Westergate.

Cunningham rose when she entered.

'My dear lady, why do you sigh? I trust I have not saddened you in any way?'

She brightened immediately.

'Forgive me, sir, for my lapse into melancholy. It had nothing whatsoever to do with you. I am truly delighted to renew our acquaintance. Your visit gives me prodigious pleasure, I do assure you.'

Just then the door-pin tirled heralding her father's arrival.

'Papa, Papa,' she called, running to open the door to him. 'Papa, we have an unexpected visitor from Virginia.'

'Oh, aye?' her father said without any noticeable enthusiasm, but he followed her through to the bedroom to be introduced. He greeted the younger man civilly enough but without any elegant gestures. Her father was a heavily built, slow-moving, dour-featured man in comparison with Cunningham's tall, lithe figure and laughing-eyed face.

'Cunningham, you say?' Ramsay chewed over the name as they settled down by the fire and he lit a pipe. 'Have you a place on the James River?'

'I have indeed, sir, Chesapeake Plantation.'

'I kent your faither.'

'You knew my father?'

'That's what I said.'

'Poor Papa has been dead these past nine years.'

'He was a good man to do business with. Hard and astute but fair. A just and intelligent man.'

'Yes, that is a very proper description of my father, sir, and I thank you for it.'

Ramsay stared from beneath bushy brows. His long wig rested on his shoulders and was topped with his three-cornered hat which he never took off in the house.

After a few puffs of his pipe, he said:

'You don't look like him.'

'Alas!' Cunningham shrugged and spread his hands palms upwards. 'That is my misfortune.'

'You look very well as you are, Mr Cunningham,' Annabella said. 'Come over to the table now and have a sup of sheep's head broth.'

Her father knocked out his pipe and joined them to intone a long, mournful grace before they could lift a spoon to the soup.

690

'I apologize for the simplicity of the meal,' Annabella said once they had come to the boiled fowls. 'If I had known beforehand of your visit . . .'

'Dear lady,' Cunningham interrupted, 'this is delicious. You have no need for apologies.'

'Or for falderals,' Ramsay grunted. 'Good plain food and lucky to have it. That's what you should be thinking, mistress.'

At least she felt fortunate in being able to offer her guest her truly delicious syllabub. The plum cake and almond biscuits were rich and tasty too and they were just enjoying these sweetmeats when the door-pin tirled through the warm, peaceful dustiness of the house.

Then suddenly a distraught Phemy burst into the room.

'Oh, Annabella, Annabella,' she sobbed, 'something terrible has happened!'

Douglas had meant to go to the counting-house after he left his wife and sister and sister-in-law to have their *tête-à-tête*. He felt more like going to bed, of course. Indeed he longed to crawl beneath the bedcovers and close his eyes and pray for relief. He felt physically as well as spiritually distressed. His legs had lost so much strength they could hardly support him and, like his hands, they feebly trembled. He trembled all over like an old man with a fever. He was absent-minded too. He tried to sound bright and normal but his inward attention kept wandering. Often he felt completely lost and bewildered.

He left the house meaning to go to work, hoping that in doing so he would please Griselle. But somehow, instead of turning down towards the Briggait and his Papa's counting house, he found that he had wandered in the other direction. He had drifted up Saltmarket Street without seeing any of its lofty buildings or long rows of arcades that afforded shelter from sun or rain. He had passed the shops and booths and little markets nestling in the background, their open windows or half-doors revealing rolls of cloth ribbed or chequered in blue or white or homely hodden grey. He had reached the Cross without even noticing the magnificent Tolbooth. Its musical chimes played *Lass o' Patie's Mill* without him hearing it.

He passed the pillared tenements of the High Street, then the more rickety semi-wooden erections. He was nearly at the college before he halted, startled, realizing for the first time where he was. One of a row of stone seats caught him just in time before his legs crumpled. He sat looking helplessly around. There was the thatched-roof grammar school where he had spent so many tormented, unhappy hours. There was the college where he had gone when he was twelve. It had been better there but the discipline had been strict. No-one dared to speak a word of their native tongue. Latin was spoken at all times by lecturers and students. 'Early to bed and early to rise' had been the motto and heaven help any student who was caught dozing in bed after five am or not in bed by nine-fifteen pm. The culprit was lashed by the Principal in the Common Hall in front of the assembled masters and students. But the severest penalties were kept for the awful crimes of robbing the college orchard or any invasion of the kitchen by hungry scholars.

There were privileges, of course. The boys were allowed to indulge in the sports of golf and archery but all carding, dicing, billiards, and the indecent exercise of bathing were strictly prohibited.

Then, of course, the civil power could not touch anyone in the university. The college held the right of final jurisdiction over its own members in all matters, civil or criminal. There had been one case in which a student accused of murder was tried before the Rector and acquitted.

Many memories of the place flooded back to Douglas. He had been relatively happy there. It was a place with a good record. Many great men had passed through its portals. He had hoped that one day George would go there and learn a profession and become not only a great man but a happy one. He had wanted George to have a good life. Often, hand in hand, they'd walked to the college and he'd said to George,

'One day you'll be a student there, my cockie.'

And he'd taken the child in to see the splendid college courts and gardens. George had been impressed.

'I'm sure I'll like it much better here than at the grammar school, Papa,' he'd said. 'I don't like it much at the grammar school; did you when you were a little boy? Oh, I am looking forward to coming here. When will it be, Papa?'

He couldn't believe that he would never see George again. The thought sent his heart fluttering up to his throat in panic. He couldn't believe how George had died. He couldn't bear to imagine how the child must have suffered.

He couldn't, he couldn't believe that he had been the cause of his son's death. The boy had loved and trusted him. He'd actually told him once. They had been talking and planning about what George would be when he grew up and George had said,

'I just want to be like you, Papa. I love you. I love you much better than Mama.'

'Now, now, Geordie,' he'd tried to chastise him, 'Mama is very kind and good to you and she loves you most dearly.'

'I know, Papa,' the child had insisted. 'But I still love you much, much better than her.'

He hadn't wanted to fail Geordie. Had he failed him? Had he actually caused Geordie to die a horrible death?

He felt sick. He rose shakily from the seat and groped back down the street again. Down past the Cross, down past the Saltmarket, round the Briggait. But he couldn't bring himself to go into the counting-house. He was not fit to touch a ledger. He was fit for nothing. He felt as if he was going insane. He was in a panic to escape from himself. He could not cope with the knowledge of what he had done.

He was at the river without knowing how he got there.

He kept thinking, 'My son, my son.'

Everyone at the table rose when Phemy burst into the room hysterically sobbing.

'For God's sake, mistress,' Ramsay shouted. 'What has happened?'

'It's Douglas. Oh, poor man. Oh, Annabella.'

'Stop blubbering,' Annabella snapped. 'Tell us.'

'He's drowned himself. He flung himself in the river. They've just pulled his body out and brought it home. I must fly back to Griselle. Oh, Annabella, I'm so sorry. Your poor brother. I know you loved him. I know how you must feel, and your poor Papa. That's why I came and told you myself instead of sending a servant. But now I must go back to Griselle. I've sent a servant to fetch Mama.'

With a stricken look at Annabella and Ramsay, she turned and fled from the room.

The front door banged and there was silence again except for Betsy haunting the kitchen with her wailing and sobbing.

'Papa,' Annabella said, brokenly. He put out his arms. Never since she was a young child had she clung to him like this and been held by him in a comforting embrace. 'Oh, Papa.'

He lowered his head against hers and as soon as she felt his tears against her face she struggled to contain her own grief so that she could comfort him. But before she could find any words, he said in a bewildered voice,

'Where did I fail the lad? Was I too harsh, think ye?'

'No, Papa. You were always kind. Only this afternoon he was telling me of your kindness in allowing him to go home because he was suffering from head-pains. He loved and admired you, Papa. Truly he did.'

Cunningham came over and put one arm round Ramsay's shoulders and the other round Annabella's.

'I wish there was something I could say or do, dear friends, to help or comfort you.'

They had forgotten his existence but now Annabella looked up at him gratefully.

'Thank you, Mr Cunningham. Perhaps you would be kind enough to pour three large whiskies. A dram might help steady us.'

'Certainly.' He hastened to do as she suggested.

Ramsay had begun to tremble. She felt his body shrink and shiver inside his clothes.

'Have courage, Papa,' she whispered. 'You will be all right.'

'But what about the lad? What about our Dougie? He took his own life. There'll be no rest for him. He'll never reach the other side. He'll be cast down in the pit of eternal damnation.'

It was terrible to see her father like this; not roaring out God's words with relish and authority, with flashing eyes and straight

694

back, but bent and querulous like an old man.

'Drink this, Mr Ramsay,' Cunningham urged. But Ramsay's hands were trembling so much, the younger man had to help the glass to his lips.

'I'd better go down the road,' Ramsay said in between sips. 'I'd better go and see the lad. Och, Dougie, Dougie, why did you commit such a terrible sin?'

'He was ill, Papa. You remember. He took these monstrous headaches. Sometimes he could hardly see, the pain was so frightful.'

'Och. Dougie, Dougie . . .'

'He would not know what he was doing. I think you would be better to go to bed, Papa. No good purpose can be served by you going down to Gibson's Land tonight.'

'We can't just stay here as if nothing's happened.'

'Mr Ramsay, Annabella is right,' Cunningham said. 'You do not look at all well. Get your servant to help you to bed. I will escort your daughter to Gibson's Land and I will offer to assist in any way I can while I am there.'

'I'm obliged to you, sir.'

'Big John,' Annabella called.

'Yes, mistress,' he answered, lumbering into the room, his face screwed up in distress.

'Help the master to his bed.'

'Yes, mistress. Come away, maister,' he said, linking arms with Ramsay and leading him from the room. 'Ye'll be all right with Big John.'

As soon as her father had gone, Annabella flung herself against Cunningham's chest and wept unashamedly.

695

Chapter 10

The church was a seething mass of humanity. It buzzed, chattered, shuffled, wriggled, pushed and threatened to burst at the seams. Ladies and gentlemen, lairds and merchants packed into the seats, peacock tails of colour in their fine clothes. Tradespeople and servants, men, women and children, and barking dogs trampled the earth and bones of the long dead deeper into the floor. The beadle roared commands for the dogs to be removed before the minister climbed the high pulpit. Some of the dogs were chased and kicked between a forest of legs. Others were heaved up and passed over heads.

Ramsay sat leaning forward, both hands resting heavily on his cane. Next to him Annabella kept her back straight and her head tipped high. Her mittened hands grasped her fan on her lap. Her face, normally pink-cheeked with the glow of health, had an unusual pallor. She had not slept well the night before, partly for thinking about her brother and the anguish he must have been suffering to have committed such a terrible act; partly because her father kept calling out and, although Big John was with him, she felt she had to dash through to his bedroom on each occasion to try and soothe away his nightmares. She had tried to persuade him not to come to church this morning but he had said,

'I've never missed a Sunday in God's house in my life, Annabella. Never missed a Sunday.'

He sounded bewildered and confused and possessed none of his normal fire or aggressiveness and the change in her father shocked her almost as much as her brother's death.

The Reverend Gowrie climbed the pulpit, his presence freezing the rabble into a silent shiver of expectancy. He was a giant of a man with coarse pocked skin, a huge beak of a nose and lips like lumps of steak. Glittering eyes stabbed this way and that and he reached forward and gripped the edge of the pulpit with such vehemence, his fists bunched up the green cloth with the gold fringes that covered it.

'A crime of the deepest dye has been committed in this town,' he thundered. 'And it becomes those who would declare the whole counsel of the Lord to bear public and solemn testimony.

'A sin has been perpetrated against God. A man of this parish has taken into his hands the decision to abandon without leave the station in which he was placed. This is an unequivocal rebellion against God, a direct opposition to His Providence, an attempt to escape from His control, an ignoble breach of fidelity to a rightful sovereign.' The black eyes narrowed, the lumps of steak under the eagle beak writhed and twisted.

'Coward! Poltroon! Deserter! That is what I say of such a man. He has put an end to every opportunity of repentance and reformation.

'Child of perdition! Death will land thee in still greater misery . . .'

Annabella struggled to control the panic of grief and distress that was threatening to engulf her. If only the tirade had been aimed at herself, she could have coped in her normal pert and self-assured manner. To hell with the Reverend Gowrie, she would have thought, and a pox on the whole town. But she did not know how to cope with such an attack on her brother. She felt shattered by the tragic occurrence of his death and was experiencing a terrifying vulnerability. She tried not to listen to the minister's diatribe but it continued to slash through her defences.

'Oh, guilty man, did you not know that "No murderer hath eternal life abiding in him"?

'The just judgement of God will increase your agonies and horrors, will banish you forever from His presence, will doom you to suffer eternal penalties without mercy and without hope . . .'

Hearing a sound at her side, Annabella glanced round and was horrified to discover her father sobbing. His shoulders were heaving and tears were spurting down his lowered face.

'Papa, don't. Please don't.' She put a hand on his arm.

'Poor Dougie. The lad never meant any harm.'

697

'I know, Papa.'

'He was always a harmless kind o' lad.'

'I know.'

She prised one of his hands off the cane, squeezed it between her own, then held it and patted it on her lap.

'But we must try and have courage, Papa. Douglas would not have wanted us to be unhappy and upset like this.'

Ramsay just kept sobbing and shaking his head. And the minister roared on and on and on until Annabella was nearly fainting with desperation to be free of his voice; away from the mob, away from the gloomy coffin of a building with its black stone walls and sickening stench of unwashed bodies.

At long last the conclusion of the sermon released her. The Reverend Gowrie raised his eyes and clasped hands heavenwards.

'May God in His infinite mercy preserve us from an infatuation so deplorable, from a crime of such complicated malignity! Let me die the death of the righteous and let my end be like His!'

For a minute or two Annabella thought she was not going to be able to stand up. Her legs were so weak they did not seem able to take her weight. Only by summoning every last vestige of will-power did she manage to rise and also to assist her father to his feet.

'We'll soon be home, Papa, and we'll have a hot toddy and we'll be all right. Come now, take my arm. Lean on me.'

Keeping her head high, she pushed a path towards the door. Outside on Trongate Street she thankfully took a big breath of fresh air. It was then she saw Letitia and Phemy and Griselle. Griselle looked dishevelled; her eyes were wide and staring and her tight mouth hung loose and out of control.

'Annabella,' she called, hurrying nearer.

As she watched her approach, Annabella thought, 'You monstrous murdering pig of a woman. You are the one who is to blame for all this. You and your cruel tongue. You and your selfish stupidity. You killed your son, your own flesh and blood. Now you've killed my brother!'

'Annabella,' Griselle repeated on reaching her. 'I have been so agitated. Indeed my agitation is all but overwhelming me.' The eyes stretched enormous and the mouth, like a smudge of jelly, could barely shiver out words. 'Oh, Annabella, I was... I *was*... nice to him, wasn't I?'

Without hesitation Annabella said,

'Of course you were, Grizzie. Of course you were. And Douglas loved you dearly. You know he did.'

Tears tumbled down Griselle's face.

'Yes, he often used to say ... he used to say ...'

'Tuts,' said Letitia, 'this is a fine kettle of fish! Folk are gawping at you, mistress. Pull yourself together and come away home. The dinner will be getting ruined. Food costs money and if there's one thing I canna thole it's good sillar being wasted.'

After they had gone, Annabella made slow progress along Trongate Street. Her father leaned heavily on her, sometimes stopping to stand looking down at the ground with an absent-minded faraway expression on his face. She felt sick with worry. It was so unlike him to behave like this.

The sun dappled the buildings on either side, sparkled window panes into diamonds, gave a golden glisten to battlements and played hide and seek among the arches of the piazzas, bathed the street in a warm amber glow that did not seem to touch Annabella and her father. It was as if they were no longer part of the scene but struggling along in a terrible no-man's-land. She felt cold.

Thankfully she turned into the close at Saltmarket Street, then climbed the tower stair. Once in the house, she helped her father off with his coat.

'Sit down now, Papa. I will go and make a hot toddy.'

When she returned he was sitting staring at the floor but after a few sips of the hot, sweet whisky he said,

'It'll have to be a private funeral. No one else will come. We'll have to bury him ourselves, too. The church won't allow him in consecrated ground.'

'Well, we shall have a private funeral. And we will bury him ourselves. Mr Cunningham will help us, Papa. He is calling again this evening. And there is Griselle's manservant. And there is Big John.'

'Where will we ... where can we ... ?'

'There is a field at the back of the house in Westergate. We will put him to rest under one of the trees there.'

'Put him to rest?' Ramsay's face threatened to disintegrate. Muscles helplessly sagged and shook. 'There'll never be any rest for that poor lad. Why did he do such a terrible thing, Annabella? Why did he do it?'

'It serves no useful purpose to talk like that, Papa. Drink your whisky and try to think and talk of other things.'

'There was always a hard bit about you. Aye, you were always a hard lassie. You were my favourite, though. Oh, aye, you were my favourite. But, och, I was fond o' Douglas as well.'

'I know, Papa.'

'But did Douglas, I wonder?'

'Of course he did. You were always kind and generous to him.'

Ramsay sighed.

'Aye, so you said.'

'This monstrous time will soon be over, Papa. You will be moving to the Westergate and the change of scene will do you good. You will feel better, I promise you.'

He nodded but did not speak and soon his shoulders drooped and he drifted into remoteness again. She sat with him for a time, stitching a piece of linen, glancing up occasionally to see if there was any change in his appearance. But he remained hanging helplessly inside his clothes without moving a muscle.

When supper time came he refused to eat anything and instead went early to bed. She was alone in her room trying to concentrate on her sewing when Carter Cunningham arrived. She rose to greet him with a welcoming smile and her hand gracefully outstretched for his kiss.

He held it tenderly against his lips. Then he asked:

'How are you, dear lady?'

'As well as can be expected in the circumstances, sir. I am prodigiously concerned about Papa, though. He is deeply dejected. It was damnable what that scoundrel of a preacher made him suffer today. I confess, sir, I was mightily distressed myself.'

'Annabella.' He took her in his arms and she hid her face against his shoulder. 'My dear, sweet girl, what can I say?

Except I love you and want to look after you and make sure that you are never unhappy again.'

'Every time I think of him lying in that house alone . . .'

'Do you want to be with him?'

Still with her face pressed close to his shoulder, she said,

'Why should he be alone? Why should he not have a wake? I cannot bear to think of him lying alone in that house tonight. Griselle has gone to her mother's.'

'Then we shall go straight away and keep an all-night vigil beside your brother. Have you a key to the house?'

She nodded against him and he dropped a kiss on the top of her head.

'Then put on your cape. We shall go now.'

Words could not express her gratitude to Cunningham for his kindness and understanding, so she kept silent as they walked down Saltmarket Street to Gibson's Land. But her silence was a warm, companionable thing. It could not be compared with the cold desolation that met them when they opened the door of her brother's house. It was like stepping into the grave. The aloneness of death was so real, so cold, so silent around her, she felt horrified and oppressed by it.

Douglas was lying in a coffin propped on top of two chairs in the middle of the bedroom. Wrapped in a dead-cloth, only his head and face showed, grey and small-looking without either wig or paint.

Annabella said,

'How could Grizzie be so cruel? How could she?' Flinging off her cape, she swirled into sudden action. 'The fire is set. Will you put a light to it, please? And light every candle you can see. I'm going to find Douglas's wig and his face paint. My brother said face paint was the height of fashion and he set great store by it. I know he would not wish to go anywhere without it.'

'Annabella,' Cunningham said gently.

'Light the fire and the candles, sir. I wish to paint my brother's face.'

Afterwards they sat beside the coffin drinking whisky and eating burial bread. Sometimes they talked, occasionally they dozed off to sleep, until the sun came up again and flickered over the paintings in their heavy gilt frames and the four-poster bed and the high-backed chairs, and the coffin, and Douglas with his powdered wig and white and strawberry-coloured face.

Big John arrived, half-carrying her father who looked like a bent and feeble old man. Letitia and Phemy and Griselle arrived too, accompanied by their servants. Little attempt was made at conversation but Letitia briskly poured out drinks and passed round cake and said:

'You'll come round to my place after the burial. I've a good meal ready. You too, Mr Cunningham. You must give us all the gossip from Virginia. I don't hear so much of it since my gudeman passed to the other side. Tuts, would you look at the corpse. I suppose that was your doing, mistress?'

'And why not?' Annabella said. 'He always wore it.'

'Aye, he did a lot o' things he shouldn't have done. Hurry up and eat your cake and drink your whisky. It's time we were getting him under the clay. If we wait much longer the whole town will be out and gawping.'

'Let them gawp.'

Letitia ignored her.

'Big John, nail him down. Come away, Ramsay. Are you going to put a shoulder to the coffin along with the other men? Grizzie, stop your snivelling. You too, Phemy.'

They carried him, not without some difficulty and jostling, down the stairs and into the waiting carriage. The women hailed sedan chairs and followed in single file up Saltmarket Street, along Trongate Street to the Westergate. Then in the open countryside beyond it, they chose a place under a rowan tree and buried him there.

'Come away now. Come away,' Letitia said, swishing her skirts over one arm and signalling to the chairmen. 'It's time we had a meal inside us.'

Annabella was thankful to be away. She felt harrowed and exhausted and did not wait long at Letitia's house. Her father decided to stay until evening and she left him drinking steadily along with Letitia and Griselle and Phemy and the old Earl of Glendinny. She doubted if he would be fit to return to his own place by evening. But Big John would either carry him back or make sure that he was comfortably settled in Letitia's for the night.

Mungo was being looked after by Betsy and Annabella was glad of the chance to relax when she reached her bedroom.

Cunningham, who had escorted her home, untied the ribbons of her hat and helped her off with her cloak.

'You look tired, Annabella. I think you should go to bed.'

'Don't leave me.'

'My dear . . .'

'Stay with me. Hold me close.'

'I want you to be with me for always. I want to take you back to Virginia as my wife.'

She shook her head

'No, I couldn't leave Papa. Not now.'

'I refuse to take no for an answer.'

'I am afraid, sir, you have no alternative. In a few weeks' time I am moving with Papa to his new house in the Westergate.'

'If you cannot or will not marry me, I will come again next year. By that time your father will be properly settled and recovered from the grievous shock of your brother's death. You will have no excuse for refusing my offer.'

'I cannot look that far forward. I can only offer you tonight.'

He took her hand and kissed it.

'It will be a memory I shall treasure, dear lady, during the lonely year ahead.'

They moved into Mungo House at the earliest opportunity and, as Phemy said, it was a blessing that they had the house to move to and all the work the moving entailed.

'It has been the saving of both of you,' she insisted. 'The colour has come back to your face, Annabella, with all your exertions and running around. And even your father is more like his old self.'

Certainly her father had regained much of his strength and was back working as usual in his counting-house. Yet he had aged. Once his back had been like an iron rod. Now the iron had melted, causing him to stoop a little and to use his cane more for support than display. His face, once dour and rigid in its expression, now had creased into lines that gave it a look of fatigue and suffering. He was still a stern taskmaster as his clerks at the counting-house well knew and he still insisted on a God-fearing routine in his home of readings and prayers.

But he drank a lot more than he used to and it was a common occurrence now for Big John to have to carry his master home from the tavern. And he did not seem to have as much strength of will or even interest in thwarting many of Annabella's ploys and plans. For instance, she had managed to purchase a spinet and have it installed in the drawing-room of Mungo House with surprisingly little trouble. Already she was taking lessons and practising diligently and with much enjoyment.

The gentleman who had kindly agreed to teach her was a most refined and accomplished personage by the name of Mr Craig. He was a leading connoisseur of the fine arts and played the fiddle as well as the spinet. He had made a visit to Italy and had the rare accomplishment of being able to speak a little Italian. He had assured her that she had a natural talent for music and that she was able to master difficult pieces with incredible speed and ease. She looked forward to the day when she would be able to entertain guests to a musical interlude, perhaps to a duet with Mr Craig playing the fiddle. As yet, she had not managed to do any entertaining. Apart from the fact that it was too soon after her brother's death for her to feel like gay parties, there was still such a lot to do to the house.

They had moved in before the painting and decorating was finished and she had had to wait until that job had been done and the paint was dry before beginning to put up the curtains. In the living-room she had hung rust-coloured curtains to match the two new upholstered chairs. The other chair was her father's old winged arm chair from their Saltmarket home. Her red silk velvet easy chair she had put upstairs in her bedroom because it didn't match the living-room colour scheme and she wanted everything new in the drawing-room. The living-room walls were panelled up to the window sill and the rest of the walls and the ceiling were painted a restful beige, and the centre of the polished wood floor was covered with a beige and rust and brown coloured carpet. She had put her little tea-table with its scalloped corners for candles in this room and the mahogany highboy with the gold handles on the drawers and a slope-fronted desk. The japanned pier glass with its raised figures of peacocks and flowers was on the opposite wall from the window and reflected the rust curtains and glimpses of the colourful sedan chairs in the keeper's yard across the narrow road at the front of the house.

It was not a large room but it was comfortable and homely. Both she and her father could relax there in the evening; he could read his Bible at the open desk or sit by the fire with a newspaper and she did embroidery or other sewing, or she wrote letters.

During the day when her father was out at work she liked to go upstairs and sit at the spinet in the drawing-room. She had furnished this room with a tall clock, a cherry red settee and chairs and gold damask curtains. Although it had the same size of window, it was a bigger room than the living-room and had white wood panelling with raised ovals decorated with the beautifully painted landscapes that were her pride and joy. She adored this room and never tired of admiring its artistic elegance.

When she wasn't admiring the interior of the house, she was gazing happily out of the window. From her bedroom she had a peaceful view of the little garden in which she had already planted herbs and roses. Then there were trees and banks of yellow broom and rolling green fields as far as the eye could see. Sometimes she could hear the cowherd's horn and the distant mooing of cows, but otherwise it was a scene of rural peace and quiet. From the living-room or dining-room windows the front looked peaceful too. There were occasional movements and sounds from the sedan-keeper's yard but the lilting Highland voices of the keeper and his chairmen proved little disturbance. Some days there would be a horse and rider gallop by, or a clanking coach and whinnying team of horses, but they were exciting diversions in an idyllic scene.

In the two cottages that flanked Mungo House lived elderly couples, respectable folk who eked out a living by selling the vegetables they grew in their back gardens. Annabella sometimes passed the time of day with them when she was out tending her herbs. It was very pleasant to potter in the garden in her wide-brimmed straw hat with the smell of flowers sweet in her nostrils and the buzz of bees and the song of birds keeping her happy company.

And of course she could be in the centre of town in no time at all if she had a fancy to do a bit of shopping or to visit Phemy or Griselle. That is, if she went by horse or sedan. By foot it was not so easy and took much longer.

Griselle had given up her house in Gibson's Land and was back in Trongate Street living with her mother. She had, by all appearances, completely recovered from her initial distress over Douglas's death and looked cheerful and well. Annabella told Phemy that she wouldn't be surprised if Griselle married again within the year. She had continued her connections with the landed gentry and still attended the games of cards and stayed overnight in the stately homes of Lord and Lady Knox and others.

She had introduced Annabella to various members of the gentry and Annabella was very excited at being included in the next weekend on the Kibbold estate.

Griselle said she was trying to persuade Letitia to agree to having a mansion built for the Halyburton family. Her brother Andrew was willing but Letitia was a stubborn woman.

'Tuts, there's nothing wrong with the home that you and Phemy and Andra were brought up in,' she kept saying. 'I don't know what's got into young folks nowadays. Your father and I were gey proud of this place when we got married and moved into it.'

'Times change, Mama,' Griselle explained. 'Everyone who is anyone now is leaving the tenements and building mansions. We'll simply need to move eventually.'

'Would you listen to that?' their leathery old maid, Kate, croaked. 'Oor Grizzie's getting above hersel'. What she's needing, if you ask me, is a skelpet bum.'

'Oh, be quiet,' Grizzie snapped irritably. 'Nobody's asking you.'

'Aye, and I'm no' too old or frail to skelp your bum either. I've done it before when you were a wee bairn and I can do it now if I've a mind to.'

'Mama, will you tell her to be quiet?' Grizzie appealed. 'This is the sort of thing I mean. There's just no peace or privacy in a cramped flat like this.'

'Tuts, Kate,' Letitia scolded, 'will you hold your havering tongue? The quicker you're away to the other side the better.'

'I'll go and meet my Maker when I'm good and ready, mistress, and no' one meenite before.'

Letitia snapped open her fan.

'Is it no' terrible what folk have to suffer from vexatious servants?'

Annabella agreed.

'I have prodigious problems with Betsy. The lazy good-for-nothing creature simply refused to wash. The other day I chased her all the way to the burn, knocked her in and flung a ball of soap after her. You might have heard her howls and yowls in the town.'

Phemy and Griselle tittered behind their fans but Letitia said,

'Tuts, Annabella, you've always had terrible wild ways. Age has done nothing to mellow you or douce you down.'

'Heaven forbid!'

'It's time you were marrying again. Has your Papa anyone in mind?'

'Mistress Letitia, I'm a mature widow-woman and I'll choose my own gudeman this time.'

Phemy said,

'Oh, Annabella, I hope you're not planning to leave us again. And your lovely mansion too. You're not still thinking of your Virginia planter, are you?'

'Mr Cunningham?' Annabella sighed. 'He is a charming man and I am catched by him, of course, but I made him no promises and I doubt if I ever will. If he resided here in Glasgow . . .' She sighed again. 'Who knows? I dare swear I would not be able to resist him. But, as it is, I am wondrously happy the way I am.' She suddenly giggled. 'Did you see the way my Lord Gilmour ogled me the other day?'

Old Kate, the hunchback servant who was still leaning on the bedpost listening intently to the conversation, let out a sudden cackle.

'That birkie's got a head like a turnip and just as thick.'

'Kate,' Letitia snapped, 'will you stop that clitter-clattering tongue of yours and away and make the tea.'

Kate shuffled from the room muttering darkly.

'I'm no' the only one with a clitter-clattering tongue, if you ask me.'

'I'm thinking of having a dinner party soon,' Annabella announced. 'A housewarming party, you could call it. You must all come, of course. Don't forget to tell Andrew.' She giggled again. 'Tell me, what other men can I invite?'

Letitia's drawstring mouth tightened.

'This isn't a respectable way to go about things. It should be left to your father to invite the men. You're asking for trouble, m'lady.'

'Fiddlesticks!' Annabella said.

Chapter 11

'How's the glass, captain?' Cunningham asked. He had climbed to the poop deck of the *Mary Heron* to have a word with Captain Daidles. He had felt singularly depressed since setting out on his journey from Glasgow. Naturally he was low in spirits at having to leave without Annabella but he suspected it wasn't only that. Perhaps the ominous weather signs had something to do with his calamitous apprehensions.

The gaunt-faced, hook-nosed Captain Daidles did nothing to cheer or reassure him.

'Dropping fast, Mr Cunningham,' he said, like a preacher at a deathbed. 'Dropping fast.'

Cunningham took a pinch of snuff.

'Then we must try and keep our spirits up, sir.'

The captain solemnly lowered his head and pointed with an upward roll of his eyes to the implacably advancing army of black clouds.

'A gale's nigh upon us.'

'Ah well, no doubt you have survived many a gale before.' He was determined at least to put on a front of cheerfulness, despite the fact that the captain was enough to depress anyone.

Captain Daidles shook a reproachful head at him.

'A severe gale, Mr Cunningham.' He swivelled slowly round to the mate and intoned sadly, 'Shorten sail, Mr Kerr. Put up the deadlights. Batten down the hatches. Take in the jib. Bend on a storm jib. Put a double reef on the main sail.'

But already the edges of the sails were cracking like pistols in the wind and humps of waves were colliding and spraying up white plumes. The ship was nervously plunging and bucking and Cunningham decided eventually that it might be wisest to return to his cabin. He found it in almost total darkness because of the wooden shutters, or deadlights as the sailors called them, that were now covering the cabin windows. A lantern hung from a hook on the low ceiling and gave a feeble light that fluttered and swooped with the movement of the ship.

With a sigh, he flopped down onto his bunk. He had been in many storms before and normally he found them stimulating and exciting. This time, he felt sad and uneasy. He tried to view his emotions objectively, to analyse them in an honest and sensible manner. It wasn't fear he was succumbing to. He had fought too many duels and indulged in too many other reckless and dangerous acts for anyone, even himself, to believe that he was a coward.

He supposed he was simply lovesick. He was sad at leaving Annabella. He had been in love many times before but he had never loved anyone so deeply and completely as he did his golden-haired, bright-eyed Glasgow girl. Somehow, without her, his vast plantation, his huge mansion, all the comforts and pleasures that his wealth provided, meant nothing. Even his gambling had become a bore. He wanted Annabella by his side to share everything with him. He realized that he could have had any unmarried lady in Virginia for the asking, indeed, many a married one as well. Virginia mothers were continuously plying him with eager invitations and hopeful introductions to their daughters. The daughters ogled him shamelessly and left him in no doubt of their availability. He was not nearly so sure of Annabella. And here, he decided, was the root of his present melancholia and apprehension. If Annabella really loved him, would she not have come back with him to Virginia in spite of everything? Or would she, should she, not have tried to persuade him to stay? He had pleaded with her. She had made no attempt to plead with him. He had made promises to her. She had made none to him. He felt that he would never see Annabella again. He sensed that her love for him was not strong enough to stand his absence. Some other man could and would steal her affections and capture her for his wife.

Panic alerted him and made him swing his legs from the bunk and sit up. If only he could get back to Glasgow. It had been madness to leave without Annabella. There were many business matters back in Virginia that needed his attention and he had been away too long already. But business was of secondary

710

importance to securing Annabella's hand in marriage.

The ship shuddered against the impact of solid green walls of water crashing down on its decks. Then there were the angry, seething sounds as the sea spewed out through the scuppers. The cabin tipped sideways, forcing Cunningham to grab onto his bunk to prevent himself from sliding down the steep incline of the floor.

With agonizing creaks and groans the ship righted itself, but another roll burst the cabin door and allowed the sea to tumble in and swish about. Swaying and staggering about like a drunk man, sometimes slipping and falling, Cunningham managed to reach the door, put his shoulder to it and secure it shut again.

Back in his bunk, he tried to ignore the pitching and rolling of the ship. He tried to concentrate on willing the storm to calm. Eventually, after what seemed endless uncomfortable hours, the weather soothed and quietened. He climbed on deck and enjoyed a few deep refreshing breaths before looking around. The captain was standing nearby morosely viewing the damage the storm had done to the sails.

Cunningham decided that it would be better not to disturb or irritate the older man with idle talk. He gave the impression, with his withdrawn moody appearance, that he was a man who preferred his own company. So, leaving the captain to brood alone, he took a stroll along the deck, picking his way between piles of rope and groups of sailors patching sails. Stopping for a while he watched with interest how neatly the men stitched with their heavy three-sided needles. They sang cheerily while they worked, their song gusting in the breeze. The wind also tugged playfully at Cunningham's plum-coloured brocade coat and lace jabot. A couple of times he had to grab his tricorn hat to prevent it from flying away.

For a time the singing and the exhilarating sea breeze lightened his spirits but it was only a temporary respite. Soon Annabella wafted back to his mind to haunt him. He thought of how long it would be before he would be able to see her again and his depression returned. Sighing with the weight of it, he went over and leaned his elbows on the bulwarks.

He didn't know how long he had been standing there, gazing

bleakly across the vast expanse of sea, when suddenly there was a shout from the crow's nest.

'A ship! On the larboard side.'

Immediately his heart raced with excitement. The ship in the distance appeared to be sailing in the direction from which they had just come. Could it be possible that it was on its way to Glasgow? If so, perhaps he could join it. Happiness nearly exploded his wits. It was as much as he could do to prevent himself from jigging with joy. He hastened eagerly, hopefully, to the captain's side.

'Maybe it's a Glasgow-bound ship, captain. I'd be mightily obliged if you'd get near enough to hail her and find out. If she is bound for Glasgow I would be glad of the opportunity to board her. There is an urgent matter I find I ought to have attended to before I left the town.'

The captain raised his glass and peered through it.

'Can't see what flag she's carrying,' he muttered.

'Could we get nearer her, captain?' Cunningham struggled to repress his eagerness.

'Oh, I dare say we could, Mr Cunningham,' the captain admitted grudgingly.

Then he called an order to the first mate without lowering the glass. Soon the *Mary Heron* was billowing and curtsying along towards the other ship.

Cunningham was already back in Glasgow in his mind. He was sweeping Annabella off her feet, refusing to take no for an answer. He had been mad to allow himself to be so easily put off in the first place. He wouldn't make that mistake twice. This time he would carry her away with him. He would make her his wife and together they would enjoy a full and happy life on his Virginia plantation.

He itched to be aboard the other ship. It must be a Glasgow-bound vessel. His prayers were so fervent surely they must be answered. He scanned it as it came nearer and was surprised when it came into full view that he could make out a long row of guns.

'It's armed like a frigate,' he gasped.

'Aye,' said the captain. 'One thing's certain, Mr Cunningham, she's not a merchantman.' He lowered his glass and called to the mate. 'Pipe to quarters!'

'Do you think she's hostile, captain?'

'I don't know, sir, but it's best to be prepared.'

Cunningham glanced around. Already sponge tubs, rammers and primers were out. Tackles were being bent and gun-ports raised. There were only a few guns, but in those powder bags and shot were being rammed home, and slow matches were alight even before the guns were run out through the open ports.

Other sailors were arming themselves with pistols and cutlasses.

'I'll go and get my weapons,' Cunningham said.

By the time he returned on deck the ship was close enough for him to see its very hostile-looking crew. He groaned. 'A damned privateer, is it, captain?'

'A damned privateer, sir,' the captain replied. The gap between the ships closed rapidly, then a voice from the privateer yelled:

'Heave-to! We're going to board you!'

'Fire!' Captain Daidles bawled at the mate.

Almost at the same time, the privateer's cannon fired a heavier broadside killing several of the *Mary Heron's* crew. Then the pirates leapt into the *Mary Heron's* rigging and began swarming down on to the decks.

Cunningham drew his sword and fought furiously. But they were coming thick and fast, fierce, wild-eyed men wearing coloured handkerchiefs and golden earrings and sashes that bristled with pistols and cutlasses. The merchant seamen of the *Mary Heron* were no match for them and were being hacked to pieces all around him.

He had taken off his coat to give himself freedom of movement. But soon the sweat was pouring from his face and body and although he had killed and wounded many of the pirates, they still kept engaging him. There seemed no end to their numbers.

Then suddenly a sharp pain in his chest made him gasp and he caught a glimpse of a scarlet stain spreading across the white of his shirt.

He remembered feeling surprise, then regret. He remembered

713

thinking of Annabella. Then he remembered no more.

The dining-room at Mungo House was radiant with many candles. It was apricot-tinted like a gilt-framed painting in orange and red and copper and rust. Warmed by the flames of the candles, the peach walls with their ornamentation of painted fruit had acquired a rich orange glow. The brocades and silks and jewels of the ladies and gentlemen round the dining-table added to the tapestry of colour. They were all bewigged and powdered and the ladies wore face patches, long tightly-laced stays and wickedly low-fronted bodices. Gowns and petticoats were embroidered with flowers and leaves, or rustic scenes of trees and hills, or vines twisting and twining. The gentlemen were resplendent in flowered silk coats and waistcoats and lace jabots and cuffs. One or two wore vivid face paint.

Even Big John who was waiting at table looked smart and colourful in a powdered wig and a pink coat and white breeches and white silk stockings.

The table was crowded with food and scarcely a spot of the tablecloth was visible. There was a roasted goose, a side of beef with frizzled potatoes, a roasted lobster, black game and partridge, brandered chickens, reindeers' tongues, currant jelly, capsicum, elder, garlic, vinegars, cheese, biscuits, goats' milk, limes and claret.

Much witty talk and merry laughter and ogling went on as well as enthusiastic eating and drinking. After the meal there were the usual rounds of toasts and sentiments followed each time by clapping or laughing.

'Here's to ye,' was the first. Followed by 'The land o' cakes'.

'May the hinges of friendship never rust, or the wings of love lose a feather.'

'Here's health, wealth, wit and meal.'

'May the mouse never leave our meal-pock with a tear in it's eye.'

'Thumping luck and fat weans.'

'May we all be canty and cosy.'

'To loving women and trusty men.'

'More sense and more silver.'

'Blithe may we all be.'

'When we're going up the hill of fortune, may we never meet a friend coming down.'

Afterwards the ladies retired upstairs to the drawing-room, their silks and brocades rustling and trailing behind them. The men joined them later and, although very merry in their cups, were able to step a minuet to the tune of two fiddles and a French horn. Next came a jig and a reel, then another minuet. Annabella also entertained the company on the spinet and Phemy sang in her sweet trilling voice:

> 'As Mally Lee came down the street,
> Her capuchin did flee;
> She cast a look behind her
> To see her negligée;
> She had two lappets at her head
> That flaunted gallantlie,
> And ribbon knots at back and breast
> Of bonnie Mally Lee.'

It was a hugely successful evening and the first of many that Annabella gave in Mungo House. She was immensely proud of the place but found it necessary to employ another servant to wait at table and help keep the house clean. Her name was Tib Faulds and she was much older than Betsy. A widow-woman, plain, agreeable and efficient in many ways, she could be stubborn and touchy in others. She had a long, horsey face and always wore a frilly mob cap into which she tucked all her hair. This made her neck appear long as well. She was given to bouts of grumbling if things didn't please her and Ramsay had chided her by reminding her that the Lord had blessed her with a good life for many years now. She had replied,

'Aye, but I haven't provoked Him any.'

She was excellent at keeping the house in order and serving at table but had not much time for and was no use at all at flipperty-gipperties, as she called such tasks as dressing or powdering Annabella's head and attending to Annabella's clothes. Annabella felt she needed a personal maid as well as Betsy and Tib, but was having difficulty in persuading her father to see the necessity.

'Oh, I do miss Nancy,' she kept sighing. 'She was an impudent baggage at times but she did my hair so well and always helped me to dress.'

Then one evening her father had astonished her by replying, 'Aye, weel might ye miss her. She was your half-sister.'

'Half-sister? Papa, what do you mean?'

He had been drunk at the time and at first she had thought he was havering. But he had looked very morose and guilt-ridden and continued.

'Aye, she was the result of a sin I committed many years ago with my servant, her mother, Chrissie Kinkaid.'

'Papa!' She was shocked but not because of his houghma-gandie with his servant. 'How could you allow your own daughter to live all these years in such menial circumstances? She ought to have been on equal terms with me. You could have employed another servant to attend to us both. You have been very remiss, Papa.'

'Ach,' her father sighed. 'That's all water under the bridge now. And you've no need to judge me, Annabella. I'll be judged and punished for all my sins when I pass to the other side and meet my Maker.'

But Annabella was no longer listening to him. Suddenly she laughed.

'Gracious heavens, it is a most astonishing thing. I must write and tell her. I wonder how she'll take it. Will she be pleased or furious? I will tell her that if she returns to Glasgow for a visit, she and her husband must stay here as our guests. What a droll occurrence that will be.'

She wondered if Nancy and her backwoods husband would know the rules of etiquette that bounded formal visits. Visits were supposed to be of a standard length; 'a rest day, a drest day and a prest day'. On the day of arrival guests were given the opportunity to rest after the fatigues of their journey. On the second day everyone wore their best full dress. On the third day it was considered proper that the guest should make as if to leave. Then the host was expected to press them to stay one more night. After the correct amount of hesitation, it was proper that

716

they should accept.

But of course, if Nancy was her half-sister, she could be classed as family and family could stay as long as they liked. And if Nancy or her husband did not know basic rules of genteel society like the one that insisted that guests should never yawn or spit, then she would soon tell them. If a gentleman felt obliged to spit, he should do so in his handkerchief and not in the room. Formal guests, of course, if they knew how to behave correctly, never entered a house wearing a cloak or a big coat or boots. But they must always wear gloves. And it was considered rude for a lady to enter a house wearing a scarf or plaid or with her gown tucked up. As for curtsying when entering a house, the curtsy ought to be slow enough to allow the company to return it. On the other hand, it should not be so slow that it wearied them.

Rules of etiquette had never bothered anyone in the tenements and folk just dropped in when and as they liked either as afternoon 'cummers' for a drink of tea and a gossip, or later to crack a hen's egg together or have a more elaborate supper. But life in the mansions was different in many ways. If Nancy came to stay she would have to tell her. Not that it mattered so much in Mungo House. Mungo House must be considered as Nancy's second home any time she came to Glasgow. But if she came and she was included in invitations to other mansions, then for Nancy's own sake, to protect her from embarrassment, she must be told the various little niceties and social rules. The chances were, of course, that Nancy would bitterly resent being told anything and they would fight like wildcats. But what did that matter, they'd fought many times before.

The more Annabella thought about having a sister, the more she liked the idea. Happiness and warm affection flowed through her veins. She felt a most fortunate woman and was truly thankful for this new blessing. She had always seemed a confident and generous-hearted person and it would never have occurred to her to be jealous of Nancy or to feel threatened by her in any way.

She wrote a long and loving letter to her ex-maid and told her of their true relationship and how delighted she was about it and how she would make Nancy and her family welcome at Mungo

717

House any time they found it possible to come. The letter went with *The Glasgow Lass* on its next voyage to Virginia and Annabella waited eagerly for a reply.

But the first news she received from Virginia was not happy. Her father came home one night in a distressed, yet excited condition and told her that his other ship, the *Mary Heron*, had been attacked by a privateer, many of the crew killed and all of his cargo stolen. The indentured servants aboard had been given the opportunity of joining the pirate ship or being left to an uncertain fate on the *Mary Heron*. The servants had decided to remain where they were and somehow they, with the wounded Captain Daidles and what was left of the crew, managed to continue to Virginia. Unfortunately, Mr Cunningham had been one of those killed.

'Oh, Papa!' Her sadness went beyond tears. 'What a waste! Such a gay and handsome man with all his life before him. Such a charming gentleman. Oh, this is a hateful calamity. I feel cruelly cast down.'

'Aye, he was a fine fellow, like his father before him. A sensible one too. In the will he made before leaving Virginia, he made you the sole beneficiary of all his money and land and possessions. Aye, it's an ill wind that blows nobody any good.'

The real impact of this news did not get properly through to her at that moment. She was too sad and distressed at the thought of Cunningham's death. A listlessness overcame her.

'Oh, Papa,' she sighed. 'I feel mightily depressed.'

'Aye, well, a jaunt over to Virginia should cheer you up. We'll all go. The *Speedwell* should be ready to leave from Port Glasgow in a few days.'

'Go to Virginia? We can't go to Virginia.'

'Why not?'

'I . . . I don't want to go, Papa. There's nothing for me in Virginia now.'

'Lassie, lassie. Did you no' hear what I said? You've a fortune over there. You've one of the biggest tobacco plantations in the colony.'

'But I don't want a tobacco plantation.'

'Well, I do.'

718

'Oh, Papa!'

'Never mind the 'oh Papa'. You do as you're bid and make yourself ready. We've important business to attend to in Virginia.'

Chapter 12

Harding had been teaching Regina a card game called picquet when her birth pangs started. They were both sitting on the settee in the drawing-room with a small table in front of them. A log fire crackled at one side, giving off a more intense light than the candles. The leather of the books lining the wall opposite the fire warmed to a ruby wine colour. The dancing orange light reflected in the gold-framed mirror giving it a dark bronze glitter. The curtains were drawn and the glow from the flames and the candles burnished the green brocade. Regina's embroidery lay on the footstool and on the open desk were some papers and a quill that Harding had been using earlier. The flower-patterned porcelain vases on the mantelpiece rippled with light, and the blue bird handles on top of their lids seemed as if they were preparing for flight. Only the tall clock in the far corner was in shadow, its brass face gloomy, its tick-tock sad and slow.

Regina put down her cards.

'What's wrong?' Harding asked. 'You've gone pale. Do you feel ill?'

'I think the birth has started.'

At least she supposed that was the explanation of the grinding, gripping pain she had felt. It had only lasted a few seconds but it frightened her.

'I'll send Westminster for the doctor.'

'We'll be lucky if we see the doctor here by morning.'

'Births usually last for hours, don't they?'

She shrugged.

'How should I know?'

'We'd better have the Negro midwife here as well. Just to be on the safe side.'

'Huh!' Regina gave a sarcastic laugh. 'I'm sure to be all right with her.'

Harding struggled to keep his temper.

'Dorcas Judy has brought hundreds of infants safely into the world and I've yet to hear of the woman who's been the worse of having her minister to them. I'll send for her.'

He went out to the hall and she heard him call for Westminster and then give him various instructions. She listened to the deep rumble of Harding's voice outside and felt a childish pique that the birth had to happen at all. She had been getting on so well with her husband recently. He had been spending a considerable amount of time with her and had even indulged her in several whims with surprising good grace. If she took a craving for peaches in the middle of the night, as she had on more than one occasion, he rose from his warm bed and actually went out to the orchard and picked her some.

He said that once she'd wakened him, he might as well get up and get them himself because he'd need a walk in the fresh air to help him to sleep again. Yet she liked to think he was doing it for her. She found herself enjoying his little attentions and sought them with all the cunning and naivety of a child. She puffed pathetically going up the stairs until he was forced to link arms with her so that she could lean on him as she slowly plodded upwards. Or he had to lift her and carry her to her room. She dropped her embroidery or her handkerchief then helplessly rocked and teetered, half-falling, half-fainting in her efforts to retrieve it until he hastened to the rescue and picked it up.

If he was too long in his office building, she would go and see him there and stand in front of his desk gazing dumbly at his quill or his ledgers until he'd groan or sigh and ask what was the matter with her now. Sometimes he could not control his irritation and would bawl:

'Jesus Christ!'

But before he could say any more, she would burst into tears and just continue to stand near him, refusing to relinquish her need of his presence. Eventually he would groan again and fling down his quill and come and take her in his arms.

Sometimes when she was getting his attention by some little ruse or other, or by acting in a babyish or petted manner, he would suddenly laugh and shake his head but it wasn't cruel laughter. She liked to imagine it was to some small degree affectionate. Pleased and grateful, she would laugh too.

Never before in her life had she been indulged or made a fuss of as she had been during her pregnancy. She enjoyed the experience intensely, greedily, savouring every delightful, astonishing moment. Now she could not bear to lose this special privileged treatment. Nor did she relish the idea of sharing Harding's attention with a baby or any other living creature. She did not want the child. She only wanted her husband.

Anxiously she watched the drawing-room door for his return and when he entered she was startled as she always was by the sight of him. He had the effect of a thunderclap on her. The sight of his huge, muscular frame, his ugly broken nose, his sensual mouth, his hard eyes frightened and excited her all at the same time.

'I told him to take my horse,' he said. 'It's the fastest.'

Another pang gripped her and switched her concentration inwards to herself.

Harding said,

'Come on, I'll help you up to bed. Dorcas Judy's coming, and Flemintina.'

She allowed him to ease her off the settee and lead her from the room and across the hall and up the stairs. She felt worried and apprehensive and she clung to him like a child. By the time they had reached the upstairs corridor, Flemintina was hastening after them and in the bedroom Harding said,

'Undress Mistress Regina and put her to bed. Dorcas Judy should be here in a few minutes.'

'Where are you going?' Regina asked.

'Back downstairs.'

'Stay with me.'

'This is no place for me now. The servants and the doctor will attend to you. You will be perfectly all right.'

'I want a glass of whisky.'

'You'd better wait and see if the midwife thinks it is safe for you to have one.'

'Damn the midwife!' A pain far worse than the other suddenly

722

jarred through her, making her moan and stoop and grab on to Flemintina for support.

Harding went out and shut the door. With beads of sweat beginning to trickle down her face, she remained in her tense stooping position, listening to his heavy tread in the corridor, then on the stairs. There was a crash as the drawing-room door shut. Flemintina cautiously began undoing Regina's gown. Regina resented the woman's help. She had chosen never to have a body servant, preferring the privacy of her own bedroom and her own person, preferring too the independence of attending to personal tasks herself. But already the pains were exhausting her and taking her breath away and she had no choice but to allow Flemintina to peel off every garment until she was completely naked and vulnerable.

'Hurry up with the nightgown,' she managed in her usual sharp tone.

Then with a breathless, determined effort, she struggled into it by herself. Before she could reach the four-poster bed, however, a pain made her whimper. Flemintina tossed back the covers, then struggled to hoist her swollen body into the bed. What a relief it was eventually to collapse back against the pillows. Yet she only enjoyed a few minutes respite before another grinding contraction riveted her whole attention and energy. Then another and another. Sweat was pouring from her face now and her red hair had darkened with moisture and was rumpling and straggling about in disarray.

'Where the hell is that bloody doctor?'

'Westminster's gone to fetch him, Miss Regina, but I don't think he'll have got there yet. It's a long ride to the doctor's house.'

'I know how long it takes, damn you. But the doctor should have been here without being sent for. He ought to have known when I was to deliver. A lot of damn good he is.'

'Yes, Miss Regina.'

'Don't just stand there,' Regina was nearly weeping. 'Do something, damn you!'

'I don' know what to do, Miss Regina.'

'Go and see if the midwife is coming. Although what good

that ignorant old witch can do me I don't know.'

Left alone in the bedroom, she writhed about the big bed obsessed with the reality of her agony, yet praying at the same time that it was only a terrible nightmare from which she'd suddenly, mercifully escape.

The world had shrunk. It was contained in four wood-panelled walls. The only objects in the world were the wash-table, and the bowl and jug that stood on it, and the lowboy with the pier glass sitting on top, and the two tall candlesticks, one on either side, and the carved kist, and the chairs, and the bedside table with the elegantly curved legs and single drawer, and the clock on top and the other two tall candlesticks, one on either side.

The world shrunk tighter. Now there was nothing but immediate, urgent agony. Sweat blurred her eyes. She began to scream. She was vaguely conscious of the green and gold silk bedcurtains, then black faces and black bodies and black hands.

'That's right, you just push hard, honey,' Dorcas Judy said.

Regina didn't know what she was talking about and didn't care. Her consciousness of pain had brought all her hatred of Harding rampaging back. It was his fault that she was suffering like this. He had caused her condition. His selfish lust had caused this incredible, never-ending torture. He had put her on the rack. He had trapped her in this torment while he sat downstairs. She was going mad with pain. He was coolly relaxing downstairs, enjoying his usual glass of whisky. Or he was sound asleep in bed. He was a bastard. She screamed her hatred. 'Bastard! Bastard!' she screamed until black hands caught her wildly thrashing face and squeezed over her mouth, all but choking her.

Until suddenly, mercifully, the agony stopped; washed away, soothed. She felt like a rag doll, without any bones, utterly exhausted. The relief was incredible. She wanted to do nothing but sleep, but first she summoned enough strength to ask,

'Is he all right?'

' 'Tain't a he,' Dorcas Judy cackled. 'It's a she. As sweet a little gal as I ever did see.'

Regina closed her eyes.

'Oh God!'

'Look at her, Miss Regina,' Flemintina pleaded. 'Ain't she pretty?'

'Take her away. I want to sleep.'

'But, Miss Regina . . .'

'Do as you're told.' The icy voice dared any further contradiction and Flemintina carried the child from the room.

Dorcas Judy dried her hands on her apron.

'Well, that's everything cleaned and tidy for the doctor comin'.'

'I don't want the doctor or anyone in here for at least four hours. Tell Mr Harding that before you go.'

'Yes, Miss Regina.'

The bedroom door opened then closed leaving silence. But outside the birds had begun their dawn chorus. She tried to think of how Harding would take the news of having a daughter instead of a son. She struggled to think of what would happen and of what she must now do. But she was too fatigued. Her mind kept drifting further and further away from her body until at last she succumbed to the luxury of complete unconsciousness.

When she awoke, she did not immediately remember what had happened. At first she hazily imagined that it was just another day of physical discomfort when she would have to drag her swollen body about. Then it dawned on her that she was back to her slim healthy shapely self again and a wave of sheer joy and gratitude washed over her. Until suddenly she remembered that her nine months of discomfort, culminating in the hours of torment of the previous night, had all been for nothing. She had not given Harding a son.

Fear alternated with fountains of panic. Somehow the fact that she was now his legal wife did not make her feel as secure and safe as she had always imagined it would. She still had fears of being discarded and left homeless and hungry and at everyone's mercy. It was as if inside she was still and always would be the child who had come home to Tannery Wynd from school one day to find no one there and the door locked against her. She was still wandering the streets belonging to no one and with nowhere to go.

She lay in limbo in the big four-poster bed, her hair flowing down over her shoulders like a burnished copper shawl until Flemintina came with the doctor, who examined her and cheerfully told her that she was perfectly all right and she was very fortunate to have had such an easy birth. Never before in her life had she hated men more than she did at that moment. She was barely civil to him and left him in no doubt that she had not the slightest desire to carry on any social conversation.

After he'd gone, she instructed Flemintina to bring her breakfast and she had barely finished some boiled milk when Harding appeared.

'How are you?' he inquired.

'Completely recovered.'

'I hear that you have refused to look at the child.'

'It is not a son.'

He sighed.

'I cannot deny I am keenly disappointed. But no doubt you will be able to have other children.'

She could hardly credit that he could talk of putting her through the dreadful experience a second time before she had even recovered from the first. She had always thought he was an insensitive brute and this proved it. But before she could make some scathing reply, he added with a smile,

'And I must say I am rather catched by my daughter.'

'Really?' she said trying to sound cool but her heart giving a flutter of interest.

'I think she looks rather like me.'

'Then God help her, sir.'

He laughed.

'You have indeed made a speedy recovery, mistress. Do you wish to see the little madam now?'

She shrugged. 'I suppose I might as well.'

He jerked his head at Flemintina who hurried away to fetch the child.

'What shall we call her?' he asked when the slave returned nursing and cooing and grinning delightedly down at the small bundle she was carrying.

'I swear she's the cleverest infant I ever did see, Miss Regina.

She's smiling at me. Yes, you are, you are so. You're the cleverest little, prettiest . . .'

'Oh, stop drooling like an idiot and give the child to me,' Regina snapped.

Once the little girl was in her arms she stared curiously down at her. The tiny red face looked as ugly as sin. She couldn't imagine how anyone could truthfully call it pretty.

'I've no idea what her name should be,' she said.

'My mother's name was Charlotte.'

'Charlotte,' Regina repeated. 'Charlotte Harding, I suppose that's as good as anything. It'll do. Do you know, I believe she does look like you.'

Just then Charlotte opened her mouth and began to howl and cry in no uncertain manner. Regina could not help laughing and Harding laughed too.

'Look at her waving her fist,' he said in a voice incredulous with pride. 'That surely is clever for a newborn infant and spirited too.'

'Yes, sir, Master Harding. Ain't nothin' wrong with her lungs neither,' Flemintina giggled. 'That Lottie, she's goin' to be a determined gal. She's hungry an' she's yellin' like mad so's we has to do something about it.'

'Lottie.' Harding savoured the word. 'Yes, we can call her Lottie among ourselves.'

He leancd over the bed and poked a finger at the infant.

'Welcome to Forest Hall, Lottie Harding.' The child's tiny fist curled round the man's finger and he cried out, 'Look at that, Flemintina!'

And the servant screeched with delighted laughter.

Regina rolled her eyes.

'Lord's sake!'

She wasn't quite sure what her reactions were to this new situation. Still feeling weak and harrowed after the trauma of the birth, she needed more time to settle herself down, to be on her own and to think.

'Dorcas Judy is waiting outside to help you with the feeding,' Harding told Regina, never taking his eyes off Lottie. 'I'll send her in.'

Reluctantly he eased his finger from the baby's hand and straightened up.

'I don't need her,' Regina protested. 'I had enough of her last night.'

'She has experience in these things. She'll know everything that should be done and the best way that everything should be done for the child's benefit.'

Depression seeped into Regina's veins weighing her down, tiring her. She leaned back on her pillows and closed her eyes.

'What's wrong?' Harding asked.

She sighed.

'I don't know. I feel low in spirits and my head aches.'

'I want no more of your tantrums, mistress. You have a child to look after now. It's time you stopped behaving like one.'

A spring of fury surged up inside Regina but it found her too feeble to continue its impetus. Tears of frustration welled up and overflowed down her face.

'Christ!' Harding aimed the word like a bullet at her before turning to Flemintina.

'I'm away for a ride round the plantation with the doctor. I hold you responsible for my daughter. See that she is properly cared for. If by any mischance the doctor is needed, send a rider after us immediately.'

'Yes, Master Harding, sir.'

Regina could not believe it when she heard him leaving, or that he had spoken to her so abruptly. She had become accustomed to being kindly treated during the past nine months. Broken-hearted sobs began to jerk from her until she abandoned herself to feeble hysteria. The child in her arms was still screaming and, unable to bear the added burden, she pushed it helplessly away.

'Miss Regina!' Flemintina sounded shocked as she scooped the infant up into her arms. Then she showered the wrinkled red face with kisses. 'What's your mammy doin' to you? Aw, you poor little thing. But don't you worry none. You're goin' to be all right. Your Flemintina's here.'

Dorcas Judy came bustling and cackling into the room then.

'Land's sake, ain't she something though?'

'Name's Lottie,' Flemintina said. 'Never seen Master so pleased with anything before. And he's told me to look after her.'

'Kissin' and cuddlin' ain't what that little missy needs right now. It's sucklin'.' She gave one of her shrieks of laughter. Then arms akimbo she viewed Regina. 'Come on now, Miss Regina. No need for you to be carryin' on so.'

'Go away and leave me alone.'

'Your goin' to be fine, just fine.'

'What are you doing?' Regina knew she could not cope with anything else but she made a desperate attempt to find enough strength to push away the hands that were now unfastening her nightgown. 'Leave me alone!' In horror she watched the two women bare her, then fasten the child's mouth over one of her breasts.

Greedily, hard gums clamped on her and drained away what strength she had left. She had not even enough energy to hate the two women for humiliating her, for standing over her gawping at her nakedness and her helplessness. But she vowed that when she had her strength back, when she was herself again, when she was safely hidden and contained inside, she would make them pay. She would make Harding pay too. She would not forget or forgive any of them. As for the child, she had no feelings for it at all. She wanted to swot it away as she would a fly or a leech. She shrank away from it inside. She did not know how to cope with the anguish, humiliation and vulnerability it was making her suffer. She just wanted to be free of it. Stiffening back against the pillows, she closed her eyes.

'Now, Miss Regina,' Dorcas Judy scolded. 'You behave yourself. 'Tain't doin' poor Lottie or yourself any good actin' like this.'

'How dare you!' she said. 'How dare you!' But tears spilled over again, making a weak fool of her, taking away from her authority.

All she could do was pray for the nightmare to end soon and when it did and she was at last alone in the room, she wept all the more. But gradually the quietness and the blessed privacy soothed her and she lay without moving, just staring at the

729

window curtains gently billowing and puffing in the breeze. A hiss of rain clouded the windows and made her think of Harding and the doctor out riding. She wondered with a pang of apprehension if Harding was wearing his heavy triple-caped riding coat and three-cornered hat to protect him from the elements. A vivid picture of him took possession of her mind, his heavy body like some giant pugilist jerking to the horse's rhythm.

She tried to blot out the picture. She tried to sleep but the image of Harding stayed in vivid sensuous colour in her mind as if it was part of her and nothing she could do would ever fade it away.

Remembering the scene earlier during his visit, she felt hurt that he had not displayed the slightest tenderness and affection towards her, far less pride. All his pride and love had been concentrated on his daughter. He had shown only cruelty and insensitivity to his wife. Indeed, he had insulted her, and in front of the servants. She would remember that. For that he would be sorry.

When the doctor came back to see her she told him that she did not feel strong enough to feed the baby. He tried to be jovial and hearty.

'Nonsense, my dear. You are as strong and healthy a young filly as I've ever had the good fortune to come across. Strong and healthy, I say.'

She withered him with a look of icy disdain.

'I do not care what you say, sir. I say I do not feel strong enough to feed the child and it is what I say that matters.'

'But . . . but my dear Mistress Harding, you are only . . . what? . . . twenty-four or twenty-five. That is nothing nowadays. Why I know of women who are feeding infants at forty. Really I do.'

'The misfortunes of your other patients do not concern me. I am only concerned about myself. Will you arrange for a wet nurse? Or must I depend on the midwife or some other servant to do what is necessary for my well-being?'

'Oh, very well,' the doctor muttered in sudden pique. 'But Mr Harding is not going to be pleased, truly he is not.'

She was sick of the sight of the useless creature. Even Dorcas Judy commanded more of her respect than him. She was glad when eventually, next day, she was finished with him and he with her and he decided it was time to terminate his visit. She did not thank him when he took his leave and Harding remarked on this later.

'It would have been civil to thank the man.'

'Thank him? For what?'

'He did his best for you.'

'Well, his best wasn't good enough.'

'Why do you sound so bitter?' Harding eyed her curiously. 'What harm do you imagine he did you?'

'I don't wish to discuss the doctor or his administrations or his lack of them. The same applies to that old harridan who calls herself a midwife. In fact, I don't want to discuss the birth or anything to do with it.'

'Most women talk about nothing else. They enjoy gossiping and exchanging stories about their childbed experiences.'

She raised a brow.

'Really? What empty, boring lives they must lead.'

A cloud darkened his eyes and he looked anxious.

'I hope you are going to be all right to Lottie.'

His anxiety made him seem vulnerable and his vulnerability pulled at her heart. She touched his hand, the contact of each finger with his skin almost painful in its pleasure.

'You love her, don't you?'

He nodded.

'Then I love her too.'

But she knew as she said the words that they meant nothing.

Chapter 13

'Now that Flemintina is the child's nurse,' Regina told the servants, 'and Jenny's working in the fields, and Old Abe's too old to work properly, I'll need more house slaves. Callie Mae, can you think of anyone who would be worth seeing? I don't want to waste my time interviewing everyone from the quarters.'

The Negroes were gathered before her in the drawing-room, Callie Mae, Flemintina, Minda, Sal, Big Kate, Melie Anne, Joseph and Westminster.

'How many were you thinkin' of, Miss Regina?' Callie Mae inquired. 'And wenches or bucks?'

'I think I'd better have another man for the house and a man to do odd jobs inside and out like fixing things and cutting grass. And one woman. Flemintina can still do other work apart from seeing to Lottie—the bedrooms, for instance. I don't like too many people about the place.'

'There's Lizzie,' Callie Mae ventured. 'She's young and quiet-spoken. Keeps herself clean and tidy too.'

'Tell her to come and see me this morning.'

'Yes, Miss Regina.'

Westminster spoke up. 'Bill's good and strong. So's Mowden.'

'Where are they just now? In the fields?'

'Yes, Miss Regina, ma'am.'

'I'll have a word with Mr Harding and see what he thinks first. That's all just now. Except for one thing. I don't want all of you petting and handling and wasting so much time with Lottie and that includes you, Flemintina. I want her properly looked after but not spoiled. Is that clear?'

There was a general murmur of:

'Yes, Miss Regina, ma'am.'

But they all lowered their eyes and Regina had the irritating feeling that they had no intention of obeying this particular order. The worst of it was, Harding encouraged the general atmosphere of adoration where Lottie was concerned. He didn't say much, he even tried to look unconcerned, but it was obvious that he enjoyed the eager chatter of the house slaves when they had some new story to relate about what Lottie had done or not done, how she'd looked, how she'd sounded, how she'd slept or not slept. She had actually heard his abrupt bursts of laughter mingled with Flemintina's high-pitched shrieks of hilarity in Lottie's room. He was besotted with the child. It was ridiculous. She wasn't even pretty with her fat face and tufty hair. Now when he came in for tea, Lottie had to be brought down to the drawing-room to sit on his knee and share a biscuit and be fed milk from a special cup.

At first she hadn't minded the sight of his big hands awkwardly holding the infant. She had even laughed at his awkwardness and taken the child, proud at being able to show him how competent she was at handling it, or how she could make it stop screaming by bringing up its wind. At first, of course, Lottie had slept most of each day and neither of them had much contact with her. But as weeks and then months passed, the little girl began to develop a personality and was wide awake for longer and longer periods and all the time demanding someone's attention. She was a plump, sturdy child with hair the same dark colour as Harding's. She had his dark eyes too but hers were large and soft and round.

At six months her fat legs were bending and bouncing on Harding's knee and determinedly clambering all over him. Her chubby hands were grabbing at him in delight, pulling at his mouth, his nose, his hair.

'Lottie!' Regina would chastise. 'Bad girl! Sit down at once and take your milk.'

'Oh, leave her alone,' Harding always replied. 'It's good exercise for her.'

Tea time was no longer peaceful. It was no longer an opportunity to have Harding to herself. No longer was there any chance to talk to him. She brushed her hair until it gleamed, dressed in beautiful gowns, wore Mistress Kitty's jewellery, but she might as well have been invisible. Harding had no eyes, no time, no interest, no attention for anyone but his daughter.

Lottie now dominated their relationship, if they had any relationship at all. When they had been married they had continued as they had done before and slept in their own rooms except on the nights when Harding came to make love to her. If it could be called making love, she often thought bitterly. He had never told her that he loved her. Certainly she had not minded the arrangement at first. Before Lottie had come on the scene, it had worked very well. She liked to have a time and an area of privacy in her life. Privacy was something she had always jealously guarded, had hugged to herself with the same secret, miserly pleasure as with the looted gold coins she had brought all the way from the Highlands after the battle of Culloden.

But now she lay alone in her bed each morning stiff and strained and resentful, listening for any sounds coming from Harding's room. She was aware that he often had the child brought to him early so that he could have a few minutes with her before going downstairs and starting his daily routine. The sounds of his deep voice, warm and soft with an affection that he'd never shown to her, filled her with anger. It was so unfair. She was his wife. She should come first in everything. Did he think she was nothing but a chattel, something with no feelings, a machine to attend to his house, his physical comforts, his sexual needs? She was a good wife. From the moment she rose in the morning until she lay down in bed every night, she worked conscientiously to be a good wife and run his house properly and efficiently. It was her life's work, her whole purpose in life to make sure that he had everything he wanted. He had wanted a child and even in that she had succeeded. She had given him a child. It wasn't her fault that the child had not been a son. But now, seeing how he behaved with Lottie, she was afraid to think of how he would be if he did have a son.

Mornings became a torment to her and she started every day with tension that more often than not developed into a headache. How dare he ignore her and lavish so much love and attention on a fat, ugly, infant who wasn't what he or the servants claimed at all? There was nothing particularly clever about anything the child did. She tried to tell him, to make him see sense and stop making such a fool of himself, not to mention completely

734

ruining the child. Once his precious prodigy began to walk and talk and be aware of the power she held over her poor doting fool of a Papa, she would lead him a merry dance. He was fast making the child into a spoiled, selfish, repulsive little monster who dominated the whole house and everyone in it. She told him so.

'I might have known,' he sneered, 'that you would be incapable of any normal feelings, even for your own child. It's a good thing the child has me. I shudder to think what a barren, loveless life she might have had with no one but you.'

'What about the barren, loveless life I've had?' she wanted to cry out to him, but the hatred in his eyes made her afraid of any further attempts to reach out to him. Eventually, however, she did broach the subject of permanently sharing a room. For long agonizing hours and days beforehand she had thought about the decision and the best manner to convey it to Harding. She had meant to be very diplomatic and choose the right moment and be at her most attractive and appealing. She had meant to catch Harding at his most intimate and vulnerable time. She had planned to make the offer to him after they had made love and were close to one another. She'd wanted to whisper that he could be with her like this every night, she'd longed to confess to him that her need to feel continuously close to him, to be part of him, outweighed even her basic compulsion to withdraw into herself.

But somehow she hadn't been able to wait for the best time and instead had blurted it out one night as they were parting at the top of the stairs to go to their respective rooms.

'It isn't right that we should be sleeping in separate rooms. We are man and wife. You may move in with me if you wish.'

His lips pulled back in an ugly sneer.

'You are a bit late in deciding what is right and what is wrong, mistress. And don't imagine that I don't know how your twisted mind reached this decision. You are jealous of your own child.'

He'd walked away to his own room without even a polite goodnight to her.

Her normal feelings of insecurity and apprehension intensified. If he did not love her, could he not fall in love with someone else?

But what could he do that would jeopardize her position at Forest Hall? She was his legal wife. He could not abandon her now. Or could he? Anxiously she leafed through the books on the drawing-room shelves in search of any legal information that might soothe and comfort her.

At other times, she squashed her anxieties, withered them, froze them and went about the business of running Forest Hall as coolly and efficiently as if nothing could possibly ruffle her. She sat opposite Harding every afternoon daintily sipping tea, a dignified outcast clinging surreptitiously to the borders of his attention with an occasional polite remark or query.

She kept telling herself that he could not do without her. For surely he loved her in his own way? In bed, what he lacked in tenderness was more than compensated for in passion. He was a passionate man and she amply fulfilled his passionate needs. Why should he want another woman? But of course, there was no other woman. The only other female in Harding's life was Lottie. At eight months, she delighted him with her ridiculous jerky, half-sideways, bottom-jerking crawl. By then, of course, she could stretch up her arms when she wanted to be lifted. At a year she was enchanting him by squealing:

'Papa! Papa!'

And of course, just as she had predicted, the child was absolutely spoiled. If she did not get all her own way, her plump face screwed up and reddened almost to purple as she yelled in outraged protest. She refused to be put down to sleep until far too late at night. Indeed she kept the same hours as Harding, only occasionally dozing off to sleep during the day when he was not there. She was fussy about her food, rejecting something she did not like, or when she had a whim not to eat at all, by upsetting and spilling the food on to the table or floor.

On one occasion when this happened, rage overcame Regina. It wasn't only because she had just had the slaves thoroughly clean and polish the dining-room floor and the dining-room furniture. It wasn't only because of Harding's loving tolerance of the child's misdemeanours, although it did occur to her, and with much bitterness, that he had no such tolerance for any of his wife's faults. What really made her lash out and strike Lottie was the realization that the child was in danger of becoming a little monster. Harding would obviously adore Lottie no matter what the child did or what she was like, but no one else would.

The astonishment with which Lottie received the stinging slap on her face registered in her saucer eyes and her moment of stunned silence. Then she let out a scream, followed by another and another during which she went rigid and Flemintina came running in panic and Harding went as white as the tablecloth.

'It's just temper.' Regina attempted to make herself heard above the din. 'There's nothing wrong with her. Be quiet at once, Lottie. At once! Do you hear?'

After Flemintina had managed to pacify her and carry her from the room, Harding said,

'Don't you ever dare lay a finger on that child again.'

'It was for her own good. Can't you see what you're doing to her?'

'I'm warning you, mistress.'

There was such venom and fury in his eyes that it was as much as she could do to prevent herself bursting into tears.

'I just don't understand you,' she managed, her voice bewildered and incredulous. 'You were so insistent before. All you wanted was a son. You wanted a son to carry on your name, you said. I'll never forget how disappointed I was for your sake when I discovered it was a daughter. Yet you've been absolutely stupid over the girl right from the start.'

'I still want a son,' Harding said. 'That does not mean I need be cruel to my daughter.'

'But you are cruel to her.'

'I am being cruel to her? *I, I* am being cruel? What are you raving about now?'

'I keep telling you. You're ruining the child. You're allowing her to have all her own way and to behave in whatever manner she fancies.'

'She's only a year old, a mere baby. What does she understand about behaviour?'

'She understands very well and she's got to be taught to behave properly.'

'By beating her, no doubt?'

'If necessary,' Regina said coldly.

'No, mistress, I would rather beat you and teach you a lesson than allow you to touch my daughter again. Do I make myself plain?'

Regina's mouth twisted.

'Oh, yes. Perfectly. You care about no one except her. She can do whatever she pleases and be whatever she pleases. All I can say, sir, is God help me if you do have a son.'

The more she thought along these lines, the more worried she became. She began to hope they didn't have a son after all. Apart from perhaps giving Harding another ally against her, a son would have more claim to Forest Hall than she would, would he not? She felt sick with anxiety. She cared for the place even more passionately than she cared for Harding. It was her home. She belonged here. It was part of her. Often she wandered about the house caressing the walls and the furniture with gentle, adoring hands. Everything about it she knew and loved. The way the chandelier in the hall tinkled airily and did a little dance in the draught; the mirror polish on the floor and banisters; the luxurious draping of the four-poster beds; the blazing log fires in every room glimmering against silk brocade curtains; the elegant dining-room with its long mahogany table and panelled walls and sideboard laden with silver; rows and rows of books making an Aladdin's cave of the drawing-room. Here she could escape alone into a hundred other worlds, worlds in which she could adventure, love and be loved, weep and laugh, lose herself and yet be safe. Often in the afternoon, after tea had been cleared away and Harding had left, or in the evening if he was occupied with Lottie, she would sit in the corner with a candle and a book, and shrink into the other world for comfort.

She loved the never-used ballroom, too, with its rows of silver-grey tall-backed chairs and its harpsichord and music stands and magnificent chandeliers.

It occurred to her, looking at the ballroom, that one day when Lottie was older, the child would need to learn how to dance and perhaps perform on the harpsichord. No doubt she would need to be given balls so that she could be introduced to and meet all sorts of people, especially beaux. That was the custom, was it not?

For the first time in many months, she felt a surge of happiness. Lottie would not be here monopolizing Harding's attention for ever. That was a fact that had not occurred to Harding. For many things and for many occasions, a young girl needed a mother much more than she needed a father. By capitalizing on this fact, she could surely win Harding round and make him more aware of her again, grateful to her, even admiring.

Cautiously, casually, she broached the subject to him.

'It is as well we have a ballroom.'

Harding raised a brow.

'Is it?'

She sighed. 'I thought such things had never occurred to you.'

'What things?'

She was sitting opposite him in the drawing-room, neatly stitching on her embroidery frame. She took her time in answering.

'You believe you are the only one who has Lottie's welfare at heart. You think you can do everything for her and know everything that has to be done. But of course you do not.'

'I have no idea what you are talking about but I suspect it is something devious.'

She shrugged.

'Oh, very well.'

After a minute or two of silence, he burst out,

'Well? Explain yourself, woman!'

'Your daughter is growing fast, sir. Are you going to allow her to throw her food around and screech like an animal forever? Are you going to have her working with you on the plantation dressed in boy's clothes? She will learn some choice language there from the overseer and the like, I have no doubt. Are you going to keep her by your side in your office and teach her how to scrape a quill across a ledger? Have these to be her accomplishments? Is that all you can offer her? May I give you a warning, sir? She will not thank you for launching her into womanhood and fashionable society with so poor a preparation.'

She saw by his face that he had taken her point. He would

739

suffer anything for his precious Lottie, even his wife. Bitterness rose like bile inside her but she lowered her eyes and swallowed it down.

'I wish to make her some pretty dresses but I need material. When can we go to Williamsburg to do some shopping? Or would it be more convenient to go to the store? Have you business to do there?'

He looked subdued, thoughtful. At last he said,

'Yes, it is time I went and settled my account there. You can come and purchase whatever you need from the store and also make a list of anything you want sent over from Glasgow.'

'I'll need linen and thread lace for underwear, and silks and taffetas for dresses and lots of pretty ribbons. When she gets older, of course, she must learn to sew for herself. I will teach her. She should also learn the social graces. I can teach her those too. But when it comes time for her to learn to perform on a musical instrument, I will have to engage a tutor. I could begin taking lessons myself just now, of course, so that I might be of help to her. Then there's dancing. That's what I meant when I said it was as well we have a ballroom. Eventually she'll want to meet people. She'll want us to give her balls, also to attend concerts and other gatherings.' She sighed. 'As you know, I have no time for such things and I'm happier without social intercourse, but for Lottie's sake I will entertain, because it is the proper thing to do. Of course, I realize she's only a baby yet.'

'But growing fast, as you say. Yes, it's right to think of her future.'

'She'll certainly need some decent dresses in the very near future. She's no better dressed than the Negro children at the moment. Flemintina doesn't care about these things. She fusses over the child and means well, of course. But she's just not capable of understanding everything that a young lady of quality will need, far less provide her with them.'

Harding did not reply but she knew she had given him something to think about and she was secretly elated. He was thinking of how much more useful and necessary his wife was to him than he'd realized.

They made arrangements to travel to the settlement and

within a couple of days had set off through the forest taking Lottie, Flemintina, Joseph and Westminster with them.

It was for the most part quite a pleasant journey with Harding and herself riding companionably in front. Flemintina and Lottie were in the carriage driven by Joseph with Westminster sitting beside him, toting a gun on his lap.

They didn't talk much, but then they never had. As they neared the settlement, however, and Widow Shoozie's tavern came into sight, Harding said,

'Gav will be pleased to see Lottie. He seems fond of children.'

'Yes, he will be happy for my sake too. I will take her straight to the store.'

Harding laughed.

'I think it would be wiser to settle in at the tavern first and have a wash and change our linen.'

'Yes, you're right. Lottie will be too tired after the journey. Anyway,' she continued, 'I must concentrate on my shopping. That's what I came for and that's what I must attend to first. Plenty of time later to socialize with Gav and Abigail.'

As it turned out, the child was so tired she fell asleep as soon as her head touched one of Widow Shoozie's pillows. They left her in Flemintina's charge and, after freshening up, they rode the rest of the way along the path to the clearing and the settlement.

Regina felt a thrill of happiness. She enjoyed so much having him to herself.

'I see there's some ships in,' Harding remarked. 'That looks like the *Mary Heron* and there's the *Speedwell*. I can't see the name on the frigate.'

Dismounting in front of the store, they tied their horses to the hitching post. Harding said,

'I think I'll take a stroll down to the wharf. I see a few planter friends there I might have a word with. You go ahead. I'll see you later.'

She nodded agreement and left him to enter the store. She had only taken a few paces inside when she stopped in surprise. There, over at the counter, talking together in between rummaging through a box of ribbons were two women, one in a plum-coloured gown with gloves of cream lace and matching lace at her elbows and bosom. Gold earrings dangled from her ears. The other woman was radiant in a turquoise taffeta hoop and silver quilted petticoat. Her hair was powdered and she was wearing face patches but there was no mistaking Mistress Annabella. The other woman was Nancy.

Regina hesitated. She had no particular wish to speak to either of them. Instinctively she shrank from social contacts. All the same, she realized that they were the only friends or acquaintances she had and in the light of what she had been saying to Harding, they could prove useful. Eventually she forced herself to approach the two women and when they noticed her, she gave a polite curtsy.

'Mistress Nancy. Mistress Annabella.'

Annabella was the first to greet her.

'Why, Regina! You are looking well. How has life been treating you? Do tell us all your news.'

'I have been married to Mr Harding since he was widowed and we have a daughter called Lottie.'

'Oh, good gracious alive!' Annabella giggled behind her fan. 'I hope you are able to manage him. I have never met such a stubborn man. Nor a . . .' She suddenly snapped her fan shut and rapped it against her lips in mock reprimand. 'I shall say no more. I dare swear you know Mr Harding well enough.'

'Indeed I do,' Regina said. 'Are you back to stay for good?'

'You'll never guess,' Nancy interrupted in her husky, amused voice. 'We're sisters! Or at least half-sisters. We've just found out. And she has fallen heir to the Cunningham plantation. I'm staying with her there now. We just sailed here today from the plantation to do some shopping. The plantation has it's own wharf and its own boat and we journey here whenever we take the fancy. There's everything at the plantation. You should see it.'

'Mungo's enjoying it,' Annabella said. 'Especially his visits to the settlement.'

'So you are staying,' Regina addressed Annabella again.

Annabella shrugged.

'It depends on Papa. I'm not sure what's happening yet. I don't want to stay. I have a wondrously handsome mansion at home in Glasgow.'

Just then a little boy joined them.

'May I watch the cockfight in front of the gaol, Mama?' he inquired politely.

Annabella flounced round, skirts rustling and swaying.

'Yes, yes.' She shooed him away with a flurry of lace at her elbows. 'On you go, do!'

But it was not before Regina was able to have a good look at the child and recognize without a doubt that he was Harding's son.

Chapter 14

Nancy murmured in a low voice to Annabella,

'I told you there was a resemblance, but you wouldn't believe me.'

Regina had gone a deathly white and Annabella pattered over in a shimmer of billowing turquoise and silver to offer her a chair. Ignoring it, Regina remained stiffly erect, although her whole world and all her plans had disintegrated. Nothing mattered any more except the fact that Harding had a son. If he found out about the boy he would make a will and leave Forest Hall to him. He would not care about her. And there would be nothing she could do. He could even bring the boy into the house now and there would be nothing she could do. She felt like an animal. All thought, all instinct now concentrated on survival. She had a vague impression of Annabella's voice trying to carry on a light, bright conversation as if nothing was amiss but she ignored it too.

Eventually Annabella gasped,

'Lord's sake, why should you look as if you've been struck by a thunderbolt? It happened a long time ago and against my will, I might add. I was mightily distressed and angry at first but, losh and lovenendie, it does nobody any good to nurse vengeful thoughts. Forgive and forget, that's always been my motto and it's one I recommend to you.'

'He doesn't know,' Regina said, half to herself.

'Oh, good gracious alive, I dread to think what Mr Harding would have been like if he had.' Annabella's eyes sparkled roguishly and she made elegant, fluttering movements with her fan. 'He pursued me with prodigious stubbornness as it was. I dare swear I could have been Mrs Harding now had I wanted to, but I did not.'

'He mustn't see the boy.'

'Huh!' Annabella flicked a glance heavenwards. 'He would

744

be the last one to notice a resemblance. Forgive me for being so blunt but I have always regarded Mr Harding as the most insensitive and unperceptive of men.'

'He is sensitive enough to his daughter. He dotes on the child.'

'Indeed!' Annabella arched amused brows. 'Well, well!'

Nancy eyed her cautiously.

'Maybe Regina's right. That man has always meant trouble. He might try to take Mungo from you if he found out.'

'Pooh! He wouldn't dare. I'd soon send him away with a flea in his ear.'

Annabella laughed, then with hoops rustling and seesawing, she turned back to the ribbon box. 'There, I have chosen mine. Have you enough there, Nancy? Regina, are you purchasing any ribbons? There are some wondrously pretty ones here.'

Regina's face hardened. How typical of this spoiled madam to think only of ribbons at a time like this. Blindly she fumbled in her reticule for the list of items she had prepared before leaving Forest Hall.

'Ah,' cried Annabella, noticing, 'you have a list. How well you are organized. Sometimes I write one,' she giggled, 'and then when I reach the store I cannot remember where I have put it.'

'Regina was always conscientious,' Nancy said. 'I used to tell you. Slow but determined. Painstaking in her efforts, I used to say.'

'So you did!' Annabella's merriment defied the sombre shadows of the store. 'And haven't your efforts been successful, Regina? Gracious heavens, fancy you being mistress of Forest Hall!' Suddenly she rapped her fan against the counter and called loudly,

'Boy! You are keeping ladies waiting.' Then turning to Nancy, 'Is there anything else you need while we are here?'

'I cannot afford any more.'

'Fiddlesticks, let Papa pay.'

Nancy groaned and rolled her eyes.

'How many times must I tell you? I want nothing from your Papa.'

'Your Papa, too.'

'I have a husband now and I'm quite content to let him

provide for me. He makes a comfortable living from the farm.'

'Fiddlesticks and poppycock! You and Morgan must stay on at the Cunningham place. It's much more comfortable.'

'Annabella!'

'Ah, here is the young fellow to serve us at last.' Annabella tossed a heap of ribbons across the counter at him. 'We shall have those. Wrap them up at once, sir.'

'I think,' said Regina, 'I will just give my list to my brother to attend to.'

'Ah, yes, Gav,' Annabella said. 'I believe Papa is well pleased with him. You are a fine pair indeed. By all accounts your brother is prodigiously conscientious too. Papa is upstairs in the counting house talking to him now.'

Regina lowered her eyes.

'Oh! Then I shall wait until he has gone.'

'Why, for God's sake? You are not his servant now. You must join us on the boat for a dish of tea and a gossip after you have attended to your business.'

'My husband will wonder where I am.'

Annabella fluttered up her hands.

'Bring him along, do.'

Annabella's flippant attitude troubled Regina. How could the stupid woman be so blind? It was vitally urgent to keep Harding away from the settlement now. She could not understand how Annabella was not able to see how desperately important this was. Regina's peace of mind, her well-being, her safety, her very existence, she believed, depended on keeping Harding as far away as possible.

'What about your son?'

Annabella dabbed daintily at one of her face patches.

'Heavens above, Regina. You haven't changed. You're still monstrously long-visaged and intense. If it will ease you, I will instruct Big John and Betsy to take him picnicking and swimming down by the creek.'

'Thank you. Now, if you will excuse me.'

They all curtsied nicely.

'You will pay us a call then?' Annabella's blue eyes twinkled over her fan.

'If my husband is agreeable,' Regina murmured, then escaped from the dark store into the bright sunlight with as much dignity as she was able.

She had no intention of even mentioning to Harding that she'd seen Annabella. Her heart thumped painfully in her chest. Her mouth and throat were parched, her hands clammy. For a few minutes she stood in the brassy heat inwardly confused, not knowing what to do. Never before had she felt so alone. Nor was it the aloneness that gave her peace and strength but a vulnerability, a helplessness.

She thought it unwise to interrupt Gav if he was talking business with Mr Ramsay so she just stood, gazing around, wondering where else she could go. The sun glittered on the river making it wink and flash like blue diamonds. The wharf was untidy with hogsheads and jostling with Negroes and sailors, unloading one of the ships. Groups of planters stood around gossiping, though there was no sign of Harding. Arching round from the river, making the shape of a slice of melon, was the giant wall of the dense primeval forest, its edges dappled with sunlight and twittering with birds. Contained between the water and the trees, the log buildings and the bald earth of the settlement hardened with heat. Cabin doors lay wide open and shadowy movement could be seen inside as housewives flitted about attending to their duties. Outside children squatted and tumbled in the dust. A crowd of men and boys had gathered in the clearing in front of the jailhouse. From the crowd came excited shouts mingled with squawks and screeches that echoed clear as bells high into the air and all around. Above everything the blazing sun sent blinding yellow flashes from a vast sky of flawless, brilliant blue.

In desperation, Regina made for Gav's house. At least she could wait there until Annabella and Nancy were clear of the store. Then she could return and make her purchases and perhaps also see Gav.

Abigail greeted her with polite words of welcome that did not reflect in her eyes or even in the hint of a smile.

'Gav is across at the counting house.'

'I know, but he is engaged with Mr Ramsay at the moment.

I mean to return to the store in a few minutes.'

'Sit down,' Abigail said. 'Can I offer you a cup of tea?'

Thankfully Regina took a seat and plucking her fan from her reticule she flapped it in front of her face.

'Yes, it might help revive me. This heat is damnable. Mr Harding hasn't called here by any chance?'

'No, I haven't seen him.'

'Oh, God!' She hadn't meant the words to escape and when she heard them she lowered her eyes and flushed with annoyance at herself.

Abigail stared at her, looked as if she was going to speak, then decided just to make the tea instead. She placed a cupful in front of Regina. At first Regina didn't notice. Her mind had wandered away down confused, distracted paths.

'Your tea,' Abigail said for the second time.

'Oh! Oh, yes.'

'Is there anything wrong?'

'Wrong?' Regina's expression turned wary. 'Why should there be anything wrong?'

'You look anxious and worried.'

'I'm perfectly all right.'

Abigail shrugged and Regina added,

'The heat is very trying, of course. It always seems hotter here than anywhere else. I shall be glad to get back to Forest Hall.' She sipped at the tea. 'I have a daughter now. Her name is Charlotte. We call her Lottie.'

'Oh?' Interest flickered in Abigail's face. 'I'd like to see her. I'm sure Gav will too.'

'I left her sleeping in the tavern. Flemintina, one of our slaves, is looking after her.'

'It'll be cooler there.'

'Yes.'

In the awkward silence that followed, Regina drained her cup, then rose.

'Thank you for the tea. I'd better go and see Gav now. I have a list of articles I want him to send to Glasgow for.'

Abigail followed her to the door.

'I like your gown.'

Regina glanced down at the bottle-green silk hoop she was wearing with its fawn embroidered petticoat.

'I wondered about the darkness of the colour.'

'It suits you.'

Regina looked up to see if there was any malice in Abigail's plain features but could detect none.

'With your vivid hair and eyes,' her sister-in-law went on, 'you don't need to bother about wearing vivid colours.'

'Come to the tavern tomorrow morning with Gav if you want to see Lottie before we return.'

'Yes, all right.'

Abigail stood in the doorway watching Regina sweep away, dust hazing behind her, until she disappeared round the side of the store.

Upstairs in the counting house Gav was alone. He had just had a long meeting with Mr Ramsay. It had not been the first and he'd gathered that Ramsay had talked with Mr Speckles too and many of his planter customers. It had been obvious to Gav from the moment that Ramsay arrived that he was not pleased with Mr Speckles, and had already received complaints and reports from customers.

Gav could not deny that Mr Speckles was spending too much time drinking. Ramsay had seen that the manager was missing from the counting house and, despite Gav's evasions about his whereabouts, Ramsay had soon found him flopped helplessly over a table in the tavern.

'He's suffering very poor health, Mr Ramsay,' Gav tried to explain. 'That's why he's taken to drinking so much. He never used to be like that. When I came here first he was most conscientious.'

'The state of his health is no concern o' mine, Gav,' Ramsay growled. 'The fact o' the matter is he's no' doing the job I pay him to do. You're doing it.'

'I'm not complaining, Mr Ramsay.'

'Aye, but plenty other folk are. They say the man's nothing but an embarrassment and a nuisance. They say you should be manager, Gav, and I'm inclined to agree with them. You've served me well, lad. Just like I always knew you would.'

'I like it here. I have a good life.'

'You've made a good life for yourself, Gav. You've worked hard and it's time you were rewarded.'

He was naturally pleased and proud at Mr Ramsay's decision to make him the official store manager. But it was a wretched situation, too, for it meant that Mr Speckles had to be sacked. Ramsay had gone to seek Mr Speckles out and tell him. Mr Ramsay had quite rightly said:

'There's no use me leaving word for him to come and see me. The man would never be sober enough to make the effort.'

What saddened Gav was the fact that Mr Speckles had, without a doubt, the consumption. He was now a shocking sight, a hollow-eyed skull over which his filthy and motheaten wig tilted loosely to one side; a bundle of long bones over which his coat and breeches sagged and flapped. He was more frightening in appearance than the living skeletons that used to be displayed at the fairs in Glasgow. He coughed up blood all the time now and it was Gav's opinion that Mr Speckles was dying. He wished that there was something he could do to help the man but knew there was not.

'Why the sad face?' Regina asked when she entered the counting house.

His expression immediately brightened.

'Regina! Come in and sit down. It's been a long time. I meant to take a trip out to Forest Hall during this past year but things have been difficult at the store. Mr Speckles hasn't been keeping well and wasn't able to be left, for one thing. It's good to see you, Regina. You're looking as beautiful as ever, of course.'

'I was over at your house and had a cup of tea with Abigail.'

He looked pleased, but before he could say anything, she passed over her list.

'Could you have these items sent over from Glasgow, Gav? And could you try your best to deliver them to Forest Hall as soon as they arrive? Most of them are for making clothes for my daughter Charlotte.'

'You have a daughter? Oh, Regina. I'm delighted for you. I'm sure Mr Harding is a very proud Papa.'

'Yes, he is very fond of the child.'

'Where is she just now?'

'At the tavern with her nurse. I've told Abigail that I'll expect you both tomorrow forenoon. I thought you'd like to see Lottie while we're here.'

'Of course. Of course. I'll look forward to it. Good God, fancy you a mother now. I'm so pleased, Regina. And I'll attend to your order right away. I'll make a point of arranging to come with it to Forest Hall. It'll be a good chance to see you again.'

She rose.

'I also want a few ribbons and other small items and some material just now. I'd better go downstairs and see what you have.'

'I'll come with you and attend to you myself. How is Mr Harding?' he asked as they made their way down to the store.

'Very well. All your family is in good health, I hope? I didn't see the children.'

'Oh, they would be playing about somewhere nearby. They are very well indeed, thank God.'

In the shop she chose her purchases and Gav promised to see that they were packed into the carriage. They had just completed the arrangement when Harding strode into the shop, dwarfing the place with his size and dominating it with his presence.

'I've just been talking to Annabella and Nancy,' he said, after a friendly greeting to Gav. 'I said we'd join them on their boat for some tea. Have you finished your business here?'

She nodded, suddenly beset by anxieties. Following Harding from the store and down to the wharf she was unaware of her surroundings, so completely was she obsessed by worry.

Inside Annabella's boat there was no one except Annabella and Nancy. The boat was beautifully upholstered in crimson and silver and a table was resplendent with a gold service and delicious looking cakes and biscuits.

She wished again that she had not chosen to wear her dark green silk. It looked dull and dowdy compared with Annabella's brilliant turquoise hooped gown and silver petticoat. With her padded, powdered hair and patches, too, Annabella looked fashionable as well as striking and vivacious.

Regina kept finding herself trapped into conversation with

751

Nancy but her attention remained riveted on Annabella, even when she was forced to look at the other woman. Surely Annabella was chattering and sparkling and fluttering her fan in a most flirtatious way at Harding? Her stomach dipped and plunged as if the boat she was sitting in had been tossed in a storm.

Suddenly Nancy murmured in a low voice,

'Regina, don't worry about Annabella. She's only teasing.'

'Indeed?' Regina said coldly.

The whole afternoon was an agony and she wished that she had never come to the settlement. Then, as if her agony wasn't painful enough she heard Harding's deep voice say,

'You must come and visit Forest Hall while you're in Virginia, Annabella. You come too, Nancy. We are hoping to do much more entertaining now that we have started a family. Isn't that so, Regina?'

Dumbly Regina nodded.

'Ah, yes,' Annabella said. 'Children do make a difference, don't they? You know I have a son, of course. He is my pride and joy, Mr Harding. A sturdy fellow of strong character and spirit who looks after me as well as any gentleman.'

'He sounds a fine young fellow.'

'Oh, he is, sir, he is. I assure you.'

'I'd like to meet him. You must bring him along.'

'Ah, but there is his education to consider and he is most diligent. I'm employing a tutor while I am here. Mr Gillespie and Mungo work together at their books for several hours every day without fail.'

'Most commendable,' Harding said. 'Bring the tutor along too.'

'You are most hospitable, sir, but I cannot make any promises. There is a prodigious amount of business to attend to while I am here. I am in a mighty bustle from morning till night at the Cunningham plantation.'

It seemed to Regina that she would never escape from Annabella's light, racy tongue. She longed to get Harding away, not only from Annabella's fluttering lashes and fan, and creamy breasts bulging up from the turquoise taffeta, but away from the

752

constant unbearable danger of Mungo's return. When the time eventually did come to leave, she was in such a state of anxiety that she hardly had enough strength to rise from her chair. But at last they were away. They were walking back up to the store to collect their horses. Then they were riding past the cabins along the path through the trees that led to the tavern.

Harding had obviously enjoyed his visit with Annabella and expressed the hope that she could be persuaded to accept his invitation to come to Forest Hall. He hoped, in fact, that Annabella would decide to remain permanently in Virginia.

'Now there's a woman who would be a great asset socially,' he enthused. 'She could help and advise you as well as Lottie when she gets older.'

According to Harding, Annabella was everything a lady should be. And there was nothing that Annabella had not done or could not do.

Even after they retired to bed that night, he was still talking about her. And it came to Regina like a poisoned arrow, twisting in her heart, that she had to face a new danger, yet one that had always been with her. She had just never recognized it as a threat until now.

Chapter 15

'Marriage with Regina, and having a family, has improved Mr Harding,' Annabella observed to Nancy after they had returned to the Cunningham mansion. 'He is not nearly so dour and brusque in appearance and manner. I dare swear I even detected a twinkle in those dark eyes of his on several occasions while I was talking to him.'

'Yes, I noticed he was amused.'

'What do you mean? You have a most irritating habit of making veiled insinuations, Nancy. In fact your tone of voice was a continuous infuriation to me when you were my maid. It always had that hint of sarcastic impertinence to it.'

Nancy narrowed her violet eyes and gave one of her husky laughs. Then she shrugged.

'You were flirting with him and he saw that you were flirting with him. That's what I meant.'

'Lord's sake!' Annabella giggled behind her fan. Then she gave a sudden nonchalant toss of her curls. 'Pox on him! Why should I feel fluttered? It is my way to be of a gayer turn. I have always indulged in a little light flirtation and teasing. I enjoy it, and gentlemen enjoy it, and there is never any harm done.'

'I know all that, but does Regina? Did you see her face?'

Annabella laughed and rolled her eyes.

'Yes, wasn't it monstrously wicked-looking. Such black smouldering glances, such rigid intensity of carriage! She will ruin her appearance with such moods, you mark my words. Wasn't it ridiculous, though, when all that was happening was a little light bantering conversation?'

'She was always a bit queer, even as a child.'

'Yes, do you remember how terrified she was of French soldiers. Remember that monstrous hullabaloo in the house when she saw Jean-Paul? I thought she was never going to stop screaming. I thought in fact, she had gone completely demented and there would be no saving of her.'

'I remember how frustrated I used to get by the way she would follow me around when I was trying to get some work done. She stuck so close on my heels, I kept bumping into her and tripping over her. I boxed her ears a couple of times but it never made any difference. She just refused to be left anywhere near a Frenchman without my protection. A pity you didn't fling her back out on the streets then instead of taking her with you to the Highlands.'

Annabella shrugged.

'The poor thing had been raped by a crowd of common soldiers. We didn't know that then or we would have understood and perhaps been a little more forgiving. That was why she betrayed Jean-Paul, of course.' Annabella sighed. 'Although my poor Jean-Paul had nothing to do with her rape.'

Nancy hesitated and twisted a lock of her black hair and avoided Annabella's eyes in embarrassment. Eventually she managed,

'You forgave Regina long before you knew what had caused her to act in the terrible way she did. You are a kind and generous-hearted woman, for all your faults, Annabella. I would like to believe Regina appreciates that but I fear she does no such thing. I wouldn't go anywhere near Forest Hall, if I were you.'

Annabella's eyes widened.

'Gracious heavens! What are you saying now? That I should be afraid of the little red-haired tramp? For I am not and never will be.' Suddenly she erupted into giggles again. 'Did I tell you about the beating I gave her the first time I saw her after that time in the Highlands? It was at a wondrously magnificent ball in Williamsburg. I don't know what came over me, Nancy. I was stepping the minuet quite happily when all of a sudden her name was announced. I looked round and there she was, practically at my elbow and as cold and stiff and aloof as she had been that day when she'd betrayed Jean-Paul. As I say, I don't know what came over me. I suddenly saw her as that filthy, repulsive, little urchin that she was and I just set upon her and gave her a good beating. I felt much the better of it, I can tell you, Nancy, and I've never regretted it. Damn it all, she deserved it, didn't she? But, oh, can you imagine how the genteel society of Williamsburg viewed the shocking disruption of their elegant and dignified assembly?'

Nancy threw back her head and enjoyed a burst of laughter.

'Of course I knew about it. Who didn't? I wish I'd been there at the ball to actually witness the event. I would have enjoyed it.'

'Yes, you would, wouldn't you, you sly bitch,' Annabella laughed.

'It's her that's the sly bitch, not me. Don't trust her, Annabella.'

'You sound like a prophet of doom. I forbid you to talk in such a morbid fashion.'

Nancy raised an eyebrow.

'Forbid me?'

Annabella's laughter danced in her eyes.

'Oh, sister, forgive me, do! It will take some considerable time to accustom myself to the idea that you are now a lady and on equal terms with me!'

Just then Ramsay entered the room accompanied by Nancy's husband, Morgan West. They were both tall men but Ramsay's age showed in his slightly stooping posture, the deeply etched lines on his face and the dark crêpy skin under his eyes. The younger man had a loose rangy frame, a tanned skin, quizzical brown eyes and brown hair tied back.

Ramsay collapsed into an easy chair with a sigh.

'Well, I'm glad that's settled.'

'What's settled?' Annabella inquired.

'The running o' the plantation.'

'Oh? You mean my plantation, Papa?'

'We'll have less o' your snash for a start,' her father growled. 'You know very well that you are neither capable nor willing to manage the business of this place. I've had to settle it.'

'Yes, Papa.'

'Morgan and Nancy are going to stay on here and manage it.'

Nancy raised a sarcastic brow.

'Are we indeed?'

Her husband shot her a warning look.

'Now don't pretend that you're not pleased. You'll live in more luxury here than you could ever have dreamed of. It's a chance in a million for both of us.'

Ramsay said,

'The tobacco crop will be shipped over to me, of course.'

'Huh!' Annabella turned to Nancy. 'Aren't men wondrously clever at arranging things?' Then she returned her attention to her father. 'You may have the tobacco crop, Papa, but I must have a regular income from it, or from the estate in some way.'

'You've never needed to worry about money before,' her father suddenly bawled, 'and you've no need to concern yourself with it now.'

'I fear I must insist, Papa, and you know very well how insistent I can be when I put my mind to it.'

Ramsay struggled to control his temper.

'Annabella, you have always been and still are a wild and wayward lassie and no' the type at all to be trusted with serious responsibilities.'

'Oh, I don't want responsibilities, Papa. Just money! And flattery will do nothing to persuade me otherwise.'

'Flattery?' her father roared. 'I'm no' a man to flatter anybody and fine you know it.'

Her eyes twinkled.

'A wild and wayward lassie, Papa? Why, I'll never see thirty again. I am a poor old widow woman.'

'This is no time for levity, mistress. I'm talking serious business.'

'So am I, Papa. And I'll fly into a pretty passion if you do not arrange that I get a regular income. I will sign no papers and agree to nothing until that is settled first.'

'Oh, very well,' her father growled. 'I suppose I might as well indulge you in this.'

Annabella fluttered her eyelashes and her fan.

'Why, thank you, Papa! You have always been most generous and kind. I am wondrously obliged to you.'

It was Nancy's turn to address Ramsay.

'Does that mean you'll be returning to Glasgow soon?'

'Aye.'

'How soon, Papa?' Annabella asked.

Her father shrugged.

'As long as we're away before the winter. It's bad enough making that journey in the summer months.'

Annabella sighed.

'Oh, it will be nice to see dear old Glasgow again and my beautiful new mansion. You must visit us, Nancy. Of course, it's not nearly as big as this place. Heavens above, this is far too big. I'm always getting lost in it and like all the mansions in the colony it's so terribly isolated. Mungo House is just perfect. It is elegant and commodious and in such a salubrious and convenient situation. Oh, I do miss it. Don't you ever miss Glasgow?'

'No, never,' Nancy said. 'But I'm curious to see your mansion and to see all the other changes that have taken place in the town.'

'And you shall see everything. Oh, we shall have such a wondrously gay time when you visit us. I shall entertain and . . .'

Her father interrupted impatiently.

'Will you be quiet, Annabella. Let them get settled in here first. This is a big place to run. They'll have plenty to occupy their time for a year or two without gallivanting over to Glasgow. You've always been the same. There's never anything in your head but wicked enjoyment.'

Annabella quickly stifled a splutter of laughter behind her fan and when her father glared at her, she covered her eyes demurely.

In point of fact, she had done nothing really wicked for an age, if she had ever done anything wicked at all, because she could never convince herself that taking a lover was wicked. As for all the many Sabbath-breaking sins like combing one's hair, or humming a merry tune, or strolling outside, or looking in a pier glass, or doing anything at all on the Sabbath except attend church, say prayers and chant hymns, she did not care a fig. Taking a lover was far more exciting and interesting. Such a delightful game. Surely it was time she had another whirl at it.

She had been so taken up with inspecting and organizing and thinking of what was to be done about the vast Cunningham plantation, she had not had any time at all for socializing and meeting potential lovers. The only gentleman she'd had any social contact with since arriving in the colony had been Robert

Harding. She thought of him in this context and was surprised to find herself feeling both thrilled and frightened. 'Damn him' she thought, immediately quelling the ripples of fear. 'No man is going to frighten me!' Yet, after all the years that had passed since that night on the Green in Glasgow when he had ravaged her, the fear she had experienced then was still there. It had been such a blow to her pride and dignity, apart from anything else. Had he forced his way into her bedroom and taken her there, it might not have been such a dreadful humiliation. But when they had emerged from the dancing assembly that night, instead of calling for a sedan to take her safely home he had swept her off her feet and carried her to the Green. There he had taken her on the filthy grass and earth as if she was a common serving wench. She had eventually escaped from him and raced home in such a state of alarm and distress as she'd never experienced before or since.

The trouble was, Mr Harding did not play the game to the normal and accepted rules.

She wondered if he had changed very much. As she had remarked to Nancy, he had improved to some degree. His manners and general deportment seemed slightly more polished and restrained and they had engaged in quite an affable and amusing conversation. There could be no denying, too, and she had never denied this inescapable fact, that Harding had an aura about him, a magnetism that was definitely sexual.

Strangely enough, she had an idea that this was what frightened her more than anything. Yet, at the same time, he was a challenge and she liked challenges. She had thrived on challenge all her life. As a young child, her Papa had first introduced her to school and said to the dominie,

'This is our Annabella, see that you thrash her well!'

But she had not been daunted even then. When the dominie had tried to beat her, she had looked him straight in the eye and warned him that if he laid a finger on her, she would see one way or another that her Papa did not pay him a penny at the Candlemas Offering. The bluff had worked because her Papa's Candlemas Offering was substantial and the poverty-stricken dominie greatly depended on it and therefore could afford to take no risks.

She had no intention of being daunted by Harding either. He might prove an interesting and exciting diversion before she returned to Glasgow. Fear rapidly rippled in again.

'Damn the bloody man!'

The words escaped out loud before she realized it and the other occupants of the room turned on her in astonishment. Fanning herself as if to faint, she tried to gather her wits together and explain her outburst.

Her father's voice was outraged.

'Devil choke you, Annabella! If that wicked outburst is aimed at me . . .'

'No, no Papa, heaven forbid! I was thinking of a rough, drunken sailor fellow who bumped into me at the settlement wharf and nearly sent me tumbling into the water. I'm still prodigiously agitated by the incident.'

'You should have told me at the time.' Her father was now outraged on her behalf. 'I would have had the scoundrel flogged.'

'You are quite right, Papa. It was most remiss of me.' She rustled to her feet. 'Will you excuse me now if I go outside for a breath of air?'

Nancy rose too.

'I'll come with you.'

As soon as they were out of hearing of the two men, they erupted into giggles and Nancy shook her head.

'How you can lie so glibly and with such an innocent face I don't know.'

'How do you know I was lying?'

'Because I know you. You were thinking of Mr Harding.'

'Gracious heavens, are you a witch? How can you know that?'

Nancy rolled her eyes.

'We were talking about the man not long before your Papa and Morgan came into the room. And I know how he troubles you.'

'Pox on him! He doesn't trouble me.'

Nancy slid her a sarcastic look. A minute or two passed as

they strolled out to the velvety green expanse of lawn, then Annabella gave a tinkle of laughter again.

'I have come to the conclusion that Mr Harding may have hidden qualities that if explored in the proper fashion might prove both interesting and stimulating,' her eyes flashed Nancy a mischievous glance as she added, 'to say the least!'

'Oh, God! Annabella, I beg you not to have anything to do with that man.'

'Pooh! Pooh! What a long-visaged coward you are. If I have anything to do with him it will be a trifling adventure, and one I will quickly forget after I return to my enjoyable life in Glasgow.'

'Annabella, I can't allow you to do this.'

'Allow? Allow? Sister you may be, but keeper you are not. I do what I please.'

'I don't want to see you get hurt—either by that man or by Regina. They are a well-matched pair, Annabella, and you are no match for either of them.'

'I am no match?' Annabella squealed incredulously and colour fired her cheeks. 'I am no match for a little gutter tramp and an ignorant boor of a man?' She stamped her foot in anger. 'I'll soon show you whether I'm a match for them or not.'

'Annabella, I'm warning you!'

'How dare you! How dare you speak to me like that, you impertinent bitch. Don't you forget that, although you have a decent Papa, your mother was a common serving-wench like yourself, and your brothers were filthy fulzie men.'

Nancy's face darkened with anger and her hand suddenly shot up and slapped Annabella across the face. With a shriek Annabella fell upon her, grabbing her by the hair and tugging her wildly about. Nancy struggled to free herself, at the same time violently kicking Annabella's shins, making her scream with pain as well as anger.

They ignored the shouts of Morgan West as he ran from the house and across the lawn to separate them. He managed to tear them apart but not without difficulty. Then holding them both by the scruff of the neck he shouted,

'Have you both gone mad? Behave yourselves at once or I'll

761

lift your petticoats and thrash the pair of you where it hurts.'

As usual, Annabella's anger disappeared as quickly as it had come. She sparkled provocatively up at her brother-in-law.

'Well, I'm willing if you are, Morgan.'

Nancy just groaned and rolled her eyes.

Chapter 16

Mr Speckles slumped helplessly in a chair by the window of the counting house while Gav's carroty head bent over a ledger nearby. Every now and again the younger man glanced worriedly over at the older one until eventually he said,

'It's just as well, in a way, Mr Speckles. You'll have more time to rest now. You can relax and enjoy life.'

'What life have I worth living, Gav? The devil has me by the coat tail, lad. I am dogged by bad luck, sir. It has always been so.'

'It all depends on the way you look at it.'

'And how do people look at me? With nothing but horror and loathing, Gav.'

'No, no . . .'

'Why, even the children despise me. Young Harding was railing at me only the other day. "Get up you filthy dog and stop your retching," he said. "You are fouling the earth that ladies have to tread on".'

Gav looked puzzled.

'You mean Mr Harding?'

'And I just thought,' Mr Speckles went on absently, 'although I did not say anything, of course. But I thought, ah, young sir, like father, like son, you both have that same brusque manner.'

'Mr Speckles, it's a little girl that my sister and Mr Harding have.'

'I couldn't get up. Not right away. "Can you help me up?" I said and he replied, "Indeed I will, sir," and kicked me hard.' Mr Speckles shook his head. 'I tell you, Gav, even the children despise me.'

'I wish I'd been there. I would have given that young sir a good kick up the backside to help him on his way.'

Mr Speckles's skull moved from side to side again, making his wig slide to a foolish angle.

'No, no, Gav, you must always be careful with good customers like Mr Harding. Mr Ramsay would not have been pleased at you if he had found that you had misused Mr Harding's son.'

Gav opened his mouth to correct the other man again but changed his mind. What was the use? Poor Mr Speckles didn't know where he was half the time, far less what he was saying. Mr Speckles was in fact a terrible problem. Because he was no longer employed by the store he was not allowed to sleep in his old room next to the counting house. That was now occupied by the two indentured servants. No one else in the settlement was willing to take him in and give him a room and he couldn't afford to live at Widow Shoozie's tavern even if she would have him.

Gav had asked Abigail if he could sleep at their place just until something else could be arranged for him, but Abigail flatly refused to have anything to do with Mr Speckles. He supposed he couldn't blame her. She had the children to consider and she had enough to do looking after them, not to mention himself.

Mr Ramsay had generously offered Mr Speckles a passage home to Glasgow in one of his ships but Mr Speckles had not as yet felt fit enough to make the long and hazardous journey. So he was sleeping rough, huddled underneath the outside stairs at the side of the store. During the day he drank at the tavern and stumbled aimlessly about the settlement, often sinking down to sprawl helplessly on the ground as bouts of coughing overcame him.

It was true what Mr Speckles said about children being unkind to him. But who the child was who had kicked Mr Speckles he had no idea, though it was easy to see why the confusion with Harding had risen in the poor man's befuddled brain. Harding had often addressed Mr Speckles in a very harsh manner.

Mr Speckles was obviously still thinking of the incident because he muttered,

'No, no. Mr Ramsay wouldn't like any of us to offend Mr Harding's son. So I didn't complain, Gav. I just looked up at the sturdy fellow, I gazed at those dark eyes and that tanned skin and black hair and I said, "Ah, how like your father you are, sir".'

'What did he say to that?' Gav asked curiously.

'He said, "You are a fool, sir, because everyone says I am not like my Papa at all".'

A bout of coughing suddenly wracked Mr Speckles and Gav hurried over with one of the pieces of rag that were kept for Mr Speckles to cough into when he was indoors. In a matter of seconds it was bright scarlet and weak perspiration was coursing down Mr Speckles's hollow cheeks.

'I'll go down to the kitchen and tell Mama Sophy to make you a strengthening gruel. Just you sit there now.'

The kitchen was a lean-to at the back of the store where Mama Sophy cooked for the store's servants during the day and slept at night. She greeted his request without enthusiasm.

' 'Tain't no use. That poor man's a dyin'. Even my gruel ain't goin' strengthen him.'

'I know, but make him some anyway. It's the only thing he'll take.'

'Apart from ale and whisky.'

Mama Sophy tutted and shook her head but she started to fuss about and prepare the gruel, and Gav returned upstairs.

Mr Speckles had nodded off to sleep in the chair so he was able to continue with some work. By the time Mama Sophy came puffing up with the gruel he had finished all he planned to do for the day and thankfully put down his quill. Normally he enjoyed his work but today, with Mr Speckles sitting in the same room muttering or coughing or sleeping, he had felt restless and disturbed. He didn't enjoy putting him out either, or leaving him crouched on the dusty earth under the stairs, but there was no alternative. The place had to be locked up.

He did what he had to and then strode across to his log cabin home. It now had three fair sized rooms. The main room was where Abigail cooked and where the family ate and sat, including the young slaves Lunesta and Little Sam. The place was plainly but comfortably furnished with a rocking chair and another chair made out of a barrel, both bright with patchwork cushions that Abigail had stitched. The table and stools he had made himself from a tree he had felled himself. The iron pots and other kitchen utensils had been fashioned by Abigail's father.

The other two rooms were used as bedrooms, one for Abigail and himself and one for Bette, Jethro, Lunesta and Little Sam.

Abigail greeted him at the door, sweet and clean in her striped cotton gown, glowing with health.

'You're late tonight. I've given the children their supper and Lunesta's put them to bed.'

Thankfully he entered the cabin and sat down at the table while his wife bustled about dishing his meal and setting it before him with a tankard of ale.

'I had a bit of trouble with Mr Speckles,' he told her in between mouthfuls of food.

'When have you not had trouble with him?' she sighed.

'He was raving on about Mr Harding's son having kicked him.'

'Lord's sake!'

'Poor devil, it's really terrible what he's suffering in mind and body. I'm at the stage now, Abby, when I'm wishing the poor fellow would die.'

'It would be a mercy if he did die.' Abigail joined him at the table. 'Mentioning Harding reminds me of their little girl. I wonder how she's getting on? She'll be walking now, I expect.'

Gav laughed.

'She was a real little madam, wasn't she? Young as she was, she had that Flemintina wrapped round her little finger.'

'And her proud Papa too, I should think.'

'Yes, he was proud of her, wasn't he? I hadn't imagined that Harding would turn out to be such a family man.

'Just goes to show, you can never tell with people.'

'Dare I say it?' Abby glanced over at him.

'Say what?'

'Regina didn't exactly appear the doting mama, did she?'

'I never for a moment expected her to. I do know my sister and she just can't show her feelings. That's not to say she hasn't got any.'

'Mmm . . .' Abigail did not look at all convinced.

'Now, don't start,' Gav warned.

'All right! All right!'

'I'll have to be going there sometime soon. There's a big order to be delivered.'

'Oh, Gav, must you?'

'Yes, I promised.'

He didn't want to go but business was business and anyway he felt he had a duty to keep some sort of contact with his sister. Not that he could honestly say that he enjoyed being with her, although he hesitated to confess this to Abigail. Regina worried him. He boasted to Abigail that he knew his sister but, in fact, he was never quite certain of her. It was true that often when she appeared cold and indifferent, he was sure she was feeling quite the reverse underneath. She had, in fact, a deep and disturbing personality. Capable of perpetrating frightening cruelties, she could also be wonderfully generous and kind. He believed she would make a good mother. She certainly didn't hover about the child fussing and spoiling and trying to make it do show-off tricks as Flemintina and Harding did. But on the other hand, she showed her daughter no ill-will or bad-temper. When Flemintina went out of the room to fetch Lottie's food, Regina held the little girl on her knee with calm, efficient hands to which the child responded by sitting quietly and patiently sucking its thumb. It showed how children could behave themselves perfectly well if treated in a sensible way. Previous to that, Lottie had been acting like a right spoiled, noisy little madam.

He wondered what effect the child had had on their marriage. At first he had been genuinely happy for Regina and believed, as Abigail still did, that Regina and Harding were well suited to one another and would be happy together in their own way. Harding wasn't such a bad fellow and Regina was obviously much attracted to him.

Yet, that last time they had visited the settlement, he had sensed that there was something wrong. Harding seemed much the same except that he was quite jovial when he was with his daughter, which had caused much amusement to both Abigail and himself. But Regina had been obsessed by some secret disturbance. Even Abigail had noticed it.

'Yes, there's something worrying her,' Abigail had said afterwards when they had been talking. 'I didn't notice anything in the tavern. She was very self-composed then, but the day before when she had tea with me here, I thought there was something wrong. I asked her, in fact, but you know what she's like. She froze me off immediately.'

That was the worst of Regina. She could never allow you near enough to be able to help her. Still, he felt he must try not to lose complete contact with her and was glad for that reason that he had to tackle the journey to Forest Hall in the near future. It was the only reason he found any satisfaction in contemplating the visit. He liked plenty of cheerful company and Abigail and he had lots of friends. They often entertained and were entertained and many a happy hour was spent over a tankard of ale or a game of billiards or box and dice. There would never be any convivial gatherings at Forest Hall, of that he was certain.

As it happened, however, he was wrong. Word had come by a slave that Mistress Annabella and Mistress Nancy had decided to accept Mr Harding's kind invitation and would shortly be arriving at Forest Hall. No mention was made of Mungo and Regina could only pray that Annabella would not, could not, bring him with her. She tried to assure herself, of course, that even if the boy did come, it need not be the tragedy she had at first imagined it might be. The boy wasn't all that like Harding. He had Harding's colour of hair and eyes, but then did not Annabella's husband, Mr Blackadder, also have black hair and brown eyes?

The shock of first seeing him and getting the idea into her head of the resemblance, and then Annabella's confession, had knocked her off balance. Everything had twisted out of proportion. Not able to live with the intensity of the emotions that had ravaged her during those few days at the settlement, her mind sought escape in rationalization.

After all, Annabella had kept the truth secret from Harding for all these years, so why should she divulge it now? What advantage would it be to her? She and her son had no need of Forest Hall for a start, and surely could be entertaining no thoughts of any claim Mungo might have on it. One day Mungo would inherit all Mr Ramsay's wealth, and now there was the vast Cunningham empire as well.

She tried to soothe herself too by remembering what Nancy had said about Annabella's apparently flirtatious behaviour with Harding. It was true, now that she had time to think calmly about it, that Mistress Annabella had always had a pert, coquettish manner.

To please Harding Regina also made a determined effort to be interested, and at least to appear to share his enthusiasm for their first serious attempt at entertaining. He had decided to make up the number to ten, including themselves, which meant inviting, apart from Annabella and Nancy, another six people. She suspected he was doing this solely to please Annabella who had never made any secret of the fact that she did not like to feel isolated and enjoyed gay company.

He sent invitations to three planters he was in the habit of meeting regularly in Williamsburg at the Public Times and often at the settlement too. The invitations included the planters' wives and were promptly accepted.

Once all the invitations had been accepted and the social occasion was a reality looming nearer and nearer, Regina began to feel confused and harassed and secretly afraid of her own inability to cope. There were not many problems with the actual house. She would move in with Harding to allow Annabella and Nancy to have her bedroom. Mr and Mrs Abercromby would have the bedroom that had once been Mistress Kitty's. Mr and Mrs Jeffries and Colonel and Mrs Washington would use the two spare rooms. It was the catering that Regina now had nightmares about. Harding kept insisting that there must be the best of everything and she spent many long worrying hours poring over recipe books trying to decide what kind of menus to plan and discussing preparations with the kitchen slaves, Callie Mae, Minda and Sal, and also Joseph, Westminster and Melie Anne who served in the dining-room.

She decided to double up the number of slaves so that her guests would each have a body slave to attend to their personal needs. She supervised the cleaning and polishing of the bedrooms and the making up of the beds. She helped Callie Mae and Minda to make cookies, sugar biscuits, slate biscuits, brandy snaps, almond biscuits, plum cake, chocolate cake and fruit tarts.

For the first main meal she decided to have two hundred oysters, beef collops, three joints of roast mutton, fricassee of five chickens, a roast goose, buttered crabs, boiled beef and fruit tarts.

The house slaves were terribly impressed and thrilled. There had never been such a stir and excitement at Forest Hall in years. For the first time they felt a bond with Regina, even if it was a tenuous one. Through her cool efficient manner they detected threads of anxiety. It made them anxious too that everything would go right and Forest Hall hospitality would be a match for any in Virginia.

Melie Anne would say worriedly:

'I think I'd better give them glasses another polish, Miss Regina. Don' they look kinda cloudy to you?'

Or:

'Joseph, you sure you done *all* that silver?'

Callie Mae would say:

'Miss Regina, ain't we got a recipe for another kinda cake? Just plum and chocolate don' seem that much.'

Or:

'Lord's sake, hope we've got enough butter and cream in that spring house!'

When the big day came, everyone was up at the crack of dawn and before long the low, mournful whine of the jack could be heard as it began to turn the spit in front of the fire to roast the meat. The whine soon rose to a louder, grating pitch, then there was a crash and a silence before the whole procedure began again.

Regina had been so busy planning menus and hurrying about supervising and helping with various tasks, she had not had any time to think about what she was going to wear. Now she began to worry about her appearance. Harding had not given her enough time to order any new dresses and she spread all her gowns and petticoats over the bed and chairs of Harding's room, so that she could examine them and try to make up her mind which she should wear first.

She felt that first impressions were most important. If the first evening, the first meal, were successful, everything would be all right. The tone would be set, everything would run smoothly after that.

She decided eventually on her flowered silk gown and white petticoat trimmed with lace and pleated at the hem. With it she wore white silk stockings and white silk slippers. For jewellery she chose diamond earrings and a diamond ring. Surveying herself in the pier glass, she felt tolerably pleased with her appearance. In the more delicate shades of the flowered silk she would not appear as dull and dowdy next to Annabella as she'd felt she had in the bottle green gown.

Flemintina was ordered to powder her hair once she'd donned a powdering gown. The slave had never done this job before and the proceedings ended with Flemintina in tears and Regina in a temper, saying that she would be whipped and then sent to the fields to work in future. Harding was forced to intervene. He sent Flemintina back to Lottie's room and bawled at one of the other slaves to come and clean up the mess of powder.

Eventually she was ready, the house was gleaming perfection, and the table was set. Of course it was far too early and afternoon tea would be served in the drawing-room first. But it made Regina feel safer to know that all the important tasks had been completed.

Then suddenly there was a cry of:

'Hello, the house!'

The waiting slaves hurried to attend to the visitors. Harding and Regina went to the front door and watched the arrival of the first coach, a very handsome green and gold four-wheeler with one footman standing at the back and another sitting at the front, both dressed in crimson and white livery, powdered wig and three-cornered hat. The carriage was drawn by four frisky horses. One of the footmen jumped down and hastened to open the door. Out stepped Annabella with a daring display of rose pink slipper and silk-stockinged leg under a foaming rose silk dress. Her face was flushed, her eyes bright, sparkling blue and her yellow hair shimmered in the sun. She was like a beautiful flower bursting into bloom from the carriage.

She pattered over to the foot of the stairs where Harding and Regina were standing, then with wide panniered skirts ballooning up, she curtsied very prettily.

Chapter 17

'You haven't seen round the house, have you, Nancy?' Harding asked after they had had a refreshing cup of tea. 'Come, let me give you a tour.'

'We shall all come,' said Annabella, jumping to her feet. 'Regina, you must show me all the changes you have made since you have become mistress.'

They went upstairs first, making the hall flare into life with their vivid gowns. Annabella glided on in front with Harding, her rosy skirts shimmering. She kept turning to talk to him with blonde curls bouncing and lashes fluttering and shoulders making coquettish little gestures.

Nancy followed with swaying sensuous movements in her striped apple green and rust gown with its low front revealing her voluptuous bosom. Regina walked with stiff dignity, edging up her delicate froth of skirts as she climbed the stairs.

'Ah, Regina,' Annabella enthused, 'how well you must have trained the slaves. I dare swear there isn't a speck of dust anywhere, and everything is so prodigiously well polished. I can see myself reflected wherever I look.'

She was thinking, however, that the place reflected Regina. Every room was indeed immaculate but they had a stiff unlived-in look. There was no warmth or personality revealed anywhere, except that of a cold and obsessive woman.

Even the dining-room was the same with its virgin white table cover, napkins and cutlery and glasses all set out in perfect formation like soldiers. Annabella fluttered around admiring the yellow pine walls and the chocolate-coloured curtains, then she suddenly swooped on one of the napkins.

'I must show you a wondrous trick with napkins. I'm sure it will intrigue you.'

And before Regina's expressionless face, Annabella proceeded with deft movements of her fingers and hands to transform all the flat napkins into elegant swans.

'My God, what a difference.' Harding was impressed. 'The table looks really interesting now.'

'And if you tell the slaves to bring a basket of fruit,' Annabella said, 'I shall build a pyramid of fruit on this silver tray.' She lifted a tray from the sideboard and made a space for it on the table. 'And flowers, ah, yes, an elegant floral arrangement in the centre of the table would be magnificent, I'm sure, and I have been told that I have considerable talent for floral arrangements.'

'You have obviously many talents, mistress,' Harding said.

'I know what I shall do,' Annabella clapped her hands. 'I shall construct floral arrangements everywhere. A wisp of fern, a little perfumed posy, a dash of colour in each bedroom would be most stimulating and inviting, don't you think?'

Harding made to say something but changed his mind and just bared his teeth in a grin of interest.

'And a glow of sunny hues in that dark corner of the hall over at the ballroom side of the staircase. How nice and welcoming that will look when your other guests arrive. Regina, hurry do, summon your slaves, tell them what we require. I will show you how to accomplish everything. We will have a mighty bustle and lots of fun.'

Regina did not move and Harding rang the bell to summon the slaves, commanding them to bring an abundance of flowers and ferns and fruit and to waste no time about it.

Regina betrayed not the slightest quiver of emotion but in fact she had never been nearer to broken-hearted tears. She had worked harder and more conscientiously in the past few days than she had ever done in her life, such was her anxiety to have everything perfect. Exhaustion, both physical and emotional, was now threatening to catch up with her. But it wasn't just tiredness or even disappointment, although her disappointment was keen enough. All her life, since leaving Glasgow, all she had gone through to build up the image and the position she now had, was disintegrating and disappearing as if it had never happened. She was a servant again with furtive lowered eyes, she was frightened and unsure again, completely at the mercy of wealthy self-assured people like Harding and Annabella.

Stiffly she followed Annabella's instructions and soon the three women, helped by a harassed crush of slaves, had completed the floral and other arrangements and changed the appearance not only of the dining-table but of the whole house. Now the royal blue of the stair carpet was picked out in the blue of wild flowers and made more noticeable. The wood floor in the hall was a garden of reflection. Even the stair bannister sprouted an artistic nosegay.

'Now I must fly and change my gown,' Annabella said. 'I still have the heat and the dust of the journey upon me. Come, Nancy, you must do the same. Your gown is monstrously creased. Don't just stand there!'

Nancy rolled her eyes and followed Annabella upstairs, leaving Harding and Regina to return to the drawing-room. Harding lit a pipe and Regina went over to stare out the window. Eventually Harding poured two glasses of whisky and handed her one with a look of disgust.

'For God's sake, can't you look a bit more cheerful? I know it's too much to expect you to exude any normal human warmth but surely you could force yourself to smile now and again for the sake of your guests.'

'I'll never forgive you.'

'Forgive me?' He looked genuinely surprised. 'Forgive me for what?'

She sipped at her whisky, grateful for its calming and comforting properties.

'Forgive me for what?' he repeated in a louder, more irritable tone. 'What the hell's going on in that twisted mind of yours now?'

'This is no time for a quarrel with guests liable to come back downstairs any minute and other guests due to arrive at the front door.'

'Does that mean you are going to nurse your grudge, whatever it is, all the time during their stay and cast an icicle gloom on us all?'

'I don't think anyone will notice what I look like or what I'm doing as long as Mistress Annabella is around.'

'Ah! Now I understand. Jealousy is rearing its ugly head

again.'

'It would fit you better, sir, if instead of criticizing me, you looked to yourself. You obviously forget that I am your wife, not Mistress Annabella, and that this is my home, not hers.'

He was prevented from answering by a cry from the front of the house that heralded the other guests. As they both left the room, Annabella and Nancy met them in the hall. Nancy was wearing a violet gown to match her eyes with a petticoat of the same colour embroidered in miniature flowers. Her black hair was padded high at the front and powdered. She was taller with more voluptuous curves, but Annabella, in high-heeled slippers and enormous hoop, was a stunning sight. Her hair was powdered high and smooth at the front and clustered with curls at the back decorated with sapphires the same sparkling blue as her eyes. Her pert face beneath the powdered confection of hair sported patches and she wore a sapphire brooch at the front of her low-cut gown which drew the gaze to the daring bulge of her breasts. All but the nipples were revealed. Her gown of rustling shimmery gold was trimmed with cobwebs of lace which also looped across the silver petticoat and trailed from the elbow length sleeves. A sapphire and diamond bracelet and rings flashed on her hand and she was fluttering a jewel-coloured fan.

Suddenly Regina felt insipid in her white gown with its delicate floral pattern and even her diamonds faded into insignificance.

'Gracious heavens!' Annabella cried. 'Who owns the splendid chariot and six I saw approaching?'

'That'll be George,' Harding said. 'Colonel Washington and his wife.'

'I shall go into the drawing-room.' Annabella manoeuvred her skirts sideways so that she could get through the door. 'You may present Colonel Washington and his wife to me there.'

Harding glanced at Regina.

'You'd better wait in the drawing-room too.'

She gave him a look that flashed like a dagger before turning away and following Annabella and Nancy.

As it happened the Abercrombies had arrived at the same time as the Washingtons and they elected to go straight upstairs to wash and change their clothes after the journey. Shortly afterwards Mr and Mrs Jeffries arrived and they also were shown upstairs and a slave sent running to fetch hot water for washing. Eventually everyone gathered in the drawing-room for introductions and refreshing glasses of whisky or brandy. The men made a leg and the ladies curtsied low. Soon they were sauntering through to the dining-room chatting and laughing at Annabella's teasing banter. Once seated between Harding and Abercromby, she chose for the most part to carry on a conversation across the table in Washington's direction but which included and interested all the company.

'Ah, Colonel Washington, not so long ago I was conversing with the master of another Mount Vernon.'

'Another Mount Vernon?' his wife, Martha, gasped. 'Surely you are mistaken, Mistress Blackadder.'

Annabella widened her eyes.

'And the master of this Mount Vernon in Glasgow is called George.'

'Tease! Tease!' accused Mrs Abercromby.

'No, indeed I am not teasing.' Annabella enjoyed a few dainty sips of wine then dabbed at her lips with her napkin. 'George Buchanan is his name. He had a plantation close to yours on the Potomac, Colonel, and was very friendly with your brother. When Mr Buchanan bought Windyedge east of Glasgow he changed the name to Mount Vernon in honour and remembrance of that friendship.'

Candles were lit as they still sat on enjoying the leisurely meal and the wine. The candle flames polished the fruit and glistened the silver of the tableware and enriched the tints of the flowers and the ladies' gowns and jewels, and the brocade of the gentlemen's coats, and gave their lace jabots and cuffs a pearly glow.

Washington and Abercromby told tales of their adventures with the militia fighting the French and the Indians. Then Annabella riveted everyone's attention again by recounting her adventures with Prince Charles Edward Stuart and his Highland army but in the manner of an entertaining storyteller. She did not harrow or embarrass the company with details like the betrayal and torture of Jean-Paul.

Washington eyed her with considerable admiration. He had a huge, muscly frame and was six feet two or more. His back was as straight as an Indian's and his blue-grey penetrating eyes were overhung by a heavy brow.

'You must come and visit our Virginia Mount Vernon, Mistress Blackadder,' he told Annabella.

She favoured him with a smile.

'I'm sure I would greatly enjoy the experience, Colonel. I always prefer originals but alas I am returning to Glasgow immediately after this visit. All the plans for the journey are made. My Papa awaits me.'

'Some other time perhaps?'

'Well, at present I have no plans for returning to Virginia but of course one never knows what changes the future might bring. Little did I ever dream, for instance, that I would ever inherit a Virginia plantation.'

Mr Jeffries peered round at her.

'The Cunningham estate is a large one, Mistress Blackadder. You will have problems there.'

She laughed.

'Not I, Mr Jeffries. My sister, Nancy here, and her husband, Morgan. I leave all the worries of running the plantation to them. Well?' She glanced from Harding to Regina in a sudden flutter of restlessness. 'Aren't we going to retire to your prodigiously beautiful ballroom for some musical entertainment?'

Regina rose politely. She had been longing to suggest that the company adjourn from the dining-room but did not get the opportunity because of the continual flow of conversation that Annabella encouraged. A quick word with one of the slaves sent him hurrying on ahead to light all the candles in the ballroom.

They had not been lit earlier because she had not expected the room to be used. Not being able to play a musical instrument herself and therefore not being able to entertain the guests on the spinet and the fiddle that were kept there, she thought it would only prove embarrassing to go into the place. She might have known, of course, she told herself bitterly, that Annabella would be more than able to charm everyone with her performance on the spinet and to accompany Mrs Jeffries who had a pleasant singing voice. Mr Abercromby, it turned out, could play the fiddle and, while he did so, Harding partnered Annabella in a minuet. Soon they were all joining in other more lively jigs and country dances.

Later that night, lying beside Harding in the four-poster bed in his room, not a word, far less a touch, passed between them. She knew he was thinking of Annabella and making love to her in his mind. Annabella's presence was so real in the bed that Regina expected her at any minute to take substance. She felt sick and disgusted, and as remote from the man at her side as if he had been transported to another world from her. There was nothing but coldness and danger around her. Her instincts for survival sharpened and long into the night she lay stiff and alert. Her mind kept tracking innumerable apprehensions and perils like beasts in the forest, never certain if she came face to face with them what she could do to defend herself.

The next day she was more exhausted than ever and she was glad when Harding took the guests out riding. At least then she could give orders to the slaves and organize the day's meals in peace. Harding had said that it was the height of bad manners not to accompany the guests but she ignored him. To confess that she was feeling confused and terrified, that she would not be able to cope with all the necessary arrangements, was to betray weakness and make herself dangerously vulnerable. She had nightmare visions of Annabella taking over Forest Hall completely and to prevent this she was determined to hang on and do all that was necessary at all costs. Insecurity mingled with suspicion and the slave who innocently remarked on how pretty all the flowers were in the house was immediately banished to the fields. Another who was overheard saying what a lively and cheerful person Mistress Annabella was suffered the same fate. The remaining slaves, nervous and unsure, whispered furtively among themselves and stopped immediately Regina came near, which made her all the more suspicious and angry.

It seemed a miracle that she was able to survive the strain of the next few days and still retain a calm and polite mask for her guests. Some degree of strain or unhappiness must have shown, however, or Mrs Jeffries was a more perceptive person than the others. On one occasion she inquired in a confidential and kindly tone if there was anything amiss and if so was there anything she could do to help. Mrs Jeffries was a timid woman overshadowed by her rather pompous and self-opinionated husband and the sympathy and pity in her expression made Regina die a thousand deaths. Were they all pitying her, she wondered, were they all thinking that Harding preferred Annabella to her and that Annabella would make a more suitable wife? With icy dignity she assured Mrs Jeffries that everything was perfectly all right.

At last the guests bid their farewells, or at least the Washingtons, the Abercrombies and the Jeffries did. Annabella and Nancy stayed a day longer and until, or perhaps especially during, the last meal before they left, Regina was in a state of tension.

Harding said,

'Next time you visit you must bring your son, Annabella. It seems strange that I have not met him yet. Does he take after you or your late husband?'

'He has my husband's colouring, Mr Harding, but I fear he takes after me in other things,' she said. 'He is prodigiously high-tempered and wilful at times.'

'If he is like you, he cannot be lacking in charm, mistress,' Harding said.

Annabella widened her eyes.

'Why, sir, I believe you nearly paid me a compliment. If you are not truly solicitous to check such pretty speeches, you will have us all in a flutter for we won't know what to make of you.'

'I only tell the truth,' Harding grinned, 'and I will tell you what I think of your son when I meet him.'

'Sometimes I think he misses a father's stern hand. My Papa spoils him, indeed he is amused when the boy copies his somewhat harsh manner. He was telling Papa not long ago of an incident in which he'd seen fit to give some unfortunate fellow a kicking. Apparently the man is a consumptive and a butt of much ridicule and harsh treatment at the settlement. I was not amused, I can tell you, and I boxed Mungo's ears. Of course he is a good boy really, and even in this matter had been concerned for the way the man was fouling the path on which ladies had to walk.'

'He sounds a devilishly fine youngster to me.'

Annabella eyed him mischievously.

'Yes, I believe the two of you would get on wondrously well.'

Regina was sitting with eyes lowered, hardly daring to breathe. Annabella was surely tormenting her, purposely dangling her on an ever-tightening noose of suspense. She sat willing the laughing voice to wither into silence, the light to extinguish in the vivacious face. But to the very last moment before she left, Annabella remained as energetic and every bit as frustrating as ever.

She even managed to catch Regina unawares and shock her just before she left. Before Regina could freeze her off, Annabella pounced on her and kissed her goodbye.

'You went to such a lot of trouble for us, Regina. I thank you for your kind hospitality.'

Then into her carriage with much bunching up of skirts and hat ribbons fluttering in the breeze, then waving from the carriage window, then a last cheery sing song of:

'Goodbye! Goodbye!'

And she was gone.

Regina's tension and strain relaxed thankfully away with the rollicking carriage as it disappeared into the forest. A silence descended like a blanket. Suddenly the place was isolated again. If you stood very still, as she was doing now, you could hear the grass sighing. Squirrels darted half way down a nearby tree, clung and stared, and darted up again.

Harding turned and without a word strode back into the house. After a few minutes she followed him, the skirt of her green gown making regular swishing sounds. Passing Melie Anne in the hall, she ordered all the flowers to be removed, tea to be served in the drawing-room and Lottie to be brought down. Not that she particularly enjoyed having the child take up so much time and attention at tea time, but she was anxious for everything to return to normal as soon as possible. Harding had been happy and contented before with the routine they had established. Surely he would be again. Not that she had forgiven him for his behaviour during the visit. She felt harrowed and wounded. All she wanted was to recover, to feel safe and secure once more.

Harding was sprawled back in his chair with a glass of whisky in his hand when she entered the drawing-room.

'Well,' he said, his dark eyes full of bitterness. 'Are you satisfied now?'

'What do you mean?'

'She's gone.'

'I believe the visit was a social success,' she said, going around plumping up cushions and ignoring his last remark. 'Everyone enjoyed themselves. Or so they said.'

'Of course they enjoyed themselves. Of course it was a social success. But they needn't thank you for anything.'

Green eyes glittered across at him like cut glass.

'I worked hard to have everything run smoothly and to have their every need satisfied.'

'You worked hard!' He sneered sarcastically. 'You did nothing to make this past week a success.'

'I did nothing?' She was so incredulous that for a moment she could not talk.

'All you were capable of was hovering in the background, like a block of ice, freezing everyone who came near you.'

'How dare you talk to me like that? You know perfectly well the amount of work and care and thought I put into the preparations for the visit.'

'The fact remains, mistress, that if it had not been for Annabella, the whole thing would have been a disaster.'

'I do not see why.'

'I know you do not see why. Christ, in your own ghastly way you're as hopeless and as useless as Kitty ever was.'

Regina paled.

'You are besotted with Annabella. Everyone saw what a fool you made of yourself in her company. They pitied me. How could I feel relaxed in such circumstances? I will never forget these past few days as long as I live.'

'Papa! Papa!' Suddenly the door burst open and Lottie

toddled in, her plump legs nearly running away with her in her eagerness to reach Harding's chair.

He swooped her up in his arms and kissed and hugged her before settling her comfortably on his knee.

'Tea, Papa, tea, Papa!' she chanted excitedly.

'Yes, here it comes.' He pointed to Melie Anne who had arrived with a tray. 'Let's see what there is. Ah! Sugar biscuits. Your favourites!'

He gave her one and she promptly held it up to his mouth so that he could share it. He took a bite and dutifully thanked her. Then Lottie held the biscuit up in Regina's direction.

'Mama?'

Regina came over and knelt down in front of the child. She took a careful bite at the biscuit. Then she kissed her daughter and said,

'Mama's good girl!'

Chapter 18

Annabella, Griselle, Phemy and Letitia crushed together at the open window of Letitia's flat in Trongate Street. They kept giving cries of protest and horror at the scene they were witnessing in the street below. A cheering crowd had gathered into a ring in the middle of which two pugilists dressed in nothing but breeches were engaged in a bare-fisted contest. After thirty odd rounds of pounding at one another, they had reduced their bodies to sides of raw beef and their faces to bloody masks. They were now staggering blindly about and slipping in their own blood.

Annabella stamped her foot and shouted:

'I cannot stand any more of this. I am going down to put a stop to it.'

'Annabella!' the other women cried out in alarm. 'You will be in danger. It is no place for a lady.'

'Then, damn it all, I am no lady for I am going down there.'

Just then their attention was caught by a single gig with a speeding horse coming at full gallop from the direction of the Gallowgate. It rushed into the ring sending earth and stones spurting up and spectators scurrying away on either side. Down from the gig jumped a man in a powdered tie-wig and lime-green coat. He took up a stance between the fighters and shouted:

'The fight is finished.'

There were immediate infuriated cries from the spectators. In answer to this, the man promptly drew a sword.

'Whoever disagrees with me, step forward,' he challenged. 'I will take great pleasure in running him through.'

No one moved.

'Then away about your business, the lot of you.'

Annabella clapped loudly and enthusiastically and called down,

'Good for you, sir! I'm glad to find there are still civilized

784

gentlemen in Glasgow.' Then to the crowd, 'Well? What are you waiting for? Do you want me to send for the military and have you flung in the Tolbooth?'

Grumbling and muttering the crowd began to disperse and the man gave Annabella a polite bow. Then he called up:

'One of these men is my brother. He was fighting to pay off a gambling debt.'

Annabella raised her hands and eyes in sympathy and the man in the lime-green coat led his brother over to the pump and splashed him with water. But blood was still pouring from his wounds when he was helped, half conscious, into the gig and driven off.

By this time a weeping woman was tending to the other pugilist as best she could and Annabella turned away from the window followed by the other ladies.

'Aye, that's the sort of thing I'll miss when we have our mansion,' Letitia observed.

'Mother!' her daughters cried out in unison.

'Tuts, I'm only telling the truth and you enjoy the street diversions the same as me. You'll be wanting a cup of tea, I suppose, Annabella?'

'Indeed it will be most welcome after all that excitement. I feel quite fluttered.'

'Aye!' Letitia was determined to press her point home. 'There can't be much to see from your window in the Westergate.'

She blamed Annabella for putting the idea into her son Andrew's and her daughter Griselle's head that they should have a mansion built outside the town. Letitia would have stuck to her guns and insisted on ending her days in Trongate Street but Andrew had said:

'Well, Mother, I'm afraid you'll have to stay on your own because I am having a mansion built and when it is ready I am moving into it. Everyone has games rooms now for billiards and cards, and a drawing-room for entertaining. It is most inconvenient to bring my friends here.'

'Tuts, your father always met his friends in the tavern or the Coffee House. We entertained here in my bedroom. What was good enough for your father should be good enough for you,

785

sir.'

She believed the new mansions were calculated for show, not convenience.

'Times change, Mother. Times change. But no one is forcing you to leave. You can stay on here or come with us. Whatever you prefer.'

She would have preferred to stay but her sight was failing and she wasn't nearly so spry as she used to be. It might prove a worry being on her own. Old Kate, the servant, had one foot in the grave herself and wasn't much use to anybody any more. So she had agreed that when the time came she would move. But she had done so with bad grace.

'Tuts, there's far too much gaming nowadays.' She shook her head as she poured the tea. 'Fancy having to get yourself half-killed to pay off gambling debts. It's disgraceful. Having a gaming-room is going to do our Andra no good at all.'

Annabella was inclined to agree with her in this. Andrew had never been very successful at anything and gaming could prove a risky diversion for him. She had already lost some money herself at hazard and far and quadrille but she didn't believe that she would ever become obsessed like some and get herself into financial difficulties. Half the time it wasn't like a game at all, or at least it did not coincide with her idea of a game. Too often the players were devilishly serious, huddled avidly together, eyes sharp or wary, fingers cautiously placing a card down or tossing it with affected negligence, or knuckles whitening with tension as they gripped them close. Personally, she much preferred musical entertainments and dancing and concerts and, of course, conversation. A visit to Robert Foulis's new Glasgow Academy of Fine Arts in the Faculty Hall at the University was also most enjoyable in her opinion. She delighted in strolling around admiring the paintings, engravings and drawings and chatting and exchanging opinions with any other ladies and gentlemen who happened to be there.

She liked to read too but literature was not a matter of widespread interest in a trading community like Glasgow. There were few books to be had. They were sold in little shops that concentrated mostly on chap-books, sealing-wax, stationery and fishing rods. Displayed alongside these items were college classics in grey pasteboard covers, devout works like *The Balm of Gilead*, Rutherford's *Letters*, Boston's *Fourfold State*, and Gray's *Sermons*.

Of course one could also get books from Robert Foulis who printed the classics and works of poets, or via the cadger from Edinburgh. But it was seldom now that anyone had to wait for special articles from Edinburgh. No one even needed to rummage through a miscellany of articles in an ill-lit booth to find what they wanted, although there were still plenty of booths supplying shoes, lanterns, stay-laces, silks and a hotchpotch of other bits and bobs. Now there were new shops in the Trongate. There was a silversmith, a haberdasher, a shoemaker, a mantua-maker, a shop that sold gloves and a shop that sold breeches. The walls of the shops were erupting with signboards. Dangling and creaking in the air from poles were red lions, blue swans, cross keys, golden fleeces, golden breeches and golden gloves. There was also a shop in which a mechanic who called himself an optician mended and sold spectacles, fiddles, fishing rods and tackle.

Annabella also enjoyed the normal gossip of ladies over the teacups and attended many merry and light-hearted tea parties and supper parties and entertained in similar fashion in Mungo House.

'I wonder who those gentlemen were?' she asked now as she sipped at the cup of tea Letitia had handed to her. 'I don't think I've seen them before. Of course I couldn't see the pugilist's face for all that monstrous blood. But I didn't recognize the other.'

Griselle said to Phemy,

'Is he not the old Laird of Meadowflat's son? Did we not meet the family at an assembly while Annabella was away?'

Phemy eagerly nodded her pocked beaky face.

'Yes, I remember. My gudeman was with me that night and he and the old Laird had such a pleasant talk.'

'Are you catched by him, Annabella?' Griselle helped herself to another piece of cake. Tall and long-boned like her mother, she had become heavier of late with puffy purple cheeks and a quivering double chin.

'Heavens no!' Annabella laughed. 'I was just curious. I thought I'd already met all the men worth meeting in the town.'

Letitia eyed Annabella disapprovingly.

'Its high time you were married again, mistress, instead of flitting about like a butterfly from one to the other.'

'Gracious heavens! Flitting from one to the other? You make it sound as if I'm enjoying a large number of lovers but I am not.'

'You've had your fair share,' said Griselle primly.

'I happily agree. And I hope I'll continue to have my fair share until I'm a very old lady. Indeed until the day I die.'

Letitia shook her head.

'Tuts, Annabella, have you no shame?'

'None at all,' Annabella confessed cheerily. 'But I must remind you that it is possible to have friends of either sex without needing to cultivate affairs of the heart.'

'I still say it's time you were safely married before you lose your looks and your chances.'

'Pooh!' Annabella said disdainfully. 'No woman with wit, a racy tongue and a capacity for enjoying life, need fear the coming of wrinkles and grey hairs.'

'I keep telling our Grizzie the same thing,' said Letitia, keeping to her original point. 'It's time she was married again.'

'It's manners to wait till you're asked, Mother.'

'Tuts, I'm sure our Andra could arrange a match.'

Grizzie cast her eyes upwards.

'Mother, Andrew hasn't been able to arrange a match for himself.'

Letitia sniffed.

'Any woman would be lucky to have our Andra. He's been well-placed since his father passed on. The only trouble is he's a wee bit shy at the courting.'

'What he needs,' said Annabella, 'is a spirited woman to take the initiative.'

Letitia sighed.

'If something isn't done soon I can see me with all three of my bairns at a loose end. Phemy's gudeman's on his last legs. It'll no' be long till she's a widow woman.'

'Mother!' Phemy wailed.

788

'Facts are facts, mistress. The Earl o' Glendinny's old enough to be your father and the Lord gathered your father in years ago.'

Just then the door creaked open and old Kate creaked in. She always wore her tartan plaid in the house now because she suffered acutely from the cold. It was draped over her head and hunchback and round her leathery long-nosed face and crossed over and fastened at her chest.

'Aye,' Letitia added when she saw the old servant, 'and here's another one living on borrowed time.'

'I'll maybe outlive yersel' yet,' Kate cackled. 'Hurry up and finish yer tea. I'm waitin' to rinse oot the dishes.'

'You'll do no such thing,' Letitia snapped. 'These are my best china cups and saucers. I'll wash them myself.' Then turning to Annabella, 'Could you go another wee drop?'

'No, I'll have to be away. I want to have a stroll down by the hiring fair before I get a chair home.'

'Very well. Kate, you can take the pot. I know fine it's the pot you've got your eye on. There's plenty left to give you and Tam a drink so there's no need to fash yourself.'

'Did you ever!' Griselle said after Kate had gleefully departed with the tea pot. 'Mother is insisting on bringing that vile old witch and old Tam with us when we move to our mansion. Isn't it diabolical?'

Letitia suddenly rapped Griselle's knuckles with her fan.

'Keep a civil tongue in your head, mistress. I'm maybe putting up with your big-headed notions of mansion houses but I will not countenance all the good old customs to be so lightly tossed aside.'

Griselle snatched up her own fan, snapped it open and agitated it in annoyance.

'Good old customs. What are those, pray?'

'Having a sense o' loyalty and some respect for a lifetime of devoted service. Old Kate and Tam have been good enough servants in their day.'

'You have given them their keep all these years, mother, and a good home.'

'Aye, and my home will be their home, mistress, until the day I die and I'll have none o' your snash. I get enough snash from them. I couldn't get rid o' the old devils even if I wanted to. They're that stubborn they just wouldn't go. Tuts, I've tried often enough. The last time I told her in no uncertain manner. We must part, Kate, I said, and she said, "Aye, mistress, and where are ye goin'? Ye'd be better to stay at home at your age."'

Annabella laughed but Griselle sighed and tutted and flicked her fan. She knew that nothing would ever change her mother. Her mother had been cast in the same stubborn mould as old Kate and Tam.

Phemy, who was a kind and gentle soul, ventured:

'Surely Mother is right? It would be unkind to turn Kate and Tam out now. Where would they go?'

'You're always the same, Phemy.' Griselle's chins bounced with annoyance. 'Why should we care about them?'

Annabella's laughter rippled out again.

'I dare swear I often ask myself that about my Betsy and Tib, not to mention Big John. Betsy is the most monstrous tearful prophet of doom you could ever imagine and the touchy vanity of Tib Faulds is downright impertinent at times. I'm looking for a personal maid now. I'm hoping I might see someone at the Fair today. You'll need more servants too when you're in your mansion, Grizzie. Do you fancy a stroll down Stockwell Street to have a look at some?'

'No, I think I'll wait till nearer the time. It'll be a good few weeks yet before we can move.'

They all rose with Annabella to see her to the door and Letitia called a warning before Annabella waved goodbye and disappeared down the spiral stair.

'You watch your reticule, mistress. Half o' that crowd at the Stockwell are no' Glasgow folk, remember. Thieves and vagabonds come flocking into the town for the Fair.'

Stockwell Street was across the road from the Shawfield Mansion in which Prince Charles Edward Stuart had stayed during his invasion of Glasgow. The street was the western boundary of the city and it formed the leading thoroughfare to the only bridge that spanned the River Clyde at Glasgow.

Fashionable tenements, some two storeys high, some three,

some four, graced the head of the street and at the foot near the river there were quaint irregular-shaped thatched dwellings with outside stairs and rickety wooden banisters. Mixed in with the handsome tenements and humble cottages there was also the South Sugar House and the rope works. The street was regarded as a most desirable town residence and many leading merchants and notabilities of the city were born and bred in the tenements in this locality cheek by jowl with the humble occupants of the cottages. It was always fairly busy with folk going to and from Trongate Street at one end, or Bridge Street which curved from the other. On Fair days however it was jam-packed. There was the horse and bestial Fair when there were endless rows of restive horses and neighing stallions or bulls and cows lowing. Or there was the Hiring Fair when ploughmen came in from the surrounding countryside and took the opportunity of enjoying much whisky and ale and merrymaking and courting of cherry-cheeked dairymaids. The country servants for hire were usually to be seen at the Trongate Street end of the Stockwell and the city servants could be viewed at the bridge end.

Annabella hadn't made up her mind, as she left her friend's close and emerged onto Trongate Street, whether she wanted to hire a country or a city servant. Country servants usually looked healthier and cleaner but she had heard that they could be very naive and more of a worry than anything else in the city.

Although the sun was shining, there was a cool breeze and Annabella was glad of her cloak. The wind frisked around her, tugging and flapping at her cloak and swaying her panniered skirts as she picked her way lightly along. A heavy cart rumbled past, then the stage coach to Edinburgh packed with loudly baa-ing lambs to be delivered at some stage on the journey. She stopped and waited under the pillared walkways until a confused drove of animals on their way to be slaughtered crushed by. Then she tripped across Trongate Street towards Stockwell Street.

Tall grey stone tenements seemed to ripple as sun chased shadow and shadow chased sun. Trongate Street was busy with people too and there was a happy festive air because it was Fair day. Gaggles of gossiping ladies with shopping baskets clung on

791

to hats and hoods, Tobacco lords, in their curled wigs and three-cornered hats and sparkling shoe-buckles and scarlet capes swirling and billowing, strolled up and down the plainstones, the special paved part of Trongate Street reserved solely for themselves. Past the equestrian statue of King William of Orange they sauntered, keeping to the right when going westwards and to the left when returning eastwards as was customary.

Other fine gentlemen in brocade coats with large cuffs and buttons astride handsome horses cantered along amid the noisy street-criers.

'Pots to mend! Pots to mend!' A man rollicked along with pots slung over his shoulders and one in his hand on which he was banging energetically with a hammer.

A woman in a white apron and gown tucked up was balancing a basket on her head and singing,

'Cherries, fair cherries!'

Another older woman awkwardly clutching her wares pleaded hoarsely,

'Buy a fork or a fire shovel?'

A man was whipping a barrel-laden mule along chanting,

'Lily white vinegar!'

Hoards of children danced and pranced around and barking dogs added to the din, especially on the east side of Stockwell Street where in front of one group of thatched cottages there were piles of empty casks and barrels belonging to a cooper who lived there. A little old woman who sold sweeties was also a great attraction.

It was in this area of Stockwell Street that Annabella caught sight of Mungo cavorting about and having a hilarious time along with a motley band of other boys.

'Mungo!' she angrily called to him. He was supposed to be in school diligently studying and it had never occurred to her that he would act in such a grossly deceitful and disobedient manner. Immediately he saw her, instead of coming in answer to her cry, he hared away in the opposite direction and was immediately swallowed up by the crowd. It occurred to her, not for the first time, that Mungo was in need of a father's stern hand. Her own

Papa was far too indulgent with him.

She afterwards discovered that Mungo had not been near the school the whole day. First he and some other boys had thrown stones at sparrows perched on trees in the vitriol dealer's yard, until the vitriol dealer, a thin curious-looking man with long legs like a spider and a face like an owl, had hastened menacingly out and chased them away. Then they had gone bird-nesting behind Virginia Street and watched a man shoot hares and partridges. From there they'd gathered in the yard of the Black Bull Inn where there was a draw-well. The well-cover was a huge oblong wooden box painted blue. Two tremendous leaden arms fixed near the top of the box hung vertically, and when water was drawn, moved from side to side like a pendulum. A thick curved spout projected from each side of the well and it was a favourite sport of boys to stop the mouth of the spout with the palm of the hand and squirt jets of water around. The well handles had great round knobs at the bottom and made a popular swing for the boys who cared nothing for the water they wasted in the process. Eventually they had been chased away by townsfolk arriving with wooden pails to collect their supplies of water. The boys had scampered from the Black Bull to Stockwell Street and the Fair.

That night Annabella soundly boxed Mungo's ears and sent him to bed without any supper. She hoped that when he went on to University, and he would be going soon now that he was twelve, he would settle down and take his studies more seriously. If he did not, she hardly knew what to do with him. He was a big sturdy lad who could be serious and sensible at times but at others could cause her much consternation with his wild and rowdy ways. She wondered if Harding had been like that when he was a child. No doubt he would have known how to deal with Mungo, but as it was she had to cope with him as best she could herself.

She decided it might be safer to take him with her when she went to stay at the Duke of Dalgleish's estate for a few days. They travelled in a new chariot and six she had bought and Big John in splendid scarlet livery sat up front. Standing at the back was Donald, the new manservant, also in a scarlet coat and white breeches.

As they galloped up the drive towards the Dalgleish mansion Annabella temporarily forgot her worries about Mungo. He was a splendid-looking young man with his richly embroidered coat and his three-cornered hat and his hair tied back and his hand resting on a gold-topped cane that her Papa had had specially made for him. When they reached the enormous residence of the Duke, Mungo jumped out and helped her to alight, and it was hard to imagine that he could ever be anything other than a perfect gentleman.

She equalled him in splendid appearance as her hair was padded and powdered and she wore patches and a luxurious fur-lined hooded velvet cloak over her wide gown of gold silk.

Both she and her son gazed in admiration at the Duke's splendid house and grounds. In their faces were visions of the balls and the banquets they would enjoy there and the riding and the hunting.

Then Mungo raised his hand with confidence and authority, and led her towards the open door.

Chapter 19

'I can't wait any longer,' Gav told Abigail. 'The weather will be too bad if I do.'

He didn't want to go to Forest Hall. He couldn't spare the time. Quite apart from his many responsibilities in the store he had his family to feed and his patch of land to attend to. Already he'd pushed back a fair amount of forest by felling trees and burning stumps.

He also hunted turkeys, otter and raccoon, caught fish, dug ginseng and hunted bees. In fact most days he worked from sunrise till dark. Not that he was complaining. He loved the settlement. He knew every occupant of every log cabin. In the settlement they were like one large family enclosed together by the boundaries of forest and river. He knew every child scampering around the store, or in the clearance in front of the gaol-house, or swimming or fishing down by the creek. He knew every ship that billowed up the river and every sea-captain and seaman who strutted ashore for a carousal in Widow Shoozie's tavern. He knew every planter who rode or sailed in for a gossip and to exchange tobacco for goods. He knew the Virginian weather, the brassy heat of summer making morning steam rise from the river, the clear crisp winters and freezing temperatures that iced over the water. He knew the variable winds. The north and north-west winds prevailed during the short winter season, while the south and south-east winds were warm, bringing sultry weather and a hazy humid atmosphere. The south-west wind was usually accompanied by gusts, hail, rain, squalls and electrical storms which could be very frightening. Many a stout ship fetched up on the shoals of the Chesapeake during a south-west gale. The settlement with its sprawl of log cabins dotted in between blackened stumps, its slippery wharf, its shimmering river, was the centre of his universe. He had no inclination to leave it even for a few days but he had promised to deliver

Regina's order, and goods for Mr Harding had also arrived in the last shipment.

Abigail said, 'Mr Harding usually comes about this time of year.'

Gav tried not to lose his temper.

'Abby, you know as well as I do he won't be coming now.'

She put a hand up to shade her eyes as if from anxiety.

'I'm never happy about you going there.'

'I know you're not, and I know why. I wish you'd try to like Regina, Abigail. Or at least not actively dislike her so much.'

She was standing at the kitchen table ironing clothes and she smoothed the iron back and forth without concentrating on what she was doing.

'I can't help it.'

'Yes you can. You just don't try.'

'She frightens me.'

'That's just because you don't understand her.'

'Promise me you won't stay long.'

He sighed.

'I promise.'

'Just the one night to rest after the journey?'

'Yes, all right.' He ran his fingers through his wiry red hair in a gesture of irritation. 'But I don't understand you, Abby. You're always so level-headed as a rule. Why on earth are you so jealous of Regina that you can't bear me to stay at her house for more than one night? You'd think she was my lover instead of my sister to hear you talk.'

Her face screwed up with worried intensity.

'I don't think it's jealousy. Not altogether. It's this apprehensive feeling.'

In a way he knew what his wife meant. He could never be quite sure what Regina was thinking or what she might do. All the same there was no need for Abigail to be so possessive and to try and stop him from going to Forest Hall. Later he tried to reassure her again but without success. Nothing he could say could make her feel any happier about the trip and eventually, despite her tense and unhappy attitude, he set out on the long trek through the forest.

He sat at the front of the covered wagon, his gun across his lap, the reins dangling between the fingers of one hand, his pipe gripped in the other. Booster rocked to and fro at his side, every now and again breaking into song to pass the time.

> 'Lord, I want to be a Christian,
> In—a my heart,
> In a—my heart.
> Lord, I want to be a Christian,
> In—a my heart,
> In a—my heart.
>
> Lord, I don't want to be like Judas,
> In—a my heart,
> In a—my heart.
> Lord, I want to be like Jesus,
> In—a my heart,
> In—a my heart.'

Puffing at his pipe, Gav thought how interesting it would be to see how Regina's little girl was progressing. Lottie must be running about and talking now. He had brought some candy that Abigail had made for her. It seemed no time ago and yet a lifetime away since Regina and he had been children themselves. He remembered how Regina always used to waken first in the morning and lightly touch him and his mother to make sure that they were still there. Her stealthy touch always wakened them and he used to be angry at this habit of hers. Looking back he realized now that Regina had been a nervous and insecure child. She'd always liked to hold his hand when they went home to Tannery Wynd in case any of the harlots who lived upstairs, or Blind Jinky and his savage dog who lived next door, suddenly appeared to menace her. Coming home from school on dark nights too she had clung nervously to his coat tails. The school had been down near the river and he had been a bit frightened himself at the noise of the clappers used by the lepers to warn of their approach as they shuffled across the bridge from the leper hospital in the village of Gorbals.

Booster was beginning to get sleepy but he still managed to keep the occasional verse going.

'Before I stay in hell one day,
Heaven shall—a be my home;
I sing and pray my soul away,
Heaven shall be my home.'

Both Regina's life and his own, Gav decided, were heaven now compared with what they had been in Glasgow. He liked old Glasgow. He had fond memories of the place as well as harrowing ones but there could be no doubt that the quality of life here and the opportunities were better. Regina and he had been ragged beggars in Glasgow. If they had stayed there how could Regina have become mistress of a large mansion house in many acres of land? How could he have become a manager with servants and slaves working under his orders? How could he have acquired his own home and land on which to produce good food and keep his family well nourished?

America was God's own country, although he had to admit next day when the wagon at last rumbled and creaked and jerked from the tangled denseness of the forest that this particular part of it was not his favourite.

The forest had been gloomy enough but Forest Hall never failed to depress him.

'Hello-o-o, the house!' he called.

He wondered if Lottie was becoming more like Regina in appearance. The last time he'd seen her she'd had Harding's black hair and dark eyes but fortunately she had Regina's even features.

Regina was writing at the desk in the drawing room when she heard Gav's call and felt an immediate surge of pleasure at the sound of his voice. She put down the quill and carefully closed the slope-fronted desk before swishing from the room. When she reached the hall, Lottie called excitedly from the top of the stairs.

'Horses and wagon, Mama.'

'Yes, it'll be your uncle Gav. Come down and say hello and curtsy nicely to him. Watch her on the stairs,' she added sharply to Flemintina who rushed to catch the child's hand.

Westminster came running to open the doors and then, along

798

with Joseph, hastened to attend to Gav's horses and wagon.

Gav took the outside wooden stair three at a time and as usual gave Regina an enthusiastic hug and kiss. As always she tutted and pushed him away.

'Lord's sake, Gav, you're getting more like an ox every time I see you.'

'It's good solid muscle,' he laughed.

'Now it is but you'd better be careful it doesn't turn to fat when you get older.'

'Where's my young niece, then? Ah!' he shouted out when he saw the little girl hurrying down as quickly as she was able, one step at a time. 'What a beauty she has become!' Indeed she looked very pretty with her dark hair done up in a feather and beads and a frock of white striped gauze over a pink slip. The pink tints showed through the thinner folds of whiteness and around her waist was tied a vivid pink sash of gauze. Beneath the dress pink silk slippers kept peeping out.

Gav stretched out his arms.

'Come on then, let's have a good look at you!'

Laughing excitedly she ran to him and he hoisted her high.

'I wonder if you like candy, eh? No, I don't think you do.'

Giggling, she nodded.

'All right.' He gave her a hug and a kiss before putting her down again. 'You shall have some because I have a box of candies almost as beautiful as yourself and all made specially for you by your Aunty Abigail. Booster!' he shouted at the door. 'Hurry up with things. There's a lady here waiting for that box with the cherry-coloured ribbon on it.'

Regina led him into the drawing-room while Lottie waited at the front door for Booster to bring her present.

'Did you get all my things, Gav?'

'Every one,' he assured her.

'Good. Can I pour you a dram?'

He nodded.

'And how has life been treating you, sister?'

'Oh, very well.'

'You're certainly looking well.'

She poured herself a drink too and with a grin Gav came over

799

and clicked glasses with her.

'Here's to us, and to our continuing prosperity, Regina.'

'Yes, brother.' She gave him a small smile. 'I'll drink to that.'

'I was just thinking while I was journeying here, how well we've got on in life. We've been very lucky.'

A flash of anger hardened her eyes.

'Luck? What has luck had to do with anything? Any good, any success in our lives we've made happen ourselves.'

'Oh, I don't know, Regina . . .'

'Well I do.'

Suddenly a deep voice from the doorway interrupted.

'What's this? Fighting already?'

'Mr Harding!' Gav strode across the room, hand outstretched to grasp that of his brother-in-law. 'It's good to see you again. But not half as good as it is to see your beautiful daughter. By God, she's really something, isn't she?'

Harding had the little girl in his arms. She was clutching a box nearly as big as herself and her father grinned at her proudly.

'You'll see a big difference in her, Gav.'

'Yes, she's fairly come on. She came racing down the stairs to meet me and I bet she can talk as well, although I haven't heard her yet.'

'Put her down, sir.' Regina said. 'She must show her manners and greet her uncle properly.'

Harding took the box from Lottie and set her down on her feet. She looked uncertainly over at Regina, then lifted her skirts and wobbled down among them, saying at the same time in an unexpected coquettish little voice. 'Welcome to Forest Hall, sir. I hope you will have a pleasant stay.'

Gav couldn't help grinning but he managed to bow very civilly in reply.

'Thank you, Mistress Lottie, you are most kind.'

'Mama, can I open the candies now?' Lottie asked.

'Very well.'

'Has a shipment arrived, Gav?' Harding asked.

'Yes, everything from cases of whisky and silver-mounted Morocco pocket-books to ivory toothpicks and gold snuffboxes. Not to mention all the pretty trifles for mistress Lottie here that

800

her fond mama ordered.'

'What's pretty trifles, Uncle Gav?' Lottie asked with a mouth full of candy.

'Lottie!' Regina rebuked sharply. 'Do not speak with your mouth full.'

Gav laughed.

'Oh, you'll soon see. But there's silk and satin and lawn and calico and gauze and lace. Your Mama must be going to make you lots of pretty dresses. There's a fashion baby too and I'm sure you're going to like it. There's a fur muff and a tortoise-shell pocket comb in a case and two of those umbrillos or umbrellas as some folk call them, a small one for you painted pink, and one for your Mama painted yellow and both decorated with feathers. They were the devil's own job to transport, I can tell you.'

'How is your family, Gav?' Regina inquired politely.

'Enjoying splendid health at the moment, thanks to God. And so is Abigail. A few months back we were worried about the children. First Bette took a fever and head pains then Jethro, but we managed to cure them all right.'

'Did you sweat them?'

'Yes, but it wasn't easy.'

'I've found tincture of saffron and sage and snakeroot is very efficient.'

'Of course,' Gav said. 'You'll get plenty of practice in doctoring with having so many slaves.'

'Lunesta and Little Sam are serving your family well, I hope,' Regina said.

'Better slaves you couldn't find in the whole of Virginia,' Gav enthused. 'They're devoted to Jethro and Bette and Lunesta's such a help to Abby too. You did us a real good turn by giving us them, Regina, and I thank you again.'

Regina shrugged.

'I'm glad they're of some use.'

Harding poured himself a whisky and refilled the other glasses.

'How long are you here for, Gav?'

'Only tonight, I'm afraid. I can't spare any more time away from the store. In fact if it hadn't been that I wanted to see you

801

all I would have just sent Tom with the wagon.'

Harding stood in front of the fire sipping his whisky, one hand in the top of his breeches. He was wearing a claret-coloured coat and a frilled white shirt which lay open revealing a broad expanse of tanned skin and black hair.

'So you're manager now, eh? Well, let's hope you make a better job of it than the drunken fool that was supposed to be managing it before.'

Gav sighed.

'Poor Mr Speckles. It's the consumption. It's been the ruination of his body and his mind.'

He was silent for a minute, regretfully remembering. 'One time he told me he had been kicked and railed at by "young Harding". I thought he meant you at first.'

Harding laughed.

'Young Harding? Thanks for the compliment, Gav.'

Rising, Regina spoke quickly.

'You'll be hungry, Gav. I'll ring for tea, or are you ready for dinner now? I could arrange to have it early.'

'I'm quite happy just now, thanks. I ate the last of my cornbread not long before I arrived.'

'What were you saying about Speckles?' Harding asked. 'He thought I'd given him a kicking? I've certainly felt like it many a time.'

'No, I discovered he meant a child. He kept insisting it was your son. I told him it was a daughter you had, but no, the poor man would have none of it. "I looked up at the sturdy young fellow," he kept raving on. "I looked at the young fellow's black hair and dark eyes and I said, oh, how like your father you are, sir".' Gav shook his head. 'I know all the children who belong to the settlement and I can't think of one who even vaguely resembles you. Of course there are others who come from time to time with planters and their friends . . .'

Suddenly Regina gave a little cry as her whisky glass fell and smashed, spurting amber fluid across the floor. 'Oh, how clumsy of me. I'm so sorry.' She cast an anguished look at Harding. 'Will you call for one of the slaves to clear this up, please? I'm afraid it will stain.' Snatching up her fan she agitated it in front of her face. Harding stared at her with hard, thoughtful eyes.

Avoiding his stare she switched her attention to Lottie who was sitting on the rug happily eating candies and listening to everything that was going on.

'Shut that box at once, you naughty, greedy girl. You will make yourself sick with eating so many. Go and get Flemintina to take you upstairs and wash your sticky face and hands.'

Lottie's eyes widened in surprise and chagrin.

'No want to go upstairs.'

'How dare you!' Regina had gone icy cold. 'How dare you speak to me in that impertinent manner. Get out of my sight at once before I give you a beating.'

Without a word Harding lifted the child and carried her from the room.

Gav screwed up his face.

'Regina, don't you think you were a bit hard on her.'

'No, I do not, sir. And I'll thank you to mind your own business. Why should you come here, stirring up trouble and ruining everything? I'll tell you why, sir. Because you are stupid. You have the brains as well as the build of an ox.'

Harding's voice levelled over hers.

'That's enough, mistress. Come on, Gav. We've time for a stroll before dinner.'

'But I don't understand.'

Gav stared perplexedly at his sister, then, as if making a decision not to query the matter further, he strode from the room. He was thinking that the sudden change in Regina's mood was so typical of her. Sometimes he feared that she was a little mad. Indeed it occurred to him that all his life he had had this secret niggling dread at the back of his mind.

Left alone in the drawing room Regina felt as though she was either going mad or taking ill. Pacing the room in extreme agitation she kneaded her hands together and struggled to gather her thoughts into some coherent order. Perhaps Harding would not remember Annabella's story about Mungo kicking a man in the settlement and so would not connect that incident with the one Gav had just spoken of. After all it was some time

803

now since Annabella's visit.

But if he had, and she was sure he had, what would he do?

Oh, why had Gav come? She didn't need him. She didn't need anyone. She had never needed anyone. As long as she was safe and secure she was all right. And she had been safe and secure in Forest Hall until he'd come. He had ruined everything she had fought and suffered to make of her life.

For if Harding knew that he had a son, there would be no telling what might happen. Harding was capable of doing anything. He would not scruple to get rid of her and replace her with the precious mother of his precious son. He had always been besotted with Annabella and if she was the mother of his child she must have felt something for him at some time. Of course Annabella had denied this but with her own eyes she had seen Annabella's flirtatious gestures and looks. Annabella had been enticing Harding all the time during her visit.

What was behind her behaviour?

All along she'd felt apprehensive about Annabella and knew that there was much more to her apparently harmless charm than could be detected on the surface.

Why should Mistress Annabella be so charming and friendly, even affectionate to her? She had been the cause of having the woman's lover tortured, horribly mutilated and killed. Forgive and forget, Mistress Annabella had said. But she had lied. It was not possible to forgive or forget such a thing. No, somehow Annabella had engineered this as an act of vengeance.

First she'd planned and succeeded in humiliating her in Forest Hall. Next she would try to take it away from her. She would try to strip her of everything, to reduce her to the terrified beggar she had once been. Well, Mistress Annabella would not succeed. Somehow she would hang on. Somehow she would find a way.

Chapter 20

How Regina survived the rest of Gav's visit she did not know. The dinner was a nightmare, although she succeeded in behaving in a calm and pleasant manner. She even managed to sit coolly sewing and smiling and joining in the conversation between Gav and Harding. Harding had never said a word about Gav's story concerning the boy at the settlement and she began to wonder if her prayers had been answered. Perhaps, after all, Harding had noticed nothing amiss.

Next day she felt somewhat easier because by lunchtime everything was still perfectly normal. Indeed, Harding had opened several bottles of wine and he and Gav had become quite merry. They saw Gav off immediately after the meal with much waving by Lottie and wishes for a safe journey by Harding and herself. She allowed Gav to kiss her goodbye and even gave him a quick peck in return.

'Are you sure you have enough food for the journey?' she asked.

He laughed.

'You're both far too kind. I've enough delicious food here for half a dozen journeys. Are you sure there's nothing else I can do for you? I'll see that all your letters are delivered, and I'll send off your order, and I'll keep those paper patterns and magazines for you, Regina. But are you sure there's nothing else?'

'Nothing I can think of at the moment.'

'Well, do try and come and visit the settlement soon.'

'I will.'

She raised her hand in a wave and he urged the horses forward. The wagon lurched and creaked and rocked away between the trees, soon to disappear.

First Harding returned to the house, then Flemintina and Lottie. Finally Regina eased up her skirts and climbed the outside wooden stairs and entered the hall. The chandelier tinkled in the breeze as Westminster shut the double doors behind her. She stopped for a minute, admiring the place, the richly gleaming woodwork, the dark blue carpet, the banisters arching round to the first floor corridor. Then she went into the drawing-room.

Harding was standing in his favourite position in front of the fire as he sipped a glass of whisky. His eyes narrowed at her when she entered but he did not speak.

'Has Flemintina taken Lottie upstairs?' she asked.

Still he said nothing. He just stared at her and every now and again took a drink from his glass.

Eventually he said:

'You knew.'

'Knew?' She raised a brow. 'Knew what? That Flemintina had taken Lottie upstairs? If I knew why . . .'

'Don't play games with me, mistress,' he interrupted. 'I have written to Annabella and asked for confirmation. I am entitled to know the truth.'

'The truth is, sir, that your only responsibility and concern should be here with your wife and daughter.'

'I am not forgetting my daughter. But if I have a son, his place is here with me where I can train him to take over the plantation.'

'If you must have a son, then I will give you a son.'

'If I have a son already, I no longer need you to give me one. I will go over to Glasgow as soon as I have a reply from Annabella. I will bring the boy back here. And I will bring Annabella back too, if she will come.'

'You cannot do that.'

'I can do whatever I like.'

'No. I will never allow it.'

Sarcasm widened his eyes.

'You will not allow it? Mistress, have you taken leave of your senses? You have as much influence over me as one of my slaves. Did you not know that?'

'I hate you,' she said.

'I know.'

'I've always hated you.' She began to tremble. 'You're a selfish, insensitive brute. I hate everything about you.'

'Ah, now, that's not quite true. There are some things about me you find irresistible. I confess I find that the same things in you have a certain mindless attraction.'

She turned away from him blindly trying to reach the door, but before she escaped she heard him say:

'It's been the only thing that's been between us, Regina. But it's a thin thread. You see, I've never forgotten my passion for Annabella.'

Upstairs in her bedroom, she wept. But after the tears had all emptied out and she was exhausted, a new resolve began to grow inside her. It would take at least six weeks for that letter to reach Annabella in Glasgow and another six weeks for a reply to return to Virginia. That gave her three months' grace. Somehow in that three months she must make Harding change his plans. She would try everything and anything. It was impossible that her position in Forest Hall should be taken from her. If Annabella came, and she would, then instead of continuing as mistress she would at best be no more than a servant in her own house. And she knew what it was like to be a servant to Annabella. She had had bitter experience of that state in Glasgow. She remembered her first confrontation with Annabella. Gav and she had been children then and wandering in Glasgow Green with the beggar Quin, when Annabella had suddenly swept towards them and said:

'You, girl! Do you know who I am?'

Nervously she had rubbed her fist against her eyes and mouth and stuttered:

'Are you . . . are you . . . ?'

'Speak up!' Annabella rapped the child's fist with her fan. 'And stop rubbing at your face in that ridiculous manner. I asked you a question. Look me straight in the eye and answer it.'

'Mistress Ramsay?'

Then she'd threatened Quin that if he didn't make sure that Regina turned up to start work next day, she would have him hanged. Mistress Annabella always made sure that she got what she wanted. Nothing ever daunted her. When she wanted to be with her French lover she had followed him from Glasgow to the Highlands and stayed with him through the battle of Culloden

807

and beyond. And she'd dragged her servants through that hell with her.

Regina closed her eyes against the memory. Oh, she knew what it was like to be a servant to Annabella all right. She was never going to be that again. She would have to leave. And that might mean leaving without as much as a change of clothing or one gold piece. Under the law she had no right to remove one glove, one handkerchief, far less any money or any children she might have. A married female, the law insisted, lost title to her clothing and other intimate possessions and forfeited any money she had brought to the marriage. Her stomach dipped and heaved at the insecurity of the prospect. But what was she thinking about? Such a thing could not happen. It was impossible. There was no reason for such a danger to arise. She had imagined everything. Her emotions alternated and confused between razor sharp alarm, woolly inability to accept the truth, and bursts of optimistic resolve to transform everything and everyone.

At every opportunity she studied books which would help her to achieve a standard of perfection in her wifely duties that Harding would be bound to admire. By her every action and attitude she would convince him that she was indispensable and irreplaceable. Handbooks like *Whole Duty of Man* and *Lady's Library* advised her that if her yoke-fellow proved unfaithful she should 'affect ignorance of it'. If he were 'choleric and ill-humoured' she should avoid any 'unwary word' and placate him with smiles and flattery. But the smiles and flattery came hard to her. In struggling to act in a way so alien to her nature she only increased the anguish of her spirit, as well as Harding's disdainful attitude towards her.

Desperately she clung to the thread he had spoken of, trying in every way to increase its strength. Her pride died a thousand agonizing deaths when she went to his room at night and allowed him to indulge in every sexual whim, knowing all the time that he was only insulting her. He would not expect his precious ladylike Annabella to behave in such a way or put up with such behaviour. Yet in her confused extremity of mind and spirit, she was not able to stop. And all the time hatred for Annabella boiled up in the background making her soul like a witch's cauldron. That spoiled, selfish, cruel madam had always been a thorn in her flesh for as far back as she could remember.

Often, as time relentlessly passed, and the three crucial months trickled away like her life's blood, she would wrap herself in her cloak and go walking on her own around the plantation. She would nurse bitter, resentful thoughts about Annabella. What had that petted creature cared when she had dragged her off to the Highlands and separated her—forever, for all she knew at the time—from her brother? She had separated her from her brother all those years ago without a qualm and she would separate her from her husband now with no more conscience than she'd had then. Annabella was a wicked woman. Someone to be guarded against at all costs.

On these lonely walks, hugging her cloak tightly around her, as if hoping it might give her protection from the fast approaching then overdue danger as well as from the elements, her mind roamed more and more back to the past. It seemed as if the present horror of her life was like a magnet drawing to itself all the other horrors she had ever experienced. She remembered the French soldiers. She remembered the harlots. She remembered the dominie at the school.

Suddenly she stopped in her tracks, wondering why she had suddenly thought of the dominie, vaguely aware that something had reminded her of him. For a minute or two she stood very still, head lowered, the hood of her cloak hiding her face. Then she retraced her steps, stopping when she came to a cluster of plants growing in the shade of an old fence amidst some rubbish. The flowers of the plant were large, bell-shaped and brownish-purple in colour. Its berrylike fruit was deep purple, almost black. She was seeing it not only growing at her feet but in her mind's eye. The dominie had shown it to all the pupils. He had told them it was commonly used by Italian women for cosmetic purposes because it could enlarge the pupils of the eyes and was thought by these women to make them appear beautiful. It was thus referred to as Herba Bella Donne and from that came the name 'belladonna'. The dominie had concluded the lesson with the warning that they must never eat the berries because they were dangerous and would make them ill.

She stared down at them. She kept being frightened by little fountains of panic. She kept thinking that the three months were up. She was existing on borrowed time. Even as she stood here, Harding might already have Annabella's letter. Already he might be riding away to the settlement and, by the same ship that had brought the letter, he would voyage to Glasgow, to Annabella, and to his son.

Annabella was a wicked, devious woman. She was making Harding prove his devotion by journeying from one end of the world to the other at the mere scribble of her quill.

All Annabella's life she had used this coquettish, teasing, tormenting manner with men. She played games with them. But Harding, fool that he was, could not see this. He refused to see it. He refused to listen to anything against Annabella. She had tried to tell him what Annabella was like but he would not listen. She had tried everything. Her mind was beginning to spin with panic. Any day now, any moment now, the letter would come and he would go running and her whole life would collapse. Yet even as she thought about Harding going to fetch Annabella she knew that she wouldn't, she couldn't, let him.

Then it came to her. If she could make him ill, if he could be sick enough not to be able to take the journey and the ship left without him, then the problem would be solved. At least it would be solved for the present, and the present was all she could cope with now. She had vague, confused ideas of nursing Harding and him being dependent on her and grateful to her and not having the heart or the conscience to leave her after all her care and devotion while he was sick.

Carefully she knelt down, gathered the berries and secreted them under her cloak. Then she returned to the house.

Blueberry tart was Harding's favourite and the belladonna berries strongly resembled them. It was easy to mix some into one of the blueberry tarts, although she had to be careful to mark the one which was meant for Harding and to see that only he ate it.

That night they sat opposite one another at the long dining-room table, and as she watched him eat the tart, she marvelled, as she had done so many times before, how ugly, yet how sensually magnetic he looked.

He ate every morsel but he gave no sign of becoming sick. Instead his eyes sparkled and he began swallowing down a great deal of wine. A kind of excitement seemed to grow in him which surprised her. He seemed to be getting drunker faster than she had ever seen him before. His face became flushed and he talked a lot in an increasingly husky, rasping voice. She could see that the slaves who were hovering in the background and to whom he kept shouting to refill his glass were getting nervous and apprehensive at his strange behaviour. Anxiety was widening her eyes too and making her heart beat faster. Suddenly he startled her by restlessly pushing from the table, sending his chair and some dishes crashing to the floor.

Melie Anne and Joseph cowered back in alarm as he lurched past them and with a drunken, staggering gait reached the other end of the table. By this time his eyes were staring like those of a madman and his pupils were widely dilated. He made a grab at her and sent more dishes flying in the process. She half rose.

'What are you doing?' she cried out.

He grabbed at her again, this time falling on top of her and making her scream out. Joseph and Melie Anne rushed to her assistance but Harding knocked the slaves aside and hauled her from her chair.

'Dance,' he croaked. 'Abigail and Gav are dancing. Everyone is dancing.'

'Oh, Mistress Regina,' Melie Anne wailed. 'What you goin' to do?'

Struggling and staggering with him she felt frightened at his madness and didn't know what to do. She tried not to cry out but his grip on her kept surprising her with the pain it inflicted.

'Dance! Dance!'

Round and round the dining-room he went, dragging her with him, crashing into all the furniture, knocking the candles over, sending bottles of wine cascading over everything and everyone. Other slaves came running through from the kitchen and the women began screaming with terror as Harding careered into the hall still gripping Regina and knocking anyone down who happened to get in his path. His voice was becoming more and more garbled and incoherent. Then, as if his throat were tightening and parching, his words disappeared into horrible whispers and finally into hoarse gasping sighs. But still he lurched about in a wild dance making her shout tearfully to the slaves to help her try and get him to bed.

It took Joseph and Westminster, with all the women, including Regina, to struggle with Harding and force him upstairs.

Even after they managed to undress him and heave his big frame into the bed and cover him with the blankets he still thrashed about. His skin, his mouth, everything about him was dry and brightly burning. She kept trying to help him to drink, struggling with him in an endless nightmare where day merged into night and night into day. She lost all count of time as cups kept being spilled over and refilled and spilled and refilled again. Sponges were dampened, and dampened again, to dab desperately over his face and neck and chest.

At long last he began to quieten. His limbs stopped their restless thrashing. She became aware of a weeping Melie Anne saying,

'Miss Regina, Callie Mae sent you this tea. Don't you think you'd better drink it? You've had nothin' all this time. Callie Mae says you're goin' be collapsin' too.' She wiped her eyes with her apron. 'And this letter came by special coach for poor Master Harding but he ain't goin' be readin' it now.'

'What do you mean?' Regina cried out as the servant put the cup of tea and the letter on to the bedside table. 'What do you mean he's not going to be reading it?'

'Miss Regina,' Melie Anne shook her head and sobbed brokenheartedly. 'We all think he's dying.'

'Nonsense!' Regina shouted at her and the other slaves hovering miserably in the background. 'Of course he's not going to die. Get out of here, all of you. Where's the doctor? I told you to send for the doctor, didn't I?' she called after the retreating figures.

'Yes, Miss Regina. Westminster went to fetch him but I guess he's not found him yet. Joseph's gone looking as well now.'

'Fetch me whisky and honey melted in warm water. Maybe that'll help.'

'Yes, Miss Regina.'

At the mention of death, panic had all but scattered her wits. She struggled to put her arms around Harding's shoulders and hold him while she stuffed more pillows behind him. Surely no one so big and hard and strong could succumb to sickness, could be destroyed by anything or anyone? It wasn't possible. He would always be with her. He would always stride about Forest Hall like a brown-skinned giant with black hair tied back and white ruffled shirt unbuttoned. He was her torment, her lover, her hell, her happiness, her husband, her whole life.

She moaned out loud in the rising panic of her realization that she loved him. Melie Anne came running with the whisky toddy, left it on the table and flew away again.

Regina was moaning and kissing Harding's cheeks and brow and mouth and neck. She felt she was going mad. She could not believe Harding was dying, yet every time she looked at the staring eyes and burning face she knew that he was.

'Robert' she called distractedly to him, desperate to bring him safely back. 'Robert, here's Annabella's letter. Robert, listen!' She snatched the letter from the bedside table, tore open the seal with trembling fingers and read:

'My dear Mr Harding.

What a wondrously pleasant surprise it was to receive your letter. When I hear that a ship or a coach has brought letters for me I am always so prodigiously thrilled, I cannot help jumping up and down and clapping my hands in excitement and joy.

And there have been so many exciting things happening in Glasgow just now. Only yesterday there was a most wondrous procession through the streets of the deacons and office-bearers of the different crafts accompanied by the members of the several incorporated trades. Oh, what a magnificent sight it was! How you would have been impressed if you had been here to witness it. The office-bearer walked at the head of each craft carrying his insignia. The masons displayed the plummet and the mallet, the wrights the saw and plane, the smith the hammer, the fleshers the cleaver, and so on. And there were also gorgeous flags and painted batons. And at the head of the shoemakers was a tall, handsome man chosen to play King Crispin and magnificently attired in a crimson-coloured robe, shining with spangles and golden ornaments and with a splendid crown on his head. How Mungo and I enjoyed it all. What a gay time we had jostling about the streets getting a good view.

Talking of Mungo, my dear Mr Harding, how strange that you should concern yourself with such a question after all these years . . .'

Through the light prattling tone of Annabella's letter Regina became aware of silence.

The hoarse rasping breathing had stopped. Robert Harding could no longer hear Annabella or Regina, yet Regina's voice trailed on like a trickle of cold water, hypnotized, unable to stop.

'. . . Of course Mungo is not your son. Definitely not, sir! What a preposterous idea! Put it out of your head at once. You will have sons aplenty, never fear. Your wife will be prodigiously fruitful, mark my words.

You are lucky to have such a beauty, Mr Harding, and one who so obviously adores you, and works so mightily hard and conscientiously at her wifely duties.

And what a delightful little daughter you have too! Cherish your wife and family well, sir, you are blessed with much good fortune in your world, as I am in mine.

Losh and lovenendie, I could chatter on all day, but the time has come to say goodbye. Dear Mr Harding, my kindest regards to you, and my most affectionate felicitations to Regina.

As ever,
Annabella Blackadder.'